All Gavril Andar has ever known of life is the sunny clime of his southern home, his beautiful mother, and his love of painting. Until his peace is shattered – and his destiny decreed – by the arrival of a group of fierce clan warriors from the north. The father he never knew – the man who ruled the wintry kingdom of Azhkendir and in whose veins ran the burning blood of the Drakhaoul – is dead, murdered by his enemies . . .

Blood. The liquid that will seal Gavril's fate. For becoming Drakhaon means not only ascending to the throne of Azhkendir, but also changing – changing, in subtle ways at first, into a being of extraordinary power and might. Becoming a dragon-warrior. One who must be replenished with the blood of innocents in order to survive.

Kidnapped by the warriors, Gavril is incarcerated in Kastel Drakhaon, with no means of escape from the isolated, ice-bound kingdom. Expected to avenge his father's death, and carefully watched by neighbouring rulers waiting for their chance to move against him, the untested Gavril must fight to retain his human heart and soul in the face of impending war – and the dark instincts that threaten to overpower him . . .

Combining the best of fantasy traditions with her own unique vision, Sarah Ash brings to dazzling life a new saga filled with epic adventure and unforgettable characters. Far-reaching in scope and imagination, *Lord of Snow and Shadows* marks the first step on a journey like no other – into a world teeming with political intrigue, astonishing magic, and passions both dark and light . . .

SARAH ASH was born and brought up in Bath. Having trained as a musician at university, she now teaches and is the author of three much-praised earlier novels, *Moths to a Flame*, *Songspinners*, *The Lost Child* and the forthcoming second book in 'The Tears of Artamon' trilogy. Sarah Ash lives in Kent.

LORD OF SNOW AND SHADOWS

BOOK ONE OF
THE TEARS OF ARTAMON

SARAH ASH

BANTAM BOOKS

LONDON • NEW YORK • TORONTO • SYDNEY • AUCKLAND

LORD OF SNOW AND SHADOWS
A BANTAM BOOK: 0 553 81470 2

Originally published in Great Britain by Bantam Press,
a division of Transworld Publishers

PRINTING HISTORY
Bantam Press edition published 2003
Bantam edition published 2004

3 5 7 9 10 8 6 4 2

Set in 10.5/12pt Times by
Falcon Oast Graphic Art Ltd.

Bantam Books are published by Transworld Publishers,
61–63 Uxbridge Road, London W5 5SA,
a division of The Random House Group Ltd,
in Australia by Random House Australia (Pty) Ltd,
20 Alfred Street, Milsons Point, Sydney, NSW 2061, Australia,
in New Zealand by Random House New Zealand Ltd,
18 Poland Road, Glenfield, Auckland 10, New Zealand
and in South Africa by Random House (Pty) Ltd,
Endulini, 5a Jubilee Road, Parktown 2193, South Africa.

Printed and bound in Great Britain by
Cox & Wyman Ltd, Reading, Berkshire.

Papers used by Transworld Publishers are natural, recyclable
products made from wood grown in sustainable forests. The
manufacturing processes conform to the environmental
regulations of the country of origin.

FOR TOM

ACKNOWLEDGEMENTS

My thanks to my editors Simon Taylor and Anne Lesley Groell for their insightful and sympathetic editing. And thanks are also due to my agent John Richard Parker of MBA for all his help and support.

LORD OF
SNOW AND
SHADOWS

WINTER GHOST SONGS

PROLOGUE

The Clan Lord lies dying, his eyes wandering, glazing over as he reaches out blindly to grasp his lieutenant's arm.

'Over . . . at last . . . old friend . . .' The hand falls away, his grizzled head lolls sideways, sightless eyes sliding upwards, clear at last, as if a dark veil has melted away.

And as his faithful friend watches, his sight dimmed with tears, he sees –

A shadow, black as a stormcloud, slowly rises from the still body of his master, lifts and gathers itself until it hovers over him: a great winged daemon-serpent, terrible and puissant.

'*Drakhaoul*,' he whispers, in awe and terror.

Now all the warriors and servants have fallen silent, watching or covering their faces in fear.

'Lead me, Drakhaoul,' the old soldier cries aloud, 'show me where he is to be found. And I will follow you, no matter how far. Take me to our new lord. Our new Drakhaon.'

I

'Shall I sit over here, Maistre Andar?'

Gavril Andar looked up from unpacking his oil paints and saw Altessa Astasia Orlova in the doorway. She was dressed for her portrait in a plain muslin dress of eggshell blue, her cloud of dark hair tied back with a single blue ribbon.

He glanced around.

'Where's your governess, Altessa?'

'Eupraxia? Oh, she's still sleeping off the effects of the fruit punch at last night's reception.' Astasia began to laugh. 'You mean – is it seemly for me to be here alone with you, unchaperoned? But this is Smarna, Maistre Andar! Surely one may relax the strict rules of Muscobar court protocol when on holiday?'

Her laughter was infectious and Gavril found himself smiling back at her.

'Was I facing this way? Or that?' She fidgeted around in the chair. 'I can't remember.'

He went over to her. 'Your head was inclined a little more to the left.'

'Like this? You'll have to help me.'

Gently he tipped her chin to the correct angle. Now her shoulders were awry. Carefully he placed his hands on her shoulders to alter the pose. As he moved her, he became aware that she was gazing intently up at him. He could feel the sweet warmth of her breath on his face. Heat flooded through him. If anyone came in and saw them in such a compromising position . . .

'And my hair?'

Gavril consulted his sketches.

'No ribbon. Loose over your shoulders.'

'But if I pull out the ribbon, I'll lose the pose,' she said with that little smile again, grave yet oddly provocative.

As he undid the ribbon he felt the dark curls against his fingertips, soft as the strands of sable in his watercolour brushes.

'How long must I sit still?'

'Long enough . . .' Gavril was concentrating on his palette, blending and mixing. The luminous dark of her eyes – so difficult to match the shade exactly. It was almost the intense purple of viola petals . . .

'If the conversation is diverting enough, I can sit for hours. Yesterday you told me all about Vermeille. That was very diverting. But you said nothing about *you*. Tell me about Gavril Andar.'

'I was hoping', he said, 'that you would tell me about the Grand Duchess's reception last night.'

'Mama's reception?' A slight flush suffused her pale face. Had she met someone special last night? 'Well, my brother Andrei flirted outrageously with

14

all the prettiest women, especially the married ones. He has no shame!'

'And', he ventured, 'was your fiancé at the reception?'

'Oh, heavens forbid, *no*!' The dark eyes blazed. He must have touched a sensitive nerve to have produced such a vehement reply.

'I beg your pardon, Altessa, but when I was commissioned to paint a betrothal portrait, I assumed—'

'A natural assumption to make. It's just that there is no fiancé as yet; this portrait is to sell my charms to the highest bidder,' she said bitterly. 'Papa sees my betrothal as a way to bring an end to a difficult diplomatic situation. He's looking for a rich and powerful ally.'

Gavril looked at her blankly.

'Haven't you heard? Eugene of Tielen has invaded Khitari. And now his warships are in the Straits. Things are looking a little . . . tricky for Muscobar. That's why Papa has stayed in Mirom.'

'I had no idea.' Gavril, like most Smarnans, paid scant attention to international politics. Smarna was a sunny summer retreat for the rich aristocracy from the northern countries, too small and unimportant to play a major part in world affairs.

'And of course, my feelings are not to be taken into consideration, oh no!'

All trace of laughter had vanished; he saw how miserable she was at the prospect of this marriage of obligation.

She glanced around guiltily. 'But you must never let slip you heard me say such a disrespectful thing. Papa would be so angry.'

'Portrait painters are trained to be discreet.'

'I feel I could tell you anything.'

'Anything?' he echoed, blushing in spite of himself.

For a moment her gaze rested on him and he felt a delicious shiver of danger. Hadn't his mother warned him? *Never become involved.* The gulf between a Grand Duke's daughter and a young, impoverished artist was so great that he knew he must never dare to think of her as anything more than a wealthy patroness . . .

And then she began to chatter again, affecting the charmingly light, idle tone of their earlier conversations.

'My dancing partners from last night. Lieutenant Valery Vassian for one, the First Minister's son. Very good-looking, but a terrible dancer.' She smothered a giggle. 'My poor toes are still bruised. And then there was Count Velemir's nephew, Pavel. He's been abroad on some kind of diplomatic mission about which he would say nothing of interest. I suspect he may be one of Papa's secret agents! I don't think I could marry a spy. One would never know if he were telling the truth . . .'

Even as she chattered on, Gavril painted as he had never painted before. Her freshness, her utter lack of self-consciousness, inspired and enchanted him. When she was in repose, he noticed a wistful expression darkening her eyes as she gazed out of the window, beyond the breeze-blown gauze curtains, to the blue haze of the sea beyond.

'Ahh. I'm stiffening up.'

'Time to take a break then,' he said, laying down his brush.

She came around to his side of the canvas.

'Well?' he said, rather more tensely than he had intended.

'I think you've flattered me, Maistre Andar,' she said after a while. 'I always thought myself a pale shadow of Mama. She is such a beauty. But you've made me look almost pretty.'

'But you *are*—' he began, only to be interrupted as the double doors opened and a stout woman hurried in.

'Altessa! How long have you been here – alone – with this man?' The governess was so out of breath she could hardly speak.

'Oh, don't be such a prude, Eupraxia.'

'If the Grand Duchess were to hear of this—'

'But she won't, Praxia, will she?' Astasia wound her arm around Eupraxia's ample waist.

'And if some impropriety had taken place—'

'You've been reading too many romances,' Astasia teased.

'That's quite enough portrait-painting for today, Maistre Andar,' Eupraxia said, ignoring Astasia. 'When the arrangement was made, I was told your mother Elysia was to accept the commission. I had not expected a *young man*. If I had known, I would have made my objections clear at the time—'

'Yes, yes,' Astasia said, 'but Maistre Andar is doing such a good job. Do take a look, Praxia. See? Isn't it coming along well?'

Eupraxia grudgingly admitted that it was a fair likeness.

'So we shall expect you at the same time tomorrow morning, Maistre Andar?' Astasia gave him a smile of such bewitching charm that he could only nod in reply.

He turned back to the canvas in a daze, still intoxicated by her fresh hyacinth scent, her smile . . .

Gavril painted until the light faded; the sun was setting and the last dying rays deepened the misty blue of the sea to lilac. He had been so absorbed in his work that he had not noticed till now that his back and arm ached. He stood back from the canvas, looking at it critically in the twilight. Yes, he had captured something of her elusively wistful expression, even though it was not yet as perfect as he could wish.

Music came floating on the drowsy summer night. Carriages were drawing up, wheels crunching over the gravel on the broad drive. Gavril took out a cloth to wipe his brush and started to pack away his paints.

Coloured lanterns glowed like little jewels on the terraces. The guests were arriving, the women dressed in bright spangled muslins of primrose, coral and turquoise, diamonds and sapphires sparkling around their throats. The men wore uniforms stiff with gold brocade and brass buttons. The night gleamed with golden candlelight, trembled with the babble of conversation and the frothy dance melodies, light as foam on the waves in the Bay.

It was time to leave. And yet he could not go, not yet, not without seeing her one more time.

Servants, resplendent in the blue liveries of the Duke's household, hurried past with golden punch-bowls, silver trays of *petits fours* and crystal dishes filled to the brim with sugar-dusted berries.

The dancers spilled out onto the terrace and

Gavril strolled out into the gardens to watch, leaning against the pillared balustrade from which the wide, dark lawns rolled down to the sea beneath. The warm night air tasted of sparkling wine, headily effervescent. Little trails of white moths fluttered around the flickering lanterns.

No-one challenged him. No-one seemed to notice that he was not wearing military uniform or evening dress.

And then he saw her, one hand resting on her older brother Andrei's arm, gazing gravely at the spinning dancers. In her gown of white organdie, trimmed with green silk ribbons, she reminded Gavril of a snow-flower, clean and pure amongst the garish costumes of the guests.

Suddenly he realized that she had seen him and was gazing at him with an intensity that made him shiver.

She moved away from Andrei, rapidly fanning herself with her white feather fan. He caught a few snatches of words as she came closer, smilingly shaking her head as attentive young men offered her ices, sherbets, fruit punch.

'So hot . . . fresh air . . . maybe later . . .'

He watched as she drifted down the marble steps onto the darkened lawns and followed.

'Altessa,' he said softly.

She turned to him. 'Gavril,' she said.

His heart beat faster to hear her pronounce his name without the formality of 'Maistre Andar' – it had a wonderfully intimate quality, as if they were equals, as if he could hope – against all hopes – that a poor painter could—

'Do you believe in fate, Gavril?' she said, softer

19

still. 'It's as if we were meant to meet. As if we were meant to be together.'

The strains of a waltz drifted out from the ballroom.

'Listen,' she said, 'they're playing "White Nights", my favourite tune . . .'

Before he knew what he was doing, she was in his arms, her head close to his and they were dancing slowly, circling on the dew-wet grass, in a pool of moonlight.

He leaned towards her – he could not help himself – and kissed her. Her lips tasted cool and fresh as her hyacinth scent but her mouth was warm. His hands touched her bare shoulders, caressing the soft silk of her skin . . .

Suddenly he felt her shiver in his arms.

'What is it?' he asked. Astasia was looking up at the sky.

'Can't you feel it?' she said. 'Like a storm coming. Far out to sea. Look . . .'

Gavril gazed out across the Bay. The moon had dimmed, as if covered by thin clouds, and the stars seemed less bright.

'Odd,' he said. He knew the moods and humours of the Bay well. And this was not the way a summer storm began.

A strange, chill little breeze ruffled the sea-pines and cedars. It seemed as if the thin veil of dark cloud was scudding along too fast for the breeze to carry it, moving almost of its own accord. A feeling of dread clouded his mind.

'You should go in,' he said suddenly.

'Altessa!'

They turned – but too late. The Orlov Guards, led

by Andrei Orlov, were running across the lawns towards them, sabres drawn.

'Arrest that intruder!'

Two burly guardsmen threw themselves onto Gavril and bore him to the ground.

'Are you all right, Tasia?' Andrei demanded. 'Has he hurt you?'

'I'm perfectly all right!' Astasia blazed back. 'He was here by my invitation. Let him go!'

Gavril struggled against the restraining arms of the two Guards. Andrei came closer and, placing the razor-tip of his sabre beneath Gavril's chin, peered down in the moonlight.

'So, it's the portrait painter.' He sheathed his blade. 'You little fool, Tasia. If you must create a scandal, at least try to choose someone of our own class.' He turned to the guardsmen. 'Throw him out. And you, painter, don't even think of coming back – or asking for your fee. Your commission's cancelled.'

'No!' cried Astasia. 'It's all my fault—'

Gavril was hauled to his feet. In spite of all his attempts to break free, the Guards began to drag him towards the gravel drive.

'Mama is making a terrible fuss. She thinks you've been abducted – or molested by some Smarnan peasant.'

'Gavril, I'm so sorry—' Astasia cried.

'Come inside, Tasia.' Andrei hurried his sister away across the lawn.

At the villa gates, the Guards flung Gavril out onto the rough gravel.

Bruised and shaken, he picked himself up, brushing the dirt from his clothes – only to find the heavy iron gates clanged shut in his face and locked.

'Hey! What about my paints?' he yelled, grabbing hold of the bars of the gates and shaking them till they clanged noisily.

One of the Guards came back and Gavril found himself staring into the muzzle of a carbine.

'Get out,' the man said in heavily accented Smarnan.

For a moment, Gavril felt a dangerous flicker of anger. Was it always to be like this? Was he always to be excluded, always the poor painter, on the outside looking in?

And then he heard a click as the Guard primed the carbine and pulled back the hammer.

'All right, all right, I'm going.' He let go of the bars and backed away.

The unlit lane which wound down the cliffside through pines and brambles to the beach far below was wide enough to accommodate the carriages of the Orlovs' wealthy visitors – and dark enough to suit his mood. Humiliated and angry, he stumbled blindly on.

How could he begin to explain to his mother that he had ruined his first prestigious commission?

The beach was deserted and silent, save for the soft lapping of the tide on the pale sands. The cloud-shadow that had scudded across the moon had gone and the waters of wide Vermeille Bay shimmered in the moon's clear light.

Gavril walked slowly along the beach. It was a magical night, a night for lovers . . .

He turned and gazed back at the Villa Orlova, gleaming high up on the cliffs above. Torchlight and lanternlight still lit the white stucco of the villa; there would be dancing till dawn.

In whose arms was she dancing now? The clumsy young officer who had bruised her toes? Or had she been sent to her room in disgrace? Was she thinking of him now? Would she remember his name when she had returned to distant Mirom? Would she remember how they had moved together in the dance as one? Or would he just be a fading memory of a sunlit summer?

Bitter resentment burned through him like a flame. He was as good as the Mirom aristocracy, no – better! How dare they humiliate him in this way?

'Astasia!' he cried aloud over the waves' soft rise and fall.

Suddenly the beach went black. Glancing up, he saw a darkness blotting out the stars, and a thin, cold wind sighed across the waves.

Must be a storm coming after all . . .

He hastened his steps, hurrying towards the path that led up to his home, the Villa Andara, at the opposite end of the Bay.

But as he moved, the darkness moved too, shifting faster than any wind-driven cloud, racing across the night sky towards him, pursuing him like a hawk wheeling over its prey.

The feeling of dread overwhelmed him, cold as a fever-sweat. He clambered up the sandy cliff-path, stumbling over the tangled blackberry briars and tree roots. Breathless and sweating, he reached the old rose garden, his mother's favourite place . . .

High above the villa the shadow-cloud hovered, black like choking smoke, leaching all the stars' brightness from the night.

What in God's name was it? And why had it pursued him so relentlessly?

He launched himself towards the safety of the villa, tearing across the lawns as though his life depended on it, hurling himself at the side door which his mother left unlocked for him.

Inside, he leaned against the door, gasping for breath. Then he shot the heavy bolts and locked the door with the key.

Now that he was inside the villa, the whole episode began to seem not only bizarre but absurd. He must have imagined it. His mind, already inflamed with anger and desire, had distorted what was nothing but a rising sea-mist into something far more sinister.

What a fool I've been . . .

He went along the passageway towards the stairs, tiptoeing so as not to disturb Elysia or their housekeeper Palmyre. But the feeling of dread still haunted him, as though the dark shadow-mist had smothered the whole house, extinguishing the light of the stars.

He reached his room and, exhausted, flung himself down on his bed, closing his eyes.

The balmy evening air suddenly breathed cold and chill.

Gavril opened one eye.

The chimney! He had not thought to block the chimney! And now the darkness had entered his room, rolling out of the open fireplace in swathes like smoke, gathering itself in great coils like a daemon-serpent, rearing up over his bed to swallow him in its gaping maw.

Gavril gave a cry, tried to roll away – and found

himself drowning in swathes of shadow.

He felt his consciousness suddenly wrenched free from the body that lay on the bed, flung far from the warm Smarnan night into a whirling chaos of cloud and stars . . .

He is in a torch-lit hall. The smoky air reeks of burned pitch and worse: the stench of spilled blood, vomit, and something else – a raw, acrid, chemical stink that makes the eyes water and the throat burn.

As the swirling smoke clears, Gavril sees a figure slumped on the tiled floor of the chamber, a figure that strives slowly, painfully, to drag itself over the patterned tiles towards the door. A dark liquid smears the tiles, staining them, steadily leaking from the slow-moving figure. Gavril can do nothing; a helpless observer, he can only watch the dying man's agonized progress.

'*Why? Why have you brought me here?*'

'*Look.*' The hoarse command reverberates in his mind, a brazen funeral bell relentlessly tolling. '*Look!*'

His gaze is forced up, away from the dying man – and he finds himself staring directly into the eyes of a golden-haired young man, eyes dark with terror and exultation as he stands over his victim, blood-stained sabre in one hand, a jewelled goblet in the other.

'This', cries the young man, emptying the contents of the goblet on the other, 'for my mother.' His voice is choked with emotion, a hatred and grief so bitter Gavril can almost taste it in the rank, death-tainted air. 'This for my sisters.'

His victim writhes around, hands upraised, fingers

25

clawing. For one moment, in the paroxysmal shudder that twists his body, Gavril sees a column of smoke arising, a spark-filled, cobalt smoke that goes rushing towards the rafters. Flames shoot out from the writhing column and the young man drops, screaming, to his knees. His arm, his hand that holds the goblet, is burning, bright with blue fire. He hurls the goblet at his adversary.

'This', he screams, 'for my father—'

The column disperses into shreds and tatters of snaking, wisping smoke. In its midst, the older man crumples, crashing back to the floor, the last of his strength exhausted. 'Who let you in?' His words rasp out on a dying whisper but Gavril recognizes the voice. It is an echo, a fast-failing echo of the stern voice in his head. *'Who betrayed me?'*

But the young man has doubled up, hugging his seared arm to his chest, too choked with pain to reply.

'No more.' Gavril tries to close his mind, to shut out the pain and terror.

A loud hammering shakes the door timbers. Now there are voices shouting, clamouring to be let in.

The young man staggers to his feet. Gavril sees the revulsion – revulsion and raw fear – in his eyes. The exultation has faded. He has never killed before.

'Here! Over here!'

Someone else is in the room. An urgent voice, low and husky, is calling from the smoke. An accomplice. The murderer is not alone.

The thuds at the door grow louder, more insistent; Gavril hears the creak of rending timbers.

'Hurry!'

The young man stumbles away from his victim, slipping on the blood-smeared tiles.

26

Gavril strains to make out where the third person is hiding – yet all he sees is a wooden panel sliding open in the painted wall.

The locked door bursts inwards in an explosion of splinters and armed men come tumbling into the room.

'*Too late . . .*' There is a mocking, ironic taint to the whispered words of the dying man.

And, as if glimpsed through his fast-dimming sight, Gavril's vision begins to break up – streaked, distorted, fading like the last shreds of the dispersing smoke.

'*Gavril.*' The voice burns through his brain, a last, desperate plea, as if dragged from the fiery depths of the abyss.

'*Remember . . .*'

Gavril opened his eyes. Watery dawn light spilled down into his room. Yet he could only lie staring into nothing, rigid, paralysed with the horror of the vision, wanting to wish it away as 'only a dream'. But how could anything so immediate, so real, have been a mere dream?

'*Remember . . .*'

The aftertaste of the vision suddenly gripped Gavril's stomach; he rolled off the bed and staggered queasily towards the dressing-room, pitching forwards over the sink, heaving and retching.

And then he heard the distant clatter of hoofbeats.

Through the receding surges of nausea, Gavril raised his head, eyes watering. He wondered if Andrei Orlov was up early with his fellow-officers for a day's hunting. And if Astasia was with her brother . . .

He stuck his head under the water tap and let the ice-cold water flow until his skin tingled with the shock of it.

The sound of horses' hooves grew louder. They were coming this way, along the upper Bay road, towards the cliffs.

He could hear shouts now, men's voices, calling to each other. Puzzled, he staggered to his feet. There came a knocking on the front door. Who was it and what could they want at this early hour?

Head pounding, Gavril made for the hall. The knocking was more insistent now. Ahead of him, Palmyre was slowly crossing the hall, yawning and wiping the sleep from her eyes.

'Palmyre!' He heard his mother's voice cry out from the upper floor of the villa. 'Don't open!'

But Palmyre had already pulled back the bolts. The door was thrown open and a group of men pushed their way past her into the hall. They were tall, tattooed with clan marks and ritual scars, their long hair braided.

'No!' Elysia screamed from the top of the stairs.

Gavril stopped where he was, staring, open-mouthed. Were they thieves come to rob them?

But the foremost amongst the intruders came forwards and flung himself on his knees before Gavril.

'Drakhaon,' he said. His deep voice trembled with emotion. 'I bring bad news. Your father—' Tears channelled down the deep-graven lines of his weatherburned face. 'Your father is dead.'

'My father?' Gavril stared down at the kneeling man in astonishment. And as he stood staring, the other men dropped to their knees too.

He turned to Elysia who had frozen, pale and silent at the foot of the stairs. 'Mother?'

'So,' she said, in a numbed, toneless voice, 'Volkh is dead.'

'Mother,' Gavril said again, pleadingly. 'Who is Volkh? Who are these men?'

'Lord Drakhaon,' the barbarian warrior said, still on his knees. Gavril saw now that, for all his rings and tattoos, he was an old man, and his braided hair was grey as iron. 'We have come to take you home.' He used the common tongue, yet so strangely inflected that Gavril wondered if he had understood him correctly.

'Home?' he repeated, utterly confused. 'This is my home.'

'Not Smarna, Lord. To your rightful inheritance. To Azhkendir.'

'Azhkendir? Surely there's been some mistake. This is my home, here in Smarna—'

'No mistake.' Tears still ran down the old warrior's cheeks; he seemed unashamed to weep in front of strangers. 'Don't you remember me, Lord Gavril? Kostya, Bogatyr Kostya Torzianin, your father's right-hand man?'

Gavril shook his head. This was all happening too fast. Maybe he was still dreaming . . .

Dreaming.

For a dizzying moment, Gavril found himself plunged back into the bloodstained hall of his nightmare, staring down at the sprawled figure, reliving those last agonizing death throes . . .

'How did my father die?' he heard himself asking in a cold, distant voice.

Kostya's expression darkened; though tears still

29

glistened in his eyes, Gavril saw now a glimmer of implacable hatred and despair.

'I failed your father, Lord Gavril. I fell into a trap. I was not at his side to defend him when he needed me. For that I can never forgive myself: that I still live when my lord and master is dead.'

'But how? How did he die?'

'He—' The old man seemed shamed even to say the words aloud. 'He was betrayed. Betrayed – and murdered.'

2

'Why, Mother? Why didn't you tell me?'

Elysia Andar stood unmoving, her back to Gavril, her hands resting on the windowsill as she gazed out over the blue waters of the Bay. She stood so still, she could have been mistaken for one of the pale marble statues that graced her terraced gardens below.

Gavril took a faltering step towards her. Still she did not turn. Tears, he could have understood. But this terrible cold, silent anger was new to him. He didn't know how to approach her. He felt as if it were somehow his fault.

White gulls swooped outside the villa's open windows, their mewing cries echoing over the Bay. The hot, dusty scent of oleanders drifted in on the golden air. A half-finished canvas stood on an easel where the light was strongest; he caught a whiff of the oily smell of the drying paints. This was the essence of his childhood memories: the hot sun of Smarna, the lapping blue waters, his mother painting, humming to herself as she worked.

And yet now it was as if he looked at it all through a dark lens that made everything warped, distorted.

'Mother?' Gavril tried a more coaxing tone. He came closer, hands hovering behind her shoulders, wanting to touch her, to seek reassurance, yet not daring to. '*Please*, Mother.' To his shame he heard his voice crack; he had not intended to break down in front of her. He had to be strong, if only to keep some semblance of sanity in the chaos that his life had become. 'I need to know.'

He heard her sigh as soft as the whisper of the waves on the gilded sands of the Bay below.

'This is my home. Smarna. Isn't it?'

'*My* home,' she said dully.

'But I grew up here. This,' and Gavril stretched out his arm, encompassing the villa and the gardens in his gesture, 'this is all I remember. Now they – they tell me I am from Azhkendir and I must leave, leave you, leave my work unfinished, to go to Azhkendir. They tell me I have inherited this title, Drakhaon – and I have no idea what they are talking about!'

Elysia slowly turned around to face him. He saw that she had been silently crying, the tears leaving glistening traces on her peach-soft skin. 'I was going to tell you,' she said, her voice stifled, 'when you come of age next year. Now, it seems, events have overtaken me.'

'But is it true?' Gavril pleaded. 'Was he my father?'

'Yes,' she said. She gazed back at him, her eyes dark, shadow-haunted. He had always cherished the image of her as serene, as sunny-natured as the

Vermeille Bay below. Kostya Torzianin's sudden, unannounced arrival had destroyed that serenity. The woman who stared at him, distractedly picking at her lace fichu with her nails, was a distortion of the mother he thought he knew. He could not remember ever seeing her look so troubled – or so vulnerable – before.

'Why did you lie to me?' It hurt him to cause her pain. But hadn't he the right to learn the truth about his birth? 'Why did you tell me you didn't know where he was?'

'You are still so young, Gavril,' she said. 'Sometimes a kind of lie is preferable to the truth.'

'And the truth is?'

'That I had to get you away from him.'

Still only these terse, enigmatic fragments.

'But why? *Why?*'

She seemed to achieve some kind of control over herself, moving suddenly to the table and the cut-glass decanter of *karvi*, the orange and caraway-perfumed liqueur she usually offered to visitors. He saw her pour herself a glass and start to take small, shuddering sips of the liqueur, as though trying to calm herself. Was it going to be so difficult to tell him the truth? Had his father been such a monster? He began to dread what he had to hear.

Elysia sat down on one of the silk couches, the glass of *karvi* still in her hand.

'What has that old man told you?'

'Kostya?' Gavril grimaced. He had been forced to listen to the stern old man's repeated insistences that he had given his dying father his oath to lay down his life for his son and bring him back to Azhkendir. Palmyre had come to his rescue; the warriors were

33

now busy eating in the kitchen and drinking their way through a keg of the household's best ale. 'All Kostya says is that I must pack my bags and make ready to leave for Azhkendir.' He wrinkled his nose. 'Do the *druzhina* always smell so ripe?'

'They all need a bath. And some fresh clothes. But that's the way of the Drakhaon's *druzhina*, as you will soon discover if you go back with him, Gavril. They are not like us. They choose to live by ancient Clan laws and Clan loyalties. Have you seen Kostya's tattoos?' She made a little moue of disapproval. 'Barbaric. Don't let them put a single Clanmark on you.'

'But my father,' Gavril said, sitting down opposite her.

'Your father.' He saw her take another sip of the *karvi*, turning the glass round and round in her fingers. Then Elysia suddenly leaned towards him, her voice huskily intense.

'I first met your father when he came here to sit for a portrait. And once he had recovered from his astonishment that the painter was a woman, we began to get to know each other. He was very good-looking then. Dashing. Rough and unpolished, by the standards of Smarnan society – but I liked him all the more for that. He had a ... a kind of raw honesty, an impulsiveness that appealed to me. Beside him, the young men in my circle seemed colourless, dull. But love made me blind, Gavril, blind to any imperfections or flaws. I could not see that your father's impulsiveness hid a terrible, destructive temper – that the fearless spirit I had fallen in love with concealed a capacity for savage cruelty.'

Gavril heard what she said but still did not

understand. 'He – he treated you badly? Did he – did he hurt you?'

He saw her try to conceal a shudder as she drained the last of the liqueur in her glass.

'What I'm trying to tell you is that your father changed. Not all at once, but insidiously, almost as though there were some slow-working poison in his veins. Or maybe he was always that way and he tried to change himself as a ploy to win me . . . and failed. Or maybe there is some malign influence at work in Azhkendir, something in the endless winters and the dark, lonely forests that sends them all mad. I don't know, Gavril, all I know is that it was no place for a little child, for my son to grow up in . . .'

'So you *left* him?'

'I ran away, yes. With you. And he sent Kostya and his men after us and they caught us in the forest and brought us back.' Her gaze had shifted from his. She was staring into emptiness . . . and through her eyes, he saw her, a terrified young woman, clutching her baby, surrounded by a ring of tattooed, fur-cloaked warriors.

'What did he do to you?' Gavril said in a whisper.

'At first he kept me locked in my room. Imprisoned. And then . . . then he came to me one night and I saw in his eyes a distant shadow of the man I had once loved. And he said, "Terrible things are going to happen here, things over which I shall have little – or no – control. I want you to take Gavril and get out. Get out now. Before I change. Before it's too late."'

'He let you go?'

Elysia nodded; her eyes had clouded with tears.

' "Before I change"? What did he mean?'

'A few days after I crossed the border, a Clan war broke out in Azhkendir. I made my way back here to Smarna with you. I had only the clothes I was wearing and a few coins in my purse. But money, generous gifts of money, began to be paid into a trust fund for you. Instructions arrived in an anonymous letter—'

'So no-one knew?'

'Everything was done using false names. Your father had made too many enemies; if anyone found out you were his son—'

'Was he—' Gavril hesitated to ask the question that had been tormenting him. 'Was he really such a monster?'

She looked him in the eyes then. Her look chilled his heart, like a jagged splinter of ice.

'Yes.'

The sunlit room seemed to grow darker, as if a cloud had drifted across the sun.

'What did he do?'

'If you really want to know, you must find out for yourself; please don't ask me to tell you. It sickens me just to think of it. Sometimes I wonder . . . if I hadn't run away, maybe I could have prevented it from happening.' She looked away, her voice hardly audible above the whisper of the sea. 'Or maybe no-one could have influenced him. But I still wake in the dark before dawn, Gavril, and I wonder – did I help make him into the tyrant he became?'

Gavril sat staring helplessly at her. Tyrant. Savage. Monster. He wasn't sure he wanted to find out any more about this man who was said to be his father.

'They called me Drakhaon. What does that

mean? You said my father's name was Volkh.'

He saw his mother shiver as he said the name. *Drakhaon*. She leaned across and took his hands in hers, looking closely down at them, almost as if she were examining them.

'Mother?' he said puzzled.

'You don't have to go to Azhkendir if you don't want to, Gavril,' she said, closing her slender, paint-stained fingers firmly around his. 'You can renounce your inheritance. Let them find another Drakhaon.'

'There is no other heir!' Kostya stood in the open doorway, his scarred, seamed face twisted with anger. 'Not while My Lord's son lives. He *is* Drakhaon. By right of birth, by right of blood—'

'How long have you been lurking out there, eaves-dropping?' Elysia rounded on him, her brown eyes narrowed. 'This is none of your business, this is between me and my son.'

'Lord Gavril,' Kostya said, ignoring her, 'I made a blood-vow to your father. I vowed I would bring his son home to his inheritance.'

'Oh,' cried Elysia, 'and what is more important? The keeping of your vow or my son's future?'

'Has it not occurred to you, Drakhys,' Kostya said, unwavering, 'that the two are inextricably connected? How can young Lord Gavril—'

'What did you call me?' Elysia said, her voice suddenly hard and tense.

'Drakhys. It is your title. As Lord Volkh's consort—'

'His consort?' Gavril heard his mother begin to laugh. Her laughter had always reminded him of the throaty cooing of the white doves in the tall sea-pines. But this laughter was harsh; mocking and mirthless. It disturbed him. 'And what of the others? Even here, in Smarna, I've heard the stories, Kostya.'

'There have been other women, yes,' Kostya said stiffly, 'but no other heir. And you were the only one he cared for, Lady. After you left he was inconsolable . . .'

'I wish I could believe you, Kostya.' Elysia turned away from him, going back out onto the balcony. Gavril saw how the dazzling sunlight turned her breeze-tousled hair to strands of antique gold. He felt a sudden stab of anguish for her. 'I wish I could believe you.'

Gavril could not sleep. Moonlight lit his room, silvering his tumbled sheets. If he slept, last night's nightmare might return to haunt him; he might find himself back in that bloodstained, smoke-choked hall.

He had not mentioned the vision to anyone. There had been fever-dreams, childhood nightmares that had woken him screaming for Elysia, but never anything as chillingly vivid as this. The voice, the presence in his room, had all been so real . . .

Murdered, Kostya had said. His father had been murdered.

I don't believe in ghosts.

And yet, hadn't a scientist at the Mirom University recently asserted that at the moment of death, some trace of energy might be etched on the atmosphere, an energy so intense that it could be measured? He and his fellow students had spent an evening hotly debating the point over several bottles of red wine in their favourite tavern down by the harbour.

He pushed aside the sweaty sheets and went out onto the balcony. The setting moon hung low over the Bay, lighting the black waters with an opalescent glimmer. From the villa's steeply terraced gardens below, the drowsy summer scents of frangipani and night jasmine perfumed the warm, dark air. This was his home.

And now he had to leave, to go north to the winter country of Azhkendir. To leave his work incomplete. To leave Astasia's portrait only half-finished . . .

Until now, he had been nothing but a servant in Astasia's eyes. Now he found himself a lord, albeit lord of an impoverished land of snow and shadows. Now he was her equal. But to claim his inheritance, he must go away from her, far away from the summer pleasures of Vermeille . . . and by the time he returned, she would be betrothed to Eugene of Tielen.

A melody began to whisper through his mind: the sweet, wistful strains of 'White Nights' which they had danced to last night.

He must go claim her as his. He would stalk past the guards who had manhandled him so brutally and demand an audience with the Grand Duchess Sofia. And if any of the disdainful Mirom aristocrats tried to stop him, he would shrug them aside, saying, 'Do you have any idea who I really am?'

He vaulted over the balcony and went running through the dark garden towards the shore.

The moonlit beach was deserted. As Gavril hurried along the glistening sands, the only sound he could hear was the lapping of the grey tide and the slap of his feet over the wet strand.

Lord Gavril, Drakhaon of Azhkendir. How he would relish the looks of confusion on their haughty faces when he revealed his true identity!

He glanced suddenly over his shoulder. Was there someone stalking him?

The beach was empty.

He followed the long curve of the Bay round towards the headland. High above him, the Villa Orlova glimmered in the moonlight amongst the dark sea-pines.

'Astasia.' He whispered her name to the night.

A sliver of moving shadow caught his eye. Instinct made him whirl around, fists clenched, ready to defend himself.

'You walk fast, Lord Gavril.' Kostya Torzianin stood behind him, arms folded.

'Kostya!' Gavril's heart was thudding, fury and fear mingled. 'How long have you been following me?'

'Quick reactions, too.' Was it his imagination, or was the old man grinning at him? 'We'll make a bogatyr of you yet.'

'A what?'

'Bogatyr. Warrior. Like your father.'

'I've told you, I'm a painter, not a fighting man.' How could he make Kostya understand? 'And I'm perfectly capable of looking after myself. I don't need a bodyguard.'

Kostya shrugged. 'As Gavril Andar, maybe. But now you are Gavril Nagarian. Lord Drakhaon. And the Drakhaon has enemies.'

Enemies. Gavril felt another shiver of unease. His father had been murdered. Had he made enemies so ruthless they would pursue their vendetta far beyond the borders of Azhkendir? What bloody legacy of violence had he inherited with this bizarre title?

'We have a long journey ahead of us, Lord Gavril. Wind and tide are set fair for Azhkendir.'

'We?' Gavril turned in exasperation on the old man. 'I'm not coming with you.'

'But you are Drakhaon.'

'And there are things I must attend to here in Smarna. I will come to Azhkendir in my own good time.'

The old warrior drew in his breath as if Gavril had stabbed him.

'Don't you understand, lad?' His eyes burned in the moonlight. 'You must come now. You have no idea, have you, of what you've inherited? *She* has told you nothing!'

Gavril turned and began to walk on along the shore, flinging back over his shoulder, 'I give you good night, Kostya.'

There was a silence then, broken only by the soft lapping of the waves on the moon-silvered shore and the sound of his own fierce breathing as he strode along at the water's edge. His fists were clenched at his sides, ready to punch anyone who dared to stop him.

Which was when he felt the blinding crack on the back of his skull and darkness came surging in, faster than a floodtide. His mind was still dazedly asking, 'Why?' as he pitched forwards.

Then it seemed as if someone reached up and squeezed the last light from the moon, leaving him crashing down, down into starless night.

3

A single lantern swung to and fro over Gavril's
head. Just watching it made him feel dizzy and sent
dull stabs of light through his head, like blunted
knifeblades. He closed his eyes, wishing the pain
would go away.

'There, lad. That's better now . . .'

Someone was speaking to him; the sound ebbed
and flowed in his consciousness with the swaying of
the lanternlight. Each word dinned in his mind like
an anvil stroke. He wanted nothing but to sink back
into the soft dark oblivion from which he had
wakened.

Instead he became aware of the noises around
him: the rhythmic creak of timbers, the swash and
splash of deep waters slapping close to where he lay.
The lantern still swung dizzyingly to and fro, swinging in time with the creak of the timbers.

'Where . . . ?' It took all his strength to whisper the
single word.

The twisted shadow of a man materialized beside him, looming over him like some creature of darkness.

'Are you thirsty? Here. Drink.' Someone raised his head, tipping a cup of water to his lips. The water was tainted with bitter spirit; he choked, peering with unfocused eyes, trying to identify the man who had emerged from the creaking, moving shadows.

'No more.' He tried to turn his head away. If only he could clear the fog from his mind, if only he could begin to think clearly, he would be able to figure out what he was doing here . . . on a boat . . . at *sea*?

'Kidnapped. I've been kidnapped!' He reared up, shaking his fist at the shadowy figure. 'You – you damned *pirate*!' The cabin spun giddily about him. He dropped weakly back onto the mattress.

'Lie still, My Lord,' said his captor tersely.

At last Gavril thought he recognized the man, from his voice and his swinging braids, grey as iron.

'Kostya? Wh . . . where am I?' Shreds of memory began to return. He had been walking along the seashore, the moon was bright on the waters and then . . .

'We left Vermeille Bay last night. In two days we should reach the White Sea and make landfall at Arkhelskoye.'

At first Gavril could find no words. Fury robbed him of speech. He had been kidnapped not by corsairs but by his father's own men.

'I told you', he said at last, 'that I would not come with you. And you abducted me.'

'Yes, My Lord.'

'You hit me over the head.' The sick headache from the blow still lowered, with the rolling menace of distant thunder. 'You almost split my skull!'

Kostya shrugged. He seemed not in the least contrite.

'Why?' Gavril managed to spit out the question at last. 'What gave you the right? To bring me against my will?'

'Because you are our Drakhaon, whether you will or no,' the old warrior said.

'And my mother?' He pictured Elysia alone, frantically searching the villa, the gardens, the empty shore, calling his name in vain. 'I don't suppose you thought to tell her of your plan? Did it ever cross your mind that she might be distressed at finding that her only son has disappeared?'

Kostya shrugged again. 'You can send word to her from Arkhelskoye.'

The swinging lantern-flame was making Gavril feel seasick again; he closed his eyes but still it etched a trail of fire on his lids.

'And how long am I to remain your prisoner?' he heard himself asking as if from a great way off. The tumult of the heaving waves seemed to be growing louder. Kostya's answer sounded as if from far away, a lone sea-mew's cry across fogbound waters.

'You are Drakhaon, Lord; you are not our prisoner.'

'It seems to me . . .' an overwhelming heaviness had begun to seep through Gavril's body, 'that the two . . . are one and the same . . .' The odd taste of the water was still bitter in his dry mouth. Drugged. They had drugged him. He tried one last time to rise up, hand outstretched in impotent anger. The

44

roaring of the foggy waters dinned in his ears and he was falling back down, down through the lightless depths of a nameless sea.

The delirious strains of a waltz whirl through Gavril's dreams. 'White Nights . . .'

He is in the ballroom of the Villa Orlova.

Dark shadow-figures flit past, their faces concealed by grotesque masks: feathered, hook-beaked like birds of prey or grinning like gargoyles. The once-rich hangings are mouldering, powdered with dust, the chandeliers with their guttering candles are draped with grimy cobwebs. But still the dancers spin dizzyingly around the mirrored ballroom to the frenetic waltz.

'Astasia!' he cries, scanning the dance floor for her. He pushes in amongst the frenzied dancers, going from couple to couple, searching.

'Gavril?'

He hears her answering cry and catches sight of her across the floor, pale in her white gown, arms outstretched.

He runs towards her – and the dancers turn on him, the leering, grinning masks looming out of the darkness as they catch hold of him, spinning him around, white-gloved fingers pawing, clawing.

'Help me, Gavril!'

Astasia, dragged away into the darkness . . .

The dance music fractures into discordant fragments, shattering like the shards of a broken mirror . . .

Gavril opened his eyes. The stench of tar, the creak of timbers, the splash of the swell of an ice-cold sea, the incessant rocking, all told him he was still a prisoner on the Azhkendi vessel, sailing ever further away from Astasia by the hour.

White light seared Gavril's eyes: thin, cold winter sunlight. He staggered as he came up on deck and felt Kostya catch hold of him, supporting him.

'One step at a time, Lord Gavril. Easy does it.'

'Where – is – this place?' Gavril covered his dazzled eyes with his hand. He felt as weak as the time he was ill with the quinsy, wandering for days in a raging fever that left him thin and unsteady as a newborn foal. But then he had been dosed with physic, not the powerful sedative drugs he guessed Kostya had used to subdue him.

The barque moved slowly forwards through the ice floes, rocking gently on a sea as pale as milk. Gavril took hold of the rail, trying to steady himself.

'The White Sea,' he murmured.

There was a crackling glitter to the expanse of water that stretched into a misty horizon. The sea glimmered with a sheen of ice. Even the air sparkled with frost.

'We passed the last merchant ships out of Arkhelskoye,' Kostya said, his breath smoking on the frosty air. 'The sea is freezing fast around us.' He leaned on the rail, frowning out at the ice-hazed horizon. 'Too fast. There's some kind of spirit-mischief at work here. Ice at sea when the berries are still red on the moors?'

'Spirit-mischief?' echoed Gavril in disbelief. This must be some old Azhkendi folk-superstition, he supposed.

Kostya gave him a long, hard look. 'Has she taught you nothing of your heritage?'

'So we're cut off.'

'Unless My Lord wishes to fly back to Smarna,' Kostya said with a wry shrug.

Gavril drew in a breath to reply. The air seared his tongue, dry and stingingly cold. The shock silenced him.

He was trapped. Trapped in a barbaric little country, far from any hope of rescue. And if the last ships had left, what means was there of getting a message to Smarna – or to Astasia?

He began to shiver uncontrollably.

'You must be cold, My Lord.'

Kostya wrapped a heavy cloak about his shoulders, a fur cloak pungent with a rank civet smell.

'There is to be a small ceremony, Lord, when we make landfall. To welcome you. To prove to your people that you are Lord Volkh's son. It is the custom in Azhkendir.'

'Proof?' Either the sedatives had not quite worn off yet or the cold had numbed his brain. He had no idea what Kostya was talking about.

'So it's true. Your mother told you nothing. Nothing at all.'

'What should she have said?' Gavril rounded on him. How dare the old man insult his mother? 'That my father never once tried to find us after she left Azhkendir? Left her to raise his son without a sou to her name?'

'You never received any of his letters?' Kostya said. There was a bleak bitterness in his voice.

'Letters!' Gavril's mind was in a whirl. 'He wrote me letters?'

'She must have destroyed them, then. Ah.' Kostya

passed his hand to and fro across his forehead as though trying to order his thoughts. 'So you know nothing of your heritage.'

'Nothing!' Gavril flung back at him. He was shaken now, wondering what terrible truth the old warrior was so reluctant to tell him. *Savage*, Elysia had said, weeping. *Cruel*.

'I knew it was wrong to let you go. I tried to reason with your father, but he was blinded by his love for your mother; he would not keep her against her will. It was always his intention to visit you on your twenty-first birthday to instruct you about your powers. But that was not to be . . .'

'Powers? What powers?'

'It should not have fallen to me to tell you.' Tears glittered once more in the old man's eyes. 'It should have been between father and son. It's not fit.'

'My father is dead. There is no-one else!'

Kostya swallowed hard. 'You are Drakhaon. The blood that burns in your veins is not the blood of ordinary men.'

'So you have told me a hundred times and more. But what *is* Drakhaon?'

'Look.' Kostya raised his arm, pointing to the barque's mainsail. On the white canvas, an emblem was painted in black and silver, an emblem that caught the light of the morning sun and glittered, cold and cruel as winter. Now Gavril could see that the emblem was a great hook-winged creature that seemed to soar as the wind caught it, swelling the sail.

'*Dragon?*' Gavril whispered, transfixed. 'But surely . . . it must be a figure of speech, a title, a . . .'

48

'You are Drakhaon, Lord,' repeated Kostya doggedly.

'But how could my father be a man . . . and a . . . a . . .' Gavril could not bring himself to say the word; the concept was just too ridiculous. Dragons were legends in storybooks for children.

'Drakhaon is not merely dragon, Lord. Drakhaon is dragon-warrior. A man who can wither his enemies with his breath, who fires the warriors of his Clan with the power of his burning blood.'

'No,' Gavril said, laughing aloud at the ludicrous implications. 'No!'

'I was there when your father soared high above the Arkhel stronghold and seared the Arkhel Clan with his breath. The night sky glittered – and our enemies died where they stood.'

'You saw what my father wanted you to see. A clever illusion, maybe. Some trick with gunpowder and poisonous smoke.'

'I know what I saw,' Kostya said, his face closed.

'But look at me. I'm a man, like any other. Where are my wings, my talons, my fire-breathing nostrils?' He could not stop the laughter now; it burned hard and mirthless in his throat.

Kostya seized hold of his hands, turning them over, thrusting them, nails upwards, in front of his face.

'Look. Look! These stains on your nails. Blue stains. See? That's one of the first signs.'

'Old paint stains, nothing more. I'm a painter, remember? Or I was until you kidnapped me.'

'You thought these paint stains? This is just the beginning.'

'You're asking me to believe that if you had not

49

come to tell me, one day I would have woken in my bed to find myself covered in scales, breathing flames and scorching holes in my sheets?'

'That is not how it happens,' Kostya said curtly.

The laughter died; Gavril stared down at his hands, suddenly sobered, as if Kostya had dashed cold water over him.

'Then how exactly does it happen?'

Kostya shook his grizzled head. 'Have you still not understood me? The Drakhaoul claimed you as its own. You are Drakhaon, whether you will or no, until your dying day. Your father's blood runs in your veins. And it is blood-proof that your people will demand to see when we make landfall.'

'What kind of barbaric custom is this?' Gavril cried, drawing back from Kostya. Were they going to sacrifice him?

'If you had been raised in Azhkendir, Lord, you would not find anything unnatural in this. But you know nothing of our ways, nothing of our history. Your history.'

'Blood, Kostya? My blood?' The anger was beginning to simmer again. 'What possible point can there be in the letting of my blood?'

'The renewing of an ancient contract, Lord. Between the Drakhaon and his Clan. A contract of mutual trust. Besides, there is a power in your blood, Lord Gavril.'

Speechless, Gavril turned his back on the Bogatyr, gazing out over the shimmering expanse of ice. White as far as the eye could see. White sea, white sky. For a moment his anger gave way to bleak despair. He was not just a prisoner of these savage Clan warriors with their crazed beliefs in dragons but a prisoner of his own birthright, condemned by the blood that pulsed through his veins to a future dark beyond his darkest imaginings.

Gavril gripped the rail as the Drakhaon's barque was brought alongside the jetty. The timbers ground against stone as sailors leaped ashore, grabbing ropes to make her fast.

Arkhelskoye was a sorry place, more a huddle of deserted wooden buildings, warehouses and customs houses than a prosperous port.

A bell began to clang from the harbour tower, an iron clamour shattering the ice-bound calm. Suddenly the shore was thronging with people. Gavril blinked. Where had they appeared from? There were women, thick shawls wrapped around their heads, rough-bearded sailors trudging through the snow, fur-cloaked Clan warriors and yet more Clan warriors.

'They have come to welcome you,' Kostya said, nudging Gavril towards the quay. Their feet crunched on tight-packed snow as they walked to the end of the jetty.

The crowd stared at Gavril in silence. Expectant silence. Now all he could hear was the thin whisper of a wind that cut like wire ... and the distant crackling of the ice.

Kostya turned to him. He had drawn a curved-edged knife from his belt. The white light glittered on the blade, as keen and translucent as ice.

'Do I have to go through with this?' Gavril asked through gritted teeth. The utter stillness of the watching crowd disturbed him. He could feel their eyes boring into him. What did they expect to see?

'Right-hander, yes?' Kostya gripped hold of Gavril's left hand, palm upwards. Before Gavril could twist away, he had drawn the thin blade across his palm. The cut stung, keen as the whisper of the icy wind.

Gavril stared down at the open wound, too surprised to cry out.

Blood dripped from his palm, a slash of dark liquid welling from his scored skin. But ... had Kostya smeared the blade with some chemical substance to alter it? Shouldn't his blood run red? This was dark, too dark for human blood. Somewhere behind the pain and outrage, his artist's mind tried to define the colour accurately. It was more porphyry-purple than crimson. No, closer to indigo than purple ...

With a grunt of satisfaction, Kostya lifted Gavril's palm high in the air, showing it to the crowd. Blood dripped onto the snow. Where it touched the snow, there was a faint sizzling sound, as though the blood were burning its way down to the soil beneath, staining the white snow dark as ink.

And now, at last, the crowd broke their silence, hushedly, excitedly nudging each other, pointing, exclaiming.

'Say these words after me,' Kostya whispered in Gavril's ear. 'With my blood.'

'With my blood,' Gavril repeated, almost speechless with anger.

'I, Gavril Nagarian, claim my birthright as Lord of Azhkendir.'

'I, Gavril Nagarian,' the knife-slash stung, cold as the icy breath of the wind on his cheeks, 'claim my birthright as Lord of Azhkendir.'

He looked up then into the faces of the *druzhina* who stood silently watching him and it seemed to him that there was a glint of hunger in their eyes, the hunger of a starving wolfpack encircling their prey, waiting for the kill.

Then the shouts of 'Drakhaon!' began. People rushed forwards, straining to touch Gavril. But the *druzhina* moved swiftly to hold them back, arms linked, forming an alley. Kostya took hold of Gavril's arm and hastily led him between the two lines towards a cluster of horses, saddled and bridled, heads down against the wind. Ears ringing from the shouting, Gavril saw nothing but a blur of staring, eager faces and grabbing hands.

As Kostya helped him up into the saddle of a sturdy black gelding, he looked back to the quay. People were pushing and jostling each other to get to the place where he had been standing, scrabbling in the snow. Dully he realized they were fighting to collect the snow that had been stained with his blood. His blood! What primitive superstition made men and women place such faith in the blood of their chosen lord?

He looked down at his palm in disbelief. The blood was clotting already in the searingly dry cold air. In the ice-light it was difficult to tell what colour it was oozing now.

'Let me bind that for you, My Lord.' Kostya pressed a linen pad onto the gash and swiftly tied it in place.

'Why didn't you warn me?' Gavril said, glaring at him.

'Gloves, Lord Gavril.' The old warrior passed him a pair of leather gloves, fur-lined, ignoring his question. 'You'll need these. We have a long ride ahead of us.' And he raised his hand in a gesture of command, impatiently signalling to the *druzhina*, beckoning them towards the waiting horses.

The crowd surged forward as Gavril's bodyguard vaulted onto the backs of their mounts with whoops and wild shouts of exultation. Kostya grabbed hold of Gavril's reins. Hooves rattled on the compacted snow, a muted thunder that shook the timbers of the wooden houses.

Gavril looked at the eager sea of faces as they swept through the crowd. One alone caught his attention. A glint of burnished gold hair, dark eyes, staring at him from a pale face with a singularly intense, unreadable expression. For one moment all the shouts and the dinning of hooves receded into a blur of sound.

A young man's face, eyes dark with pain and horror . . .

Gavril swung around in the saddle, scanning the following crowd. But the face had vanished and the townspeople were dropping behind, only a few energetic ones still pursuing them, waving and shouting his name.

They had been riding north across the moors for two days now since they had disembarked at the port of Arkhelskoye. Inland from the bleak ice-bound coastline, the snows had not yet settled on the bracken-brown moorlands.

At first Gavril had been sunk too deep in despair to notice anything but the bitter cold and the desolation. Hunched in his thick fur cloak, he rode along the moorland tracks in a drugged daze, shoulders braced against the gusts of icy wind that buffeted them.

But as the last effects of the sedation gradually lifted from his mind, he found himself going over and over what had happened in Arkhelskoye. Again he felt the blade bite into his palm, saw the blood sizzle into the snow, staining it with drops as dark as midnight. The knife-cut, tightly bound, still stung beneath his leather riding gloves every time he adjusted the reins.

It was a clever trick to impress the crowd, he allowed, now that he could be more rational about what had happened. Kostya must have used some secret dye on the knife-blade to change the colour of his blood. Maybe it was even a side-effect of the sedative. As for the other talk of dragons and flying . . . he was certain it must be metaphorical. Much as past warrior princes had been named 'the Bear' or 'the Hawk', so the lords of Azhkendir must have gained the title of 'Drakhaon' for their ruthless skills in battle.

Gavril glanced uneasily at the *druzhina* riding on either side of him. Their dour silence was less a trial than a relief. He was in no mood for conversation. They might call themselves his bodyguard but he knew himself their prisoner. Besides, he had not forgotten the look in their eyes when Kostya held aloft his bleeding hand to the crowd in Arkhelskoye. That strange look, hunger and terror intermingled. What was in his blood that they both desired and feared?

A sudden gust of wind swept across the purpled moorlands and Gavril began to shiver. Days away from the sun-gilded shores of Smarna . . . would he ever feel warm again?

In the far distance lay a range of jagged mountains he heard Kostya call the Kharzhgylls. Kostya told him – in one of his rare communicative moments – that they were making for his father's kastel which lay on the borders of the vast forest of Kerjhenezh. On the open moorlands the only trees they passed were single and sparse-branched, but now the wind-bent clumps increased to small groves, and from small groves to bristling woods.

That night they camped in a sandy clearing and the *druzhina* built a small fire of cones and pine twigs. They had nearly used up their store of provisions; all that remained were hunks of stale black bread, strips of dried fish and the water in their flasks. And when Gavril suggested calling at a farmhouse or village to buy food, Kostya turned such a strange look on him from beneath his bushy, iron-grey brows that he did not dare repeat his question.

Whilst Gavril helped water the horses at a nearby stream, Kostya sent the younger men of the *druzhina* in search of wild mushrooms, herbs and pungent berries in the wood. Soon he was brewing a savoury, salty fish broth in which to soften the stale bread.

Gavril sat gazing into the flames of Kostya's fire. He was too exhausted to find the energy to be angry with his abductors any more; his whole body ached from the long hours in the saddle. He reckoned he could feel every muscle in his thighs and calves. Now all he could think of was a bath: a long soak in a hot, steamy tub.

Kostya spooned some of the broth into a bowl and handed it to him; Gavril cupped the hot bowl in his hands, breathing in the savour of wild herbs in the steam. He had not realized till then how ravenous he was.

The *druzhina* ate in silence, draining the bowls to the dregs with satisfied grunts, then wiping the clinging drops of broth from their moustaches with the backs of their hands.

Gavril watched them with a kind of fascinated disgust. Was this what his father had been like? Rough-mannered, taciturn, and battle-scarred? What had Elysia seen in him to make her leave her home and family in Smarna for this wild, desolate place?

He mopped the last of the broth from the sides of the bowl with the bread.

Thinking of Smarna only brought Astasia back into his mind. For a moment the firelit glade blurred as tears filled Gavril's eyes. He had not even been given the chance to send word from Arkhelskoye as Kostya had promised. Was he to be trapped here until the ice melted in the spring? By then she would be married, beyond his reach for ever. Furiously, he blinked the tears away. Tears were no use. He must start to plan his escape.

Kostya hunkered down in front of the fire beside him, stretching his scarred, knotted hands out over the flames to warm them.

'Tomorrow we reach your father's kastel,' he said, 'and you come into your inheritance, Lord Gavril.'

Gavril's wits were sharper now that he had eaten.

'This initiation I must undergo,' he said drily. 'What does that entail? More blood-letting? More conjuring tricks?'

Kostya gave him a long, appraising look; Gavril suddenly felt like a young, raw recruit whose pretence of bravado has been exposed as sham.

'It is a ceremony or a contract,' Kostya said at length, 'between the Drakhaon and his *druzhina*. Do you think that hardened warriors like these would be impressed by conjuring tricks?'

'If I agree to go through with this ceremony,' Gavril said wearily, 'then I want my freedom. I want to be free to come and go as I please. To go back to Smarna.'

'That would be unwise in the circumstances, My Lord.'

'Unwise! Didn't my father meet my mother when he was travelling abroad?'

'Your father had no blood-feud to settle when he met your mother.'

'Blood-feud?' This time it was Gavril who looked searchingly at the old warrior. 'What blood-feud?'

'Whenever a Clan Lord dies dishonoured in Azhkendir, murdered in bed or in his own hall,' Kostya threw a handful of pine cones on the glowing embers of the fire, 'his Clan are blood-bound to find the murderer and exact their revenge.'

'Revenge?' Gavril echoed, dreading what must come next.

'If the murder is not avenged, the spirit of the Clan Lord cannot rest in peace. The land begins to die. Crops fail. Winters never end.'

The cones crackled and spat, drops of crystallized resin flaring up into little flames, giving off the bitter sweetness of burning incense into the black night.

'And the honour of vengeance falls, by right of blood, to the Clan Lord's eldest son.'

'You mean me? I must kill my father's murderer?' Anger flared again, impotent, cold anger. 'Is that what this is about? You've kidnapped me to perpetuate your barbaric blood-feud?'

Smoke billows across his sight, blue smoke, spangled with iridescent firesparks. A young man's face, blood-smeared, turns towards his, eyes dark with pain and horror . . .

Gavril felt the old man's hand on his shoulder, gripping hard, steadying him.

'Are you all right, Lord Gavril?'

Gavril shook his head, trying to clear his sight. The only smoke he could see now was the twisting woodsmoke from their fire, grey and dull.

'But – no-one knows who the murderer is. You told me so yourself.'

Dark eyes staring at him from the crowd at Arkhelskoye with a singularly intense, unreadable expression.

'We'll twist a few more tongues.' Kostya turned his head aside and spat. 'People talk . . . sooner or later.'

That acrid stink of chemicals, the vial of liquid, his father's shuddering cry, 'Who let you in?'

'No assassins will come near you, My Lord. You will be well protected in Kastel Drakhaon.'

Well protected?

The sliding secret panel, the low voice whispering, 'Come this way . . .'

Gavril sat, hugging his knees to his chest. However faithful the *druzhina* professed to be to their Lord Drakhaon, someone within the kastel had betrayed his father. Someone who hated all of the Nagarian blood with an unrelenting, unreasoning hate. Someone who was waiting for him.

4

The youngest and most insignificant housemaid of Kastel Drakhaon came hurtling along the painted corridor, not looking where she was going. Coming towards her was Sosia the housekeeper, weighed down by a pile of clean linen. Kiukiu skidded to a halt – but too late to avoid a collision. Sheets, pillowcases and towels cascaded to the floor.

'Clumsy child!'

A sharp slap to the face; Kiukiu ducked – but not quite fast enough. Her cheek stung.

'Sorry, Auntie Sosia.' Kiukiu dropped to her knees, trying to help Sosia pick up the spilled sheets.

'You'll have to mind your manners, my girl, when our new master arrives. Best stay in the kitchen out of the way. He won't want—'

A bell began to tinkle. Sosia looked up.

'What does *she* want now?'

The bell went on tinkling; a high, insistent, irritating sound. Lilias's bell; Kiukiu pulled a face.

Beautiful Lilias, indolent and heavy with child. Refusing to leave her rooms. Demanding attention at all hours of the day and night. Sosia's slaps might sting, but her anger was soon forgotten. Lilias never forgot a transgression, no matter how small.

Sosia shoved the sheets into Kiukiu's arms.

'Well, I can't send you to see to *her* wants, can I, not after last time? Where's that good-for-nothing maid of hers?'

The bell continued its insistent, petulant tinkle.

'You'll have to make up the bed for Lord Gavril.' Sosia pushed herself up again, shaking the creases from her grey skirts. 'I'll go see to My Lady Lilias. Oh – and don't you dare touch anything. Just make the bed. And go.'

Since the time she was old enough to take up service, Kiukiu had been sent to clean the grates and lay the fires in the kastel bedchambers. She had lugged the heavy buckets of sea-coal and logs up from the outhouses, she had swept and scraped the ashes from the grate, rubbing the iron firedogs clean, day after day. But it was an honour to be allowed into the Drakhaon's chamber, to perform even the most menial task – a fact which Sosia never let her forget, reinforced with many cuffs, slaps and beatings. But Kiukiu never minded being accorded this particular honour, because it meant she could sneak a look at the portrait.

She wandered around, drifting a duster over the dark carved wood of the brocade-curtained bed, the tall chest of ivory-inlaid ebony, the lower chest encrusted with carved dragons, all sharp spines and curved wings, until . . .

Until she reached the portrait. It was set in a

simple frame, so unostentatious that you could have passed it by were it not for the vivid quality of the painting. Whoever the artist was, they had captured a moment in time so intensely that whenever Kiukiu looked at it, she felt as if she were gazing through a window into another world.

The portrait showed a boy of nine or ten years, head slightly turned as if someone had just called his name. His wind-ruffled hair was dark brown, lit with little tips of golden bronze. Behind him, Kiukiu could see a white balcony – and beyond that the blue of the sea. The boy's sunburned features were regular, strong-boned. His expression was serious – though there was something in the way the artist had painted his eyes, the little quirk at the corner of his mouth, that suggested the seriousness was assumed for the solemn occasion of the portrait and that an infectious grin was about to break through. And those eyes – they seemed to follow her when she moved away. Blue as the misty sea behind him, shaded by curling dark lashes and strong, dark brows, there was a luminous gleam to those blue eyes that was so lifelike it made her catch her breath.

When no-one was around, she used to speak to the boy. Who else was there to confide in? Sosia was too busy with the affairs of the household to trouble herself with the feelings of the youngest, lowliest servant-girl. Lilias had taken an instant dislike to her. Lilias's maid, Dysis, ignored her. Ninusha and Ilsi, the other housemaids, were always flirting with Lord Volkh's bodyguards, giggling over secrets together . . .

So Kiukiu spoke to the Lord Drakhaon's son. She knew that the boy in the portrait was Lord Volkh's son, Gavril, and that he had been sent away before the Clan Wars, a few months before she was born. Which would make him about twenty years old, she reckoned on her fingers, as she was so nearly eighteen.

'Why have you never come home, Lord Gavril?' she whispered, lovingly dusting the frame. 'Till now?'

The painted sea shimmered blue, an achingly deep, beautiful blue. Kiukiu had never seen the sea, but if it was anything as blue as in the portrait, she thought she would never want to be anywhere else. If you stared for long enough, it seemed as if the painted water began to ripple, to move . . .

Kiukiu forced her eyes away, focusing on the boy's face.

'They say your mother wouldn't let you return.'

The boy gazed silently back with his clear, sea-blue eyes.

'Because of what Lord Volkh did to her.' Her voice was barely a whisper. Even though the Lord Drakhaon was dead, she still feared him. And dead in such a horrible fashion, burned by an alchymical poison, slashed and stabbed till his blood soaked through the floorboards of the Hall . . .

She shuddered. Best not to think of it.

'Is that bed made up yet, Kiukiu?'

Kiukiu started, startled by Sosia's sharp voice from the corridor outside.

'Nearly finished,' she lied, shaking open the crisp folds of fine, bleached linen. The chill, sombre air of the bedchamber filled with the fragrance of summer-dried lemon balm as she spread the sheet on the mattress and carefully tucked in the corners. Then she plumped up the soft goose-feather quilt and arranged the pillows.

A little door behind the brocade-canopied bed led to the Drakhaon's dressing-room and garderobe.

Better leave some clean towels . . .

Kiukiu slipped inside the little room. Here stood a vast armoire of dark-stained wood containing the Drakhaon's clothes, dwarfing the wash-bowl and jug on its stand. What would become of all those fine linen shirts, those fur-lined winter jackets of black leather stitched with metallic thread, those rich brocade coats, trimmed with the softest velvet?

Dead men's clothes . . .

Lord Gavril would never want to wear them, no matter how expensive the cloth . . .

Kiukiu carefully placed the towels by the wash-bowl and straightened up, catching sight of a fragment of her reflection in the full-length, gilt-framed glass mirror that stood behind the armoire, still draped in a dark cloth, a funeral custom of Azhkendir.

She knew well enough the old stories told around the kitchen fire at night, superstitions about the souls of the departed. Stories that said the restless dead could use the shadows of their reflections in mirrors and glass to clothe themselves, could return to haunt the living.

But Lord Volkh had been laid to rest in the Nagarian mausoleum with all the funerary rites due to a Drakhaon of Azhkendir. And Lord Gavril would be here by evening.

Kiukiu whisked off the mourning cloth and folded it into four. She sneaked a glance at herself and, in case Sosia came in and caught her preening, gave the glass a perfunctory polish with the cloth.

Did she really resemble her mother, long-dead Afimia? Whenever she asked Sosia, Sosia would nod and then let slip ambiguous little snippets such as, 'Of course poor Fimia's hair was so much lighter than yours . . .'

But all Kiukiu could see in the mirror was a homely kind of face. Strong cheekbones, a broad brow, long straight hair that was more wheaten gold than pale barley, plaited and tucked away beneath a bleached linen kerchief, and freckles. Try as she might to rub them away with herbal concoctions, they stubbornly remained, dusting her sun-browned skin like specks of golden pollen. No lady of quality had freckles. Lilias's skin was pale as early almond blossom, unblemished, translucent. Even now that Lilias was so heavily pregnant, her complexion had retained its becoming pallor. Her rich chestnut hair was sleek and glossy – and so it should be, Kiukiu thought scornfully, after the hundred brushstrokes Dysis had to administer every day.

Now the dressing-room looked a little less dour but it was hardly a suitable apartment for a young man. Even Lord Volkh had spent little time here, working late in the night in his study in the Kalika Tower. Kostya said that the Drakhaon liked to study the stars from the roof of the tower, that he and Doctor Kazimir were often to be found together, charting the constellations with the doctor's telescopes.

But all that had been before. Before their quarrel, before the terrible events that followed . . .

Kiukiu felt a strange, sudden chill in the little room. She shivered involuntarily, rubbing her arms, feeling the skin rough with goosebumps.

She sensed that there was someone else behind her, and yet there had been no sound of footsteps or a door opening.

'Who's there?' The question came out sharp-spiked and tense.

'*Kiukirilya.*'

'Ilsi? Ninusha? If this is a joke—'

The room darkened as if winter fogs had drifted in from the moors. The damp-cold air tasted of the lightless dark of winter and despair.

'*Turn around, Kiukirilya.*' The words resonated in her mind like the sombre din of the funeral bells in Saint Sergius's monastery, tolling out across Azhkendir for their dead lord.

'No,' she said in a small voice, resisting.

'*Help me, Kiukirilya.*'

Slowly, unwillingly, she turned around. The mirror had become a yawning portal of rushing darkness from which wisps of fog escaped, colder than winter's chill. And framed in the centre of the portal stood a tall figure of a man, a warrior, his hands reaching out to her through the swirling mists. The terrible burns of the alchymical poison still disfigured his face, stains of dried blood marked the gaping wounds through which his life had leaked away . . .

'Lord Volkh?' she whispered. Her tongue was frozen with fear. She was talking with the dead.

'*My son Gavril, I must speak with my son.*' The words shivered into her mind, bitter as hoarfrost. How could she hear him so clearly against the chaotic roar of the darkness?

'*Bring me through, Kiukirilya.*'

'M-me?' Her heart seemed to have stopped beating. 'Why me?'

'*Because you have the gift.*' Blue, the spirit's eyes were, intensely blue as starfire on a winter's night. '*You have the gift to bring me through.*'

'I – I can't bring you through, Lord Drakhaon.' She wanted to back away but his gaze held her frozen to the spot. What gift did he mean? She had no special gifts; she was only a serving-maid. She fought to close her mind to the relentlessly tolling voice, to turn away from the lifeless stare of those compelling blue eyes. 'I d-don't know how.'

'*For my son's sake. I must warn him. Before it's too late.*'

'Warn Lord Gavril? Is he in danger?' Those ghost stories told around the kitchen fire on winter nights still niggled at the back of her memory. Something you were not supposed to say, to do, in the presence of a revenant ... But the chill fog seemed to have seeped into her memory, and there was nothing in her mind but smoke and shifting shadows.

'*Kiukiu. Use your gift.*' A spectral hand reached out towards her, frail as a skeletal leaf blackened with glittering frost. '*Help me.*'

She reached out to touch the revenant's hand. What was she doing? Something at the back of her mind cried out to her to stop before it was too late ...

She stood on a bare, scorched plain, dark storm-clouds scudding fast overhead, distant bleak foothills, gullies of grey scree, all empty, desolate, lifeless ...

'Where have you brought me?' she cried but her voice was drowned by the howl of the wind. Stinging grit gusted into her face, a hailshower of burning dust. 'What is this terrible place?'

'*Look.*'

Through her dust-stung eyes she began to make out a slow stir of movement in the plain. As she stared, she saw they were human forms, some crawling laboriously, mindlessly onwards across the barren plain, others so exhausted they had collapsed, lying half-buried in dust, grey statues of petrified lava.

Pity and horror wrung her heart. But at the same time she knew she must escape before she found herself drowning in the stinging dust. She forced herself to turn away, straining back towards the distant glimmer of light.

'*Don't condemn me to eternity here.*' The revenant still held fast to her hand, gripped it with a desperate strength and would not let go. '*Bring me through, Kiukirilya!*'

'I can't, I daren't—'

Then they were falling, tumbling back down through a turbulence of boiling thundercloud and whirling, sere-cold wind . . .

Her whole being fought the pull of the darkness. She wanted to let go, to shake herself free of the revenant, but still it clung on.

The mirror frame glimmered ahead, a portal limned in stardust.

She strove towards the daylight, the shadow clinging fast to her hand. It was like swimming up through the cold, heavy waters of the Silver Lake in the forest, kicking free of the treacherous pull of the hidden currents. One more effort and she would reach the surface . . .

Suddenly she felt herself tumbling out onto the floor of the dressing-room. Her head hit the floor – and the room about her seemed to explode into little stars of pain.

'Kiukiu. Kiukiu!'

Someone was shaking her. She wished they wouldn't. It only made the aching in her head worse.

'Don't . . .'

She looked up and saw Sosia's face frowning down at her.

'What happened?' Kiukiu asked, trying to sit up. Her head only ached more; a dull throbbing spread from the back of her skull to her temples. She closed her eyes again.

'What happened? I come in to find why you're not in the kitchen and there you are, stretched out on the floor and the mirror broken. Now you tell *me* what happened, my girl! Is it your monthlies?'

'No, Auntie.'

'Look at this mess! Glass everywhere. You're lucky you didn't cut yourself.'

Kiukiu blinked. Shards of mirror glass lay on the floor, on her skirts.

'You'll have to do extra work to pay for this, Kiukiu. Mirrors don't come cheap!'

'I – I'm sorry . . .'

'Have you eaten? I can't have my girls passing out. Not today of all days, when Lord Gavril is expected. You've got a nasty bruise on your head; go and dab some of my witchhazel on it before it swells up into an egg.' Sosia gave Kiukiu her hand and pulled her to her feet. 'At least you had the foresight to faint after you'd finished changing the bed.'

Kiukiu looked about her warily. What had happened? Had she brought the shadow through? Did the dressing-room feel any different? Colder, maybe; the kind of unearthly cold that made the little hairs rise on your arms. And was there a slight taint of gravedust in the air?

But everything looked just as it had before – except for the shattered mirror.

'Fetch your dustpan and sweep up this mess.'

It must have just been a trick of her imagination, a vivid illusion brought on by a blow to the head.

'Don't dawdle, Kiukiu!' called back Sosia sharply. 'There's work to be done.'

'Coming . . .'

Kiukiu hesitated – then took up the carefully folded cloth and draped it over the mirror frame. Just in case . . .

'What's the matter with you, Kiukiu?' Ilsi glanced up from the herbs she was chopping – but not at Kiukiu, over her head, catching Ninusha's eye. 'Cat got your tongue?'

Kiukiu, cheeks hot with the steam rising from the beetroot soup she was stirring on the great cooking range, sensed that Ilsi was out to cause trouble. Ilsi and Ninusha found Kiukiu-baiting a perpetual source of amusement. Kiukiu had patiently endured their taunts since they were children. She had always been the odd one out when it came to games and choosing friends. Their scornful teasing had caused her many tears when she was little, the youngest, unwanted one, tagging along behind the older kastel children, begging to be allowed to join in.

'I'm tired,' she said, squeezing some lemon juice into the rich, red soup. She hoped that would stop them pestering her. Besides, her head still ached.

'Sosia's favouring her sister's child again,'

Ninusha said to Ilsi. Talking about Kiukiu as if she were not present was another childhood torment that had carried over into adulthood. 'Letting her prepare Lord Gavril's bedchamber. Such an honour.'

'Lord Gavril. They say he's not much above twenty. Good-looking too.' Ilsi gave a coquettish little shake of her fair curls, twisted into bunches like yellow catkins.

'Think you can compete with Lady Lilias?' Ninusha said with a giggle. 'What's the odds that she'll be fluttering her lashes at Lord Gavril within a day of his arrival?'

'Lilias?' Ilsi gave a snort of laughter as she scraped the chopped herbs into the bowl of salad leaves. 'She's as fat as a farrowing sow these days. He won't give her a second glance.'

'And won't she just hate that?' Ninusha said, breaking into delighted giggles.

'Ninusha!' cried Sosia, appearing with a tray which she put down on the table with a crash. 'What possessed you to sprinkle cinnamon on the Lady Lilias's dish of *sutlage*? You know she can't abide the smell or taste of it! Whatever were you thinking of? Now she's in a temper and blaming me.'

'Must've forgotten,' Ninusha said with a shrug. 'Everyone else has cinnamon on *sutlage*. Why does *she* have to be different?'

'Pregnancy affects you that way,' Ilsi said. 'My mam said she couldn't be in the same room as anyone who had eaten garlic when she was carrying me. But I love garlic!'

'You'll just have to prepare some more.'

'Pregnant women and their stupid little fads.

That's the fourth bowl she's pigged today. She'll turn into *sutlage* if she goes on eating so much of it. White and glutinous . . .'

'Perhaps she'll stay fat after she's had the baby,' Ilsi said with a malicious little smile. 'Lolling around all day, making us wait on her hand and foot. Who does she think she is? He never married her. She was only his whore.'

'Ilsi!' Sosia slammed her fist down on the kitchen table, making the pots rattle. 'That's enough. I won't have idle gossip in my kitchen. You're here to work, not chatter.'

Kiukiu glanced up to see Ilsi pull a sour face at Sosia behind her back.

'Here's Lady Lilias's pudding.' Ninusha slopped some cold *sutlage* into a clean bowl and slammed it down on the little lacquer tray.

'Don't forget the chopped pistachio nuts,' Sosia said, not even glancing up from the pastry she was rolling.

Kiukiu was looking longingly at the rejected bowl, with its brown sprinkling of powdered cinnamon. To throw it away would be a wicked waste. She loved the smooth, creamy taste of the ground-rice dessert; she loved the subtle sweetness of the precious rose-water Sosia used to flavour it. No-one would mind, surely, if she just took a spoonful or two . . .

'Talking of greedy pigs,' rang out Ilsi's voice spitefully, 'look at Kiukiu. Caught with her nose in the trough!'

Guiltily, Kiukiu gulped down a mouthful of pudding, wiping the back of her hand across her mouth as if she could erase the sweet, sticky traces of her crime.

'You know the rules of my kitchen, Kiukiu,' Sosia said, shaking her rolling pin at her. 'No women servants to eat leftovers from the Drakhaon's table until the men have had their fill. Have you any idea how much rose-water costs these days? Or pistachios? Or lemons?'

'No supper for you tonight, Kiukiu,' whispered Ilsi.

'I could make rose-water,' Kiukiu protested. 'It can't be that difficult.'

'Don't change the subject,' Sosia said. 'Besides – where would you find the rose petals? And when was the last time roses bloomed without blight at Kastel Drakhaon?'

'It just looked so good,' Kiukiu said contritely, 'and I was *so* hungry.'

'So hungry,' mimicked Ninusha.

'Listen!' Sosia lifted one floury hand for silence. 'Horses.'

Kiukiu, glad of the distraction, ran to the window, opened the shutter and peeped out into the dark courtyard.

Torches flared; the black shadows of mounted warriors came clattering in over the cobbles beneath the archway.

'The *druzhina*,' she cried excitedly. 'Lord Gavril's here!'

'Out the way!' Ilsi and Ninusha elbowed her aside, eagerly peering out into the night.

'Silly girl, it's just the vanguard,' Ilsi said. 'There can't be more than twenty riders. Look, Ninusha, there's Michailo! Michailo! What's the news from Smarna?'

Kiukiu, standing on tiptoe behind the two maids,

saw the young man leap down from his mount and wave.

'Lord Gavril will be here within the hour. Tell Sosia.'

'You look well, Michailo,' Ilsi said, simpering.

'I'm famished!' cried Michailo, laughing. 'Tell Sosia we're all famished.'

'You hear that, Sosia?' Ilsi said. 'Within the hour!'

'Ilsi, put this dish of carp in the bake-oven. Watch it like a hawk and don't let it burn. Ninusha, finish this pie off for me. And Kiukiu – you'd better take this bowl up to my lady's rooms now before her bell starts jangling again,' Sosia said, wiping her hands on her apron.

'*Me?*' Kiukiu said, horrified.

'Give it to Dysis. My lady need never know who brought it.'

'Make sure you don't spill it, Kiukiu,' mocked Ilsi.

Flustered, Kiukiu took up the tray and set out towards the Lady Lilias's rooms. The dark-panelled corridors and echoing hallways of the kastel which had been empty and silent for weeks were now filled with men; warriors tramped up and down the polished stairs, the air echoing to their shouts and the clatter of their boots. Only the most trusted members of the *druzhina* were allowed in the Drakhaon's wing of the kastel; Volkh personally selected those who stood guard. But since the Drakhaon's . . . Kiukiu shuddered, hardly allowing herself to even think the word . . . since his death, the old guards were gone. Put to the question first by Bogatyr Kostya, then brutally executed. No mercy shown.

If any of them had been part of a conspiracy, none had revealed it. They had gone to their deaths tight-lipped, silent – except to declare on the scaffold that they deserved death for not protecting their lord in his hour of need. His murder dishonoured them. And what was one of the *druzhina* without his honour?

So she hurried past the warriors, eyes cast down, careful that she did not trip and spill Lilias's sweet rice *sutlage*. The honeyed scent of the beeswax polish she had rubbed into the panelled walls was overlaid by the musky animal smell of men. The invasion was at once alarming and exhilarating. Yet she knew no-one would notice her; she was only dumpy, frumpy Kiukiu, after all, not dark, languorous Ninusha or fickle Ilsi – or Dysis with her charming Mirom accent and refined manners.

Long before she reached Lilias's room she could hear the petulant tinkling of Lilias's silver bell. The Drakhaon had given his mistress fine rooms on the first floor of the kastel, overlooking the neglected kastel gardens with a view to the distant mountains beyond.

She reached the door to Lilias's anteroom.

Please let Dysis open, she prayed as she tapped at the door.

From behind the heavy door she thought she caught the sound of a woman's voice raised, harsh and shrill, ranting.

She tapped again, a little louder this time.

From within came the sudden sound of smashing crockery.

Kiukiu stepped back from the door. Perhaps she should go away . . .

The door opened a crack. To Kiukiu's relief, Dysis's face appeared. But the maid's face was flushed, her little lace coif, usually perched neatly on her immaculately arranged hair, was awry, stray wisps of brown hair escaping from the lace.

'*Sutlage* for my lady,' gabbled Kiukiu, thrusting the tray forwards. 'Without cinnamon.'

'It's true, isn't it?' Dysis said, her voice a little breathless. 'The new Lord Drakhaon is here.'

'Within the hour. So Michailo says.'

Dysis's pretty mouth briefly twisted into a grimace; she took the tray from Kiukiu and closed the door before Kiukiu could say any more.

As Kiukiu turned to go back to the kitchens, she heard a muffled shriek – and then another crash, sharp with the shards of shattering porcelain.

Kiukiu winced as she crept away. All that sweet, rich pudding wasted, reduced to a splatter of slimy, sticky mess to be painstakingly wiped away by poor Dysis.

Poor Dysis? She stopped, wondering at herself. She had never pitied Dysis before. She had always envied Dysis her elegant Muscobar ways, her pretty looks, her efficiency and neatness. What did it matter that her mistress Lilias happened to be difficult to please? Surely the rewards of service to the Drakhaon's mistress outweighed the discomforts. The discarded clothes alone must make it worthwhile, the silk gloves, the lace petticoats, the gowns worn once or twice then tossed aside! Kiukiu looked sadly at her patched, stained gown, a hand-me-down from Sosia, which had faded from brown to an indeterminate shade of grey with many scrubbings. She had another gown, more discreetly patched, kept for 'best'. It had once been blue, a clear sky-blue like flax-flowers . . .

'Kiukiu! What're you dawdling up here for?' Sosia was standing in the hallway below, glaring up at her. 'Get back to the kitchens and baste the roasting fowl. Lord Gavril won't want to eat a plateful of dry leather!'

'I've had tables set in the panelled Dining-Room.' Sosia's voice was becoming cracked and hoarse with issuing orders. 'Kiukiu – go and make sure Oleg's drawn ten flagons of barley beer, as I told him. Make sure he's not still in the cellar, sampling the new keg. Tell him to get upstairs and brush off the cobwebs.'

Kiukiu sighed and opened the door to the cellar, only to hear Sosia saying, 'To wait at table – Ninusha and Ilsi.'

Ninusha and Ilsi. Not Kiukiu.

'Sosia, can't I help?' she said plaintively.

Sosia gave a sigh. 'What are you still doing here? Go get Oleg. And no, you can't wait at table, Kiukiu, and you know why.'

Because I'm too clumsy, Kiukiu thought angrily, fumbling her way down the dank cellar steps by the greasy rope rail.

At the bottom of the stone stairs a lantern hung, faintly illumining the clammy air which was stale with the smell of old ale.

'Oleg?' Kiukiu called into the darkness, a little uncertainly. Dusty webs clung to the stones. There were great granny spiders down here as big as her fist; she had seen them.

Around the corner of the archway, she came upon

the massive barrels of oak; beer on one side, the smaller barrels of rich, red wine imported from the sun-baked vineyards of Smarna on the other.

Oleg, the Drakhaon's butler, stood with his back to her, surreptitiously sampling the beer from the furthest barrel. Obviously he had not heard her – or Sosia.

'Oleg!' Kiukiu said again.

He started, turning around with a telltale froth of beer-foam whitening his grey moustaches.

'Kiukiu,' he said, grinning leeringly at her. 'You won't tell Sosia, will you?'

'She wants the flagons in the Lower Hall. Ten.'

'She's a slave-driver, that woman. Ten flagons! Come here and give your old Uncle Oleg a hand, Kiukiu, there's a good girl.'

Kiukiu came forwards reluctantly. Being alone with Oleg in the cellar where no-one else could hear made her feel very uncomfortable. She didn't want to be pawed by the lecherous old man. Besides, he was not her uncle. He was no relation to her at all.

'You lift that flagon for me, girl, my back's playing me up . . .'

A gust of his beery breath, stale as the cellar air, made her wrinkle her nose in disgust. She bent to pick up the brimming flagon and felt his hands on her buttocks. She took in a deep breath then stepped backwards, stamping down her heel on his foot, hard. Beer slopped onto the floor.

'Ouch! What'd you want to do that for?'

'Don't touch me!' she hissed, retreating. 'Don't ever touch me again!'

'I was only brushing off a spider. A big one—'

'Tell that to Sosia.'

'There's another nine flagons here—'

'You'll just have to carry them yourself.'

She reached the stairs and, hitching up her skirts with one hand, began to climb up, staggering under the weight of the heavy flagon.

'Hard-hearted whore,' Oleg was muttering to himself, loud enough so that she could hear. 'Just like her mother. Cold as you please to honest men.' He had reached the bottom of the stair and was teetering drunkenly upwards behind her. 'Yet slut enough to open her legs to any passing Arkhel Clansman.'

'What did you say?' Kiukiu turned slowly around, gazing down at Oleg.

'You heard me.' His face was twisted now with a vindictive snarl. 'Your mother Afimia. Arkhel's whore.'

'She was *raped*!' Kiukiu shrieked. 'She didn't have any choice!'

Suddenly the day's accrued insults were too much to endure. She swung the flagon – and emptied it over Oleg's head. For a moment he stood, mouth open, drenched in the flood of beer. Then as his bellow of outrage echoed around the cellar, she turned and fled, sobbing, towards the kitchen, tearing past Ninusha and Ilsi, towards the back door into the stableyard – and the night.

Kiukiu crouched in the darkest corner of the stables, her apron clutched to her mouth to try to stifle the choking sobs that shook her whole body.

She was sick of her life at Kastel Drakhaon. She was sick of being the butt of Ninusha's and Ilsi's spiteful jokes, of being fumbled by lewd old men like Oleg, of Sosia's shrill nagging. There was not a single soul in the whole kastel who cared for her, to whom she could go and pour out her heart. She was just a nuisance to them, a thing to be used and abused.

All her life she had been told how grateful she should be to Sosia for taking care of her when Afimia died, how a life of servitude was the best a · poor bastard child, misbegotten spawn of the enemy Clan, could ever dare to hope for.

Well, she had dared to hope. There had to be more to life than the drudgery of the kitchen and scullery. And she would run away to find it. She wouldn't stay to be maltreated any longer.

The cold night was suddenly splashed bright with torchflames; Kiukiu heard the kastel gates grind open and the iron clatter of hooves on the cobblestones. She knuckled the tears from her eyes, feeling a gust of frosty night air stinging her wet cheeks.

Run away without even catching one glimpse of Lord Gavril?

She crept to the stable entrance, peeping out into the night. Even though her thoughts were in turmoil, she forgot her unhappiness as she searched amongst the dismounting warriors for the boy from the portrait. Shadows and torchlight twisted and flickered in the darkness, men shouted to each other – and for a moment, she was certain she had missed him, certain he must have gone ahead into the kastel.

And then she saw him.

He stood gazing about him, the one still figure amidst the moving warriors, the tossing horses' heads, watching, assessing, his face betraying no emotion. By Saint Sergius, Kiukiu whispered in her heart, he is every bit as handsome as I thought he would be. Those eyes, can they really burn so blue? Was Lord Volkh ever so good-looking? It must be his mother's warm Smarnan blood. His skin seems to glow gold in the torchlight, the gold that comes from the warm kiss of the summer's sun, not the harsh burning of the winter's wind or the cruel dazzle of the high snowfields . . .

At his side stood Bogatyr Kostya, stiffly protective, gesturing to him to ascend the wide stone stair that led up to the front door. In the dark, Kiukiu thought, Lord Gavril would not see that the stairs were cracked with frost, the grey stone mottled with lichen and stained with weather.

What must he be thinking? she wondered as the *druzhina* drew their sabres in salute as Lord Gavril slowly climbed the steps. He was so young when he was taken away from Azhkendir. Does he remember anything of this place? Does he remember anything of his father? Then she shuddered. What had Kostya told Lord Gavril of the Drakhaon, his father? Could he have any idea?

And then, as the heavy front doors to the kastel closed behind Lord Gavril and the *druzhina* came tramping into the stables to rub down their horses, Kiukiu slipped silently into the courtyard.

The night air was crisp. Frost was already glistening on the damp cobblestones. Kiukiu shivered, clasping her arms tight to herself.

Winter was coming. If she ran away tonight, she would freeze to death in a ditch. No, better to endure Sosia's anger one more night. And she would endure it willingly if only to snatch another glimpse of Lord Gavril.

5

Dish after unfamiliar dish was presented to Gavril:
a hot, red soup in which great daubs of soured
cream floated; cold jellied carp; salmon baked in
papery pastry with bitter, aromatic leaves and
rice . . .

But he was too weary to take more than a mouthful of each course, slowly, mechanically chewing,
hardly tasting the food, longing to escape the intense
scrutiny of his father's household. All he really
wanted was a hot bath.

'Lord Gavril is tired after the long journey,'
Kostya said. 'My Lord, let me escort you to your
bed.'

No hope of escape, even now. Kostya had not let
him out of his sight once since they arrived.

As they reached the head of the stairs, Gavril saw
two of the *druzhina* had taken up positions outside
a dark carved door at the end of the landing.
And as they saw him, they struck their chests with

their fists in salute and flung open the door for him.

'So I'm still your prisoner,' he said, his voice dry with bitterness.

'It is for your own safety, My Lord,' said Kostya. 'We have lost one Drakhaon through our own negligence. We must not lose another.'

As Gavril entered the room, he heard the door close behind him and a key turn in the lock.

No hope of a bath tonight. He would have to sleep as he was, dirty, stinking of travel. He sank onto the bed and started to tug off his riding boots. He wrinkled his nose in disgust as his feet emerged, the socks stiff with grime and sweat, almost glued to his feet.

He lay back on the bed, curtained by the sombre brocades, dark as his own despair. Locked in, like a criminal in the cells.

'In my father's bedchamber,' he said aloud softly. The room betrayed little of its previous occupant. The tapestries, like all the others in the kastel, showed hunting scenes. The sheets smelled crisp and fresh, faintly perfumed with the leaves of dried summer herbs. A little fire crackled in the grate, warming the chill of the room. It could have been any wealthy landowner's bedchamber for all that it told him of Lord Volkh Nagarian.

And then he caught, through heavy lids, the glint of firelight on a portrait on the wall.

Curiosity overcame tiredness. He forced himself from the comfort of the bed to inspect the picture – and found himself staring at his childhood self. Young Gavril. Ten or eleven years old. And the picture was so vividly painted that he knew it could only be his mother Elysia's work.

Had she painted it because his father had requested it of her? Or had she painted it as a reminder, a poignant message to Lord Volkh saying, 'Don't forget you have a son who is fast growing up'?

All these years he had believed his father had taken no interest in him. He had even secretly wondered if his father had abandoned his mother because of him. Some men were like that, Elysia said, moving on to the next conquest when the demands of domesticity became too constricting.

Now he saw that his father had kept his picture here in his bedchamber, the first thing he saw when he awoke each morning, the last before he closed his eyes to sleep.

Tears suddenly pricked his eyes, stingingly hot.

'Father,' he whispered.

But if he had hoped to find some further connection with the father he could not remember, he had found none. There was nothing here but a void.

He must escape. As soon as it was light he would begin to make his plans, observing, watching for any weakness, no matter how small, in the defences Kostya had set up 'for his own safety'.

Gavril slowly undid the buttons on his jacket and shrugged it off, letting it lie on the floor where it fell. Then he snuffed out the oil-lamp and crawled onto the bed. The flickering fireshadows gradually dimmed as the glowing coals crumbled to ash, and he slept.

The diamond-paned windows of the Drakhaon's bedchamber looked out not over the inner courtyards of the kastel, but over swathes of moorland and brooding forest stretching far into the hazy distance where the horizon was crowned by jagged mountains, half-wreathed in swirling cloud. Beneath the fast-scudding cloud, Gavril caught a shimmer of fresh snow on the peaks.

He unhooked the catch; opening one window, he felt the fresh air cold on his face, faintly tinged with the aromatic fragrance of oozing pine sap.

No way of escape here; there was a sheer drop of twenty feet or more to the yard below. Stories of prisoners knotting sheets together to improvise a way of escape came to mind. He might reach the ground, but at the entrance to the courtyard he could see guards patrolling the walls; he would never get past his own bodyguard.

There came a sharp rap at the door.

'Lord Gavril? Are you awake?' Bogatyr Kostya's voice was powerful enough to carry across a parade-ground. Gavril hastily closed the window.

A key turned in the lock and servants came in, bowing and murmuring greetings, one bearing a bowl of hot water, another a tray of food.

'Lord Volkh always took his first meal here,' Kostya said, 'whilst we discussed the day's arrangements.'

Gavril looked at the breakfast tray: a bowl of a thick porridge; a pewter mug filled with strong spiced ale; and a hunk of coarse bread with a slice of hard-rinded pungent yellow cheese. Soldiers' rations. He was used to croissants and a bowl of hot chocolate, with maybe a fresh apricot or two picked from the espaliered trees in the villa gardens. His stomach had still not recovered from the unfamiliar food last night. He turned away from the tray.

'I sent word of your arrival to Azhgorod last night,' said Kostya. 'The lawyers are on their way here for the reading of your father's will. As soon as you are ready, My Lord, you must authorize the reopening of the Great Hall.'

The walls leading to the Great Hall were lined with hunting tapestries; Gavril saw scene after gory scene of blood and slaughter: the lolling heads of butchered stags, bears and wolves filled each stitched canvas.

Kostya halted before a pillared doorway. The way was barred with planks of wood nailed across the doors. Two of the *druzhina* stood on guard outside.

'Open the doors,' said Kostya.

The warriors glanced at each other – the first time Gavril had seen any of the *druzhina* hesitate to execute a command – then took their axes to the planks, levering and hacking until, with a splintering crack, the wood came away and the doors swung open.

'Now the shutters,' Kostya said.

Gavril watched with a growing sense of unease. That queasy feeling of dread had returned, like a cold, sick fever. He did not want to cross the threshold. He wanted to turn and run, to find the crisp brightness of the autumn day outside.

'Come, My Lord,' Kostya said, ushering him over the threshold.

No torches lit the Great Hall, guttering their smoke into the shadows. But beneath his feet Gavril saw the same black and ochre patterned tiles which in his vision had been slimed with blood.

He was standing only a few feet from where his father had lain dying.

If he closed his eyes, he could see again the flash of spangled light that seared the eyes, could smell again the reek of burning flesh, could feel the dying man's last, agonized gasps as his consciousness faded . . .

'*Remember.*'

He opened his eyes. Etched against the daylight a figure of shadow wavered, tall, broad-shouldered.

The air breathed cold as winter fog; there was an unpleasant, mouldering taint to it, like decaying leaves and chill earth.

'*Gavril.*'

'Father?' Gavril whispered.

'*My son.*' The revenant's voice shuddered through him, each word a sliver of ice. Then the revenant suddenly crumpled to the floor, a figure sprawled in the ungainly attitude of death, dark blood leaking like ink onto the tiles from the slack mouth.

A second shadow came billowing like curling smoke from Lord Volkh's breast until it towered above Gavril, blotting out the daylight, the shadow of a great daemon-serpent, hooked wings outspread, darker than a thundercloud.

Sick and faint, Gavril felt himself swaying, falling . . .

Strong hands gripped his shoulders, supporting him.

'Steady, lad,' muttered Kostya's voice in his ear.

Gavril blinked. *There's nothing there. Look.* In the daylight, he could see that the tiles had been washed clean. But Kostya and the young guard who had let them in were staring at the same spot, transfixed.

'This is where he died, isn't it?' Gavril said shakily.

'Aquavit for Lord Gavril!' barked Kostya, recovering. 'Hurry, Michailo!'

The young guard went running out, and returned with a metal flask, which Kostya thrust into Gavril's hands.

'Drink.'

Gavril put the flask to his lips and took a mouthful. The aquavit burned his throat like fire. Cleansing fire. Coughing, eyes watering, he handed the flask back to Kostya, who took a long swig himself before passing it to the young guard who had brought it.

'This is bad, very bad,' Kostya muttered. It was the first time Gavril had seen him disconcerted.

'You saw it too?'

'I saw what I saw. And you, Michailo?'

The young man started; beneath his sunburned cheeks, Gavril noticed that he had turned as pale as whey.

'I saw My Lord Volkh as he was when he was alive. May the Blessed Sergius preserve me from such a sight again. The dead should not walk with the living.'

'My father's ghost?' Gavril said softly. He did not believe in ghosts. But there had been something here in this room for which he could find no other name.

'Once a spirit-wraith has been called back into our world, it is very hard to persuade it to return,' Kostya said.

'And who could have summoned it?' said Michailo.

'I aim to find out,' Kostya said darkly.

Gavril's eyes kept returning to the distinctive patterns on the tiles, the black serpent, wings spread against the ochre background. How could he have dreamed all this so accurately? And the painted panels and beams, the wreathing carved friezes of ivy in which bright-beaked wooden birds nested?

Why? he silently asked his dead father. *Why have you laid this burden on me? I didn't ask to be born your son. I didn't ask to be Lord of Azhkendir. Why must I inherit your feuds, your hatreds, your vendettas?*

The wall behind the dining-table was hung with spiked oval shields, each one painted with the black and silver device Gavril had first seen darkening the barque's mainsail: the winged serpent. And beneath the shields hung a gold-framed portrait draped with black funeral cloths and crowned with dried sprigs of rosemary and rue. No flowers for a dead Clan Lord, only his weapons, polished to lethal brilliance, laid reverently in tribute.

'Lift the cloth,' Kostya said, gently pushing Gavril forwards.

Gavril pulled the cloth to one side and, mouth dry with apprehension, gazed upwards.

The portrait showed a man in the prime of life, dark-haired, dark-browed, gazing back at Gavril with eyes of the same brooding intense blue as his own. But there the resemblance ended; the Drakhaon's long, curling hair and beard were of a black so glossily dark the painter had picked out the little highlights in cobalt, an artist's trick Gavril had learned from Elysia. But this was not Elysia's work. Everything about this portrait of Lord Volkh Nagarian spoke of power and control; the proud gaze, the unyielding stance, the grim, firm-set mouth. The Drakhaon was sombrely dressed in black; his only concession to ornament was a blue-stoned signet ring on his gloved left hand and the embroidered device of the winged serpent in silver and sapphire threads on the left sleeve of his jacket. On his head he wore a hat trimmed with sable fur. Behind him, the artist had detailed a wintry landscape: a snow-covered vista of forests and mountains stretching into infinity, implying that the Drakhaon's domains were too vast to portray.

'This is not the picture my mother painted,' Gavril said, unable to take his eyes from the likeness. 'What happened to her portrait?'

Kostya gave a little shrug. 'In an attic, a cellar . . . There was a time when your father could not bear to have anything near him that reminded him of her.'

'Are there no more recent portraits than this?'

Kostya did not reply. Gavril turned around and saw that the old man was evidently struggling to find an answer to his question.

'Well, Kostya?'

'Lord Volkh took a dislike to having his portrait painted.'

'But why?' Gavril asked, puzzled. 'Was there some reason? You said there was a war, a bitter Clan War. Was he scarred in the fighting? Disfigured?'

'He was . . . not the same,' Kostya said obliquely. 'It . . . altered him.'

'What do you mean?'

'My Lord, there are many people waiting to meet you. There will be time in plenty to talk of your father later.'

It was as blatant a change of subject as Gavril had heard since he arrived. Looking at the old warrior's face he saw that Kostya was not going to answer his question.

'Indeed, Kostya, you are right. I have been impatiently waiting to meet you, Lord Gavril.'

A woman's voice, sweet as lavender honey, made Gavril start.

'Who gave permission for *you* to be admitted?' Kostya said gruffly.

All Gavril saw at first were green eyes, green as forest glades, and the sheen of glossy chestnut hair. Then the woman moved slowly towards him through the shaft of bright daylight and he saw that she was pregnant, heavily pregnant.

'Aren't you going to present me, Kostya?' the woman said, smiling.

Kostya cleared his throat.

'Lord Gavril, this is Madame Lilias Arbelian.'

Gavril came down from the dais, his hand extended. To his surprise, Lilias dropped to one knee and instead of shaking his hand, kissed it, the pressure of her lips warm on his skin.

'Please. There's no need . . .' Embarrassed, Gavril leaned forwards and raised her to her feet.

'So you're his son,' Lilias said, gazing intently into his face. 'Elysia's boy.' Although she still smiled, Gavril saw that her bewitching green eyes had filled with tears. As she straightened up, he noticed she wore a black mourning ribbon about the pale porcelain column of her neck. Who was she, what was her place in the household? Gavril glanced at Kostya for help but Kostya had turned away, his back stiff with disdain.

'You – you have the advantage over me, madame,' Gavril stammered.

'Oh, Kostya,' said Lilias, her tone sweetly chiding, 'did you forget to tell Lord Gavril about me? I was your father's mistress, Gavril.'

'Whore,' Kostya muttered through his moustaches.

Gavril stared at her, tongue-tied. He should have known there would be other women in his father's life; who could expect a Clan Lord to stay celibate for so many years? If only Kostya had warned him.

'Your journey must have been tiring, Lord Gavril,' Lilias said. 'When I first came to Azhkendir from Mirom, the voyage took eight days. Such terrible storms! I was utterly exhausted—'

'Shouldn't you be resting?' Kostya interrupted.

'Such concern over my welfare! I'm touched, Bogatyr,' said Lilias in her sweetly honeyed voice. 'I merely came to invite Lord Gavril to take a dish of tea with me. I thought we should get to know each other better, My Lord. There is so much to talk about.'

'Thank you,' Gavril said warily.

'Tomorrow afternoon, then? About four?'

'Four.' Gavril heard himself accepting her invitation even though Kostya was frowning at him and shaking his head.

'I look forward to our meeting, My Lord. I want to get to know all about you.' Lilias gathered her full skirts and curtseyed to him, before turning to leave.

'So you've seen nothing unusual, Lilias?' Kostya said.

She stopped. 'What should I have seen?'

'Lord Volkh.'

Lilias's serene smile faded. 'Don't play word-games with me, Kostya. Say what you mean.'

'My meaning is', Kostya said with some savagery, 'that his ghost appeared here in this hall today. In the very place where he died. A foot or so from where you are standing.'

Gavril saw Lilias delicately flick the hem of her gown away from the place which Kostya was pointing at.

'Why should that concern me?' She looked up at Kostya, staring at him as though challenging him to answer her question directly. 'I don't believe in ghosts.'

She turned away and went sweeping from the Great Hall.

Kostya muttered something under his breath.

'Kostya,' Gavril said. 'Why didn't you tell me? She's carrying my father's child, isn't she?'

Kostya muttered again, inaudibly.

'Kostya! Tell me the truth.'

'The truth?' Kostya shook his battle-scarred head. 'When it comes to My Lady Lilias, no-one knows the truth. But I ask you, Lord Gavril, does she look like a woman in mourning? Oh, she made a fine fuss the night of your father's murder, shrieking and wailing like a madwoman. But she's put off her mourning clothes soon enough.'

'And if her child is a son? Won't he be a rival claimant?'

'Son, daughter, it doesn't matter; your father made you his heir. And he never married Lilias, no matter what she claims. By the ancient laws of Azhkendir, you are his only son. He never divorced your mother.'

Gavril's head had begun to ache. So many threads left untied at his father's death.

'I'll send your apologies later this afternoon,' Kostya said.

'Surely that would be discourteous?'

'There are more pressing matters to attend to! She's only a woman. She should know her place.'

'Lord Gavril,' Sosia came hurrying in, 'the lawyers have arrived from Azhgorod.'

'Was it just a dream?' Kiukiu kept asking herself as she raked the embers of Lord Gavril's fire into her dustpan. The new Drakhaon was downstairs, reopening the Great Hall; she must work fast to prepare a new fire in readiness for his return.

She had slept badly, tossing and turning on her little bed all night. Each time she closed her eyes, she saw again the desolate plain and the pitiful lost souls crawling aimlessly through an eternity of swirling, stinging dust. Her head was still sore to the touch but Sosia's witchhazel had soothed the bruise. Yet how could a mere blow to the head produce such terrifying visions?

She took up her little brush and began to sweep the grate clean of cinders. The ash drifted into the pan, grey as the bitter dustclouds of that windswept plain.

He said I have a gift. The gift to hear the voices of the dead? She dropped her brush with a clatter and looked round guiltily, hoping no-one had heard her. The thought was not a comforting one.

If I have this gift, then why haven't I ever seen any ghosts before?

She stood up, her pan full of ashes. She would

have to go fetch fresh coals and kindling to lay a new fire.

And then she noticed the door to the dressing-room was slightly ajar.

And if I did bring Lord Volkh's ghost through, why has no-one else seen it?

She hesitated. The temptation to check the dressing-room was overwhelming. It would only take a minute or so: all she needed was to convince herself that it had been a trick of the mind.

She tiptoed across to the dressing-room. As she entered she noticed Lord Gavril's travelling clothes, washed, ironed and folded by Sosia. The smell of Sosia's best soap perfumed the air. Already the room felt completely different from yesterday.

Pensively she fingered the frame of the broken mirror. Yesterday it had become a doorway to another world and now it was just a piece of wood.

If she had really brought a ghost through from the world beyond, it was no longer confined here in this room. And, with the mirror-portal shattered, how was she to send it back?

The servants were in a huddle as she came into the kitchen, all talking in hushed voices. Half-rolled pastry lay abandoned on the pastry slab, peeled apples for a pie were turning brown. No-one was working.

'Michailo saw Lord Volkh.'

Kiukiu froze in the doorway.

'Where? Where did he see him?'

'In the Hall. In the shadows. Where Lord Volkh – *you know*—'

'And how can we be sure Michailo hadn't been at the aquavit?'

'Because the Bogatyr has seen it too.'

Kiukiu felt faint and cold. So it hadn't been a dream. She had brought Lord Volkh's spirit-wraith back from the Ways Beyond.

'But why does the Bogatyr think one of us summoned it?' Ilsi's voice, sharp even when whispering, rose above the others. 'No-one knows how to do such a thing.'

If she tiptoed through very softly, maybe no-one would notice her—

'*Kiukiu!*' Sosia had spotted her. She stopped, not daring to look around.

'Yes, Auntie?' she said in a small voice.

'The Bogatyr wants a word with you.'

'Me?' She tried to shrink into the corner. 'Why me?'

'You haven't been a bad girl, have you, Kiukiu?' said Ilsi in a silly, singsong voice. Ninusha began to giggle. 'If you've been a bad girl, the Bogatyr will have to punish you.'

Kiukiu began to shiver. She was afraid of the Bogatyr. She remembered the screams and agonized cries of the men he had had put to the question. The *druzhina* could inflict pain in any number of cruel and ingenious ways.

'Come with me, my girl.' Sosia seized hold of her wrist and began to pull her. 'And put that coal-bucket down.'

'I don't want to come.' Kiukiu tried to pull away but Sosia's grip was tight as pincers. 'I haven't done anything wrong.'

Sosia, tight-lipped, half led, half dragged her towards Bogatyr Kostya's quarters.

The Bogatyr was waiting for them. When the guards on the door let them in, he said brusquely, 'Let no-one else in. We are not to be disturbed.'

A little whimper of fear came out of Kiukiu's lips. He looked so fierce, so unforgiving. She had never been brought before him like this; Sosia usually dealt with all matters of discipline below stairs.

'Someone has summoned up Lord Volkh's spirit-wraith,' he said. 'Was it you?'

'Me?' Kiukiu's legs were trembling. 'Why me?'

Instead of answering, he looked accusingly at Sosia.

'Does she know?'

'How could she?' Sosia said scornfully. 'She knows nothing. I've kept my counsel all these years, just as you made me swear to.'

Kiukiu stared from one to the other, confused. What was she supposed not to know?

'Look at the girl, she's simple; she has no idea what you're talking about.' Sosia smiled at Kiukiu but Kiukiu could sense the tension behind the smile. 'Simple but loyal-hearted, isn't that right, Kiukiu?'

'Well, Kiukiu?' His eyes burned into hers.

Fear locked her tongue.

'A straight answer, girl,' he barked.

'I'd never do anything to hurt Lord Gavril,' she burst out. 'Never!'

There was a silence. She could feel sobs welling up inside her but she fought to hold them back; if she wept now, he might take it as an admission of guilt.

'Very well,' he said. 'But if I find you have been lying to me, things will go ill with you. Understand me, girl?'

She nodded.

'Now get out of my sight.'

Outside his room, the tears began: helpless, stupid tears. She stuffed her apron in her mouth to stifle them, angry with herself for being so weak and frightened.

'Dry your eyes.' Sosia bustled up beside her. 'There's work to be done.'

Kiukiu nodded, wiping the wetness from her cheeks with the back of her hand.

'What did he mean, Auntie,' she asked, hurrying to keep up with Sosia's brisk pace, 'when he asked, "Does she know?" Know what?'

'Nothing that need concern you.'

'And why is it so bad that the ghost is here? Perhaps all it wants is to bring the murderer to justice. Perhaps—'

Sosia stopped suddenly, spinning around and wagging her finger in Kiukiu's face.

'Now listen to me, Kiukiu. There's been a lot of foolish talk in the kitchens since Lord Volkh's death. If you want to keep your place in this household, you'd do best to stop asking silly questions.'

Oris Avorian, Lord Volkh's chief lawyer, rose to his feet, raised the rolled document so that all could see, and broke the great seal of black wax.

The Great Hall was filled with people: grim-faced *druzhina*, servants and serving-maids, all were waiting silently to hear their dead lord's will.

Gavril sat in the centre of the dais, flanked by Kostya and Lilias, who had put on a sombre black gown for the occasion. Lilias's maid, Dysis, stood behind her mistress's chair, eyes demurely lowered.

Now that it had come to the moment, Gavril felt

numb. He just wanted the ceremony to be over.

' "The last will and testament of Volkh Nagarian, Drakhaon and rightful Lord of the Land of Azhkendir. I, Volkh Nagarian, being of sound mind and body . . ." '

Gavril let his gaze wander over the silent assembly, watching the sea of faces of his father's household.

' "My lands, my monies and all my estates pass by right of birth to my only son and heir, Gavril Andar." '

Not even the faintest murmur of dissent greeted the announcement and yet Gavril sensed a growing tension within the hall.

' "To Bogatyr Kostya, my faithful lieutenant, counsellor and friend, I bequeath my battle-sabre . . ." '

Gavril heard a muffled snort; glancing uneasily to his side he saw that Kostya had drawn out a hand-kerchief and had noisily blown his nose.

' "Every man in the *druzhina*, from the humblest keep-boy to the master of horse, is to be paid a deathgift in gold coins, one for every year he has been in my service in recognition of his loyalty and valour . . ." '

Now the murmuring began; Gavril saw the men turn to each other, nodding and counting on their fingers.

' " . . . and to my only son and heir, Gavril Andar, I also bequeath a casket. This casket must be opened by Gavril and Gavril alone and the contents of this casket are never to be revealed to another living soul." '

The small casket stood in the centre of the table.

It was a singularly plain piece of workmanship; fashioned out of dull-sheened wood, reinforced with tooled iron at the corners. If it held treasure, its outward appearance gave no hint of its contents. And yet Gavril could not keep his eyes off it. As the lawyer droned on, he found he kept staring at it, wondering what lay within that was so secret, so personal that no-one else should see it.

'". . . and to my charming companion Madame Lilias Arbelian, I leave a pension of five hundred gold coins a year until her death. If she chooses, she may continue to live in the West Wing – or if she prefers, she may ask my son Gavril to establish her in my mansion in the city of Azhgorod."'

'Well?' a voice demanded tensely in the silence. 'Is that all?'

Gavril, jarred from his reverie, glanced up to see Lilias staring at the lawyer, her face white.

'That concludes the reading of the will,' the lawyer said in measured tones, ignoring her.

'Is there no codicil? No later additions?' She leaned forwards on the table towards him, her eyes narrowed. 'Are you *sure*?'

'Perfectly sure,' the lawyer said coldly, rolling up the parchment.

'Then I challenge the validity of this document.' She turned to the household, one hand raised imperiously. 'He told me he had changed the will. When he knew I was carrying his child. He told me!' Her voice began to crack.

'Lord Volkh has bequeathed you a very generous legacy, madame,' Avorian said coldly. 'I beg you not to excite yourself in your condition. Think of your child.'

'I won't let this matter rest,' Lilias said. 'I shall inform my lawyers in Mirom. I shall contest the will. Come, Dysis.' And Lilias gathered up her sombre skirts and swept from the hall, Dysis pattering along behind.

The instant the doors had banged shut behind them, a frantic gabble of conversation broke out, everyone talking at once.

'That woman's nothing but trouble,' Kostya said. 'Pack her off to Azhgorod, Lord Gavril, before she causes any more mischief.'

'Why was she so convinced my father had changed his will in her favour?' Lilias's behaviour perplexed him: at one moment, she was all charm and Mirom refinement, the next, a grasping, calculating schemer. 'Is it possible she's right and there is another will?'

'All things are possible,' Kostya said morosely.

The reading of the will was followed by another dinner of interminable length. Gavril had little appetite for the rich food Sosia had prepared and sat, crumbling a bread roll with his fingers, waving aside dishes of wild cherry soup, venison and jellied carp, as he kept wondering what secrets his father had concealed in the wooden casket.

At last the lawyers retired to their guest rooms. Gavril rose, one hand on the wooden box, hoping at last to escape to his room and discover what his father had concealed inside. But Kostya gripped hold of him by the arm so firmly that he could not pull away.

'The will has been read, Lord Gavril,' he said sternly. 'There is one duty still to be performed.'

One more duty. Was there no end to this day?

Torchflames lit the Great Hall and flickered across the tattooed and battle-scarred faces of the massed ranks of the *druzhina*.

'There is a debt of honour to be paid,' Kostya said. 'By the ancient laws of our Clan, you must now track down your father's murderer, and exact vengeance.' He took up Volkh's gleaming battle-sabre and presented it, hilt first, to Gavril. 'Blood for blood.'

'Blood for blood,' came an answering murmur from the warriors.

Gavril took the sabre, bracing himself to sustain the weight of the heavy curved blade. 'I'm no fighting man,' he said defiantly, 'I'm an artist. I wouldn't even know where to start.' And he dropped the sabre back down with a clang on the table.

The murmuring began to grow louder.

'You dare disgrace your father's memory here, in the very place where he died?' cried one of the warriors. Gavril recognized the flax-fair hair of the guard Michailo who had been in the Hall when his father's ghost appeared.

'Silence!' Kostya rounded on the young man. 'Is it Lord Gavril's fault he has not been trained as a warrior? His father's blood runs in his veins – is that not enough?'

'Prove it,' shouted out another warrior.

'Give us proof!' shouted Michailo. 'Drakhaon! *Drakhaon!*'

One by one, the *druzhina* took up the chant until the whole hall echoed to their stamping and shouting, to the metallic din of sabres banged against shields and boots.

'I will help bring my father's murderer to justice and a fair trial,' Gavril cried. 'But I will not perpetuate this ancient blood-feud—'

His last words were drowned in a storm of jeering.

'*Enough!*' Kostya placed a hand on Gavril's shoulder. At first Gavril sensed reassurance in the grip of iron – and then he realized Kostya was also restraining him. Had he tried to run, he could not have moved.

'Drakhaon!' chanted the *druzhina*.

'Proof of blood, My Lord.' Kostya turned back to the *druzhina*. 'A chair for our Lord Drakhaon!'

As Gavril was forced to sit in his father's great carved chair, Kostya drew out his knife. Gavril tried to struggle up but Kostya pressed him down again.

'What are you going to do?' Gavril hissed.

'A few drops of blood to gain their lifelong loyalty – is it so much to ask?'

'It's barbaric!'

'Blood for blood,' Kostya said. 'The ancient contract between Drakhaon and *druzhina*. A time will come, My Lord, when you will be glad you went through with this ceremony.'

As if in a confused and dark dream, Gavril saw him bring the glinting blade across his wrist, saw the dark blood begin to drip out. And through the strange, thin, pulsing pain in his wrist, he saw a thin, blue vapour arising from the dark blood, as though it burned with a heat of its own.

Michailo dropped to his knees before him and pressed the oozing wound to his lips.

Gavril, stunned into silence, could only stare at the young warrior as he drew back, lips moistly stained with his blood, one hand pressed to his heart in sign of fealty.

One after another, the *druzhina* knelt before him and kissed the bleeding wound on his wrist. And with each warrior's bloodkiss, a distant murmur at the back of his mind grew until it surged like the roaring of an autumn stormtide on the Vermeille shore.

Suddenly hot and faint from loss of blood, Gavril felt as if he were falling deep into drowning waters. The red torchlight flickered and grew dim . . .

Were they going to let him bleed to death?

Kostya pressed a pad onto the edges of the cut, swiftly and skilfully binding it firmly in place.

'I can hear voices . . .' Gavril murmured, 'in my mind . . .'

'The ritual blood-bond between Drakhaon and *druzhina*. Sealed in your blood.' Kostya took up a ring of ancient keys, rusty and intricately forged, from his belt. 'These are the keys to Kastel Drakhaon. Take them; they are yours. Now you are free to go wherever you will.'

6

'There's nothing to discuss, Madame Andar,' said the Grand Duchess Sofia. 'Your son Gavril was employed to paint a portrait of my daughter, not to attempt to seduce her.' She fanned herself lethargically with a lace and ivory fan. Even though all the balcony doors were open, a hot, dry breeze stirred the muslin blinds and the once-famed beauty was wilting in the last warmth of the Vermeille summer. 'I'm surprised you have the audacity to come here to plead his case!'

'Your Grace.' Elysia Andar stared glazedly at the Grand Duchess. She had hardly slept since Gavril's disappearance and she found it difficult to think with any clarity. 'My son has disappeared.'

'Disappeared?' the Grand Duchess said with a frown. 'What precisely do you mean?'

'My son has never gone away from home before without telling me where he is going.' Elysia struggled to keep her voice steady. 'I – I fear he has been kidnapped.'

'Your son kidnapped?' The Grand Duchess fanned herself with a little more vigour. 'Has there been a ransom note?'

'No.'

'Then how can you be sure?'

Elysia sighed. It was such a long and complicated story she was certain the Grand Duchess would never have the patience to hear her out.

'Your Grace,' she said, 'let me complete the portrait of your daughter. I have never yet let a patron down. It is a matter of professional pride.'

'I don't want this portrait to be a slipshod piece of work,' the Grand Duchess said petulantly. 'It is to impress her future husband.'

'Have I ever disappointed Your Grace in the past?'

'I suppose you'll be wanting your money now so you can pay off these kidnappers?'

Elysia felt herself flush; the Grand Duchess seemed to take pleasure in reminding her of her lowly status. Years of accommodating to the demands of difficult patrons had still not taught her to shrug aside the humiliation.

'I wish to request a different form of payment.'

'Oh?' said the Grand Duchess suspiciously.

'I wish to petition the Grand Duke about my son.'

'The Grand Duke does not concern himself with such matters. Surely it is a matter for the local militia.'

The heat was beginning to affect Elysia too. She steeled herself. She was going to have to reveal the truth.

'But when the Grand Duke learns who my son is—'

'A young painter, madame! Who has probably gone off to indulge a young man's appetites with women of questionable virtue.'

'Women of questionable virtue?' A dark-haired young man burst in from the balcony. 'Quite my favourite kind!'

'Andrei.' The Grand Duchess snapped her fan shut and shook it at him, tutting. 'Must you be so coarse?'

The rising sense of despair was almost more than Elysia could bear. For the past week she and Palmyre had fruitlessly searched the taverns and ateliers of Vermeille. No-one knew where Gavril was. The only possible explanation was the sudden disappearance of Kostya, the *druzhina* and the Azhkendi barque.

'Besides,' the Grand Duchess said, 'we sail for Mirom at the end of the week. As I told you, there is the matter of Astasia's betrothal to be arranged. And this heat has become too oppressive to bear . . .'

'Poor Mama.' Andrei seized the fan and began fanning his mother.

'Then let me come with you,' Elysia said impulsively.

'Why? I tell you, madame, that my husband will not be interested.'

'My son', Elysia said, 'is heir to Azhkendir.'

'Azhkendir?' Andrei repeated. Elysia saw mother and son exchange glances. 'But what has become of Lord Volkh?'

'Has the news not reached Muscobar? Lord Volkh is dead.'

'And how, madame,' said the Grand Duchess, 'are you so well-informed of affairs in that backward and barbaric country? When we received Lord Volkh at court last year he made no mention of a wife or a son.'

'I was his wife,' Elysia said, refusing to be put off by the Grand Duchess's imperious manner. 'We separated when Gavril was a little boy. I have been living quietly here in Vermeille ever since.'

'Gavril the painter?' Andrei began to laugh. 'Wait till I tell Tasia. Her artist with the soulful sea-blue eyes – the one who was thrown out by the White Guard the night of the ball – is a lord!'

'Even if your extravagant claim is true, I still don't understand how the Grand Duke can assist you,' complained the Grand Duchess.

'Don't be so unimaginative, Mama,' said Andrei. 'If I were to go missing, what would you do?'

'My dear, I'd leave it to your father to sort out.'

'Just when we had established the Treaty of Accord with Azhkendir?' The laughter had gone from Andrei Orlov's voice; suddenly he was serious, incisive. 'Azhkendir is all that stands between us and Tielen. If Madame Andar's son has been kidnapped by political extremists – or Prince Eugene's agents – Muscobar could find itself in a tricky situation.'

'I have no idea what you're talking about, Andrei,' said the Grand Duchess in tones of bewilderment.

Andrei strode across the salon and seized Elysia's hands.

'Come with us to Mirom, Madame Andar. I will send word ahead to Papa, advising him of the situation.'

Elysia stood staring at Gavril's portrait of Astasia. Even though half-finished, she could see it was the best piece of work he had ever achieved. Technically it was superb – but it was the way he had gone beyond technique to capture an elusive, wistful quality in the young girl's face that impressed her so forcibly. Her eyes blurred with tears until she could no longer see the portrait clearly.

All the last week she had not allowed herself the luxury of tears; she had kept herself busy with ceaseless searching, ceaseless questioning. She had not slept much, either, sitting on the balcony, staring out hour after hour at the starlit waters of the Bay, worrying and conjecturing.

It was totally out of character for Gavril to go away without leaving her a message. He had left Vermeille countless times, on solitary fishing trips or coastal treks with his student friends. She had never feared for his safety till now.

Staring blindly through her tears at Astasia's portrait, she realized she was not certain what frightened her most: the thought that Volkh's enemies might have kidnapped him, or the realization that the *druzhina* wanted to make him Drakhaon – to change her charming, loving boy into a ruthless tyrant like his dead father.

'Madame?'

Elysia hastily wiped the tears from her eyes and looked around. A dark-haired girl stood in the doorway.

'You must be Altessa Astasia,' Elysia said.

'I – I am so sorry to hear about your son,' the girl said haltingly. 'Andrei has just told me.'

Elysia nodded. She might have been deceived but she was certain from the pallor of Astasia's face that she had also been crying. Was this the reason for

Gavril's inspired portrayal? Was the Grand Duchess right? Had the relationship between painter and sitter deepened into something far more intimate?

'I will complete the portrait,' she said. 'Her Grace tells me it is to be a betrothal gift to your fiancé.'

Astasia said nothing, but a bitter little sigh escaped her lips.

'Well,' Elysia said, opening her box of paints, 'shall we start?'

'Madame is leaving so soon?' Palmyre cried. 'And travelling alone?'

'Dear Palmyre.' Elysia looked up from her packing. 'I don't think you could describe accompanying the ruling family of Muscobar as travelling alone.'

'But you'll be all on your own in that great cold, draughty city.' Palmyre had found the last days as taxing as her mistress; her ready, kindly smile had faded and she looked tired and careworn.

'I need you to stay and take care of the villa.' Elysia clasped Palmyre's hands. 'Just in case *he* returns. It could happen. I want someone to be here for him whilst I'm away.'

'Oh, madame. You've been so brave.' Palmyre squeezed her hands warmly in return. 'You can count on me. I'll keep the place in good order. You mustn't worry about things here. Now, have you packed that shawl, the lacy wool one? The nights are cold in Mirom.'

'Yes, yes.' Elysia turned back to her trunk. 'Where did I put that hairbrush . . . ?'

There was still an hour or so before the barouche Elysia had ordered was due to take her to the Villa

110

Orlova. She entered Gavril's room. Everything was just as he had left it, clothes flung carelessly down on the floor, the covers on his bed rumpled. Unfinished sketches littered his desk along with pencils, charcoal and pastels.

He would never have gone away without his sketchbook and pencils. Since boyhood he had always taken a sketchbook with him; he had been a compulsive sketcher, always with a stub of pencil in his hand, always doodling on any available scrap of paper.

She kneeled down and began to pick up the discarded clothes. Until now she had not wanted to touch anything, to maintain the illusion that Gavril had only just left the room and would – at any moment – return.

Now, without thinking, she found herself stroking a crumpled shirt against her cheek.

The collar betrayed a rim of grime and the cuffs were frayed.

'Where are you, Gavril?' she whispered.

As her barouche swept into the grounds of the Villa Orlova, Elysia found herself surrounded by chaos and confusion; servants and guards swarmed to and fro, carrying luggage in and out of carriages.

Elysia climbed out onto the gravel drive and stared about her, perplexed.

'Madame Andar!' A young officer in a dazzling white uniform came hurrying up; not till he had reached her did she recognize Andrei Orlov, his wild dark curls slicked down with pomade, plumed helmet tucked under one arm.

'What is going on, Altessa?'

'I am afraid you find us in some disarray, Madame Andar. We have had to alter our travel plans. We shall be returning to Muscobar overland.'

'Oh?' Elysia said, unsure if this were good news or not.

'You may have heard that Prince Eugene's fleet has been on manoeuvres in the Straits? There's been a little misunderstanding over the matter of the herring grounds.' How reassuringly he spoke, Elysia thought, already well-trained in the use of the gilded lies of diplomacy. 'A disputed treaty. I'm sure it will all be settled soon.'

Elysia nodded. Somewhere out in the Straits the navies of Tielen and Muscobar were blasting each other to matchwood with cannon.

'Such a silly business.' The Grand Duchess appeared on the steps, leaning on Astasia's arm. 'And for this we have to bundle ourselves into carriages. In this heat!'

'Never mind, Mama, you know how you hate the sea,' said Astasia.

'But it's so humiliating,' complained the Duchess, 'to be obliged to alter one's plans all because of *herring*. And you, Andrei, now you tell me you're going to join the fleet? How could you upset your poor mother so?'

'I must do my duty, Mama!' Andrei said gaily.

'But this isn't a game. You could get killed!' The Grand Duchess dabbed at her eyes with a tiny lace handkerchief.

'There's always been an Orlov in the navy, Mama. Besides, the uniform of rear-admiral impresses all the girls!' And, flashing his mother a wicked grin, Andrei swung nimbly up into the saddle.

112

'If only we could arrange a match for you with Prince Eugene, Astasia,' murmured the Grand Duchess, 'and bring all this unpleasantness to an end.'

Astasia pulled a face behind her mother's back.

Gilded carriages, drawn by teams of six white-plumed horses, clattered along the stony roads through the fields and olive trees, escorted by a troop of the White Guard, harnesses jingling, their helmets and breastplates dazzling in the sun.

It was hot, dusty and very dry. Elysia gazed listlessly through the window of the carriage and saw the farmworkers in the fields sweating to bring in the last of the harvest. As the road climbed slowly into the foothills, the charred cornfields and olive groves gave way to vineyards. But the dust still blew into the carriage, drying her mouth and throat, making her eyes sting.

There had been some confusion in etiquette as to where to place Elysia in the ducal party. As portrait painter, her place was with the servants – yet as wife to the late Drakhaon, she was only a little lower in rank to the Grand Duchess herself. Eventually they had put her in the second carriage with Astasia, her governess Eupraxia, and the ancient Countess Ilyanova who was deaf as a post.

'Look, Tasia, there goes your brother,' Eupraxia exclaimed for the third time, pointing out of the window and waving. 'Yoo-hoo, Andrei! Now he's saluting us. How handsome he looks in his uniform.'

'I don't see why he should be allowed to ride and not me,' complained Astasia.

'My dear, it is not seemly.' Eupraxia, suffering from the heat, began to dab at her temples and neck with a handkerchief impregnated with a sickly sweet floral water.

'Seemly,' repeated Astasia in disgusted tones. 'A word I place in the same category as obligation and filial duty.'

Elysia turned her head to look out of the window, hoping Eupraxia would not attempt to bring her into the conversation.

'Especially the kind of filial duty that could compel me to marry a pompous bore from Tielen.'

'Is that any way to speak of a prospective husband? And in front of Countess Ilyanova?'

'She can't hear a word,' Astasia said. 'Can you, Countess?'

'Oppressively hot, my dear,' said the Countess, nodding her wizened head and smiling.

'Why did Mama suggest Prince Eugene? He's killed off one wife already.'

'The poor woman died in childbirth,' Eupraxia protested.

'And he must be well past thirty. Middle-aged. I'll bet he has a receding hairline and a paunch by now.' Astasia turned to Elysia, pleading, 'Oh, dear Madame Andar, couldn't you make my portrait exceedingly ugly? Give me a squint and a dowager's hump? And a gap in my front teeth?'

'Have you ever been introduced to Prince Eugene?' Elysia asked, unable to prevent herself from smiling.

'Three or four years ago.'

'So he might wonder how you had come to acquire so many imperfections in so short a time?'

'But suppose Mama persuades Papa to approach Prince Eugene? Why must I be a pawn in this game of strategy?'

'It isn't your place, Tasia, to question your parents' decisions,' Eupraxia said sternly.

The carriage wheels encountered a pothole and they were all flung violently to one side.

'And I hear that Tielen is infested with mosquitoes every summer,' Astasia said, righting herself. 'Didn't the Prince have the marshlands drained for the building of his palace at Swanholm? And didn't hundreds of workers die of the sweating sickness? How could I live in a place that's been the cause of so much misery?'

But Eupraxia had closed her eyes and appeared to be sound asleep; Elysia wondered how many times the governess had resorted to this strategy to avoid Astasia's awkward questions.

Astasia gave a sharp sigh.

'Madame Andar,' she said after several minutes' silence. 'Do you truly believe your son has been kidnapped?'

'I don't know what to believe,' Elysia said, startled at the sudden change of conversation. 'But I hope that the Grand Duke will use his influence to help him.'

Astasia was gazing at her, her dark eyes intense.

'But you think he is still alive?'

'My husband had many enemies who wished him dead. But Gavril—' Her voice faltered in spite of herself.

The girl put out one delicate hand, laying it on her arm in a gesture of sympathy. 'My dear Madame Andar, I'm so sorry, that was insensitive of me.'

Elysia saw with a shock of surprise that Astasia's eyes were brimming with unshed tears. Now she was sure of it: Astasia Orlova entertained genuine feelings for Gavril.

'I promise you', Astasia said in a low voice that burned with emotion, 'that I will persuade Papa to do all in his power to ensure your son's safety.'

Elysia nodded, biting her lip. But in her heart a little voice whispered, *'If it is not already too late . . .'*

7

Gavril took the little key Avorian had given him, turned it in the lock, and opened the lid of his father's wooden casket.

No glint of gold or jewels met his eyes. Only a paper, carefully folded, tied with silken ribbons and sealed.

And when he tore open the seal and unfolded the paper, he saw that it was not meticulously penned by an anonymous legal clerk but written in hurried, erratic strokes that were difficult to decipher, as though dashed off in desperate haste:

To my only son, Gavril.
If I am dead when you read this letter, Gavril, you will already be becoming Drakhaon. Look at your nails. Can you see blue ridges thickening above the quick?

Gavril glanced down at his hands. He placed the

letter down on the bed and raised his hands to the oil lamp, intently examining his fingernails. There were the faint, darkish shadows Kostya had shown him, barely discernible above the quicks ... but ridges?

Gavril picked up the letter again.

Look closely in the mirror. Your brows. Are they thicker? Are there stray hairs that are more blue than black? Examine your moods of the last few weeks. Have you lost your temper? Have you felt surges of irrational anger? Have the dark dreams begun yet? If you have experienced any of these, my son, it has begun. And there is no reversing it.

Gavril wanted to stop reading – but he could not drag his eyes from the page. And as he read on, he began to hear again in his mind that hoarse voice speaking the words, chill as a winter's night:

You may dismiss as merely fanciful the stories my people tell of dark wings beating overhead in the night or the mist that settled over the Arkhel lands, the mist that sparkled like shattered stars – and withered all who breathed in its poisonous vapours, both man and beast alike. But it is the gift and the curse of the Drakhaons to wield such devastating forces, and my people will fear and respect you for the burning Nagarian blood that runs in your veins and the Drakhaoul that inhabits the darkest recesses of your soul.

What they will not tell you is that there is a terrible price to pay. Every time you let the

Drakhaoul within you take possession, you will become less human. Poisons are released into your blood: poisons that will change you, both in body and soul.

Have they told you the legend of the Drakhaons' Brides? Monstrous though the tale may seem to you, there is a horrible truth in it. For the only way to retain our human appearance is to accept the Drakhaon's traditional tribute and ingest fresh human blood. Innocent blood. At first, Gavril, I confess that I was forced to comply with tradition. And then, sickened by the inhuman practice, I refused to continue.

No matter what pressures and persuasions my people may use upon you, you must resist the urge to use your powers with all your strength.

I captured one of the Spirit-Singers, the Guslyars of the House of Arkhel, in the hope that he might be persuaded to exorcise the creature. But, blinded by Clan loyalty, he refused to comply with my wishes. He paid the ultimate price for his obstinacy.

I have spent these last years searching for a cure. For a way to halt the cruel degeneration that has altered me – even as it did with my father and his father before him – whilst I still have some shreds of humanity left. So that I can bequeath to you, my son, a possibility of hope that things may be changed for you and your children.

To this end, I have brought Doctor Altan Kazimir to Azhkendir. Doctor Kazimir is a distinguished Doctor of Science with a reputation in Mirom for using unconventional methods. To him and him alone I have entrusted the secrets of my powers – and my weakness. Together we are working to determine if the degenerative effects of the Nagarian blood can be arrested – or, at least, effectively repressed.

No-one else must ever know. Because of this, I have taken the precaution, as has Doctor Kazimir, to encrypt the results of his experiments and observations. When he has completed his work, the results and the code to break the encryption will be given to my lawyer, Oris Avorian, and sealed with these papers in this casket.

Codes? Encryptions? Gavril held the letter up to the lamp, looking for hidden script that remotely resembled scientific formulae or encoded writings. But there was nothing to be seen but his father's handwriting.

Pools of early morning sunlight, emerald and blood-ruby, glimmered on the polished wooden floor of the tower-room from diamond-paned windows, each ornamented with borders of painted glass: twisting garlands of ivy and wild-rose.

'This is the Kalika Tower,' Kostya said as he ushered Gavril in. 'Your father liked to work here undisturbed. We've left it just as he left it . . . that night.'

Papers tied in neat bundles were piled on one corner of the desk; a map lay spread out, pens, rulers and an open inkwell close by, as if Lord Volkh had just walked out of the room and might return at any moment.

Gavril went to the desk and feverishly started to leaf through the papers, hoping to discover the encryptions. But all he found was page after page of estate accounts.

Where could his father have left them, if not in his study?

There were books too, ancient volumes with yellowed pages. Gavril picked one up, shaking it to see if any hidden papers fell out. The title proclaimed it to be *Through Uncharted Seas: a Sailor's Account of a Perilous Voyage of Exploration.* Another book was entitled *Travels in the Westward Isles* and a third, with a red ribbon used as a page marker, *Ty Nagar: Land of the Serpent God.*

'What was my father doing in here?' he asked, distracted from his search. 'Was he planning a journey?'

'Maybe.'

'And this, what's this?' Gavril bent over the outspread map. 'A star chart?'

The penmanship on the map was intricate, neat and skilful; different coloured inks marking out constellations and planets. So his father had been in the process of making a detailed map of the winter skies above Azhkendir? This scholarly activity seemed strangely at odds with Volkh Nagarian the savage warlord.

'Why was my father making this chart?'

Kostya shrugged. 'What your father did here was his own business. Although of late, he and Doctor Kazimir liked to watch the stars from the roof; the telescopes are still up there, behind the battlements.'

Kazimir. The Mirom Doctor of Science mentioned in his father's letter.

'I don't believe I've met Doctor Kazimir yet,' he said as casually as he could.

Kostya's face darkened.

'We're still searching for him. God knows why your father brought him here all the way from Mirom. He was reputed to be a great scholar. Scholar!' Kostya spat. 'He turned out to be a great drinker. And womanizer.'

'And what was Doctor Kazimir's area of expertise?'

Kostya shrugged again. 'Making foul smells and smoke. Sometimes the East Wing stank like a latrine. And then there were the noises. Whistlings. Bangs. As if he'd let loose all the fiends from hell.'

'East Wing? I haven't been shown an East Wing.'

'It's been empty since the last Arkhel raid,' said Kostya cryptically. 'That was why your father gave it to Doctor Kazimir. So he could work there undisturbed.'

'But what was he doing in there?'

'It was good enough for me that My Lord chose to employ him. I never questioned My Lord's motives. All I know is that things went from bad to worse when Kazimir came.'

'What things?' Gavril would not be fobbed off this time by Kostya's hints and allusions.

'Lord Volkh's temper, for one. At first he spent long hours with Kazimir, doors locked, no-one to be admitted. Then one day, everything changed. There was a quarrel. A terrible quarrel. He told Kazimir to go before he set the hounds on him. Before he strangled him with his bare hands.'

'And Kazimir went?'

'Ah, but *did* he?'

'You think he's still here in Azhkendir? Why would he stay here?'

'She has friends. Allies.'

122

'She? Lilias? They quarrelled over Lilias?'

'He was seen. Leaving her chambers. She denied it, of course. But once My Lord found out . . .'

Gavril nodded. He had not missed the unspoken allegation in Kostya's words. Whose child was Lilias carrying? His father's? Or the absent Kazimir's?

'So Doctor Kazimir is a suspect in my father's murder?'

'He had motive enough.'

'How old is he, this Kazimir?' Gavril asked, trying to make the question sound casual.

'Somewhere between thirty and forty,' Kostya said, scowling. 'Difficult to tell with these scholars. All that peering at books in libraries gives them a pallid, unhealthy look.'

Not a young man, then. Certainly not that gold-haired young man from his vision, with eyes seared with hatred and fear. But his unseen accomplice, maybe . . .

'And have his rooms been searched?'

'They were one of the first places we looked. No trace, of course. We searched *her* rooms as well. She wasn't pleased.'

'Show me the roof.'

As soon as Kostya's back was turned, Gavril swiftly slipped pen, ink and paper into his jacket. At least he now had the means to write a letter.

A little arched doorway led to a winding spiral stair; as Kostya had warned, the steps were narrow, uneven and worn smooth. It was necessary to lean into the wall against the roughness of the stone to avoid slipping.

A draught of cold wind slapped Gavril in the face as Kostya opened the door at the top. Breathless from the climb, Gavril stepped out onto the lead lining – and gasped at what he saw.

They were on the roof of the tallest of all the kastel towers and spread beneath them, stretching far into the cloudy distance, was a dizzying prospect of Azhkendir.

'Your father's lands, Lord Gavril,' Kostya said. 'And now all this is yours.'

Gavril went to the high battlements and leaned his elbows on the gnarled stone, gazing out at his inheritance.

'All this?'

It was a wilderness. Mountain and moorland, forest and fell, with little sign of human habitation. Overhead, wind-driven clouds scudded through a grey and louring sky.

Even as he stared out, a feeling of desolation overwhelmed him, chill as the wind, grey as the colourless sky. How could he ever hope to live here? Where were the vivid colours of the Smarnan landscape, the constantly shifting play of the sunlight on the sea? There might be some technical challenge for a painter in charting the earthy tones of the outcrops of craggy stone or mountain screes – or the pine greens of the forests – but the wintry bleakness of the scene repelled him.

I feel no link with this place. I don't belong. My mother's southern blood burns too strongly in my veins. Oh for the warmth of the sun . . .

Four telescopes, their weather-dulled metal glinting in the cold light, had been placed at each of the four walls of the tower. Volkh the warlord indulging his hobby as amateur astronomer. It didn't quite seem to tally.

'Tell me more about my father. Tell me about the Clan War.'

Kostya was staring out towards the mountains, his back to Gavril.

'Azhkendir was always divided. By the time Lord Volkh became Drakhaon, only the Clan Arkhel stood against him. And Lord Stavyor Arkhel, in his mountain stronghold, was invincible. See that forked mountain, there, to the right of the ridge? That was where Kastel Arkhel stood. And Azhkendir was divided into factions: Arkhel against Nagarian. Civil war.'

'Was there no hope of negotiations? Or a peace treaty?'

Kostya turned and looked at him, frowning.

'You've much to learn about Azhkendir. That's not how we settle matters here. Your grandmother, Drakhys Marya, was killed in the raid on the East Wing. Your father was only a boy at the time. He barely escaped with his life. How could he forgive Stavyor Arkhel for murdering his mother?'

'So my father attacked Lord Stavyor?'

'Years later your father retaliated. As Drakhaon he had . . .' And Kostya hesitated, as though searching for the right words. 'He had a singular advantage. No mercy was shown. Stavyor and his family and followers – all were destroyed.'

'His family? My father had Stavyor's children killed?'

'You think that Stavyor Arkhel would have spared you and your mother if he had been the victor?' Kostya said harshly. 'Yes, they were all killed and the kastel burned to the ground.'

Echo of a young man's voice, choked with

125

emotion, sobbing out those words of hatred and exultation over the dying man's body . . .

'*This for my mother . . . my sisters . . . my father . . .*'

'Did Stavyor Arkhel have a son?' Gavril whispered. 'A year or so older than me?'

'Jaromir,' Kostya said. 'What of it? He was killed with his sisters.'

For a moment Gavril caught a glimpse of a cruel and savage light in Kostya's eyes. Kostya must have been there at his father's side in the massacre. His hands were also stained with the blood of the Arkhel children.

And then the full import of the echoing mindvoice hit him with the shattering force of winter lightning.

Stavyor's son Jaromir was not dead. He had 'seen' Jaromir kill his father.

8

A flock of wild swans wheeled up into the air from the grey mists covering the waters of the ornamental lake.

Prince Eugene of Tielen reined in his bay mare Cinnamor on the grassy promontory high above his palace of Swanholm and gazed down at his creation. Falling birch leaves covered the frost-crisped lawns with a coverlet of faded gold, drifted like yellow butterflies about his head. The cold air of early morning smelled of mouldering leaves and woodsmoke.

He had brought the architects for his new palace all the way from Bel'Esstar and they had designed him an impressive building of pale stone, marble and glass: simple, yet magnificent in its formal park setting. Where once his father's favourite hunting lodge had stood in a valley of birch and alders, an elegant house had arisen, flanked by kitchens, stables, servants' quarters and the barracks of the

Royal Bodyguard. Even now, workmen were still busy in the East Wing, its gently curving colonnade mirroring the completed West Wing, and the ring of their hammers echoed across the quiet parklands.

It was a palace fit for the man who dreamed it was his destiny to reunite the divided princedoms of Rossiya into one powerful empire.

It was a palace fit for an emperor.

Yet the nearing of its completion only served to remind Eugene all too painfully of an absence in his life. Together they had pored over the plans and drawings, discussed features, details. The black and white floor tiles of the entrance hall had been his idea, rejecting the architects' more fanciful suggestions. And he should have been here now to see the workmen finishing their long years of labour, to stroll along the polished parquet floors, to admire the soft brocade hangings of ivory, green and gold – shades he had chosen to reflect the leaves and bark of the birch trees in the park. But his personal daemons had tormented him to the point when even the pleasures of Swanholm Palace could no longer distract him from his desire for revenge. One morning, news had come from an unexpected source – and after that, there was nothing Eugene could do to keep him in Swanholm. Since his departure, in spite of Eugene's extensive network of intelligence agents, the subtle enquiries made of all the foreign ambassadors, even in spite of Magus Linnaius's most ingenious scrying, his trail had gone cold.

But then, Eugene reflected, everyone he cared for had deserted him. One could not plan one's life by relying on the constancy or affection of friends, wives, lovers . . .

The thin autumn sunshine brightened a moment, flooding the wooded gardens with a wash of pale gold.

Distant laughter, a child's laughter, joyous and carefree, disturbed his reverie. There, on the lawns below, was his daughter Karila, playing catch with her nurse Marta. A gilded ball spun to and fro through the air between them.

The frail little girl managed well enough with her twisted leg, but the doctors had told him that even if she survived childhood, she would be crippled for life.

If only he could play with her as light-heartedly as Marta did. But he must maintain a distance. To get to know her, to love her too well, would only tempt the fates again. Every time they were together, every time she snuggled up close to him, he glimpsed that malign shadow-spectre hovering behind her, waiting to snatch her as it had snatched her mother.

'Papa! Papa!' Now she was waving at him. Sunlight glinted in her curls which were fair as catkin pollen, the same delicate shade as her mother's had been. He waved back. She started out eagerly towards him, arms outstretched – and, betrayed by her crippled leg, pitched forwards on the grass.

Cinnamor gave a nervous, jittery whinny.

'What's up there, girl?' He patted her neck to try to reassure her but she did not respond, shaking her head from side to side and rolling her eyes.

Now he looked – and looked again, hardly believing what he saw. Through the rising mists a wolf was loping towards his little daughter: a great, shaggy beast with an ill-kempt coat streaked with the lurid yellow of sulphur.

129

No ordinary wolf. A Marauder.

Cinnamor let out a whicker of terror and reared up, iron-clad hoofs beating the air.

Eugene squeezed his heels into the bay's side and urged her down the precipitous side of the hill.

On the green lawn below he saw Marta run to Karila and clutch her in her arms.

Leaning low in the saddle, Eugene steered Cinnamor straight towards Karila, plunging into the mists.

A shrill, high scream pierced the chill air, a child's scream.

If anything has happened to her ... Eugene reached down for his hunting pistols. Cinnamor was slowing, flakes of foam flying from her mouth, unable to sustain the mad gallop much longer.

Scuffing up great clods of earth and grass, the mare skidded to a halt on the lawn.

The Marauder crouched in front of Karila and Marta, spittle trailing from its jaws, poised to spring.

Raising the pistol, Eugene took aim and fired. The ball caught the creature in the side of the head as it leaped, flinging it across the lawn; its flailing limbs juddered once or twice and then it lay still in a puddle of blood and spilling brain.

Karila let out another cry and buried her face in Marta's shoulder.

Eugene jumped down from the saddle and ran over to his daughter. He took her in his arms, feeling her cling to him as if she would never let go.

'It's all right, Kari, it's all right now,' he whispered. Her clothes were soaked with dew.

Guardsmen of the Royal Bodyguard, alerted by

the shot, came running out from the palace across the lawns.

'Are you all right, Highness?' a young lieutenant cried anxiously. One of the bodyguards grabbed hold of Cinnamor's reins and was patting her, speaking softly to calm the jittery mare.

'Take the little one inside and put her in some dry clothes.' Eugene placed Karila in Marta's arms.

Marta was staring at where the attacker's body lay.

'What *was* it, Highness?' she asked shakily. 'A . . . a werewolf?'

Eugene looked too. In death, the Marauder had reverted to his human form, limbs lying awkwardly splayed, skull split open by the pistol-ball.

'My daughter will catch cold,' he said shortly. 'Take her inside.'

The Guardian of the Marauders came hurrying over, his flintlock primed.

'Look,' Eugene said grimly, pointing at the twisted corpse on the grass. 'Why did you let one escape? It attacked my daughter. I want an explanation.'

'News, Highness!' General Anckstrom, Eugene's chief of staff, came hurrying down the steps towards him, his aide-de-camp hovering behind. 'News from Azhkendir.'

Azhkendir. Eugene felt his heart twist in his breast. 'Shall we go in?' he said, making a supreme effort to conceal his feelings in front of his men.

Eugene's study was an austere room, furnished as if for a campaign with regimental colours, maps and weapons. The only concession to ornamentation were the gilded coronets set in the plaster ceiling mouldings. Eugene and Anckstrom went to sit at the desk; the aide-de-camp stood stiffly to attention in front of the doors.

'Magus Linnaius was right,' Anckstrom said. 'Volkh is dead.'

'Dead?' Eugene struck his fist on the desk, making the silver inkpots tremble. 'How?'

'Assassinated,' Anckstrom said bluntly.

'And the assassin?'

'Escaped.'

'Thank God. Thank God.' Eugene realized that he had not taken a breath until that moment. The secret torment that had gnawed at his soul over the past weeks abated a little. 'And has any claim been made to the throne?' he asked, unable to hide the tension in his voice.

'Ah. There the matter seems to become much more complex.'

Eugene raised one eyebrow questioningly. Anckstrom noddded to his aide-de-camp.

'We are not to be disturbed. Not by anyone.'

The aide bowed and left the study. Anckstrom waited until the doors clicked discreetly shut before swinging round to face Eugene.

'Volkh's son is alive. If our information is correct, he has been made Drakhaon.'

This morning all the pieces of Eugene's complex strategic gamble had been in place. Now he saw his carefully laid plans crumbling away. Everything had hinged on Azhkendir.

'Why', he said eventually, 'were we not informed about the son?'

Anckstrom's eyes were fixed on the polished

parquet floor. 'Our agents did not – erm – consider him a threat.'

'You mean our agents were unaware of his existence.'

'He's just a boy. Apparently his mother has raised him to be a painter, like herself. Anyone less suited to the task of ruling Azhkendir I can hardly imagine—'

'And Jaromir?' Eugene said, unable to keep the rawness from his voice. 'What's become of him? He's thrown himself into the dragon's jaws.' The thought that his young protégé might be trapped in Azhkendir, lying burned by Drakhaon's fire, slowly dying alone . . .

He stalked away from Anckstrom, hands clasped behind his back, trying to control this sudden uncharacteristic swell of feelings.

On the further wall two portraits hung, side by side. The first was of his wife Margret. Margret, dead at twenty years, giving birth to poor, lame Karila. Margret, forever young, sweet-faced and smiling, in a striped summer gown, daisies in her pollen-bright hair, the canvas giving no hint of the cruel fate which would take her from him. Beside her hung the portrait of a young man with hair of dark gold, dressed in the grey and blue uniform of the Royal Dragoons, whose haunted eyes betrayed him as one who has looked on horrors no-one so young should have to endure.

'Oh Jaro, Jaro,' Eugene said under his breath, 'why did I let you go?'

'He knew the risks,' Anckstrom said bluntly. 'He chose to go. Nothing you said would have kept him here. Once we had that particular piece of intelligence from *our source*, he knew it was time to make his move.'

Eugene nodded, only half hearing.

'So we call off the invasion?' Anckstrom, thick brows knotted in a frown of concentration, was gazing down at the desk on which a map of the whole continent lay outspread.

'No.' The military strategist in Eugene re-awoke. He walked swiftly over to Anckstrom's side. 'We're going to destroy this young Drakhaon – and put Jaromir in his place. Who then will stand between us and Muscobar? But we must move fast or winter will confound all our plans.'

'So you're willing to risk a direct confrontation?' Anckstrom said, still frowning.

'What did you tell me? "He's just a boy." If he's just a boy, he won't have come into his full powers yet. And with our Marauders we're easily a match for his *druzhina*.'

'But the Marauders are still unproven, unreliable. Look what happened this morning—'

'This morning was an unfortunate error.' And then, seeing no change in Anckstrom's dour expression, 'Anckstrom, I want a message sent to all our troops on the Azhkendi borders: "Stand ready." As for the Marauders . . . I'll go consult Linnaius.'

Magus Kaspar Linnaius, Court Alchymist and Royal Artificier, had recently taken up residence in his new rooms adjacent to the library in the West Wing. Eugene's father, Karl the Navigator, had tempted the scholar to Tielen from the Thaumaturgical College in Francia with the promise of alchymical laboratories, a high-ranking position at court and – perhaps most significant of all – no interference. There had been growing hostility to the work of the alchymists in Francia and, not long after Linnaius left for Tielen, a surge of religious bigotry had closed the college and seen the magisters tried in ecclesiastical courts – then executed for heresy. A more enlightened attitude prevailed in the colder climes of Tielen: the princes had long encouraged the arts and sciences in equal measure.

For the last six months, Linnaius had been working with Eugene on a unique military experiment, the Marauders: a company of warriors from the northern steppes of Tielen transformed by skills Linnaius had learned and adapted from a tribal shaman.

To create the Marauders, Linnaius had visited gaols and barrack-prisons, assembling a group of convicts, all young and fit. Faced with the choice of the gallows or Linnaius's experiment, all had readily agreed to take part.

At first, the Marauders had been comfortably housed in the new palace barracks. Well fed and clothed, they submitted daily to Linnaius's thaumaturgical procedures. Early on, two broke their contract; both had been shot as they tried to sneak away through the parklands with a sack of palace silver. After that, no-one else rebelled. But of late, a change had come over them. The Marauders began to snarl and snap at their keepers, almost as if the lupine nature of their transformation were beginning to overmaster their human traits, and Eugene had been forced to order them to be confined.

As Eugene climbed the wide stone stair that led to the Magus's rooms, his mind was still in turmoil. Had they created a team of uncontrollable monsters, too wild to respond to commands? Now he feared that the whole experiment had been proved a failure and he would be forced to destroy them.

Linnaius's door swung silently open as Eugene reached the top of the stairs and he saw the Magus, his long wisps of silvered hair tied back with a black silk ribbon, standing on the threshold.

'You assured me, Magus, that the Marauders were responding to your commands,' Eugene said as the door silently closed behind him. He had almost grown used to Linnaius's ability to anticipate his visits. 'You assured me they were ready for active service. And now—'

'Now another has absconded,' the Magus said, nodding.

'Absconded? It attacked Karila!' Eugene was still shaken by the encounter – and even more disturbed by his own reaction. 'How can we send them into Azhkendir when they don't respond to our commands?'

'So, you still plan to infiltrate Azhkendir,' said Linnaius, steepling his fingers. His voice was soft and contemplative, colourless as drifting ash.

'There is a new Drakhaon,' Eugene said.

'Ah . . .'

For a moment, Eugene wondered if he was right to place so much trust in the Magus's powers. Was the elderly scholar losing his faculties? No-one had any idea of Linnaius's exact age. He was tall, lean and clean-shaven, the skin stretched so tautly on his face that the bones of the skull protruded, as if countless years devoted to the rigorous study of the science of magic had honed away all softness of flesh, leaving only smooth sculpted bone.

'And there is still no news of Jaromir.'

'Jaromir . . .' A veil descended across the Magus's eyes, thin as spidersilk. Eugene tried to suppress a shudder; he had seen this trick before when the Magus withdrew into his own thoughts. Experience had taught him to be patient.

Suddenly Linnaius blinked and focused his gaze on the Prince again. He rose and beckoned Eugene towards his laboratory. He paused at the open doorway and snapped his fingers. Eugene sensed, rather than saw, the air ripple as an invisible barrier was drawn aside. Passing through, he felt the hairs on the back of his neck prickle – a disconcerting sensation – as though they were brushed by unseen fingers.

The laboratory beyond was scrupulously neat, glass phials and jars arrayed in ranks on the shelves.

'Is he still alive?'

Linnaius took a gold key from about his neck and unlocked a little ebony cabinet. The laboratory grew dim as if clouds had suddenly drifted across the sun, and a soft humming vibration began to emanate from the black depths of the cabinet. A dark light glowed within.

Taking care not to reveal what was inside, the Artificer carefully removed a tiny glass phial in the shape of a lotus-flower, cupping it between his spindly fingers. A faint gleam – dark, tenderly red as heart's blood – lit his hands.

'Our last link,' Linnaius said softly. 'And the only one of the enchantments I placed upon him that has remained untouched by Azhkendir's malevolent atmosphere.'

Eugene, overcome with yearning, found himself stretching out his hand towards the little glass, as if touching it could restore something of lost Jaromir. But Linnaius slowly shook his head.

'As long as this flame still burns, you will know he is alive.'

'It burns so faintly,' Eugene said, his voice trembling. 'What does it mean?'

'It is best not to conjecture. Conjecture can lead to false hopes – or delusions of despair.' Linnaius replaced the lotus-glass in the ebony cabinet and, as he locked it, the darkness slowly bleached from the room and the low hum died to silence. Eugene found himself narrowing his eyes against the daylight which now seemed piercingly bright. Etched on his sight was Jaromir's faint life-flame; wherever he looked, he saw its crimson shadow.

Eugene was at dinner with his chiefs of staff and Chancellor Maltheus when Marta appeared.

'Highness.' She bobbed a curtsey. 'The little one is not well. She's asking to see you.'

'The Prince is busy with matters of state,' Chancellor Maltheus said coldly. 'He will come when he can.'

'I wouldn't have disturbed the Prince,' Marta insisted, face flushing a bright pink, 'but his daughter is very sick.'

Eugene felt a sharp stab of anxiety. Karila ill again. And just at the time he was planning to leave Tielen.

'I'll go see Karila,' he said, rising from the table. 'Excuse me, gentlemen.'

He followed the nurse out into the candlelit corridor, soon outstripping her in his haste.

'Has the doctor seen her? What does he say?'

'Another sweating fever.' She was out of breath from hurrying to keep up with him.

'She was playing near the lake again. It's too damp there, she must have caught a chill. You must keep her in the orangery in the cold months.'

'I try, Highness. But the sunlight is also good for her. I do my best but . . .'

He dashed up the wide curving stair that led to the nursery wing, taking two steps at a time.

Karila's bedroom was painted cerulean blue pricked out with little gold stars and moons. But in spite of the scented candles burning to perfume the sickroom air, he noticed the all-too-familiar smell of illness again. In the bed, beneath the gold coronet and lace hangings, lay his daughter, all curled up under her mussed sheets like a drowsing kitten. He put out one hand to stroke her brow and felt the fever-heat and tendrils of hair damp and lank with sweat. At his touch Karila murmured in her sleep.

'She's burning up. Are you sponging her down with cool water?'

'Oh yes.' Marta bobbed another curtsey. 'And giving her two sips of willow-water every half hour. Just as Doctor Amandel said.'

'Papa.' A little croaking voice issued from his daughter's throat. Eyes, overbright with fever, glistened in her flushed face.

'How do you feel, Kari?'

'My throat hurts.' She held out one hand to him and – after hesitating – he leaned over and took it, feeling the hot, sticky fingers curl about his. 'And my head feels funny. All wrong.'

'You must sleep. When you wake tomorrow, you'll feel much better.' How he hated to hear himself speaking words of reassurance in calm, measured tones when inside he felt such turmoil.

'I dreamed there were shadows in the bedroom. There. At the foot of the bed.' The fever-bright eyes widened in fear. 'Winged. Like dark dragons with fiery eyes. They burned me with their breath. If I sleep again, they'll be there, waiting for me.'

Dragon-shadows. He shivered. What did she mean? What had she seen?

'It was just a dream,' the nurse said, smoothing the rumpled sheets.

'Stay with me, Papa.' The pressure on his hand increased. 'Tell me a story. The Swanmaiden . . .'

'My dear, I have guests. Important guests.' Such a weak excuse. But the longer he stayed, the more the buried memories of Margret's last illness began to surface.

'His Highness is a busy man, Karila,' Marta said briskly. 'Say good night to your father and settle down. I'll tell you the Swanmaiden's tale.'

He glanced gratefully up at her.

'Good night, Kari. Sleep sound.' He leaned over and briefly brushed her hot forehead with his lips.

'Night . . .' she murmured, lids fluttering closed.

Maltheus had conducted the chiefs of staff from the dining table to the Walnut Anteroom where *digestifs* were being served; Eugene accepted a little glass of clear aquavit from a servant and swallowed it down.

'Well?' Maltheus said.

'Another chill.' Eugene beckoned the servant to refill his glass; the clean taste of the aquavit cleared his head of the lingering taint of the sickroom.

'There's nothing for it. You must marry again.'

'Must I?'

'Karila is sickly. A sweet child, but hardly one capable of ruling Tielen. You need an heir, Highness.'

'Yes, yes. All in good time.' Eugene set the glass down. 'At this moment we have other concerns. What news from the Straits?'

'Admiral Janssen reports no significant losses,' said Maltheus, helping himself to more sloe brandy. 'The *Helda* lost her mainsail in the most recent exchange of fire. But we sank two of the Muscobar fleet and holed a third.'

'That'll make the Grand Duke sweat!' said Anckstrom with a chuckle.

'Indeed,' Maltheus said drily. 'And to that end, I suspect, we have a visitor. The Muscobar ambassador is waiting to see Your Highness.'

'Count Velemir?' Eugene said. Was there news at last from Azhkendir?

'He says he has come with a proposition. He's waiting for you in the Malachite Room.'

A fire was burning in the marble fireplace of the Malachite Room, casting warm shadows on the dark sea-green brocaded walls.

Count Velemir was standing before a great naval battle canvas depicting the triumphant defeat of the Francians by the Tielen fleet commanded by Prince Karl off the Saltyk Peninsula. The sea boiled with fire and the red-streaked sky was dark with the smoke of the Tielen cannon.

He turned as Eugene entered and bowed.

'An impressive piece of work, Highness.' He spoke the Tielen language with just the slightest hint of a Muscobar accent. 'Designed, no doubt, to strike fear into the hearts of the enemies of Tielen.'

'Commissioned to celebrate my father's first naval victory,' Eugene said, affecting a careless tone. In spite of his lifelong schooling in self-restraint and fortitude, he longed to cry out, 'You've brought news of Jaromir at last?' Instead he merely gestured to the Count to come to sit opposite him beside the fire. 'This room is full of mementoes of his life. I like to think of him watching over me, approving what I have done with his old hunting lodge.'

'And what a magnificent achievement Swanholm has turned out to be, Highness. Such refined taste. Such elegance.' In all their meetings Eugene had never once been deceived by the ambassador's urbane manner; he saw beneath Velemir's cultured façade a sharp and devious mind, always ready to turn a difficult situation to his own advantage.

'So what is this proposition you have come to make me?'

'Marriage. The Grand Duke proposes a match between Your Highness and his daughter, the Altessa Astasia.'

'Marriage?' Eugene echoed. This was not at all what he had expected and for a moment he found himself thrown completely off course. Could this be the Duke's admission of defeat in the Straits? Or just another stalling tactic?

142

'A delightful girl, just nineteen summers old, strong, healthy – and very attractive.'

'Nineteen.' Margret had been just eighteen when they married, he a dozen years her senior. There would be a greater gap between Astasia and himself. Damn it all, he was old enough to be her father. 'Another child bride.'

'A portrait is nearing completion, Highness. I think you will not be disappointed.'

Eugene nodded absently. He had more troubling matters on his mind.

'A union between the royal houses of Muscobar and Tielen. What better way to bring peace to the continent? What better way to put the unpleasantness over the herring grounds behind us?' Velemir was still the consummate courtier, ever ready to charm. But Eugene was in no mood to be charmed. He had been patient long enough.

'News,' he said, leaning forward into the glare of the flames. 'You promised me news.'

Velemir's pleasant expression faded. 'Of our mutual friend? No further news. All we know is he never reached the Council in Azhgorod to make his claim to the throne. Neither did he make it to Arkhelskoye in time to catch the last boat out.'

'You promised me your agent in Azhkendir would keep us informed,' Eugene said, his voice dangerously quiet. 'You gave me your word, Velemir.'

'My agent has been unable to keep contact with the young man in question. And, I might add, recent circumstances have placed my agent in a very delicate situation. Communication is . . . difficult.'

'Even though Magus Linnaius entrusted you and your agent with his most sophisticated intelligence artifice.' Frustration – and the certainty that Velemir was not being as open with him as he should – hardened Eugene's voice. 'You underestimated the *druzhina*'s cunning, Velemir. I'm disappointed in you. If we had known—'

'You wouldn't have let Jaromir go?' There was the slightest tinge of irony in the Count's voice.

Eugene let a sigh of frustration escape. 'Who am I trying to fool? Nothing I could say or do would have prevented him going to seek out Volkh. He was like a caged bird, beating at the bars of his gilded cage, burned up with grief and frustration. Now I fear—'

'That the *druzhina* have captured him?'

Jaromir interrogated, tortured, left to die in chains in some vile Azhkendi dungeon . . . The fear flared again in Eugene's breast.

'The House of Nagarian has been a constant threat to the peace and stability of the whole continent. We must crush this young serpent in his lair. And if Muscobar will not help, then I swear on my father's name I will take action myself.'

'How can Muscobar help you, Highness,' Velemir said with a shrug, 'when we are tied by the Treaty of Accord the Grand Duke signed with Lord Volkh?'

'Volkh is dead,' Eugene said coldly. 'The treaty is null and void. You will remind the Grand Duke of that fact, Ambassador.'

There was silence a moment except for the hiss and crackle of the flaming logs in the grate.

'So what answer shall I convey to Grand Duke Aleksei, Highness? Do you accept his proposition?'

Eugene sensed – with some satisfaction – the

slightest suggestion of desperation colouring the ambassador's carefully chosen words.

'Can we hope for a peaceful conclusion to this unfortunate disagreement in the Straits?' Velemir added.

'I will give it all due consideration.' Let the Grand Duke and his ministers sweat a little longer, Eugene thought. Now that Muscobar's most powerful ally, Volkh, was dead, Aleksei Orlov was doubly vulnerable. 'I will let you know my decision as soon I have discussed the matter with my ministers.'

Velemir's face darkened as he realized he had been dismissed, but Eugene saw him swiftly conceal his disappointment in an elaborately courtly bow.

9

Every time Kiukiu closed her eyes she saw Bogatyr Kostya loom out of the smoky shadows, staring at her with eyes of stone, finger jabbing accusingly.

'*You lied to me. You summoned Lord Volkh. Now you must send him back.*'

'But I don't know how—'

She woke shivering, her linen shift soaked with perspiration. She sat upright in her narrow bed, hugging her knees to her, trying to still the shaking.

The little room was dim with the half-light before dawn, a fusty, dusty light. She blinked – and it was as if the dust of past ages had settled on her lashes, veiling her sight. One thing alone was clear: she must try to send Lord Volkh's spirit-wraith back to the Ways Beyond before anyone discovered the truth.

But how can I send him back without the mirror? And what if he refuses to go?

* * *

Kiukiu waited, hiding beneath the stairs, until she saw Lord Gavril escorted from his chamber by the Bogatyr. As they descended, she heard the Bogatyr insisting upon an important meeting with the Azhgorod lawyers. If she was lucky, the bedchamber would be empty for at least an hour.

Once inside, she made loud noises scraping out the grate, clattering the dustpan and brush so that anyone passing outside would know she was busy at her work. And all the time that she worked, she could sense the little doorway to the dressing-room behind her. Such an innocuous-looking little door – and yet in her mind it loomed vast as a portal to hell.

At last the grate was cleared and fresh kindling laid. She sat back on her heels and wiped the back of her hand across her brow. Hot work, clearing grates.

She listened. No-one was about. No-one would know if she slipped into the dressing-room for a few minutes.

'Lord Volkh?' she whispered as she entered. 'My Lord?'

What was she doing, calling on a ghost as she might call Sosia's cat? The little room had lost all its charged atmosphere, it was just a dressing-room again. She closed her eyes, searching in her mind for any trace of Lord Volkh's presence. But there was no response, no prickle of fear or recognition . . .

A sound from outside startled her.

Someone was in the bedchamber. Someone who – from what she could hear – was rifling through the Drakhaon's possessions.

And they don't know I'm here.

Kiukiu crept through the doorway and stayed, hidden behind the bed-canopy, biting her lip so as not to breathe.

Who is it? What are they looking for?

Curiosity overruled caution. Kiukiu knew she should not peep, but she could not stop herself. Silently, she drew back a fold of the heavy dark brocade and saw . . .

A woman in a jade-silk gown bending over the unlocked dragon-chest, a woman who was feverishly sifting through the contents, a woman whose luxuriant chestnut hair glinted in the dim light.

Lilias.

Kiukiu closed her eyes in dread. If Lilias knew she had been observed . . .

'Not here. Not here!' Lilias was muttering to herself now. She pressed the lid shut and locked it again, using a little key on a chain around her neck.

She pushed herself up to her feet, moving slowly, laboriously. 'Then where, *where*?' she whispered, one hand on her swollen belly, as though talking to her unborn child. She looked up at the portrait of the boy and – to Kiukiu's astonishment – spat at it. The genteel Lady Lilias, spitting like a common village drudge . . .

'Don't think I'm going to give all this up without a fight. When my son is born, then we shall see who is truly Drakhaon.'

There was such malice in her voice that Kiukiu shrank back inside the doorway.

Best not to have looked. Best to stay quiet, not move, not give myself away.

Lilias gathered the loose folds of her green silk

gown about her and Kiukiu saw her lift the corner of one of the great gold and crimson hunting tapestries on the far wall. A little door slid open behind . . . and Lilias bent to enter, letting the tapestry fall back behind her.

A secret door. Kiukiu stared, her mouth open. She knew there were secret passageways in the kastel, but she had never before been aware that there was one right here, in the Drakhaon's bedchamber. She had dusted and polished so close to it and never known . . .

'Kiukiu!' shrilled Sosia.

Kiukiu opened the door a crack and looked warily out.

'Better hurry,' said one of the guards on the door with a grin, 'or she'll box your ears!'

She nodded. As she reached the stairs, she grabbed up a handful of skirts and ran down to the hallway, the sound of her footsteps echoing and re-echoing up into the rafters.

And as she ran, she kept silently repeating to herself, 'Best forget, best forget . . .'

Best to forget all about it.

Kiukiu carried her empty bucket across the weed-grown cobbles to the coalhouse in the kastel outbuildings. Here the green boughs of the great forest of Kerjhenezh overhung the ramshackle roofs of the stores and granaries, whispering and sighing in the breeze, wafting a faint breath of pine resin across the twilit courtyard.

She was shovelling the precious coal into her bucket when she heard the cry. An eerie, keening sound that raised the hairs at the back of her neck.

Ghost spirit of the forest. The stalking beast whose fangs dripped blood.

It came again – high-pitched, inhuman – the cry of a creature in pain.

Kiukiu dropped the shovel and began to run towards the sound of the cries, through the kitchen gardens towards the old walled orchard. She came stumbling in between the bent, weathered apple trees to see a man kneeling, stout stick raised, over something that shrieked and struggled, caught in the fanged jaws of a poacher's trap.

'Let it *alone*!' Kiukiu cried, launching herself across the frosty grass. She hurtled into the man with full force, knocking him over. Only then, as she rolled clear of him, she saw who she had felled. It was Oleg, the butler.

Oleg gave a winded groan and began to fumble for his stick. Panicked, Kiukiu edged away across the grass, slippery with frost-blackened windfalls. Was there still time to make a grab for the stick? She had meant to save the creature in the trap, but now it looked as if Oleg was about to attack her.

'Come here.' Oleg rose unsteadily to his knees. He let out a rumbling belch; his breath stank of stale beer. 'Come here and I'll give you a good thrashing.'

'Help!' Kiukiu yelled at the top of her lungs. 'Help me!' She grabbed up her skirts to run – but her toe caught in the hem and she came crashing down onto her knees. Oleg lurched towards her, jabbing the end of his stick in her face.

'They bring bad luck, Arkhel's Owls. Cursed creatures. Kill 'em and string 'em up to rot, I say.'

'*Help me!*'

'Who's going to hear you, you silly little bitch? Someone needs to teach you a lesson.'

He swung the stick back to strike.

'No!' Kiukiu flung up both arms to cover her face.

'Who's there?'

Oleg hesitated, distracted, looking round.

There were footsteps, running through the orchard towards them. Kiukiu looked dazedly up to see Lord Gavril beneath the ancient apple trees. His eyes burned like blue flames in the gloom.

'L-lord Drakhaon.' Oleg dropped the stick.

Lord Gavril advanced on Oleg, one hand outstretched, finger pointing. Oleg began to tremble.

'You. Go. *Get out.*'

'M-my Lord—' Oleg, face suddenly pale as alefroth, turned and went loping clumsily away, leaving the stick where he had dropped it.

'Are you all right?' Lord Gavril kneeled beside Kiukiu. 'Did he hurt you?'

Kiukiu stared up at him, dizzy with gratitude and relief. Lord Gavril had saved her from Oleg! Her heart sang silently within her.

'Thank you, My Lord,' she whispered.

'Who was that man? What was he doing here?'

A bloodchilling shriek came again from the trap. Kiukiu jumped up, brushing the moss and dead bracken from her skirts.

'He's called Oleg. He was going to kill it,' she said, pointing to the trap. 'I couldn't let him do it.'

The creature was a writhing ball of speckled snow-white feathers against the dark brambles. No blood-boltered fiend, just a young bird, injured and terrified.

151

'Ohh,' Kiukiu said softly. 'Poor thing. Poor little thing.'

'What *is* it?'

'See those ear-tufts? I think it's a young snow owl. But they rarely nest this far from the mountains . . .'

The bird hissed at her from a sharp-curved beak. It was nearly exhausted from its struggles and its feathers were bloodied and torn, but it was still ready to fight to defend itself.

'We'll have to prise the trap open.' She was untying her apron. If Sosia found out what it had been used for, she would beat her, but there was no alternative.

'There, there,' she crooned to the owl as she edged forwards across the crushed bracken. 'Hush now. We'll soon have you out.'

She held out the apron. Good, thick-woven linen. Tough as a sack. She hoped it would protect her from the sharp, snapping beak.

'Here.' Lord Gavril had retrieved Oleg's stick.

'When I put the apron over its head, My Lord, you open the trap.'

Brilliant owl-eyes blazed defiance. Gavril knelt beside her and the terrified bird tried to jerk away again. Hastily she threw the apron over its head.

'Quick!' Its struggles beneath the coarse cloth were frantic as Lord Gavril fumbled with the iron teeth of the trap, trying to find the spring. 'I – can't hold it – much longer—'

'I *am* hurrying!'

With a sudden clang, the trap sprang open and Kiukiu swiftly drew out the owl. For a moment it went limp – whether due to loss of blood or relief, she couldn't tell. She took a look at the injured leg. 'It's lame.'

'It'll never survive if we leave it here.'

'Then I'll care for it.' She began to wrap up the little creature again, swaddling it like a baby.

'The hunting dogs'll sniff it out and kill it. If Oleg doesn't find it first. What does he have against snow owls?'

She looked up at him. Didn't he know? Had no-one told him?

'They still call them Arkhel's Owls, My Lord. They were the emblem of the House of Arkhel.'

'Arkhel's Owls,' Lord Gavril said pensively.

'They bring bad luck, My Lord. Bad luck for our House. Your father's men kill them whenever they find them.'

'Bad luck?' he echoed. His eyes had reverted to their normal sea-blue again, calm waters now after the storm.

'Poor little abandoned orphan,' Kiukiu crooned to the owl, trying to stroke it. 'Ow!' She snatched her hand away, shaking her fingers. 'It pecked me.'

Lord Gavril began to laugh. 'There's gratitude for you.'

'But where shall we keep it? Till it can fly again?'

'We? You're involving *me* in this?'

She grinned back, forgetting for a moment who he was, relishing the conspiratorial closeness.

'I can see that it would be foolish to take it back into the kastel. Is there somewhere in the gardens – a toolshed, a disused aviary?'

'The Elysia Summerhouse!' Kiukiu said, triumphant. 'No-one ever goes there now, the floor's all rotted away.'

'Elysia?' His eyes clouded over. 'That's my mother's name. Was it her summerhouse? Did he build it for her?'

He seemed to be talking to himself, thinking aloud, not anticipating an answer. Which was just as well, Kiukiu thought, as she had no idea who had built the summerhouse – only that it was a ruin, swathed in ivy and brambles. An ideal house for an owl.

'And you – what's your name?' he asked.

'Kiukiu.'

'Kiukiu?'

She felt herself blushing with pleasure to hear him say her name out loud.

'Does it have a special meaning?'

'Oh, it's just what everyone calls me. It's short for Kiukirilya.'

He nodded. 'Quite a mouthful. No wonder everyone shortens it.'

The Elysia Summerhouse had six sides, with a veranda around it. The delicate curving roof was ornamented with a little spire with a weather-vane fashioned out of wrought iron like a barque in full sail.

Once, Kiukiu reckoned, it had been prettily painted with white and green paint. But neglect and the ravages of the Azhkendir winter had stripped all but the stubbornest traces of paint from its trelliswork.

'Watch where you tread, My Lord,' she cautioned.

She wasn't sure if he had heard her; he was staring up at the ruined fretwork that decorated the veranda.

'I wonder . . . did she used to sit here in the summertime?' His face had become wistful.

Kiukiu swallowed. She so wanted to be able to say 'yes' and console him. 'I don't know, My Lord, I wasn't born then.'

'Of course not.' He seemed to collect himself. 'I'll go look for something to splint that leg.'

Lord Gavril soon reappeared with a short, straight twig from which he stripped the bark with a little pocket-knife, snapping it to make a little splint.

'Now all we need is something to bind the leg to the splint, some twine, string . . .'

'Here.' She untied the blue ribbon securing one of her plaits and handed it to him.

'Now hold it tight. It'll struggle. I'll fix this as fast as I can.'

Kiukiu held the owl in the apron. It felt warm and soft beneath the linen; she was half afraid she might smother or crush it if it fought her.

'Keep firm hold,' Lord Gavril muttered. She watched as he bound the broken leg with deft fingers.

The light was fading, the last of the daylight bleeding from the sky in streaks of fiery crimson; Kiukiu wondered how he could see what he was doing in the fast-gathering gloom.

'It's done. You can let it go now,' he said, letting out a slow breath of relief.

Kiukiu eased the apron away from the feathery bundle and hastily drew back in case the owl decided to attack her again. But it merely ruffled its feathers as if deeply offended, and hopped in an ungainly, lopsided way into the darkest corner of the summerhouse.

'If it survives the next two days, it'll be fine,' Lord Gavril said, pushing his hair from his eyes. 'As long as that brute Oleg doesn't find it.'

Kiukiu gazed at him, smitten. He had rescued her from 'that brute' Oleg. She owed him. She wanted to help him in return – even if she put herself in danger.

'My Lord,' she began. 'There's something else. Something you ought to know.'

'Well?' he said.

'There's a secret door in your room.'

'In my room?' Suddenly he was all attention. 'Where does it lead, this secret door? Out of the kastel?'

'I don't know. But I – I saw someone use it to get into your bedchamber.'

'Someone? Who?' he asked, frowning now.

She swallowed. To tell him would be to take a dangerous path from which there was no turning back. And yet not to tell him . . .

'Lilias,' she said softly.

'Lilias? In my bedchamber? Doing what?'

'She was looking for something.'

'Did she find it?'

'No. She unlocked that chest, the dragon-chest. She seemed very angry. And I heard her say – oh dear.' Kiukiu clamped both hands to her mouth. She had said too much. Suddenly she was frightened.

'What did she say?' The warmth had faded from his eyes.

'Promise me, My Lord, promise me you'll never tell anyone.' Even now, her common sense was screaming at her not to say any more, to protect herself.

'You have my word as Drakhaon.'

She knew then she could not help herself, she would walk through fire for him.

'There was something about not giving up without a fight. And then she said, "Wait till my son is born. Then we'll find out who is really Drakhaon."'

'Ah,' he said.

Darkness seeped into the summerhouse; the owl rustled its feathers in the shadows, letting out a soft, trilling hoot.

Lord Gavril glanced round, almost as if glad for the distraction.

'What shall we give this poor creature to eat till it can hunt for itself again?'

'I can filch some little bits of raw meat from the kitchen,' Kiukiu offered. 'Sosia won't notice.'

'And water. We must leave it water.'

'What shall we call it?' Kiukiu was glad not to be talking of Lilias any more. 'It must have a name.'

'We don't even know if it's male or female.'

'What about Snowy, then?'

'Too predictable.'

'Blizzard?' Ideas came crowding into her mind. 'Icefeather? Snowcloud?'

'Snowcloud.' He repeated the name slowly, pensively. 'A good name. An evocative name.'

'Your name is Snowcloud,' she told the owl. It did not seem in the least impressed.

'You go back first, My Lord. Best we're not seen together.'

At the door of the summerhouse he paused and looked back.

'You're not afraid, then?'

'Afraid, My Lord?' She wasn't sure what he meant. 'Of Arkhel bad luck?'

'Of me,' he said quietly. And before she could answer, he walked out into the dusk.

Next morning Lord Gavril was still in bed when Kiukiu crept in with her bucket of coals.

'I've come to do your fire, My Lord. I didn't mean to disturb you, I can come back later . . .'

'No. Come in, Kiukiu.'

She was shocked to see how pale he looked; there were dark shadows beneath his eyes, as if he had not slept all night.

She hurried across the bedchamber to the grate and hastily began to scrape out the ashes of last night's fire. She could not help but notice how golden-brown his skin was where the white cambric nightshirt gaped open at the neck . . .

What was she thinking of? Her cheeks burning, she tried to concentrate on the task in hand.

'How is Snowcloud?'

'Still alive, My Lord.' Kiukiu carefully laid the last coals on top of the carefully constructed pile. 'He tried to peck me when I brought fresh water and food.' She lit the kindling, then took up the bellows, coaxing the tiny flame. 'But the frost was very harsh last night. The water I left was frozen over. Perhaps we should take some straw for it to sleep in?'

'But it's a snow owl,' he said absently, as if his mind were elsewhere. 'Aren't they used to the cold? Better used than we are?'

He was right, of course. What must he think of her? It was just that every time she gazed into those sea-blue eyes, she forgot what she was talking about.

He threw off the bedclothes and swung his legs out of bed.

'Show me the hidden door, Kiukiu.'

'N-now?' She had told him about it; wasn't that enough?

'What better time?' He was alert now. 'The guards outside think you're busy lighting the fire. Who will know?'

'But you're not dressed,' she said, blushing.

'Easily rectified.' He grabbed a pair of breeches and began to pull them on; hastily she turned her head away.

'There!' He had put on the fur-lined black jacket which had been left slung over the dragon-chest. 'Will that do?'

She wavered before the great hanging tapestries. Was it the one with the bowmen shooting down a stag? Or the one next to it with the falcons?

She raised the tasselled and braided edge of the tapestry. A plain little door was set in the wall behind.

'It's here.'

The heavy tapestry smelled of dust; her arm was beginning to ache with the weight of holding it up and the gilded threads felt as scratchy as strands of coarse string.

Lord Gavril put out his hand and tried the handle; the little door swung slowly inwards with a creak. Beyond lay a narrow stone passageway that wound away into utter darkness.

Kiukiu shivered.

'Where does it go?' Her voice echoed back to her from the cold passageway beyond.

'Let's find out,' he said. 'Fetch a candle, Kiukiu.'

'Suppose it goes straight to My Lady Lilias's rooms?' Kiukiu said, horrified at the thought. 'Straight to her bedchamber?'

'Then perhaps she'll entertain us to breakfast.' The blue eyes flashed with grim humour.

As Kiukiu crept along the cold, dark passageway behind Lord Gavril, she realized she had completely forgotten they were master and servant. He treated her as if she were his equal, and yet he was lord of all Azhkendir. She must never let herself forget again. It was just that he was so . . . nice.

'Mind your head,' he whispered, 'the passage's getting lower. And narrower . . . Ah.' He stopped. The pale candleflame wavered in a gust of fresh, freezing air.

'What is it, My Lord?'

'Two tunnels ahead. And some kind of grating. That's where the air's coming from. And the spiders.'

'Spiders.' She pulled a face.

'Generations of spiders. My guess is that the tunnel to the right is the one Lilias used. It's much cleaner than the left-hand one.'

'I should have brought my broom,' Kiukiu said, trying to sound nonchalant.

'Kiukiu, you don't have to come any further.'

'Oh, I'm coming, My Lord, broom or no. I've got to make sure you get safely back.'

'And protect me from the spiders.' She could hear self-mockery in his voice now.

'Oh – I didn't mean—'

'My guess', he said, turning into the left-hand tunnel, 'is that this one leads to the East Wing.'

His voice came back hollowly to her, muffled by the dusty darkness ahead. Strands of powdery webs tickled her face, clinging to her hair and hands.

'Pah!' She spat out a wisp of spidersilk that clung to her mouth.

'Another door.' She heard him rattling the handle. 'Locked.' He fished out a ring of keys from his pocket. 'Here, hold the candle, Kiukiu.'

As he tried key after key, half-forgotten fragments of stories began to swirl like wisps of moor-mist around Kiukiu's mind. Stories of the lost brides of past Drakhaons, walled up in towers and left to die, of unfaithful wives incarcerated with the rotting corpses of their murdered lovers. Tales of gouts of black blood dripping through into the rooms below from hidden chambers above, the muffled, agonized cries of the tortured heard through walls a handspan thick . . .

And all in the East Wing.

Several neglected chores began to nag; suddenly the prospect of scrubbing a tubful of washing seemed infinitely preferable to waiting in this cold, spider-infested labyrinth.

She shifted awkwardly from foot to foot.

'Perhaps I should go back—' she whispered.

'Ah!' Lord Gavril said triumphantly. The key had turned in the lock – and the ancient door slowly opened.

'Sosia'll be wondering where I am,' she said, hating herself for sounding so faint-hearted.

'I'll tell Sosia you were working for me. I'll think of some excuse or other – she won't dare to go against the word of the Drakhaon, will she?'

His face, in the flickering candlelight, was twisted into a smile of wry self-deprecation.

'No,' she said unhappily.

A shaft of daylight, pale as milk, lit the passageway ahead. Lord Gavril, leading the way, stumbled and almost fell, putting out one hand to save himself.

'Take care,' he said. 'The floorboards are rotting away.'

Kiukiu looked down and saw that he had nearly put his foot right through a worm-eaten board. A musty smell of decaying wood rose from the hole.

'Didn't Sosia say Doctor Kazimir was overfond of his liquor?' Lord Gavril said, testing the floor ahead, one step at a time. 'It's a wonder he didn't fall and break his neck.'

Lord Gavril reached the source of the light: a great oriel window, boarded and bricked up, with just a few cracked panes at the top still letting in the daylight . . . and the rain.

'Look,' Kiukiu said, awed, forgetting all about Sosia. She could see now that they stood on a balcony with an ironwork balustrade that ran around three of the four sides. Opposite them a dilapidated marble stair curved drunkenly downwards to the ground floor, which was tiled with the same patterned tiles as those to be found in the Great Hall.

There had been plaster on the walls, and in places fragments of fine gilt mouldings still remained; the rest had faded to a chalky grey and was marred by great, dark blotches of damp and a telltale rash of mould.

Lord Gavril set off towards the stairs and almost

tripped as something small and furry shot out from under his feet and went squeaking away into the shadows.

'Mice?' Kiukiu placed her hand on her chest, trying to still the panicked thudding of her heart. 'Or rats . . . ?'

'What a dismal place,' Lord Gavril said, his voice echoing around the cavernous hall. 'If I were Doctor Kazimir, which of these rooms would I have chosen as my laboratory?'

He had begun to open the dark doors that led off the landing, one after another. Kiukiu hovered behind him, unwilling to look inside, dreading that she might glimpse the remains of some nameless atrocity committed by Lord Gavril's ancestors. Bloodstained spectres of mutilated brides floated through her imagination, drifted their skeletal fingers through her hair, whispered her name with dust-choked charnel voices . . .

'If you are gone too long, My Lord, the Bogatyr may come looking for you,' she said.

He did not reply. She turned around – and found herself alone. He must have gone into one of the rooms.

'Lord Gavril?' she said in a small voice.

Then she heard a hollow footfall coming from inside one of the open doors. She crept on tiptoe across the dusty boards and peeped inside.

'Look. Look at this,' he said in soft, awed tones.

The walls were lined with shelves; just like Sosia's pantries, Kiukiu thought. And on the shelves were jars: each with gilded labels with black, curling writing on them. But as Kiukiu could not read, the letters meant nothing to her.

Lord Gavril was standing at a long table, examining the clutter of strange objects ranged along its top. Glass phials, jars and alembics, some with murky liquids still inside, were connected by a complicated system of tubes, pipes and coils.

Kiukiu couldn't help giggling.

'So that's what Doctor Kazimir was up to,' she said. 'No wonder he was always drunk!'

'Hm?' Lord Gavril was gently blowing the film of dust from an open ledger.

'It's a still! Oleg's got jars and pipes like this in the cellar. He makes aquavit and plum brandy – strong enough to rot your entrails, Sosia says.' She ran one finger along the rim of the table and absently examined the grey dust-stain it left. He did not answer; he was thumbing feverishly through the pages of the ledger which were filled with a fine, spidery handwriting.

'Look at this mess!' She reached the end of the long table where the neat arrangements of pipes and bottles ended in chaos. Smashed glass littered the floor and strange stains of green and acid-yellow had corroded the wood. More livid splashes stained the floor and the walls. It was as if someone had dashed the construction to the floor in a fury.

Lord Gavril closed the ledger, sending up another little puff of dust into the air.

Kiukiu sneezed.

'I have all I need for now,' he said tersely.

'We're going?'

He shut the door carefully behind them.

'The candle's burning low,' Kiukiu said, shielding the wavering flame with her hand as another damp draught set it wildly flickering.

'Lead the way, then.'

When they reached the great door that led back to the secret passage, he put down the ledger to find the keys.

'What's this?' He straightened up, holding out his hand for her to see what he had picked up.

It was a slender glass phial, barely the length of her little finger.

'For perfume?' she said. 'Or one of the essences Sosia uses to flavour puddings: vanilla, almond, rose?'

'But why here? And look, there's some residue.' He sniffed the phial, pulling a sour face. 'It smells acrid. Not the least like perfume . . .'

'*Poison* . . .'

Kiukiu felt herself racked by a sudden bitter chill; glancing up, she saw – behind Lord Gavril – a man, standing watching them, a shadow dimly etched against the pale shaft of frosted daylight.

Lord Gavril whipped around.

'Father! Wait!' he cried. His voice came echoing back in shivers of sound.

But even as Kiukiu forced herself to look again, she saw that the revenant had gone.

'Must have been a . . . a trick of the light,' she said.

He said nothing. When she dared to look up at his face she saw that his eyes were set, staring grimly into the empty passageway.

'*You* saw him too.' She felt cold and sick. The air, when she tried to take in a breath, tasted bitter as winter-frost.

He weighed the little glass tube in his palm. 'Of course. There must be another passageway that leads from here to the Great Hall.' He seemed to have forgotten she was there. 'A whole network of passages – even one that leads out into the grounds, outside the kastel walls . . . Kiukiu!'

'Yes, My Lord?' She gazed up into his eyes. So blue, she could drown in them. The fear and the cold receded.

'I want you to give me your word. That you'll say nothing of what has happened here today. My life – and yours – may depend on it.'

The earnestness of his voice, the intensity of his blue gaze, mesmerized her. She looked down and saw that his hands were on her shoulders.

'I give you my word,' she said.

His hands – touching her! As she led the way back down the grimy passageway away from the door, she felt so light, so airy, she could have danced.

You didn't have to ask me to swear secrecy, My Lord. Can't you see that I am utterly devoted to you?

10

On the fifth evening the Orlov carriages rattled across a broad fertile river plain towards the setting sun and the distant shimmering mirage that was Mirom, capital city of Muscobar.

As they drew near, the mirage became stone, and the light of the setting sun gilded the spires and painted onion domes of Mirom's monasteries and cathedrals. Elysia leaned close to the dusty window to gaze out. She had never visited Mirom in her life and she wanted to see if the city lived up to the many reports of its wealth and splendour.

Centuries ago, Mirom had been the capital of the powerful empire of Rossiya. Once, before the downfall of the imperial family, the emperors had held court here. On the death of the last emperor, Artamon, his sons had scrapped like dogs for the throne – and eventually the empire had been divided up amongst their warring families: Muscobar; Smarna to the south; and Tielen, Azhkendir and

Khitari to the far north. The Grand Dukes of Mirom still claimed blood descent from the Great Artamon, though genealogists disputed the claim.

Stiff though she was and weary from the rigours of the overland journey, Elysia was enchanted with her first view of the city of Mirom. The cathedral domes were bright with coloured swirls of mosaic tiles in rich reds, purples and blues, and bristled with golden spires.

The great gateway under which they passed bore the Orlov crest: two proud sea eagles, wings outstretched, emblazoned in blue, white and gold.

And then they were in the city, clattering over cobbles, as, flanked by the White Guard, the carriages rolled towards a broad tree-lined boulevard.

'Home at last,' cried Astasia. And then she let out another piercing sigh.

'And not before time,' said Eupraxia. 'How wearisome this journey has been. The sea-route is much more pleasant.'

'Praxia, you know Mama was seasick last time we came by sea. Perhaps Prince Eugene has unwittingly spared her.'

Elysia was still looking out of the window. In the mellow dusk, lamplighters were lighting the streetlamps which glowed along each side of the wide avenue. The carriage-wheels ran more smoothly now, as if rolling on soft-milled gravel. Ahead lay high walls interspersed with ornately spiked iron-work railings; in the centre were gilded iron gates which also bore the Orlov crest finely worked in metal.

In the wide avenues Elysia saw people stopping beneath the trees and staring. But she had heard no cheers of welcome, only the incessant clatter of the horses' hooves and the jingle of the harnesses. Perhaps the comings and goings of the ruling family were a commonplace event to the people of Mirom . . .

Then the carriages wheeled through the gates and into the vast courtyard, making straight for the central building. It was not until they drew close that Elysia saw a second archway constructed in the palace itself and realized they were about to drive through into an inner courtyard.

'Home at last,' Astasia said again as the carriage juddered to a halt. She flung open the door and leaped nimbly down before one of the liveried servants had hurried forwards to help her. 'Eupraxia, make sure Madame Andar is made comfortable. See she has rooms in the West Wing near to your own. I have things to do.' And she went running off before Eupraxia could stop her.

Eupraxia shook her head, tutting fondly. 'Still rushing round like a giddy schoolgirl. What will Prince Eugene think? What kind of a bride will she make?'

Elysia was staring up at the painted stucco façades of the Winter Palace: walls of grey and blue, pillars and carvings highlighted in cold, winter white. Inside the tall windows she caught the glitter of glass crystals in chandeliers and polished mirrors. A palace of ice and snow, she thought. I only hope its inhabitants haven't hearts of ice as well.

'A word of advice, Madame Andar,' Eupraxia whispered in her ear. 'When you are preparing for your audience with His Grace the Grand Duke, make sure you wear appropriate court dress. It would be deemed an impropriety to appear inappropriately dressed.'

Court dress? Elysia took out the few clothes she had brought with her, shaking her head over each as she laid them on the bed. There was nothing remotely grand here. Her life in Vermeille had not included balls or imperial receptions. Vermeille was a republic; a revolution long before she was born had ousted the ruling family and established a democratically elected council.

Perhaps she could borrow a court gown? She had no wish to offend the Grand Duke by dressing inappropriately and thereby prejudicing Gavril's cause . . .

'How ridiculous!' she whispered, furiously casting down the last gown on the bed. 'My son's future is at stake, and here I am having to worry about *dresses.*'

There was a discreet tap at the door and Eupraxia appeared, bearing a little tray. A delicious smell wafted from a porcelain bowl on the tray as Eupraxia set it down.

'Astasia thought you might need some refreshment, madame, so I've brought you some *bouillon* to restore you after the journey.'

'How thoughtful,' Elysia said distractedly. 'But right now, Eupraxia, what I most need is some advice. Which of these gowns is closest to court dress?'

Eupraxia looked down at the dresses and Elysia saw a little frown furrow her plump, pleasant face.

'Oh dear.'

'None of these?'

'Well, perhaps this one, the russet velvet. But it is considered a discourtesy to His Grace to appear in his presence plainly dressed; one must look as if one has spent the greatest time and trouble to look one's

170

best. But as long as you wear your jewels with it . . .'

'Jewels?' Elysia stared at Eupraxia. What would they think of her? She had no jewels; she had sold the sapphires Volkh had given her on their wedding day to pay for their passage back to Vermeille. All she had kept was a single ruby, Volkh's first gift to her, dark as blood. She had not worn it in over fifteen years but somehow had found herself unable to part with it, even when times were hard. Now she took it out and strung it around her neck; against her creamy skin it looked like a crimson teardrop.

The marble floor was so highly polished that Elysia could see her reflection in it. Gold-swagged mirrors and varnished maps painted in rich colours adorned the panelled walls, and at the centre of the room stood a wide desk fashioned out of walnut, each leg carved as a gilded sea-eagle.

A white-haired man sat writing at the desk; he was in plain court dress with a blue ribbon bearing an order of gold about his neck. He looked up as she entered, frowning a little.

'Drakhys,' he said, rising.

Elysia winced. 'I do not choose to be called by that name,' she said coldly.

'Madame Andar, then.' Although his cropped hair and neat-trimmed beard were white, the grey eyes observing her gleamed with a keen, youthful intelligence. She felt uncomfortably as if she were being assessed. 'Let me welcome you on behalf of His Imperial Grace the Grand Duke to the Winter Palace.'

'I was told I was to be granted an audience with His Imperial Grace.'

171

'And indeed, Madame Andar, you are, you are. Let me introduce myself: Vassian, First Minister of Muscobar.'

Flustered, Elysia dropped into a curtsey, one hand to her breast.

'I beg your pardon, Your Excellency, I misunderstood.'

He gestured with one hand for her to rise.

'My dear madame, you have been through a difficult time. I am here to listen to your tale and to discuss in what ways we might be able to help you. But first . . .' With another curt gesture he signed to the hovering servants to leave the antechamber. 'Now we are alone. You can say what you will without fear of being overheard. Please be seated.'

Elysia sat down on the gilt-framed chair on the other side of the ornate marquetry desk.

Vassian listened to her account without comment, his hands folded on the desk-top.

'And when I went into his room next morning, he was . . . gone.'

'And you believe your late husband's bodyguard have kidnapped Gavril?'

Elysia nodded. She could feel tears pricking at the back of her eyes yet her pride would not allow her to weep in front of Vassian. She sensed he would take it as a sign of weakness.

'There is another, darker possibility for which you must steel yourself, madame. Your husband made many enemies within his own country – and without as well. Someone might have taken this opportunity to rid Azhkendir of the Nagarians for good.'

Elysia took in a breath to try to steady her voice.

'I am all too aware of that possibility. That was one of the reasons I took Gavril away from Azhkendir.'

'And all youthful japes and misdemeanours have been discounted? There is no woman involved?'

'None, I assure you,' Elysia said, rather more sharply than she had intended, and saw the ghost of a fleeting smile pass over the First Minister's impassive face. 'I'm not saying Gavril has been a saint, Your Excellency. But all his usual haunts have been checked and double-checked. None of his friends or drinking companions has seen him.'

Vassian leaned forward across the desk.

'Let's assume he has been taken to Azhkendir. Had you considered the possibility that – knowing all too well your feelings towards your late husband – your son is afraid of telling you he wishes to be made Drakhaon?'

'Gavril left all his paints and sketchbooks behind. He never goes anywhere without them,' Elysia insisted.

'Are you aware that Lord Volkh came here to Mirom about eighteen months ago to discuss a treaty of mutual benefit to our countries?'

'I told you, Your Excellency, we did not communicate.'

'It was a little diplomatic coup for which I take full credit.' Vassian examined his nails as he spoke. 'The Treaty of Accord. For years we had been trying to establish relations with Azhkendir, remote and inaccessible as it is. In the light of our present . . .' and he hesitated as though searching for the right word, '. . . difficulties with Eugene of Tielen, I can assure you we are still most interested in maintaining good relations with Azhkendir.'

'I don't see how this helps my son,' Elysia burst out.

'You may recall, madame, that the southern mountains of Azhkendir form a natural barrier between our two countries. Look.'

He smoothed out a map on the desk, pointing to the long southern range of mountains which separated Azhkendir from Muscobar.

'The White Sea to the east of Azhkendir is already filled with ice. And now we hear that the Saltyk Sea on the western shores has frozen over too.'

'You're saying that he is a prisoner?'

'A prisoner of the elements, madame. The Grand Duke has much influence in this hemisphere – but even he, I fear, cannot command the snows to thaw or the ice to melt.'

Elysia stared at the crude jagged lines of the mountain peaks; the cartographer had evidently not been able to gather enough information about Azhkendir to map the contours accurately.

'So what am I to do?'

'Azhkendir is, as I said, of great significance to us,' Vassian continued, rolling up the map. 'Our relations with Eugene of Tielen of late have not been as cordial as we would wish. He has amassed a vast fleet in the Straits. Azhkendir is all that stands between Eugene's armies and Muscobar. We can only hope that this forthcoming wedding proposal will serve to—'

There came a discreet tap at the door.

'Yes,' rasped Vassian.

'His Excellency, Count Velemir,' announced a liveried servant.

Elysia turned around in her seat to see the

newcomer. The Count was wearing a fur-trimmed coat of black velvet cut like a military greatcoat. He walked with the aid of a gold-topped ebony cane yet Elysia saw with a portrait painter's astute eye that he was only in early middle years. He was clean-shaven, with his brown hair combed severely back, military-fashion, from a weather-tanned face. He smiled as Vassian introduced them, kissing her hand, and she noticed that his eyes were a warm tortoiseshell brown.

'You have news for Madame Andar, Velemir?' Vassian said.

'Indeed I have.' Velemir sat on another of the gilt chairs opposite Elysia. 'News that will serve to reassure her, I trust.'

'News of Gavril?' Elysia was all attention now.

'Your son is, as you guessed, in Azhkendir. He disembarked at Arkhelskoye where he was welcomed by the townspeople. He then set out for Kastel Drakhaon where your late husband's will was due to be read.'

'But how can you be sure?' Elysia cried, not certain whether she felt relief or dismay that her fears had been confirmed.

'It is my business to know these things,' the Count said calmly. 'I am on my way now to relay the information to the Grand Duke. If you would care to accompany me, Madame Andar, I will present you to His Grace.' He rose and offered her his arm; after a moment's hesitation, Elysia rose too, placing her hand on his arm.

'We will talk again soon, madame,' Vassian said, picking up his pen. It seemed as if he had already turned his mind to other matters.

'So you have recently returned from Azhkendir, Count?' Elysia asked boldly.

'Indeed no, madame, but I have been on official business to Tielen.' He stopped. They had reached a long, mirror-lined gallery whose tall windows looked out onto a formal garden where fountains spouted amongst clipped hedges of box and yew. 'I must congratulate you, Madame Andar.'

'Congratulate me?' Elysia looked into the weather-browned face but saw only the Count's charming smile.

'You had us quite baffled. News from Azhkendir travels slowly at best, and much is garbled when it reaches us. Some rumours gave out that you were dead. We had no idea you and your son had been living in Vermeille for so many years.'

'Even when I accepted the commission to paint Altessa Astasia?'

He laughed softly, patting her hand. His laugh was smooth and dark like strong, sweet coffee. 'Ah, then, then we began to make connections. Shall we take a turn about the Rusalki Garden?'

The Rusalki Garden was filled with the sound of splashing waters; formal beds of topiaried box and yew surrounded a great fountain. As they walked along the alleyways Elysia saw a fine mist shimmering in the cold, dull air above the fountain from which carved river-nymphs arose, water spouting from their cupped hands, making green-copper streaks on their bare marble breasts.

'Tell me about your son, Gavril. Will he make a good Drakhaon?'

Elysia stopped, swinging around to face the Count.

'Can there be such a thing as a good Drakhaon, Count?'

'We know so little about the House of Nagarian,' the Count said with a shrug. 'We understood that Lord Volkh had developed powerful weapons to defend his lands ... yet when he and his entourage arrived in Mirom, his bodyguard were only armed with axes and sabres!'

Elysia glanced at the Count, wondering why he was pursuing this line of conversation. What did he aim to learn from her?

'Count Velemir,' she said, looking him directly in the eyes, 'I left Azhkendir just before my husband destroyed the Arkhels. He revealed nothing of his military secrets to me.'

'But young Gavril – he has had no military training, has he?'

'My husband wanted him to attend the Academy in Mirom, but I refused to let him go.'

'You think for yourself, madame,' the Count said. 'A quality I much admire in a woman.'

Elysia – to her chagrin – found that she was blushing. What business had she, blushing at an idle compliment like a schoolgirl?

They stopped beside the central fountain; the splashing waters almost obscured his voice.

'Elysia,' he said suddenly, catching hold of her hands. 'We may talk freely here; no-one can overhear us. I have some important information for you. Your husband came to Mirom for a secret purpose. We are still not entirely sure what that purpose was, only that a Doctor of Science from Mirom University accompanied him back to Azhkendir.'

'A Doctor of Science?'

'One Altan Kazimir. Now I have it on good authority that the doctor has recently arrived back in Mirom. I can only suppose that his employment came to an end when Lord Volkh was murdered.'

A lead at last! Elysia was so excited that she began to babble questions.

'Has this Doctor Kazimir resumed his work at the university? Can I go find him there?'

'My dear lady, I beg you to proceed with a little caution. Altan Kazimir has so far resisted all attempts to reinstate him. In fact, it seems as if his experiences in Azhkendir may have disturbed his reason. He refuses to talk to his old colleagues and keeps himself barricaded in his apartment. However, another fugitive from Azhkendir may fare better . . .'

'You think he might listen to me?'

'If you can convince him that you understand what he has been through . . .' He pressed her hands warmly between his own. 'But take care, Elysia. He is in a volatile, unpredictable state.'

'Volatile or no, I must speak with him,' Elysia said.

'If you are determined to take the risk, I can provide a plain-clothed escort. But remember, he will not even listen to you if he thinks you are not alone. He trusts no-one!'

'I think I know how to be discreet, Count.'

'Still so formal!' he said teasingly.

'So, when can I go?'

'And so eager!'

'Gavril is my only child.' To her annoyance tears had begun to blur her eyes again. And she had wanted to show Velemir how strong she was.

'Here in Mirom it is never done to put one's own

desires before the imperatives of duty,' he said sternly. 'In simpler terms: you must be presented to the Grand Duke.'

'Oh!' Elysia's hand flew to her mouth. Another gaffe in court etiquette. 'I didn't mean—'

'Of course you did not,' Velemir said smoothly, 'and you must think me a boor. There is a pattern to court life not unlike that of a formal dance; once you have learned the steps it all becomes intelligible.'

'Then please, dear Count, teach me the steps.'

'That is a singularly fine ruby you are wearing.'

Elysia's fingers flew to her throat, instinctively covering the jewel. 'A gift from my late husband.'

'You will forgive me, but . . .'

'I feared as much. It's too unsubtle.' Elysia let out a sigh of vexation. He must think her so provincial. 'I only brought it in the hope I could sell it to raise money for Gavril. Then Eupraxia insisted I should wear jewellery for the audience, and this is all I have.'

'I hope you don't think it presumptuous of me, but I know the court jeweller Maximov very well. He could be persuaded to transform this rather . . . rough-cut stone into something in gold and tiny rubies, perhaps with earrings to match? The Grand Duchess favours a six-petal rose design this year.'

'You're very kind, Count, but—'

A little clock on a nearby tower struck the hour in a pretty tinkle of chimes. Church and monastery bells echoed without in a darker resonant clamour.

'Come with me; it's time for today's audience.'

As they approached the audience chamber, Elysia heard a great murmur of voices and the sound of a

179

string quartet. Servants flung open double doors of white and gilt, announcing loudly above the music, 'The Drakhys of Azhkendir with His Excellency, Count Velemir.'

The murmur of voices stilled as everyone turned to stare. Elysia quite forgot her anger at being announced as Drakhys as Count Velemir led her into the chamber. Everyone was staring at her in her simple velvet gown; staring and – she was certain – whispering behind gloved hands and fans. Even the vast portraits of Orlovs dead and gone seemed to glare disapprovingly at her from the brocade-hung walls.

The audience chamber glittered with gold; from the painted ceilings to the plaster mouldings, every surface looked as if it had been inlaid with gold leaf or gilt. And the Duke's courtiers glittered too; Elysia was dazzled by the sparkle of jewels. Every woman present seemed to be wearing diamond chokers and tiaras, sapphire earrings and emerald rings. She felt as if she were a sparrow sneaking into an aviary of bright-plumaged exotic birds.

As Velemir led Elysia into the chamber, the courtiers drew back to let them pass and ahead she saw two gilt chairs set on a blue-carpeted dais, guarded by two of the White Guard. Draped across the less ornate of the two chairs was, she saw, the indolent figure of Sofia, the Grand Duchess. Beside her a broad-shouldered man, resplendent in a blue uniform glittering with medals, sat glowering at the chamber.

'Your Grace.' Elysia sank into a curtsey.

'Who's this, Sofia?' Grand Duke Aleksei grunted. Close to, Elysia saw the lines of worry creasing the

Duke's face and the artful way strands of greying hair had been combed to conceal his baldness.

The Grand Duchess gestured vaguely in Elysia's direction.

'Elysia Nagarian. The portrait painter.'

'Please rise, madame.' The Grand Duke waved one white-gloved hand. 'Welcome to our court. I'm glad to see that the Count has been looking after you.'

As Elysia rose, she noticed that First Minister Vassian had appeared on the dais and was whispering to the Grand Duke. She risked a quick, interrogatory glance at Count Velemir but he was watching the Grand Duke.

'Vassian has just told me that your son is to be made ruler of Azhkendir.'

'Made, Your Grace? *Forced*,' Elysia said sharply. 'My son was taken from our home against his will.'

There was a little stir amongst the nearest courtiers; she could not be certain whether they were shocked that she had spoken so boldly to the Duke or shocked at what had happened to Gavril.

'The news of Lord Volkh's assassination was most disconcerting – especially so soon after the signing of the Treaty of Accord. Mirom has no wish in these uncertain times to see its allies overthrown. However,' and the Grand Duke seemed to be looking directly at Count Velemir as he spoke, 'until we ascertain that the assassination was an internal matter, Mirom must rest neutral, madame. If there is proof that external factors were involved – say, one of Eugene's agents – then we will unite forces with your son and retaliate.'

This was not at all what Elysia had expected to

hear. Military action, involving Gavril? All she had wanted was help to extricate him from Kostya's clutches. For a moment the glittering room dimmed about her; she faltered and felt Count Velemir's arm supporting her.

'But I only meant—' she began.

A crash of breaking glass interrupted her. The music stopped jaggedly in mid-phrase. Instantly the White Guard went running to the windows; the Grand Duke rose to his feet.

'Keep down, Your Grace!' Velemir leaped onto the dais to protect the Grand Duke and Duchess, a flintlock pistol in his hand.

'Down with the Orlovs!' a muffled voice shouted. 'Free Muscobar from tyranny!'

'What in the devil's name—' bellowed the Grand Duke.

There seemed to be a scuffle taking place; Elysia, too surprised to think of her own safety, stared as the White Guard hauled a shabbily dressed man up into the audience chamber through the smashed window and flung him on the floor before the dais.

Velemir lowered his flintlock until the muzzle rested on the man's forehead.

'Identify yourself,' he said in a quiet voice.

The man shook his head. One of the White Guard kicked him in the side.

Elysia winced.

'Your name,' Velemir said again. There was a small but audible click as he cocked back the hammer, readying the weapon to fire.

'Stepan,' the man muttered.

'Search him,' Velemir said.

More of the White Guard came running in; they

held the man down and, in spite of his struggles, roughly searched his clothing.

'What's this?' one of the Guard demanded. He brandished a knife in front of the man's face.

'I'm . . . a cobbler . . .' The man spoke thickly, half-choked by the stream of blood pouring from his nostrils. 'It's a . . . leather knife . . .'

'Cobbler! An assassin, more like.'

'Take him away,' Velemir said impassively. 'Question him. But go easy. I want names this time. And double the guard. I want to know how this self-styled cobbler got inside the gates.'

The Guards hauled the man to his feet and dragged him away; Elysia could not help but notice the trail of blood spots left in his wake on the marble – and the speed with which the liveried servants swiftly polished them away. She felt shaken, unsettled by the whole incident.

'Today's audience is at an end,' announced the major-domo.

'But wait – I haven't—' Elysia spun around to see the Grand Duke escorting the Duchess from the room. 'Count Velemir. What did the Duke mean about retaliation? I must speak with him again.'

'Tomorrow, my dear Madame Andar,' the Count said, smiling. He seemed utterly unruffled. Behind him, repair work was already taking place, broken glass being swept up, carpenters and glaziers taking measurements of the shattered panes.

Elysia stood watching them, confused and angry. What had she stumbled into? What was happening in Mirom? No-one seemed to understand her concerns. No-one understood – let alone cared about – the danger Gavril was in.

I I

A shaft of dazzling morning sunlight pierced the brocade curtains of Gavril's bed.

Gavril instinctively covered his eyes with his hands. His nails bit into his skin. With a yelp he lowered his hands and saw that his jagged fingernails had a dark glitter to them, as if dusted with spangles. And they were indigo now, right down to the quicks. More like talons than human nails . . .

He stared down at them, revulsed yet fascinated. Why had the discoloration progressed so rapidly? Were other changes taking place, subtler changes of which he was not yet aware? This odd feeling brought memories of childhood illnesses, of waking to find his throat sore, his body covered in a rash of red spots.

Suddenly he was gripped with a compulsion to look at himself.

'Ready for your morning ablutions, My Lord?' enquired a quavering voice. Gavril flung open the curtains, wincing at the brightness of the light. Old Guaram stood there, towel draped over his shoulder, a razor in one hand and a bowl of soapy water in the other. Every morning he had brought hot water and shaved Gavril – another ritual which Gavril had inherited from Volkh.

'I'll shave myself today, Guaram,' Gavril said curtly.

'But how, My Lord?' The old servant looked bewildered. 'How will you see what you are doing?'

'You will bring me a mirror.'

'A mirror?' Guaram shook his head vehemently. 'I always performed these services for your father. It would not be right for My Lord—'

'I want a mirror, Guaram. You can shave me if you wish, but I want a mirror.'

'The water will be cold, My Lord—'

'Now, Guaram!'

'Very well, My Lord.' Guaram shambled away, muttering to himself and still shaking his head. He did not reappear for a good quarter hour, but when he came he was carrying a small hand-mirror.

'At last.' Gavril snatched it from him and gazed down at his reflection. The face he saw frowning back at him was still recognizably his own – even if the brows seemed darker and the narrowed eyes more hooded, more wary. But he was not in the least reassured by what he saw. He might still look like Gavril Andar outside, but he did not feel the same inside. He felt restless and off-colour.

As if he no longer belonged in his own skin.

'Tell me about my father, Guaram.'

'I attended Lord Volkh for over forty years, My Lord.'

'And is it true? That his hair was more blue than black? That the pupils of his eyes became like snake's eyes, just slits? That—'

'My Lord was Drakhaon,' Guaram said with a shrug.

'But how did he look at my age?'

'That is too long ago for old Guaram to remember clearly.' Guaram gave him a wide, toothless grin. 'I am eighty this year, My Lord. And I am becoming forgetful. Now as this second bowl of water is getting cold . . .'

Gavril resignedly let Guaram shave him, inwardly fretting through the procedure, wanting the old man to be done and leave him in peace. At last Guaram gathered up his barber's tools and shuffled away, leaving Gavril staring at his smooth-shaven reflection in the hand-mirror.

What is happening to me?

He stuck out his tongue; it looked dark, slightly furred, as though after a night or two of drink and dissipation. But there was nothing to explain this inexplicable sensation of . . . *wrongness*.

Gavril flung on his clothes and, taking the mirror with him, hurried over to the Kalika Tower where he had hidden Kazimir's ledger and the little phial the night before.

No-one challenged him – but he had the distinct impression that the servants and *druzhina* he encountered in the passageways were all staring at him and whispering to each other after he had passed. He took the precaution of locking and bolting the door after him.

Then he took out some clean sheets of paper from his father's desk and propped the mirror up on some books. He inscribed the date at the top of the first sheet and the words 'Self-Portrait 1'. Then with feverish pen-strokes, he began to sketch his reflection in ink. When he had finished, he set the portrait to dry.

As he looked down at what he had drawn, he could not remember ever having produced such sombre work before, full of shadows and jagged pen-strokes.

Every day he would come here and sketch another self-portrait. And if there were any gradual process of degeneration or change taking place, the portraits would provide a tangible record.

'What shall I call this? *Transformation*?' he muttered. '*Disintegration*? Or – *Birth of a Monster*?'

Late afternoon light from the moorlands, filtered by the coloured lozenges of glass in the windows, tinged the study walls with wine-rich stains. Gavril still sat at his father's desk, poring over the pages of Doctor Kazimir's ledger. And the more pages he turned, the more his desperation grew.

Some of the symbols here he recognized – for sulphur, for volatile alkaline salts – but others were as unfamiliar as the curling, intricate script of the Djihari. Page after page of incomprehensible formulae, many dashed out with only the occasional irritated comment scribbled in the margin, betraying Kazimir's frustration. Many of the later pages were almost indecipherable, as if some caustic substance had splashed onto the ledger, eating away both ink and paper. In other places, the black of the ink had discoloured and leaked, creating strange blotches of sepia brown, blue and purple.

What had been in the little phial? Poison – or traces of Kazimir's elixir that could halt the physical and mental degeneration?

Gavril held the phial up to the light, squinting into the glass tube at the dried blue stains, cautiously sniffing.

He had even begun to wonder if the scientist had unintentionally poisoned his father. Kazimir had been working for a wealthy, intimidatingly powerful patron desperate for a remedy for a fast-worsening condition. The temptation to hurry the process, to experiment and take risks, must have been overwhelming. But the entries in the ledger did not read like the writings of a man with a grudge.

The passage that had intrigued him most described an experiment using 'Drakhaon's blood'. But acid or damp had eaten away one side of the page, leaving a tantalizingly incomplete account. It seemed that Kazimir had been using his father's blood – but in what quantities and to what precise purpose, he could not be certain.

Eyes aching from trying to decipher the blurred text, Gavril laid the ledger down. The only one who could help him was Kazimir himself. And no-one knew where he had gone. Except maybe . . .

'*Lilias*,' he said aloud.

It was time to accept her invitation to tea.

'Welcome, My Lord.' Dysis ushered Gavril into an oriel-windowed room, lit by the low, rich light of the dipping sun. 'My mistress is waiting to receive you.'

The walls were hung with subtly dyed silks in peony shades of cream, rose and moss. There was no trace here of savage hunting tapestries. Little cushions, fringed and tasselled, were strewn over the long, low sofas. Porcelain bowls, white, gold and pink, filled with sugared almonds and crystallized rose and violet petals, were placed on the mosaic tops of little tables; Lilias obviously had a sweet tooth. And a volume or two lay open beside the bowls of sweets, as if Lilias had been disturbed at her reading; the uppermost book was the fashionable *Autumn Leaves* of the Muscobar poet and philosopher Solovei.

'Please sit, My Lord.' Lilias was reclining on a sofa. She was wearing a long, loose-fitting gown of turquoise silk intricately embroidered with peacock eyes and fantails. 'Make yourself comfortable.'

Gavril remembered salons like this in Vermeille: bowls of scented tea, almond *petits fours*, witticisms, discreet laughter drifting from the shaded terraces. In Vermeille he would have been able to relax and enjoy the flirtatious glances, the clever wordplay. But this was Azhkendir and there was too much at stake; he had hazarded a great deal on the outcome of this meeting.

'I have jasmine tea or vervain. Which would you prefer?'

'Jasmine.'

Lilias lifted a little teapot and poured the pale, fragrant tea into a porcelain bowl. Leaning forwards, she handed the bowl to Gavril.

'Take care. It's very hot.' Her fingertips brushed his as he took the bowl from her. A single jasmine flower floated on the surface of the steaming liquid.

'We need to talk, Madame Arbelian,' he said.

'I'm glad you see it that way too.' Lilias smiled at him. The strident, needy tone he had heard at the reading of the will had been smoothed away. 'But please don't be so formal. Call me Lilias.'

'Only if you will call me Gavril.' He had learned how to play these little exchanges of gallantry on summer evenings at the soirées of Elysia's friends. He had enjoyed their gently seductive teasing, their playfully adoring looks and sighs. There it had all been a flattering, pleasurable game. But now he was in no mood for playing games.

'So, Gavril,' she said, 'where shall we start?'

He took in a deep breath. 'How did my father come to employ Altan Kazimir?'

'Your father was in Mirom on state business. To sign the Treaty of Accord with Muscobar. He met Kazimir at the university, I believe. They shared a passion for astronomy. The nights are so clear in Azhkendir and the constellations are, they tell me, easier to chart.' She had shown no reaction to the name of Kazimir. 'Have you ever been to Mirom, Gavril?'

Gavril shook his head.

'Oh, you must visit Mirom. It is such a beautiful city. But then, it's my home; for me it is the most beautiful place in the world. I imagine you feel the same way about Vermeille?' Lilias smiled at him again. 'Your father attended a reception at the Winter Palace. I happened to be there with Count Velemir, an old friend of mine. When I was introduced to your father there was ... an instant rapport. When he asked me to come back to Azhkendir with him, naturally I accepted.'

Velemir. He had heard that name before. But where?

'You gave up Mirom society to come here?'

'One can grow tired of so many balls, ballets, concerts,' she said lightly. But Gavril saw that though her lips smiled, her eyes were shadowed, giving nothing away. Had she left Mirom to escape a tiresome relationship . . . or a court scandal? There was more, so much more, to Lilias Arbelian than she was prepared to reveal to him.

'It's ironic, isn't it?' she said. 'You and I, both strangers in a strange land.'

The sun was setting, its red light burning through the oriel windows like autumn bonfires.

'I want to find Kazimir, Lilias.'

'And you think *I* know where he is?' One plucked eyebrow rose eloquently upwards. 'Kostya's been slandering me again, hasn't he? Oh, I was lonely, I don't deny it. Altan Kazimir was lonely too, so far from his friends and colleagues in Mirom. You've only been here a few days, Gavril. When the winter sets in, this draughty kastel can feel like a prison.' Her eyes brimmed with sudden tears. 'Was it so wrong to spend time together? To have a friend of my own to talk of happier times in Mirom?'

'So you have no idea where he went?' Gavril was determined not to let her distract him from the purpose of his visit.

'My guess is he returned to Mirom. He was lucky to escape with his life. Kostya sent the *druzhina* after him.'

'Mirom.' The mood of despair was descending again, dark as a winter fog. Mirom was – if Kostya was to be believed – as inaccessible as Vermeille until the thaw came.

'And Kazimir never talked of his work with you?' He could feel a muscle had begun to twitch to the

side of his mouth. *'No-one else must know.'*
Recklessly, he ignored his father's warning. 'He never discussed the elixir?'

'With me?' Lilias set down the little bowl of tea. A sudden horrible thought crossed Gavril's mind. She had not even tasted her tea and it was so exotically perfumed that the strong flavour could easily have disguised the bitterness of poison. 'Why?'

He swallowed hard, his mouth dry with apprehension. Was this how the assassin had disabled his father, leaving him weak, vulnerable to attack? And hadn't Lilias – for all her pleasant small-talk – stated quite openly that she expected *her* child to inherit?

'I – I need the elixir,' he said hoarsely.

'But I thought you knew. Your father destroyed it,' she said, staring at him. 'The night of the . . . the misunderstanding. He went storming into Kazimir's laboratory and smashed every bottle, every phial. He accused Kazimir of trying to poison him.'

Gavril stared at her, speechless. So it was his father who had destroyed the elixir in a fit of jealous rage. His last hope of finding a cure in Azhkendir was gone.

'Ah,' she said softly. 'Now I understand. It's started, hasn't it?'

'How can you tell?' he asked, as softly as she.

'Oh, little things that remind me of Volkh. It's not just your hands, your hair, your eyes. There's a kind of . . . darkness about you.'

'You must be mistaken,' he said coldly.

'Why fight it, Gavril?' Her voice had become softer, almost seductive. 'Think of the power you have inherited. Power that could make you master of the whole continent.'

'I don't want that kind of power!' Gavril cried.

'Then you are as much of a fool as your father.' For a single moment, all pretence melted away and he glimpsed an unmistakable glint of contempt in her languorous green gaze. 'Volkh could have conquered Tielen, Khitari, Muscobar; he could have crushed the Grand Duke and ridden into Mirom in triumph. But what did he do? He denied his true nature, he denied his powers. And that was his weakness. The fatal weakness that led to his downfall.'

'But he was a monster.'

'Power can be quite an aphrodisiac, Gavril.'

Gavril stared at Lilias, at a loss for words. If he was not mistaken, his father's mistress was making him some kind of sexual overture. There was nothing more to be gained from this meeting. If he had hoped to forge some kind of truce between them, he had failed.

'More tea, madame?' Dysis appeared in the doorway.

'Did I ask for more tea? I think not!' Lilias snapped.

Gavril, grateful for the distraction, curtly thanked Lilias for her hospitality and withdrew.

'You must excuse my mistress, My Lord,' Dysis whispered as she opened the outer door for him. 'These last days of pregnancy have made her very irritable. She says things she would not normally dream of saying . . .'

Outside, a servant was lighting oil lamps in the shadowed passageway. Autumn nights came on fast in Azhkendir.

A stormwind had begun to whine outside the

kastel, rattling shutters and gusting spatters of sleet against the window panes. Gavril stopped at a narrow window and gazed out into the rapidly darkening night, his breath clouding the cold glass.

A few streaks of blood-red light still gashed the night sky, casting a lurid glow across the distant ridge of jagged mountain peaks. The prospect chilled his spirit.

'There's a kind of darkness about you . . .'

Was it true? Was it so obvious? Was it already too late to stop it happening?

Back in his chamber he poured water from the jug into the bowl and splashed his face. As he plunged his hands into the clear water, the darkness of his fingernails caught his eye. The stains of blue were still there, dark as bruising.

He thrust his hands into the water again, frantically scrubbing at his nails with a sliver of soap. When he raised his fingers from the bowl, he saw that all his efforts had been to no avail: each fingernail was still as blue as ground cobalt.

With a cry of frustration, he took up the empty water jug and brought it crashing down on the floor. Fragments of pottery and water spattered the dressing-room.

Shaking with rage, he stood staring down at the shattered jug. What was happening to him?

Gavril leaned his burning forehead against the cold, rough stone of the wall, trying to conjure up memories of Astasia Orlova, her voice, the scent of her hair . . .

Memories of a time when he had never heard of Azhkendir.

'Astasia,' he whispered.

By the light of a little lantern, he sketched swiftly, several times stopping to dash down his pen and crush the paper in his hand and start again.

But at last the obsessive penstrokes began to shape a portrait that pleased him: the outline of her face, her sweet, dark eyes with their silky lashes, her mouth, gravely smiling – then curving upwards with spontaneous pleasure when she spoke of dancing...

If Kazimir had gone back to Mirom, then Mirom was the place he must go.

He piled on extra layers of clothes against the bitter cold and lay down on the bed to wait for midnight.

'Gavril...'

The air in the bedchamber had turned freezingly cold. Gavril blinked in the darkness, knowing he was no longer alone.

'You still do not understand, my son.'

The stern voice shivered through his mind. The tall spirit-wraith materialized at his bedside, a shadow towering over him, limned in silver moonlight.

'Watch – and learn.'

And then, as if a dark gauze has been peeled away from his vision, Gavril sees he is in the hall of the East Wing. The oriel window is whole; vast gold-framed paintings hang on the walls.

Smoke begins to drift into the hall below.

Men are shouting, women screaming.

'They're in! They've broken in!'

'Where's Volkh? Get him to safety! For God's sake get him out of here!'

Two women come running into the hall. One carries a little child in her arms.

'Volkh! Where are you?' cries the other. 'Dear God – where is he? Have they found him?' Her voice breaks with anguish.

'Drakhys, you must hide.'

The little child starts to cry. The woman clutches him closer to her.

'Please come with me, Drakhys. Come now.'

'I can't go without Volkh. I must know he is safe.'

The glass in the oriel window shatters. Men clamber in, men with torches and bloodstained sabres. In a blizzard of wings, great white owls swoop into the hall, screeching and shrieking.

'Go, My Lady!' begs the woman with the child.

Men of the *druzhina* hurry in, wielding sabres and axes. Metal blades clang and clash. The great owls come scything down on them, tearing at their heads and shoulders with hooked claws and beaks.

Smoke billows into the hall; the invaders have set torches to the tapestries, and the glow of flames reddens the smoky air.

The *druzhina* are falling back now, outnumbered. One warrior starts to scream, a horrible, shrill sound, as a snow owl claws his face, beak pecking at his eyes till the blood streams down like crimson tears.

'Make it stop, Father,' Gavril pleads. 'I've seen enough.'

'*No, not enough, not nearly enough.*' The harsh voice is suddenly choked with emotion.

A man stands in the broken frame of the great window, watching as, one by one, the *druzhina* fall. His hair glints in the torchlight, burnished dark gold.

With a curling whistle, he raises his arm and the owls fly to him, perching on his wrist, his shoulders. Now their white feathers are bloodied and tattered, but their great golden eyes gleam like burning stars through the smoke.

Gavril cannot take his eyes off the man. There is a radiance about him, an unnatural golden glimmer. When he moves forward, his eyes gleam with the same blank, gold light as the owls'. He moves like a man possessed.

'Where is your son, Drakhys?' he asks. His voice echoes with the cold, cruel ring of metal. With a shock, Gavril sees that he is no scarred warlord but young, scarcely older than himself. 'Give him to me and I will spare your household.'

The Drakhys, who has stood immobile with shock, suddenly bends down and seizes a pike from the hands of one of her dying *druzhina*.

'Give my son to you, Stavyor Arkhel?' Her words burn with scorn. 'I would rather kill him myself.'

From elsewhere in the kastel come distant screams and the crackle of flames.

'It is not your fault you have borne a monster, Drakhys. But monsters must be destroyed. I cannot allow your boy to grow to manhood. He must die.'

'Do what you want with me,' the Drakhys flings back, 'but you will never make me betray my son.'

'So be it. Kill them. Kill them all.'

And Stavyor Arkhel turns away with a shrug.

Smoke billows up, clouding Gavril's sight. By the flamelight he sees the Drakhys retreating, trying to defend herself and her companion from the advancing Arkhel warriors, fiercely jabbing and swinging the pike like a scythe. But they are outnumbered.

And when the Arkhels seize the child from the mother, when she begins to scream, he cannot look any more and, tears streaming down his cheeks, hides his face in his hands.

Then comes the silence.

Reluctantly, Gavril forces himself to look, peering between his fingers.

The two women lie sprawled on the tiles below, the child beside them. A little boy, Gavril sees now, with barley-fair hair. Daylight illuminates a scene of carnage: cinders and smoke choke the air, bodies lie stiffening in their own blood . . .

'No more,' he says again, his voice breaking. 'Please, Father.'

'*Watch*,' comes back the inexorable reply.

A man hurries into the hall below, stumbling in his haste, a young soldier, one of the *druzhina*, with barley-fair hair. When he sees the women and the child, he drops to his knees. He picks up the child in his arms, cradling it, hugging it to his breast, weeping, crying. But although Gavril can see his mouth working, shouting out words of grief and fury, he can no longer hear a sound. The ghost-images begin to waver, to evaporate like moorland mist. When Gavril blinks his own tears away, he sees nothing below but darkness and the faint, fast-fading traces of moonlight.

'Who were they?' he asks aloud, his voice still unsteady, although he has already guessed the half of it.

Beside him he can still sense the stern presence of his father's spirit-wraith, a glimmering shadow.

'*Marya Nagarian, my mother. And her companion Zabava Torzianin.*'

'Torzianin? But isn't that Kostya's name?'

'*Zabava was his wife. The boy was little Kostya, Kostyushka, his only son. Now do you understand?*'

Gavril nods miserably. 'And you?'

'*I ran back from the safety of the passageway to call to my mother, to beg her to hurry. But I was too late.*'

The bitterness in his father's voice makes his heart ache.

'*They murdered her, Gavril. The Arkhels murdered my mother.*'

'No more, Father.'

'*You know Jaromir Arkhel is alive. Seek him out. Kill him. Before he kills you.*'

'Enough!' Gavril cries, his voice echoing, raw in his own ears. 'No more Seeings. Let me be. Let me be!'

After a while he raised his head. He was alone. It was well past midnight. The only sounds still audible in Kastel Drakhaon now were the whine of the wind from the moors and the distant, monotonous tread of the sentries on night-watch.

If he was to get away before the kastel woke to a new dawn, he must hurry. Taking a lantern, he raised the hunting tapestry and opened the secret door.

Darkness entombed him, smelling of dust and mould. He faltered a moment. And then, by his lantern candle, he saw the traces of his and Kiukiu's footprints in the dust on the floor of the secret passageway.

A rush of chill air hit him as he entered the cavernous hallway of the East Wing. A faint trace of moonlight, pale as phosphorus, outlined the great window, shining through the broken panes onto the tiled floor beneath.

The light from his lantern illuminated traces in the dust below. Footprints . . . and stains. A telltale little trail of brown spots leading away into the gloom. Old bloodstains?

Lantern held low to illuminate the tiles, he began to follow the trail of blood.

Beneath the stair there were other doorways, boarded up, grey with dust-clogged cobwebs. One door alone was slightly ajar. Gavril gave it a little push; his hand came away powdered with grime, but the door creaked inwards.

The passageway beyond was blind, with no windows or vents to give light or fresh air.

If the ceiling caves in, I shall be crushed . . . and no-one will reach me in time to pull me out.

He was beginning to sweat; the palms of his hands were damp and clammy. The lantern-candle was burning dangerously low, the wick was puddled in a pool of hot wax.

And then by the failing candlelight he saw an iron ladder.

Freedom.

Craning his neck, he saw a trap-door above him. Setting the lantern down on the earthern floor, he climbed up the ladder and pushed the heavy trap-door with both hands until it began to open.

Fresh night air flooded into the stale atmosphere of the tunnel. Gavril pushed back the door further until he could look out.

Two golden eyes blazed into his and he almost fell back down into the tunnel.

A low, curling hoot greeted him.

'Snowcloud?' he whispered, grasping the rim of the trap-door to support himself. By the waning moonlight he saw that he was in the Elysia Summerhouse.

He had struggled for so long through the clammy, claustrophic darkness of the tunnel that he was certain he would emerge on the other side of the kastel walls.

Snowcloud gave another soft, hooting cry and began to move jerkily across the boards towards him.

Gavril put out one hand to stroke the owl's soft white plumage, and then hesitated.

Snow owls. Arkhel's owls. A man with golden-glimmering eyes, cruel and unseeing . . .

'But you're just a little one, Snowcloud, you haven't been trained to maim and kill.'

Only now did he recall the full horror of the Arkhel raid on the kastel.

The little child lying so still, the blood trickling through his fair hair. Kostyushka. Kostya's only son.

The waste and the pity of it overwhelmed him. He put his head in his hands and wept.

A while later, maybe a long while, he raised his head and saw that the night sky was slowly lightening along the eastern rim. In the tunnel below, his candle guttered a thin trail of smoke and went out.

He must find a way to end his father's torment, to stop him reliving the horrors that had scarred his life – and now threatened to scar his own.

Exorcism. Surely there must be some holy ritual that would bring peace to a troubled spirit?

Abstractedly he ran his fingertips over

Snowcloud's ghost-white plumage. After a while, to his surprise, the owl suddenly hopped onto his wrist, balancing there as if it had been born to it. The thin talons bit like wire through his jacket cuff into his skin . . . but the wonder of holding the wild creature, of sensing its trust in him, made the discomfort easy to ignore.

There seemed a peculiar irony in the situation; the heir to the Clan Drakhaon adopted by one of Arkhel's Owls.

'You and I, Snowcloud,' he whispered, 'if we're to survive, we have to find a way to escape from Kastel Drakhaon.'

Dawn mists were already rising from the ruins of the neglected gardens, tinged with the musty smell of mould and fungi. Rose briars, red with late rosehips, choked the crumbling stone arches and arbours, their thorns tearing at Gavril's clothes as he made his way down the overgrown path towards the stables.

He would just take a horse and ride out across the moors towards Azhgorod. Let them try to stop him! He was Drakhaon, his word was law.

A blackbird flew up out of the brambles, shrieking a warning cry.

The rising mists had begun to swirl more thickly. Gavril felt an intense chill seeping into his bones, a black, aching chill that invaded his mind as well as his body.

Someone was coming towards him through the mists. A tall figure that seemed to drift rather than walk. With a sick feeling in the pit of his stomach, Gavril recognized who – or what – it was.

'*A harsh winter is coming...*' The voice that breathed from the tall figure barring his way was brittle with black ice.

A hand stretched out towards him, insubstantial as a skeletal leaf, and the chill increased, numbing his whole body.

'No!' Gavril cried, twisting away. 'Let me be, Father! Leave me alone!'

He put his head down and ran.

Where the shadowy figure had passed, he saw as he ran that the wet grass was white, rimed with bitter frost. And all the rich red rosehips had turned black, withering on the briar.

'You're out early this morning, My Lord.' Kostya stood at the entrance to the stables, arms folded, breath clouding in the frosty air. 'So early that your bodyguard don't seem to recall you leaving your room.'

Had the spirit-wraith woken Kostya, sent him to prevent his escape?

'Didn't you see him?' Gavril's teeth had begun to chatter. 'My f-father? In the garden?'

'I saw nothing.'

'Look, Kostya.' Gavril stabbed one finger back towards the frost-blackened garden. 'Can't you see? The frost seemed to ... to seep from him like poisonous breath. Even the trace of his footprints: frost-burned into the grass.'

Kostya frowned. 'As I feared,' he said, taking hold of Gavril's arm, leading him towards the side door into the kastel.

'Feared what?' Gavril let himself be led; he was so cold now, he could hardly feel Kostya's fingers gripping his arm. 'What does it mean?'

Kostya pushed him inside, stamping the hoarfrost from his boots on the flagstones. 'You, boy!' He whistled to one of the scullions who was scurrying down the corridor. 'Fetch us some hot spiced ale. And be quick about it!'

The fire was lit in the grate in the Dining Hall; Kostya brought Gavril close to the sizzling pine logs. As Gavril stood over the blaze he felt his numbed fingers and toes slowly begin to thaw.

The boy came in with mugs of steaming ale and Kostya handed one to Gavril.

'Get some of that into you, lad. You look shrammed.'

Gavril took mouth-searing sips of the mulled ale until the warm spices burned their heat into his chill body.

Kostya stretched his scarred, knotted hands out over the flames to warm them.

'Your father's spirit-wraith is trapped here and rages against its imprisonment. Now its rage has turned against the land that holds it prisoner. I warned you, My Lord. Now crops will fail, winters never end.'

Gavril gazed out beyond Kostya through the window at the black shimmer of frost enveloping the kastel, filtering out the morning sunlight. Only a few days ago he would never have believed what Kostya was telling him. The rational Gavril would have dismissed it as superstitious folklore.

'You say someone brought my father's ghost through. There must be some way to send it back. Some form of exorcism.'

'Exorcism?' repeated Kostya in tones of horror.

'Surely you have priests here in Azhkendir who would perform such a ceremony?'

'But you are talking of your own father—'

'Yes. *My* father.'

'And I have told you, My Lord, that here in Azhkendir it is the custom for the firstborn son to avenge his father's death. That is the only way to lay a restless ghost.'

Kostya's attitude grated on Gavril's nerves. The sleepless night, the frustrations of the long and hazardous crawl through the secret passageways, the horrors of the massacre, all had eroded what little patience he had left.

'And in Smarna we have a priest say prayers for the souls of the dead and sprinkle holy water to cleanse the place.'

'It is not our way,' grumbled Kostya.

Black, cold anger gripped Gavril.

'Who is Drakhaon, Kostya?'

'You are, Lord.'

'So you keep telling me. Then why', and Gavril went up close to Kostya, almost spitting the words in his face, 'don't you obey my orders, Bogatyr?'

Kostya did not reply; Gavril saw for a moment the stubborn resistance fade and a look of uncertainty flicker in his eyes.

'You spoke of a monastery in the forest. Would the monks perform the ceremony for my father?'

'I could speak with Abbot Yephimy,' Kostya said grudgingly. 'He might be persuaded to come here. But I tell you, Lord Gavril, no form of exorcism will work. Your father's spirit-wraith is too strong, too full of anger. Nothing will appease it – nothing but the blood of his murderer.'

'Must I repeat myself?' Gavril said, his voice cold and hard. 'Send word to the Abbot. Straight away.'

'I'll send one of the *druzhina*.' Kostya walked away, muttering under his breath. At the doorway, he turned and said accusingly, 'What use is a gaggle of white-bearded priests? A warlord should be honoured in blood.'

12

There was still no news from Azhkendir.

Eugene woke to a grey dawn and the realization that he could delay his invasion plans no longer.

He went to the Hall of Arms before breakfast. Sabre practice every morning was regarded as an anachronism by many of the younger officers. His troops were equipped with the most advanced of alchymical weapons – why did they still need to learn to wield a sword?

But Eugene, trained by his father Karl, still delighted in the art of the sabre, relished the discipline it instilled where mind and body worked as one. To encourage the dissenters, he established contests with generous prizes and golden trophies for the most skilled swordsmen – and now even the most sceptical competed every season with enthusiasm to win the top awards.

There was always something strangely calming in practising the routines and rituals of the blade. No time to brood over the progress of his troops, feverish Karila or lost Jaromir, only the cut and thrust of the steel. And when he entered into a bout with the *maître d'armes*, cadets and officers alike gathered to watch them.

He had spent hours here with Jaromir, trying to draw the deep-buried anger out of the boy, to train him to hone and use it like a well-tempered blade. But every time Jaro took a sword in his hand, he began to battle daemons, the shadows that haunted his dreams. He became wild, vengeful, erratic. Many times Eugene walked away from the hall, despairing of ever making a swordsman of his protégé. But as Jaromir came to trust him, he had seen the boy develop a kind of grim pleasure in the rituals of the sabre contest.

Yet this morning as Eugene reached the Hall of Arms, he sensed a dangerous sizzle of tension in the air.

A bout was in progress between two of his household cavalry, and as he drew near to the watching cadets and officers, he saw instantly that what had begun as a friendly contest had turned sour.

He recognized the more aggressive of the two combatants from his untidy shock of pale hair, so blond it was almost white: Lieutenant Oskar Alvborg, an able bladesman whose promise was marred by a tendency to recklessness. He already sported sabre-scars across his forehead and left cheek, trophies of honour from illicit barracks duels.

Now Alvborg drove his opponent across the floor with a merciless determination, each sabre-stroke striking silver sparks that glinted in his pale eyes.

The other, Eugene saw now, was Nils Lindgren, a

stolid officer from a humble background who, lacking Alvborg's noble blood, had worked his way up through the ranks. It took merely a few seconds for Eugene to see that Lindgren was in trouble. Losing ground, step by step, to Alvborg's lightning-slashes, he was putting all his remaining strength into defending himself.

Some other matter must lie beneath this: money lost at cards, or rivalry over a woman . . .

The breathing of the two men rasped hard and fast in the cold hall. Lindgren slipped – and Alvborg's sabre whistled within a hair's breadth of his chin.

Lindgren righted himself with a grunt. Sweat glistened on his forehead, dripped down his nose and chin. His eyes were narrowed in a look of puzzled outrage.

Eugene glanced at the *maître d'armes,* who gave a quick, terse nod. The *maître* stepped forwards, baton raised.

'Alvborg, Lindgren, put up your swords!'

Alvborg seemed not to hear him. His sabre flashed in a wide scything arc. The *maître* ducked out of the way just as the blade keened through the air and nicked Lindgren on the side of the chin. Blood spotted the floor.

Eugene had seen enough. Sabre in hand, he moved swiftly out, placing himself in front of Lindgren, facing Alvborg. A rash move for a less gifted swordsman – but a calculated risk for one of his experience.

Alvborg was so caught up in his blood-frenzy that his sabre had struck and seared off Eugene's blade before he saw who stood in his way.

'Highness,' he said, slowly lowering his sabre.

'I will not have duelling in my palace, Lieutenant,' Eugene said coldly.

Alvborg's pale, proud eyes stared back unrepentantly.

'A few days in confinement will cool your hot blood. Take him away.'

For one moment Eugene glimpsed in Alvborg's pale eyes the impulse to evade arrest, to attack the one man who stood between him and his quarry. Slowly, he extended his hand.

The hall fell silent. Everyone was watching.

A convulsive little flicker of rage twisted Alvborg's face – and then, as quickly, changed to an arrogant grin as he lowered his blade. Wiping the bloodied tip on his sleeve, he presented his sabre, hilt first, to Eugene.

Two of the household bodyguard came forwards to escort Alvborg from the hall.

Eugene turned to Lindgren. The young man had pressed a handkerchief to the gash in his chin and a bright stain of blood was leaking through.

'And you, Lindgren, what have you to say for yourself?'

'I am as culpable as the lieutenant, Highness,' Lindgren said, eyes lowered. Beneath the brown of his tanned skin, he had turned milky pale. 'I deserve to be punished too.'

'This is your first offence, hm?' Behind Lindgren's back, Eugene saw the *maître* nod in confirmation.

'Then take this as a warning. If you're ever caught duelling again, you'll be demoted to the ranks. If you want to put your blade skills to better use, Tielen has enemies in plenty to defeat. Now go get that wound cleaned up.'

'Thank you, Highness.' Relief infused the young man's pale face with a healthier colour.

A junior officer came hurrying up, smartly clicking his heels together as he saluted and presented him with a folded paper.

'A message from the field marshal for Your Highness.'

Eugene took the letter, handed his sabre to his valet and retired to the side of the hall where Anckstrom was presiding over a lively bout.

Snowed in by blizzards of unusual ferocity. Unable to comply with your orders until the weather breaks. Await further instructions.

Karonen, Field Marshal.

Frustrated, Eugene crushed the paper in his fist and lobbed it into a nearby brazier.

'Azhkendir,' said Anckstrom with a shrug. 'What did I tell you? We're wasting valuable resources – and valuable men.'

'And if we delay much longer, we will have a full-grown Drakhaon to deal with. We must move now, Anckstrom, or risk losing everything.'

'Well, Magus?' Eugene could no longer disguise his impatience. 'What's happening on the Saltyk Sea?'

'Patience, patience, Highness . . .'

On the table stood a plain silver bowl of clear liquid. Linnaius passed his long, slender fingers over the bowl several times. Eugene blinked – and found he was gazing down onto a rocky shore. This trick of Linnaius's never ceased to astonish him. But instead of the rise and fall of the waves, there was nothing but ice, translucent grey, green and white crests and sheets of ice. A frozen sea, frozen beneath a cloudmist of falling snow. Just to gaze on its bleakness made him feel cold, achingly cold.

'And inland?' he said.

Linnaius's fingers moved again across the skin of the water; the image shivered and broke into shifting fragments, re-forming into a mist of cloud and snow. The bowl shimmered with drifting wisps of grey. Behind the drifting mists a smudge of darkness hovered, ominous as a thundercloud. Intermittent glitters of lightning, white-blue, lit the darkness.

And then – unmistakably – lightning-eyes flickered suddenly from the turbulent snowclouds, chill and foreboding as winter.

'What is that?' Eugene whispered.

The Magus snatched his fingers away as if they had been singed.

'A powerful spirit-wraith is abroad, freezing the seas and wreathing the country with impenetrable snowstorms.'

'A spirit-wraith?' Eugene could not hide the scepticism in his voice. 'Surely this is nothing but a freak winter storm.'

'The Azhkendi shamans use the crudest and most dangerous methods – they summon the spirits of the dead from the Ways Beyond to do their bidding. And the spirits of the dead are not always as biddable as they would wish.'

'Spirit-wraith or not, I have sent word to the troops to stand ready. There's never been a better time to take Muscobar. But I cannot invade with the navy alone. I need Azhkendir! And I need Jaromir in Azhgorod, at the head of the Council. Magus—'

Eugene hesitated. Kaspar Linnaius was the only man in all Tielen who intimidated him. In his presence he felt like a stuttering schoolboy; even in conversation he could sense the elderly scholar's immense powers. 'Can you subdue this spirit-wraith?'

'No, Highness,' replied Linnaius, giving him the mildest of smiles. 'The magical sciences I practise are refined, sophisticated. I hesitate to include the dark forces abroad in Azhkendir in the same category.'

'Then we must devise an alternative strategy.' Eugene fought back the growing sense of frustration. He was not used to feeling so powerless.

'Are you truly determined to pursue this course of action, Highness?' asked Linnaius, suddenly fixing him with his clear, unsettling stare. 'Will nothing dissuade you?'

'Jaromir needs my help. If we strike now, we can draw the young serpent's fangs.'

'But until the blizzards and fogs clear, the risks to you and your troops are too great to entertain.'

'Then we must send in a different kind of army,' Eugene said. 'The kind of advance guard that can cross a frozen sea and will pay little heed to the weather.'

'Ah,' said Linnaius. 'My Marauders.'

A fierce snarling could be heard as they descended the rough steps towards the inner stableyard. The whole area had been converted into a cage with double iron bars to contain the Marauders. Eugene and Linnaius halted and gazed down; in the yard below, ragged-clothed men prowled around. A powerful stench rose from the cage: urine, rotting meat and an unmistakably feral odour.

'But this is a disaster!' Eugene said. 'This will never work! Look at them—'

'If anything the experiment has worked a little too well, Highness,' Linnaius said calmly.

'How so?'

'Don't be deceived by their human appearance. They have the souls of wolves. They have all but forgotten they were men. To effect the transformation you desired it was necessary to take their human cruelty and cunning and meld it with the wolves' voracious hunger. Now they do not just kill for food, they kill for sport.'

'They seem to have lost the power of speech, Highness,' said the Guardian, Eugene's Captain of the Hunt. 'We've tried to make contact with them, but every time our attempts send them into a kind of frenzy. They only understand food – and blows.'

And as if to prove the captain's point, one of the men, his yellow beard and hair shaggy and unkempt, hurled himself at the bars, grabbing the iron and shaking it frenetically, as if he could break through. His eyes gleamed in his unwashed face with an unnatural sulphurous light.

Disappointment and frustration overwhelmed Eugene again. The experiment was a failure.

'If they have no speech, how can they be expected to obey orders? Loose this ragged crew on the Azhkendi borders and we'll never see them again.'

'They will listen to me.' The Magus had focused all his attention on the occupants of the cage. 'Within that unprepossessing human frame the wolf-shadow lies dormant.' Slowly he raised his hands, like a diviner seeking water. 'Watch what happens when I wake it.'

Suddenly the nearest prisoner was seized with a convulsive spasm, thrown to the ground, his limbs and torso writhing so violently that a cloud of dust spun around him.

A long, chilling howl echoed around the yard and Eugene felt the hairs at the back of his neck prickle at the sound.

Feral eyes gleamed as the dust settled. No longer an unwashed, unkempt man, a steppe wolf came loping forwards, shaking the dirt from his shaggy coat. The other men growled, baring their teeth.

'Ugly brute,' Eugene whispered, staring in fascination into the sulphur-bright eyes.

'This is our pack leader. His name is Loukas.'

Suddenly the wolf gathered itself and sprang at the bars, snarling and snapping its yellowing teeth. Eugene stepped back.

'Loukas,' the mage said softly, 'show His Highness some respect.'

Loukas lowered his shaggy head. Slowly, eyes still gleaming, he backed away, tail between his legs.

Linnaius turned to Eugene.

'But can you be sure this wild beast will take the pack where we want it to go?'

'Loose them on the ice and they will find their way to their prey. Especially if they are hungry enough,' Linnaius said. 'They are wolves. They are used to harsh conditions. Though with respect, Highness, this is not your usual style, to send assassins in the dark.'

'And with respect, Magus, this young Drakhaon is not my usual adversary. We must fight sorcery with sorcery.'

A polite cough alerted Eugene to the arrival of his Chief Private Secretary, Gustave.

'An incoming message, Highness. From Mirom.'

'At least the Muscobar lines of communication are still functioning,' Eugene said with a grimace.

He hurried to Gustave's office and sat down at his desk, drawing the Vox Aethyria in front of him; Gustave hovered behind, ready to assist.

Linnaius's invention, the Vox Aethyria, had proved invaluable in all Eugene's recent campaigns. With these ingenious devices Eugene had been able to keep in communication with his commanders – even over vast distances. The principle, Linnaius had explained, was quite simple: it was merely a question of splitting crystals into two identical component parts, so that they resonated to the same aethyric frequency. Once the crystals were in tune with each other, they worked by sending a series of sympathetic harmonic vibrations through the aethyr. The artificier's skill lay in fashioning the crystal glasses so that they would transmit and receive these infinitesimally small vibrations. Though Eugene was certain that, as with all Linnaius's 'simple' devices, the Magus had added some subtle touch of alchymy all his own.

Now he waited tensely for his informant to reply, tapping out a tattoo on the desk-top.

With a rough crackle, a faint voice began to issue from the Vox Aethyria:

'*I am delighted to inform Your Royal Highness that Elysia Andara, once wife to Volkh Nagarian and mother of the new Drakhaon, Lord Gavril Nagarian, has arrived in Mirom.*'

Eugene frowned, turning the crystal rose around to speak. 'To what purpose, precisely?'

'*It seems she has come to ask for help in extracting*

216

her son from the clutches of Bogatyr Kostya. And she has specifically requested that I introduce her to Doctor Kazimir.'

Eugene leaned closer to the device. 'Kazimir? The inventor of the antidote?'

'I will keep you informed on the progress of these meetings. Oh – and I thought Your Highness would be interested to learn that she has entrusted to our care a certain antique jewel given her by her late husband.'

'An antique jewel?' Eugene could not disguise a sudden surge of excitement. 'Can you be certain—'

'Without a doubt, Highness, it is the finest ruby I have ever seen – save one in the Grand Duke's treasury. We have here another of Artamon's Tears.'

Eugene went across the courtyard to the workshop where the most skilled craftsmen of the Goldsmiths' Guild had been busy at work for months on a unique commission.

Alongside their tools and magnifying glasses on the workbenches lay ancient woodcuts, engravings and jewel-bright miniatures. All depicted the last emperor of Rossiya, Artamon the Great, wearing the imperial crown.

As Eugene entered, Paer Paersson, Eugene's master goldsmith, rose and bowed, presenting him with a golden diadem.

'Look, Your Highness. We have fixed the Tear of Khitari in its setting.'

Eugene took the crown and rotated it slowly, silently admiring the intricacy of the craftsmanship. Delicate strands of gold had been fashioned into the forms of heraldic creatures, claws clutching three great blood-red rubies: three of the legendary Tears of Artamon, from three of the five countries that made up ancient Rossiya. When Artamon died and the empire fell, his warring sons had divided the jewels of the imperial crown between them. And the legend had arisen that no man could unite the broken empire until the emperor's crown was made whole again and the five Tears of Artamon were united in one diadem.

Eugene, the rationalist, held no belief in legends, but he recognized the symbolic power that lay in the reforging of the ancient crown.

A swan held the Tielen ruby, a merman the gem from Smarna and a phoenix the Khitari stone, latest of his acquisitions.

The Smarnan ruby had been acquired by his father Karl when the deposed prince, Giorgo of Smarna, had fled a violent revolution, only to die in exile in Tielen, a broken man, rejected by his countrymen in favour of a republic.

'Fine work, Paer,' Eugene murmured, turning the crown around in his hands again to the last two empty settings. Muscobar and Azhkendir. Azhkendir and Muscobar . . .

'Would you like to try the crown on, Highness?' Paer asked, squinting at him through his jeweller's eyeglass, still screwed into one eye-socket.

'No. I'll not tempt the anger of the gods,' Eugene said, smiling as he handed him back the heavy crown. 'Let's wait till we have the last two jewels. And I anticipate that won't be too long now.'

Artamon's Tears. Called, so the legend said, for the tears of blood shed by the emperor at the heartless behaviour of his ungrateful sons.

'Thank the gods I have only a daughter.'

13

'Snowcloud . . . Snowcloud . . .'

Kiukiu heard the scratch of sharp claws on wood and a white shadow appeared in the twilight, moving jerkily towards her across the rotting boards of the summerhouse.

'Food, Snowcloud.' Kiukiu put down the scraps of meat, grain and bacon rind she had scavenged from the kitchen – and hastily withdrew her hand as the hooked beak descended, pecking greedily.

She watched, crouched down, trying to assess if the damaged leg was healing. It might be a trick of the fading light but Snowcloud seemed to be growing larger. The rich food was obviously doing him good. But the more food he ate, the more he would need to sustain his size . . .

'Somebody might notice what I was at,' she told it, 'and then what would happen to us both?'

Telltale stains of owl-droppings marked the

boards and little tufts of white down had drifted into the dusty corners.

The owl finished its meal and shook its beak. Tentatively she put out one hand and stroked the soft feathers. For the first time it did not jerk away or try to peck her.

'Have you come to trust me?' she whispered. 'Oh, Snowcloud. As soon as you can fly, I'll have to let you go. You must learn to fend for yourself.'

The owl put its head on one side and regarded her with its great golden eyes. In the darkness they gleamed like fire-lit amber.

'It's almost as if you understand what I'm saying.'

Kiukiu had never had a pet of her own, although she had once tried to nurse a succession of little animals back to health. First there had been the fledgling sparrow that had fallen from its nest. The poor scrawny little creature had not lasted more than three days even though she had lavished all her attention upon it. Then there had been a baby mouse – but Adzhika, Sosia's sharp-eyed pepper-spotted cat, had caught it and bitten its head off; Kiukiu still shuddered to think of it. Adzhika had also polished off two shrews and a broken-winged blackbird she had adopted. But now, looking at Snowcloud's cruel hooked beak and razor-sharp claws, Kiukiu reckoned it was more than a match for Adzhika.

'I must go back now,' she told Snowcloud. 'Maybe tomorrow you'll be ready to fly away . . .'

Kiukiu slipped silently out into the darkling garden. It was bitterly cold now that the sun had set, and the overgrown path was slippery with frost. The gleam of the lamps in Lilias's oriel window guided her through the darkness.

Huh! Only time I've had reason to thank *her* for anything, she thought.

Rose brambles tore at her skirts; she brushed them aside. She must find a way to tell Lord Gavril about Snowcloud; if it weren't for his intervention, the owl would be dead. Perhaps they could set Snowcloud free together . . .

She ducked under the archway into the kitchen courtyard and opened the door a crack, peering warily down the ill-lit passageway. It was empty. She rubbed the soles of her boots on the edge of the step so that she should not bring in garden mud and went in, carefully closing the door behind her.

'There you are, Kiukiu!' Ilsi suddenly stepped out from the dairy larder, blocking her way. Kiukiu turned to flee and saw Ninusha had appeared from the laundry room. She was trapped.

'Cold tonight, Ninusha,' Ilsi said. 'Freezing cold – unless you've got someone to keep you nice and warm.'

Kiukiu gazed at her, mystified.

'Don't you want to tell us, Kiukiu?' A hard, teasing little smile curled Ilsi's lips.

'Tell you what?' Kiukiu's heart had begun to thud. What had they seen? Had they followed her?

'About your admirer. Your secret admirer.'

'*Me?*' Kiukiu could feel her cheeks going red. They thought she had been out with a boy?

'So, who is he, Kiukiu?' Ninusha moved closer, swaying her hips suggestively from side to side. 'Aren't you going to share your little secret with us?'

'Don't try to pretend,' Ilsi said, 'because I saw you. Slipping out at twilight, going down towards the old summerhouse. Not the place I would choose myself for a romantic tryst, but it *is* secluded.'

Kiukiu swallowed hard, her throat tight with apprehension.

'So go on, Kiukiu, tell us. Who is he?'

'I – I can't.'

'Why ever not?' Ilsi's eyes glittered, bright as needles.

'I – made him a promise.' It was true in a way. As long as her foolish tongue didn't betray her, blabbing out the very thing she was trying not to say.

'Him!' cried Ilsi triumphantly. 'So you admit it!'

Whatever she said now, they were out to prise the truth from her, she could see it in their eyes. Flustered, she tried to back away down the passageway, hoping Sosia would hear and come to her rescue.

'Let's guess who it is.' Ilsi's smile hardened. 'Not old beer-breath Oleg!'

'It had better not be your Michailo,' Ninusha said, advancing menacingly on Kiukiu.

'Michailo? With Kiukiu?' Ilsi spluttered with laughter. 'No, it's one of those pimply boys, isn't it, Kiukiu, one of the *detsky*, the little keep guards, with fluff on their chins and squeaky voices—'

'How much did he pay you for a fumble, Kiukiu? Or did you let him have it for free?'

Kiukiu kept backing away but still they came after her, their hateful voices whining like stinging gnats in her ears.

'A slut. Just like her mother,' Ninusha said contemptuously.

'Like mother, like daughter. Whore.'

Kiukiu gasped. They could insult her, but her mother's memory was sacred. How dare they call her mother a whore?

'You'd better not let Sosia hear you,' she said.

'Why not? It's true, isn't it?' said Ilsi.

Kiukiu launched herself at Ilsi. Ilsi screamed, thin and high, as Kiukiu thudded into her, bearing her, kicking and scratching, to the floor in a tumble of boots and petticoats. Ninusha threw herself onto Kiukiu – and Kiukiu felt Ninusha's fists violently pummelling her back.

'Stop this at once!' Someone thrust the sharp bristles of a broom in Kiukiu's face, prising her and Ilsi apart.

Kiukiu – through a tangle of messed hair – saw Sosia standing over them, wielding the broom. Behind Sosia in the passageway she could see grinning, leering faces: the potboys and scullions, nudging and jostling each other to get the best view.

'On your feet!' Sosia's voice cracked, hard as a whipstroke. 'All three of you!'

Kiukiu stumbled to her feet. Her lip was bleeding. Ninusha and Ilsi helped each other up. Ilsi's face was white with rage except for a fast-darkening bruise around one eye.

I got her! Kiukiu raised her hand to her mouth, wiping away the blood. *I gave her a black eye! That has to be worth a beating.*

'Whatever are you thinking?' Sosia's voice dropped to a whisper, viciously sharp as her kitchen knives. 'Brawling in my kitchen like fishwives. I want to know who started it.'

'Kiukiu,' Ninusha and Ilsi said, in one voice.

'Kiukiu. Is this true?' Sosia stood in front of

Kiukiu. 'Look at me, girl, when I'm talking to you! Did you start it?'

Thoughts skittered through Kiukiu's panicked mind. If she told Sosia how the fight started, she'd reveal she'd been to the summerhouse. And if Sosia prised the truth from her, Snowcloud was as good as dead.

'They called my mother a whore,' she mumbled. Her lip was swelling up.

'You called my sister a whore?' Sosia planted herself in front of Ilsi, hands on hips.

'I feel a little faint.' Ilsi sagged against Ninusha.

One of the scullery boys sniggered. Sosia turned on him. 'You! Have you nothing else to do? Go scour those soup pots clean. Back to work, all of you!'

'And she called me a whore too.'

'For what reason?'

'Ilsi saw her,' Ninusha put in defensively. 'Sneaking out to meet some boy. When she was supposed to be drawing water.'

'Is this true?' Sosia demanded.

Soft white feathers, stained red, fluttered through Kiukiu's thoughts like a bloodstained blizzard. *Must protect Snowcloud.* She mumbled an unintelligible response.

'Ilsi, Ninusha, go and get yourselves cleaned up. I'll speak with you two later. The roast pheasant needs basting – see to it. And check on my corn bread in the second oven. It'll burn if it's left much longer. Now, as to you, Kiukirilya, you're coming with me.'

Sosia only ever used her full name when she was in trouble. Kiukiu trailed behind as Sosia marched tight-lipped through the kitchen. They were going to Sosia's room and that could only mean a beating.

Sosia shut the door after Kiukiu and locked it.

'Sit down.'

Kiukiu, head still down, sat obediently on one of Sosia's hard-backed chairs. When she was younger, Sosia had often beaten her for disobedience: the ruler on the knuckles for clumsiness, the stick across the legs for answering back. The punishments had seemed harsh – she could still remember the fierce sting of the stick – but once administered, they had been over, the incidents never mentioned again.

She held out her hands, bracing herself, squeezing her eyes shut. Nothing happened. She looked up and saw to her surprise that Sosia was dabbing at reddened eyes with the corner of her apron.

Her aunt was weeping.

Kiukiu stared at her, shocked. Sosia never wept. Was she so mortified by her niece's behaviour that she was reduced to tears of shame?

'I – I'm sorry, Auntie Sosia,' Kiukiu ventured.

'It was a mistake to keep you here, I said so all along,' Sosia said in a dark, hard voice. 'But who else was there to care for you? What with your poor silly mother driven out of her wits.'

'She was never a slut!'

'No. Afimia may have lacked one grain of sense in her pretty head but she was never a bad girl. Sweet-natured, yes. But irresponsible, foolish—'

'So why did they call her that? Just to provoke me?'

Sosia looked up at Kiukiu. The expression in her eyes made Kiukiu shiver.

'You had to know the truth one day. And now that Lord Volkh is dead, maybe it's time to tell it. Your mother wasn't raped by the Arkhels. She met your father by chance in the forest and – silly girl – she fell in love with him.'

'With Lord Arkhel?' Kiukiu whispered.

'With one of his followers, Kiukiu; pay attention!' snapped Sosia. 'His name was Malkh. That's all I know.'

'Malkh.' Kiukiu repeated the unfamiliar name to herself. She was the daughter of a man called Malkh.

'They found him in her bed one night. Dragged him out, put him to the torture. To make him betray his master, Lord Stavyor. Then they killed him. They made her watch. I'll never forget his screams . . . or hers.' Sosia's eyes had gone cold and dark as moorland mists. 'I thought she would miscarry. But though her wits never returned, she carried you to nine months. After you were born, she just faded away. She would sit singing to you in a strange, soft voice, singing and smiling, smiling and singing . . . my poor sweet-natured Afimia. When the winter snows came, she wandered out into the forest, saying she was going to meet your father. No-one thought to stop her, they just thought she was talking her usual nonsense. They found her the next day, frozen to death. You were just a few months old.'

Kiukiu sat staring at Sosia. She could feel tears pricking in her eyes, but they would not come. She was numb, cold as her long-dead mother. She could see the endless canopy of snow-laden forest branches, feel the sting of the bitter cold, the crunch of hard-frozen snow beneath her trudging feet . . .

'I had to fight for you, Kiukiu. For your life.'

'What?' Kiukiu blinked away the white chill of the snow-mantled forests.

'The *druzhina* wanted you dead.'

'Because I was an Arkhel bastard-child?'

'They urged Lord Volkh to have you killed.'

'A baby. What harm could a little baby have done?'

'Babies grow up.'

'So why did Lord Volkh spare me?'

'He said a curious thing. It was late at night and you were kicking and cooing in your crib near the fire when he came in. His face was dark as thunder. I was so terrified I didn't know what to do. His hand was outstretched and I feared, I feared he was about to—'

'To do what?' Kiukiu could see terror gleaming in her aunt's eyes, pale as the glow of the long-ago firelight.

'Be thankful, child, that you never had to see the Drakhaon wield his powers.' Sosia gave a dry little shudder.

The last time Lord Volkh had tried to summon his powers, Kiukiu thought, shuddering too, he had been so weakened by poison that they had failed him.

'But all he did was touch your face. Those powerful fingers gently stroking the cheek of a child in a cradle. And he said . . . I've never forgotten what he said.'

Kiukiu found she had been unconsciously touching her cheek, as if trying to recall that long-ago firelit night. Strange benediction . . .

'What did he say, Auntie?'

'He said, "There will be no more songs for the House of Arkhel. But one day, perhaps, this child will use her inheritance for the good of my House."'

'My inheritance?' Kiukiu shook her head, utterly puzzled. 'What inheritance? What did he mean?'

'Does one question the Drakhaon?' Sosia said sharply. 'I did not dare then; I would not dare to presume now. It was not often in Lord Volkh's nature to show mercy. Never forget that he spared your life. You have a debt of loyalty to the House of Nagarian . . .'

'To Lord Gavril,' Kiukiu murmured, almost to herself.

'But there are members of his household with long memories, Kiukiu. Now that Lord Volkh is gone, there is no-one to protect you. There are those in the *druzhina* who still regard you as a threat.'

'Me?' Kiukiu stared at Sosia, astonished. 'A threat?'

'Bogatyr Kostya still suspects you. He thinks you sympathize with the Arkhels.'

'How can I?' The unfairness of the suspicion astounded Kiukiu. 'I didn't know!'

'So I told him when he came storming round after Lord Volkh's death, looking for you.'

'Kostya c-came looking for me?' Kiukiu felt her throat go dry with fear. The *druzhina*, enraged beyond reason with grief for their lord's death, could have imprisoned her, tortured her – and all because she had Arkhel blood in her veins.

'He has a long memory. That's why I've had to go on telling the lies.' Sosia began to weep again. 'Dishonouring your father's memory. Saying he violated your mother. When he was just a reckless

228

young fool, head over heels in love with the wrong girl. With my poor Afimia.'

Kiukiu could only nod her head, overwhelmed by conflicting emotions. It was a kind of consolation to know now that she was not the product of a random act of violence but a child of love, doomed love. But she could not begin to take in the full import of Sosia's tale. She only knew nothing would ever be the same.

'And now you must forget everything I've told you.' Sosia wiped her eyes on the edge of her apron.

'Forget?' Dismayed, Kiukiu rose to her feet. 'Why must I forget?'

'Because of Bogatyr Kostya. And all the others who hate the very name of Arkhel.'

'But I would never have harmed Lord Volkh!' Kiukiu cried. 'You know that, Auntie Sosia, you know I—'

'*I* know it,' Sosia said. 'But if you want to stay here, you'll have to work extra-hard to prove your loyalty. No slipping out for a quick kiss and a cuddle. That sort of carrying-on can be mis-interpreted. Besides, after what became of your mother,' she said sternly, 'I hope you have the sense to stay well away from young men, Kiukiu.'

Kiukiu hung her head. She hoped Sosia would assume she was ashamed. She hoped there would be no more questions about where she'd been and who she'd been with.

'Yes, Auntie, I promise. I'll go back to the kitchens now.'

'One more word of warning,' Sosia said, catching hold of her by the wrist. 'That Ilsi's a tricky piece of work. I'd have dismissed her months ago if she weren't such a good little cook. She doesn't like to be crossed. I'm not saying she didn't speak out of turn; she had no business to talk to you like that. But you attacked her, Kiukiu. She won't forget that in a hurry. She'll do all she can to get back at you. Be on your guard, girl. I won't always be around to defend you.'

Kiukiu dazedly stared at her aunt. Ilsi had never been her friend – but her enemy? Would Ilsi be watching her all the time now, waiting to catch her out? A feeling of dread seeped into her stomach. She didn't want to have to face the other servants in the kitchens. She wanted to go and hide in her room, to burrow into her bed and pull the covers up over her head.

Little light filtered into the basement, even at midday. In the perpetual gloom of the scullery, Kiukiu found it hard to tell whether the piles of plates she had been set to wash were clean or not. Her hands were wrinkled and swollen with repeated plunging into the greasy water. But she endured Sosia's punishment without complaining; at least being confined to scullery duties meant she did not have to meet Ilsi or Ninusha . . . just yet.

Malkh. I am the daughter of a man called Malkh. She tried to push what Sosia had told her last night out of her mind but his name kept returning, like a monotonous refrain. She wished Sosia had not told her. For every time she remembered his name, she remembered that he had died in agony, tortured by the *druzhina* into betraying his own Clan . . .

I am the daughter of a traitor called Malkh.

She scrubbed angrily at the trencher she was

holding. Why wouldn't the dried-on stains of sauce come off?

'*There will be no more songs for the House of Arkhel . . .*'

She plunged the trencher back into the water.

'Ugh.' Now the water was not just greasy, it was cold. She would have to pour it away and heft in the bucket of hot water she had set to heat on the scullery range. She would have to grate some more soap into flakes, trying not to skin her sore and swollen knuckles.

What had her father been to Lord Arkhel? Had he held some special position of trust in the Arkhel Clan? Why had Lord Volkh spared her life? What was this inheritance of hers he had been so at pains to preserve?

That's quite enough! she told herself. Her head had begun to ache with unanswered questions. *Time to think later. Just finish the dishes.*

The tread of feet on the courtyard gravel put all thoughts of her father out of her mind. Visitors? Sosia had not mentioned visitors. They could not have come on horseback for she could hear no jingle of harnesses or grate of shod hooves.

She stood on tiptoe at the sink, craning her neck to peer up out of the scullery window.

Sandalled feet. Long, grey robes the colour of dusk.

'Monks?' she said out loud. And at least a dozen of them, all wearing the cowled habits of the Monastery of Saint Sergius. Had they come to bid welcome to Lord Gavril?

A cold draught suddenly chilled her. One of the scullions must have come in with another pile of washing-up.

'Close the door!' she called without turning round.

The chill intensified. The twilight shadows darkened.

Someone was there, darker than the clustering twilight shadows.

'*Kiukirilya.*' The voice shivered in her mind, harsh as winter frost.

'M-my Lord Volkh?' She was trembling as if with intense cold. And now she dared not turn around, she dared not look on the face of the revenant.

'*The monks have come to send me back.*'

'*What do you mean, My Lord?*' she whispered, her face still averted.

'*Exorcism, Kiukirilya. Don't let them do it. Once I am gone, who will protect my son?*'

'H-how can I stop them?'

'*You were born with the gift.*'

'The gift? I d-don't even know what it is, let alone how to use it.'

'*Your father's gift. In you it is raw, untrained. But even an untrained Guslyar is more powerful than a whole choir of chanting monks.*'

'Guslyar?' The unfamiliar title meant nothing to her. 'What is a Guslyar?'

'*Praise-Singer. Ghost-Singer. You come from an unusual family, Kiukirilya. Your forebears could spin songs that bridge this world and the Ways Beyond. They could summon the souls of dead warriors to possess the bodies of the living. Sing for me, Kiukirilya.*'

'Sing?' Kiukiu was stupefied. 'I can't sing.'

'*You brought me back. Make me powerful. Sing me into a living, breathing body.*'

232

A stab of fear pierced Kiukiu, sharp as an icicle. 'I . . . can't do that.'

'Kiukiu?' shrilled Sosia from the corridor. 'We're out of serving-platters!'

Kiukiu blinked. With one convulsive shudder, the revenant had vanished. She was alone, staring into empty air.

'Where are those clean platters, Kiukiu?' Sosia came in, banging the door open. Then she stopped, hugging her arms to herself. 'Brrr! Have you had a window open? It's freezing in here. Cold as the grave.'

The distant sound of chanting wove its way like drifting smoke down into the kitchens.

Kiukiu stopped scrubbing, up to her elbows in greasy water, to listen.

The monks' chant was so calm, so remote, that it lulled her tired mind into a trance. She felt as if she were floating upwards, far above the dark branches of the forest, up into the grey twilit skies towards the great expanse of white ice.

Ice. So pure, so cold . . .

A rattle of pots broke the trance. Kiukiu plummeted rudely back down to earth. Little Movsar had come struggling in with his arms full of cooking pans.

'How many more?' Kiukiu asked in disbelief. She wiped the back of her hand across her face. The fingers were red and swollen. In the morning the skin would be cracked and chapped.

'Sosia says this is the last.'

''Bout time too,' Kiukiu grumbled.

'Monks have big appetites.'

'And I thought they were s'posed to be frugal.'

'Chanting's hungry work,' Movsar said with a wink before he scurried off.

Kiukiu looked at the pans. She looked at the dirty water.

The distant singing still wreathed through the autumn dusk.

'*Your forebears could spin songs that bridge this world and the Ways Beyond . . .*'

She started, checking guiltily behind her.

But there was no wraith-chill to the air, only the crisp tang of twilight.

'*Make me powerful. Sing me into a living, breathing body.*'

What had Lord Volkh meant? What had he intended? Had he wanted to possess one of the household, to live again in a new body? How could such a thing happen? And what, Kiukiu wondered wearily, became of the original owner of the repossessed body? Where did that spirit go?

It was rapidly becoming too dark to see what she was doing. Snowcloud must be starving hungry by now. He was always hungry, gobbling up in beakfuls the little scraps Kiukiu brought each day. A good sign, she supposed. A keen appetite must mean he was building up his strength. But how was she to get him his scraps if she was still confined to scullery duties? The stacks of dirty pots and dishes had all arrived scraped clean of food debris.

She went to the door and peeked out into the passageway.

All clear.

She edged out, back to the limewashed wall, making for the slop bin at the kitchen entrance. All scraps of food not deemed suitable for the soup-pot were thrown in here and carted away to be fed to the kastel pigs.

Shadows moved across the wall, distorted by the flickering flames in the range. Ilsi was complaining in a thin, strident voice. Kiukiu took a breath and plunged her hand into the slop bin. Her fingers closed on the cold fatty slime of bacon rinds. Grabbing the biggest handful she could, she fled before anyone noticed her in the doorway.

The twilight air was already tainted with frost; she paused a moment on the doorstep to check no-one had seen her and then hurried out over the slippery cobblestones.

The autumn moon was rising. Kiukiu looked up as she pushed open the rusted iron gate to the gardens and shuddered; the slender crescent glinted copper, like dried blood on steel. When the moon cast a bloodstained light on Azhkendir, it was said to presage a terrible disaster.

Guided by the coppered moonlight, she flitted silently down through the overgrown gardens towards the summerhouse.

'Dinner's on its way, Snowcloud.'

And then just as she reached the warped summer-house door, she heard a woman's voice.

'What are you doing here? Do you want to get yourself killed?'

Kiukiu hesitated; she knew she should not eavesdrop yet she was desperately anxious to make sure her beautiful Snowcloud was not discovered.

'I had to see you again, Lilias.' It was a man's voice answering, young and hoarse with emotion.

Lilias. Kiukiu froze. What was Lilias doing out here

in the dark, keeping a secret tryst with a man whose every nuance of voice betrayed his love for her?

'Why didn't you go back to Swanholm, Jaro? As we agreed?'

Jaro? Kiukiu repeated to herself. Who was Jaro? No-one in the kastel bore that name.

'You saw what *he* did to me. I crawled out into the forest. A charcoal-burner found me and took me to the monastery. If it hadn't been for the good brothers, I would have died. By the time I reached Arkhelskoye, the port was ice-bound.'

'And so you came back here? Are you quite *mad*?'

'I can't stop thinking about you, Lilias. If that's a kind of madness, then yes.'

'Our business is concluded.' Lilias's voice was cold as frost. 'You got what you wanted. And so . . . so I thought . . . had I.'

'You told me the son was no real threat. A painter, not a soldier. You told me his mother had poisoned his mind against his father. You said he would never come to Azhkendir.'

'Kostya had other ideas,' Lilias said.

The son. Up till now Kiukiu had not understood what was being discussed so furtively. Now she began to realize she had stumbled on something so treacherous that she had endangered her life just by listening. Crouched down in the frosty garden, clutching the cold, coagulating scraps of bacon fat for Snowcloud, she badly wanted to run away – but dared not.

'So you and the child—'

'Have been awarded a paltry pension. Paid off like a common whore. Thank you for your services,

Madame Arbelian, which are no longer required.'
Lilias spat out the last words.

'And all our plans—'

'He'll come looking for you. The *druzhina* are
working on him already, wearing his resistance
down. Sooner or later the Drakhaon blood will
prevail. So you have a choice. Kill him now, before
he gains his full powers, or go. Leave Azhkendir.
Never come back.'

'Kill him now?' the young man echoed. Kiukiu
heard the uncertainty in his voice.

'There's another passageway that will take you
directly to his bedchamber. Remember?'

Kiukiu clapped one hand to her mouth, trying to
keep from gasping aloud.

'There . . . there has to be another way,' the young
man said eventually.

'There is no other way. You destroyed the
serpent, now you must destroy its young before it
learns to bite.'

Kiukiu began to back away over the frost-brittle
grass, one step at a time. The food scraps dropped
from her hand, and she turned and began to run.

Halfway up the overgrown path she stopped. She
was shaking, but whether from the intense cold or
from fear she could not tell. The garden shimmered
with hoarfrost under the blackness of the star-
powdered sky.

Her word against Lilias's. Who would believe her?
By the time she had brought help, Lilias and her
accomplice would have disappeared from the
summerhouse. Dysis would vouch that her mistress
had spent all evening reading in front of the fire.
Kostya would punish her for wasting his time. But

237

Lilias, secure with her alibi, would know. The instant she accused Lilias she was as good as dead.

Lord Gavril will protect me . . .

But Lord Gavril needed her protection so much more than she needed his. At this very moment, an assassin might be creeping along the underground passage, making for his bedchamber to lie in wait for him . . .

Thoughts drifted wildly about her brain like little flurries of snow.

Think! Think!

As she drew closer to the kastel, she could hear the serene chanting of the monks wafting out into the night. Lord Gavril was attending the ceremony of exorcism in the Hall. There was no way she could attract his attention without alerting the *druzhina* or disrupting the ceremony.

'*Once I am gone, who will protect my son?*'

Suddenly she knew what she must do. She must stop the exorcism ceremony. She must find a way to keep Lord Volkh's spirit-wraith in this world, where it could watch over Lord Gavril.

Candles had been lit all around the Great Hall; the darkness trembled with their golden flames.

Kiukiu balanced on tiptoe in the bramble-tangled ruins of the frostbound garden, nose just above the level of the stone sill, peering in.

Abbot Yephimy stood in the centre of the Hall, at the very place where Lord Volkh had been found dying. But Kiukiu saw that the abbot of the forest monastery was not some withered elderly cleric as she had imagined but a robust, broad-shouldered man in middle years who, in spite of his grey robes

238

and long beard, looked more like a warrior than a monk.

Lord Gavril sat at the table on the dais beneath his father's portrait, watching. His face was sombre, shadowed, unreadable. Kiukiu's heart ached for him. She had caused him so much trouble...

One of the monks brought over a tall tripod on which rested a green bronze dish, smeared grey inside with powdered ashes. Abbot Yephimy placed the likeness of a man shaped out of yellow beeswax into the bronze dish, resting it on a bed of incense embers.

'Hear me, Volkh, Lord Nagarian. We have sung the Chants of Valediction. When this waxen body is consumed, you will pass beyond the bournes of this world and never return.'

The monks began to sing again, their chant a deep droning resonance.

'*Kiukirilya.*' The spirit-wraith's voice echoed faintly in her mind. The drifting smoke swirled more thickly. And in the smoke Kiukiu saw a shadow-shape was forming, raising insubstantial hands towards her, clasped in a pleading gesture. '*They mean to send me back. Stop them.*'

'How?' she cried aloud. 'I don't know how!'

The wax figure had begun to glow on the incense embers, more golden than the myriad candleflames glittering in the Hall.

'*Hurry...*' The voice was fading fast, a dying whisper.

Grasping hold of the creeper, Kiukiu pulled herself up and banged hard on the window.

'Help! *Help!*' she cried, clinging on till the wiry vine-stem burned her palms.

Inside, the singing faltered, heads turned towards her, monks, *druzhina*, even the Abbot. She saw consternation in their faces, and then outrage. The Bogatyr came hurrying across to the window. She let go and dropped to the ground just as he tugged the window catch open and leaned out. The shimmering candlelight wavered and dimmed as the flames shivered in the blast of cold air.

'What in hell's name—'

'Intruder!' she gasped, waving her hand vaguely towards the garden. 'Intruder in the grounds!'

'Search the gardens!' the Bogatyr shouted.

Druzhina came running, stumbling over each other in their haste, seizing torches, crowding to the window. In the commotion, Kiukiu saw the tripod knocked to the floor, the ashes spilled over the glowing wax figure. And then she was thrown to the ground as the men jumped down into the rose bushes and went running down the gardens.

The Bogatyr caught hold of Kiukiu and dragged her up into the Hall. 'Where, girl? And what were you doing out there alone at night?'

But behind him she saw a stormcloud of bitter incense-smoke hovering like a milling beeswarm above Abbot Yephimy's head. 'Look, Bogatyr.'

'*Yephimy!*' Lord Volkh's voice trembled like rolling thunder through the kastel. '*Leave this place. Go back to Saint Sergius.*'

The Bogatyr let go of her. His face had turned pale.

'Lord Volkh,' he whispered.

A wind gusted through the Hall, a chill charnel wind, dry as dust. Candles crashed to the floor.

'Enough!' Yephimy struck his abbot's staff three times on the echoing stone floor.

'*Leave me be, Yephimy.*'

Kiukiu saw that Lord Gavril had risen from his chair, was standing staring as the swirling incense-smoke became the shadow of a man, tall, broad-shouldered, dark hair silver-brindled with age.

Yephimy raised his staff high above his head. 'Be gone, Volkh!'

The charnel wind swirled, howling about the Hall. The central lantern swung wildly, jerkily, as on a storm-tossed ship. The monks cowered back, calling the sacred name of the Lord God to preserve them from harm.

'*Go!*' commanded Yephimy in the blast.

Lord Gavril suddenly shouted out over the roaring of the wind. He launched himself forwards, throwing himself on top of Yephimy, bearing the Abbot to the ground.

And the madly swinging, jerking lantern snapped from its chain and came whistling down to crash where Yephimy had been standing.

Stillness after storm. No whirlwind, no turbulent voice shrieking. But laughter. Laughter as dry as wind-scattered pyre ashes.

And like cinders blown on the wind, the echoes dispersed, disintegrated . . . and disappeared.

14

The exorcism had failed.

Gavril stood in the Great Hall, staring numbly at the marks of ash and melted wax staining the tiled floor.

All his plans had centred on laying his father's spirit to rest. But instead of fading peacefully away, the wraith had only grown stronger, more wrathful, than before.

Gavril sank down onto the dais and covered his face with his hands. How could it all have gone so wrong?

The monks were purifying the Hall, burning sweet angelsmoke in their censers and sprinkling the air with holy water.

'Lord Gavril.'

Gavril looked up to see Abbot Yephimy.

'You saved my life.'

Gavril nodded, still too heart-sick to speak.

'Your father's spirit-wraith is far more powerful than I had anticipated.'

'Was that . . . abomination really my father?' At last Gavril found words, stumbling words to articulate the bitterness choking him.

Yephimy nodded. 'I have observed this phenomenon before. The wraith becomes the embodiment of the dying person's last conscious thoughts. And a violent death produces a violent wraith, obsessed with its own fury, obsessed with revenge. And now I fear . . .'

'Now?'

'I fear', the Abbot said grimly, 'that I have unleashed a force of elemental rage. Until last night the wraith was trapped within the boundaries of the place where it died, unable to roam abroad. But now it has burst free. It is too strong for me to exorcize.'

'My father was a cruel man. I wish I were not his son.' Gavril had blurted the words out before he had thought what he was saying. But they were words from the heart. Why should he go on pretending?

'My Lord—' the Abbot began.

'What's all this commotion?' Lilias swept into the Hall, with Dysis bobbing anxiously at her heels. 'Are we being raided? Why are there men swarming about the grounds?'

'Madame, please don't excite yourself,' begged Dysis. 'Think of the baby.'

'One of the servants thought she saw an intruder in the garden,' Kostya said.

'And which servant was that?'

'Kiukiu.'

Kiukiu? In all the commotion he had not even noticed who had interrupted the ceremony; he had only heard a girl's voice screaming outside.

'And have you found anyone so far?'

'No,' said Kostya brusquely.

Lilias let out a little laugh of disdain. 'I could have told you not to waste your time! That girl is soft in the head. She's scared of her own shadow.'

'We can't afford to ignore any report of intruders – however unlikely.'

'Indeed,' Lilias said with a cryptic smile. 'Vigilant at all times, Bogatyr. It would be scandalous for a second tragedy to follow so fast on the first.'

Kostya scowled at her. 'Shouldn't you be resting, madame?'

'How can I rest with this constant noise? And all because one silly girl was scared by a shadow—' Lilias broke off, grimacing as she pressed one hand to the side of her belly.

'Madame,' said Dysis, reaching out to support her as she swayed on her feet, 'the Bogatyr is right. You should be resting.'

'If any harm comes to my baby because of you and your investigations—'

'Please, madame. Come and lie down. I'll make you a nice, calming tisane.'

Gavril watched Dysis lead Lilias away. Lilias had not left her rooms for days, not since the reading of the will. Why had she come now, so near her time, why had she not sent Dysis to find out what was happening? Of course, it could just be the whim of a pregnant woman . . .

The daylight seemed to dim – and glancing at the tall windows, he saw little flecks, white as drifting petals, slowly spiralling down from the leaden sky.

'Snow,' he whispered, transfixed. He could only remember one winter snowfall in temperate Smarna and that had been many years ago. 'It's started to snow.'

Snow swirled around the Kalika Tower, great gusts of flakes billowing like foam-crested breakers, whipped up by a bitter, howling stormwind.

Gavril stood staring at the chill white turbulence. The storm had raged since morning and showed no sign of abating. He sensed a dark, brooding spirit stirring the eddies of snow, a bitter anger animating the blizzard that battered the walls of the kastel.

'Father,' he said aloud. He flung open the stained-glass window and, gripping the sill, leaned out into the blast. *'Father!'* he yelled into the screaming of the wind. 'Make it stop! Tell me what you want!'

Freezing snow spattered him, numbing his face and hands, soaking his windblown hair.

A sudden gust caught him, flung him back, propelling him right across the floor. The tower trembled, the window blew inwards, coloured glass shattered against the stone wall.

Dazed, he opened his eyes. A tall figure, dark as thundercloud, towered above him, filling the room, wreathed by whirling snow.

'*You know what you must do.*' A voice crackling with ice and thunder made the whole room tremble.

'There has to be another way,' Gavril said stubbornly.

A buffet of wind, sharp as a blow to the head, slammed him back hard against the wall.

'Why?' Gavril whispered, breathless and bruised. 'Why treat me this way? You're my father.' Dizzy, ears ringing, he found himself sliding back down to the floor, unable to keep upright.

245

The fierce assault of the blizzard suddenly ceased. From the hovering snowshadow blotting out the daylight, Gavril heard a slow, sad exhalation, like the eerie whine of the wind over the frozen moors. And on the exhalation came words, weary, desolate words that made his heart ache.

'So . . . cold . . . So . . . very . . . tired . . . Help me, Gavril. Help me end it. Set me free.'

Gavril felt a sudden stab of pity. There was still a trace of humanity in this cold, wrathful snow-spirit.

'I want to help you. But there has to be some other way. I promise you I will do all in my power to bring Jaromir Arkhel to justice, but – don't ask me to kill him.'

'*There is no other way.*'

Volkh's shadow collapsed inwards into a spinning cone of cloud and snow. Gavril was hurled backwards as the stormshadow burst out of the tower room, on a trail of shrieking wind.

'My Lord! My Lord!' There came a frantic hammering on the door. Gavril crawled over and pulled himself up to his feet, trying to turn the great iron key. As the door opened, he collapsed onto his knees.

Kostya caught hold of him and helped him into a chair.

'You've taken quite a beating there, lad,' he said. He took out his handkerchief and, scooping up a handful of melting snow, made a compress and pressed it to Gavril's forehead. Gavril winced.

'Tsk, tsk.' Kostya was clicking his teeth in disgust as he stared at the chaos the wraith had caused in the study. Books had been torn from the shelves and tossed haphazardly down; now they lay in disarray, their spines broken, torn pages fluttering in the draught from the shattered window.

'And this room was always your father's favourite,' Kostya said, almost to himself, absently gathering the scattered papers.

'Whatever was here just now seems to bear little resemblance to my father.'

'Didn't I warn you?' Kostya said with a laconic shrug. 'The wraith is out of control. Fury drives it, makes it strong. Soon it will not even remember its name, only its hunger for revenge – and ultimate oblivion.'

Amongst the snow-wet papers in Kostya's hands Gavril caught sight of his sketches of Astasia. He sprang up from the chair.

'Give me those,' he said, grabbing them from Kostya. They were all but ruined. The inks had run and blotched, distorting the image of her face to a nightmare caricature, a leering succubus with eyes weirdly blurred and shadowed, mouth dribbling leaks of dark liquid. Choked, he cast them down on the desk. Even his most cherished memories had been violated.

'Lord Drakhaon! Bogatyr!' Now there were more voices outside. One of the *druzhina* came running up the stairs. 'Visitors. From Azhgorod.'

'In this weather?' Kostya said.

'It's Lord Stoyan,' the man stammered. 'There's news. Bad news.'

'The Drakhaon!' barked Kostya as Gavril came into the Hall.

A richly dressed man, in robes of jewel-dark brocades trimmed with fur, stood with his retainers, who were stamping snow from their boots and warming their hands at the fire. There was a rancid smell of snow-wet fur drying. When they saw Gavril, all went down on one knee, clutching their fur-rimmed hats to their breasts.

'Lord Boris Stoyan,' Kostya announced. 'Head of the Council of Boyars in Azhgorod.'

Lord Stoyan, a heavy-set man with a flowing brown beard, came forward and bowed, the heavy gold chain about his neck clinking as he lowered his head.

'My Lord, we had hoped to welcome you to the Council in Azhgorod after the mourning for your father was over,' the Boyar said. His voice was deep, rich as a good vintage wine. 'But we have been forced to intrude by events . . . very grave events.'

'You must be chilled to the bone, My Lord, after such a journey,' Gavril said. 'Spiced ale for our guests,' he called to Sosia.

Kostya conducted Lord Stoyan to the great polished table on the dais and pulled back the carved chair beneath Lord Volkh's portrait for Gavril.

'Well?' Kostya demanded brusquely, taking his place at Gavril's right hand.

'There's been what I can only describe as . . . a massacre.'

'What d'you mean, a massacre?' Kostya said, suddenly all attention.

'Last night. In the stronghold of Kharsk – which has always been loyal to your House, Lord Drakhaon.'

'Are you implying there's an Arkhel connection?' said Kostya, leaning forward, his eyes bright and fierce.

Lord Stoyan shrugged expansively, his gold chain clinking as he moved.

'Some say it was a pack of wolves, others say it was mercenaries, secret Arkhel sympathizers, maybe. I think you should come and see for yourself, My Lord. If there's a band of renegades at large, we need to find and destroy them.'

'Casualties?' Kostya asked.

'Too many to count. Mostly women and children.'

Gavril had sat listening in silence, wondering what was expected of him.

'Hot spiced ale, My Lords,' announced Sosia. She approached the dais, Ninusha following. Distracted, Gavril watched Ninusha silently flirt with Lord Stoyan's retainers as she poured ale for them, darting little provocative glances at them from under thick, black lashes.

'So where is Kharsk?' he asked as the men drank.

One of the retainers unrolled a creased vellum map on the table before him. It was crudely painted in faded inks, with childlike kastels drawn to represent towns; it showed none of the penmanship of his father's map in the Kalika Tower.

'A day's journey from here to the east of Azhgorod.' Lord Stoyan pointed. 'Across the shores of Lake Ilmin.'

There lay the city of Azhgorod, bristling with spires and towers. And at the far end of long Lake Ilmin, Gavril saw clearly outlined the southern mountain pass that led down into Muscobar.

'The people of Kharsk have begged for your protection, My Lord.'

Gavril turned to Kostya.

'Then we must go to Kharsk – and straight away.'

* * *

Gavril went racing up the stairs. After last night's vigil, he had felt weary and dispirited but the thought of freedom – of a kind – had given him new energy.

He flung open the doors of his bedchamber.

'My Lord,' a voice whispered.

'Kiukiu?' He stopped on the threshold, puzzled. The room looked empty.

The great hunting tapestry that concealed the secret door moved, and Kiukiu crept out. Her hair was dishevelled, escaping in wisps from her plaits and her eyes were huge, dark-shadowed in a wan face. She looked as if she too had not slept all night.

'What were you doing behind the tapestry?'

'Keeping you safe, My Lord.' She stumbled a little and he caught hold of her arm, guiding her towards a chair.

'Or hiding from Kostya?'

'He told you?'

'You saw an intruder in the grounds. The *druzhina* searched till dawn. They found no-one.'

'But were they looking in the right places?' she asked, distractedly trying to weave the escaping wisps of hair back in place.

'Kiukiu, you disrupted the ceremony.' He kneeled beside her. 'Why? Why did you do it?'

'Because there *was* an intruder.' She gripped the sides of the chair. 'He was in the summerhouse. With Lilias.'

'Why didn't you say so?'

'Because she mustn't know I overheard.'

He could see now she was shaking. He went to the table where Sosia had left his breakfast tray and

250

poured her some ale. She took the mug with trembling hands and drank a little in short, shuddering sips.

'What did you overhear?'

She looked up at him, her eyes wide with fear.

'Lilias. Telling him to come here by the secret passageways – and kill you.'

'Kill me?' The news confounded him; he didn't know what to say. 'Who was this man?'

'I – I don't know for sure. She called him Jaro.'

'Jaromir.' All Gavril's elation vanished, as if stormclouds had come scudding up again to blot out the pale sun. 'Jaromir Arkhel here.'

'Arkhel?' Kiukiu repeated in a hushed voice.

Dark eyes, staring at him from a pale face, staring with a singularly intense, unreadable expression.

'I don't think he planned to kill you,' Kiukiu's words broke in on the darkness of his thoughts. 'He said he had only come back because he wanted to see *her* again.'

Lilias: the assassin's unseen accomplice, the low voice calling from the secret panel in the Great Hall . . .

'I think he's in love with her, My Lord.'

'And so you came up here to try to stop him.' Gavril looked at Kiukiu with new respect. 'That was a brave thing to do.'

'I had to hide from the *druzhina*.' Kiukiu took another shaky sip from the mug. Her voice was stronger now. 'Besides, I wasn't certain he would come.'

Gavril sat back on his heels, trying to make sense of Kiukiu's information. So Lilias and Jaromir were lovers. What had they hoped to achieve from the

251

assassination? To be joint rulers of Azhkendir? And whose child was she carrying – Arkhel or Nagarian?

'Lilias,' he muttered, 'always Lilias.' His past conversations with Lilias flashed through his mind; he saw again the delicate cups of scented tea, the perfumed flavour so strong it could easily have concealed the bitter taste of poison. To know that she wanted him dead clarified matters. But how could he prove her guilt?

'We need evidence,' he said to Kiukiu. 'If you accuse her, she'll just laugh in your face and call you a liar. And after that your life won't be worth a fig.'

'Evidence?' she said, crestfallen. 'What kind of evidence?'

'Kiukiu,' he said. 'I have to go away for a day or two. With Lord Stoyan.'

He saw her eyes widen with alarm.

'But suppose Jaromir Arkhel is in hiding out there, lying in wait for you?'

He found her concern for his safety touching. He put one hand on hers.

'I want you to be my eyes and ears whilst I'm away. Don't endanger yourself needlessly, but listen out for anything unusual.'

'You can count on me, My Lord.' She smiled up at him bravely, her grey-blue eyes warm, almost . . . adoring.

'What's happened to Snowcloud?' he asked, abruptly changing the subject.

'He's not flown yet.' She got up from the chair to place the empty mug back on the tray. 'I was going to feed him when I – when I heard the voices.'

She seemed to have no concerns about her own safety.

'You must be careful, Kiukiu,' he said. 'Whilst I'm away, there'll be nobody to protect you.'

'I'll be careful.'

A flake or two of snow still spiralled down from the louring sky as they set out along the forest-track.

Gavril rode with Lord Stoyan and Kostya; the Boyar's retainers and ten *druzhina* completed the party. Kostya had left Michailo in command of the kastel, bringing his older, more experienced warriors to protect his master.

Branches grey with hoarfrost brushed their heads; Gavril leaned low in the saddle to avoid them. Beyond the lane that skirted the kastel there seemed to be a pale haze, lying low like driftfog over the moors.

The track slowly wound upwards through the last, sparse pines straggling along the rim of Kerjhenezh.

The moorlands were blank with snow. Where there had been purple heathers and coppery bracken, there was nothing but whiteness.

There was a kind of an irony, Gavril thought bitterly, that the first time he escaped the confines of Kastel Drakhaon, Azhkendir was choked with snow, the ways barely passable. There seemed little hope now of making a bid for freedom over the mountains. His father's spirit-wraith had seen to that.

He was trapped in winter's prison.

They weathered the night in Lord Stoyan's kastel whilst fresh blizzards battered the walls.

In the morning Lord Stoyan led them to a frozen lake where the green-grey ice was so thick, the horses walked across as safely as if it were firm ground.

On the far side of Lake Ilmin, Gavril saw wisps of smoke rising into the still air. As they rode nearer, he saw a little fishing village of wooden huts behind beds of frozen reeds.

'No-one to greet us?' Kostya said, rising in the saddle to scan the shore. 'Hallo, there!' he cried. His voice echoed across the desolate landscape. A few birds flew squawking from the reedbeds, the flap of their wings sharp as gunshots on the chill air, but no-one called back.

'Is this Kharsk?' Gavril asked.

'Another few leagues eastwards to the stronghold at Kharsk, My Lord. This is Ilmin. And something's not right here, not right at all . . .'

Wooden boats lay abandoned on the shore, draped with nets and floats. Only the wind sighed through the reeds, rattling the ice-dry stems.

'Hallo!' cried Kostya again. He turned to the *druzhina*. 'Search the huts.'

The whine of the wind chilled Gavril to the bone; he pulled his coat closer, gazing uneasily at the empty village.

'Here! Over here!' The shout came from behind the huts.

Kostya swung down from his horse and, drawn sabre in hand, hurried away. Gavril followed.

He was unprepared for the sight that met his eyes. Bodies. Women and children, little children, lying sprawled and still in frozen snow stained rust-red with blood.

And as he drew reluctantly closer, he could see that they bore terrible wounds, bloody, ragged wounds to the limbs and throat . . . almost as if their attackers had savaged them.

He wanted to turn away from the horrible sight but could not.

'What in God's name happened here?' he said in a whisper.

'Assassins that maul innocent women and children, that kill for pleasure but steal nothing . . .' Kostya's strident voice was muted. He was bending over the torn body of a little child and Gavril saw with sudden anguish the pale hair spilling onto the bloodied snow as Kostya, with gentle hands, tried to straighten the twisted limbs. 'What's the sense in that?'

'Kostya—' he began and then fell silent, remembering that Kostya had no idea that he knew what the Arkhels had done to his little son Kostyushka. Sickened by the carnage, he turned away, taking a swig from his flask of aquavit to try to steady his stomach.

'This looks like wolves' work, My Lord.' Lord Stoyan, grim-faced, came to stand at Gavril's side.

A shout came from one of the huts.

'Survivors, Bogatyr!' called Askold, one of Kostya's lieutenants.

They crowded into the little hut, stooping to enter by the low doorway. It was dark inside, the air pungent with the smell of dried fish. As Gavril's eyes became accustomed to the dingy light, he saw a wizened old woman cowering in the corner, clutching a young girl-child to her.

'She says it was wolves, Bogatyr,' said Askold.

'What kind of wolves?' Gavril demanded. 'How many?'

The old woman was muttering to herself in some kind of Azhkendi dialect; Gavril could hardly make out what she said.

'She says "their eyes burned like marshfire", Lord Drakhaon. They came by night over the ice. Too many to count.'

'We need more details!' Kostya struck his fist against his palm.

The old woman stared imploringly at Gavril above the child's lolling head.

'Aquavit?' Gavril said, handing her his flask. She seized the flask and gulped down the fiery liquid as if it were water.

'Where are your other menfolk?' Kostya asked.

The old woman shook her head and mumbled a half-coherent reply.

'Seems some went to market in Azhgorod. She thinks they were caught in the blizzard. They should have been back by nightfall. The women were out with torches looking for them when the wolves struck.'

'And which way did they go, these wolves?' Kostya persisted.

She shrugged and began to rock the limp child against her shrivelled breast again, crooning a tuneless lullaby. Only now did Gavril realize with horror that the child was dead.

He beckoned Kostya outside. The *druzhina* were moving the bodies, covering them with sheets from the huts. He could not look. His eyes filled with useless tears. Blinking them away, he said, 'These wolves are wanton, vicious killers.

We must go after them. We must destroy them.'

'We must be on our guard, My Lord,' Kostya said. 'Snow wolves kill for food, not for sport. They rarely leave the mountains. Whatever these may be, they're not normal wolves. I smell Arkhel sorcery here.'

'You told me all the Arkhels were dead.'

'Kharsk is Nagarian. All the strongholds on the southern side of the moors are Nagarian. But to the north . . .'

Gavril fell silent, staring out across the frozen lake. He had not mentioned to Kostya anything of what Kiukiu had overheard. Now he began to wonder if Jaromir Arkhel had been raising a band of supporters to strike back at the Nagarians.

Was this the beginning of another Clan War?

15

'This is the last food I can bring you, Snowcloud.'

With a shudder of wings the owl dropped down to perch on Kiukiu's arm and pecked the titbits from her palm.

'It's too dangerous for you to stay here. You've got to go.'

In the fading light she noticed little pellets on the floor of the summerhouse. Regurgitated compressed remains of indigestible bone. Owl pellets.

'So you've learned to hunt for yourself! Clever boy!' She tickled the soft feathers around his ear-tufts. 'Now all you've got to do is fly.'

He was a wild creature, for all that he had learned to come when she called, and he needed his freedom.

She set him down and took out Sosia's best vegetable knife which she had smuggled out of the kitchen. 'Now hold still, Snowcloud.' The little splint Lord Gavril had made had worked loose; it took only two swift cuts to remove it. Snowcloud shook his feathers, ruffling them up into a snowy froth. Another cut and the tether was off.

'You're free,' she said, straightening up. The owl made no move. 'Come on, Snowcloud, fly away.' She clapped her hands. The owl blinked but did not stir. She offered her arm and he hopped up, clinging on with wiry claws that pierced the thick cloth of her sleeve. She moved slowly to the door, the owl balancing on her wrist.

'It's dark now; owl-time,' she told him. 'Time for you to go home.'

She tried to raise her arm in one sweeping movement to encourage him to lift off but he still held on, his claws gripping deeper into her flesh.

'Come on, you silly owl,' she urged. 'If you stay here, you'll be caught and killed. And I couldn't bear that.'

Almost as if in reply, the owl turned his head right around and nibbled with his beak at her neck in a friendly, familiar way.

'One more night then,' she whispered reluctantly, ruffling the downy feathers with her finger. 'But tomorrow you must go. No more titbits. You've got to fend for yourself.'

Kiukiu yawned as she huddled in front of the kitchen range, knuckling the sleep from her eyes.

'What's this? You're sitting here idle?' Sosia demanded as she bustled past.

'Lord Gavril's away so I . . .' mumbled Kiukiu.

'Then you'll have to do Lady Lilias's fires today.'

'Lady Lilias? No. Oh, no.' Alarmed, Kiukiu shook her head. 'She hates me. She won't want me anywhere near her.'

'We're short-staffed. Ninusha's in her bed with the stomach gripes again. I need Ilsi with me in the kitchens. It'll have to be you.'

'Why can't Dysis do it?'

'Dysis is a lady's maid. Apparently lady's maids in Muscobar don't dirty their hands with fire-making,' Sosia said acidly.

A little while later Kiukiu ventured along the corridor to Lilias's rooms and tapped tentatively at the door.

'Hallo. Hallo! Can you hear me? This is Dysis. Please respond!'

Kiukiu could hear Dysis's voice, but who was she speaking to? She tapped again, louder this time. There was silence, and then Dysis snapped, 'Come in.'

Kiukiu went in, glancing nervously around; to her relief, Lilias was not in her sitting-room. Dysis was standing by the mantelpiece, dusting one of Lilias's ornaments: a delicate crystal sculpture which was usually encased in a domed glass cover.

'Come to do the fires,' Kiukiu mumbled.

'Well, you'd better get on with it, then,' Dysis said crisply, replacing the glass cover. 'Start in here. My Lady is still in bed.' She went over to the window-seat and took up her embroidery.

Kiukuiu had never looked out from Lilias's rooms on to the gardens before. But as she knelt down, she noticed that now that the leaves had fallen, the Elysia Summerhouse was just visible. Had she been seen, creeping out at twilight to feed Snowcloud?

The thought was so alarming, she forgot what she was doing, losing her grip on the dustpan, dropping it with a clatter in the fireplace.

'Who's making all that racket, Dysis?' complained a woman's voice from the bedchamber. 'I'm trying to rest in here.'

'Sorry,' Kiukiu whispered.

Dysis said nothing but narrowed her eyes at her above her embroidery.

'It's no good, Dysis, I can't sleep.'

Kiukiu glanced up to see Lilias standing in the doorway of her bedchamber.

'What is *she* doing in here?' The petulantly weary tones hardened as Lilias saw her. 'Looking for intruders? Haven't you disturbed my sleep enough this week, Kiukirilya?'

Does she know? Kiukiu cowered on her knees in the cinders. Has she guessed?

'Why is *she* here and not Ninusha?'

'Ninusha's sick,' whispered Kiukiu.

'More's the pity. Ah!' Lilias stopped, clutching at her belly. Kiukiu saw her face contort in an expression of disbelief. 'My waters,' she whispered. 'My waters have broken.'

'What?' Kiukiu said dumbly. Her brain refused to work; the sight of Lilias doubled up with pain terrified her. She didn't know what to do.

Dysis dropped her embroidery and hurried forwards to help her mistress.

'Why are you still standing there?' she hissed, supporting Lilias. 'Get help!'

Help? Kiukiu, flustered, began to back towards the door. What kind of help did Lilias want? A mop to wipe up the waters?

'*Hurry!*' cried Lilias and then let out a cry of agony so piercing that Kiukiu fled into the corridor, leaving the door wide open behind her.

261

'Help, help, Lilias is ill!' she cried.

'The baby!' Lilias's voice carried after, a banshee wail, echoing high into the stairwell. 'The baby's coming!'

'Sosia! Sosia!'

As Kiukiu went running down the stairs, she saw that more snow had begun to fall in silent spirals, dusting the frost-blackened garden with white.

'What's the matter this time, girl?' Sosia appeared in the hallway, drying her hands on her apron.

'The b-baby,' Kiukiu stammered, waving her hand towards Lilias's rooms. Another blood-curdling shriek came from above.

'By all the saints,' Sosia said, starting towards the stairs, 'she's in labour!'

The cursing and shrieking went on from behind Lilias's apartment doors well into the night. Ilsi had control of the kitchens and, in Sosia's absence, made Kiukiu's life miserable, ordering her to draw bucket after bucket of water from the well to heat on the range.

As Kiukiu was struggling back with the third bucketful, she caught sight of Ilsi gossiping with Michailo.

'Listen to her yell!' Ilsi said scornfully as another distant shriek penetrated the house. 'You'd think no woman on earth had ever had a baby before.'

'They say Nagarian babies are harder to deliver. They say they fight their way out.'

'Who says this one's a Nagarian?' said Ilsi with a sly smile.

* * *

About one in the morning, the shrieking stopped. A while later a weary Sosia came out onto the balcony, carrying a tightly swaddled bundle.

Kiukiu and the other servants gathered in the hall below with a few of the *druzhina*.

'Michailo,' she called down, 'send a messenger to Lord Gavril that Lilias has had a son, a fine son. She's calling him Artamon.'

She raised the bundle high – and from inside came the unmistakably powerful yell of a newborn baby. Kiukiu craned her neck to look at the baby, but he was too well-wrapped to see. All around her she could hear muttered comments from the other servants as they strained to get a glimpse of little Artamon.

'Artamon,' grunted old Guaram. 'Does she think he's going to be emperor?'

'Is he dark?'

'Is he fair?'

'Is he a Nagarian?'

'How can you tell? Tell for sure?'

Four, five, today made six days Lord Gavril had been gone. Kiukiu counted under her breath as she hefted a heavy coal bucket up the stairs to Lilias's rooms. Kostya had sent word to the kastel that they were hunting a vicious pack of snow wolves.

She scratched on the door and, when there was no reply, let herself in.

A white-painted cradle had been placed near the dying embers in the grate.

Kiukiu peeped over the rim of the cradle. The baby stared up at her from his warm cocoon of blankets. His little fingers curled and uncurled as if they wanted something to grasp hold of.

Her heart melted. He might be Lilias's son, but was that his fault? With his wild wisps of red-bronze hair and his stubborn little nose, he was already his own person.

'Hallo, Artamon,' she whispered. The little fist waved back in response to her voice. Tentatively she put out a finger – and felt tiny fingers close about it, stickily warm and astonishingly strong for one so small.

'I've got to get on, little one,' she said regretfully, withdrawing her finger and stroking his downsoft cheek. 'You need a good fire to keep you nice and warm.'

She went over to the grate and, kneeling down, was soon busy scraping out the cinders.

A choking, gurgling sound came from the crib. Not the contented noise of a well-fed baby, something more ominous. Alarmed, Kiukiu dropped her dustpan and shovel and, wiping her hands on her skirt, hurried over to the crib.

The baby had been sick. She could smell the sweet, fetid smell of the milky vomit before she reached him. But he had wriggled himself into an awkward position, one where he was inhaling the regurgitated milk – and choking.

Kiukiu plunged her hands into the crib and swiftly lifted him up, patting him hard to clear his airways, feeling his little body convulse with the effort to breathe again ...

'What are you doing!'

Lilias stood on the threshold, her face distorted.

'Put him down! At once!'

'But he—' Kiukiu began. At last the baby managed to gasp a gargling yell.

Lilias rushed across and snatched him from her.

'What were you doing! Smothering my son – the Drakhaon's son!'

'I tried to save him—' Kiukiu cried, almost speechless at the unfairness of the accusation.

'Save him?' Lilias clutched the baby to her so tight that he began to wail. 'You tried to kill him! I saw you!'

Ilsi and Ninusha appeared in the doorway, curious to see what the noise was about.

'He was choking on his own sick, look, there's sick on his sheet, I was only—'

'Choking? What kind of feeble excuse is that? You were shaking him.' The louder Lilias's voice became, the louder little Artamon wailed. 'The girl's not only weak-brained, she's malicious too. Malicious enough to want to harm my child. Unless of course,' and her voice dropped as she rocked the baby up and down on her shoulder, 'someone put her up to it.'

'Why won't you listen?' Kiukiu began to cry too. 'I love babies. I don't care who its mother is, I'd never want to harm him, I swear it—'

'I caught her leaning too close over the baby's crib once before,' said Ilsi. 'When she saw me, she leaped back. I thought it was suspicious.'

'Yes,' said Ninusha, backing Ilsi up as usual, 'I saw her too.'

'You never—' gasped Kiukiu.

'Deny it,' Ilsi said with a cold little smile.

'I do deny it!'

Now there came the sound of footsteps hastening down the corridor, voices shouting out.

'Where is she? Where's Afimia's girl?'

Oleg burst in, closely followed by Sosia with

several of the *druzhina*, Michailo to the fore. Oleg threw down a handful of white feathers on the floor. Kiukiu let out a soft little cry. There was blood on the feathers.

'Snowcloud,' she whispered.

'She's been rearing one of those cursed creatures in the summerhouse. One of Arkhel's Owls!' Oleg shook his fist at her.

'And she told us she was seeing a boy!' Ilsi said, her voice dry with scorn.

'Bad blood will always out in the end.' Oleg spat on the floor. 'Arkhel blood.' Lilias glared at him, drawing the hem of her robe closer to herself.

'It was only a baby owl,' Kiukiu said, dropping to her knees to touch the blood-smeared feathers, letting them drift through her fingers. 'It hadn't harmed anyone – and now you've killed it.'

'We should have known no boy would want to have frumpy, dumpy Kiukiu,' Ninusha said spitefully. 'We should have guessed she was up to something.'

'Did you have to kill him?' Kiukiu cried.

'Kiukiu,' Sosia said in a hard, flat voice, 'you're in terrible trouble. Why did you lie to me?'

Kiukiu stared at Sosia through her tears. Lord Gavril had gone to Kharsk. Who would speak up for her in his absence?

'I didn't exactly lie, Auntie.'

'First the baby, now this.'

'And who knows what else was going on in the summerhouse,' Lilias said in tones of ice.

'No-one rears Arkhel's Owls as pets. They're hunting birds – and we all know what Arkhels use them for,' Oleg said in a growl.

'But Lord Gavril helped me rescue Snowcloud. Ask Oleg. He was there!' Kiukiu protested. 'We were going to let him go when his leg was better.'

'And what would Lord Gavril want with an Arkhel's Owl?' Oleg spat again. 'She's lying. She's in league with someone. Someone from outside.'

'My great-niece has always been a little . . . simple-minded,' Sosia intervened. 'She meant no harm—'

'No harm? Have you forgotten what happened in the East Wing, woman?' Oleg grunted.

'Kiukiu must go,' Lilias said. 'Michailo?'

Michailo had been watching, contributing nothing, arms folded across his chest.

'Kostya left you in charge of the kastel,' said Lilias. Suddenly her green eyes brimmed with tears and her voice began to tremble. 'Send her away. I'm afraid for my son.'

'But the winter snows have started—' said Kiukiu.

'I don't care where she goes, I won't have her near my baby.'

Kiukiu saw Michailo glance at Lilias, who melted into tears as she cradled her child. She saw him swallow hard.

'Kiukiu,' he said.

'Yes?' she whispered.

'You must leave the kastel.'

'But I tried to save the baby—'

'I am commander here in the Bogatyr's absence.' Michailo's face was expressionless. 'You are dismissed from the Drakhaon's service.'

'Think yourself lucky.' Lilias stared at her over her baby's head, her green eyes narrowed, sharp shards of river-jade. 'In Mirom wicked servant-girls like you are sentenced to years of picking oakum. Their heads are shaved. Most die of dysentery before their sentences are up.'

'In Mirom I'd get a proper hearing,' Kiukiu burst out.

'You have half an hour to collect your belongings,' Michailo said. He moved now, going to Lilias's side. 'Please don't distress yourself so, Lady,' he said in a softer voice.

Kiukiu turned to Sosia. 'Auntie—'

Sosia looked down at the floor.

'I can't help you this time, Kiukiu.'

'But where can I go? Can't I shelter in the barn till the snows stop?'

'You will be escorted out of the kastel grounds. Do not return on pain of death. Remember,' Michailo said in a low voice, 'and remember well, Kiukirilya. In Lord Gavril's absence, I have charge of Kastel Drakhaon. Now go, collect your possessions – before I change my mind.'

Kiukiu clapped one hand to her mouth to try to stifle her sobs and ran out of the room. As she passed them, she could sense Ilsi and Ninusha watching her in silent, gloating triumph.

Her mind was all of a panic. If Lord Gavril were here . . .

But what was the point? He was miles away. There was only Sosia – and Sosia had washed her hands of her. She had spoken up for her so many times; but against Lilias, she was powerless.

Kiukiu passed a window and saw the distant gleam of the snows blanketing the moors. The sky was grey, promising more snow. Where could she go? She had spent all her life at the kastel. She had no family but Sosia.

She hurried down the stairs to her little room and tore the worn blanket and sheet off the bed. The blanket would have to serve as a cloak. She began to throw her few possessions into the sheet: her comb, blue hair ribbons, thick darned socks . . .

'Kiukiu.' Sosia stood in the doorway. Her face was pale, her lips paler still. She looked old and ill. 'Why did you do it? Why?'

'I was saving the baby; he was choking on his sick,' Kiukiu said. 'But *she* hates me, she used it against me—'

'The owl, Kiukiu. Have you no sense? In the massacre those cursed creatures attacked our men, women and children. They are not *ordinary* owls.'

The thought of Snowcloud lying dead, bleeding in the snow, made Kiukiu begin to sob again. 'Lord Gavril helped me rescue him. Why doesn't anyone believe me?'

'Go to the village,' Sosia said briefly. 'Ask at the inn for Piotr. He'll give you work. Mention my name.'

'But it's a day's walk on foot to Klim.'

'Then you'd better hurry. Here's bread and cheese for your journey.'

Kiukiu tied the blanket about her neck and waist and slung her knotted sheet over one shoulder.

'Wait.' Sosia untied her woollen kerchief and wrapped it around Kiukiu's head. 'To keep you warm.'

'Sosia!' bellowed Oleg. 'Where's that good-for-nothing niece of yours?'

Kiukiu shuddered. 'Don't let him near me. Please,

Sosia. He – he'll interfere with me. You know what I mean.'

Sosia gave her a nod. Then she hugged her swiftly, pushing her away as Oleg and two of the *druzhina* loomed in the doorway.

'Take care,' she whispered to Kiukiu.

'Come on, girl.' Oleg grabbed hold of Kiukiu by the arm, dragging her to the door.

'Where d'you think you're going, Oleg?' Sosia, arms folded, blocked his way.

'Seeing this girl off the property.' Oleg was breathing heavily in a way that made Kiukiu's flesh crawl; his body stank of sweat and stale beer. She had no doubt that he intended to do her harm.

'You were supposed to have moved ten kegs of ale for me yesterday. And those flagons of cider . . .'

'Can't they wait?'

'You dare ask me to wait?' Sosia demanded tartly.

Kiukiu felt the grip on her arm relax. She pulled free and darted out into the passageway. The two *druzhina* were after her in a moment and she felt their hands clamp on her shoulders. She twisted but they held firm, almost dragging her along.

To her shame, she saw that the whole of the kitchen staff, right down to the lowliest scullion, were standing, watching her humiliating departure from the kastel, Ilsi and Ninusha to the fore. No-one spoke but Kiukiu was certain she saw Ninusha smirking. Ilsi's eyes burned brightest, sharp with malicious triumph.

Who would make Lord Gavril's fires when she was gone? Who else knew how to smooth down the clean sheets and plump the feather pillows just so? Tears threatened to flow again, bitter tears – but she blinked them away, refusing to let Ilsi and Ninusha relish their victory.

As the two *druzhina* marched her past the stables, she couldn't help looking with a shiver at the marauding crows and kites that had been killed and nailed up to rot, mouldering trophies of tattered feathers and curled claws. Snowcloud would soon join them, his once-beautiful white down stained with brown blood . . .

Kiukiu stood forlornly in the trampled snow gazing back at the dark towers of the only home she had ever known.

And now she was an outcast.

'Lord Volkh,' she called softly. 'Can't you help me? There's no-one else. I helped you, I stopped the exorcism—'

She listened intently. But the only sound was the soft, sad whine of the wind.

Even Lord Volkh had abandoned her.

16

Kiukiu shouldered her bundle of possessions and set off down the lane without another backward glance. Here, at least, the snow was well-trodden by the *druzhina*'s horses – but at the end of the lane, at the edge of the kastel grounds, lay open moorland.

A little track wound across the moors to the distant village of Klim. The pines were thinning out now and the protection which the forest trees had given her from the keen wind would soon be behind her.

She came down the lane and stopped. An icy-breathed wind sighed through the pine needles, rattled the leafless branches of the last remaining trees.

A white desolation stretched ahead as far as she could see. The dark green gorse, the bronzed fronds of bracken, all had disappeared beneath the snow. There was no sound except the incessant sighing of the wind, a desolate, lonely whine. And there was no break in the grey canopy of cloud overhead, no hint of sun or thaw. Even the track was difficult to make out now that it was covered with drifts of snow.

Must keep moving, Kiukiu told herself. She put her head down and trudged out into the powdery snow. The wind whined about her ears; she was glad of the warmth of Sosia's scarf.

After a while, she stopped, breathless and weary. Her feet were beginning to feel wet; the snow had worked its way into all the cracks in her old boots and melted, seeping up into the soles.

Am I going the right way? She shaded her eyes against the snowlight; even though there was no visible sun, the whiteness was dazzling, making her eyes ache. All the usual landmarks looked different – or had vanished, blended into the monotonous snowscape. The Kharzhgylls should be on her right side, with the biggest peak, Arkhel's Fang, in the centre.

But as she peered across the snowfields, all she could see was a dull mist where the mountains should be. And if she was on the right path, shouldn't she have come to the shepherd's hut by now?

She felt a sudden pang of apprehension. If she had lost her way, she could wander into one of the moorland quagmires and never be found again. Or freeze to death . . .

'Stop scaring yourself!' she told herself fiercely. 'Just keep walking. You'll come to Klim soon enough.' She wrapped the old blanket more closely about her. After a while she began to mutter rhythmically to keep her feet moving, 'Lord Gavril will save me, Lord Gavril will save me . . .'

As she tramped doggedly onwards, it began to seem as if the light were slowly fading and the snowmist was rolling closer, blotting out everything but the immediate surroundings. She had no idea how long she had been walking now, only that her bundle seemed to weigh more than when she had set out . . . and her feet were not only wet but sore.

Up ahead she saw a standing stone looming out of the mist.

Eat something, she decided. A lighter bundle would help. She rested her back against the lichened boulder and untied her bundle, pulling out the bread and cheese Sosia had given her. It was not until she began to eat that she realized how hungry she was; she tore into the rye bread, relishing the taste, the chewy crust. Even the cheese – the hard, pungent ewe's milk kind, usually used for toasting – tasted delicious. *Better save some just in case* . . . She looked down regretfully at the last of the loaf and a corner of cheese and then stuffed them back in the bundle.

Just in case I don't reach the village? She pushed the thought away. *Must keep going.*

She slung the bundle over her shoulder and forced herself to start out again, away from the shelter of the boulder.

The mists seemed to have rolled in more thickly and even the track was becoming difficult to make out. Sometimes she found herself blundering into snow-covered bracken brakes. Her legs were aching now . . . and her feet were numb with cold.

Reach the village soon. She kept the picture of the village in her mind, imagining arriving at the inn, knocking the snow from her boots, opening the door and feeling the glorious warmth from the fire enveloping her, seeping right down into her frozen toes . . .

Was it growing darker? There would be lights in the village, lamps lit in the little houses, she would soon see them glowing in the mist . . .

Kiukiu stumbled on a stone and when she righted herself her stubbed toes hurt in spite of the numbness, bruised and sore. She was tired now, tired enough not to walk with a regular swing any more. Bone-tired. And cold. She shivered in the intense, aching cold.

Keep on walking – it can't be far now. Stubbornly she kept on even though it was fast growing too dark to see. Only the white shadow of the snowfields still glimmered, stretching away into the moonless dark, endless and empty as the White Sea.

The little whispers of doubt that she had tried to ignore began to clamour in her mind.

Lost. She was lost on the moors. She would never reach the village, the snow and the intense cold would gradually freeze the last of her strength. She would sink down into the drifts, dying here alone. They would never find her body until the spring thaws, if the wolves didn't find it first . . .

Stop thinking like that! She must find shelter, huddle up for the night in her blanket and wait till dawn.

Shelter. She could hardly see more than a yard or so in front of her. There was no shelter, only bracken and stone outcrops and the slow-rolling snowmist.

Something cold and feather-light brushed her cheek. First one soft, chill kiss, and then another and another . . .

It had begun to snow.

* * *

Kiukiu stumbled blindly on, head down, through the softly falling snow. Just putting one foot in front of the other took all her energy now. She no longer knew which way she was going. Sometimes she thought she saw figures in the swirling white flakes, and then the wind would whip them away. Snow-mirages, white on the blackness of night.

Can't – keep – going. Must – rest.

But where could she find shelter, out here on the bleak moorlands? There was not even a dry-stone wall to act as a windbreak.

'Ghost-singer . . .'

She heard voices in the wind, soft as the whispering snow.

'Who's there?' she called hesitantly.

'Guslyar . . .'

Was she imagining the voices? Little eddies of snow, whipped up by the wind, whirled about her and were blown away into the darkness.

'Is there anyone there?' Snow blew into her mouth, melting to icewater, sending shivers through her aching body. 'Please? Anyone?'

Now she could hear faint singing, an eerie sighing, desolate music, cold as the drifting flakes.

How could there be people singing out here, so far from shelter? She shook her head, trying to clear the persistent sound.

Suddenly a memory flung her way back into the warm kitchen at the kastel. She could only have been four, five years old. She kneeled, nose pressed to the cold pane, smearing the glass with her hot breath. Outside the snow twirled and swirled, wind-spun eddies of chill white down.

'The old snow woman's plucking her geese again,' said Sosia, at the cooking range, busily stirring vegetables into soup.

As Kiukiu stared out, she saw figures amidst the snow, vague and insubstantial, wreathing in a swirling dance. Their wild hair spun about their slender bodies like spirals of frost-hazed mist. And then it seemed as if they saw her at the window, for the dance ceased and they clustered together, stretching out fingers as thin as icicles, their eyes huge and dark as the moonless sky.

'Auntie,' Kiukiu had called. 'Who are they? Those people outside?'

'No-one outside in this blizzard,' Sosia replied distractedly, concentrating on the soup.

And then she had heard the voices. Wisps of sound at first, cold and brittle as hoarfrost, then the singing grew stronger, wilder. The music was so beautiful that it made her heart ache. She had never heard anything so beautiful in her life.

And before she knew what she was doing, she was getting down, walking towards the door, wanting to go out into the snow . . .

She ran smack into the legs of a tall man who stopped and caught hold of her.

'Where are you off to, little one?'

It was one of the *druzhina*, Yuri, Auntie Sosia's elder brother.

'Outside. To join the singing.'

'There's no singing outside. Only blizzard.'

He picked her up and carried her back into the kitchen, dumping her on the table.

'But the dancers—'

'Haven't you ever heard of the Snow Spirits?' He

crouched down so that his head was on a level with hers. 'The spirits of people who died out on the moors in the snows? They come back with the blizzard every winter and they sing to lure the living to their deaths in the snow.'

'What nonsense are you filling her head with now?' Sosia cried, turning around from the bubbling pot. 'There's no such thing as Snow Spirits. It's just a silly tale.'

Just a silly tale . . . Kiukiu repeated to herself now, trudging doggedly on. *No-one there. Only the wind.*

Pale faces, white as mist, loomed out of the swirling snowflakes. Spindle-thin fingers, translucent as icicles, plucked at her hair, her clothes.

Voices breathed in her ear, whispering of the cold caress of the snow.

'You're not there!' shouted Kiukiu. 'I don't believe in you. You don't exist!'

A thin, high voice began to sing in the mist. It sang of snowfilled wastes, the white vastness of the ice-bound sea. The songline was pure as clear ice and bitter as eternal winter.

Kiukiu was desperately tired now. She stumbled, nearly fell. She tried to block the song from her mind.

Many voices joined the one. '*Rest*,' they sang. '*Let us wrap you in soft snow, let us sing you to sleep.*'

'I can't hear you,' Kiukiu cried. How did they know all she wanted was to stop and lie down? She could no longer feel her feet. Her throat and lungs burned with the cold, dry snow air. But if she stopped it was as good as giving up . . .

Her foot caught in a knotted clump of heather. She pitched forwards, putting out her numbed hands to try and save herself. Too late. Snow Spirits wreathed around her, hands linked in a swirling, spinning dance. She was trapped.

'Help me!' she called vainly into the darkness. She tried to push herself back up but the snow clung to her clothes, weighing her down as still the spirits circled, closer, closer . . .

Faces glanced down at her, white as death, cruel and bleakly beautiful as mountain snow. Chill fingers caressed her, each drifting caress numbing her blood until she cowered, shivering uncontrollably in the wet snowdrifts.

'Help me!' she called again even though she knew there was no-one to help her.

'*Sleep,*' sang the sweet, cold voices, stroking their chill fingers through her hair.

Kiukiu saw a dark doorway slowly opening before her. With growing dread she recognized the yawning blackness beyond. It was the portal to the Ways Beyond, the portal she had last crossed with Lord Volkh's spirit-wraith clinging to her. Now it yawned open for her alone.

'No!' she cried, furious that she should have to die like this. 'I'm not going to go through! It's not my time yet! I have to protect Lord Gavril. I gave my word—'

'*Why go on suffering?*' whispered a single voice close to her ear. '*Give in. Let go. Is life so sweet?*'

Kiukiu sank back into the snow, exhausted. The black portal towered above her. She was too weak to resist it. Already she could feel the dark leaking into her mind, filling it with death-cold shadows. As she sank back into the snow, her will begin to waver. The darkness was surrounding her, numbing all her senses. All she could hear was the whispering chant of the Snow Spirits. She was fading . . .

Dying.

17

The warship *Sirin* rocked at anchor on the broad River Nieva, her sails furled. A cold, gusting wind whipped the river water into choppy waves.

The White Guard lined the quay as the ducal party, well wrapped against the wind in furs and cloaks, left the Winter Palace by the Water Gate. There were few onlookers; only a vast flock of grey and white seagulls floated on the water.

'Gulls in the city,' Eupraxia said as she and Elysia watched from an upper window. 'It must be stormy out in the estuary.'

Andrei Orlov, dashingly arrayed in his naval uniform of royal blue, gold buttons gleaming in the cold sunlight, drew apart from the ducal party and saluted his father and mother.

'Oh,' sobbed Eupraxia into her handkerchief, 'my little Andrei. Look how handsome he is.'

Suddenly the Grand Duchess hastened forwards and flung her arms around her son.

Perhaps she has a heart after all, Elysia thought.

'Why must he go?' Eupraxia whispered. 'He's only a boy. Suppose Prince Eugene's fleet attacks them? Suppose the *Sirin* sinks? Suppose . . .'

Astasia was hugging her brother now. Elysia saw him gently disengage her arms from about his neck and kiss her on both cheeks. Then, with a final wave of the hand, he climbed down into the rowing boat that was bobbing ready beneath the quay, and the sailors began to pull across the choppy water towards the *Sirin*.

Elysia heard a few ragged cheers from the onlookers and a military band played – rather badly – the national anthem as Andrei scrambled up the ladder and reached the deck. An answering salvo from the *Sirin*'s cannon sent a cloud of seagulls screeching up into the grey sky. The anchor-chain began to grate as the sailors laboured at the capstan to wind up the heavy anchor.

'So few of the city people to see him,' mused Elysia.

'People are afraid to show their support,' said Eupraxia with a sigh. 'It's those wretched intellectuals at the university. Intellectuals! Insurgents, I call them, filling people's heads with their scurrilous nonsense. Free speech, indeed!'

Sails were unfurled and slowly the great ship began to slip away.

'Madame Andar?' A liveried servant appeared, presenting her with a letter on a silver salver.

She tore it open and saw only the laconic message:

I have traced our friend K. This man will bring
you to me. Come incognito.

F.V.

* * *

An unmarked carriage waited at a side entrance of the Winter Palace; Count Velemir helped Elysia in and climbed in after her.

'Where are we going?' Elysia asked as the carriage pulled away over the cobbles.

'Our friend Kazimir has lodgings down by the docks. Not a very salubrious area for a respectable woman to explore alone.'

'The docks? Why is he not at the university?'

'As I warned you, Elysia, Altan Kazimir is a changed man. Suspicious of his own shadow, edgy, unpredictable. He seems to believe that there is a price on his head.'

Elysia nodded. No-one escapes Azhkendir unchanged, she thought – but did not say so aloud.

'In order not to alarm the good doctor unduly, you will have to enter the street unaccompanied. Help will be close at hand, should you need it. I have placed a man or two in the vicinity.' He leaned across and took her hands in his. 'I would not put you at risk, Elysia, for all the world – but there is no other way.'

The little carriage had turned off the wide avenue and was proceeding down a steeply winding street, overhung with dilapidated buildings that blocked out much of the daylight. Raucous street cries could be heard now and pungent smells began to penetrate the carriage: frying onions; smoking fish; rotting refuse.

'Kazimir lodges above the Sign of the Orrery. It is a tavern on the corner of the quay; you cannot miss it. We will set you down before the quay and we will wait for you there. But if Kazimir turns violent, just open a window, any window, and cry out, "Azhgorod!" '

'Now you're really beginning to alarm me,' Elysia said, essaying a smile. The smell of herring from the smoke-houses was beginning to make her feel a little queasy.

She climbed down from the coach and gazed uneasily around her. She had taken the precaution, as he had advised her, of wearing a broad-brimmed hat with a veil. A new smell assaulted her nostrils: the stink of boiling pitch. Out in the middle of the river she could see a little island where many fine ships were moored for repairs. The boisterous wind was blowing tar-fumed smoke directly towards the quay.

Wrapping her veil more tightly about her face, she ventured out along the quay, head down. She had to pick her way across mud-slimed cobbles where gulls fought over fish guts discarded by the herring-wives who clustered together to do their messy work, chatting and laughing raucously. This, at any rate, was no different to the harbour in Vermeille.

When she passed two sailors staggering along, propping each other up, yelling a shanty, she knew she must be near her goal. Gazing upwards, she saw the Orrery sign flapping wildly overhead in the gusts of wind.

She pushed open the door. The dark taproom was filled with a haze of pipe-smoke that made her eyes water. Men turned towards her, staring.

'What do you want?' A thin-faced woman appeared, carrying mugs of ale. She glared at Elysia.

'Doctor Kazimir.'

The woman gave her a quizzical look. 'Out the

back,' she said. 'To the left just before the yard.'

Elysia hurried through the taproom and almost ran headfirst into a burly sailor hitching up his trousers, coming in from what the woman had euphemistically called the yard.

Elysia shrank back to let him pass. When he had lumbered by, she saw, with relief, a blue-painted door to her left. Lifting the latch, she went through and found herself at the foot of a narrow wooden stair.

'Doctor Kazimir?' she called, wishing her voice sounded less hesitant.

There was no reply.

At the top of the stairs was a little door; the landing ceiling was so low she had to stoop to knock.

'Go away!' came a man's voice from within.

'Doctor Kazimir, I've come a very long way to see you.'

'Go away!' repeated the voice irritably.

Elysia tried the door latch but it was locked. She would have to try a different tack.

'My name is Elysia Nagarian. Bogatyr Kostya Torzianin has kidnapped my son Gavril and taken him to Azhkendir.' What was she doing, shouting her most intimate secrets through a wooden door to some eccentric scientist who had barricaded himself in?

'What's that to me?'

'I—' She stopped a moment, almost speechless with frustration. 'I hoped you could help me. There's no-one else in all Mirom who knows anything about Azhkendir.'

There was a silence on the other side of the door.

'You're alone?'

'Yes,' she said, trusting there was nothing sinister implied in his question.

There came another silence – and then she heard the sound of furniture being dragged across bare boards. Chains clinked, bolts were shot, and at last the door opened a little way and a bespectacled man peered out at her from the gloom.

'You'd better come in.'

Elysia squeezed inside – and could not help noticing how Doctor Kazimir put his head outside, checking the stair before closing the door, standing with his back to it, as if to prevent anyone else getting in.

Elysia raised her veil and looked at him quizzically. She hoped that she had not just walked into a madman's trap.

'I – I've got little in the way of refreshment to offer you, madame.' He edged away from the door, his movements nervous and uncoordinated. 'Not even tea. Only vodka.'

Elysia shook her head. 'Nothing, thank you.'

He reached for a half-empty bottle of vodka and poured himself a glass, swallowing it down in one gulp.

'You – you must excuse me. This is not how I usually entertain visitors. P-please sit down.'

The dingy room was meagrely furnished; the table was covered with a clutter of glasses and empty bottles. The clean smell of spirits did not quite obscure the stronger smell of unwashed flesh.

As Elysia sat down on a rickety chair, she noticed a battered travelling trunk in one corner, half open, spilling out dirty linen and books. Doctor Kazimir had either recently arrived, or not bothered to unpack.

'How did you find me?' he asked warily. His voice, though light and a little tremulous, was not unpleasant. If he shaved, Elysia thought, looking at the several days' growth of fair stubble, if he let the barber attend to his long, straggling hair, he would prove quite well-favoured.

'I have connections at court,' Elysia said equally warily.

Doctor Kazimir sat down at the table opposite her, one hand clutching the vodka bottle, the other his empty glass. He began to speak; yet due to his agitation, the words came out in a rush.

'I – I must tell you, madame, that when I left Azhkendir, Lord Volkh was alive. The news that he had been killed was a shock to me, a total shock. We did not part on the best of terms, you see, and now I regret that. Not only because the *druzhina* put a bloodprice on my head but because your husband was in his own way an honourable man, forced to bear an intolerable burden—'

'This is all well and good,' Elysia said patiently, 'but it is my son's plight that brings me here.'

'Your son. I never met your son.' Kazimir raked one hand through his lank fair hair. 'You must understand, Madame Nagarian, that I was on my way to Arkhelskoye when the news of Lord Volkh's murder broke. Suddenly I was a wanted man! I was forced to disguise myself and seek the first passage out – on a fur trader's vessel. The smell of the stinking hides clings to me still—'

'So you can't help me.' Elysia, who till this moment had been clinging on to this one vain hope, felt herself engulfed in a wave of hopelessness. She rose, pulling the veil down to conceal the tears that had begun to well in her eyes.

'No, wait!' cried Kazimir, leaping up. 'I am ashamed, madame, to receive you in this fashion. What must you think of me? It's just that I have been in constant fear for my life since the news broke, moving from one filthy tavern room to another—'

'So?' Elysia said coldly.

Kazimir lifted the bottle and shakily began to pour another glass; the bottle rattled against the glass and the spirit spilled onto the table.

After another gulp, he began to speak. 'Your husband wanted to find a cure. He wanted to become human again. He wanted to stop – or even reverse – the unusual condition he had inherited. He believed from his researches that the Drakhaons were in some way related to reptiles or serpents. The old legend . . .'

'The first Volkh Nagarian was called the Son of the Serpent,' murmured Elysia.

'And that maybe the lethal venom with which he killed his enemies could also be used to produce an antidote.'

'An antidote?'

'You had not seen him for many years?'

'No.' For a moment she saw him again, saw those broodingly dark eyes, burning unnaturally blue in the darkness of their bedchamber. And she heard again his voice shiver through the icy Azhkendir night, the cry of a beast cursed with a human soul.

'He was . . . extraordinary.' The doctor slowly shook his head, as if what he had seen was still beyond his comprehension. 'Such a rare condition.'

'How . . . rare?' Elysia was thinking of Gavril, not Volkh, now. For all these years she had been silently watching him, hoping against hope that the telltale signs of his father's deformities had not begun to manifest themselves.

'I have spent my life trying to explain and explore the mysteries of the natural sciences, madame. But I had never before encountered a condition such as this – one which *defied* scientific explanation. I could have spent a lifetime researching it. But Lord Volkh did not have a lifetime. He wanted a cure.'

'Is such a thing possible?' Elysia had wanted to leave. Now, against her better judgement, she found herself compelled to listen to Kazimir's tale. If there were the slightest hope . . .

'We began to experiment with the . . .' and Kazimir's voice dropped, as if he were afraid they were being overheard, 'the venom. In minuscule doses. A process of desensitization, if you care to call it that.'

'And what effect did it have?' Elysia found that in spite of herself she had drawn closer to the doctor.

'The desired effect. The physical changes began to be reversed. But as I had suspected, the more human Lord Volkh began to look, the more his powers dwindled. The elixir I developed restored his humanity but left him weak, unable to transform himself.'

Elysia shuddered, remembering the nightmare she had tried to block from her mind all these years. Transformation. That was a rational, prosaic way of describing something so darkly visceral, so profoundly terrifying, that it had deprived her of speech for several days. Volkh had warned her that there was a side of his life that she could never share – and she, foolishly, had thought he referred only to his military campaigning, never imagining . . .

'Of course, at the time I could only see the advantages of my discovery. I never imagined, madame, that anyone would use my elixir to assassinate Lord Volkh.'

'Assassinate?' His last words jolted Elysia from her reverie. She looked up to see Altan Kazimir staring at her, his eyes wild and grim. 'You believe someone stole your elixir to kill Volkh?'

'They think it was me!' he burst out. 'They think that because we quarrelled I bore him a grudge. They think I wanted Lilias all to myself—'

'Wait a moment.' Elysia held up a hand, trying to stem the flow. 'Who is Lilias?'

Kazimir tipped the bottle into his glass again, shaking it till the last few drops were gone.

'His mistress,' he said thickly.

'Oh.' Elysia sat down again. Silly, really, to imagine that Volkh would not look for love elsewhere after she had left him. Why should he still pine for her, inconsolable, all these years? Hadn't she found companionship with Lukan?

'We were just lonely, Lilias and I,' Kazimir mumbled into the glass. 'Two strangers in a strange land. I never intended—'

'Be that as it may,' Elysia said briskly, 'how effective do you judge your elixir to be? If it could reverse the deterioration in a man of Volkh's age, could it prevent it completely in a younger man?'

'Your son?' he said, trying to focus on her above the rim of the glass. 'It depends. If he has never . . . been transformed, then there might be a chance. But the elixir must be made from the venom in his own bloodstream and it must be very carefully diluted and monitored. What worked for the father could well kill the son.'

'Was there any of the original elixir left in Kastel Drakhaon?' Elysia cried, alarmed.

'I don't know. I was obliged to leave so fast I had only my valise with me; there was no time to go back and collect my papers . . .'

'But suppose Gavril found your papers, suppose he tried to recreate the elixir—'

'Madame Nagarian, please don't distress yourself.'

'You must help him,' she said.

'Me? Return to Azhkendir?' Kazimir began to laugh in a strange, high voice. 'Never.'

'Altan! *Altan!*'

Someone stormed up the stair. The door burst open and a dark-haired man came in, out of breath. Elysia rose, fearing some kind of trap.

'Who is *she*?' he demanded, stabbing his finger at her.

'A f-friend,' Kazimir said, waving a hand vaguely in the air.

'Who sent her? How did she know how to find you here?'

'I was just leaving,' Elysia said, wondering if she could reach the window in time to yell for help if the newcomer attacked her.

'What do you want with him?' The man stared at her, eyes dark with suspicion.

'That's my business,' she said, staring back.

'*His* agents are on the quay. You'll have to move on, Altan.'

'Can't keep running,' Kazimir said, his words slurring. 'Too tired.'

'Drinking again?' The stranger snatched the glass from his hand. 'What use are you to us when you're drunk all the time?'

'I'm sorry, Matyev. Really sorry.' Kazimir seemed on the verge of tears. 'I'm such a stupid fool. I had it all – in the palm of my hand – and I just threw it away.'

He crashed forwards onto the table suddenly, insensible.

'Altan?' Matyev shook him; the only response was a shuddering snore. Matyev slowly lowered him back down. Kazimir's fair hair spilled onto the stained oilcloth tabletop.

'One of the best minds in Mirom, and look at him. Drunk as a pig.' He looked up at Elysia, glaring. 'Whatever your business is, lady, it's over for today. Doctor Kazimir's not at home to visitors.'

'When can I—'

'Just go.'

Biting back her frustration, Elysia turned on her heel and hurried away.

Outside the wind had changed direction and a bitterly cold gust tasting of snow and salt almost blew Elysia's flimsy hat from her head. She grabbed hold of it with both hands and marched blindly out along the cobbled quay. She was angry now, angry with Kazimir, angry with herself for feeling so powerless. She stopped a moment, gazing out at the tall ships on the river, sails filling with the autumn wind.

There must be a way to get a warning to Gavril.

The rumble of carriage wheels over the cobbles startled her. Horses snorted just behind her, stamping their hooves, breath misting the cold air. The carriage door opened and Count Velemir leaned out, offering his hand.

'We had quite given you up. I was about to send one of my men in to find you.'

Elysia's face was burning from the cold sting of the wind. She clambered up into the carriage and the coachman drove off at a brisk pace.

'Inadvisable to linger here,' the Count said, settling back in his corner of the carriage. 'How is our good friend Doctor Kazimir?'

'Rather the worse for drink.'

'I hope the meeting did not prove too disagreeable. There are several degrees of inebriation . . .'

'When I left him he had reached the degree of insensibility,' Elysia said wryly.

'So your visit was a disappointment?'

'Not entirely. It seems that Lord Volkh had engaged Doctor Kazimir to find a cure for his . . . condition.'

'His condition?'

Elysia looked into the Count's shrewd brown eyes and sighed. In all the years since she had fled Azhkendir she had never once tried to explain what she had seen there.

'We live in a rational age, Count. You will find it difficult to believe what I am about to tell you.'

'Try me.'

'Lord Volkh believed himself the last of an ancient race. He was both man . . . and dragon. Drakhaon. But every time he was possessed by the dragon-spirit, he became progressively less human.'

'He looked human enough to me,' Velemir said. His expression had become unreadable; Elysia could not tell if he believed or was just humouring her.

'He was skilled at concealing his deformities. Though there were other ways of maintaining his human appearance . . .' Elysia faltered. There were parts of that time in Azhkendir that were still too painful to talk about.

'The reports of searing blue fire, the creeping mist that kills all who breathe it—'

'All the Drakhaon's doing.'

'And we had thought Lord Volkh had developed some revolutionary form of weaponry.' Velemir began to laugh. 'No wonder Azhkendir has remained impregnable all these years!'

Elysia suddenly wondered if she had revealed too much. Velemir had charmed the facts from her with his sympathetic manner, and now it could be used to harm Gavril. Why should she trust Count Velemir?

'Why so quiet, Elysia?' he asked, solicitous again. 'I wasn't laughing at you, I assure you.'

'I told you all this in confidence,' she burst out, 'because I believed it would help Gavril—'

'And I told you, Elysia, that Muscobar needs Azhkendir as an ally.' Velemir took her hand in his own, pressing it warmly. 'There are troubled times ahead.'

Elysia became suddenly aware of muffled sounds of shouting outside the carriage.

'Troubled times!' Velemir repeated. He let go of her hand and rapped on the carriage roof. The coachman drew the carriage to a halt and opened the communicating window.

'What's going on?'

'Some kind of gathering in front of Saint Simeon's, Excellency.'

'Can you make out what they're shouting about?'

'Sounds like . . . "Free Stepan the Cobbler".'

'You'd better turn the carriage around and take us back by the Water Gate.'

'Yes, Excellency.'

Velemir settled back on his seat. Elysia saw that the warmth had faded from his eyes; he now seemed distant, cold.

'Damned insurgents,' he muttered.

'What is their complaint?' Elysia asked.

'Their leaders have convinced them that if the Grand Duke were to abdicate and let the people govern themselves there would be more bread to go round.' Velemir began to drum his fingers on the arm-rest. 'As if matters were not complicated enough. Their petty grievances will soon be forgotten if matters come to a head. Then they'll be begging the Grand Duke to protect them, singing his praises in the streets, cheering the White Guard—'

'What matters?' Elysia said sharply.

'The Grand Duke is weak. His foreign policy is at best capricious, in spite of all Vassian's efforts. The people despise him.'

Elysia stared at him, astonished to hear him speak so bluntly of his master. 'Is not such talk treasonable, Count?'

'Not a jot. I am a patriot after my own fashion,' Velemir said with a shrug. 'I want only what is best for Muscobar. And I will say – and do – what I must to keep my country safe.'

The carriage was moving alongside the river

again; a brown river fog drifted across the wide waters, dulling the painted façades of the grand riverside terraces to a uniform drabness.

'So Astasia must marry a stranger to protect her country. A man twice her age. A man she dislikes.'

The Count shrugged. 'Astasia has always known she must put her duty to Muscobar first. She is an Orlov.'

Astasia arrived late for her final portrait sitting, her pale cheeks flushed with delicate colour, an early blush rose, pink on ivory.

She fidgeted around on the chair, fingers darting to play with her hair, her sash, her *décolletage*. Eventually Elysia laid down her brush.

'Altessa. Is something troubling you?'

'I've been to see Papa. I suggested that instead of marrying Prince Eugene I should be formally engaged to your son, now that he is Drakhaon.'

The paintbrush dropped from Elysia's hand. Paint spattered the floor and the hem of her dress. She knelt down, hastily dabbing at the polished boards with a rag, trying to collect herself.

'And what did your father say?' she asked warily.

'That it would be *difficult* to withdraw the offer he had made to Prince Eugene,' Astasia said, eyes dark with anger. 'Difficult! He has no consideration at all for my feelings.'

'My dear,' Elysia said, taking in a deep breath to steady herself, 'what I have to tell you now is not common knowledge. The Nagarian family has . . . an inherited condition. It is passed on from father to son. And at present there is no reliable cure for it.'

'A medical condition?' Astasia looked confused. 'Like haemophilia? I could learn how to manage haemophilia. I'd do all in my power to help Gavril, Madame Andar. I'm not afraid of illness.' And then when Elysia did not, could not, reply, 'Oh, do you mean madness? Dementia?'

'Not precisely,' said Elysia unhappily. It had been hard enough to tell Count Velemir; now she could hardly bring herself to talk of it.

'But you married Lord Volkh!'

'Like you, Altessa, I was young, idealistic. I believed that our love was so strong that nothing would shatter it. And then ... then he began to change.'

A swirl of memory fragments suddenly clouded her mind: young Volkh, darkly and dangerously beautiful; a winter wedding in Azhgorod with snowflake-confetti spiralling down as the great bells of the cathedral dinned out their sonorous, sinister peal; the jagged towers of Kastel Drakhaon looming black against the snowy sky ...

'Change? How, change?' demanded Astasia.

'If I were to tell you, my dear, you would think I had lost my reason.'

Astasia let out a little cry of vexation. 'I thought you – of all of them – would have understood!' And she ran from the room.

Elysia spent the next day immersed in her painting. Whilst she was busy with the technical concerns of the canvas, touching up the last details, she could block everything else from her mind.

At last, at about four in the afternoon when the last of the natural light had faded from the room, she lit the candles and stood, wiping her brushes, looking at the finished work with a critical eye.

Yes, Gavril would not be displeased with the way she had completed his portrayal. If only he were here to see it completed . . .

Elysia sat down in the window seat, resting her cheek against her hand, and stared out at the twilit gardens below, half-wreathed in drifting river fogs.

'Elysia . . .'

She looked round to see Velemir standing watching her.

'So the portrait is finished.'

'The portrait? Yes; it's ready to be framed.'

'It's very fine.' The Count walked around the canvas, inspecting it from another angle. 'How well you have captured the young lady's dreamy, capricious nature. You have a true gift, Elysia.'

'It's mostly Gavril's work.' Elysia glanced again at the wistful expression on Astasia's face and felt a sudden pang of regret. If she had known this portrait was to be the prelude to consigning a young girl to a loveless marriage . . .

'I have something for you.' He drew a crimson velvet box from his jacket and opened it, presenting it to her. Inside, nestling against the soft velvet, lay a gold necklace, exquisitely fashioned, with rubies cut into tiny rosebuds. Two matching drop earrings, set in gold filigree, completed the set.

'The ruby?' she said, amazed. 'But this – this must be worth far more than one single stone.'

'Here.' He lifted the necklace and fastened it around her throat; she shivered at the touch of the cold metal until she felt the warmth of his fingertips, almost caressing the nape of her neck.

Overcome with conflicting emotions, she drew away, gazing down at the delicate workmanship.

'Do you like it?' he said.

'It's beautiful.' She nodded, trying to find adequate words to express her pleasure. 'But your jeweller must have worked night and day to finish this so quickly.'

'We never concluded our conversation, Elysia.'

'There were too many interruptions,' she said with a sad smile.

'I thought we might finish it over dinner.'

'Dinner?' Since they arrived she had forgotten about formal meals; she had not had much appetite and had been sustaining herself on tea, fruit and bread and butter. Now she realized that she was very hungry. 'Thank you, Count.'

'If we are to have dinner together,' he said, offering his arm, 'you must remember to call me Feodor.'

The Count's apartments were more soberly decorated than the rest of the palace: the panelled walls were painted a cool, pale grey and the polished boards were covered with carpets woven with patterns of black and gold.

Instead of floral tapestries, Velemir had covered the walls with paintings. There was nothing pretty or frivolous here: no languorous nymphs, no frothy-petticoated girls on swings. Instead there were stark seascapes, riven with storms, and bleak winter pictures: icefloes, snowflats, all coloured by dark and louring skies.

'I hoped my little collection might intrigue you.'

'Indeed, yes,' Elysia said, examining the canvases with interest. 'I am unfamiliar with these artists. The brushwork in the snowscenes is particularly fine.'

An exquisite crystal structure stood on the black

marble mantelpiece. It was encased in a glass dome, like a clock, and although Elysia could discern no moving parts, it still emanated a curious impression of hidden motion, almost a faint hum. Fascinated, she stood looking at it, trying to figure out how it worked.

'And this pretty toy, what is this? A new kind of pendule, a timepiece?'

'A gift from Tielen, from happier times . . .'

'It's very unusual. Does it strike the hours?'

'Let me offer you a glass of Smarnan wine,' he said, as if he had not heard her last question, 'to make you feel at home. I always keep a case or two in my cellar. I think its warm palate is filled with Smarnan sunlight, don't you?' He poured two glasses of light amber wine from a crystal decanter.

'Let's drink a toast – to your son Gavril's safe delivery from his Azhkendi captors.'

The Count said nothing else of Gavril during supper until a cream-filled meringue dessert overflowing with tart red berries had been served and his manservant had retired to prepare coffee.

Velemir pushed away his plate and dabbed a trace of cream from his lips.

'You were telling me about Kazimir. I'm afraid we completely misread his intentions. We feared he might be selling military secrets to Azhkendir.'

'Kazimir a traitor?' Elysia laid down her dessert fork, her meringue untouched.

'He was working on a highly classified project at the University of Mirom. But there was an argument between him and his colleagues, and he stormed out.

When Lord Volkh approached him, he had not been seen in the university for some weeks. You can understand now, Elysia, why we were obliged to keep an eye on him.'

Elysia said nothing. The taste of the wine had made her wish she was back in Smarna, standing on her balcony in the delicious cool of an autumn evening, listening to the waves on the beach far below. She wanted to feel the warm breeze on her face, to smell the autumn roses in her gardens, not the ever-present stench of fish, tar and tanning. She was wishing she had never come to Mirom.

'I have reached the conclusion', she said, 'that if there is nothing Muscobar can do to help my son, then I had better make arrangements to return home.'

'Is my company so uncongenial?' he asked in mock offence. 'Or is the meringue not to your taste? Tell me what you like to eat, and the kitchens will supply it.'

'No, no,' she said, unsure whether to be flattered or annoyed by his attentions. She could not read him; one moment he was remote and inscrutable, the next solicitous, charming.

'Tell me what you want, Elysia.' He reached across the little table and took her hands in his. There was a strength and a warmth in his grip that seemed to belie his chameleon moods. She did not withdraw her hands.

'I want to know my son is safe.'

'Ah, but is that all you want?'

'No. I want him out of Azhkendir, away from the influence of Bogatyr Kostya. Gavril is not anything like his father. If they try to make another Volkh of

301

him, I fear it will destroy him.' She bit her lip to stop the tears from flowing again. 'He is a caring, sensitive boy, Feodor. An artist.'

'In the carriage today you mentioned that Kazimir had found a cure for your late husband's condition?'

'Some kind of elixir', Elysia said, nodding, 'that reverses the detrimental effects of the inherited condition. That makes the sufferer human again.'

'My dear Elysia,' Velemir said, refilling her glass with the pale amber wine, 'it seems from all you have told me that it is essential – for the health and well-being of your son – that Doctor Kazimir should administer his healing elixir as soon as possible.'

'Oh yes, yes,' Elysia cried, 'but how can it be done? He refuses to return to Azhkendir. And now that the ice has set in, it will be months—'

'Not with the assistance of Eugene of Tielen. His Artificiers have designed vessels, ice-yachts, which can easily traverse the winter ice that divides the two countries.'

'But you said there could be war with Tielen!' Elysia gazed at him, bewildered.

'And there could as easily be peace if Astasia agrees to become his bride. I am in constant diplomatic communication with the Tielen ambassador. And I believe the Prince might be agreeable to helping you, Elysia.'

18

The swirling snow-song of the Snow Spirits lulled Kiukiu into a blank, white daze. She felt herself moving slowly forwards over the snow.

Skeletal ice fingers beckoned her, caressed her, chilled her flesh until she could feel no cold, could feel nothing any longer but a profound numbness.

The shadowdoor gaped open. Beyond it veils of darkness swirled and billowed. The singing had become wordless, each interweaving line a tendril of icy wind, reaching out to ensnare her, to draw her into the darkness. It was the barren breath of the wind as it stirred the frozen reeds. It was the song of the emptiness of the eternal snowflats.

And now she was gliding, gliding towards the mouth of the shadowdoor—

A faint yik-yik-yikking cry broke the Snow Spirits' glacial song.

She halted, listening.

'Who's there?' she called. How weak her voice

sounded. Even if anyone heard her, she would be past help before they found her. 'H-hallo?'

Something came flapping out of the darkness, its golden eyes blazing.

Kiukiu looked up and saw a snow-white owl hovering overhead. Behind it, others materialized, a flock of great owls, their golden eyes bright as torch-flames in the snow.

'Snowcloud?' she whispered. 'But you're dead; Oleg killed you. Am I dreaming, or am I dead too?'

The snow was falling heavily now, large white flakes, soft as owl feathers. Kiukiu felt her eyes closing again, unable to stop herself slipping back into the cold stupor that had numbed her weary body.

'Well, My Lords?' a querulous voice called. 'What have you found? It had better be worth my pains, dragging me out on such a night.'

Dreaming . . .

'Away with you, you greedy Snow Spirits. Shoo, shoo! There's nothing here for you. It's Malusha talking to you, now. And when Malusha talks, you listen, you obey!'

The chill chanting ceased.

There was a malevolent hissing and a bitter-cold swirl of wind whisked around her as the black door-way collapsed in on itself.

Then there was nothing but snow.

Something sharp and hard grated against Kiukiu's cheek. 'Too tired, Snowcloud,' she murmured apologetically. 'Just can't . . . go on . . . any further . . .'

'Who's this, then, little lord?' The voice was closer now. Someone was bending over her, touching her cheek with callused fingers. 'Friend of yours?

304

Why, it's a girl. Wake up, child. Wake up!'

Kiukiu opened her eyes a little and blinked the snow from her lashes.

A wild-haired old woman was staring into her face with eyes that were as golden-bright and mad as the eyes of the snow owls clustering behind her.

'You can't stay here, child. You'll freeze to death. Up you get now and come with me.'

'I – c-can't.' Kiukiu could no longer feel her legs.

'Nonsense! Lean on me.' The old woman put her arm around Kiukiu and tried to pull her up. 'Oof! You're a great sturdy girl, too heavy for me. You're going to have to do the work yourself.'

Kiukiu struggled to her knees.

'My sleigh's here. Just a little farther, child. Blizzard's whipping up – we must get to shelter.'

Out of the snowmists, Kiukiu could just make out a dim lantern glow. Painfully she forced herself to crawl through the snow towards the light until she saw the lantern hung from a little sleigh covered in furs, owls perching on its top. A sturdy, shaggy-coated moorland pony was standing patiently waiting, head down against the snow.

The old woman got into the sleigh and leaned down to give Kiukiu her hand. Her clothes water-logged with melting snow, Kiukiu clambered awkwardly up into the sleigh.

'Wrap these furs round you.' The old woman took up the reins and flicked them, making clicking sounds to the pony. 'Off we go, Harim.'

Slowly, bumpily, the sleigh began to move across the snow into the darkness. Teeth chattering, Kiukiu huddled down into the furs. The snow owls took off, flapping overhead, their great wingstrokes fanning the fast-falling snow.

Numb with cold and exhaustion, Kiukiu lost all sense of time. Soothed by the rhythm of the pony's steady trotting, the swishing of the snow, she lapsed into a trance. It seemed that the little sleigh had been travelling through the winter darkness for ever when it suddenly drew to a stop.

'Here we are,' the old woman said, hopping down and unhooking the lantern. Kiukiu was too weak to ask where 'here' was; she let the old woman lead her. She had a vague impression of passing beneath a tall archway, crossing a snow-covered yard and ducking down to enter a low door. Inside, she saw firelight.

'Sit yourself down and get warm,' the old woman said, tossing some more sticks onto the fire. 'I'm off to stable old Harim.'

Kiukiu slid down on the hearth, raising her frozen hands to the blaze. But as her fingers and toes began to thaw, pain burned through them. She had forgotten how the cold could cause irreversible damage even as it numbed hands and feet. Melting snow dripped down her cheeks from her wet hair; she tried to pull off Sosia's headscarf but her fingers would not obey her.

An old iron cooking pot, blackened with fire and age, hung on a tripod over the flames. Kiukiu thought she could recognize a faint but mouth-watering waft of vegetable soup. Only now did she realize she was ravenously hungry.

'Just in time!' The old woman reappeared, stamping the snow from her boots. 'The blizzard's set in. Even My Lords and Ladies won't hunt tonight.'

'I must thank you,' Kiukiu stammered. 'You saved my life.'

'The little lord was most insistent,' the old woman said, coming closer to stoke the fire. Her eyes gleamed bright in a face as wrinkled as a winter apple. 'Friend of yours, is he?'

For a moment Kiukiu was not sure what her rescuer was talking about.

'You mean Snowcloud?' she asked, understanding.

'Snowcloud? Is that what you call him?' The old woman cackled as if Kiukiu had made a joke.

'His leg was broken,' Kiukiu said, indignant that her special name should be mocked. 'We nursed him back to health. But – but how did he know I was in danger? How did he tell you?'

'What is your name, child?' enquired the old woman, ignoring her questions. 'And what were you doing out so far from shelter?'

'My name is Kiukirilya but everyone calls me Kiukiu.'

'There is something about you . . .' The old woman was staring at her intently, the firelight glinting in her bright eyes. Then she turned away, muttering to herself, 'No, no, it cannot be. No.'

'What is your name?' Kiukiu ventured.

'Malusha.' The old woman seemed to recover her composure. 'Old Malusha. Mad Malusha.'

'And you live out here on the moors all alone?'

'Alone?' Malusha cackled again. 'With all My Lords and Ladies to care for?'

Something stirred up high in the rafters. Kiukiu looked up and saw a snow owl perched above her head on bare rafters stained white with owl droppings.

307

'The owls?' Kiukiu said.

'My Lords don't usually choose to roost in here, they prefer the tower. But they were curious tonight. They wanted to inspect our guest. But we're forgetting our manners; you're soaked to the skin. You'll catch your death, child. Take off those wet things.'

Only now did Kiukiu realize she had left her bundle of possessions out on the moors.

'Here's an old shift of mine and a dry blanket.' Malusha shuffled over with a folded pile of clothes. 'You can change by the fire.' When Kiukiu hesitated, she said indignantly, 'Don't be so modest, I won't look.'

Kiukiu wriggled out of her damp clothes and hurriedly shrugged on Malusha's coarse old linen shift, wrapping the blanket about her as a shawl. Last of all she set about peeling off the soggy woollen stockings. Her feet emerged, swollen and blue. At the least she would have agonizing chilblains – if she didn't lose any toes to frostbite.

'Put these on.' Malusha brought her a pair of thick woollen socks. 'And now let's have some tea. Tea will warm us up.'

A little later, Kiukiu sat, a bowl of green tea in her hands, beside Malusha on the hearth in the glow of the fire's blaze.

'Now tell me, Kiukiu,' Malusha said, 'what were you doing out on the moors in the first snows?'

Kiukiu sighed. She had not the strength to pour out the whole story tonight.

'I was going to Klim,' she said.

'Klim! You were going in the opposite direction,

child. If Lord Snowcloud hadn't found you, you'd have frozen to death. The Snow Spirits were hungry tonight. And where were you coming from?'

'Kastel Drakhaon.'

'Kastel Drakhaon!' Malusha's eyes blazed, bright as the owls'. 'So you're one of Volkh's minions?'

'Lord Volkh', Kiukiu said, alarmed by the old woman's reaction, 'is dead.'

'And what business does one of Volkh's minions have rescuing Arkhel's Owls?' Malusha asked, thrusting her face up close to Kiukiu's.

'They threw me out for rescuing him!' Kiukiu cried. She began to sob. 'I thought he was dead. Oleg told me they'd killed him.'

'My little lord flew here last night. Seems he heard the call of one of my young ladies and found her irresistible.'

Oleg had tricked her. Had he found the white feathers shed by Snowcloud and smeared blood on them to make the *druzhina* believe his story? Or just to cause her pain?

'So you've a kind heart in spite of where you were raised, child.' Malusha was still staring at her, looking so keenly that, in spite of her tiredness, Kiukiu felt acutely uncomfortable.

'No, no,' the old woman muttered. 'Impossible. More tea, child?' She took the bowl from Kiukiu's hands and hobbled over to the fire to refill it. Kiukiu gratefully swallowed down more of the warming tea. This time it tasted more fiery, as though Malusha had added ginger and hot spices to the dried leaves. Heat sizzled through Kiukiu's veins, warming fingertips and toes, making her cheeks burn. A delightful drowsiness followed;

all she wanted now was to sink back in the blankets and sleep away the troubles of the day.

'That's right, child,' Malusha crooned. 'You're tired, you must sleep. We'll talk in the morning.'

Kiukiu dreams:

She is walking through a forest of slender birches, past tall, silver trunks, beneath delicate leaves that sway and sigh in the breeze. Faint amidst the sighing of the birch leaves comes the sound of music, distant notes, water-clear like the patter of falling rain.

In a clearing carpeted with dry fallen birch leaves, soft and silvered with age, a woman sits, playing a stringed instrument. The woman's head is bent over the strings; the dark folds of her headdress shade her face.

Kiukiu comes towards her and the music stops, mid-phrase, like a question.

'Who are you, child?' the woman asks, her head still bent, her voice low and sweet like a wood-dove's.

'My name is Kiukiu—'

'That is your name. But what is your parentage, who was your father, your mother?'

The breeze stirs the strings, a strange, wild breath of sound.

'My mother's name was Afimia. And my father – my father—' Kiukiu can hardly say it. 'My father was called Malkh.'

There is the harsh discordant sound of snapped strings – and the woman casts down the instrument.

'Malkh, Malkh, my golden boy,' the woman whispers, rocking to and fro in grief.

The birch forest is growing rapidly dark and

the gentle breeze has become a cold wind. Silver leaves begin to stir and eddy in the harsh gusts.

'You knew my father?' Kiukiu asks, chilled to the bone.

The woman raises her head and Kiukiu finds she is staring into the tear-streaked face of Malusha.

'Knew him? He was my son.'

19

'Welcome, Gavril,' Lilias said, smiling. She lay on her silk-draped bed, propped up on pillows. Beside the bed was set a cradle, draped with folds of crisp white linen. A subtle seamstress – Dysis? – had embroidered the Nagarian crest on the linen in threads of gold and blue.

'Congratulations, Lilias.' Gavril could not bring himself to smile back at her.

'Don't you want to see my son? Your half-brother Artamon?'

Half-brother? Gavril approached the cradle and looked inside. He had never had a brother or sister. The pink little scrap of a thing that lay curled asleep inside did not look much of a threat. Neither, he thought, did the baby look anything like a Nagarian with its wisps of red-gold hair. Or an Arkhel. If anything, little Artamon favoured Lilias's colouring. He felt a sudden pang of pity for the sleeping child, innocent and unaware of the snake's nest it had been born into.

'Sleeping so peacefully. And yet,' and a darkness shadowed her face, 'he had such a narrow escape.'

'What do you mean?'

'A horrible thing happened. I still find myself shaking when I think of it. One of the servants tried to kill him.'

'One of the servants?' Gavril had a sudden sick feeling of apprehension; what unpleasant revelation was she leading up to? He had noticed an unusually subdued atmosphere in the kastel. 'Who would want to kill a baby?'

'The girl was never right in the head. She should never have been left alone with the baby. But don't worry, My Lord, the matter is dealt with.'

'Dealt with?' Apprehension turned to dread. '*Who was it?*'

'Why, Kiukiu, of course. I thought you might have guessed from my description!'

Gavril felt his heart lurch painfully in his breast. He had warned her to be careful of Lilias. But Lilias was clever. Too clever for good-hearted, loyal Kiukiu.

'Kiukiu isn't the kind of girl to harm babies,' he began. 'Are you sure you aren't mistaken?'

'I caught her trying to smother my baby!' Lilias's green eyes glistened with sudden tears.

'But why would she do such a thing?'

'Because she has bad blood in her! Did you know her father was an Arkhel? Not a lord, of course, but one of their shamans.'

Gavril stared at her in dismay. He did not for one moment believe that Kiukiu would have tried to harm the baby – but for now he found himself outmanoeuvred.

'And where is she now?' he asked.

'Oh, she's gone.'

'Gone!' His heart gave another lurch. 'Gone where?'

'I had her thrown out. I couldn't risk her being anywhere near my baby.'

'By what right', he said coldly, 'did you have one of my servants dismissed without my authorization?'

'Michailo authorized it. Kostya left him in command of the kastel. There was more. An owl. She was keeping an owl – an Arkhel's Owl – as a pet! She was lucky to be dismissed without punishment.'

Worse and worse. They had found Snowcloud.

'And when did all this happen?'

'Yesterday.'

'You sent her out into that blizzard?'

'Was it my fault the weather changed?'

'And has no-one gone to look for her?' Gavril turned and went striding out of Lilias's bedchamber, letting the door bang behind him. He didn't care if he woke the baby. He only knew that Kiukiu had been made to suffer on his account. Lilias had found a way to rid herself of Kiukiu – a way that worked all too well to her advantage.

'Sosia!' he shouted. He was Drakhaon; the whole household would pay if Kiukiu had come to any harm.

'My Lord?' Sosia came up from the kitchens; her face was wan and drawn.

'Why did you let them dismiss Kiukiu? Send her out into the snows?' He could hear his own voice, hot and rough with anger.

'I – I had no alternative, My Lord.' Sosia looked frightened.

'Where did she go?'

'I told her to go to the village. To Klim. I have family there, at the tavern.'

'Michailo!' The anger was building inside him; he made an effort to contain it. '*Michailo!*'

'My Lord?' Michailo appeared on the balcony overhead; Gavril could see the glint of his fair hair in the gloom.

'Assemble a search party. Get blankets and aquavit.'

'Why, My Lord?'

There was something in Michailo's tone of voice that rankled, almost a hint of insolence.

'You dare question my orders?' The words rasped out. 'Do as I say.'

There was a small pause.

'Very well, Lord Drakhaon.'

Gavril struck his clenched fist against the panelled wall. Fixed shields and crossed sabres rattled. Suddenly the household sprang into life; orders were bellowed, men of the *druzhina* came running past, grabbing axes, buckling on sabres. Gavril watched them with a kind of grim satisfaction, following them through to the courtyard where he saw them leading their horses from the stables. The cobbles were dirty with muddied slush and hard-trodden snow.

'Who are we to search for, Lord Drakhaon?'

'For the serving-girl Kiukiu. She went towards Klim.'

He saw the warriors exchanging glances.

A tow-haired stable-boy tried to sidle past; Gavril

recognized Ivar and caught hold of him by the shoulder.

'Saddle me a horse. I'm going too.'

He saw Michailo mutter something to his men.

'Do you have a problem with that, Michailo?'

'With respect, Lord Drakhaon,' said Michailo, looking him straight in the eye, 'there must be other more important matters than searching the moors for one insignificant servant-girl.'

'No-one in my household', Gavril said, returning the stare until Michailo sullenly looked away, 'is insignificant, Michailo.'

The stable-boy led out a black gelding. Gavril, eyes still fixed on Michailo, swung up into the saddle.

'Lead the way, Michailo.'

Gavril's horse laboured to the brow of the hill, snorting out steam from his nostrils. Below them the moors stretched away into the misted distance, a glistening sheen of white snow, white as far as Gavril could see.

'How far to the village?' he asked Michailo.

Michailo shrugged. 'In good weather, an hour or so on horseback.'

'But Kiukiu was on foot.'

Michailo shrugged again and clicked his tongue to his horse. Down the stony track they went, down towards the endless expanse of whiteness. There was not a stir amongst the windless branches, not even the bark of a distant rowan-deer or the flutter of a bird's wings.

So quiet. And so very cold. The lonely prospect

crushed Gavril's hopes. Had Kiukiu made it to the village before the blizzard swept across the moors? There was no shelter here, just an endless expanse of windblown snow.

They rode on, the horses stepping up to their fetlocks through the snow. The wind, sharp as a saw's blade, whined across the moorlands. The six *druzhina* put their heads down, uncomplaining. Gavril felt unrepentant for bringing them out in such weather. They were pledged to serve him. But Michailo's blatant show of arrogance had unsettled him; the intimate looks passing between the young man and Lilias had not escaped him. What had they been planning?

At last Gavril thought he could just make out a faint dark smudge rising above the skyline against the dazzle of the snow. Shading his eyes, he realized the smudge was smoke rising from hidden chimneys.

They came to the brow of a slope and there, below them, lay a little compound of wooden houses nestling around a chapel. Tiny figures moved to and fro through the snow-bound lanes. As they approached he could hear voices: children screaming and shouting as they played – and the lowing of cattle, herded into the barns for shelter.

'*Druzhina!*' One child spotted the riders and ran down the little street, calling out, '*Druzhina!*' Other children gathered in a doorway, peering warily out at the riders from beneath shawls and close-wound woollen scarfs.

'Minushka! Danilo! Come in at once.' A woman appeared and snatched up two of the children, dragging them into the house. Gavril did not miss the look she gave them; at once fearful and resentful. The *druzhina* inspired awe – but not affection – in their neighbours.

Michailo dismounted and flung the reins of his horse to his companion.

'Landlord! Piotr!' he shouted.

The door of the nearest wooden house opened and a thickset bearded man appeared, bowing.

'Welcome, My Lords.'

Gavril caught a waft of warmth from a fire within. He longed to dismount and go inside to thaw his cold hands and feet.

'We're looking for Sosia's niece. Kiukirilya.'

The landlord looked blankly at them.

'I haven't seen our little Kiukiu in over a year. Why, My Lord?'

'Are you certain?' Gavril urged his horse forwards.

'Would I lie to you, My Lord?' Piotr stared up at him and Gavril saw a sudden look of fear shiver across his face. 'You are Lord Volkh's son,' he whispered and dropped to his knees.

'Get up, Piotr,' Michailo said irritably.

'If I'd known you were coming, Lord Drakhaon—' Piotr babbled.

'Kiukiu is missing,' Gavril cut in. 'She set out to come here a day and a night ago, and you say she never arrived?'

'Never, My Lord.'

'Where else could she be?'

'There is nowhere else. Nowhere between here and Azhgorod.'

'A farm, a homestead on the moors, that might have given her shelter?'

Piotr shook his head.

'I'll get a search party together,' he said. 'Come in, My Lords. You must be frozen to the bone. Dmitri!' Piotr whistled and a lanky, raw-boned youth appeared. 'Hot caraway ale for My Lord and his men.'

Inside the tavern a log fire was blazing in a bright-tiled stove; two old men were huddled close to the stove but they hurriedly shuffled away as the warriors came in. Dmitri ladled out mugs of steaming ale from a pot on the stove for Gavril and the *druzhina*.

'All this for one foolish girl,' muttered Michailo, blowing the steam from the top of his mug. But before Gavril could remonstrate with him, a group of men came tramping in, stamping the snow off their boots. All were wrapped in furs and animal-skin cloaks, and carried sticks, axes and clubs. To Gavril they looked more like brigands armed to go raiding than a rescue party.

'Wolves,' one of them said. 'Steppe wolves from Tielen. Broke into my neighbour's yard last night, killed half of his sheep. They haven't ventured this far since Drakhys Marya's time.'

'I've never seen snow like this,' Piotr said, blowing on his fingers. 'This is the worst I can remember.'

'Steppe wolves here?' Gavril saw again the twisted, torn bodies of the women and children of Ilmin, scattered in the bloodstained snow.

'We have our own wolves up in the mountains, silver-haired snow wolves. But these vicious brutes come from the steppes of Tielen. Over the ice. Yellow-fanged, yellow-haired, they'll tear a man to pieces if they're hungry enough.'

Kiukiu, struggling through the snows alone . . .

'Let's go,' Gavril said, making for the door.

Michailo gulped down the last of his ale and waved the *druzhina* to follow him.

'My Lord,' Piotr said quietly to Gavril as he reached the horses, 'things don't look too good. Steppe wolves, blizzards . . . Don't raise your hopes.'

As they rode out of the village, some of the children ran alongside, waving to the search party as they trudged along behind the *druzhina*'s horses.

'Go back!' Piotr shouted to them. 'Stay in the village. Stay where it's safe!'

On the brow of the hill, the wind scythed in again, cold enough to take the breath away. Gavril gazed about him at the glittering snowfields. He wondered how anyone would know how to find their way to Klim when all landmarks except the distant jagged range of mountains were covered in snow.

'Is there anywhere she could have found shelter between Klim and the mountains?' Gavril asked, shading his eyes.

'Only the old witch's place,' Piotr said. One of the men made a sign with his fingers and spat in the snow.

'Witch?' Gavril echoed.

'Wisewoman. Mad as a bat. Lives on her own on the edge of the Arkhel waste.'

'But still—'

'Here. Here!' shouted out one of the search party.

Gavril jumped down from his horse and went running over to look. The man was digging in the snow; under the light surface powder-snow, Gavril saw the sodden folds of a piece of material appear. He kneeled down to help dig, all the time fearing that beneath the drift a frozen human face would appear.

But all that lay beneath the drift was a crumpled square of material, an old threadbare sheet, that spilled a few objects as they pulled it out, brushing away the snow.

Gavril picked up the contents. And as he touched them, a sick, desolate feeling numbed him. So few possessions. So little to leave behind. Thick socks darned and redarned with gypsy-bright wools, an ivory comb with broken teeth, the remains of a half-chewed piece of black bread, blue ribbons . . .

Blue, her favourite colour. Gavril began to dig in the snow with gloved hands.

'These are her things. Where *is* she?' he said between gritted teeth.

'This looks bad,' Piotr said.

'Help me dig!' Gavril cried. The men from the search party looked down at their feet, unwilling to meet his eyes.

'There's no point, My Lord,' Piotr said bluntly.

'But there's no body. Without a body, how can we be sure?' insisted Gavril.

'You heard what was said, My Lord. Steppe wolves.'

'But there are no remains.' Gavril had begun to sense an unfamiliar pulsing in his temples, dull as the thud of a heartbeat but faster, more insistent. 'We should search for evidence.' Irritated by their complacency, he went further away, scuffing up the snow, forcing himself to look for what he most dreaded to find: bloodstained scraps of clothing, a hank of fair hair, fragments of bone . . .

'We're wasting our time,' broke in Michailo.

'She'd never have survived this long out here in the snows.'

'Michailo's right, My Lord,' broke in Piotr. 'The sun'll set soon. We should turn back now. '

The dull pulsing intensified. 'But if Michailo had waited for my return,' Gavril said in a low voice, 'this would never have happened.'

'I was placed in command,' Michailo said self-righteously.

'You know how treacherous the weather is in winter. You sent her to her death.' A voice at the back of his mind was urging self-control – and yet the bitter grief that had come rolling up like a dark fog almost obliterated it.

'My Lord, look at the sky. We can't stay out here – or we'll risk the same fate.'

Gavril glanced up. The clouds fast-scudding from the mountains had an eerie yellow cast to them. A distant low moan shivered across the snowflats – and was answered by another closer by. The sound, eerily inhuman, made Gavril's flesh crawl. Wolf-howl.

'That wasn't the wind.' His horse gave a nervous whinny and tossed its head, pawing restlessly at the snow. 'Was it?'

'Your horse can scent them,' Piotr said uneasily.

'We're more than a match for any wolf pack,' one of the younger *druzhina* boasted. 'Our horses can easily outrun them.'

'Oh yes?' Piotr said. 'So you'd ride off and leave us to fend for ourselves?'

'Give me her things,' Gavril said. He crammed Kiukiu's few possessions into his saddle-bag. 'Now let's be on our way.'

As he remounted, another howl quivered through the air. The men on foot shouldered their weapons and stolidly began to trudge back, following their footprints in the thick snow.

One lone girl, stumbling exhaustedly through the snow, had proved easy prey for a pack of marauding wolves. But a band of armed men . . . Gavril put the thought from his mind. He could only think of Kiukiu. He gazed out over the bleak landscape as he rode. He could not forget what Michailo had done. Michailo would pay.

He looked up at Michailo, riding ahead, nonchalant and relaxed in the saddle. His eyes narrowed against the glare of the snow. He hated the man. Hated his arrogant manner, his sullen comments, the way he tossed his flax-fair braids . . .

The pulsing in his temples had begun again. The more he thought how much he hated Michailo, the more the blood burned in his head.

He could not remember ever hating anyone so vehemently before. Disliking, maybe, the odd difference of opinions, but *hate*?

A lurid snow-light suddenly lit the far-distant mountain peaks, briefly gilding them a sulphurous yellow. Flakes of snow began to drift down, a few, chill white petals from the ash-grey sky. The last sunlight suddenly disappeared and the moors were swathed in gloom.

A long, low howl trembled through the air. Other voices answered, eerily close.

'The village!' cried Piotr, his voice sharp with alarm. He began to run; Michailo and the others kicked their heels into their horses' sides, urging them back. 'The children!'

Gavril followed.

The *druzhina* reached the ridge above the village, reining in their horses, hooves scuffing up showers of powder-snow.

The little gaggle of children were still playing, engrossed in a game of catch. They glanced up as the men came riding back.

'What are you doing out here?' shouted Piotr. 'The wolves are coming! Go in, go in!'

The children spilled down the ridge towards the village, shrieking in fear.

'Go get torches!' Michailo ordered, following them.

Gavril heard a shrill little scream. One of the children, the little boy Danilo, had gone sprawling headlong in the snow.

A dark, snarling creature leaped out of the shadows, teeth bared, right in front of the child.

Gavril spurred his horse down the hill towards Danilo, intending to scoop him up onto his saddle. But the horse shied, rearing up into the air. Gavril lost his grip on the reins and fell off into the snow.

Winded by the fall, he struggled to his feet. He could hear the child whimpering.

'Danilo!' he cried. 'Get behind me!' But Danilo just lay where he had fallen, paralysed with fear.

A wolf crouched, yellow teeth bared, poised to attack.

Eyes gleamed in the twilight, orange, feral eyes. Wolf-voices bayed and yelped. Not one wolf – but a whole pack of them.

This is how she died. The wolves killed her, tore her apart . . .

Gavril flung himself in front of Danilo.

The young girl stumbles in the snow. The beasts encircle her, leap on her, pull her down. And then there is nothing but the sound of screaming and the gobbling, growling sounds of the beasts as they ravage her living flesh, slobbering over the fresh carcass.

Now Gavril no longer felt afraid. He felt himself possessed by a terrible, burning anger. Anger for Kiukiu, his Kiukiu, dying alone and in such terror. The anger caught fire in his mind. Flames flickered across his sight: red, orange, white. Blue.

Blue, phosphorescent blue of starfire on freezing winter nights, starblaze of burning, brilliant blue . . .

Through the shimmering blur of fire he saw the creature gather itself to spring.

The wolf leaped into the air. Instinctively Gavril raised his arm to protect himself.

He heard the snap of ragged fangs, sharp as daggers, smelled the hot, rank stink of its carnivore's breath.

Flames shot from his outstretched fingers, glittering blue as cobalt.

The twilight exploded into a dazzle of shattered stars.

The wolf's shaggy coat caught fire.

Blinding blueflare, brighter than lightning.

Burning, the wolf dropped into the snow, writhing and making horrible whining sounds. And in the flames, Gavril saw for a moment – but how could it be? – the black shadow of a burning man, clawing and twisting in agony. Then the dazzle of the flames dimmed. Slowly the blackened paws moved aimlessly . . . and stilled.

Now there was only choking smoke and a vile smell of burning fur.

What had he done? For a moment his whole body had convulsed in that one cataclysmic burst of power. Now he felt utterly drained. His knees buckled.

'My Lord, My Lord—' Voices were calling his name.

He toppled forwards into the snow, and the last sparks of Drakhaon's Fire were extinguished in a black tide that overwhelmed him, dragging him down to oblivion in its lightless depths.

20

Kiukiu woke with a start.

A cold snow-light filtered in from slit windows set high in the rough walls of the hut.

At first she had no idea where she was – and then, seeing Malusha stooped over the fire, stoking it with fresh wood, she began to remember.

'Snow's stopped for a while,' Malusha said without turning around. 'I've made porridge. Want some, child?'

Porridge. Kiukiu's empty stomach rumbled; embarrassed, she pressed her hands on it to silence it.

'Yes, please. I'm starving.'

Malusha brought over a bowl filled with steaming barley porridge and a spoon.

'Eat it from the outside in or you'll burn your tongue. I've stirred in a spoonful of heather honey to give you strength.'

Kiukiu breathed in the honey-scented steam

hungrily. She was so ravenous she didn't care if she burned her tongue to swallow down some of the delicious porridge.

She looked up into Malusha's face – and her dream came back to her so vividly it seemed as if it had been more than a dream. She set down the porridge bowl and reached out for the old woman's hand.

'I – I had a dream last night,' she said.

'Ah.' Malusha sat down beside her. She did not withdraw her hand.

'You were in my dream. You asked me who my parents were. You said – you said Malkh, my father, was your son.'

The old woman's bright eyes clouded suddenly with tears.

'You remember the dream,' she said, squeezing Kiukiu's hand. 'You remember!'

'Are you my grandmother?' Kiukiu stammered.

'If Malkh was your father, then I am, child.'

'How can it be?' Kiukiu was wary now. 'They told us all the Arkhel household were killed.'

'All but me, Kiukiu, all but me.' Kiukiu saw the shadow of the bleak years of solitude and suffering darkening her grandmother's eyes. 'All but me and My Lords and Ladies. Someone had to care for them.'

'The owls.'

'When I first saw you, there was something familiar about you, child.' Malusha gently stroked Kiukiu's cheek, gazing at her face as if she could not stop looking at her. 'Now, in the daylight, I can see it. You have your father's eyes . . . and something of his chin, his cheekbones. Strong features, strong personality.'

'But the dream. How did you – how did I—'

'You have the gift,' Malusha said. She laid her gnarled hand on Kiukiu's forehead. 'That was what finally convinced me. I thought the gift would die with me, the last of our line. Our little Lord Snowcloud must have sensed it . . .'

'You are my grandmother,' Kiukiu said wonderingly. This should have been such a sublimely happy moment – and suddenly there were tears streaming down her cheeks.

'Hush now, child.' The old woman leaned forwards and hugged her. 'Dry your eyes and eat your porridge; it'll go cold and there's nothing worse than cold porridge.'

Kiukiu, swathed in Malusha's blanket, began to look about her. There were little hints of a once-prosperous life in the cottage. The walls were bare – yet the bed in the corner was covered with a patchwork quilt of rich cloths: Kiukiu could make out velvets and threads of gold in the squares of material. A metal jug by the fireplace was swan-necked, too elegantly fashioned for a peasant's cottage. And there was a lacquer chest at the bottom of Malusha's bed. In the firelight's glint, Kiukiu could see it was kin to the dragon-chest in Lord Volkh's room – although instead of dragons, golden owls adorned its lid and sides.

Now that she was fully awake she could hear the distant clucking croon of hens; somewhere beyond the firelit room there must be the barn where the pony was stabled.

'How do you manage here, Grandmother?' Kiukiu ventured. 'So far from the village?'

'I've enough for my needs,' Malusha said. 'A well of clean water, a few apple trees. There's lingonberries to be gathered on the moors, and wild mushrooms.'

'But weren't all the Arkhel lands withered by the Drakhaon? They told us they were laid waste, that nothing will grow there.'

'Child, you'd have had to walk for three full days to reach Arkhel's domains. But yes, my home was once in Kastel Arkhel. Guslyars were valued members of Lord Arkhel's household. But everything – and everyone – was destroyed by Lord Volkh.'

'How did you escape?'

'I was away from Kastel Arkhel that night, searching for my boy. I knew something terrible had happened to him.' Malusha's eyes darkened. 'He hadn't told me much about your mother – only that he had fallen in love. I shouldn't have left My Lord Stavyor. But what was I to do? Malkh was my only son, I had to go find him.' The old woman fell silent, staring at her hands which were crossed in her lap.

'They say my mother was never the same after my father—' Kiukiu hesitated, 'after he died. Even after I was born. I don't really remember her. My Auntie Sosia brought me up.'

'Your mother? Oh, for a long time I hated your mother.' Malusha looked up at Kiukiu and Kiukiu felt a sudden chill that was nothing to do with the snow. There was still a lingering shadow of that bleak, unreasoning hatred that allowed no forgiveness. 'I called down every curse I knew on her head for leading my boy to his death.'

'She didn't mean to get him killed,' Kiukiu said hotly. 'She loved him. And they made her suffer for loving him.'

'And you, child?' Malusha slipped her gnarled fingers under Kiukiu's chin, turning her face to hers. 'Why were you allowed to live? An Arkhel child in the Drakhaon's household?'

'I don't know.' Kiukiu looked away, embarrassed by her grandmother's intense scrutiny. 'I don't know.'

For the next few hours Kiukiu pottered about helping her grandmother. That was what, Kiukiu reasoned, she was best at: kitchen chores. She swept up the dust with a broom, she drew water from the well outside, kneaded dough for bread and set it to rise in a warm place near the fire.

Malusha watched her, nodding her head from time to time. She seemed weary now, as if the shock of finding her granddaughter had exhausted much of her energy.

'You're a good, useful girl, Kiukiu, and no mistake.'

'You've lived here all alone, all these years?'

'Not alone, Kiukiu, I've had my duty to My Lords and Ladies here to keep me busy.' There was a strange, fey glint in Malusha's eyes now as she pointed to the rafters where some of the snow owls were roosting, hunched white shadows high overhead. 'There were still songs to be sung in praise of My Lords' hunting exploits and My Ladies' broods of owlets. I've nurtured a whole dynasty of Arkhel's Owls here, no thanks to the Drakhaon's men.' Malusha made the sign against evil and spat eloquently three times.

'But . . . no other people?' Kiukiu, who had spent all her life in the kitchens, surrounded by people, could not begin to imagine such a solitary existence.

'Oh, now and then there's a farmer stops by or a pedlar-woman going to Klim. They give me things in exchange for my skills; a sack of flour here, a length of cloth there. I get by.'

Kiukiu was growing weary; she had set the bread to bake and had chopped some vegetables Malusha gave her from her home-grown store to make soup. She sat down in front of the newly laid fire and warmed her fingers and toes at the blaze.

'Where's Snowcloud?' she asked.

'Roosting, where else? It's day; My Lords and Ladies of the night won't stir till the sun sets.'

'Tell me, Grandmother,' Kiukiu sat back on her heels, face glowing with the fire's blaze, 'tell me about the Guslyars.'

'You've had no training, child, have you?' Malusha sighed. 'Where to begin? A Guslyar should be trained from childhood in her art. I fear it may be too late for you. My mother started training me when I was four.'

'Too late?' Kiukiu tried not to sound too disappointed, but the thought that by an accident of birth she had been deprived of the chance to develop her gift was devastating.

'You know no more of the art than any other Nagarian.' Malusha's voice had become dry, deprecating.

'That's not my fault! And how can I know if you won't tell me?' Kiukiu burst out.

'All this talking has dried my throat.' Malusha got up stiffly, awkwardly, as if her bones had become set in the hunched sitting position. 'I need some tea.'

Kiukiu watched her grandmother taking pinches of dried leaves from earthenware pots, muttering to herself as she poured hot water onto the leaves, pressing them with a spoon to release the flavour.

A curiously fragranced steam wafted towards Kiukiu as Malusha brought over two bowls of tea. She sniffed suspiciously. This wasn't the kind of tea Sosia brewed in the kitchen.

'What's in this?' she demanded.

'Special herbs,' Malusha grunted as she eased herself back down beside her. 'To ease my aching bones. To keep the cold from getting into yours.'

Kiukiu took a tentative sip and pulled a face.

'It tastes odd.' And then the bitter taste altered on her tongue, releasing unfamiliar savours that were both sweet and tantalizingly elusive. It was as if the tea reminded her of some lost childhood memory.

'Ah. That's better,' Malusha said after taking a long sip. 'Now, where were we?'

'Guslyars,' Kiukiu said. Her voice sounded different – muzzily distant as if she were trying to call through thick, swirling mists.

Malusha set down her tea bowl and went to the lacquered chest. Throwing the lid open, she took out what looked at first to Kiukiu like a large rectangular wooden tray. She settled herself down with it on her lap and Kiukiu saw now that it was an instrument, many-stringed, its case intricately painted and gilded with patterns of animals, birds and flowers. The metal strings, even though unplucked, gave off a slight shimmer of sound as though vibrating in sympathy with Malusha's breathing.

'This was my mother's gusly.' Malusha ran her hard, curved nails over the strings, releasing a wild quiver of notes that set Kiukiu's flesh tingling. 'Needs tuning.' Malusha plucked at the strings, head on one side, twisting the metal pegs that glinted like gold, adjusting the pitch until it reached her satisfaction.

'I've never seen – never heard – anything quite—' Kiukiu stammered, overwhelmed.

'How could you?' Malusha snapped. 'This is Arkhel magic. Subtle magic. What would the House of Nagarian understand about subtlety?'

'Play for me, Grandmother.'

'What shall I play? I know. A song to welcome home young Lord Snowcloud.' Malusha bent her head over the strings and began to play.

Kiukiu listened, entranced. The little flurries of notes evoked fast-falling snow. And suddenly she was flying through the snow-spun darkness, soaring and swooping, her senses alert to the tiniest sounds of the moorland night.

As the last notes died, she realized she was gazing down at herself and Malusha from the rafters. Slowly, softly as a falling feather she floated down, and found herself looking at her grandmother through her own eyes again.

'I was flying,' she whispered. 'Was that you, Grandmother, or the tea?'

'Tsk, child, a little of both.' Malusha laid down the gusly. 'And a little of your own gift. Look at me.' Malusha placed her fingers on Kiukiu's cheek, staring into her eyes as she had done the night before. 'You've been out of your body before, haven't you?'

'Only once.' Kiukiu looked away, ashamed.

'And how did that come about?'

'Lord Volkh,' Kiukiu whispered. 'He made me bring him through the mirror. From the Ways Beyond.'

'You've travelled that dark road? Unguided, untrained? Alone?' Malusha shook her grey head. 'Child, child, what a foolishly dangerous thing to do. But then, how were you to know?'

'To know what?' Kiukiu said, alarmed now.

'A Guslyar can use her gift in many ways. But others can take advantage of her – and each journey she makes into the Ways Beyond drains a little more of her life-force. It is not a journey to be lightly undertaken.'

'Life-force? You mean strength?'

'Each time you return, you return a little more diminished, leaving a little more of yourself in the world of spirits.'

'But why do you have to go there at all?' Kiukiu shuddered, remembering the chill winds sweeping the bleak plain where she had found Lord Volkh.

'You've heard one of our other names? Ghost-Singers? Did no-one ever tell you how the Arkhels became so powerful?'

Kiukiu shook her head.

'There were many hero-warriors amongst the ancestors of the House of Arkhel. Bogatyrs, golden knights, who once ruled Azhkendir in ancient days. Before battle the Ghost-Singers summoned the spirit-wraiths of the ancient heroes to possess Lord Arkhel and his Clan warriors. Fired with the strength of their ancestors, they were invincible. And no-one knew, no-one guessed the secret until . . .'

Malusha's voice died away, her eyes staring into the distant shadows.

'Until?' prompted Kiukiu uncertainly.

'Destroy the Singer, and you leave the Arkhels vulnerable. Unprotected by the ancestor warrior-spirits, open to attack. Not even My Lord and Lady owls could save them.'

'The Singer?' Kiukiu understood now. 'You mean my father.'

'I mean my poor Malkh.'

'But what about you, Grandmother? Why didn't you—'

'Because I was his mother,' Malusha snapped. 'I was out searching for him on the moors when I should have been at Kastel Arkhel. When the sky grew dark and the Drakhaon swept out across the moorlands towards the mountains, I knew too late that I and my son had failed. Failed in our duty to the Lords of Arkhel. Beneath that terrible shadow, I fell to the ground and wept. I could do nothing, nothing but watch. I saw the distant flare of blue fire, I saw the glittering cloud that enveloped the kastel – and I felt them die, so many extinguished, all at once. I felt their deaths even from so far away, like a dark wave engulfing me. When I came back to myself, I was alone and the day was spent.'

'But could you and my father have withstood the Drakhaon's powers?' Kiukiu whispered. 'Wouldn't you have been destroyed too?'

'Aye, and that would have been a merciful thing. But then who would have cared for My Lords and Ladies? And who would have been here to rescue you from the snows?'

Her grandmother's logic was a little skewed but

Kiukiu could see that, in a way, it made sense.

'Some nights, when the loneliness is hard to bear, I go down those mist-shrouded, winding paths into the Ways Beyond,' Malusha said distantly, as if she were talking to herself. 'But ghosts make sad company . . .'

'You went there looking for my father?'

'When I could not find him in the land of the living, I knew where I had to look. We said a kind of farewell to each other.'

'He wasn't in that . . . that terrible place of dust and ashes?'

Malusha leaned across and squeezed Kiukiu's hand.

'No, child, he passed across that barren landscape long ago. As a Guslyar he knew how to find the Ways that lead Beyond. But wretched souls, such as Lord Volkh, weighed down, blinded by their burden of cruelty, cannot see where the true paths lie.'

'I couldn't see any paths.'

'Because you have not been trained. But now that will change.' Malusha turned Kiukiu's hand over, raising it to inspect her fingers. 'Good, long fingers. Strong fingers. But your nails, child! All worn and chewed. A Guslyar needs nails of iron to pluck these metal strings.'

'I had to wash dishes,' Kiukiu said. It seemed a feeble excuse.

'You'll have to use these.' Malusha fished out some pieces of curiously fashioned metal and slipped one onto Kiukiu's index finger. 'These are plectra. Until your nails grow strong and hard, you'll have to practise with these.'

'But why do Guslyars need to play songs? I didn't

make any music before Lord Volkh appeared in the mirror.'

'Mirrors? Pah,' Malusha said dismissively. 'Crude peasant magic. A Guslyar uses music for many purposes. The first is to sing the Praise Songs, the *bylini*. Each Lord of Arkhel has his own Praise Song. I shall teach you all the Songs of the House of Arkhel. And then there is the *other* music.'

'Other music?' Kiukiu echoed.

'We can make the sound of the gusly act as a bridge between our world and the Ways Beyond.' Malusha plucked two of the strings, setting up a weird and disconcerting resonance that seemed to pulse to the core of Kiukiu's body. 'We can summon spirit-wraiths by the sounds we make with our voices and these strings. These sounds send us into the trance-state where we unlock the hidden portals and travel the Ways unknown to ordinary men, the Ways untravelled by the living.'

'You said you went to find Malkh, my father. Can I find him too? And my mother?'

'Child, child, have you not heard a single word I've been saying? Every time you walk those paths, you shorten your own lifespan. You must be properly trained before you venture out on those uncharted paths again. Or the Lost Souls will drain you of your life-force, and you will have no strength to return to your body.'

'You mean I have to learn to play first?' Disheartened, Kiukiu looked down at the strings. How was she ever to make sense of them all?

'You have a lifetime's work to make up. So we'd better get started!'

* * *

At sunset Kiukiu went to feed Harim the pony. She was glad to escape Malusha and her scolding for a little while. She was well used to scolding, but her brain was dizzy with all the instructions her grandmother had given her in her first gusly lesson. 'Hold the instrument this way, your left-hand fingers are here, no, *here* . . .'

Her arm ached from the unfamiliar weight of the gusly and her fingers were sore. Her mind jangled with the discordant sounds she had made. It was a relief to come outside and listen to the quiet.

She ventured out beyond the gateway to the edge of the moorlands. It had stopped snowing and the setting sun had stained the snowfields with a glitter of pale fire. The intense cold took her breath away. Now that the wind had dropped, it was so quiet. It was as if she were the last living being in this winter wilderness.

She turned to go back into the warmth of her grandmother's cottage.

Suddenly the twilight sky flashed blue, intense lightning blue. The air shuddered and crackled. The ground shook beneath her feet. In his stall she heard the pony whinnying in terror. The snow owls burst up out of the tower in a flurry of white wings, shrieking and jickering.

Malusha came running out of the cottage. Kiukiu moved towards her, clutching at her in her fright. Her grandmother's face had turned grey.

'Grandmother,' Kiukiu stammered. 'What was that?'

Malusha could not speak for a moment. Her lips moved but no sounds came out. One hand waved feebly in the direction of the moors. At last the words began to come, faint yet tainted with a virulent and bitter hatred.

'Hoped – never to have to see *that* again in my lifetime—'

'What, Grandmother?'

'Arkhel's bane. Drakhaon's Fire. Your young Lord Gavril is no longer human, Kiukiu. Nagarian bad blood will out, sooner or later. He has become truly Drakhaon.'

21

Madame Andar-Nagarian,

I must apologize for my behaviour; it was quite unpardonable. To make amends, I wish to propose a meeting at the Tea Pavilion in the Water Gardens at three today.

Altan Kazimir

Elysia glanced around again. She had gone out unaccompanied on the pretext of needing to purchase some new oil paints. Yet since she left the shop with her purchases, she had been certain someone was shadowing her.

Now that she had reached the Water Gardens, she hurried along the winding paths, following the signs to the Tea Pavilion, hoping she had been mistaken. Frost still dusted the frozen grass. The last of the autumn leaves were slowly drifting down from the bare branches; as she reached the lake, she saw the Tea Pavilion, a graceful summerhouse painted a delicate shade of willow green, standing beside the grey, still waters.

The Tea Pavilion was busy and the scent of roasting coffee beans warmed the steamy air. To Elysia's astonishment, many of the customers were eating ices in spite of the frosty temperature outside; she saw glass after glass of pale green pistachio, apricot and vivid pink raspberry being eagerly consumed as she gazed across the room, searching for Doctor Kazimir.

She caught sight of him in a window-seat overlooking the lake, staring into the distant reed beds, lost in thought.

'Doctor Kazimir?'

He started. Below the window black swans glided past on the lake.

'Madame.' He rose to his feet. 'I'm so glad you came. I wanted to apologize.' He was neatly dressed today, clean-shaven, with his fine fair hair combed back off his face. With relief she saw there was no sign of the drunken, dishevelled Kazimir she had met above the Orrery tavern. She prayed this meeting would prove more fruitful than the last.

'No need to apologize, Doctor,' she said. 'You have been through a terrible ordeal. And I caught you at an inopportune moment. I should have sent a letter. It's just that I've been so worried about Gavril.' She sat down at the little table. 'And I must confess, what you told me about your discoveries did little to allay my fears.'

'Will you try the ices, madame? They're the best in Mirom.'

'Ices?' Ice cream had been the last thing on

Elysia's mind. 'Oh, yes, thank you,' she said distractedly.

A waitress came past and Doctor Kazimir beckoned her over. 'Two sundaes,' he said. When the waitress had gone, he leaned forward and said in a low voice, 'There is something else you should know.'

'I'd hoped there would be more to this meeting than ices,' Elysia said, unable to resist smiling.

Kazimir glanced around, as though checking they were not overheard. The general noise of conversation and clinking spoons on glasses was enough to afford a little privacy.

'I may have mentioned Lilias Arbelian—' he began but broke off as the waitress appeared with two glass dishes filled with scoops of the brightly coloured ices.

'You said she was Volkh's mistress,' Elysia said bluntly. She picked up her spoon and began pressing the pistachio ice with it.

'I'm sorry I was so unsubtle.'

'No, no. Plain speaking. That's what I prefer.'

'What I didn't tell you', and Kazimir leaned forward across the table, 'is that she was working for Velemir.'

'Count Velemir?' Elysia said, genuinely surprised.

'Ssh.' Kazimir glanced around uneasily again. 'His agents are everywhere.'

'You mean she was officially representing Muscobar's interests in Azhkendir?' Elysia sampled the red raspberry sorbet; the flavour was both sweet and refreshingly sharp.

'Lilias?' An ironic little smile twisted Kazimir's lips. 'Good heavens, no, there was nothing official about Lilias. I mean she was sent to spy.'

Elysia laid down her spoon in the saucer. So the charming Count Velemir was Muscobar's spymaster. Suddenly she found she had lost her appetite for ice cream.

'You didn't know, madame?'

'No.' All Velemir's talk of diplomacy and embassies was merely a cover; how could she have been so blind? She tried to dismiss the sense of betrayal from her mind, but somehow she felt cheapened, naïve. 'But what was so important to Muscobar about Volkh?'

'His powers, of course.'

'I don't understand.'

'They thought your late husband had developed a weapon of massive destructive potential. They heard the stories of explosions, blue fire, hundreds, thousands dead. So they were more than a little perplexed when they heard the true explanation.'

'It does defy rational analysis, doesn't it?' Elysia said wryly.

'They had hoped for the recipe for a new kind of gunpowder that could be manufactured here and used to defeat Eugene's armies. Instead they were spun fairy-tales about flying dragons and shapeshifting wizards.'

It was all so ludicrous that Elysia wanted to laugh; she clapped one lace-gloved hand to her mouth to hold the laughter in.

'But your son, Gavril. He is in a decidedly tricky situation.'

Sobered, Elysia nodded.

'Did I tell you Lilias was pregnant?'

'Pregnant? With Volkh's child?' The possibility had not occurred to Elysia till now. She was not sure how she felt about the news.

'Well, no-one was entirely sure whose child, including Lilias herself.' Kazimir's expression had become cold and distant but Elysia sensed a slow simmering of suppressed emotion. 'But she made certain everyone thought it was Lord Volkh's.'

'You think it might be your child?' Elysia said, with a sudden rush of understanding.

Kazimir did not reply but beckoned the waitress over. 'Vodka,' he said.

'And for madame?' the girl asked.

'Nothing else for me, thank you,' Elysia said with a sigh. Vodka again. Was this where the conversation ended, just when it was beginning to prove fruitful?

Kazimir was silent until the vodka came in a slender glass bottle; he poured a measure and swallowed it in one gulp. Elysia watched, not knowing what to say.

'Lilias is a dangerous woman,' he said at last. 'Manipulative, clever – and very beautiful.'

'You are in love with her.'

'Was,' he corrected.

'In what respect is she dangerous?' persisted Elysia.

'She's ambitious. She wanted to be Drakhys, mother to the heir of Azhkendir.'

'And still spying for Muscobar? Oh, please!'

'I said she was dangerous. Dangerously fickle. Now that Lord Volkh is dead, do you think her aspirations have changed? Her son is to be Drakhaon.'

Kazimir reached for the bottle again but she put out her hand, covering the top. She wanted him to be lucid, not to slide back into inebriated incoherence. To her surprise, he did not protest.

'I should never have let myself be tempted. I should have been stronger. But she was lonely and I was lonely. You know what a dismal place Azhkendir can be in winter . . .'

'Yes,' Elysia said, remembering. 'I can see it would have been indelicate of you to stay.'

'I begged her to come away with me. But she refused! She didn't love your husband. She admired him, in her own warped kind of way, for his power – and his cruelty. Oh yes, that appealed to Lilias. But love?' His voice trembled. 'She doesn't understand the meaning of the word.'

He pushed back his chair, turning away from Elysia to gaze out over the mist-grey lake. Elysia thought she saw the glisten of tears in his eyes. In spite of herself, she found that she felt a little sorry for him.

'She must be a bewitching woman, this Lilias,' she said softly.

'And that is why your son, madame,' he said, clearing his throat, 'is doubly in danger. He is a threat to her ambitions.'

'Are you saying she is ambitious enough to try to kill my son?'

'I believe she used me, manipulated my affections, with the sole purpose of gaining access to the elixir. And then I believe she used it to poison Lord Volkh.'

'*Lilias?*' Elysia exclaimed.

'Now I've alarmed you. I'm so sorry. That was never my intention, madame, I assure you, I only wanted to—'

'Yes, yes.' Elysia nodded, angry with herself for

showing any sign of weakness. 'But you haven't really answered my question, Doctor Kazimir. How can *you* help Gavril?'

'Altan!' A man's voice rang out above the buzz of conversation. Heads turned to stare.

Elysia looked up and saw to her annoyance that the man she had met in Kazimir's room was forcing his way towards them. Matyev.

'Altan, where the hell have you been? Had you forgotten the meeting? Of the *philosophical* society?'

'Oh, sorry, Matyev, I must have lost all—'

Matyev picked up the vodka bottle; now he set it down hard on the table.

'And you've been drinking again! What use are you to our philosophical society if your brain's soggy with alcohol?'

Matyev had ignored Elysia during the whole exchange. She looked coldly at him.

'M-may I present Madame El—'

Matyev turned to stare at Elysia.

'We've met,' he said curtly, turning away.

'Elysia Andar,' Kazimir finished.

Matyev turned back. 'Andar? You are the portrait painter from Vermeille,' he said, eyes burning. 'You work for the Orlovs.' The scornful way he pronounced the name left Elysia in no doubt of his feelings. 'The Gardens are crawling with *his* men. How can you be sure she's not in his pay as well?'

'If you have an accusation to make, sir, at least make it to my face,' said Elysia, affronted by Matyev's belligerent manner. 'Do I take it to mean that you suspect me of some kind of double-dealing? Because – let me assure you – my meeting with the

347

doctor here is of a purely personal nature. And none of your business!'

'Madame is a friend—' Kazimir began.

'Altan, Altan, why still so naïve? Friend? When she keeps company with Butcher Velemir?' Matyev's voice trembled with anger. 'Haven't you heard, man? Stepan is dead.'

'D-dead?' Kazimir looked up, stricken.

'Stepan?' Elysia murmured.

'The official version is that he hanged himself in his cell. But they won't let anyone see the body, not even his wife Natalya. I say *they* put him to the question – and botched the job.'

'Do you think he talked?' Kazimir said, suddenly agitated, shaking hands reaching for his glass. 'Mentioned n-names?'

'Listen, you drunkard.' Matyev's hand clamped down on his wrist, stopping him raising the glass to his lips. 'Are we going to let this pass? Another "suicide" in custody? Another unofficial execution?'

'The regime is corrupt, we all know it,' Kazimir said. 'But what can we do?'

'Do? What can we do?' Matyev repeated in a harsh parody of Kazimir's tone of voice. 'I've just come from Stepan's house. Natalya's distraught, half-mad with grief. Four children to raise and her husband dead.' He glanced up and glared at Elysia. 'And now I suppose you'll go running back to your friends at court and blab all this out?'

'I can see why you have no reason to trust me,' Elysia said with chill disdain.

'You're in a privileged position. You could be of use to us.' Matyev's voice dropped, low and confidential as he leaned towards her across the table.

'You know details, intimate details of the Orlov household. Who will leave the palace, by which gate, at which times—'

'Matyev, no!' Kazimir interrupted.

'You're asking me to betray the confidentiality of a patron?' Elysia said, her voice brittle with contempt. 'Do you think I have no professional ethics?'

'You see?' Matyev said with a shrug which said all too obviously what he thought of her professional ethics.

That was enough. Why should she stay only to be insulted? Matyev might be passionate about his beliefs, but he was a boor. Elysia rose. 'It's getting dark; I must be going.'

'M-madame, I—' Kazimir struggled to stammer out an apology.

'Thank you for the ices, Doctor,' she said crisply. She had no wish to hear his excuses. She had wanted his help, and he had let her down. 'They were most . . . refreshing.'

She had the distinct impression as she threaded her way through the crowded tables that Kazimir had made a blundering move to come after her, but that Matyev had held him back.

Twilight had faded into night and the Water Gardens were shrouded in the gloomy autumnal fog that Elysia had already come to associate with Mirom. She shivered, pulling her cloak up to cover her mouth so that she did not breathe in too much of the damp, chill air.

That infuriating man Matyev! Twice now he had interrupted her meetings with Altan Kazimir – and twice now she had come away frustrated, with only glimmers of answers to her questions.

Lamps had been lit along the paths, but their thin light illumined little. As she hurried under the black, dank foliage and dripping branches, she began to wonder if she had taken a wrong turning. She had been walking briskly for some minutes and had come no closer to the gates.

Surely they would not lock the Water Gardens with so many people still inside the Tea Pavilion?

A man loomed up out of the fog. She slowed her pace, glancing behind to see if there was anyone else on the path. To her dismay, she realized she was quite alone. She turned around and began to hurry back the way she had come.

The man's pace hastened to catch up with her.

The path divided into two ahead; she grabbed her skirts and broke into a run, taking the left fork.

Mustn't panic. Try to retrace steps – find the Pavilion – be safe there.

She had lost all sense of direction now, but she could see the glow of a lamp up ahead. She began to hurry towards it – and ran straight into the arms of the shadow who was pursuing her.

'Steady there,' he said. The dim lamplight illuminated the warm brown eyes of Feodor Velemir.

'Count Velemir?' she cried. And then anger replaced relief and she shook herself free of his steadying grip. 'What were you doing! Following me?'

'Protecting you, madame,' he said with a wry smile.

'Am I so important that the spymaster of all

Muscobar must devote his valuable time to following me?'

'Ah. So Kazimir told you.'

'I wonder why you never thought to do so yourself.' To her annoyance she found she was trembling like a frightened schoolgirl. *Pull yourself together!* she told herself. Was she trembling with fear – or anger? 'But was it really me you were protecting? Or were you trailing someone else?'

He did not answer.

'I came to you for help, Count. I have answered all your questions with complete candour. And in return I have received nothing but evasions.'

Still he said nothing. The fog seemed to grow more dense around them. Then he said, 'Tell me what it is you want, Elysia.'

'I want to return to Vermeille. My work here is done. It's obvious to me that no-one here can – or will – do anything to help Gavril. Perhaps one of your agents, Count, could send word to my housekeeper, Palmyre, to tell her I am coming home?' And, pulling her hood closer about her head, she set out again along the path.

Velemir hurried after her, blocking her way again.

'Do you doubt me, Elysia? I made you a promise – and I always keep my word.' He spoke in a low, intense voice that sent a shiver through her. 'But these matters take time. And there have been distractions. Unwanted distractions.'

'What do you mean, distractions?' she said, exasperated. 'If you mean what happened to Stepan—'

'Stepan?'

Shadows loomed up out of the fog, people coming towards them from the Pavilion.

Suddenly he swept his arm around her, pulling her close as if about to kiss her. His breath was warm on her cheek, faintly sweet with anise. Too surprised to twist away, she heard him whisper, 'Forgive me, Elysia.'

The men walked on past – and when the sound of their footsteps had died away, he took her arm and began to hurry her along the path.

'Isn't it customary for the woman to slap the man's face in these circumstances?' Elysia said breathlessly.

'It was unpardonable of me to take such a liberty.' He spoke to her in a quiet, intimate voice, more the tone a confidant or lover might use. 'It was essential that I should not be recognized. Here, of all places.' He stopped, his hands still enclosing hers. 'Listen to me, Elysia. I don't know what you've heard or who told you. But I beg you, do not condemn me until you have learned all the facts.'

'Facts!'

'My carriage is waiting at the gates of the Gardens. The fog is growing thicker by the minute. At least let me take you back to the palace in comfort.'

Elysia sat in silence as Count Velemir's carriage rolled away from the Water Gardens into the drifting fog.

'You met our friend the doctor again?' Velemir said.

'Since you know everything about my comings and goings,' she began, 'it is hardly necessary for me to confirm or—'

'What's that noise?' Velemir raised the carriage blinds and leaned out.

Elysia listened. It was the same roar of shouting she had heard outside Saint Simeon's, the roar of an angry crowd.

'The street's blocked ahead,' the carriage driver called down. The carriage slowed to a standstill. 'Hundreds of people.'

Elysia looked out from her side of the carriage. The foggy darkness had turned from black to flickering red and gold. Torches. They had run into a torchlit procession.

'They've filled the Palace Square, Excellency. We may not get through.'

'Drive on, coachman!' Velemir ordered. 'I want to see what this is about.'

The shouting was louder now, the glow of torches brighter. Elysia thought she could identify words and a name.

'Stepan! Stepan!'

'Stepan the cobbler?' she said. 'The one who died in your custody?'

'Stepan the assassin,' Velemir said coldly. 'Remember? He tried to stab the Grand Duke.'

The street wound down towards the Winter Palace. The coach slowed to a crawl as they reached the square in front of the palace. People pushed around them, past them. From the coach window Elysia could see that the square was filled with a vast crowd, many bearing flaming torches whose glare cast red shadows on the white stucco walls of the palace. More ominous still, behind the high palace railings – behind the elaborate ironwork grilles with their spread-winged sea-eagles – the White Guard were ranged. The shouting of the crowd had become deafening.

'We shouldn't go any further,' Elysia whispered.

'Look.' He had not heard her. 'There's the ring-leader.'

As she followed his gaze she saw a man climbing up to stand on a herring-barrel outside the main gates, immediately beneath the gilded Orlov crest. The shouting slowly stilled as he raised his arms and some of his words carried to them across the square.

'Our brother Stepan dared to strike a blow for his comrades.'

'Stepan!' roared back the crowd.

'Now we must strike a blow for him. To honour his memory.' The rough, strident tones were familiar. She recognized him.

'Matyev,' she said under her breath. So this was their 'philosophical' society meeting. What had Kazimir got himself mixed up in? Was this the reason for Velemir's interest in the scientist? The fact that he kept company with insurgents? Or was mildly spoken, short-sighted Kazimir one of the rebels behind this uprising?

'You know this man?' demanded Velemir.

She could have bitten her tongue. Why had she spoken his name aloud? But his attention was already diverted.

'What's going on?' he muttered. 'What's Roskovski playing at?'

'Who is Roskovski?' Elysia asked, noticing a ripple of movement along the line of the White Guard behind the palace railings.

'He's giving the order to load and prime,' Velemir said, craning out of the window.

'To fire on the crowd?' Elysia said, horrified. 'It'll be a massacre.'

'You're right. Something has to be done.'

Suddenly he threw open the carriage door and jumped out. He clambered up onto the driver's seat, seizing the whip and reins from the driver.

'Feodor!' she cried.

'It's all right, Elysia, I'll take care of you.' The next moment, Elysia felt the carriage jerk forwards.

'Way! Make way!' Velemir shouted.

Elysia sat, tightly clutching hold of the strap as the carriage gathered speed. People in the crowd, taken by surprise, hastily jumped out of the way.

What was Velemir planning to do? Ram the gates? The carriage rolled from side to side, jolting and bumping over the cobbles. She could hear the outraged cries of the people in the crowd, could feel the thumps and thuds of stones and missiles hurled at the moving carriage.

'Hold your fire!' Velemir's voice rang out above the din.

The carriage swerved round in a tight arc, rocking wildly. Elysia's head cracked against the back seat. Dizzied, she realized that they had come to a standstill right in front of the railings. And then she heard Velemir's voice ring out again above the crowd's jeering, clear and strong as a brazen bell.

'Colonel Roskovski. *Hold your fire!*'

Elysia peered out of the little front window. Velemir was standing up on the driver's seat right above her head, facing the crowd.

'Who the hell are you?' barked a voice from behind the railings.

'Feodor Velemir!' Velemir replied. The name went rippling through the crowd on a low whisper, brushwood catching alight. 'And you can charge me with insubordination later, Colonel. But I will not let you fire on these good people. If they have grievances, we should listen to them.'

'I have my orders. Get out of the way, Velemir.'

'Feodor! They're going to fire,' Elysia cried.

'The Grand Duke cares about these people, Roskovski. *His* people. If one – just one of this crowd – is harmed, it will go ill with the soldier who fired the shot. I give you my word.'

'There he stands, Feodor Velemir, in his fine clothes!' Matyev cried to the crowd. His face, in the flaring torchlight, was contorted with fury. 'Why should you listen to him? All the Orlovs have given you are lies – and more gilded lies!'

'Stand clear, Count!' ordered Roskovski.

Velemir clambered down from the coach. Elysia watched in astonishment as he walked up to the railings as nonchalantly as if he were out for an evening stroll.

'Shoot if you must, Roskovski,' Velemir called out. He swung around, his arms flung wide as if embracing the crowd. The gesture was sublimely theatrical – and impossibly gallant. 'But you'll have to shoot me, too.'

'Down with the House of Orlov!'

'Justice! Justice for Stepan!'

What am I doing here? Elysia wondered. *Why did I ever come to Mirom?* She was almost beyond terror, possessed by a strangely detached sense of calm.

'Justice!' Velemir cried. 'I promise you justice!'

'Feodor, they'll tear you to pieces,' she whispered.

A stone whistled through the air, striking him a glancing blow on the temple. He staggered then righted himself again.

She held her breath, fearing a hail of stones, fearing to see him tumble to the ground, bloodied and battered.

The crowd's shouting slowly subsided until she could hear nothing but the crackle and spit of the burning pitch on the torches.

And in the silence there came another order, roared from behind the railings. The line of glowing matches went out, one by one.

'Tell your men to stand down, Colonel!' Velemir commanded. 'It's over. These good people will go home in peace – and I will personally hold an investigation into Stepan's death. I give you my word.'

'Your word!' Matyev echoed. He spat. 'Word of the Orlovs' spymaster. Worthless. No, worse than worthless.'

'You have grievances,' Velemir said, ignoring Matyev. 'We will meet and you can tell me your grievances. Together we can work to put them right. We can work together to build a new understanding. A new Mirom.'

Another man had appeared beside Matyev and was whispering urgently in his ear. There was something familiar about him. Elysia craned her head to try to see if she recognized him – and caught a glint of torchlight on the glass lenses of spectacles. Altan Kazimir? She prayed it was not, but the likeness was undeniable.

'Tomorrow, at ten in the Senate, I will meet with you and your representatives.'

Behind Matyev the great iron gates of the palace swung slowly open.

The carriage began to move forwards. Elysia saw

the silent line of the White Guard standing behind the railings. She waited, tensed, for the first stone to crash onto the carriage, for the first protester to break from the cover of the crowd and launch himself towards them. But no-one moved.

When she looked back to catch sight of Matyev, he – and his accomplice – had vanished into the crowd.

22

Gavril's head hurt. Ahhh, hurt came nowhere near; it throbbed, pounded, hammered . . . The pain flared purple and black like a thunder-filled sky. He couldn't remember so bad a hangover since his graduation night at the College of Arts . . . and he could remember little enough of that uproarious student riot of drinking.

He tried to open his eyes. Daylight flooded in, cruel, bright daylight, sharp as citrus juice. He shut his eyes again. Now he felt sick. A terrible, gut-aching sickness.

He retched, wincing and groaning as each heave only made his head pound more.

A viscous slime came up, vile, black and stinking of pitch.

What had he been drinking? He flopped over on his back, exhausted. And when had this drinking bout occurred? His mind was still blank. Why couldn't he remember what had happened? Had there been some kind of celebration? The waves of nausea still surged. The foul taste still tainted his mouth and throat. It was as if he were trying to expel some noxious poison from his body

Poison.

Terrified, he tried to open his mouth to cry for help. Had someone slipped him the same poison that had paralysed his father, leaving him helpless?

Where were the *druzhina* when he needed them?

He rolled over onto his stomach and began to squirm his way across the floor like a serpent, mired in his own slime.

'Help . . . me . . .' His voice sounded as if from far away, a pathetic whisper.

If only he could remember what had happened to him, if only his memory were not a blank. All he could see was mist, clouds of black, drifting moor-mist . . .

It was as if he had contracted some deadly wasting sickness, as if his whole body were corroding away. He half expected to look down and see his skin flaking off and noisome pus-filled fluids leaking through beneath . . .

Not black mist . . . but smoke, billowing smoke.

'Help me . . . Kostya . . .'

His throat burned now from the retching, as if he had vomited up some caustic liquid. His voice when he tried to call out again for help was seared to a smoke-dry whisper.

'Thirsty . . .'

His body was all burned-up, a charred shell. He craved water.

Why did no-one hear him? Why did no-one come?

He managed to drag himself forward another foot

or so only to collapse again. His hand clawed uselessly at the floor.

He found himself staring at his own hand as it
scrabbled ineffectually to grab hold of something –
anything – for support. The nails gleamed blue-
black like chips of coal, hard and ridged as talons.

Now he could only stare at his hand, mesmerized.
Had there been a fire? Was that why he could only
remember clouds of billowing smoke? Was that why
his whole body felt so alien to him? Had he been
burned in the fire?

Hangover, poison, fire . . . None of it added up or
made any sense.

All he knew was that he would die of thirst if no-
one came soon.

But now the thirst whispered to him of other
liquids, delicious beyond imagining. He had never
known thirst or hunger like this before in his whole
life.

The pounding in his head had become a thunder
of drums. All he wanted now was for the black
smoke to envelop him, to smother the last breath
from him and put him out of his misery . . .

'My Lord?' A head appeared above his, warrior
braids swinging about a weather-beaten, grizzled
face. It was a face he had never thought he would
feel glad to see. Until now.

'Kostya?' His lips felt parched dry, his tongue
swollen. The name came out in a croaking whisper.
'What's – happened – to me?'

'You must drink, My Lord. And plenty.'

Gavril felt someone raise his head and the rim of
a cup was pressed against his sore mouth. A cool
liquid splashed into his mouth; he tried to gulp it

361

down, trickles leaking down his chin, onto his neck and chest.

'Enough.' He turned his head away. 'Where – am I?'

'Klim,' Kostya said. 'In the tavern.'

'Feel – so – ill.'

Kostya stroked the hair from his forehead. Even so gentle a touch from the old warrior made a shiver of nausea ripple through Gavril's body.

'This is a proud day for us.' Kostya's voice was unsteady, and when Gavril tried to focus on his face, he saw that Kostya's eyes were glistening with tears. 'Now you have shown them. Shown the doubters you are truly your father's son. Now no-one will dare oppose you.'

The old man's words came and went like wisps of half-heard music drifting from an open window. Gavril could only see darkness and smoke, could only feel the next dark surge rising to engulf him.

'It will pass, lad,' he heard Kostya saying from beyond the darkness. 'And then we will talk of the future.'

He walked through a drifting smoke of dreams, searching in vain for water to quench his burning thirst.

A pool glimmered in the smoke. Dropping to his knees, he bent towards its glassy surface, hands extended to scoop up the cool water.

And saw eyes, blue as lightning, staring at him.

'Water alone will not quench our thirst, Gavril.'

Gavril halted, staring. The dry, subtle voice had spoken quite clearly – but all he could see was the reflection of the glittering blue eyes, blue as distant starlight in the dull pool.

'Who's there?'

'*You woke me, Gavril Nagarian.*'

'Who are you?' Gavril whispered.

'*I am your guardian. You are my host.*'

'I don't understand.'

'*Look into the pool. This is how I once was – and how you will become when I have refashioned you in my likeness.*'

The image rippled, slowly clearing. A creature stared back at Gavril, dark-winged, hook-clawed, its muscular body covered with the dull glitter of sapphire scales. A tumble of wild hair, blue-black, framed a strangely elongated face dominated by the gleam of those watchful, inhuman eyes.

A creature of air and darkness, a winged daemon-lord, cruel and powerful.

Gavril shook his head. 'I'm dreaming.'

'*Soon your dreams will become reality. Soon, Gavril.*'

Gavril opened his eyes to a cold dawn. He was lying in fresh linen on a bed in a bare room. Open shutters let in a grey snowlight, crisp and clean. He blinked. His head no longer pounded, his stomach had stopped churning. He felt cleansed – and empty.

Someone must have bathed him, washed the vomit from his hair, the shitslime from his body.

And he could remember nothing of it, nothing at all.

There was no taint of sickness in the room, the chill air smelled faintly of pine logs and snow. His breath, when he exhaled, made a little puff of steam.

He swung his legs out of bed.

'Feeling better, Lord Drakhaon?' Kostya appeared with a bowl of porridge. 'Now you must eat to build up your strength again. Hot porridge and honey. Honey for strength, oats for stamina.'

Gavril nodded. He wished Kostya didn't sound as if he were talking of one of his horses. But he was ravenous and bolted down the porridge.

'Now tell me what I am doing here,' he said, setting the empty bowl aside. He still felt a gnawing emptiness, although the porridge had filled his belly. More of a craving than an emptiness . . .

'You remember nothing?' Kostya said. 'Nothing of the steppe wolves?'

'Wolves?' Gavril said uneasily. Something nagged in his memory. A vivid flash of fur, claws and gnashing teeth.

'You and the search-party were attacked on the moors. A pack of steppe wolves. You used your powers, My Lord.' Kostya's voice trembled. He seemed almost overcome with emotion. 'You destroyed the wolves.'

'*I* did?' Fragments of memory spun in his brain, little firesparks that fizzled to smoke. Nothing made sense still.

'Even in Kastel Drakhaon we saw the flare light up the sky, felt the earth tremble. And so I came here straight away, knowing you would need me.'

'I used my powers?' Gavril had gone cold and faint. What was it his father had written in the secret will?

'*No matter what pressures and persuasions my people*

may use upon you, you must resist the urge to use your powers with all your strength.'

'You destroyed the wolves.' Kostya put his hand on Gavril's shoulder. 'Now no-one dare question your right to rule Azhkendir, Lord Gavril.'

'Every time you let the Drakhaoul within you take possession, you become less human. Poisons are released into your blood: poisons that will change you, both in body and soul.'

If only he had had the self-control to contain his anger, to fight the wolves with fire and man-made weapons . . .

'For now you must rest, My Lord. When you are feeling better, we will return to Kastel Drakhaon.' Kostya pulled the blanket around Gavril, tucking him in as if he were a child. Then he rose to his feet. 'I had the girl's things placed in here. Piotr said you wanted to return them to Sosia.'

The girl's things? Now Gavril remembered what the whole wretched expedition had been about. He looked where Kostya was pointing and saw the pitiful heap of Kiukiu's abandoned possessions.

Kiukiu, his one true friend and ally in all Azhkendir, was dead. He was alone now.

He lay back staring at the beamed ceiling. Tears leaked from his eyes.

He had to get away. He had to find Doctor Kazimir before this Drakhaoul within him burned away the last of his humanity.

The snow-wind whispered like wraith-pipes, thin and reedy, about Gavril's head as he and Kostya rode back onto the moors. Fresh snow had fallen in the night and the search-party's tracks had been covered with new, soft white flakes.

'You have no need to do this, My Lord,' Kostya said.

'I have to see where it happened.' Gavril was gazing around the bleak snowflats, looking in vain for some landmark to trigger a memory of the attack. Though the sky loured a pale dismal grey overhead, the reflected light off the snow hurt his eyes. He still felt drained and ill. He still craved . . . if only he could identify what it was his body demanded. Wine and aquavit had made his sensitive stomach cramp. Warmed milk had only made him sick again.

The damp snow-wind seemed to penetrate even the thick fur of his cloak, sending his body into little fever chills. He pulled the cloak closer, shivering and miserable.

'Here, My Lord!' Kostya had ridden ahead, up towards the brow of the little ridge.

Gavril's horse seemed reluctant to go any further, stamping the ground and shaking its head, snorting its refusal in gusts of steam from flared nostrils.

'He can still smell the wolves,' Kostya said, dismounting.

Gavril followed him on foot through the fresh snow to the top of the ridge. There he stopped, staring. Beneath the fine white granules of powdery snow, there was a bare crater. The ground was charred, bushes seared to stubs and stumps, bracken and heather burned to ashes. And in the snow-dusted ashes Gavril could just make out the blackened bones of wolf carcasses. Yet when he bent down to examine them, he saw not the long jaw-bones of a wolfish predator but an unmistakably human skull.

'*I* did all this?'

Now that he stood here, jagged fragments of memory returned: the glint of snarling fangs, the hot, fetid stink of feral breath. He saw himself thrown from his horse, sprawling headlong in the snow as the wolf paused to spring. He tasted the rank savour of fear again at the back of his mouth.

And then came the recollection – oh, so brief but so intense – of a moment of transformation, mind and body melded into one paroxysmal burst of energy.

After that there was nothing but a searing dazzle of blue in his mind and a chaos of shouting voices.

'You destroyed the whole wolf-pack,' Kostya said, clapping his arm about Gavril's shoulders.

Gavril looked dazedly at him out of the chaos of smoke and voices.

'These were not wolves but men.' He turned to Kostya. 'How can that be?'

'There's been some Tielen shape-shifting mischief at work here.' Kostya spat into the snow. 'Someone must have sent these creatures to find you, My Lord.'

'You mean to . . . assassinate me?'

'That's very much how it looks.' Kostya kicked at a ribcage and it crumbled away into sooty cinders.

'But who would have done such a thing?'

Kostya shrugged.

A group of women and children waited in the cold, to wave them farewell.

A small boy ran up to Gavril, cheeks burnished apple-red by the wind.

'Drakhaon—' he piped.

Gavril recognized Danilo, the child he had saved from the wolves.

'Thank you for rescuing me.'

So close to Danilo, Gavril suddenly became aware that there was an extraordinarily luminous bloom to the child, a gilded aura that seemed to breathe from every pore. A delicious freshness emanated from the boy's body. Gavril could see the blood coursing in the child's delicate veins, could smell its life-giving fragrance. Before he knew what he was doing, he had begun to stretch out one blue-clawed hand towards the child's slender neck to draw him closer . . .

Brown eyes stared trustingly up at him, wide and innocent.

What in God's name was he doing! Trembling, Gavril hastily withdrew his hand.

'Good boy,' he said in a choked voice, dry as cinders. 'Go back to your mother.'

Danilo scampered back and hid behind his mother's skirts.

'Why?' Gavril said as they rode away, his voice harsh with self-disgust. 'Why the child?'

Kostya glanced at him and Gavril saw his eyes were cold as honed steel in his scarred face. 'This is how it is. You must learn to accept what you are. You must learn to be Drakhaon.'

'How did my father live with it?'

Kostya looked at him warily.

'This terrible craving. How did he control it? How did he—'

'There were times', Kostya said flatly, 'when he had no control.'

The words burned into Gavril's mind. *No control.*

'What did he do? Did he go out and just take what he needed? How...' And he faltered, his imagination conjuring obscenely vivid images: crushed tender young flesh, warm blood flowing, red as summer rose-petals ...

'In the old days, there was a tribute paid to the Drakhaon. Young girls. The Drakhaon's Brides. That was put a stop to by your grandmother Marya.'

Gavril gripped hold of Kostya.

'Tell me what my father did.'

A sad look dulled the old man's eyes.

'He went out hunting. He took what he could find.'

'Young girls? Children?' Gavril gripped Kostya tighter, claw-fingers biting into the old man's bony shoulders.

'Only when he was half-mad with the hunger. And afterwards ... afterwards he was sick with self-loathing. He would lock himself away for days. I would hear him weeping and beating his fists against the walls.'

'How often?'

'As often as he used his powers.'

'And did no-one come looking for these ... lost children?' Gavril could hardly say the words.

'No-one dared to say a word against him. He was Drakhaon. Sometimes it was said a wild beast had mauled them in the forest, sometimes that they had died of a virulent wasting sickness.'

'And the children in Kastel Drakhaon? Were they spared?'

'The only way to protect them is the bloodbond.'

'Even little Artamon?'

'No need. Artamon is Nagarian, like you.'

Gavril slowly loosened his grip on Kostya's shoulders.

All his dreams of a life with Astasia Orlova now seemed like a cruel delusion. Once she learned the truth of his monstrous heritage, she would run from him, just as Elysia had fled his father.

Out of the mists he thought he glimpsed Astasia, hovering like a Snow Spirit, dark eyes staring down at him in horror and loathing.

'Welcome back, Lord Drakhaon.' Sosia stood on the kastel steps to greet him, clutching a woollen shawl tightly to her. Her voice spoke the customary words of greeting but her eyes betrayed her agitation.

Gavril swallowed hard. He had been dreading this moment. He dismounted and whilst one of the stable boys held his horse's reins, he undid the saddle-bags, taking out the damp bundle of Kiukiu's few possessions.

Sosia still hovered on the top step as though unwilling to move closer to see what he had brought back to her.

'I know,' she said in an unsteady voice. 'Michailo brought the news. The steppe wolves got her. Got my Kiukiu.'

Gavril could not find any words to say to comfort her; he placed the little bundle in Sosia's arms.

She nodded, then turned and walked away. He noticed then how stooped she had become, how slowly and uncertainly she moved, almost as if grief had aged her overnight. Had she been hoping against hope as he had for some last-minute miracle?

Gavril followed, fired with a grim purpose.

Kiukiu's death would not go unpunished. Those responsible would pay dearly.

Starting with Lilias Arbelian.

With Kostya at his shoulder, Gavril hammered on Lilias's door. Then, without waiting for anyone to answer, he turned the handle and flung the door wide open.

Dysis was sitting at her embroidery. As the door burst open, she jumped up with a little shriek, the bright silks falling from her lap to the floor.

Gavril strode on past her towards the doors to Lilias's chamber.

'Wait, My Lord—' Dysis ran to block his way but he moved more swiftly, throwing open the double doors.

Lilias and Michailo were sitting on one of the silk couches, deep in conversation, auburn and flax-fair heads so close together they almost touched. They sprang apart as Gavril came in and Lilias rose to her feet.

'Lord Drakhaon,' she said formally, although her green eyes glinted.

At the sight of her, so beautiful, so unrepentant, he felt the dark and dangerous anger began to simmer again. He clenched his fists, willing it away.

'I want you to pack your bags and leave my house, Madame Arbelian,' he said with equal formality. 'You will be gone by first light tomorrow.'

'You're turning me out?' she said. 'By what right—'

'I am merely fulfilling the conditions of

371

my father's will. I suggest you don't even try to charm or wheedle your way out, this time.'

'If this is about Kiukiu,' Michailo said, rising from the couch, 'then I don't see why Madame Arbelian should be punished. The girl tried to smother little Artamon. She had to go.'

'In all this we have heard only Madame Arbelian's version of events.' Gavril turned to stare at Michailo. 'Were you here, in this room, when it happened?'

Michailo held his gaze a moment – and then, slowly, sullenly, his pale blue eyes looked away.

'Michailo,' Kostya growled. 'Out. Now.'

Michailo looked as if he were about to answer back – and then thought better of it. He saluted Gavril and then turned to leave with a defiantly insolent swagger. Kostya, shoulders stiffly squared, marched after him.

There came a small, hiccoughing sound from the crib in the corner and Lilias moved to pick up her baby, cuddling him close. Suddenly Gavril was seized with an inspiration. She had schemed and plotted against him. Now it was his turn to play her at her own game.

'Perhaps I've been too hasty,' he said, forcing himself to hide his anger. 'The winter weather is so severe. And your little son is so young, so vulnerable. I'd like you to stay here until the blizzards die down.'

She stared at him. He saw with bitter satisfaction that he had caught her off-guard. She had not expected this. At last she said, eyes narrowed to slivers of jade, 'You are very gracious, Lord Drakhaon.'

'I shall send word to Azhgorod so that your house will be prepared for you – made warm so that little Artamon doesn't catch a chill.'

'My Lord is too generous,' she said, unsmiling.

He turned to leave – and at the door, stopped, as if suddenly remembering.

'Oh, and as I was not here at the time of his birth, I will arrange for a gift to be sent to Saint Sergius so that the monks may say prayers in thanksgiving for your safe delivery and ring the bells for the birth of your son.'

This time she said nothing. If what Kiukiu had overheard was right, Abbot Yephimy had been sheltering her lover, Jaromir Arkhel. Now, he calculated, she would live in constant dread that Jaromir would risk his life to see the child – and in coming back, expose her treachery. He would have a watch kept on her rooms, day and night.

Kiukiu's death would not go unavenged.

The Drakhaon's rooms were cold, the fire in the grate unlit. Tending the Drakhaon's fire had been Kiukiu's task.

Gavril stared at the empty grate, remembering how he had first met her. Little details seemed so poignant now that she was gone – like the way she had smudged a soot-smut on her nose in trying to rub it away. He had not realized how much he missed her till now.

Disconsolate, he went into the dressing-room to strip off his stained travel clothes. A bath, a long hot bath to ease away the aches of the winter ride, was what he longed for. But as he stripped down to his shirt, he began to notice little discoloured marks on his arms and shoulders, blue-flecked, like bruises – yet no bruise ever glimmered like these. They were more like the scales of a snake.

Dear God, was it not to stop with the fingernails and the face?

He heard the outer door open and close – and froze, hoping no-one would enter the dressing-room and see him naked. Then he heard the clank of a bucket and low scrape of a shovel. Someone had come to make up the fire.

Hastily he searched for clean clothes, pulling on a linen shirt to conceal the telltale marks of his blood-inheritance.

'What're you moping about like a wet washing day for, Ilsi?'

'None of your business, Ninny.'

'Don't call me that. And hand me that kindling.'

There were voices, girls' voices, inanely bickering in his bedchamber. He hoped they would light the fire quickly and go away.

'Ninny. Ninny Ninnyusha.'

'Just because your handsome Michailo hasn't talked to you in over a week . . .'

'He's been busy.'

'Yes,' in a smirking tone, 'with My Lady Lilias.'

There was the sound of a sharp slap, followed by an aggrieved little cry.

'He hasn't.'

'Has so. I saw him sneaking out of her rooms early one morning when Lord Gavril was away.'

Gavril began to listen with attention, his earlier irritation forgotten.

'I don't believe you.'

'Sosia sent me to do her fires. And I saw

him. Why don't you go watch for yourself if you don't believe me?'

'I will, then. I will so.'

Ninusha's snide comments might be no more than kitchen gossip, sharp-barbed to wound her friend's feelings, but Gavril saw a way he could put the situation to good use. Taking up his wallet, he pushed open the dressing-room door. The gossips dropped shovel and tinder in the grate with a clang and sprang to their feet.

'We didn't mean to disturb you, My Lord. We didn't know . . .'

Gavril recognized the two maids now; dark Ninusha with the languorous eyes and tart-tongued Ilsi, her pretty face pinched in a sulky frown.

'So you've also been working in My Lady Lilias's rooms?' he asked, affecting a careless tone.

Ninusha pulled a face; Ilsi nudged her sharply in the ribs.

'I want you to tell me if you notice anything – or anyone – out of the ordinary.'

He saw the maids glance uncertainly at each other.

'Here's money for your pains,' he said, 'and there'll be more if you have anything to report.'

Ilsi darted forwards and took the coins from his hand, as delicately as a little bird pecking crumbs. For a moment a strange sensation swept through his whole body and he found himself wanting to reach out, to seize her slender wrist and pull her back towards him . . .

'Dismissed,' he said, turning abruptly away. They scurried off and he heard the door click shut behind them. He put one hand to his burning forehead and found it was damp with pearls of sweat.

There had been an irresistible perfume in the room, the fresh scent of young, sweet flesh and blood.

Drakhaon's Brides.

An unnatural chill lingered in the Kalika Tower as if the spirit-wraith had left behind some ineradicable taint of winter. The broken windows in the study had been mended with plain glass yet the room was still as cold as the snow-encrusted gardens far below.

Hidden in a drawer in the desk lay the self-portraits Gavril had sketched before the coming of the steppe wolves. Now he took them out and gazed at them, comparing them to his reflection in the mirror.

Trick of the winter light or had his face altered again?

He stared at himself in the glass, frowning. His brows had become even thicker and more slanted, dark midnight gashes across his temples. And his eyes ... He leaned closer into the glass, almost squinting in his efforts to see more closely. His pupils had narrowed, and there was a glint of gold flecks in the striated blue of the iris.

Inhuman eyes. Drakhaoul eyes.

Had he begun to see the world differently through these alien eyes? Did the light fall differently, were the shifting colours and shadows of his world subtly altered? Still staring, he reached for the pen and inks and began a new sketch.

When it was finished, he set down his pen and waited for the ink to dry.

What he had drawn both appalled and fascinated him. It was a distortion, almost a caricature, of the earlier self-portraits – except there was no humour, not even of a maliciously capricious kind, in the portrayal.

The face with its brooding serpent's eyes glowered back at him from a cross-hatched background of shadows.

It was a face to terrify children, a daemon-face, cruel and alien. And this was just the start. What his father had written down was true, the process would only accelerate from now on.

The more his powers increased, the more monstrous he would become.

Astasia would no longer recognize him.

He sat in the cold staring at the portrait until it was too dark to see any longer.

'My Lord! My Lord!' Someone was tapping insistently at the door. He got up and went to open it to see Ilsi on the spiral stair outside, clutching a lantern.

'You said,' she said in little gasps, 'if anyone came—' She had been running.

'Who is it?' he said; the words came out more roughly than he had intended, and he saw her flinch.

She shook her head. 'Don't know. Don't know how he got in. Thought it was Michailo – but I've never seen him before—'

Gavril's heart began to beat overfast; had his ruse worked?

'Go get Kostya. Tell him to meet me outside her rooms. And hurry.'

'Just you try to stop me!' He caught a spark of malice in her eyes as she pattered away, fleet-footed, down the spiral stairs.

* * *

Jushko One-Eye, Kostya's taciturn second-in-command, was waiting outside Lilias's rooms with four of the *druzhina*.

'The Bogatyr's on his way, My Lord.' Jushko silently opened the door to let Gavril into the antechamber. Two *druzhina* stood guard outside, two followed them inside.

'Where is Dysis?' Gavril whispered to Jushko.

'In safe-keeping.' Jushko went to one of the candle-sconces on the wall and twisted it to one side, revealing a peephole cut in the panelling.

Gavril came forward and peered in.

Lilias's room was warmly lit by firelight and scented candles which let drift a drowsy scent of sweet summer meadows. Lilias was sitting on one of the sofas, her loose silk gown drooping off one shoulder, feeding her baby. Firelight gleamed on the soft curves of her bare shoulder and breast, glinted russet in her unbound hair. Gavril felt his face begin to burn; he turned away, ashamed to be playing the voyeur.

'When I heard about the child, I had to come.' A man spoke, his voice huskily deep. Gavril turned back to the spyhole, straining to see and hear. 'Did you really expect me to stay away?'

'And are you insane? If you're caught, it'll be the end for us both.'

'At least let me see him. Hold him.'

Lilias began to laugh, a low, throaty laugh that seemed to tremble on the verge of tears.

A man moved into Gavril's field of vision, a tall man, wrapped in a long, dark caped coat. Gavril felt his heart miss a beat; he knew him now.

Jaromir Arkhel.

23

Gavril watched as Jaromir Arkhel moved into the warmth of the firelight and gazed down at Artamon. He put out one hand gently to stroke the baby's cheek.

'He resembles you, Lilias,' he said. His voice shook.

'What did you expect? Scales? Claws?'

'That's not what I meant and you know it,' he said, less gently. Artamon stirred, as if sensing the tension, and whimpered. 'Is he *my* son?'

Gavril heard Jushko's sharp intake of breath.

'Why couldn't you wait?' she said. 'As soon as the snows stop I am to leave for Azhgorod. Why endanger us all_by coming here? They are watching my rooms, day and night.'

'You haven't answered my question.' There was a roughness in Jaromir's voice now that betrayed raw emotion, barely suppressed.

'I'm told that Nagarian children show no sign of

their inheritance till puberty.' Lilias went to lay Artamon down in his cradle, more intent, it seemed, on tucking in the embroidered sheets than on her conversation with Jaromir.

'Don't you *know*, Lilias?' Jaromir went up to her and placed his hand on her shoulder, gently turning her around to face him.

So this was Jaromir Arkhel, the man he was blood-bound to kill? Gavril saw only a tall, gaunt young man, whose dark eyes had haunted his dreams ever since the Drakhaoul first possessed him.

'Jaromir,' Lilias said, 'you have powerful friends. Why haven't they come to your aid?'

'Jaromir?' muttered Jushko. 'An Arkhel name . . .'

'Can you be sure your last communication was received?' Jaromir said. 'If they've heard nothing from us, they must believe we are dead.'

'We've both tried, Dysis and I, day and night, but since the snows started, nothing seems to work any more.'

A sudden gust of wind battered the kastel and in the grate the log-fire began to crackle and spit sparks.

'*It* is blocking us.' Jaromir shivered, glancing uneasily over his shoulder towards the window. 'Do you have any idea what we unleashed when we – we did what we did?'

She held up a hand as if to silence him. 'Please. No more of these archaic Azhkendi superstitions.'

'Can't you sense it, Lilias? There will be no end to this bitter winter until I am dead.'

She let out a little exclamation of annoyance.

'If you won't take action, then I must. I have my son's interests to consider now.'

Her son's interests. Gavril's throat tightened, knowing she meant his death.

'I've heard enough.' Jushko drew his sabre. 'Now!' He kicked the door to Lilias's salon open and ran in, followed by the waiting *druzhina*. 'Arrest them!'

The baby let out a terrified yell and began to cry, a high, breathless sobbing.

Behind Lilias, a small secret doorway lay open, the gold and magenta tapestry that had concealed it pulled to one side. Jushko and the two *druzhina* struggled to haul out their quarry from the secret passageway.

Gavril watched as Jaromir was dragged back into the chamber. He saw how the *druzhina* caught hold of him by the arms, yanking them behind his back, roughly forcing him down onto his knees.

'Here he is, My Lord,' Jushko said, breathless but triumphant. He jabbed the point of his sabre under Jaromir's chin until Jaromir sullenly raised his head. 'I believe this is the one we've been looking for.'

'How dare you invade my privacy, Jushko?' Lilias spoke, her voice low yet controlled. 'Where is Dysis? What have you done with her?'

'Take them away for questioning,' said Jushko, ignoring her.

Two of the *druzhina* went towards Lilias.

'Don't you dare to touch me!' she spat, drawing away from them. 'I am a citizen of Muscobar. A visitor in your country. I have rights. I demand to see a lawyer.'

'Let her go.' Jaromir spoke for the first time. Gavril could see a tiny trickle of crimson on Jaromir's neck where Jushko's blade had drawn

381

blood. 'Whatever your charges are, she is innocent.'

'Did I say you could speak?' Jushko struck Jaromir with the back of his hand. Jaromir's head snapped back with the force of the blow. 'Keep silent.'

Artamon yelled even more furiously. Gavril's ears began to ring with the sound.

'Take the woman to the Bogatyr's rooms for questioning,' Jushko commanded. 'Under armed guard.'

'Lord Gavril!' Lilias cried as she was hustled past him. Her green eyes glistened with tears. 'Don't let them hurt my baby.'

Gavril looked away.

'At least let me have Dysis.' Tears spilled out, down her pale cheeks. 'Don't leave me all on my own with your soldiers, My Lord. Please.'

Gavril, distracted, half-heard himself saying, 'Very well. Let the maid be brought to Madame Arbelian.' All he could think was that Jaromir Arkhel was his prisoner. Now there was no escaping the blood-curse his father had placed on him. He stood alone in Lilias's empty room, paralysed, unable to move.

What, in God's name, would the *druzhina* expect of him now? To take part in some archaic ritual, a barbaric duel to the death? He shuddered at the thought.

In the hallway below, he could hear Kostya briskly issuing orders.

'No-one allowed in or out but myself. No matter what story she spins, no matter what excuse, "My baby's sick, dying . . ."'

'What have you done to my mistress?' Dysis

hurried up, escorted by Michailo and several of the *druzhina*. Her usually neat clothes were in disarray, locks of brown hair were escaping from her lace coif.

'Michailo?' Kostya broke off in the midst of his orders, frowning. 'I put you on keep-watch. What are you doing here? You were forbidden kastel duties.'

'Are you all right, My Lady?' Michailo asked Lilias, ignoring Kostya.

'Back to the keep!' thundered Kostya. 'Till you've learned some respect.'

'I'm taking no more orders from you, old man,' Michailo said. 'Let her go.'

'You young fool—'

Gavril heard the rasp of steel. Then a sharp retort. Light and fire exploded in his mind.

Pistol shots. How could there be pistol shots in Azhkendir where he had never yet seen a single firearm?

Flares of violent red splashed across his vision, fire and blood. Darkness gusted, cold as winter stormclouds through his mind.

A terrifying void gaped at his feet.

He blinked – and found the whole kastel was in disorder. Maids were screaming, men of the *druzhina* clattered up and down the stairs, brandishing sabres and axes.

Now the shouts were coming from outside the kastel. Gavril ran to the window to look down on the courtyard.

A sleigh sped away across the snow, drawn by two sturdy horses. Behind it galloped a small escort of horsemen.

Druzhina were leading out their horses from the stables, scrambling up into the saddle, spurring after them.

'She's escaped,' Gavril said under his breath.

'Lord Drakhaon!'

In the hall below, he saw several of the *druzhina* leaning over a prostrate form. A slowly pooling stain of red leaked out onto the black and white tiles. As he leaned far out over the stair-rail he saw from the iron-grey braids that it was Kostya.

He flew down the stairs towards the gathering crowd.

'Let me through!' They drew aside when they heard his voice. 'What's happened here?'

Sosia was crouched beside Kostya; she had lifted the Bogatyr's head and was supporting it on her knees. From the grey pallor of his battle-scarred face, from the blood trickling at the side of his mouth, Gavril could see he was badly wounded.

'How could Michailo do such a thing?' Sosia said, her voice tight with unshed tears. 'To his own commander?'

'Where's the surgeon?' Gavril cried. 'Bring the surgeon here!'

'Lord Gavril?' Kostya's hand reached out and gripped his. His eyes opened but they were unfocused. 'She's gone. I tried to stop them . . .'

'Don't try to talk,' Gavril said. 'Save your strength.' His voice trembled; he made an effort to steady it. 'And that's an order, Bogatyr.' Now he could see that blood was oozing from a hole in Kostya's side, the ruined fabric scorched and burned. Whoever had fired had done so at close range.

384

The surgeon came hurrying up, shooing the crowd out of the way.

'What's this, Bogatyr?' he said briskly. 'A pistol-wound?' He began to peel away the layers of blood-stained clothing.

'Never held with all those newfangled gunpowder contraptions,' grumbled Kostya weakly. 'No honour in them. Weapons for cowards . . .'

'Who brought pistols into Kastel Drakhaon?' Gavril turned to the watching servants. As he looked up at them, he saw the apprehension in their faces, saw them draw back. He realized they were afraid of him.

'That . . . cursed . . . Muscobar whore . . .' Kostya said from between clenched teeth.

'*Lilias* shot you?'

'We'll have to move him, My Lord,' the surgeon said, keeping one hand on Kostya's pulse. 'He's losing blood too fast.'

'Not Lilias . . .' Kostya's voice was fading. 'Michailo . . . betrayed me . . . divided the *druzhina* . . . broke the bloodbond . . .'

'Easy now, Kostya,' Gavril said, squeezing his hand.

'Shameful . . . way to die . . .' Kostya whispered.

'No talk of dying here!' the surgeon said. 'And no more talking, Bogatyr. Save your strength.'

Four of the *druzhina* lifted Kostya and carried him away.

Gavril stood watching them, his heart chill and heavy. First Kiukiu, now Kostya. Lilias had worked a subtle kind of destructive mischief in his household, attacking those closest to him. Now who was there left to trust?

A smothered sniffing sound distracted him; in a doorway he saw Ilsi weeping into her apron.

'Don't cry; the Bogatyr is strong, he'll pull through,' he said, trying to sound reassuring.

'I'm not crying for Kostya, I'm crying for Michailo, the deceiving, two-timing bastard!'

'Stop snivelling, Ilsi!' Sosia came out of the kitchen carrying a bowl of steaming water in which pungent wound-herbs were steeping. 'Take this to the Bogatyr's chamber – and don't spill it.'

'Lord Drakhaon.' It was Jushko; his usually impassive face was twisted into a scowl. 'We've failed you, My Lord. He's given us the slip. Got away. In the confusion.'

'The prisoner?'

'The gold-haired Arkhel. The one she called Jaromir.'

'You let him go?'

'When the Bogatyr was shot, My Lord—'

'There are other casualties?'

'We've two *druzhina* dead, that's Nicolai and young Boris; both cut down in the stables. Three others wounded, not counting the Bogatyr. I reckon that about twenty or so have followed Michailo.'

Two dead. So it had been their deaths that had flared blood-red through his mind, disorienting him, bringing him to the brink of the abyss.

'We'll track them down,' Jushko said grimly. 'They'll pay the price. And after we've done with them, no-one in Azhkendir will ever dare betray the Clan again.'

'And this Jaromir Arkhel went with them?'

'No, My Lord. We're searching the grounds for him now. Though we did find this.' He held out a little pistol, exquisitely fashioned for so lethal a weapon, the handle inlaid with mother-of-pearl, the muzzle stained black with burned powder.

Gavril took it and examined it. Michailo would never have thrown it away if he had fresh powder or shot. Perhaps, in his ignorance of firearms, he had neglected to bring fresh supplies with him?

He hurried back to Lilias's rooms and began to search, pulling out drawers, throwing open chests, tossing their contents on the floor. In vain. Until he remembered the baby's crib. The last place anyone would think to look . . .

Concealed beneath two soft down mattresses he found the box, rosewood, inlaid with mother-of-pearl and silver. And inside, nestling in the grey velvet lining, a little phial of gunpowder and one single bullet.

As he loaded the little pistol, his mind moved on one matter alone.

The *druzhina* had failed to find Jaromir Arkhel the first time. But they had been searching the grounds and outhouses. Any fugitive who knew the hidden passageways could lie low in any of the ruined rooms in the East Wing, deep inside the bowels of the kastel, until the search was called off.

Snowlight filtered into Doctor Kazimir's abandoned laboratory, turning the dust to glittering powder-frost.

Gavril moved noiselessly through the empty rooms, examining the dusty floor for any traces of an intruder. Finding nothing, he hurried on towards the Hall.

The blizzard had blown snow through chinks in the boarded windows to lie in little drifts on the floor.

From the upper gallery he leaned over the rail and saw – with bitter satisfaction – the unmistakable pattern of footprints leading away below the ruined stair.

Carefully edging his way down the precarious sweep of the broken staircase, he checked again for prints in the chill light. Bending down, he saw the marks of a man's boots in the wet snow. Fresh marks. His hand crept to check the little pistol which he had concealed in his jacket pocket. Lilias had – unwittingly – given him one significant advantage over his quarry.

The wet trail of prints led him to a low doorway so obscure he had completely missed it on his last exploration. He would have to go mole-blind into the darkness, with no lantern to give his quarry warning.

He squared his shoulders and drew out the pistol, gripping the handle with sweating fingers.

The tunnel wound on into earthy blackness. Doggedly he moved onwards, one hand feeling his way along the rough wall, the other clutching the pistol.

And then a glimmer, faint as a daystar, wavered far ahead. He began to hurry, moving gladly towards it without thought of anything but escape from this claustrophobic tomb.

Daylight pierced the darkness like a shard of ice. This tunnel, unlike the one that ended so abruptly beneath the summerhouse, had been more subtly engineered and wound gradually upwards until he could see a grating – the source of the light overhead.

Gavril moved warily now, placing one foot before the other as stealthily as he could, listening for the slightest sound.

His adversary could be waiting for him in the darkness. It could all end here in one swift, assassin's blow.

Metal rungs in the wall led up to a trap-door; it required all his strength to lift it, putting his shoulder into the task. Emerging from the tunnel headfirst, he felt a rush of cold air, snow-chilled.

He was in what looked at first glance to be an abandoned watchpost, an old tower whose mossy stones were smothered with ivies and old man's beard.

Gavril pulled himself up out of the tunnel and heaved the rotting wooden trap-door back in place. Close to the trap-door he noticed a rusting brazier choked with fresh cinders; when he tested them, some were still warm to the touch.

Someone had been hiding out in here, sheltering from the blizzard.

Heart beating fast, he hurried to the doorway.

The tunnel had brought him to a ridge on the edge of the forest. He was gazing down at the sprawl of buildings that was Kastel Drakhaon. Below he could see sentries patrolling the boundary walls, the watchtowers, the black pennants fluttering on the weather-vanes, smoke rising from the chimneys.

He wanted to shout aloud in sheer frustration at the fate which had doomed him only to find an escape when it was too late to be of any use to him.

Snow had covered the forest, muffling it in a white winter's cloak. Gavril's breath clouded the cold, still air as he searched for prints. The birds were silent; only the meandering trails of tiny claw-marks in the snow hinted that they had been out scavenging for food.

Soon he found what he had been searching for: fresh bootprints winding away from the watchpost deep into the forest.

For a moment he hesitated. He was in the forest alone and with only a single bullet for self-defence.

And then that chill, weary voice sighed again through his mind:

'*So . . . cold . . . So . . . very . . . tired . . . Help me, Gavril. Help me end it. Set me free.*'

Gavril buttoned the collar of his fur-lined jacket against the cold and set off in amongst the trees, eyes fixed on the trail of prints.

The snow was so thin here beneath the thick canopy of the branches of the great trees that the trail of prints was petering out, difficult to distinguish in a carpet of old pine needles, dry leaves and moss. And for the last hour or so the trail had led upwards, a slow ascent through mountain firs and whispering pines.

Frustrated, Gavril halted and leaned his aching back against a knotted pine trunk. He was thirsty now and his feet were sore from tramping through the forest over tree roots and pine cones.

To have come this far, only to lose the trail . . .

Disheartened, he sank down, back sliding against the rough trunk until he was sitting on one of its gnarled roots. He had not taken as much trouble as he should to mark his way; now the light was beginning to fade.

He began to suspect that Jaromir Arkhel had purposely led him on this wild-goose chase to shake him off his trail. Jaromir had been born in this wild country; he must know it as intimately as Gavril knew the coves and cliffs around Vermeille Bay.

Damn it all! Gavril struck his fist against the pine trunk. He had not come this far to be Jaromir Arkhel's dupe.

Somewhere on the borders of his mind he could sense a dull confusion of voices; the *druzhina* were still at large, searching the snow-bound moorlands for Lilias and Michailo.

'*We will always know where you are . . .*'

Did they know precisely where he was now?

And if he needed them, would they come to his rescue in time?

Gavril tramped on towards the fading light until he saw that what he had thought to be the brow of the incline he had laboured up was the rim of a steep escarpment.

Above and beyond loomed the grim shadow of a jagged mountain peak, half-hidden in snowclouds. He stood on the brim of a deep drop; the land fell away beneath the ridge in gullies and grey screefall. Behind him the dark green of the forest went rolling away into the distance – but immediately below lay an endless expanse of bleak moorland, powdered white with snow. And on the far western horizon, the angry flames of the setting sun pierced the louring pall of grey.

The prospect was at once so desolate yet so starkly beautiful that Gavril stood staring down at Azhkendir, all fatigue and frustration forgotten.

He was alone. There was no sign or sound of life in this still mountainscape, not even the cawing of crows or mountain choughs.

Was this where the Arkhel lands began? Was this the wasteland his father had created in his devastating quest for revenge?

And then he heard the sound of a distant bell tolling from deep in the forest below. Puzzled, he gazed back over the forest trees, searching in vain for a sign of a bell-tower or spire. If it were the sound of the monastery bells, the buildings must be hidden close by in the heart of the forest.

Better to make his way towards the sound of the bell and ask the Abbot to give him refuge for the night. But how far could he trust Yephimy, knowing he had sheltered the very man who was now his quarry? For all he knew, this could be another plot to lure him to his death . . .

He turned back to the drab mountainside, scanning the rocks one last time.

He looked and then looked again, blinking, in case his eyes had betrayed him in the failing light.

Something – no, someone – was moving against the sheen of snow, slowly, steadily progressing upwards.

Gavril let out a shout.

The figure paused a moment, glancing back over its shoulder. And then it continued its unhurried ascent, as if ignoring the fact that he was in pursuit, confident that it would elude him.

Gavril forgot that his legs and back ached, forgot the brooding despair that had haunted his progress through the forest.

So Jaromir Arkhel thought he could best him!

Did he think he was some soft southerner, too scared to save his own skin to venture into mountainous terrain?

And then the need to concentrate on finding a firm foothold amidst the treacherous shale drove all other thoughts from his head. Now as the gully narrowed, it became a matter of clinging to the jagged rocks to pull himself up, hand over hand.

Even though the last rays of the sinking sun still lit the western sky with a flare of fire, night began to darken this side of the mountain. And with the night came the cold, intense and penetrating. Gavril struggled up to the top of the gully to find that the snowfield above and overhanging rock buttresses were glistening with fast-freezing ice crystals.

And yet, in spite of nightfall, Jaromir Arkhel still toiled on upwards across the snow.

Gavril's laboured breath gusted in puffs of steam on the chill air. His ribs were sore. He stared at his quarry, now little more than a blurred shadow against the dull sparkle of snow. Jaromir Arkhel must be making for a hut, a mountain refuge, hidden high above the snowline. Why else would he be trudging on upwards into the night?

At this moment, he was aware that Gavril Andar the painter would have shrugged, turned away and gone home. But this new Gavril could not go back. He could only go on.

The snow was not as thick here as it had looked from the forest ridge; it had settled in crevices, sheening the rocks with a glisten of white. As night's cold intensified, it was rapidly freezing underfoot. Now he began to understand why Jaromir had been moving so slowly. But he was used to climbing slippery rocks; even though those in Vermeille Bay were treacherous with the slime of seaweed and algae, they were no less difficult to negotiate.

As he moved doggedly on, teeth clenched against the burning cold of the night air, he realized he was gaining on Jaromir. His quarry was slowing, tiring. The distance between them had halved.

He stumbled, clutching at an overhanging rock to steady himself.

One foot slid out over the edge.

His heart thudded as dislodged stones went spinning away from beneath his dangling foot into the gully below, rattling far down into the darkness.

He forced all his strength into pulling his whole body back onto the rock. He slumped there, cheek against the rough granite, clutching the contours of the rock.

Narrow escape.

The air seemed thinner here. His head was spinning. When he gazed back down at the darkening moorlands, the dizziness increased.

Steady there, steady . . .

He forced himself to control his gasping breaths, to look upwards, not at the dizzying drop below.

So close now.

So close he could see his quarry clearly against the snowfield. His hand crept to the pistol's handle. At this distance he reckoned he could easily pick him off. If . . .

A sudden gust of wind came shivering from out of the night. Its keen bite woke him, cleared his head.

He primed the pistol and set off again, head down against the wind, tramping on upwards.

'*Jaromir!*' He had shouted the challenge aloud

before he knew what he had done. The name echoed around the mountain like a trumpet call to battle.

He saw the toiling figure up ahead halt and look round. But then – almost as if thumbing his nose at his pursuer – he merely turned away and carried on.

A flare of rage blurred Gavril's sight.

'It's over, Jaromir Arkhel!' he shouted, hastening his pace. His words came echoing back, ringing with ice and fire. He raised his arm, taking aim, closing one eye as he took a step forwards. 'It's—'

His feet slid from under him.

The shot – a crack as loud as splintering ice – went wide.

This time he couldn't save himself. The pistol fell from his hand and went bouncing away down into the ravine. He grabbed in vain at the icy rock and felt the jagged stone grazing his fingers, sharp as razors.

He tried to cling on but the burn of the ice was numbing his bleeding hands. Blood smeared the clear sheen of ice. Even as his dangling feet fumbled for a foothold, his numbed fingers lost their grip.

And then he was sliding, clutching helplessly at the ice-sheened stone, tumbling down, down – till he plummeted over the edge.

Into the void.

24

It had started to snow again. Kiukiu lay huddled under blankets beside the embers of the dying fire. A blizzard howled about the chimney and stray flakes were sucked down to sizzle amongst the embers. She thought she could make out another sound behind the wind's howling, the distant, eerie song of wolves, prowling for prey. Although she knew she was safe, protected by the thick, rugged stones of the cottage, she still shivered to hear that desolate sound. Even the owls shifted uneasily from claw to claw on their rafter perches high above.

She could not sleep. Her fingertips were scored raw from the wire strings of the gusly, and her head jangled with the clumsy, tuneless sounds she had made. She had worked hard to try to please her grandmother, but each lesson always ended with Malusha's sighing. A lifetime's work to make up. What if she wasn't good enough? What if Malusha gave up on her? What if—

Kiukiu's mind jittered from one worry to another. What was happening back at the kastel? Was Lord Gavril safe? Had he come looking for her? That cataclysmic blue blaze, lighting the dusk sky like the ripple of northern lights – had that truly been his doing? She shifted onto her other side, pulling the blankets up over her head, but still she couldn't sleep. Malusha's words kept repeating in her mind, a dull, distant chant:

'*Your young Lord Gavril is no longer human, Kiukiu. Nagarian bad blood will out, sooner or later. He has become truly Drakhaon.*'

She had tried to reason with her grandmother, had tried to explain that Gavril was different from the other Drakhaons, but Malusha was resolutely deaf to her pleading. She had even, in a moment of vexation, rapped out, 'If your Lord Gavril is such a hero, then go back to him, young lady! See if he is as kind to you now that the Nagarian blood has caught fire in his veins. See if he can resist the urge to put you to *other uses*.'

'What other uses, Grandma?' Kiukiu had asked.

'Heavens, child, you grew up in Kastel Drakhaon and you ask *me* to tell you?' Firelight flickered on Malusha's lined face. 'Have you never heard of the Drakhaon's Brides?'

'Sosia said it was all nonsense to frighten wicked children,' Kiukiu said defensively.

'The Drakhaons cannot keep their human appearance for long without young, fresh blood. You know the old dragon tales. The maiden sacrifices, the children found dead in the forest—'

'But Lord Volkh found a cure,' Kiukiu insisted. 'He brought a man from Muscobar, a scientist—'

'A *what*?' Malusha screwed up her eyes in a frown of incomprehension.

'A learned doctor. And he made up some kind of elixir which cured Lord Volkh. Only it reduced his powers as well . . .'

'That's as may be,' Malusha sniffed, 'but you saw what I saw, plain as plain. Drakhaon's Fire. Your Lord Gavril doesn't seem much interested in using that elixir.'

Kiukiu opened her mouth to argue, and then shut it again. What was the use? Malusha hated the Clan Nagarian and would hate them to her dying day.

'And you should hate them too,' Malusha said. Kiukiu jumped. How had she read her thoughts? 'They took your father and mother from you.'

'My father.' Kiukiu was grateful to change the subject. 'You said you would teach me how to seek out my father.'

'Pfft!' Malusha made a little noise of contempt. 'You are not going to meet your father until I've made a proper Guslyar of you. Besides, you haven't the skills yet. You must practise, practise, practise. Why are we wasting time talking, child? Get back to your exercises.'

A blizzard howled about the little cottage, fierce gusts of wind rattling the shutters and doors.

Kiukiu winced as she plucked at the cruel wire strings of the gusly. Little drops of red shimmered on the strings; her fingertips had begun to bleed again. She blinked back tears of pain and frustration. It was so *hard*. Learning to find the right notes was difficult enough but the mental challenge combined with the constant bleeding of her raw fingers made it almost impossible to pluck the strings.

'It's no use!' she cried, pushing the instrument of torment aside so roughly that the strings let out a mocking little jangle of sound. 'I can't do it. I shall never be able to do it. It hurts too much.'

A sudden violent gust burst the door open, slamming it against the rough-stone wall. Startled, she leaped up and ran to force it shut. The wind moaned in the chimney as snow spattered down onto the fire, dampening the flames. And it seemed to her now that she could hear words in the blizzard wind as it stormed across the moors.

'That's no ordinary storm,' Malusha said, pulling her patchwork shawl closer about her shoulders. 'That's the raging of a spirit-wraith out of control. Can't you sense it?'

'Lord Volkh?' Kiukiu said in a whisper.

'Who else?' Malusha went over to stoke the failing fire.

'So it's all my fault,' said Kiukiu miserably. 'Can nothing be done to stop it? Even Abbot Yephimy and all his monks failed.'

'Well, of course they failed.' Malusha turned, the flaring firelight emphasizing the scorn in her eyes. 'They were not the ones who brought the spirit back, were they?'

Kiukiu began to understand. 'You're saying I must do it?'

'It's that or seek out and kill his murderer.'

'His murderer?' Now Kiukiu could only think of the overheard conversation in the summerhouse; even if Jaromir had fought Lord Volkh face to face, Lilias was part of the conspiracy. And much as she hated Lilias Arbelian, she had no desire – or stomach – to kill her.

'Blood will lay one ghost, but only create another. That's not our way.'

'But I don't know where to start.' Kiukiu held up her swollen, scored fingers to the firelight. 'And how can I try when my fingers just won't heal?'

'Then we must harden your fingertips first.' Malusha took out an earthenware pot of a creamy ointment and began to rub it gently into the cuts. 'You can do little until they are healed.' Kiukiu bit her lip, trying not to cry out as the ointment burned its way into her raw flesh.

'At least this way the only blood on my hands is my own,' she said, attempting a wry smile.

Kiukiu lost count of the days she had spent with her grandmother. The endless winter snows blotted out the passing of time; the short daylight hours seemed to flicker past so swiftly.

Her raw fingertips began to heal. Her nails grew and Malusha made her paint them every night with a foul-smelling unguent to strengthen and harden them. And as the pain of playing the sharp strings grew less, Kiukiu's skills increased. Now she could remember the whole sequence of note patterns Malusha had patiently taught her.

She still fumbled some of the individual notes – but as Malusha had also taught her to relate each of the seven fundamental pitches to the vibrant colours of the rainbow, she would murmur as she played, 'Blue – yellow – blue – red . . .' And after a while, the colours would vibrate in her mind as vividly as the sounds, creating starbursts of intense rose-crimson, dazzling sun-yellow or piercing azure-blue. Outside the winter landscape was a dull shimmer of white, but in Kiukiu's soundworld, the colours were as bright and clear as summer.

One bitter-cold morning Malusha opened the old lacquer chest and took out a rolled scroll of vellum, soft and creased with age. She spread it out on the floor and Kiukiu saw that it was dark with writing in a strange and antique script. Illuminated letters, jewelled with tiny birds and flowers, were dotted here and there amidst the slanting pen strokes.

'Now it is time for you to learn the names and lineage of the House of Arkhel. Off you go, here at the top.'

Kiukiu stared unhappily down as her grandmother stabbed one gnarled finger at the unfamiliar letters. Malusha had never thought to ask her if she had learned to read.

'What's the matter, child?' Malusha said sharply. 'Can't read?'

'Not well,' Kiukiu said in a shamed whisper. 'Sosia started to learn me my letters, but she was always so busy . . .'

Malusha let out a little sigh of exasperation.

'Then we shall have to do it all by rote. At least you should know Lord Stavyor first and his poor, dead children. Such beautiful daughters, such brave sons . . .' She began to recite in a low, singsong voice a list of names, making Kiukiu repeat them back to her.

'Dead, all dead,' Malusha whispered under her breath. 'Even my little Jaromir whom I sang to sleep in his cradle when his mother was too sick to nurse him . . .'

'Jaromir Arkhel?' Kiukiu stared at her grandmother. 'But he isn't dead.'

'Child, don't be foolish. They were all killed.'

'It's true,' Kiukiu said staunchly. 'I've *heard* him speaking. I almost caught sight of him.'

'It must be some pretender, some impostor—'

'He mentioned a monastery. Saint Sergius. Said the monks sheltered him.'

'Why do you only tell me this here, now?' hissed Malusha.

Kiukiu fell silent. She had her reasons.

'Surely,' she said hesitantly, 'you would have seen him with his father in the Ways Beyond, if he were dead?'

'Child, child, he was only a boy, no more than nine years old. His father's spirit is bound to reside with the other ancestor-warriors in the Hall of Arkhel. There are no children in that place. D'you understand me, Kiukiu? Lord Stavyor believes all his family died that night of fire and devastation.'

Kiukiu's dreams began to be woven through with little threads of glittering sounds, evanescent wisps of melody that melted away as soon as she awoke. When she told Malusha about them, her grandmother nodded her head for a while, eventually contenting herself with saying, 'Good, good, good.'

'Why can't I remember them?' Kiukiu said, frustrated.

'Oh, you will one day, child, you will. These are dream-songs. They emanate from the Ways Beyond.'

'From the *dead*?'

'Is that so very difficult to accept?' Malusha's eyes had become dark and deep as a forest pool. 'Soon we will go across together.'

'To find my father?' Kiukiu cried excitedly.

'Not yet, not yet. It is still too soon.'

'Why can't we go find him?'

'Because—' Malusha let out a grunt of irritation. 'Because he doesn't know you exist, child. You were born after his death, remember?'

'But surely my mother—'

Malusha laid a hand on Kiukiu's arm. 'He has no knowledge of your mother.'

'What do you mean?' Kiukiu stared at her. 'My mother is dead. I'd assumed she – I mean, they—' She broke off, too distressed to finish.

'I told you, child, that your father had moved far into the Ways Beyond. He has little memory of earthly matters – and little interest in them. That is how the dead are.'

Kiukiu suddenly burst into tears. 'I'd thought – at least if they can't be with me – they're together. And now you say – all these years – they've been apart—'

'There, there, child, don't upset yourself so.'

'But where is my mother? Suppose she's in that terrible place of dust and ashes? Suppose she's lost, looking for my father, wandering year after year over that endless scorching plain?'

'Time is different in the Ways Beyond. Time has no meaning. You will see for yourself . . .'

Kiukiu blew her nose. 'I've got to find her. I've got to go find my mother.'

'Don't even consider it!' Malusha said sharply. 'I

warned you, Kiukiu, didn't I? You have the gift to leave your body and wander the Ways Beyond, but you must use it sparingly. If you stay too long, your life-force will slowly seep away until you become a Lost Soul, eternally trapped between life and death, a sad, pathetic remnant. And every visit you make will age you in this world. It is *dangerous*.' And then she sighed. 'I will take you there, child. If you will only promise me not to attempt the journey on your own yet. Not till you have acquired all the skills – and practised them.'

'So,' Kiukiu said, sniffing loudly, 'where do I start? How do I start?'

'There is a tea which relaxes the body and lets the mind roam free.' Malusha went over to the fire and started to spoon dried leaves into a pot, pouring on hot water. A fragrant aromatic steam, slightly bitter, filled the room. Kiukiu's nose twitched.

Malusha brought over two little cups. The hot liquid inside was green and smelled – Kiukiu sniffed, wrinkling her nose – yes, it smelled of forest rain and bark, earthy and bitter.

'We are merely going to initiate you into the House of Arkhel, no more than that, a brief visit,' Malusha said, sitting down next to Kiukiu, cross-legged. 'First you place the gusly on your lap, so.'

Kiukiu copied her grandmother.

'Now, the tea. Drink it down in one gulp. That's right.'

Kiukiu pulled a face. The bitter tea burned her throat – and then the fumes, green and cleansing, seemed to rise in a gentle cloud.

'Listen to the notes I play and copy them, one at

404

a time. Let the vibrations die before you pluck the next string.'

Kiukiu concentrated hard. The pattern of notes her grandmother was playing tolled with the solemn sonorities of clanging bells. The vibrations set shivers of colour in the air, shadow-shimmers of sound. Her mind began to vibrate in time with the slow, solemn procession of notes, the colour-flares rippled and burst, rippled and burst like the dazzle of sun through fast-falling rain.

Now she was floating, moving up through a glittering veil towards a radiance so intensely bright she was blinded . . .

Her senses deserted her, she was blind, deaf, dumb, tumbling through utter darkness.

'*Grandma!*' she cried in panic but her voice made no sound – and there was no-one to hear her.

Then she was blinking in the light of an unknown sun that filtered down through the whispering silver leaves of tall birch trees. She turned round and round, her feet moving on the soft carpet of fallen leaves.

Ah yes, I have been here before.

Such a consoling place, hushed, muted, peaceful. The softsilver light lulled her, quelled her fears.

'This way, child. We must not linger.'

Her grandmother had appeared beside her, but she was no longer grey-haired and stooped. She was a tall young woman with thick brown hair braided with ribbons and feathers falling down her back.

'Grandma? You're – young!'

'My spirit is young,' Malusha said.

Yet when Kiukiu tried to look into her grandmother's face, her features seemed to alter, just as if she was seeing child, girl and older woman all mingled into one.

'Follow me.' Malusha set off at such a vigorous stride that Kiukiu had to hurry to keep up. But even though she knew she was walking, she had the oddest sensation that she was travelling at a far greater pace, floating above the fallen leaves until the birch trunks blurred into a tapestry of silver and grey.

Ahead Kiukiu saw the dim outline of a great gateway appear, gleaming golden through the mists. And beyond the gateway she saw a hall, thronging with warriors in burnished bronzed armour: men, women, fierce-eyed like birds of prey, beautiful and cruel.

'Who are they?' she whispered.

'This is the Hall of Arkhel,' Malusha answered. Her eyes were bright with a fierce pride. 'Here are the true heroes of Azhkendir, Kiukiu.'

The air dazzled with a light like the fire of the setting sun. And yet Kiukiu sensed a darker taint to the golden glory, the crimson of human blood, blood shed in battle. A distant roar echoed in her ears, a roar of fighting, the anguished cries of the fallen and dying. These hero-warriors of the House of Arkhel had lived by the sword and now they were bound for eternity to wait here until their deeds of blood were expiated.

'Do you see him? There?'

Kiukiu saw a tall man with hair of dark gold standing apart from the rest of the company. And as she looked she felt bleak despair and loneliness overwhelm her, cold and dark as moorland mist.

'Lord Stavyor. Last Lord of Arkhel.'

'Why is he so sad?' Kiukiu whispered. Even looking at him made her shiver.

'Because he could not save his people from Lord Volkh. Because the Arkhel lands are laid to waste.'

'Malusha.' The voice was stern, piercing as grey steel. Lord Stavyor stood before them, lean and austere. Kiukiu dared to glance up into his eyes . . .

A wave of blue flame, cold and glittering like starfire, rips through the air, searing flesh, blood, bone in its pure, devastating power.

'Kiukiu!' Malusha said sharply. She snapped her fingers in front of Kiukiu's nose.

Kiukiu jerked awake. She had seen Lord Stavyor's death, the moment of his annihilation.

'Forgive her, My Lord,' Malusha said, 'she is a novice. This is Kiukirilya, my granddaughter.' Kiukiu noticed a little tremble in her grandmother's voice. Was Malusha proud to have a grandchild to present to her dead lord? 'Bow, child,' Malusha whispered, 'but don't look at his eyes. Never look in their eyes.'

Kiukiu hastily obeyed.

'So,' Lord Stavyor said dully. 'The House of Arkhel has a new Praise Singer. But what is there to sing of? All my children are dead. My house lies in ruins—'

'She brings news from the land of the living, My Lord. News of your son.'

'Your son Jaromir is alive,' said Kiukiu.

'Alive?' Stavyor's voice quivered with sudden emotion. 'How can that be?'

'I don't know how,' Kiukiu said, 'I only know that he is alive.'

'Didn't I tell you, My Lord, that there was reason for hope?'

'Jaromir alive,' Stavyor repeated, 'and a young Guslyar here to serve him. Kiukirilya.'

'My Lord?' Kiukiu shivered. The last spirit-wraith to call her by her full name was Lord Volkh. Why did she feel she was betraying him? Wasn't she of the Arkhel Clan by birth? All her life she had been treated like dirt because of the Arkhel blood in her veins . . .

'You must find Jaromir, Kiukirilya. You must help him raise an army.' Lord Stavyor's voice dinned in her mind, harsh as the brazen clash of sabre-blades. 'You must help him take back Azhkendir and crush the House of the Serpent.'

'Me?' said Kiukiu weakly.

'The House of Arkhel waits for you to summon them.' One lean hand swept across the Hall and the fierce-eyed warriors who all had fallen silent, watching, listening. 'With you to help him, who can stand against us?'

Suddenly he reached out and – before she could stop him – drew her to him and kissed her forehead.

The kiss burned into her mind like a brand of gold.

Jangled clash of swords, shards of gilded light shattering the air. A host of dead warriors rise from the dust, hovering about her. Eyes gleam in the shadows, unnatural eyes, cruel and bright, predatory, unblinking.

Owls' eyes.

'Now you are mine,' he said. 'Now you belong to the House of Arkhel.'

But I am pledged to help Lord Gavril . . .

The shimmer of the armour, the bloodfire radiating from the fierce faces of the warriors, all had begun to dazzle Kiukiu's senses. And worst of all, the nagging suspicion that – in accepting Lord Stavyor's kiss of initiation – she had betrayed Gavril Nagarian. She had taken the first step on a path that would lead her further and further from him, making them enemies. A step that would only perpetuate the ancient feud between the two Houses.

'Malusha,' she murmured, slowly sinking back. She was falling, falling back into darkness. 'Help me . . .'

'Catch hold of my hand.' She heard Malusha's voice as if from very far away.

Rushing darkness enveloped her, and her last memory was of a strong grip seizing her wrist, tugging her back towards a distant glimmer of light.

Kiukiu squinted at her reflection in the polished bronze plate that served Malusha as a mirror. She was certain there must be some mark on her – she could still feel the imprint of Lord Stavyor's lips, a burning, tingling heat. But all she could see was her forehead, smooth and unmarked, tickled by tendrils of wheat-gold hair escaping from her thick plaits . . .

The bronze reflection shivered, like still water rippling, stirred by a sudden breeze – and another face stared at her from burnished shadows, a proud, stern face whose cold, golden eyes seared into hers.

'*Take me to my son, Kiukirilya, let me see him . . .*'

'M-my Lord Stavyor?'

'*Bring me through, Kiukirilya.*'

She gasped aloud – and tried to drop the mirror. But her fingers seemed welded to the metal. She could not move or look away from the staring eyes.

'*Take me to Jaromir.*'

'No – I cannot – I haven't the skill yet.' She tried to squeeze her own eyes shut, but a will stronger than her own compelled her to keep them open. 'Grandma—' Kiukiu croaked. But Malusha had dozed off in her chair by the hearth and seemed utterly oblivious to the danger.

From the rafters high above there came a sudden enquiring hoot. Snowcloud came flapping down from his perch and settled on her shoulder, his claws clamping like iron wire into her flesh.

'*Your spirit-familiar awaits me.*' Golden eyes in the mirror, golden owl-eyes beside her. Too late she understood what he intended.

'Snowcloud – oh no—'

And then her mind was wrenched open and darkness flowed through.

25

The servants were snuffing out the candles in the Palace of Swanholm. A restless wind shook the last dry leaves from the birches in the darkened parklands outside. It moaned around the chimneys, sending draughts whistling along the corridors.

Karila lay sleepless in her golden swan-headed bed, tightly clutching the covers to her. Voices. There were voices in the wind, she was sure of it, wild voices that whispered of mischief and destruction.

The little flame of her nightlight wavered in the cold draught. Suddenly it went out.

Karila gave a faint cry and huddled down under the soft wool blankets. Doors rattled. Her shutters burst their latch and banged open. How could she sleep with all this noise?

She threw off the covers and trailed over to the window.

Rain and sleet spattered her window-panes.

Gazing out at the stormy sky, she saw lightning crack open the clouds, illumining the darkened palace with dazzling white.

Black against the lightning's silver flash, she saw a figure of a man standing below in the courtyard, oblivious to the wind and rain, one arm upraised, fingertip pointing to the turbulent sky.

Thunder rolled, far away. And the wind came rushing across the parklands, straight towards the solitary figure.

'Who are you?' Karila murmured. 'And what are you doing?'

The temperature plummeted; the window-pane steamed over with her breath. Shivering, Karila rubbed a peephole with the hem of her nightgown. Her skin was chill with goosebumps, but she could not tear herself away.

The wind whirled around the rooftops. The man below stood his ground, his gown, his white wisps of hair, blown hither and thither. She saw him describe a single circle in the air with his finger and then extend his arm, pointing far away from the palace.

And at once the wind tore away across the parklands; she could see the trees bending and swaying drunkenly in its path, stormclouds scudding away towards the distant coast.

The man stood a while longer, watching its progress. Overhead a paring of crescent moon appeared, shedding a meagre light on the courtyard below.

Karila knuckled her eyes. No, she was still awake and what she had witnessed astounded her. Someone in the palace had the power to summon up the wind and send it to do his bidding. Such terrible power . . .

The man slowly lowered his arm and turned away, merging into the shadows. But not before Karila had seen quite clearly who it was.

'Magus Linnaius,' she whispered.

Eugene set down the morning's despatches. His armies were prepared for the invasion and now the news from the Northern Front had – for the first time in many years – made him doubt his tactics.

He went over to his study window and stood frowning out over the parterres and parklands of Swanholm. Fallen leaves lay everywhere, blown down by the night's storm.

Two gardeners walked slowly out to rake the leaves from the gravel paths. One, carrying a little pair of shears, trimmed a wayward twig or two from the neat box-trees as he walked.

Eugene felt a sudden pang of envy; how satisfying to be a gardener with one's whole world bounded by ironwork fences and ditches, measured by the rhythm of the passing seasons, no longer burdened by the cares of statesmanship . . .

The morning's despatch only confirmed the messages received earlier by Vox Aethyria.

The eastern skies over Azhkendir had turned black, and lightning streaks of white and blue fire had sizzled and rippled like the northern lights.

There was a soft tap at the door and Kaspar Linnaius came in.

'That was quite a storm last night, Magus,' said Eugene, gesturing to the leaf-strewn lawns. 'It must have caused havoc in the Straits.'

'I trust all our ships were safely in harbour, Highness?'

'I have word from Admiral Janssen to that effect, yes. But I imagine', and Eugene could not resist giving the Magus a sidelong glance, 'that the Muscobar fleet may not have fared so well. However, it was not the storm that made me send for you. What do you make of this?' He handed Linnaius the despatch. 'Not only has Gavril Nagarian inherited his father's dark powers, he has learned how to use them.'

'So it appears,' said Linnaius, scanning the despatch.

'And your Marauders—'

'My Marauders are dead. Destroyed.'

Eugene glimpsed a cold shadow pass across Linnaius's mild gaze. And he felt a surge of hope: the Magus would not let this slight on his professional skills go unpunished.

'The fault is partly mine. I underestimated Gavril Nagarian. But I need a diversion, Linnaius, something to keep him distracted for the time it takes to move the Northern Armies into Azhkendir.'

Linnaius nodded. 'So you are still convinced that this is the strategy most likely to succeed, Highness?' The simple question, asked in such a seemingly casual manner, only reinforced Eugene's sudden crisis of self-doubt.

'We've given the Muscobites every reason to believe we're about to invade by sea. The last thing they expect is an overland invasion from the north.' Eugene looked the Magus directly in the eyes. 'I've ventured everything on this, Linnaius. I can't afford to fail.'

'Eugene of Tielen.' Eugene signed his name with a flourish on the officer's commission. He never objected to carrying out the regular duties incumbent upon a military commander, yet today his restless mind kept wandering from the task in hand. Since the news from Azhkendir, he had not slept well.

He was damned if he would let all his dreams of empire be frustrated by one man.

The next document bore the name Count Oskar Alvborg: the charges included duelling, gambling and insubordination.

'What's this, Gustave? A court martial?'

'Count Alvborg is awaiting sentence in the barracks prison, Highness.' Gustave handed Eugene the official seal of the commander-in-chief of the household cavalry.

'Oskar Alvborg,' murmured Eugene, remembering.

The spectators in the Hall of Arms fall silent. The duellist removes his mask. Pale, proud eyes stare back at him unrepentantly.

One such as Alvborg might be persuaded to risk his life for a second chance.

Eugene rose, letting the seal drop onto the desk.

'Hold that order, Gustave.'

The unannounced arrival of the Prince at the barracks prison caused a flurry of panic amongst the guards and gaolers. His Highness was promptly conducted to visit Lieutenant Alvborg.

The bare brick walls of the cell were dimly lit by daylight from a high open grille.

'Surely officers usually buy themselves a few

comforts: fire, candles, a book or two?' Eugene asked, surprised at the starkness of the conditions Alvborg had been enduring.

'Aye, Highness, but it seems this one has gambled the last of his money away.'

Eugene nodded; this information only served to confirm he had chosen the right man for the mission he was planning.

The gaoler opened the heavy door and barked out, 'His Highness the Prince!'

The prisoner, who had been sprawled on his wooden bed, glanced up, eyes squinting into the sudden stark daylight.

'Welcome, Highness, to my humble lodgings. If I'd known I was expecting such an august visitor—'

'Show some respect to His Highness!' The gaoler grabbed hold of Alvborg and hauled him to his feet.

'Leave us,' said Eugene. 'We are not to be disturbed.'

'I'll be outside if you need me, Highness.' The gaoler retreated, grumbling under his breath.

'D'you know what this is?' Eugene thrust the court martial order before Alvborg's face.

'My reward for five years' service to Tielen?'

Eugene ignored the jibe. 'Gambling debts; duelling. Frankly, Alvborg, you've set a bad example to the younger soldiers and you deserve this court martial. You've abused your position.'

'I don't deny it,' Alvborg said. He shook a wayward lock of pale hair out of his eyes. He seemed unrepentant.

'And yet in action you're a damned good soldier.' Eugene threw down a handful of despatches on the narrow bed. 'I've read the reports.'

416

'So?' Alvborg said with a careless shrug.

'I'm offering you the chance to redeem yourself. To escape the court martial, the disgrace, the debtor's prison . . .'

He sensed he had Alvborg's attention now.

'I'm sending an advance party into Azhkendir.'

'And the assignment is?'

'To distract the Drakhaon and his *druzhina*.'

'A suicide mission, then,' Alvborg said drily.

Eugene forced a smile. 'I see you haven't lost your sense of humour. You'll need it.'

'So – apart from certain death, what's in it for me?'

'Complete this mission successfully and I'll pay off all your debts.'

For a brief moment the mask of indifference slipped.

'And get me back my mother's estates?'

The crack of a lash and muffled cries came from the prison yard outside; punishment was being administered to a malefactor. And Eugene thought he glimpsed Alvborg wince.

He nodded.

'What if I refuse?'

'Your court martial is still scheduled for tomorrow morning.'

Alvborg was silent a moment, arms defensively folded across his chest.

'What's to stop me absconding?'

Eugene did not dignify the question with a reply, merely turning to call back the gaoler.

'Wait.'

'You dare tell *me* to wait?' Eugene fixed the young man with a look of chill disdain.

'I'll do it,' said Alvborg. 'Your Highness,' he added.

'Decoys,' Alvborg said. The firelight glinted in narrowed eyes as he studied the map spread out on Eugene's desk. 'Or easy targets, for the Azhkendi barbarians to pick off one by one.'

'On the contrary.' Eugene gazed back at him, still wondering if he had chosen the right man for the task. 'Your mission, Lieutenant, is to stay alive. You're no use to Tielen if you get yourselves killed.'

'That is why', said a disembodied voice, 'His Highness has asked me to entrust you with my latest invention.'

Alvborg jumped.

Linnaius emerged from the firelit shadows.

Alvborg swore under his breath. He seemed shaken.

'Effective, isn't it?' Linnaius said, with the slightest hint of a smile. 'You had no idea I was there, did you, Lieutenant?'

'How did you pull off that little trick?'

'Shadowsilk.' The Magus turned away – and merged with the shadows again. In the firelit darkness, it was impossible to tell whether he was still in the room or not.

'Extraordinary,' Eugene said softly. The Magus reappeared, shaking his head as though shrugging off a hooded cloak. 'What is this remarkable shadowsilk, Linnaius?'

'Suffice it to say that it is not woven in the conventional manner, Highness, and that each cloak takes much time and craft. I have manufactured enough for a dozen, no more.' Linnaius offered

Eugene the cloak to try: a shimmer of shadow draped across his outstretched arms.

When Eugene wrapped the evanescent cloth about himself, he felt a shiver of the Magus's sorcerous glamour that set the hairs on his body prickling. The sensation was not in the least pleasurable. He shrugged off the cloak, relieved not to have to wear it a moment longer.

'But if we're to be fried alive, what use is this clever little conjuring trick?' Alvborg said.

Now Eugene was certain: the nonchalant drawl the young man affected hid genuine apprehension.

'The aim of your mission', he said, 'is to tantalize the Azhkendi forces, to distract them, to lead them astray.'

Alvborg turned to him, one eyebrow sceptically raised.

'Even though we have no accurate charts or maps and it's perpetually blizzarding—'

Eugene nodded. 'This mission will prove a considerable test of your ingenuity, Lieutenant. You will cross the Saltyk Sea not at the narrowest point from the tip of the isthmus here,' he pointed to the coastline, 'but twenty miles further north. If our intelligence is correct, you will make landfall near the fishing port of Narvazh. I want you to be sure the people of Narvazh see you before you move further up the coast.'

'And if we're challenged?'

'You retaliate. Azhkendi casualties will bring the *druzhina* swarming like flies to carrion – which is exactly what we want.'

'And if we run head-on into the Drakhaon himself?'

'Magus.' Eugene turned to Linnaius. 'You've prepared a device for the lieutenant to use if he finds himself and his men in an extreme situation?'

'To be used only in the direst need,' Linnaius said. 'A different kind of ammunition for your carbines.' He undid a soft leather pouch belted around his waist and placed a small pointed metal capsule on the desk. The metal gleamed dully in the firelight like pewter and it gave off a low buzzing sound like a drowsy bee.

Alvborg extended his hand towards the capsule – and then sharply drew it away, as if he had been stung.

'That's no ordinary bullet. What the deuce is it?'

Linnaius smiled. 'The alchymical elements contained within are extremely volatile, Lieutenant. When they are exposed to the element of air, they create clouds of a noxious gas that will confuse your enemy, giving you time to escape. Make sure that you and your men do not breathe in the fumes they give off when they explode.'

'Why?' Alvborg said.

'The fumes contain an alchymical poison. Breathe in a little and you suffer confusion, dizziness, sickness. Breathe in a little more and your lungs are seared.'

'Clever. Clever – and cruel.' Alvborg nodded. Eugene could not tell from his expression if he approved or disapproved. 'And how long, Highness, are we to carry on this game of cat and mouse?'

'As long as you can hold out, Lieutenant – longer still, if you wish to receive your full reward.'

Two Tielen ice-yachts skidded across the grey ice. Though it was midday, the frozen Saltyk Sea was shrouded in freezing snow-fogs and the sun could not be seen through cloud.

The navigator crouched over his compass, shouting out instructions to the helmsman. Beneath the yacht's smooth-honed keel, the thick ice creaked and groaned and the wind gusted noisily in the single canvas sail.

Alvborg looked at his men who sat huddled together against the cold, clutching their carbines in gloved hands.

Poor deluded fools. Who in their right mind would volunteer for a desperate mission like this? Hugging his heavy greatcoat closer to him, he crossed his arms and stared out into the rolling fogs.

What the devil had made him agree? At this moment the disgrace of court martial and debtor's prison seemed quite an agreeable alternative.

'Something's wrong with this compass, Lieutenant!' yelled the navigator above the wind.

Alvborg fought forwards against the buffeting gusts to peer down at the compass; the needle was swinging wildly around beneath the glass case.

'Where's Azhkendir?'

The navigator shrugged.

Damn it all, hadn't Magus Linnaius warned him they might encounter such a problem? But the Magus had shrouded the warning in obliquely mystical talk of inexplicable climatic phenomena emanating from Azhkendir.

'My grandfather used to say', began one of the soldiers lugubriously, 'that the Azhkendi protect their shores with the spirits of dead warriors. If you don't starve to death going round in circles, they lead you astray to where the ice is thin and drag you under.'

'Tales to frighten silly children,' Alvborg said with a weary sigh. Why had he been cursed with a bunch of superstitious idiots to command? 'Besides, His Highness is relying on us. There's no turning back now. We don't even know which way *is* back.'

26

Elysia gazed down from her window. The crowds still surrounded the Winter Palace, their pitch torches a blur of flame in the foggy Muscobar night.

Matyev's voice kept echoing through her mind. All his talk of philosophical societies had been nothing but a blind; he was a revolutionary, one of Velemir's 'damned insurgents'. So, she saw now, was Altan Kazimir.

And what was she? An artist, a freethinker from a country that had deposed its prince and substituted a democratically elected government. Matyev had been right; her sympathies should lie with his cause, not with the aristocrats. And yet here she was, inextricably involved with the ruling family.

And the only man in all Muscobar who could save Gavril had allied himself with the opposing side.

* * *

'Madame Andar! You've got to help me!'

Elysia looked up from her packing to see Astasia, back pressed against the door as though to prevent anyone from entering. Didn't anyone knock in the Winter Palace?

'What are you doing? Why are you packing?'

'My work here is finished, Altessa. I'm going home.'

Astasia ran across the room to her side.

'Madame Andar. I can never love Prince Eugene. I love your son. What shall I do?'

Elysia continued to fold her clothes and place them inside her trunk.

Astasia seized hold of her hand. 'Can't you take me with you to Smarna? Can't you smuggle me out, disguised as your maid? Please say you will!'

Elysia gently extracted her hand from Astasia's. 'Dear Altessa, that kind of disguise only works in absurd romances and operas. This is real. You can't escape this marriage, but perhaps you can make it work to your advantage.'

'No!' cried Astasia. 'Now you sound just like *them*. And I'd thought you were different. Like Gavril . . .'

Count Velemir appeared in the doorway.

'Altessa,' he said, 'I thought I might find you here. Your mother is looking for you.' He looked weary, his face grey except for the angry gash where the stone had struck him.

'Let her look,' Astasia said and for a moment Elysia glimpsed a little of the Grand Duchess in her daughter's petulant expression.

'It was Madame Andar I came to see,' the Count said.

'I won't marry Prince Eugene. I can't go through

424

with it! And you can tell Mama I said that.' Astasia burst into tears and ran from the room, slamming the door.

'Do you have any coffee?' Velemir said, easing himself into a chair.

Elysia, suspecting he had not just come for coffee, abandoned her packing. 'There's still some in the pot. Do you take sugar?'

'Thank you. But no cream.' He drank two cupfuls without speaking. 'I've been up all night.' He drew one hand ruefully over his chin, feeling the stubble. 'I apologize for appearing before you unshaven.'

'I don't think any of us have been able to get much sleep.'

He was silent a moment, studying the coffee grounds in his cup.

'So why did you come to see me, Count?'

'To ask you if you would consider changing your plans.'

'What, stay here?' Elysia returned to her packing. 'To be threatened by revolutionaries, shot at by the Palace Guard? No, thank you.'

He set down his coffee cup and said, 'I have news.'

She turned around. 'Of Gavril?'

'Of Azhkendir. It is reported by my agents on the northern borders that several nights ago, about sunset, a blue light lit the whole sky over Azhkendir and the ground shook.'

'Winter lightning.'

'Or Nagarian lightning.'

The folded clothes she was holding dropped to the floor.

'Gavril,' she said, stricken. 'Oh no. Not Gavril.'

'You remember my initial suggestion? That you should go to Tielen? Of course, the official reason for your visit would be to formally present your portrait of the Altessa Astasia to Prince Eugene.'

She hardly heard him at first. All she could think was that Gavril, in spite of all she had done to shield and preserve him, had given in to the malign influence of his Nagarian blood.

'I don't see', she said at last, her voice stifled, 'how my going to Tielen would help in any way.'

'Doctor Kazimir will accompany you.'

She stared at him.

'He would never agree.'

'Oh, I think he may find he has no choice but to agree.' Velemir pushed himself to his feet.

'No choice?' Elysia caught a sinister undertone to his words.

'The good doctor should be more careful about the company he keeps.'

'Last night?' she said. 'In the square? But he tried to calm the situation, he tried to restrain Matyev.'

'I had Kazimir arrested at dawn. The charge is insurrection. Treason. Plotting against the Grand Duke. The usual sentence is death – by hanging.'

Elysia stood motionless, staring at the Count.

'B-but he is the only one who can help my son.'

'It's time', Velemir said, turning towards the door, 'to find out if Kazimir is really as dedicated to the revolutionary cause as his friend Matyev thinks.' He turned back, offering her his hand. 'Come, madame. I need you as witness to this little negotiation.'

* * *

The Count led Elysia through cold subterranean tunnels whose walls were lined with brown bricks, glistening with water.

They emerged in a dark and dingy room which stank of mould and stale urine.

'What is this place? It looks like a prison,' Elysia said, staring around her with distaste.

'Hush.' He beckoned her through a low, narrow archway.

Elysia reluctantly followed the Count and found herself in a little observation chamber with an iron grille set in the wall.

The room beyond the grille was dark and windowless, lit only by one bright-burning lamp. Two men sat on opposite sides of a table. One was writing in an open ledger. The other sat facing the grille. He was drooping in his chair; his arms appeared to be tied behind his back. Lank locks of fair hair hung across his face.

'And the last time you spoke with the insurgent Matyev was in the Tea Pavilion?'

The man mumbled an inaudible reply.

The interrogator raised his pen. This seemed to be some kind of signal, as two men appeared out of the shadows and lunged at the prisoner, tugging his hair and jerking his head back.

Elysia stifled a cry. It was Kazimir. But Kazimir without his glasses, Kazimir with a bruised and bloodied face, peering myopically at his interrogator.

'What have you done to him?' she whispered angrily. But Velemir affected not to hear her, focusing all his attention on the interrogation.

'So why, Altan Kazimir, was it you were seen – by many witnesses – talking with the insurgent

427

Matyev in front of the Winter Palace last night?'

'Not talking, warning—' muttered Kazimir.

'Warning him?'

'That he was a bloody fool,' Kazimir said thickly.

The interrogator nodded to the two men standing beside Kazimir. The next instant one grabbed hold of the doctor whilst the other hit him across the face. Elysia, outraged, clutched at Velemir's arm.

'Make this stop, Feodor. It's barbaric!'

Velemir turned to her.

'Do you want to save your son, madame?' he asked coldly.

Kazimir sagged in the grip of his tormentors.

'Tell us the truth, Doctor Kazimir,' said the interrogator. 'Confess. You are part of a conspiracy to overthrow the House of Orlov. Your extremist sympathies are well-documented. For some years now you and your so-called philosophical society have been plotting with the rebel Matyev to assassinate the Grand Duke. Why don't you just admit it?'

'I have been in Azhkendir,' Kazimir said faintly. Blood trickled down one side of his mouth. 'How could I have done all these things so far from Mirom?'

The interrogator took out a pile of documents and began to read aloud:

'"How can we be said to have freedom of speech when the presses are censored? How can our voice, the true voice of the people, be heard when we are gagged? This censorship must end and the tyrants who impose it must be removed from power."' He laid down the papers on the table and turned to Kazimir. 'Your words, Doctor Kazimir? Do you deny you wrote this seditious pamphlet?'

'No, I – I wrote it . . .'

' "The tyrants who impose it must be removed from power." Dangerous words.' The interrogator moved close to Kazimir, spitting the words in his face. 'An incitement to assassination, no less.'

'That was not my intent.' Kazimir tried to move his head away.

'You'll have to do better than that, Doctor, if you're to escape the scaffold.'

'The scaffold?' Kazimir's face twisted, crumpled – and suddenly he began to weep, his shoulders sagging.

Elysia turned to Velemir to protest – and found she was alone behind the grille.

'Well? Do we have the names of the other conspirators yet?' Velemir appeared in the cell.

'Not yet, Excellency.' The interrogator bowed to the Count. 'But we have a confession. Kazimir admits he wrote these pamphlets.'

'I see.' Velemir's face was shadowed, giving no hint of expression. 'You can leave me with the prisoner. I shall continue the interrogation alone.'

Elysia leaned closer, biting her lip in her agitation.

'You know me?' Velemir said, seating himself opposite Kazimir.

'Count Velemir.' Kazimir's sobs slowly subsided. 'Spymaster to the House of Orlov.'

Don't insult him, you fool! Elysia wanted to grasp the grille and shout aloud. *He's here to try to save you!*

'Spymaster, if you will,' Velemir said, smiling affably, 'Foreign Ambassador is my official title. And I'll be going on a little trip soon, Doctor Kazimir, to Tielen. I'd like you to accompany me.'

429

'Tielen?' Kazimir said, sniffing. His face was streaked with blood and tears.

'If you stay here in Mirom, you'll be hanged for a traitor and a conspirator.' He leaned toward the prisoner. 'My dear Altan, I'm offering you a chance to save your life.'

'Why Tielen?' Kazimir said suspiciously.

'Tielen lies adjacent to Azhkendir and you have unfinished business there, I believe.'

'Unfinished? I'm a wanted man there. Wanted for Lord Volkh's murder.'

'Tielen or the gallows. It's your choice, Doctor,' said Velemir, turning to leave.

Kazimir started up. 'W-wait.'

Velemir turned back, one brow raised.

'Tielen.' The words were scarcely audible. 'I'll go to Tielen.'

'Well, madame?' Feodor Velemir said. He was smiling. 'Have I convinced you? Will you go to Tielen too?'

'Was it necessary to interrogate Doctor Kazimir quite so brutally?' demanded Elysia.

'My dear Elysia, by the laws of Mirom, the man deserves to die. In the circumstances, we treated him with extraordinary civility.'

'But he has committed no crime!'

'He has incited others to open rebellion. A revolution we can ill afford at the present time—'

'Count Velemir!' A man stumbled in, his clothes and face filthy with mud and dust.

'Gennadi? What's happened?' Velemir said.

'My – Lord—' The man was so out of breath that only a dry croaking sound issued from his lips.

430

'Terrible – storm in the Straits,' he managed. 'The *Sirin*—'

'The *Sirin*?' Velemir gripped hold of Gennadi by the shoulders.

'Gone down, with all hands.'

Elysia clapped her hands to her mouth. The *Sirin* was Andrei Orlov's command.

'Survivors?' Velemir demanded. 'There must be survivors!'

'They're searching. But the sea's still rough, and they were far from shore.'

'The Grand Duke must be told at once. Madame Andar, please accompany us.'

Elysia, bewildered, followed Velemir as he hurried towards the royal apartments. But it seemed as if the news of the *Sirin* had preceded them. Everywhere doors were opening, servants and courtiers milling in the echoing corridors, all talking together in hushed, anxious voices.

The Grand Duke and Duchess were at dinner in their private apartments with Astasia, Vassian and other court officials. Velemir flung open the double doors and went in. Elysia, caught in the mêlée of courtiers, heard the Grand Duchess's anguished cry before she could push her way through.

Astasia was standing, staring at Count Velemir.

'Andrei?' she whispered. 'Drowned?'

The Grand Duchess gave another choked cry.

'Send more search-parties!' ordered the Grand Duke. 'He could have been washed ashore on any of the beaches. He's a strong swimmer, our Andrei.'

'Andrei,' echoed the Grand Duchess, beginning to sob into her napkin. The Grand Duke reached out blindly for her hand.

Courtiers rushed to and fro in confusion; some called for the captain of the White Guard to organize a search, others surrounded the Grand Duchess, putting a glass of brandy to her lips, fanning her, easing her into her chair.

Elysia could not bear to think of so many lives lost in the cold, churning seas. She could not bear to remember how Andrei had smiled and waved as he went to board the *Sirin*, the vivid enthusiasm of the young and the fearless lighting his dark eyes. He had so reminded her of Gavril . . .

'This is all my fault,' Astasia said softly. Her lower lip trembled.

'How so, my dear?' Elysia asked, taking her hand and pressing it gently.

'Oh, Madame Andar, if only I'd agreed to the marriage with Prince Eugene sooner, then none of this would have happened and Andrei would still be alive. Now it's too late—'

'We don't know for sure—' began Elysia, hating herself for saying the meaningless words.

'I shall never, ever forgive myself!' cried Astasia, running from the dining-room.

27

The darkness is flecked with specks of gold. Gold specks spin, meld together, forming a disc, pale gold as the harvest moon. Not one disc – now twin full moons glimmer in the night sky. Moons – or eyes?

Owl eyes.

Kiukiu groaned. Her body felt as if it had been ripped apart. Every sinew ached.

Snowcloud was sitting on the back of a chair staring intently at her.

She knuckled her eyes. Such a horribly vivid dream. Lord Stavyor had taken possession of her. She could still feel the cold, cruel anger of her Arkhel master, seeking to impose his will on her, forcing her to—

But no, it could only have been a dream.

'*Free . . .*'

The word sighed through the firelit room so softly that she was not sure whether she had imagined it.

'Grandma?' But Malusha was still sleeping

soundly under her brightly coloured rug of patches.

'*Alive.*' The voice was clearer this time. And there was no doubting where it came from.

'*Wings.*' The owl stretched out one powerful white wing, retracted it and extended the other. '*Fly. I can fly.*'

She jumped up, alert now.

'Snowcloud?'

'*You – will – address me*', the creaking voice issued from the owl's beak, '*as – My Lord.*'

For a moment Kiukiu found herself completely speechless. Her owl had answered her back. She was not certain if Snowcloud had articulated actual words, or if she had heard the owlspeech and understood it for the first time. Didn't Malusha call the owls 'My Lords and Ladies'?

'M-my Lord Snowcloud?' she stammered eventually.

'*Must you be so stupid?*' the owl snapped back spitefully. '*Don't you know me? Stavyor Arkhel?*'

At once all Kiukiu's delight and amazement melted away. It had been no dream. Lord Arkhel had used her to return to the world of the living. She had tried to resist him, but he had been too strong; his will had overmastered hers.

How dare he! Panic and anger clouded her mind. *Must send him back. But how, how?*

She began to edge towards Malusha's bed.

'Grandma?' she hissed. 'Wake up.'

The owl rose off its perch, wings slowly beating, making an attempt to fly in her face. 'No!' She gave a shriek, flinging up her arms to beat it off.

Snowcloud twisted awkwardly in the air, tumbling towards the floor, only just managing to right himself as he skidded into an ungainly landing. A few downy feathers floated down.

'*You will learn to treat me with respect,*' he said aggrievedly.

'What's all this commotion?' Malusha sat up suddenly in her bed, clutching her quilt to her. Then she saw Snowcloud and her eyes narrowed. 'Lord Stavyor,' she said quietly, 'it's not yet time. You must go back.'

'*Do you presume to tell me what to do?*'

'This young owl has not been properly trained, My Lord.' Malusha swung her feet out from under the covers. 'You will only harm yourself – and your host.'

'*I want to see my son.*'

Overhead the rustling and low crooning of the other roosting owls grew louder.

'Didn't I warn you, Kiukiu?' Malusha was tucking a shawl around her nightshirt; her voice was low and angry. 'Never look in their eyes.'

Now Malusha was blaming her – as if she'd had any choice in the matter!

'He made me!' Kiukiu burst out. 'He was in the mirror, the bronze mirror—'

'*Don't send me back!*' The cry tore out of the owl's throat. The other owls above jickered and shook their wings.

'It is deepest winter, My Lord.' Malusha, muttering to herself, shuffled towards the fireplace. 'Your owl-host would not last more than a day in this bitter weather. We must wait for the thaw.' She took hold of the gusly and struck a shivering ripple of notes.

'*No!*' The owl's scream, a cry of rage and defiance, made Kiukiu clutch at her ears.

Malusha had begun to sing, a low, insistent

chanting, plucking at the deepest string until her voice and the string's dark vibration mingled and became one. The air trembled. A fissure began to gape open. The deep, thrumming note had opened a doorway into the void filled with rushing darkness that Kiukiu recognized with growing terror.

Stavyor-Snowcloud recognized it too and flung himself upwards, great white wingbeats stirring the gaping air.

'He's getting away!' Kiukiu cried.

All the owls were gripped with Snowcloud's panic now, whirring around like wild-clawed fiends, feathers and owlshit dropping down onto the room below like snow.

'Ugh!' Kiukiu grabbed a cloth, flinging it over her head for protection. In the confusion of flying feathers she thought she saw Snowcloud dash through the owl-hole in the roof. Others followed, screeching and hooting.

With a small, sucking sound the doorway collapsed in on itself.

Malusha laid down the gusly. She put her wrinkled hands to her head and rocked to and fro for a moment as if about to faint.

'Grandma?' whispered Kiukiu, creeping close. 'Are you all right?'

'I wasn't strong enough,' Malusha said dully. 'He resisted me. He fought me and he won. The dead should not control the living so easily. Am I losing my powers? Am I too old?'

'This is all my fault,' Kiukiu said. She felt shaky, near to tears. 'I was weak. He took advantage of my weakness.' If Malusha wanted to punish her, she deserved punishment.

Malusha leaned towards her and took her hand, squeezing it between her own.

'Weak? No. If anything your powers are too strong, child.' She shook her head. 'I should have known Lord Stavyor would try to use you. Even as a child he was always headstrong, wilful. I should have protected you better. I should have been more vigilant.'

'What will he do to Snowcloud?' demanded Kiukiu.

'He will drive him to fly to the limits of his own strength – and beyond.'

'I can't let him do that.'

'Snowcloud is an Arkhel Owl. He is strong, bred to fight in battle. Bred to fight as host to a warrior spirit-wraith.'

'But – but I thought those were just old stories, Grandma. Legends. Put about to scare the Nagarians.'

'And now you have seen the truth of it.'

'Owls trained to maul and maim in battle?' It seemed obscene to Kiukiu that such beautiful, noble creatures had been subjugated to the Arkhels' will and used as killing-machines. 'I have to save Snowcloud. He will go mad with Lord Stavyor lodged in his head.' And then another thought, worse than the first, gripped her. 'He said he wanted to see his son. But suppose – suppose he has gone to seek out Lord Gavril instead?'

Malusha shrugged. 'My throat is dry. I need some tea.' She moved slowly towards the fire, tutting as she tried not to step in the mess left by the owls.

'Grandma.' Kiukiu followed her. 'Lord Gavril helped to rescue Snowcloud. He wouldn't know, until it was too late—'

Malusha ladled water into the pot and put it to heat over the flames. 'Fire's burning low. We need more kindling.'

'Grandma!'

Malusha turned to her, brown eyes gazing at her critically. 'You still speak like a Nagarian, Kiukirilya.'

'Is that my fault?' Kiukiu blazed. 'I was raised a Nagarian. I was taught to hate the Arkhels. And besides,' her voice dropped, 'you've got to believe me, Grandma, Lord Gavril is *not* like his father.'

'The Drakhaoul has taken your Lord Gavril as it took his father before him. If you go back to Kastel Drakhaon, you'll be in for a rude shock, child.'

Why didn't Malusha understand? 'But I have to put things right. First Lord Volkh, and now Lord Stavyor. You have to teach me, Grandma. Teach me how to send them back.'

'Very well.' Malusha turned her back to the fire. 'But it's a dangerous business. The spirit-wraith will fight you. It will do all in its power to stay with its host – and even if you drive it out, if your will is not strong enough, it will possess you instead.'

'How can I track him?' Kiukiu persisted. 'How can I be sure which way he's gone?'

'Your only hope is to take My Lady Iceflower with you. The two were getting on very nicely together before Lord Stavyor appeared; I have hopes of chicks in the spring. She'll know which way he's gone.'

Kiukiu glanced uncertainly up at the rafters. She had never known any other owl but Snowcloud, and from down here all the snow owls looked dauntingly fierce, their talons cruelly hooked and barbed.

'First my tea,' Malusha said, 'then I shall teach you the Sending-Song.'

The fire burned low as Malusha played and Kiukiu imitated her as best she could. There was a sequence of notes to be learned but the art, Malusha showed her, was in a subtle retuning of the strings of the gusly. The slow, deep vibration of each plucked string seemed to bleed the brightness from the flames of the fire, to draw the winter shadows closer. Every dark pitch had to be matched with a long, low, ululating sound in the throat, closer to weeping than to singing. A hypnotic funeral chant, Kiukiu thought, at once peaceful and remote, a meandering path of sound leading far, far away, beyond a dim, distant horizon.

'You will weave the spirit-wraith within one of these chants. It will find it irresistible. Once you have trapped it and bound it you'll be able to lead it back into the Ways Beyond.' Malusha's voice droned on; Kiukiu fought the growing urge to close her eyes. 'But be careful that it doesn't drag you with it, child, for it won't go peacefully. It will fight you. All the way.'

Kiukiu shook her head, trying to clear her thoughts. The notes still reverberated in her mind, each one as dark and sombre as an autumn twilight.

'Now,' Malusha said, rising to her feet to go to stoke the fire, 'you must practise.'

'The sleigh is ready.' Malusha placed her hand on Kiukiu's shoulder. 'I want you to wrap yourself up warmly. I've put in food and a little flask of cloud-berry brandy for emergencies – but you will need a clear, keen head if you're to entrap My Lord Stavyor. Oh – and your mittens, child. What use is a Guslyar whose fingers are so chilled she cannot tell one string from another?'

In the yard, Harim the pony stood patiently waiting, harnessed to the sleigh. On the rail perched a white owl, regarding Kiukiu with its head inclined a little to one side. The owl was smaller, slighter, more elegantly groomed than Snowcloud.

'You must be Iceflower!' Kiukiu cried.

The owl retracted its head as if affronted at her crude greeting.

'My Lady Iceflower,' she hastily corrected herself.

'My Lady will lead you to Lord Snowcloud. Let her guide you through the snows.' Malusha tucked Kiukiu in amongst the furs and blankets she had piled in the sleigh, placing the gusly beside her. Then she leaned across and, to Kiukiu's surprise, gave her a kiss on the cheek. 'Now be off with you all.' She whispered in the pony's furry ear and patted him on the rump.

Obediently, Harim set off at a slow trot, the runners of the sleigh grinding over the snowy cobbles of the yard.

At the gateway, Malusha stood, clutching her shawls to her against the snow-wind's icy breath. Kiukiu heard her murmuring a slow, mumbling chant beneath her breath. As they passed beneath the gateway she felt the invisible veil of protection part to let them through. And then the cruel wind off the moors hit her like a whip. Turning to wave to her grandmother, she saw that Malusha and the walls of the cottage had completely vanished into the snowmists.

Even though it was day, the skies were dark and threatening as thunder. A thin, dismal light shone through chinks in the snowclouds.

'Which way, Lady Iceflower?' she asked the owl, whose neat white feathers were being ruffled by the wind.

The owl haughtily lifted her head, turning it a quarter to the left.

'You're certain?'

The owl turned her head right around and gave her a look of such chilling contempt that Kiukiu instantly pulled on the reins, turning Harim's head to the left. Soon they were skimming over the frozen snowflats.

Exhilarated by the cold and the speed of the sleigh, Kiukiu tossed back her head and – because she couldn't help herself – let out a loud whoop.

The owl gave her another disdainful look.

'So? Who's about to hear us?' Kiukiu cried.

28

'Hold on. Hold on, now.' Someone was speaking in a low, insistent voice.

Pain – agonizing pain – exploded like firecrackers through Gavril's body. A restraining hand gripped his arm.

'Don't move. Lie still.'

Through wavering lids, Gavril saw a figure bending over him in the night. Behind him shimmered a vast wall of rock and ice, glittering against the starry sky.

'Jaromir?' he whispered to the shadowed face above him.

And then another surge of pain swept sickeningly through him, and the night and his rescuer blurred into one cresting dark wave.

'So. You're awake,' said Jaromir Arkhel.

Snow mists still swirled in front of Gavril's eyes. Through the haze of concussion, he saw

Jaromir gazing impassively down at him.

'Where . . . am . . . I?'

'In the monastery refuge. On the mountain.'

'I . . . remember falling. Thought I would die.'

'A ledge broke your fall. I heard your cry for help.'

'*You?*' Gavril struggled to sit up – and gave a gasp as a stab of excruciating pain shot through his right side and arm. 'B-but why?'

'I think your shoulder's broken. I've bound it,' Jaromir said impassively. 'You were lucky. It could have been so much worse.'

Another wave of sickness washed over Gavril. Suddenly he found himself retching uncontrollably. Jaromir produced a bowl and held his head until he was done.

'I'm – sorry.' Shamed, Gavril lay back, shakily wiping the spittle from his mouth with his good hand.

'Drink this.' Jaromir held a cup to his lips. 'It will help control the nausea.'

Gavril gazed up at him, suddenly riven with mistrust. He was at Jaromir's mercy. Jaromir could poison him here, and no-one would ever know how he had died.

'The monks gave it to me to take when the pain was too much to bear.'

Gavril reluctantly drank down the draught. He had expected it to taste bitter, but the monks had masked the bitterness with a pleasant syrup of green mallow and ginger.

'Now you will sleep, and heal the faster for sleeping,' Jaromir said.

The draught was already working; his lids were

drooping, the pain in his shoulder dulling to a bearable throb. And yet there was something still troubling him . . .

'B-but why?' he said, his voice sounding thick and drugged in his own ears. 'Why not just leave me to die?'

'Why? Oh, I have my reasons. You are much more use to me alive than dead on the mountain, Lord Drakhaon. Much more use.'

A girl stands alone in the middle of the darkened ballroom. She is weeping.

Moonlight silvers the broken glass in the panes, the dust powdering the cracked floor, the grimy cobwebs hanging like streamers from the chipped plaster. Moonlight lights her cloudy dark hair, her white organdie ballgown – all torn to tatters.

'Astasia,' Gavril cries. 'Astasia!'

Slowly she turns, slowly she raises her face from her hands.

He is gazing at a blank. Where her features should be, there is nothing but a void.

Gavril, drowsy and feverish, lost count of the hours; days and nights passed as he wandered through troubled dreams.

When he came back to himself it was dark. He could just make out Jaromir kneeling over the smouldering eye of the fire, stirring a pot that hung suspended above the flames. A thin, savoury steam wafted out. Gavril's stomach rumbled at the scent of the broth. He was ravenously hungry.

He shifted a little and pain flared through his right shoulder, tingling down his arm to his hand.

Looking down he saw that Jaromir had strapped his right arm across his chest, and that the straps pinned him to the narrow wooden bed on which he lay.

'So I'm your prisoner.'

'Hostage.' Jaromir threw a handful of pine cones onto the fire; the flames crackled and spat sparks into the darkness.

'And your terms?'

'I'd have thought you'd have worked that out for yourself,' Jaromir said drily. 'Your life for hers.'

'Lilias? Didn't you know? She got away. Michailo rescued her.'

'But your *druzhina* went after her. Your *druzhina* will catch up with them. They will not treat them kindly.'

'They would never dare harm the baby. They still believe Artamon to be my father's son.'

'And you?'

'The *druzhina* will track me down,' Gavril said, ignoring Jaromir's question. 'They'll find me.'

Jaromir shrugged.

'Let them come. If they want you alive, My Lord, they'll have to let me go.'

Gavril felt too weak to argue. He lay back, closing his eyes.

'You should eat.' Jaromir went to the pot and spooned some of the contents into a bowl. Gavril could smell herbs, mingled with the stronger savours of leek, celery and onion.

'Shall I help you?' Jaromir set down the bowl and unfastened the restraints. Then he hoisted Gavril up into a sitting position, lifting a spoonful of broth to his lips.

I won't be spoonfed like a baby. Gavril glowered at Jaromir. 'Let me do it myself.'

'As My Lord wishes.' Jaromir placed the spoon in Gavril's left hand.

The broth, with pearly grains of swollen barley and chunks of potato, tasted delicious, even if in his clumsiness he spilled some down his chin.

'So,' Gavril said, to the shadowy figure who sat staring into the flames, 'why did you do it? Why did you kill my father?'

Slowly Jaromir turned his head around to look at Gavril, but did not reply.

'I know it was you. I've known it was you since the night he died – although I didn't guess your name until Kostya told me what my father did to your family.'

'How?' Jaromir said at last. His voice was hoarse. 'How could you know?'

'A kind of . . . vision.' Gavril did not want to say the name of the Drakhaoul aloud for fear of waking it.

'And did your vision also show what your father did to my family?'

'No.'

'I was at Saint Sergius the night it happened. Suddenly the sky was filled with a glittering blaze of blue fire, too bright to look upon. It was so beautiful – as if a star had burst in the sky and rained down its glittering dust on the land beneath. The mountains trembled. And as the monks and I ran outside, I saw—'

'What did you see?'

'A great winged daemon, blacker than shadow, wheeled over the forest, swooping low over the monastery towers and spires, as if seeking me out to destroy me. To sear me with its fire.'

'My father,' Gavril said under his breath.

'I flung myself on the ground. I was so terrified I thought I would die of fear.' Jaromir drew his knees close to him, as if hugging in the years of hurt. He seemed unwilling to continue. Eventually he said, 'If Yephimy had not stood over me, defending me with his staff, I would have been destroyed that night. And many times afterwards I wished I had.' His voice dropped to the ghost of a whisper. 'I still hear the sound of the beating of its wings in my dreams. I still see the blue, inhuman gleam of its eyes, blue – and gold.'

Blue – flecked with gold – like his own. Gavril had seen just such eyes in the mirror.

'Though those dreams are not the worst. The dreams that are hardest to bear are the ones where I hear my sisters laughing as they play, and my mother comes running to greet me, arms wide, smiling, as though all was as it had been . . .'

Gavril looked at Jaromir; his face was little more than a shadowed blur in the dying fireglow but he thought he saw a single tear roll silently down his cheek.

'And when the shadow of its passing had lifted from the valley, when the clouds of smoke had rolled away, my father's great kastel was a smouldering ruin, filled with a grey, poisonous dust. They were all dead, my mother, my father, my little sisters . . . Our lands were charred to cinders. Not one living creature survived.'

Jaromir let his head drop forwards until his forehead rested on his knees.

'You had motive enough to kill my father,' Gavril said in the silence. 'But Lilias – what does Lilias Arbelian have to do with it all?'

Jaromir did not answer.

'And why didn't you use her pistol? Wouldn't it have been easier just to shoot my father than to have to confront him, man to man?' There had been plenty of time to think as his shoulder mended. And there was still so much that Jaromir had not told him.

The fire was burning low. Jaromir jabbed suddenly, angrily, at the glowing cones, setting off an explosion of sparks.

'I wanted to see him face to face. I wanted him to know who he was dealing with. I wanted him to die knowing who had killed him – and why.'

There was such a bitter ferocity in Jaromir's voice that Gavril was stunned into silence.

'Or perhaps I was seeking something else. To die by Drakhaon's Fire, like the others . . .'

A branch snapped in two, sinking into the embers with a sighing hiss. The room grew darker still; the snowchill seemed to be slowly seeping up through the cold flagstones.

Jaromir stood up, shivering in the sudden draught.

'We need more wood.' He went outside, his shadow flickering along the fire-stained wall.

Gavril lay back, listening to the moan of the wind. As his eyelids began to close, he wondered how far he could trust Jaromir. His instincts told him that Jaromir was a man of integrity, an educated man who had lived abroad, far from Azhkendir's malign influence.

An uneasy kind of understanding was developing

between the two of them which – had they not been born into opposing Clans – might have ripened into a strong and enduring friendship.

But then there was the matter of Lilias . . .

The last cones on the fire fizzed, sending up a shower of cindersparks.

He opened one eye and saw that Jaromir was bending over the fire, feeding it with fresh kindling.

Then he straightened up and began to shrug off his jacket, deftly using his left hand to untie the fastenings. He took up a small earthenware pot and pulled out the stopper, releasing a waft of a clear, aromatic smell, sharp as wintergreen.

Feigning sleep, Gavril watched through half-closed lids, curious to know what he was doing.

Peeling off his loose shirt, Jaromir began to dab the contents onto his arm, wincing as the healing unguent seeped in. And in the dying firelight Gavril saw the terrible burns that had shrivelled his right arm and hand, searing the skin to a dark, angry crust.

The assassin drops, screaming, to his knees. His hand that holds the goblet is burning, bright with blue fire. Drakhaon's Fire.

Jaromir had suffered for his crime – and would continue to suffer every day of his life. Maimed, burned, he would carry the scars to the end of his days. Wasn't that, in its own way, punishment enough?

Jaromir seemed ill at ease next morning, restless, constantly going outside the log-hut to scan the valley below.

'They should have traced you by now,' he said,

coming in again, snowflakes melting to waterdrops in his dark-gold hair.

'The *druzhina*?' Gavril forced himself up into a sitting position. He had slept badly and the constant nagging pain in his shoulder had made him irritable, edgy. 'Don't you think I would have called them if I knew how? If there's a way to do it, Kostya has not taught me.' And perhaps Kostya is dying, he thought, and they are rudderless, divided, with Drakhaon and Bogatyr gone . . .

'There's been fresh snow. Our prints have been covered up. I hope they haven't concerned themselves with . . . other matters first.'

'Lilias?' Gavril said.

Jaromir did not reply.

Realizing he had touched on a sensitive nerve, Gavril said, 'You think they've caught her? They're interrogating her?'

Suddenly Jaromir snatched up his greatcoat, saying, 'I'm going to Yephimy. He will negotiate with your *druzhina*.'

'Ironic, isn't it?' Gavril said from his pallet. 'You and I. Equal now. Left-handed. What a fine duel to the death that would make.'

Jaromir turned back. His face was drawn.

'Call them,' he said, 'your *druzhina*. I don't want your death. I just want to know she and the child are safe.'

'And I told you, I don't know how to call them,' Gavril snapped. He had been trying to ease himself into a more comfortable position, but whichever way he shifted, the shattered shoulder-bone only ached the more.

'You're still in pain.' Jaromir reached for the

earthenware bottle, pulling the stopper out with his teeth. 'Let me give you some more of the monks' draught.'

'So you can keep me half-drugged? No, thank you.' Gavril shook his head. 'I want my wits about me.'

Jaromir shrugged and pushed the stopper back in.

'You and Lilias.' Gavril stared at the firelit shadows flickering across the hut roof. 'How did that come about?'

'We were passengers on the same ship bound for Arkhelskoye. There were terrible storms and our ship ran aground. We ended up in a little fishing-port to the north of Smarna, waiting for the storms to subside.'

'My father's mistress. Rather an unlikely form of revenge?'

'Revenge?' Anger glimmered in Jaromir's eyes. 'Is that how it seems to you? That I merely used her to get to him?'

'Isn't that what it was?'

'Maybe that's how it started. But then we found we had so much in common. Her early life was hard, a constant struggle against poverty, a merchant father who drank his family into debt and the work-house. There's a resilience about her . . .'

'And she is also remarkably beautiful.'

A whirling gust of wind rattled the turfs on the roof and made the fire splutter.

'It's started to snow again,' said Jaromir, piling more pine cones on the fire. Gavril sensed that he was unwilling to discuss his feelings for Lilias.

A sudden insistent tapping began on the shutter. Jaromir tensed, his sound hand closing around

451

the stout mountaineer's staff he kept beside the fire.

'What can that be?' Gavril said uneasily.

Jaromir moved silently to the shutter, peering cautiously through a crack to see what was outside. 'Well, well . . .' he said under his breath, reaching up to unlatch the shutter, letting in a blast of cold air. 'Look what the storm's blown us.'

On the sill perched a large snow owl, ragged and weatherbeaten, its white feathers bedraggled.

'Snowcloud?' Gavril said in disbelief. He forced himself up off the pallet and went across to the owl. Now he could see that one of the owl's legs was crooked, as though it had been broken and had mended a little awry.

'Is it you, Snowcloud?' Gavril murmured, remembering the forest clearing – and Kiukiu, eyes ablaze with anger, trying to protect the owl from Oleg's club. 'Have you come to find me?'

'You recognize this creature?'

'I rescued him from a trap.'

And still the owl lingered on the sill, staring at him with unblinking golden eyes.

'You, a Nagarian, rescuing an Arkhel's Owl?' Jaromir asked drily.

'The name I grew up with is Andar,' Gavril said brusquely. 'Not Nagarian.'

With a screech Snowcloud suddenly launched himself off the sill and flew straight at Gavril, knocking him off balance.

Gavril flung up his sound arm to protect his face.

Snowcloud came at him again in a flurry of white feathers, strong wingbeats beating against his head, forcing him down onto his knees. Furious screeches of anger tore from the owl's throat.

'Snowcloud!' Gavril cried. 'Don't you remember me? I saved your life!'

Hooked claws locked into his sound shoulder as Snowcloud gripped hold and began to peck at his head with an iron-sharp beak.

Anger and pain seared through Gavril, and he felt the sudden warning flare of the Drakhaoul awakening deep inside him.

'Get – him – off me!' he shouted, rolling onto the floor of the hut. White feathers flew about the hut like blizzarding snow.

Jaromir seized the mountaineer's staff and struck at the frenzied owl. It dropped to the floor of the hut and went limp, great wings splaying out like a white-feather cloak, carelessly flung down.

'Thank you.' Gavril pulled himself to his feet, leaning on the table with his sound hand.

'I fear I may have killed your owl.' Jaromir kneeled down beside the owl and reached out his hand to touch it.

Snowcloud's limp body twitched, spasmed violently. Jaromir gave a hoarse cry and fell flat on his back, as if some invisible force had knocked him over.

The owl lay still again.

'What happened?' Gavril asked uncertainly. 'Jaromir!'

Jaromir groaned and a convulsive shudder, violent as an epileptic fit, shook his whole body.

'Jaro. Are you all right?'

The fit ceased.

Jaromir sat up. His eyes blazed golden in the dimness of the hut.

'*At last*,' he said. But his lips hardly moved – and

the voice that issued from his throat was harsh and unnatural.

Gavril took a step back.

'Who are you?' he said in a whisper.

'*I know you. You are Volkh's son,*' Jaromir said in the unnatural voice. '*I should have had you killed at birth.*' The golden eyes gleamed, cruel and predatory.

'Jaromir?' Gavril cast around for a weapon, any weapon with which to defend himself.

'*I am Stavyor. Stavyor Arkhel. Come back from the dead to send you to hell, Drakhaon's child.*'

29

'It's no good, Lady Iceflower.' Kiukiu sank down on a boulder. Her lungs ached, her head spun. And it had begun to snow again. She could go no further without a rest.

Lady Iceflower fluttered down onto a nearby boulder and made twickering noises of impatience.

'It's all right for you, you can fly.'

Kiukiu had been trudging up this winding, treacherous mountain path all morning. Iceflower had seemed so certain they were on Snowcloud's trail that she had been flapping around Kiukiu's head, hooting excitedly.

'If we were back down in the forest, you'd be mobbed,' Kiukiu told her sternly. 'Daring to show your owl-face in daylight, indeed!'

The owl twisted her head right around and gave her a defiant stare.

Kiukiu turned her back on her and gazed out at the dreary landscape, half-gauzed in a thin veil of falling sleety snow. She had never ventured up into the mountains before. Indeed she had never been further than the Nagarian estates in her whole life until Lilias turned her out. Up here in the mountains she sensed the desolation of the snow-crusted wilderness as if the taint of the Drakhaon's poison-breath still lingered in the air, dulling her spirit, diminishing her will to go on.

And if Snowcloud's trail led her to Jaromir Arkhel, what would she say to him? 'Hallo, I'm Malkh's daughter. Yes, that's right, Malkh who betrayed your father. Malkh who broke under torture and blabbed all the battle plans to Lord Volkh . . .'

Such thoughts seemed unworthy, a betrayal of her father's memory.

She reached into her woven bag and took a swig from the precious flask of cloudberry brandy Malusha had given her. The sharp, sweet taste refreshed her a little. She stood up, hefting the gusly in its rough-woven cloth bag onto her back again.

'Must keep going,' she said, more to herself than Iceflower. After all, this journey was nothing but a matter of physical endurance. She was sturdy, strong, she could tramp on for hours. The real test of her courage would come when they tracked down Snowcloud.

No. Must put that out of mind. Deal with Lord Stavyor when I find him. One problem at a time.

Iceflower launched herself off her rock and floated out above the valley on ghost-feather wings.

Kiukiu gazed upwards at the low clouds – and the shadow of the mountain peaks that loomed behind

– and tramped off after her, up the stony, slippery path.

The gusly weighed heavily now, the straps cutting into her shoulder. From time to time, if Kiukiu put a foot wrong or slithered on loose scree, the strings gave a metallic shudder, as if offended at this rough treatment. And in spite of the intense cold, her face felt as if it glowed with the effort of toiling on upwards.

This search was taking far longer than she had planned. It was well past noon now, she judged, and soon it would be getting dark. Where would she find shelter on this bleak mountainside? She should have come better prepared.

Hope I've left Harim enough fodder.

She had left the pony in a sheltered gully, with his blanket tucked over his shaggy coat to keep out the worst of the night's wintercold.

Her back ached with carrying the gusly. She was going slower and slower now. She knew she must stop soon, if only to put down her load and stretch the stiffness out of her spine. She was well used to hard work and heavy burdens; she'd carried enough heaped coal scuttles, flour sacks and buckets of water in her time at Kastel Drakhaon. But she'd never been obliged to carry one uphill in the freezing cold for mile after endless mile.

She swung the gusly bag off her shoulder and lowered it onto the snow-covered path. Fresh snow – on compressed snow. No prints. What was she expecting? She gave a little snort.

Who but I would be stupid enough to come all the way up here on a fool's errand into nowhere?

Iceflower suddenly swooped down and alighted on her shoulder. Kiukiu staggered and righted herself.

'Don't startle me like that!' she cried. Her own voice echoed back to her, brittle with the chill resonance of ice.

Iceflower gave her a resentful little nip – not sharp enough to draw blood but sharp enough to hurt.

'Ow! And don't peck me.'

Iceflower nipped her again, no less sharply.

'What *is* it?'

Iceflower flew up into the air, spiralling round above her head.

'You've traced Snowcloud?' Kiukiu forgot all about titles in her excitement. 'Up here? Where? Show me.'

Iceflower flapped off into the fast-gathering gloom.

'Wait!' cried Kiukiu. She bent down and heaved the gusly bag back up onto her shoulders. 'And this'd better not be a false alarm,' she muttered, setting off after the owl.

There it stood, a little mountain hut, constructed of tarred wood and stone, its low turfed eaves almost reaching down to the ground. A thin trail of woodsmoke wisped upwards into the dusk from the chimney. The first sign of human habitation she had seen for days.

Kiukiu watched Iceflower swoop silently across the snowfield and alight on the roof.

'Here?' Kiukiu called softly to the owl. 'Are you sure?' The owl did not budge.

Now that it had come to it, Kiukiu felt an

overwhelming reluctance to go any further. She was to be tested to the limits of her abilities as a Guslyar, maybe beyond. She was not sure she was good enough to fulfil the task ahead of her. And if she failed . . .

It has to be done. And as there's no-one else to do it but me . . .

Hitching the gusly bag under her arm, she sighed and started out towards the hut.

Iceflower gave a sudden cry of alarm and shot up into the air.

'What is it?' Kiukiu cried.

From inside she could hear voices, men's voices arguing. Lord Jaromir was evidently not alone.

She hurried forward across the thick snow and pounded on the door with her mittened fists.

'Let me in!'

From within came the smash of breaking crockery. She tugged at the latch and shoved the door open.

A man stood with his back to her; as he heard her come in, he spun around and she saw he gripped a stout stick.

Mad, moon-gold eyes blazed at her from the fire-lit shadows of the hut.

'*Go away.*' The voice that issued from the man's throat was slurred and hoarse, but Kiukiu knew it for Lord Stavyor's.

'Oh no,' she whispered. Behind him she saw the white form of Snowcloud lying broken on the floor. 'What have you done, My Lord?'

'*You won't stop me now.*'

But now that her eyes had grown more accustomed to the murky darkness of the hut, she saw another man sprawled on the floor. A flame sprang up in the dying fire, glinting blue in his tumbled hair, and she knew him.

'Lord Gavril!' she cried, tears burning her eyes. She turned on the man with the stick, no longer afraid but angry almost beyond words. 'If you've killed him—'

'*Silence, Guslyar.*' The possessed Jaromir began to move towards Lord Gavril, lurching grotesquely, jerkily, a life-sized marionette animated by an unaccustomed hand. '*Let me finish what I have started.*'

Hands shaking, she dragged out the gusly from her bag.

There was no time to think clearly. She only knew she had to weave a shroud-web of sounds for the Sending and bind Lord Stavyor's spirit fast before leading it back towards the Ways Beyond.

As the first sonorous notes reverberated around the hut, she saw the possessed Jaromir grip the stick tightly and lurch towards Lord Gavril again. She wanted to cry out a warning to him, but she knew she must concentrate all her efforts into her Sending-Song. She struck a dark shiver of notes and saw the possessed man halt, the raised stick frozen in his hand.

'*Stop. I command you to stop!*'

Kiukiu forced her voice to resonate with each sombre note she plucked from the strings. Each note trembled through her body like a fever.

Jaromir swung round towards her. The golden eyes burned defiantly into hers. Obstinately, she plucked another long filament of notes, matching her voice to the deep, dusky threnody she was spinning. He was fighting her with every ounce of his will. She must pluck the metal strings louder, stronger, she must show she was not afraid. Now each time she touched the strings, the harsh metal bit into her fingers; each note was agony.

'*Stop*...' The stick dropped from Jaromir's fingers to the floor. He sagged – and fell to his knees. '*No – Kiukirilya – let me stay with my son*—'

Kiukiu felt herself slowly moving towards the dark heart of her Sending-Song.

'*Come with me, Lord Stavyor.*'

Now she hardly felt the pain of the lacerating strings as the notes throbbed louder. The shadows in the hut wavered, merging together into one darkness as the doorway to the Ways Beyond began to open.

'*No*...' Jaromir's body suddenly slumped onto the floor as she drew Lord Stavyor's spirit-wraith out.

'*With me, My Lord.*' She was strong now, her will was stronger than his. She had bound him – and as the portal opened in front of them, she led him towards it.

There, as she had seen it before, was the path winding away into the infinite beyond. The path glimmered in the darkness. Her song became calm, each note a step further along the path away from life.

'*Take care, child, for he will fight you every step of the way*...'

She glanced behind her. She was leading, he was slowly following. The fierce gold of his eyes dimmed as they passed further away from the shadow-door. He moved like one walking in a dream, his gaze distant, sad.

She sensed there was no fight left in him, only a quiet resignation.

It was so quiet here. And she was so tired. She longed to rest, to let the calm embrace her, lulling away the hurts and heartbreak of the past months. A soft light, gilded spring sunlight, filtered down through silver-green leaves.

When she looked around again, he had drifted silently away.

And there was something she had to remember to do.

But now it didn't seem to matter that much. It was so peaceful here, so very, very peaceful . . .

30

The fire had almost burned down to cinders and the mountain hut was dark and chill.

Gavril lifted his head – and cursed as the pain hit him.

He stared dazedly around him, wondering if he were still unconscious or hallucinating. Jaromir lay on the floor as if dead; beside him was the still, broken body of Snowcloud. And slumped in a corner, a young woman sat, fair head drooping, fingers on the strings of a large wooden zither.

'Kiukiu?'

He moved closer, staring in disbelief. Was he seeing ghosts everywhere? She was so like dead Kiukiu . . .

He put out one hand and gently touched her shoulder. She murmured something inaudible but did not wake.

His fingers touched her fair hair; it was the same rich shade as hers, the ripe gold of summer wheat.

Yes, it was she, he was certain of it, and felt his heart twist in his chest, torn between joy and anguish.

'Kiukiu!' He spoke her name louder. She seemed locked in some kind of trance, deeper than sleep. He pinched her cheek. Still no response.

'Kiukiu, come back.' He kneeled before her, stroking her face. 'It's me. Gavril. Can you hear me?'

Her lashes fluttered, and she opened her eyes, gazing into his as if she had been very far away.

'My Lord?' she murmured. 'You're safe. You're safe now. I've sent *him* back.'

An extraordinary confusion of feelings swept through him. She was alive. And he was more glad than he had ever imagined he could be to see her. He forgot the headache, forgot his sadness for Snowcloud. He wanted to hug her.

'We thought you were dead,' he stammered out. 'We thought the steppe wolves had got you.'

'And I thought you were dead when I saw you lying there and I was so angry—' Now the words came tumbling out.

There came a groan from beside the dying fire. Jaromir slowly got to his feet, steadying himself with one hand. Gavril glanced around, fearing to see the golden blaze of spirit-possession distorting his face, but Jaromir's eyes were dark again, dulled with confusion.

'What – happened here?' Jaromir swayed a little on his feet and then sat down.

'What do you remember?' Gavril asked warily.

'White wings – the owl. Then – nothing. There's a darkness in my mind. Like fog. And somewhere someone was singing. Slow and sad . . .'

'That would have been me,' Kiukiu said.

Jaromir lifted his head and stared at her through narrowed lids.

'And who are you?'

'Kiukirilya, Malkh's daughter,' she said in a small, steady voice.

'Malkh?' he repeated. 'Malkh, who betrayed my father?'

'Is that what they told you, My Lord?'

Gavril, sensing tension, moved to put more wood on the embers of the fire.

'That's what Abbot Yephimy told me. Volkh's men caught your father in the grounds of Kastel Drakhaon and tortured him. He broke and revealed everything to Volkh: the plans my father had drawn up to take Kastel Drakhaon, the night of the attack – everything.'

Kiukiu let out a small, tired sigh. 'I never knew my father.'

'You're a Guslyar?' Jaromir said, pointing to the instrument on her lap.

She nodded.

'A Guslyar?' Gavril repeated under his breath, remembering his father's will. Volkh had believed in the power of the Guslyars.

Jaromir went over to Kiukiu and touched the strings, which gave off a soft shimmer of sound. 'They told me you were all dead.'

'My grandmother is still alive.'

'What, old Malusha?' He sat down beside her and Gavril saw his face suddenly alight, eager. 'I used to listen to her tales when I was little. How my mother loved her songs! Malusha was such a wonderful singer – and the stories she spun—' He broke off as if the memory was suddenly too painful to continue.

Kiukiu a Guslyar . . . Gavril still stared at her as if seeing her for the first time. Was there a hope, the faintest of hopes, that she could help him rid himself of the Drakhaoul?

'How did you find us?' Jaromir asked.

'We followed Snowcloud.'

'We? Your grandmother's here?'

'No.' A look of weariness suddenly washed across Kiukiu's face. 'Lady Iceflower. Snowcloud's mate . . .' Her head drooped forwards again.

Gavril started up from the fireside.

'Is she all right?'

Jaromir leaned forwards to listen to her breathing. 'I think she's fallen asleep.'

Gavril and Jaromir sat opposite each other beside the fire. Silence hung in the air between them, an awkward, uncomfortable silence that Gavril was in no mood to break. He had wrapped Snowcloud's stiffening body in a piece of sacking and Lady Iceflower stood a silent, respectful guard over it. Kiukiu lay sleeping, strands of her wheat-gold hair spilling out from beneath the blankets they had tucked around her.

Outside, the snow had begun to fall again.

'In Tielen they have a saying "sleeping like the dead",' Jaromir said softly.

'She travelled a dangerous road to send your father's spirit back,' Gavril said. 'And a painful one. Did you see her fingertips? The strings were wet with blood.'

The silence fell again between them, cold as the empty snow wastes outside.

'Your owl,' Jaromir said eventually. 'I didn't mean to—'

'It was no longer Snowcloud,' Gavril said abruptly. 'Your father's spirit had sent it mad.'

'In the morning we can make a cairn. There's no earth up here for burying.'

Gavril nodded. He was still staring at the sleeping Kiukiu. He had not forgotten the heady rush of emotion that had overwhelmed him on seeing her. He had called it gladness, joy, relief at knowing she was alive. But deep inside him, a small, insidious voice whispered that he was deceiving himself. There had also been the stirrings of some stronger, darker feeling.

He hastily turned his head away. He had promised his heart to Astasia Orlova. But now Astasia seemed no more than a distant, impossible dream. When he tried to remember her face, her voice, he saw only a shadow-girl, insubstantial and unreal.

He ventured a glance at Jaromir who sat hunched, staring into the fire, his burned arm and hand hanging useless. Jaromir Arkhel had suffered enough at the hands of his father's Clan. If Kiukiu could lay Volkh's ghost, the blood-curse would be lifted from both their heads – without another drop of blood being shed.

Hope glimmered, a tiny crocus-flame of clear light, in the darkness.

And then he remembered the power and fury of the revenant, the way it had flung him across the tower room in Kastel Drakhaon. If it could attack him with such violence, what would it do to Kiukiu?

No, he had no right to ask her to risk her life, her

sanity – her very soul itself – on such a dangerous mission.

He would have to find some other way.

'I've never seen anyone heal so fast,' Jaromir said in puzzled tones as he examined Gavril's shoulder. 'Is it your Drakhaon blood?'

Gavril was testing how far he could move his right arm before the first telltale warning twinge told him to stop. 'Only a few days,' he said, flexing his fingers, 'and look!' He was astonished at the speed at which the damaged bone and sinews were knitting back together; perhaps there was some advantage to his blood-inheritance after all.

Kiukiu sat suddenly bolt upright, the blankets dropping from around her.

'Harim!' she said. She looked as if she was still half-asleep, her hair all mussed, her eyes unfocused. Then she saw Gavril. 'How long have I been asleep?'

'Who is Harim?' asked Gavril.

'My grandmother's pony. I left him in a gully before I started the climb up here.' Clutching a blanket around her, she wandered over to the shutter and opened it. 'Look. It's been snowing all night.'

'If he's out of the wind, he'll weather the storm. Those moorland ponies are very tough,' Jaromir said.

'But I promised her I'd take good care of him—'

'You'll have to wait till the snow stops. Have some porridge. You must be hungry.'

Jaromir handed her a bowl of porridge sweetened with a spoonful of heather honey; she bolted it down enthusiastically.

There was something different about her, Gavril thought, watching her, an almost indefinable quality of . . . *strength*. Yes, there was strength but also a new vulnerability. And her face had changed, the softness of early youth had gone. He wished he had a pen and paper to capture what he saw.

'Still no word,' Jaromir said, edgily.

'It's been snowing all night,' said Gavril.

'You must call your *druzhina*. Summon them. I can't bear to stay here and not know how she is.'

'And I told you, I don't know how.'

Kiukiu had been glancing from one to the other, evidently puzzled by the exchange.

'What's happened whilst I've been away?' she asked.

'Lilias,' said Gavril. 'Michailo helped her escape – and shot Kostya.'

Kiukiu's grey-blue eyes widened. 'The Bogatyr's dead?'

'We don't know for sure,' Gavril said uneasily.

Jaromir rose to his feet in one sudden restless movement, knocking over his stool. 'If they won't come to me, then I'll have to go to them.'

'And they'll kill you,' Gavril said. 'At least up here you have the advantage. When they come for me, you can bargain more effectively.'

'But right now we have no dialogue, no bargaining, nothing!' Jaromir struck his sound fist on the table, making the porridge bowls rattle.

'Then I'll try,' Gavril said grudgingly. He tried to empty his mind, listening intently for the distant murmur of voices he had first heard the night of the blood-oath.

'*We will always know where you are.*'

But all he could hear was silence, a rushing, empty silence, like the wind-stirred darkness at night.

'It's no good,' he said, shaking his head. 'I haven't been trained how to do it. Or if Kostya is dead, the link is broken.'

'Can I help, My Lord?' Kiukiu hefted up the gusly onto her lap. She plucked a low note or two and he saw her wince as her scarred fingertips brushed the cruel metal strings. Before he knew what he was doing, he had reached across and gently covered her injured fingers with his own. He saw her glance up at him, startled.

'You're hurt,' he said. 'You must let your fingers heal first. Lord Jaromir has a medicinal salve which the monks make. It might help.'

Jaromir nodded and brought over the earthen-ware pot. As he opened it, the soothing, aromatic scent filled the air, sharp as witchhazel, sweet as mallow.

'It smells like the moorlands in spring,' she said, taking in a deep breath.

'It smells sweet,' Jaromir said, 'but it stings like hell.'

Cautiously she dipped her fingertips into the green salve and grimaced as it began to bite. She shook her fingers furiously as if to shake the pain away.

'Try again,' Jaromir said to Gavril in a low voice.

Gavril went to the door of the hut and opened the top half, gazing far out across the cloud-shrouded valley.

'*Kostya,*' he called silently to the bleak mountains. '*Jushko! Can you hear me? It's me, Gavril. I'm trapped, injured – and I need your help.*'

And this time he thought he sensed a faint answer,

bleak and ominous as the distant flicker of winter lightning. Had he made contact at last? He waited, but there was nothing else.

He turned his back on the winter wastes and closed the door.

'Well?' demanded Jaromir.

'There was something there, this time ... but so far off, I couldn't tell if it worked.'

A sudden violent gust of wind made the whole hut shudder. The door blew inwards, banging on its hinges. Gavril whirled around. The sky had gone leaden-dark, and the temperature plummeted. He hurried to the doorway and gazed out.

The wind came shrieking back up the valley, wild as a tornado, tearing at the roof of the hut as if it meant to wrench it apart.

Overhead turbulent stormclouds churned, grey, shot through with sudden flickers of violent white lightning. Claps of thunder made the ground shake beneath his feet.

'Where did this storm come from?' cried Jaromir above the din.

'This is no ordinary storm!' Gavril shouted back, gripping the doorframe to keep upright.

Jagged hailstones came pelting down, slivers of ice as sharp as broken glass. The wind spun around the hut again, a high, menacing whine.

He had called – and *something* had answered him, some dark, savage force of winter ...

'Get back inside!' He pushed Jaromir back into the hut.

'What the hell's going on?' Jaromir twisted around, eyes blazing.

Kiukiu stood, white-faced in the hut, clutching her gusly to her. Lady Iceflower perched on her shoulder.

'It's Lord Volkh,' she said.

Thunder crashed again overhead. Dazed, ears ringing, Gavril heard a sudden rending sound. Looking up, he saw that a gaping hole had appeared in the roof.

'We must get out!' he cried.

Lightning almost blinded him. Silver fire crackled in the wooden roof as the turfs caught alight. The hut was ablaze.

'Run!' he cried.

The snow outside glittered with hailstones. They ran, sliding and slipping over the carpet of crushed ice, as lightning bolts sizzled around them and the turbulent wind roared on, tearing at their clothes and their hair. Behind them the hut flamed like a pitch torch.

Lady Iceflower fluttered above them, battered by the violence of the wind, blown helplessly hither and thither. Torn feathers fluttered down, white amidst the lacerating blast of the hail.

Jaromir suddenly stopped, flinging his arms wide, gazing up at the cloud-racked sky. 'Here I am, Volkh! Why don't you strike me dead? Finish what you started!'

Gavril turned. The rain of hail-shards grazed his skin, cold as frozen steel. The mountainside trembled with lightning and glistening hailstones.

And then he glimpsed in the lightning's shadow a tall figure, dark as thundercloud, towering above Jaromir.

'Father!' Gavril yelled with all the force of his

lungs. He started back towards Jaromir. 'If you kill him, you must kill me too!'

'Leave me!' Jaromir cried. 'Let it end here!'

A spiral of cloudshadows spun up about them. His father's wraith, eyes cold as lightning-silver, loomed above them.

'*Then you both will die.*' A voice of thunder made the rocks tremble.

Gavril steeled himself, eyes squeezed tight shut, waiting for the final blinding bolt of power.

And then another sound ripped through the roll and rumble of thunder, sharp as the shattering of glass, a tumbling cascade of plucked notes.

'Volkh!' A girl's voice rang out, clear and challenging. 'You made me bring you through into this world. Now I have come to send you back.'

Another cascade of notes followed, ending in one long, low pitch so deep it was darker than a moonless sky.

'*No!*' The spirit-wraith's cry echoed around the mountains like a thunderclap.

Gavril dared to look up.

Kiukiu sat on a rock, amidst the turbulence of the swirling snow, eyes closed in calm concentration, hands slowly moving across the strings of the gusly.

White lightning crackled about her head – a lethally dazzling corona – but it did not burn her.

And from her still figure, a low, deep humming sound emanated, serene as the summer drone of wild bees.

Slowly the savage fury of the storm began to die down. Thunder rumbled fitfully in the distance. And from the grey sky, snowflakes fell softly instead of vicious hail.

The flames in the hut were smothered in billowing smoke, gradually fizzling out, extinguished by the wetness of softly falling snow. Now all that could be heard was Kiukiu's voice, spinning out each dark thread of sound into the snow-chilled air until the ancient stones of the mountain resonated with her singing.

Gavril crouched in the snow beside Jaromir.

'What's happening?' he said under his breath.

'She's making a Sending-Song for your father.'

'He'll fight her.'

'She's strong. She can do it. Can't you feel it in the air?'

Gavril glanced up at the sky. Jaromir was right. There was a subtle change, as if the harsh bitter-cold of the past weeks was slowly melting away. The snow had stopped. Even the clouds seemed higher, whiter. And as Kiukiu's measured chanting continued, the fogs began to lift from the valley below, evaporating as they watched. A faint, pale brightness lit the clouds overhead.

'The sun?' Gavril said in disbelief.

Kiukiu's voice was becoming quieter, more drowsy, tailing off into long silences. Eventually there was nothing but silence.

'Kiukiu?' Gavril said.

Still she sat there, motionless, eyes closed, head drooping, her hands on the strings, just as they had found her the night before.

'*Kiukiu.*'

He hurried over to her and gently touched her shoulder. Slowly she slumped forward – and if he had not caught her, she would have toppled onto the snow.

'Help me!' he cried. Between them they held her, he and Jaromir. Her head lolled forwards. Overhead the clouds thinned, parted and a thin wash of blue sky appeared.

'What's the matter with her?' Gavril said in anguish as the sunlight glimmered gold in her hair. 'Why doesn't she answer?'

'Malusha once told me', Jaromir said, grim-faced, 'that it is always dangerous for a Guslyar to venture into the Ways Beyond. Sometimes it is too difficult to find the way back.'

Gavril looked down at Kiukiu's golden head lying against his shoulder. He saw the little spots of scarlet staining the white snow, and the blood staining the strings. 'No, Kiukiu,' he whispered into her soft hair, 'you must come back. Come back to me. Please come back.'

31

All night long lights burned in the Winter Palace as couriers, sailors and ambassadors came and went. Before dawn the Grand Duke set off on the royal barque to lead the search for his missing son.

Elysia found it impossible to sleep. It wasn't just the constant commotion, the rattle of carriages and horses' hooves over the cobbled courtyards; it was the thought of the foundering ship and the drowned men that kept her awake. She had lived most of her life by the sea and knew all too well its treacherous nature; one of her earliest memories was of hearing the wailing and keening of women in the harbour as the drowned bodies of a fishing boat crew were brought ashore. The memory chilled her still as it had terrified her then, seeing a limp, dangling arm swing loose from under the wet sail-shroud draped across it. Her first encounter with death . . .

At dawn she rose, splashed some water on her

face and forced herself to pack the last of her belongings.

There came a little tap at the door and Astasia appeared.

'What are you doing?' she cried. Her face was wan; the fresh rose-tint Gavril and Elysia had striven so hard to capture in paint had vanished. 'You're not leaving?'

'I have been invited to Tielen,' Elysia said, 'to present your portrait to Prince Eugene.'

'But you're my last link with Gavril—'

'Dear Altessa,' Elysia said, closing her valise, 'have you considered your position? If your brother is not found – though I pray he yet may be – as your father's only surviving child, you are heir to all Muscobar. You have more pressing affairs to consider than my son.'

'I know, I know.' Astasia pressed her fingertips to her forehead as if it were aching. 'Already Vassian has been to see me, talking of duty and obligation. He says there's nothing I can do to save Andrei. But if I marry Prince Eugene, I will save my country from all-out war. Isn't that a kind of blackmail?'

'Yes,' said Elysia. 'I suppose it is.'

'Though if I were to marry Gavril . . .'

'Muscobar would still have to answer to Prince Eugene. And Azhkendir would be dragged into the conflict too.'

Astasia let a choked little sigh escape her lips.

'Why does it all have to depend on me?'

On the quay Elysia and Count Velemir watched as Astasia's gilt-framed portrait, well-wrapped in cloths, was carried on board the barquentine, the

Alkonost, that was to carry them to Tielen. A fresh breeze was blowing off the Nieva and Elysia pulled her cloak closer to her, shivering.

Elysia noticed a dark plume of smoke rising above the rooftops.

'Is that a house on fire?' she asked Count Velemir who stood silently beside her, leaning on his cane.

'I fear it is the Senate House,' he said.

'But I thought that the Senate was the one place where the people could express their views—'

'Apparently Matyev's supporters think firing the Senate a suitable way to express their anger at the arrests. They say that free speech has been stifled, so what is the point of a Senate House?'

At that moment Elysia noticed the arrival of a small carriage with barred windows. She caught a glimpse of the pale face of Altan Kazimir peering out; the instant he saw her, he turned his head away. Guilt washed over her. He had seen her with Count Velemir. He knew.

'You saved his life,' Velemir said in her ear. 'He should thank you. On his knees.'

'How long did you say the voyage would take to Tielen?' Elysia asked, wanting to change the subject.

'With a fair wind behind us, two days at most.'

As the Nieva broadened out into a wide estuary, the fresh breeze became a gusting wind and the calm river waters became choppy, crested with churning foam.

Elysia stood on deck grasping the rail, relishing the wild breath of the wind. She did not care that her hair was whipped free of its confining pins. She

478

could see warships ahead, guarding the entrance to the river, their white sails billowing full, their Muscobar flags blue against the grey of the sky. Ahead lay the open waters of the Straits ... and Tielen.

'You're not affected by the motion of the waves, then?' Velemir joined her, clapping one hand to his fur-rimmed tricorne to stop it blowing away, the other to the rail.

'I was born and raised by the sea,' she said, having to shout above the creaking of the ship's timbers and the roar of the wind in the sails.

'Not far from here is where the *Sirin* went down,' he said. 'Several leagues to windward there's a treacherous reef where the currents flow strongly. We think her captain lost control of the ship in the storm and she was blown onto the rocks.'

'A terrible business,' she said, sobered. 'And is there still no news?'

'One or two bodies have been washed ashore along the coast. Some wreckage as well. But the storm was so violent, so sudden, the *Sirin* was smashed like matchwood and its contents spread over a great distance.'

'What are those ships on the far horizon?' she asked, shading her eyes against the fierce-gusting wind.

'The Tielen fleet,' Velemir said with the glimmer of an ironic smile. 'We are about to cross the contested fishing grounds.'

'Will they fire on us?' she said, alarmed.

'We are flying the flag of diplomatic immunity. After all, we are harbingers of a new peace.'

The ship pitched and a spurt of freezing cold

spray showered them; she stepped back, pulling her cloak closer.

'You will catch cold, Elysia,' he said. 'Come below. I've set my valet to make us some tea.'

Elysia had to duck her head low to enter the cramped cabin the captain had allocated to his passengers. In a corner Yashvil, Velemir's valet, had been brewing up tea in a little samovar.

'Drink it and enjoy it whilst it's hot,' Velemir said, passing her a steaming cup. 'If the sea gets any rougher, Yashvil will have to douse the fire.'

There was plum jam to sweeten the strong black tea.

'Or a dash of vodka?' Velemir said, offering her a little silver flask. She shook her head.

The cabin door opened and two of Velemir's men led in Doctor Kazimir. He walked with a strange, shuffling gait – and Elysia saw to her chagrin that his ankles were shackled as if he were a convicted criminal.

'And tea for the doctor too, Yashvil.' Velemir handed his servant the flask. 'He might appreciate a drop of this to keep out the cold. I'm off to see the captain.'

Altan Kazimir moved slowly, as though barely awake, mechanically spooning jam into his tea and stirring, staring at the dark liquid. His lip was badly swollen and when he raised the cup, she saw him wince as he tried to drink, some of the tea dribbling down one side of his mouth. In the half-light it was difficult to see clearly, but his face seemed to be marked with dark stains of bruising. They had mended his spectacles after a fashion, but they sat awry on his nose, one lens marred with a spider's-web tracery of cracks.

'Doctor, I hope you understand this was not my idea,' she said. 'I would never have sought to compel you—'

He stared down at his tea, eyes half-closed, as if the thin daylight in the cabin were too bright.

'Do your injuries still pain you? Shall I ask for some witch-hazel? I have arnica in my travelling case.'

'Is he gone?' he said in a dry whisper.

Yashvil had followed his master and they were alone in the little cabin. She could hear voices above on deck.

'He's out of earshot.'

He opened his eyes again, staring at her through his twisted, cracked spectacles.

'Be careful of Velemir. Very careful.' He spoke in a rapid undertone. 'He knows far more of Azhkendir than he has told you. When I was at Kastel Drakhaon, *she* was still in regular communication with him.'

'Lilias? But how?'

'A remarkable device. To the uninitiated eye, it appeared an exquisite ornament – like a clock – and indeed, she often referred to it as her Mirom chronometer.'

'Like a clock?' Elysia repeated, remembering the elegant glass-cased timepiece she had seen gracing Count Velemir's mantelpiece.

'But she couldn't fool me. I've seen plenty of chronometers in my time, I've taken them apart and reassembled them, but this was a device so advanced, so sophisticated, it was beyond my comprehension. It had a smell of alchymy about it.'

The cabin door opened again and Velemir came in.

'I thought you might want a change of clothes, Doctor, so I had my agents collect your valise from your lodgings.'

'How kind,' Kazimir said with a grimace, 'and I suppose you had your agents rifle through it at the same time, searching for incriminating evidence?'

'But of course,' said Velemir.

Elysia slept badly. She tossed and turned on the tiny bunk, alternately too hot and too cold. The mattress was flat and lumpy, and she had a horrid suspicion that there were small, biting creatures lurking in the horsehair stuffing. There were draughts and the window-panes rattled in their frames as the ship groaned and creaked.

She kept seeing Kazimir's damaged face, hearing his weeping. If he knew she had seen him humiliated and broken, she feared he would never trust her again. Worst of all was the feeling that she was in some obscure way responsible for his arrest and maltreatment, guilty by association with Velemir and his spies.

Yet surely Kazimir's politics were the sole cause of his present misfortune . . .

What's the matter with me? She sat upright in the bunk, clutching the covers to her. Am I beginning to think like Feodor Velemir?

She lay back, trying to empty her mind of thoughts, trying to picture the soft indigo of the Bay waters at midnight, trying to breathe slowly and rhythmically with the remembered rhythm of tidefall . . .

She is walking beside the Bay in the moonlight, her feet scuffing through the soft, moonwhite sand. The sky glitters with stars, brilliant white, ochre and blue, diamond-facets against the velvet dark.

'*Mother! Mother!*'

She starts, hearing Gavril's voice calling her name. She forgets he is a grown man, she hears only the child, frightened and helpless, calling for her.

A tower blocks her way, a tall tower, black against the stars.

'*Mother – help me!*'

High above her she sees a boy imprisoned, clutching at the bars of a window.

'*Gavril?*' *she says, not understanding.*

'*Don't come too close. Don't look at me. Please.*' *He flings up one arm to cover his face, turning from her, as though in shame.*

'*But how can I help you?*'

'*Set me free. Make me human again.*'

The moonlight shines out from behind a cloud, bright as a beaconflare, illumining the face at the barred window.

Dazzling reptile eyes gleam like starfire, slanted and inhuman, from a head covered in scales of glittering malachite. Nostrils flared. Wild locks of windblown hair, a shock of blue and jet . . .

A monstrous face. An inhuman face. She can only stare and stare, horrified.

'*My son. What have you done with my son, you monster?*' *she stammers out at last.*

'*Mother,*' *the monster cries, stretching out cruel claw hands to her in anguish, '*don't you recognize me? I am Gavril.*'*

32

The *Alkonost* made landfall at the port of Haeven at dawn on the third day out from Mirom. Carriages were waiting to take the party from Mirom to Prince Eugene's palace at Swanholm – and an escort of immaculately uniformed soldiers, their tricorne hats decorated with cockades of pale blue.

They passed through forests of silver-barked birch trees and skirted the edge of still, blue-watered lakes. Every time they clattered past a farm or through a village, Elysia noticed that the people would leave their tasks and stand silently, respectfully, by the side of the road. Were they cowed by the presence of Eugene's cavalry, she wondered, or was this the local custom?

As the light faded from the distant misted hills, the escort lit torches and placed lanterns on the carriages to illuminate their progress.

'We are not far now from Swanholm,' Velemir said.

Elysia nodded. She had been thinking of Gavril. Flashes from her dream kept intruding on her thoughts. Where had such grotesque images come from? She had only once glimpsed Volkh in his altered form – for he had gone to great pains to conceal that aspect of himself from her. And at too great a cost. When she had learned what he had done to keep his human form, she had run from him and barred her door. Even now, so many years later, the memory of his bitter confession made her feel ill with revulsion.

She prayed that it was not too late to start to administer Kazimir's elixir. She prayed that Gavril had not already committed some terrible atrocity which would haunt him for the rest of his life. That would poison any chance of future happiness, as it had with Volkh.

The gracious sweep of the curving wings of colonnades of the Palace of Swanholm was lit with bright flambeaux.

Elysia had been nodding off to sleep, lulled by the jogging of the carriage, but when Velemir gently touched her shoulder, pulling up the blind to show her the sight, she stared in wonder.

The still, black lake waters were streaked with the fiery reflections of the flambeaux. And behind the lake, the palace stood, the flames warming its cool stone with gentle fire.

'It seems to . . . glow,' she said.

'In spite of what Astasia may have told you,' Velemir said wryly, 'you will find the Prince a most cultured and enlightened man.'

The carriages followed a long, winding drive

down behind the hills so that the palace was hidden from sight. But, Elysia noted with surprise, the glow in the sky lingered.

'Welcome, Madame Andar,' said Prince Eugene.

Elysia sank into a low curtsey. 'I am not dressed for a formal presentation, Your Highness.'

Prince Eugene took her hand and raised her to her feet.

'You have just had a long journey,' he said in the common tongue. 'You must be tired. Tomorrow morning – when you have rested – you can present me with the portrait.'

He was broad-shouldered and tall, at least a head taller than Velemir. Astasia had been unjust in her description: he was not handsome, Elysia allowed, but neither was he ill-favoured, with a strong chin and jutting nose, his fair brown hair cut short in military fashion. But although his lips were smiling as he greeted her, she caught a chill from shrewd, sad grey eyes that reminded her of bleak winter skies.

Plainly and unostentatiously dressed in a dark grey uniform coat, the Prince made only one concession to decoration: a golden medal, shaped like a sunburst, on his left breast.

'Count.' He turned to greet Velemir who bowed, hand on his heart. 'We are so very sorry to hear about the loss of the *Sirin*. I have ordered my men to search Tielen's beaches in case anyone – or any debris – is washed ashore. But in the meantime, please convey our deepest condolences to the Grand Duke and Duchess.'

* * *

486

The next morning Elysia was woken early by the tap and ring of hammers. Looking out of her window, she saw workmen busy on the opposite wing of the palace; the night had hidden their scaffolding and ladders.

After a light breakfast of rolls, fruit and coffee, she sat to await the summons to attend on the Prince, trying to order her thoughts.

A light tap at her door announced that her wait was over.

'His Highness is awaiting you, madame.' A white-wigged servant, in a yellow and white striped coat, ushered her out of her room.

The palace smelled of fresh plaster and paint. And as she followed the servant along the corridors, she looked with admiration at the way the architects had used pale woods, mirrors and glass to enhance the effects of light in the palace; it was almost like walking through the facets of a glass crystal.

And then in the distance she thought she heard a child's carefree laughter echoing down one of the corridors.

'There are children in the palace?' she asked in surprise.

'His Highness's daughter, Princess Karila, madame,' the servant replied.

So Astasia – hardly more than a child herself – would find herself cast in the delicate and difficult role of stepmother.

'And will we meet the Princess?'

'She is only seven, madame. The Prince does not judge her yet ready for social occasions.'

The portrait stood on an easel, the cool light of late autumn falling on Astasia's delicate features.

And the Prince was standing looking at it, pensively stroking his chin.

Hearing her enter, he turned around to greet her.

'It's a very fine piece of portraiture, madame. I must congratulate you.'

'Mostly my son Gavril's work, Highness,' she said.

'So natural. And . . . lifelike?'

Elysia detected a slight hesitation, as if the Prince thought it indelicate to ask the artist outright if the portrait were idealized or true to life.

'There is no flattery here,' she said bluntly. 'Astasia is a sweet-natured and attractive young woman.'

Gavril, I'm so sorry to do this to you, she said in her heart. But Astasia was never destined to be your bride . . .

'She likes balls, music, dancing, yes? Will she not find Swanholm rather quiet after life in Mirom?' A slight frown darkened his grey eyes. 'Dull?'

At that moment Count Velemir came in with Altan Kazimir. Elysia was glad not to have to answer the Prince's question. The doctor's injuries had been tended to and he had been fitted out in clean clothes; only his spectacles had not been mended.

'Highness, may I present one of Mirom's most eminent scientists?'

'Doctor Kazimir!' Eugene cried, going to shake Kazimir's hand. 'What an honour to meet you.'

'The – the honour is mine,' murmured Kazimir dazedly.

'The Count has told me a little about your work; I should like to hear more.' Eugene was suddenly animated, enthusiastic, in sharp contrast to his earlier mood. 'But there'll be time for that later. We have more pressing matters to deal with. Your son, Madame Andar.'

'Yes?' she said uneasily.

'Come, look at the route I have planned for you.' He spread out a map on the desk. 'We will travel to the northern coast and the isthmus. The snows have not reached Swanholm yet. But you will need to be warmly dressed; the inland sea is quite frozen over. I will arrange for fur-lined cloaks, gloves and hats to be delivered to your chambers.'

'Is it safe to travel across the ice?' Elysia said, looking down at the map. Even though the Saltyk Sea narrowed to a wide channel at the point Eugene was indicating, where a strip of land jutted out from the Tielen coast, the distance between the two countries looked – she judged – at least twenty leagues.

'Quite safe, I assure you, madame. And you, Doctor, you have agreed to cure Madame Andar's son of this distressing affliction?' Eugene turned to Kazimir. 'To that end, Magus Linnaius has agreed to let you use whatever supplies you require from his laboratories.'

'Magus?' said Kazimir in tones of distrust. 'But surely these are alchymical laboratories? I employ properly tested scientific methods and materials, not magical mumbo-jumbo.'

Elysia gazed at him, aghast. How could he speak so insultingly to the Prince, his host?

But Eugene threw back his head and laughed. 'I can see the sparks will fly when you and Linnaius meet. Wonderful! Two opposing intellects arguing the relative merits of their disciplines.'

'And I must also point out', Kazimir said stiffly, 'that for the elixir to work, I will need to take fresh samples of blood from the Drakhaon. That means returning to Kastel Drakhaon. And as I have repeatedly reminded the Count, I am a wanted man in Azhkendir. If I am caught, the *druzhina* will hack me to pieces first and ask questions later.'

'Perhaps if Madame Andar were to write some kind of safe-conduct, signing herself as Drakhys Elysia?' said Velemir.

Elysia shot him a frowning look, unhappy at the idea of being forced to use her title. 'But as I shall be with him, I can vouch for him—'

'And if you are separated?' added Velemir.

'Do any of those Azhkendi brutes know how to read?' muttered Kazimir.

'I make the suggestion merely to allay your anxieties, Doctor,' Velemir said amiably.

'Well, Velemir?' Eugene said as soon as they were alone, trying to hide the tension in his voice. 'Do you have it?'

Velemir drew a little velvet bag from his inner breast pocket and handed it to the Prince.

With careful fingers, Eugene drew the stone from the velvet and held it up to the light. Still warm with the heat of Velemir's body, the heart of the ruby seemed to glow, transmuting the wintry daylight to a blood-red flame.

'It is the Tear of Azhkendir, isn't it?'

'Yes, oh yes,' Eugene murmured, turning the jewel in his fingers. 'And Madame Nagarian was unaware of its value?'

'Utterly unaware. She described it as a gift from

Lord Volkh. I believe she intended to sell or pawn it to buy passage to Azhkendir.'

'And she accepted the substitute without dispute?'

'She believes the necklace she is wearing to have been made from Lord Volkh's ruby. Why should she be dissuaded? Ignorance is bliss. This way, we are all content.'

Eugene looked round and caught a hint of a little smile of self-satisfaction on the Count's face.

'You are an artist in dissimulation, Velemir,' he said.

Velemir bowed, as if acknowledging a compliment.

'And now . . . there is only one Tear left to win.'

Elysia sat at a little escritoire, pen poised above a sheet of smooth cream paper, staring out across the park. She had already written a short formal introduction for Kazimir, signing her Azhkendi title with reluctance:

> To whom it may concern: the bearer of this urgent letter is my special envoy. I have satisfied myself that he was in no way involved in the assassination of my late husband and he must be given safe conduct to my son, Gavril Nagarian.
>
> Elysia Nagarian, Drakhys

The letter to Gavril was far harder to write.

Dearest Gavril,

We have so much to talk of. I cannot wait to see you. I have missed you so much! Please, please find it in your heart to forgive me for withholding the facts about your inheritance from you. It was wrong of me, I see now. You needed to know about your father. Now all we have to do is to hope and pray that Doctor Kazimir can cure the condition you have inherited from your father and enable you to lead a happy and normal life again.

Your loving mother,
Elysia

There came a rap at the door and Velemir entered, dressed in his travel clothes.

'For your letters.' He laid a small folder of soft dark leather on the desk.

'What's this?' She turned it over, revealing two white and gold sea-eagles emblazoned on the leather.

'A diplomatic bag bearing the Orlov crest. I felt the Tielen arms would be inappropriate in the circumstances – the doctor might find it a little difficult to explain.'

Elysia sprinkled a little sand to dry the ink and gently blew it off the paper. Then she folded the letters and slid them inside the soft leather, tying the folder with a blue ribbon.

'You must give them to Kazimir yourself.'

'Are you not coming with us, then?' she said, surprised.

'I have just received an urgent communication from the fleet. It seems some more wreck debris from the *Sirin* has been washed ashore in southern Tielen. Bodies. They need me to go – to identify, if necessary—' He broke off.

'Oh.' Elysia placed her hand on his. 'Such a sad task.'

'And such a fine young man. Headstrong, yes, but full of promise.'

Elysia nodded. The news only served to lower her mood, increasing her apprehensions about the journey she was about to undertake.

'So I must abandon you for a little while,' he said. He took both her hands in his and kissed them. 'It is a brave thing you are doing, returning to Kastel Drakhaon when you have such unhappy memories of the place.'

'I would do anything to ensure Gavril is safe,' she said fervently.

'I know.' He released her hands and withdrew.

When he had gone, she wondered why she felt so strangely bereft. Now that she was close to seeing Gavril again, she had no real need of the Count's aid any more.

So why these confused feelings? Had she – in spite of all her misgivings – developed some kind of attachment to Feodor Velemir?

Altan Kazimir was escorted by the Prince's guard to the Magus's rooms. A heavy carved door confronted him, decorated with a grotesque brass door-knocker moulded as a head of one of the Four Winds, cheeks puffed out, eyes crossed, hair wildly blown.

He lifted the knocker and rapped. The heavy knocker caught his finger on the rebound. Silently cursing, he lifted his hand to his mouth, sucking it to ease the pain.

The door swung silently open – and Kaspar Linnaius appeared in the doorway.

'Come in, Doctor Kazimir.'

A slight, stooped elderly man in scholar's robes stood before him, looking on him with pale, mild eyes. Could this be the infamous Magus Linnaius

493

whose controversial experiments had provoked such a violent reaction in Francia that his college had been razed to the ground and all his colleagues executed?

'I realize that as a doctor of natural sciences, you may not recognize the methods I practise.'

'Indeed I do not,' Kazimir said stiffly.

'And yet we might have much to learn from each other?'

'I doubt it.'

'Perhaps you would like to see my laboratory?' The Magus raised his left hand – and an open doorway appeared behind him.

Altan Kazimir gazed around the Magus's laboratory – and caught himself staring in astonishment and envy. The most sophisticated chymical scientific apparatus lined the shelves. There were filtration devices far more complex than those he used in the Mirom University. And yet all this sophisticated equipment was being put to a quite different use – a use of which he not only disapproved but did not begin to understand.

'His Highness has spared no expense in the creation of this laboratory,' Linnaius said, a little smile playing around his lips.

'So I see.' This made Kazimir even more uneasy; was it merely a smile of condescension, or did it conceal some more sinister intent?

'We have a little task for you, Doctor.'

'T-task?'

'I owe His Highness an infinite debt of gratitude. His father saved me from persecution – and death – in Francia. You will understand, Doctor, that I wish to do everything in my power to preserve His

Highness's life – especially from the threat of attack by the Drakhaon.'

'You mean the elixir?'

'But the elixir takes some weeks to work effectively, yes? That is what our agent in Azhkendir reported. We do not have weeks. That is why I have prepared *this*.' Linnaius went to a little cabinet and removed a slender phial whose contents exuded a slight phosphorescent glimmer. 'You will proceed exactly as if you were preparing the elixir, Doctor. You will take samples of the Drakhaon's blood and be seen to be using them in your experiments. But instead you will administer, drop by drop, this tincture I have prepared.'

'You mean me to poison him?' Kazimir said, aghast.

'This will merely subdue the daemon-creature that inhabits his body.'

Kostya's stern face flashed before Kazimir's eyes. 'If they suspect, they'll rip me to pieces!'

'I had not yet finished,' Linnaius said, mildly reproving. 'You will then escape the kastel, bringing with you the phials of the Drakhaon's blood you have drawn, so that the Prince and his men may be protected from the Drakhaon's Fire.'

Kazimir's palms were damp with perspiration.

'I – c-cannot do it—'

'Oh, you'll do it, Doctor,' Linnaius said smoothly. 'For if you do not make the rendezvous with His Highness's messenger, you will not receive the anti-dote to the slow-acting alchymical poison which is even now infecting your blood.'

'P-poison?' Kazimir clutched at his collar which suddenly seemed too tight, tugging it loose. A collar-button pinged onto the floor. 'But – how?'

'When you trapped your finger in the door-knocker, I believe you sucked it to relieve the pain? The substance was transferred from the metal to your finger, and thus to your mouth.'

Kazimir stared dumbfounded at his bruised finger. He felt cold all over.

'I'm dying,' he whispered.

'You will only die,' Linnaius said, still smiling, 'if you fail to comply with our instructions.'

The great horse-drawn sleds sped over the sunlit snow, bells jangling. Elysia, well-muffled in a soft, fur-lined grey woollen cloak, gazed out from under the hood at the winter landscape, glittering white under a pale blue sky.

At last, she thought, at last the endless waiting is nearly over.

Her heart beat in rhythm with the horses' galloping hooves; the ice-cold wind took away her breath, leaving her feeling faint yet exhilarated with anticipation. She willed the horses to go faster, faster.

At last she was nearing her goal. Soon she would see Gavril again.

Let it not be too late, she prayed, to save him.

They stopped in a little town at midday to change the horses, and warmed their hands in the local tavern on mugs of hot rowanberry cordial. To eat, there was smoked fish and smoked cheese on rye bread with large slices of pickled cucumbers. Elysia found the strong, coarse flavours rather unpalatable, but she chewed the tough bread dutifully.

Kazimir eyed her warily over the top of his

steaming mug, as if wanting to talk. She glanced around the tavern room; Prince Eugene's guards were joking and laughing together. She moved closer to Altan Kazimir.

'Your spectacles have been mended,' she said.

He pulled a wry face. 'Is there nothing Prince Eugene can't fix? Yes – he had the lens replaced for me and I swear now I can see more clearly than before. Too clearly, perhaps.'

'How so?' Elysia said.

'Well, where is the Count, for a start? How convenient that he was suddenly obliged to attend to urgent diplomatic matters. And then there's the Magus Linnaius.'

'You still don't trust him?'

Elysia saw a strange look pass across Kazimir's face, like clouds scudding across the sun.

'He's been most generous. He's given me all the equipment I could ask for: phials, pipettes, measuring flasks.' His tone had altered and his gaze kept flicking above her head, as though fearing they would be overheard. 'He's even given me chemical powders and elemental compounds—' He broke off suddenly, his eyes fixed, staring at the doorway.

Elysia, puzzled, followed his gaze, wondering what could have caused him to react so dramatically.

An elderly man had appeared in the doorway; he nodded amiably to the guards, exchanging a word or two with them.

'Who is that?' she asked, curious.

'The most dangerous man in all Tielen,' Kazimir said. He was shaking. 'Kaspar Linnaius.'

* * *

As the sleighs approached the isthmus, the sunlight faded from the sky. A penetrating wind whined dismally in their ears beneath a pall of grey snow-clouds. The air smelt bitter: sea-salt and snow.

They spent the night huddling round the stove in a weather-boarded inn – cheerfully decorated, like so many of the wooden houses in Tielen, in a child's paintbox colours, red, yellow, blue and green – whilst the wind roared and buffeted the building.

Next morning Elysia saw what the night had hidden from them: the inn stood on a windswept headland and below, stretching away into a grey and impenetrable fog, lay the ice. A sparsely pebbled beach led down to a frozen sea, pale as jade. It was as desolate a landscape as she had ever witnessed.

The guardsmen had gone down onto the shingle at first light to assemble the ice-yacht, rigging up a sturdy mast above the runners and fixing the canvas sails to it, tightening ropes and checking the tiller.

Elysia approached the officer supervising the work.

'Why not take the horse-sleds onto the ice?' She had to shout to make herself heard over the roar of the wind.

'Too heavy, madame. The ice is not uniformly thick and appearances can be deceptive. We cannot take the risk.'

'But the wind is so wild here, it could easily blow the craft off-course.'

'There's a knack to the steering. Don't worry. My men have been practising.'

'And that mass of cloud and fog. Can they steer through that?'

'I have been observing that phenomenon for some time, madame.'

An unfamiliar voice, soft yet penetrating, startled Elysia. She turned around to see Kaspar Linnaius standing behind her on the hard-packed snow where she was certain there had been no-one before.

'And I believe there is a change underway, at long last. Look.'

The fog where he was pointing had begun to churn and swirl as if stirred by a distant gale, and as Elysia watched, wisps broke away from the cloud-mass, dispersing and melting.

'Magus Linnaius,' she said slowly. 'Is this your doing?'

'Oh, no, not in the least,' he said. 'This comes from within Azhkendir. Shaman's work. Crude, dangerous necromancy, but it works singularly to our advantage.'

'We're ready, Magus!' One of the guardsmen came running up over the icy shingle, sliding and slithering about as if he were on a skating-pond.

Elysia watched as the guardsmen carried Kazimir's case of chymical equipment down to the yacht and settled it in, cushioned in furs. The doctor followed, shivering, pulling his fur-lined coat closer around his neck. He looked miserable; shaking with cold and apprehension.

Elysia felt sorry for him; she found herself planning how Gavril might reward Kazimir for his pains: gifts of money to enable him to travel far from his troubled past and start a new life . . .

What was she doing, daring to dream of the future? They hadn't even left the shores of Tielen yet!

Once they had reached Azhkendir – once they had found Gavril – then and only then could she allow herself to look forward again.

She gathered up her skirts and followed Kazimir down the treacherously icy path to the wind-racked beach.

The wind dinned in the ice-yacht's sails, making the canvas crack like a whip.

'Why don't you just wave your hand and transport us there magically, Magus?' Kazimir said caustically to Linnaius.

'Oh, please, young man. I haven't devoted my life to studying the Artificier's art just to perform conjuring tricks,' said Linnaius, mildly reproving. 'But I have devised a compass for you which will enable you to steer the craft as accurately as you can to landfall. With a good wind behind you, you may reach the other side in a few hours. But the Prince has provided victuals – and a tent – in case you land far from human habitation. And a few of my slow-burning fire-sticks so you don't freeze to death tonight.

'Fire-sticks?' Kazimir said, frowning.

'One of my favourite artifices. I think you'll find them rather an amusing little conceit,' said Linnaius. Was he smiling? Elysia wondered. 'And it'll give your enquiring mind something to puzzle over during the long winter night.'

Four of the guardsmen pushed the craft out onto the ice and grasped the mooring ropes hard as the wind filled the sails, almost tugging it out of their grip.

Kazimir staggered after them, head down in the wind, almost slipping on the ice. He floundered, grasping at the craft to steady himself, and managed to haul himself over the side, landing head-down.

Elysia moved forwards to follow him, and one of the guardsmen put out his hands to steady her.

'Thank you. I could do with a helping hand,' she said.

The guardsman did not let go of her arm. Another moved rapidly to hold her other arm.

'What's this?' she said, confused.

'You are to stay, madame. The Prince's orders.'

'But – but I was promised!' Elysia burst out. 'That was the whole reason for my coming – to see my son!'

'I'm sorry, madame, but those are our orders,' the guardsman said politely. 'Perhaps His Highness thought it was too dangerous for you . . .'

'Dangerous!' Elysia cried. 'I don't care about the danger—'

'Ready to cast off!' shouted an officer above the blast of the wind. Elysia flung herself forwards, trying to twist free of the guardsmen's restraining grip.

'Doctor!' she screamed into the wind. 'They won't let me come!'

She saw him turn around, puzzled. She tried to break free, slithering over the icy pebbles . . .

And saw Magus Linnaius lift one hand in a gentle, twisting movement, as though pulling an invisible force from thin air and directing it towards the craft.

Suddenly the ice-yacht was tugged out of the guardsmen's hands and went speeding away across the frozen sea. A hissing, scything sound came back to them, wood and metal runners skimming over the ice – and Kazimir's long-drawn-out yell of alarm.

Elysia slid to her knees on the shore, staring in disbelief as the tiny craft dwindled until it was only a dark speck, gliding on towards Azhkendir without her.

33

Kiukiu stood, arms outstretched, her back to the portal, blocking the way back onto the snowy mountainside.

'*Witchchild!*' Volkh loomed over her. His eyes burned with the bitter brightness of a midwinter blizzard. '*Let me back! We have a bargain, you and I!*'

'You are never going back, Volkh!' she cried, angry beyond fear. 'Your place is here, with the dead.'

'*Then I will take your place.*' He reached out to clutch her in his chill, clawed hands. She shut her eyes, dreading what he might do to her, dreading the cruel kiss of winter that would freeze her soul for all eternity.

But the cold embrace never came. Fearfully she opened her eyes – and saw Volkh convulsed, jerking as if in a violent fit. Shreds and tatters of snowcloud and mist spun about him and went whirling away into the vast emptiness of the Ways Beyond.

'My Lord?' she said tentatively.

Volkh slowly raised his head, gazing at her. The winter-madness had left him. Now she saw him as a man, dark-browed and proud, the sombre Lord Drakhaon who had been her lord and master.

'Is it over?' he said in puzzled tones.

'Yes,' she said. 'It is finally over. You are free, My Lord.'

The bleak plain on which they stood slowly melted away. Kiukiu felt the gentle brush of leaves on her hair. Looking up, she saw they stood on the edge of a grove of birch trees. A distant sun gleamed through mists.

'Free?' he repeated, as though hardly able to believe what she had said. 'At last?'

Blue eyes, a darker reflection of Gavril's, gazed into hers. For the first time she saw how much Volkh resembled his son. For the first time she glimpsed the earnest, ardent young man he had been before the Drakhaoul had begun to corrupt him, to change him to its own likeness. And a profound sadness overwhelmed her – sadness at the thought of a life corrupted, warped from its original path, and the countless other lives it had ruined.

'You will find peace here,' she said, remembering what Malusha had taught her, her voice unsteady. 'Go, Volkh Nagarian. Go in peace.'

'Yes,' he said, dazedly. Silver-gold leaves whispered, stirred by a soft breeze. 'In peace . . .'

He turned and walked away amongst the eternal trees.

The whitewashed monastery room was dim with a fast-dwindling twilight. A sudden soft breath of

504

wind rattled the open shutter, tinged with the faint mould-odour of fallen leaves from the great forest outside.

Kiukiu lay as one dead on the little wooden bed.

Gavril reached for the tinder-box and lit a candle; it gave off a dark, honeyed smoke, perfuming the room with a memory of summer.

From one of the towers a bell began to clang to call the monks to their evening devotions, a deep, solemn note that was soon answered by other higher-tongued bells, setting up a repetitive metallic clamour.

Gavril watched Kiukiu's still face intently, but she did not stir, even when the loud jangling of the bells began.

He got up and paced around the room, frustrated and angry with himself that there was so little he could do. Abbot Yephimy had tried to reach her, but his efforts had failed. Now the monks were saying prayers for her as if she were already dead.

Gavril kneeled beside her and stroked a stray lock of pale gold from her smooth forehead.

'But you're not dead, are you, Kiukiu, just very far away . . .'

Not dead yet . . . but the longer her spirit was lost in the Ways Beyond, the harder it would be for it to return. And all the time it was gone, her body was slowly slipping into a decline.

'I won't let you waste away,' Gavril whispered into her ear.

A whole day had passed since Jaromir set out in search of Malusha, hoping that the pony Harim would find his way home across the moors. Gavril had wanted to go with him, but Jaromir had

505

reminded him that the sudden appearance of a Nagarian lord would be seen by the old woman as a threat.

In the warm candlelight, Kiukiu's skin seemed to glow with a faint translucence. Her face was a serene void.

She had hazarded so much to exorcize his father's ghost. Too much.

A girl is weeping.

Kiukiu sees a young woman, standing shivering on the edge of the trees, her arms clasped tightly to her, as if she were freezing cold.

Some instinct drives Kiukiu towards her – even though she knows she must not linger in the Ways Beyond.

'What's wrong?' she asks.

'C-cold. So cold.' The girl's fair hair gleams in the light of the distant sun. 'Where is he? I c-can't find him.'

'Who are you looking for?'

'They killed him. Broke his fingers, tore out his nails, tortured him . . .'

Kiukiu draws closer still. She recognizes this young woman. She sees in her features a reflection of herself.

'Where are you, Malkh? I've been searching for you so long – and now I can't find my way back home.'

'Would you like me to help you?' Kiukiu says gently. *Mother*, she says softly in her heart.

'Yes.' The girl nods. 'Oh yes. But it's so cold—'

'The sun is shining. Can't you feel its warmth?'

Slowly the girl raises her head, eyes squinting into the light as if emerging from darkness.

'Warmth,' she says slowly, wonderingly. 'Yes. Oh yes. Now I can feel it.' Her hands drop down to her sides. She has stopped shivering. She gazes at Kiukiu from a wan, sad face.

All the long-buried anger Kiukiu has endured at being abandoned by her poor, mad mother vanishes. She sees only a young girl, not much older than herself, broken by events beyond her control.

'Come with me, Afimia,' she says, wanting to heal Afimia's hurt and confusion. 'We're going to find your Malkh.'

'Where is she? Where's my granddaughter?' demanded a querulous voice.

Gavril awoke with a start. He had fallen asleep in the wooden chair beside Kiukiu's bed. The door burst open wide and a wild-haired old woman marched in. On seeing him, her face darkened in a snarl of such virulent hatred that he shrank back, alarmed.

'How dare you!' she said in a hiss. 'How dare you sit in the same room as my beautiful girl? You're not fit to clean her boots.' And she spat on the floor at Gavril's feet.

Jaromir appeared in the doorway.

'Now, Malusha, you promised me,' he said, gently chiding. 'Lord Gavril is quite different from his father. You'll see.'

'Different, pah!' Malusha spat again. 'They're all the same, the Drakhaons. Can't you smell the darkness in him, My Lord? Can't you see the Drakhaoul curled around his heart? Sooner or later, he'll turn for the bad. *They* always do.'

Darkness. Why could she only see darkness in him? Hadn't he sat at Kiukiu's bedside day and night, speaking to her, holding her hand, trying to call her back?

'If it hadn't been for your cursed father, she wouldn't have wandered so far away.' Malusha laid her hand on Kiukiu's pale forehead, closing her eyes as if listening. 'And I don't know if I can reach her now. Or if she'll come when I find her. You can get out, both of you.' Malusha unslung the gusly she had been carrying on her back. 'Off with you. Leave us alone.' Already her gnarled fingers were quietly testing the strings.

'But—' Gavril began.

'Go.'

Jaromir beckoned him outside and shut the door.

In the darkness of the cold stone passageway outside they heard the first urgent ripple of notes, a wave crashing on a distant beach. More waves followed, a stormtide of fierce, elemental sound.

And then Malusha's voice drifted out to them. Gavril had expected the old woman's voice to sound feeble and cracked. He had not thought to hear such strong, deep singing, such power.

Maybe there was still a chance . . .

The birch leaves glimmer above her head, silver-grey and gold in the hazy light.

Kiukiu wanders on through the forest. She is looking for someone. But she has been wandering for so long now that she has almost forgotten who he is . . . and why she has to find him.

Afimia trails after her.

'So peaceful here . . .' she whispers.

The soft, calm light has lulled her; her footsteps gradually slow.

'Don't wander away, Afimia. Stay with me.'

'Why the hurry?' Afimia asks dreamily.

A bird is singing in the tracery of branches high above her head, a little ripple of notes, like drops of falling water.

Singing . . . It was something to do with singing . . .

Through the slender trunks Kiukiu catches sight of the gleam of water. A lake, a vast grey lake, stretches far into the distant mists. Its still waters lap slowly against a gently shelving shore.

A man, his back against a birch-trunk, is sitting, staring out into the mists.

Kiukiu ventures closer. He doesn't look round. He doesn't seem to know – or care – that she is there.

Now she can see he is young, maybe no more than twenty-two, twenty-three, with straight, fair-brown shoulder-length hair. And there is something familiar about his face, although she cannot quite say what it is: the strong chin and cheekbones, maybe . . . and the wide forehead?

'I think I know you,' she says tentatively.

He doesn't even look up. And now she is sure of it and with it comes a strange pain about her heart. And she had not thought she could feel pain in this place.

'Your name is Malkh,' she says. 'Malkh the Guslyar.'

He glances up at her. Grey-blue eyes, as clear as

her own, look at her as though she were almost invisible.

'I came here to forget that name,' he says after a while, a long while. His voice is light and pleasant, a singer's voice. But his gaze drifts away from her as if he has already lost interest in her.

Kiukiu kneels down beside him.

'I'm your daughter,' she stammers out. 'Kiukiu.'

He shakes his head slowly. 'You are mistaken. I had no children.'

'I was born after you died. My mother was Afimia. You must remember Afimia.'

And at last a faint shadow flickers across his face.

'Afimia?' he repeats.

'Please remember,' Kiukiu says, anguished that he shows so little reaction. Yes, Malusha did warn her to expect this, but she had so hoped she might be able to bring about some kind of reunion.

'There was a girl. Her hair was your colour, maybe lighter when the sun caught it . . .' The effort of trying to remember seems almost too much and he lapses back into silence again.

'She is here. With me.'

'Afimia is here?' Again that brief flicker of interest.

'Look.' Kiukiu beckons Afimia towards her. In the gold-dappled shade of the leaves, she looks more wood-spirit than human, her wide eyes as wild and nervous as a faun's.

'Malkh?' Afimia says uncertainly. Kiukiu looks imploringly at her mother – and suddenly sees a blood-stained splash of memory, a glimpse of a man's torn and mutilated corpse hung up to rot in the kastel courtyard.

'*Never look in their eyes*,' Malusha's voice breathes in her memory.

'Afimia.' Malkh rises slowly to his feet.

'Th-they killed you.' Afimia stares at Malkh warily. 'And all because of me. If I hadn't begged you to stay—'

'We are beyond death here. Here, none of that matters any longer.'

'Malkh,' Afimia says again. She is smiling. Her wan face is radiant, transformed. 'It *is* you.'

Malkh moves towards her. Their figures seem to blur, to merge together for a moment, one indistinguishable from the other.

'Be at peace,' Kiukiu murmurs.

Together, they drift away from Kiukiu along the shores of the lake, into the sun-gilded mists.

All grey and silver here, touched with gold. Muted colour, soft wash of grey water lapping on a silver-sand shore, soft whisper of breeze through silvered leaves . . .

'Well, here you are at last, child!'

Kiukiu looked up. A woman was walking along the lake-shore towards her.

'Time to go back, Kiukiu.'

Kiukiu gazed up at the woman. She had no idea what she was talking about.

'Go back where?'

The woman hunkered down beside her. 'Kiukiu, don't you know me? Heavens, child, you've only been here a short while, has this place worked its charm on you so soon?'

'This place?'

'These waters are the Waters of Forgetfulness. It's

a place of healing. But it's not your time yet, child. You must come back with me now.'

Kiukiu shook her head.

'I don't want to go. It's so quiet here, so peaceful . . .'

The woman gave a sigh of exasperation. 'The longer you stay out of your body, the harder it will be for you to return. And your body will age and wither. Come *on*, child. Don't you want your life? Isn't there anyone else back there who needs you, cares for you?'

'There was someone . . .' Kiukiu stared out into the pale mists, trying to remember.

'Think!' the woman said sharply. 'The last person you saw before you came here!'

Blue eyes, blue as the sea in a far summer country.

'Lord Gavril,' she murmured.

'Well, if that's it, then it must do,' muttered the woman. 'Lord Gavril. Fix your thoughts on him, Kiukiu.'

A blinding dazzle of snow and lightning flashed across her mind. The grey mists vanished. She *remembered*. She looked at the woman and saw it was Malusha.

'Grandmother? Why are you here?'

'At last!' Malusha grabbed her by the hand, tugging her to her feet. 'Come, we must hurry. If we linger here, we'll both forget why we came. And then there'll be no going back.'

'But – my father. I found him. I have to—'

'Later, there's time for that later,' Malusha urged, pulling her up the bank and away from the shore. 'Look ahead, Kiukiu, into the trees. Keep looking ahead. Somewhere near here there's a portal.'

Everywhere Kiukiu looked she could see nothing but birch trees, a bewildering maze of silvered trunks. No sign of a portal. Panic gripped her. They would never find the portal, they would be for ever wandering through this endless forest of eternal trees, hopelessly searching . . .

Malusha pulled her to a stop and sharply slapped her cheek.

'Ow!'

'That's for thinking such foolish thoughts. Think them here – and they become true. We are going to find the portal. We are going *home*.'

Kiukiu nodded, face stinging.

If Malusha had not been with her, she would have missed it. It shimmered in and out of her vision, a distant mirage, an ephemeral veil of golden motes briefly glimpsed as the sun slants down through a dusty window or a leafy forest clearing.

'Hurry!' Malusha grabbed her hand more tightly, head down, running towards it as if it might disappear at any moment.

As they ran, Kiukiu became aware of shadows slinking alongside, increasing their pace as they increased theirs.

'Something's following us!' she cried.

'Don't look round.' Malusha's grip on her wrist tightened. 'Don't look back. Just run.'

Shadows. Starved of life, starved of love. Kiukiu could see the Lost Souls in her mind's eye, could see their empty, cold eyes, their clawing hands, could sense their terrible hunger.

They want me. They want my life-force. They'll never let me go!

Breathless, gasping, they reached the portal and Malusha struck it with her clenched fist. The shadows were gaining on them, Kiukiu could sense them gathering, clustering together. Hungry hands reached out, grabbing at her, pawing her legs, trying to hold her back.

'Don't let them follow!' Malusha cried as the portal suddenly gaped open. She caught hold of Kiukiu and shoved her through.

And then Kiukiu was hurtling helplessly through chaotic darkness, utterly lost, utterly alone.

34

'Now you truly are . . . your father's son . . .' Kostya, lying propped up on pillows, just managed to whisper the words, and Gavril had to lean close to catch what the old warrior was saying. There was a rank, rusty smell on his breath, old blood and pus mingled. 'Jushko told me. Jaromir Arkhel is destroyed, and your father's spirit is at peace.'

'You're not to tire him, My Lord,' Sosia said, bustling in with a bowl of hot water. 'He needs his rest.'

'Stop fussing, woman,' whispered Kostya with a brief glint of his old ferocity.

The wound seemed to have drained all the old warrior's strength and vitality; his lean face had become emaciated and his scarred hands lay listlessly on the bed covers. His breathing was shallow and from time to time a rattling cough shook his whole body, leaving him grimacing with pain.

'Jushko's a good man,' Kostya said after a while.

'He'll make a good Bogatyr. Not much to say for himself, but he knows his men. And he's loyal. He'd give his last drop of blood rather than betray you, My Lord.'

'What's this talk of Jushko?' Sosia said briskly. 'You're My Lord's Bogatyr, Kostya.'

'I'm no use to you like this, My Lord,' Kostya said, turning his head away. Gavril heard the catch in his voice. 'And you're going to have need of a Bogatyr. Michailo won't give in without a fight. For all we know he's gathering his own little army out there, planning his campaign . . .'

'Rebellion?' Sosia said, stopping in her tracks. 'Civil war?'

'You must crush him, My Lord,' Kostya said, trying to sit up. 'Put down the rebellion. Stop *that woman* from gaining power. She's using him. Like she used your father—' He slumped back onto the pillows, coughing.

Sosia came hurrying over, clutching a bowl and cloth.

'That's enough excitement for now,' she said firmly, wiping his mouth. Gavril saw the rusty stains of brown blood on the cloth – and the sad, resigned glance she gave him over Kostya's bent head as she wrung the cloth out in clean water.

'I'll leave you to rest now, Kostya,' he said, not knowing what else to say. He leaned forwards and placed a hand on the old man's shoulder.

'Don't want rest. Rest is for old men,' muttered Kostya. 'Damn that Michailo to all the torments in hell for putting me here.'

'I'll see you out, My Lord,' Sosia said loudly.

Outside Kostya's bedchamber, she turned to

Gavril. 'You see how it is, My Lord? He's putting up a fight, but for the first time in his life, he's losing. And he doesn't understand why.'

'Sosia,' Gavril said, 'I have news for you. But for your ears only.'

Sosia gave him a vexed look. 'I can't leave him alone. He might need something.'

A new kind of relationship had evolved between Sosia and the Bogatyr, Gavril saw now, a change in the balance of power – and dependence. Kostya needed Sosia, and Sosia liked to be needed.

'Then call one of the girls to sit with him.'

'Very well, My Lord.'

Gavril led Sosia to a little antechamber and shut the door, hoping no-one would listen at the keyhole.

'You'd better sit down,' he said, gesturing to a chair.

'Why?' Her face creased with alarm. 'Not more bad news?'

'Good news,' he said, waiting until she had settled herself in the chair. 'Kiukiu is alive.'

'Alive?' Sosia's face went white, and then red with shock. 'B-but the wolves—'

'You must tell no-one else. It must be our secret. For her sake.' Now he found that even speaking Kiukiu's name aloud was a kind of torment. He believed that in leaving her in the monastery he had put all thoughts of her from his mind – and now all he could see was her face, her grey-blue eyes gazing into his, still clouded with all she had endured in the world of the spirits for his sake.

'How can she be alive? You found her things on the moors—'

'I haven't heard the full story yet. But she is safe

and in good hands. I wanted you to know. And I wanted you to keep it secret until—'

A piercing scream slashed through the quiet of the kastel.

'What was that?' Sosia leaped up from her chair and hurried to the door. Gavril followed.

One of the maids was running along the upper landing. Gavril could hear her high, terrified sobbing for breath.

'Whatever is the matter?' Sosia gathered up her skirts and set off up the stairs.

'Witchcraft!' the girl cried out, stumbling past.

'Some girlish foolishness, My Lord,' Sosia called down. 'If you'll excuse me, I'll go sort things out.'

Gavril nodded. Sosia seemed almost glad of the distraction, glad not to have to talk any more of Kiukiu. He went back into the antechamber and stared out of the window at the neglected gardens, glistening white under their thick covering of snow. Although no more snow had fallen and the sun's faint gleam had penetrated the last thin veils of cloud, it would take the spring thaw to melt such a heavy snowfall.

Michailo could not have gone far in such difficult conditions. Not with Lilias and little Artamon to consider . . .

'My Lord?' It was Sosia again. 'I think you'd better come with me.'

Sosia had assembled the household servants in the kitchens; all stood meekly waiting for him in a line, heads bowed, like errant schoolchildren.

'Ilsi has something you should hear, My Lord,' said Sosia. 'Well, come on, girl!'

Ninusha pushed Ilsi forward.

'They say that I'm losing my mind, My Lord. But I heard what I heard. In *her* rooms. Didn't I always say she was a witch?'

'She's talking of Lilias,' said Sosia.

'I was in her rooms, putting on the dustsheets, covering everything up, just as Sosia told me to. After all, My Lady left in such a hurry, she didn't even take her jewels with her.'

'You were trying them on, weren't you?' Ninusha burst out. Ilsi flashed her a venomous look.

'And . . . I heard this voice.' She placed one hand on her heart, as if it were still beating too fast. 'Speaking – all wavery-like and indistinct – from behind me. And I knew I was alone. I was so terrified, I almost passed out.'

'Get to the point, Ilsi,' said Sosia sternly.

Ilsi shot Sosia a resentful little glance.

'I was just getting to it. There *wasn't* anyone there. The voice was coming from that clock thing she has on her mantelpiece. The one in the glass case that she was so touchy about. Remember? "Don't touch that, you clumsy country girl!"' She mimicked Lilias's voice.

'A voice coming from a clock?' Gavril said wearily; he was beginning to think this was another waste of his time. 'It must be some kind of mechanical toy – or a music box. Maybe you jogged it and set off the mechanism?'

'It spoke to me,' insisted Ilsi. 'Or rather to her. It kept saying, "Lilias, are you there? Dysis, where's your mistress? Please respond."'

'Witchcraft,' whispered Ninusha, languorous eyes widening. 'Daemon voices. *Her* familiars.'

'Show me,' Gavril said.

'You must be careful, My Lord, it might be a trap—'

'Just show me.'

Dust sheets were draped over the striped silk sofas, velvet stools and marquetry card tables in Lilias's salon. Only the ornaments on the marble mantelpiece had not yet been covered up.

'There, My Lord,' said Ilsi, pointing.

A domed glass case enclosed the mechanism; a glittering device of crystal and intricately crafted metals. Gavril had, like Ilsi, assumed it was a clock. But on closer inspection, he realized it was like no clock he had ever seen. Cautiously he tapped the glass. With a click, the front opened, sprung on invisible hinges. Inside the device glittered even more brightly. Now he could detect a faint hum – barely more than a vibration – emanating from the mechanism. Fascinated, he leaned forward and listened.

'What *is* it?' he murmured, more to himself than the others present.

The humming was growing louder; more of a crackling.

'Take care, My Lord,' Sosia said nervously.

'*Lilias. Lilias. Can you hear me? Respond, please.*'

Ilsi gave a little shriek. Gavril stepped back, astonished. The voice – indistinct and crackly – had issued from the mechanism.

'*Respond.*'

'Answer it,' Gavril whispered to Ilsi.

'I – I can't!'

'Say you're Dysis.'

520

'Please don't make me, My Lord—'

'You must,' he said, catching hold of her hand and dragging her forwards.

'But won't it know? That I'm not her?'

'*Respond!*'

Gavril gripped her wrist harder. 'Speak to it.'

'Ha-hallo?' Ilsi quavered. 'I'm D-Dysis.'

'*At last. All these weeks – and no answer. I feared the worst.*' A burst of crackling almost obscured the faint voice. '*Can you still hear me?*'

'Ask who it is,' Gavril murmured in Ilsi's ear. He could feel her trembling.

'Who's speaking?'

'*Feodor, who else? Listen, Dysis, now that this infernal interference has cleared at last, I have vital news for your mistress—*' Another loud burst of crackling cut across the voice. '*. . . Lord Gavril . . . his mother Elysia.*'

'What!' Gavril felt a shiver of apprehension go through him.

'P-please repeat,' stammered Ilsi.

'*Tell Lilias that Prince Eugene has Elysia Andar in his keeping. She must persuade Lord Gavril to—*'

Gavril pushed Ilsi to one side.

'You're talking to Gavril Nagarian now. What has happened to my mother? And who are you?'

There was a silence, punctuated by crackling.

'Reply!' Gavril cried.

'*Altan Kazimir is our envoy,*' came the indistinct response. '*You will find him at Narvazh. You must do as he instructs. Make sure your men don't harm him, but bring him directly to you.*'

'Kazimir? Doctor Kazimir?' Gavril repeated.

'*You must do exactly what Kazimir tells you. Or it will go ill with your mother.*'

The crackling suddenly ceased as the glittering artefact fell silent.

'Hallo. Hallo!' Gavril shouted. No response. His overriding impulse was to dash it to the ground, destroying its crystal perfection.

He looked up and saw Ilsi staring at him, face white as her starched linen apron.

'Your mother, My Lord—'

'How can my mother be in Tielen?' Gavril said, utterly bewildered. 'She's in Smarna, hundreds of miles away. What possible reason would she have to go to Tielen?'

'Perhaps they had her kidnapped?' whispered Ilsi, wide-eyed.

Shadowy figures stealing through the moonlit grounds of the Villa Andara, the sound of shattering window-glass, a woman's terrified scream . . .

Even the thought of his mother's abduction filled him with a cold, irrational fury.

'Call Jushko to me!'

So Lilias was a spy. That at least made sense – of a kind. But on whose behalf had she been working? She was from Muscobar, not Tielen.

What had been going on in the world outside all the time he had been cut off here in this winter wilderness?

'My Lord.' Jushko appeared in the doorway. 'What's Ilsi babbling about?'

'That mechanism', Gavril pointed to the mantelpiece, 'is not a clock but some kind of communication device. Someone called Feodor has just told me that my mother is being held

522

as a hostage by Prince Eugene of Tielen.'

'What?' Jushko stared at him in evident disbelief.

'And Doctor Kazimir is at a place called Narvazh with further instructions.'

'Kazimir at Narvazh?' repeated Jushko. 'So he and Lilias were working for Tielen all along, eh? Pair of vipers, the two of 'em. Sooner we catch My Lady Lilias, the better.' He went up to the mechanism and peered at it suspiciously. 'But your mother – what proof do we have they've got her? Did you hear her voice, did she speak to you?'

'You're saying it's a bluff?'

'Of course it's a bluff!' said Jushko.

Gavril heard the undisguised scorn in Jushko's voice. Jushko had given him the seasoned soldier's interpretation of Prince Eugene's tactics. Even if not intended as such, it felt like a slight, yet another *druzhina* criticism of his weakness as leader.

'Don't believe a word – until she's spoken to you and you're certain it's her.'

'If only I could re-establish contact . . .' Gavril probed and pressed the crystal device, trying to coax it into life again. 'There must be some trick to this.' A faint thrumming pulse began in his temples. 'Damn it all to hell, I can't make the cursed contraption work!'

'A bluff, I tell you,' repeated Jushko.

'But what if my mother *has* been kidnapped?' Gavril felt the faint thrumming quicken to an ominous throb. Pacing the confines of Kastel Drakhaon, waiting for the *druzhina* to find Altan Kazimir would drive him mad.

'Jushko, I'm taking a scouting party to look for Kazimir and I want you to accompany me.'

'Yes, My Lord!' Jushko said.

'And as for Lilias and her part in this conspiracy – I want her brought back alive for questioning. Alive – and unharmed.' Gavril pressed a hand to his throbbing forehead. 'Station a man here by this device. At the first sign of further communication, he is to contact me.'

Gavril smelt the familiar tang of sea-brine on the biting wind.

'The sea! We can't be far now.'

He urged the *druzhina* onwards. The growing sense of foreboding had driven him relentlessly across the snowy moorlands, barely stopping to rest the horses, even riding at night by the thin light of the setting moon. Jushko had sent scouts on ahead to Narvazh to search for Doctor Kazimir, but as yet no-one had reported back.

Now Gavril spotted one of the scouts returning at the gallop across the snow, crouched low in the saddle as though to avoid enemy fire.

The scout wheeled his mount around and the horse skidded to a halt, hooves scuffing up lumps of snow.

'Narvazh – attacked—' His words came out on clouds of steam. 'No sign – of Kazimir—'

'Attacked!' Gavril felt a shiver of fury, hot as fever, burn through his body. 'Who attacked them? Are the attackers still there?'

The scout, trying to catch his breath, shook his head.

'On to Narvazh!' Gavril cried.

Narvazh lay huddled beneath them in a narrow cove, a scatter of grey-stone fishermen's cottages and fish-gutting sheds, braced against the bitter winds that swept across the Saltyk Sea.

Gavril and his *druzhina* dismounted on the clifftop and stared down at the little port. The wind off the frozen sea battered them, stinging ears, eyes and nostrils. There was no movement below, no wisps of smoke rising from the stunted chimneys, but on the wind, Gavril thought he caught a distant sound of coughing.

The scout beckoned them to lead their horses down a winding cliff-path. As they entered the village, they saw overturned barrels of salt fish leaking their contents onto the rocks.

'This feels wrong,' Jushko muttered. 'Just like walking straight into a trap.' He sent two men back up the path to keep watch.

A door banged suddenly, slammed by the wind. Jushko whirled around, sabre-blade hissing from its sheath. The *druzhina* froze where they stood, axes and crossbows at the ready.

'Come out!' Jushko shouted. 'Show yourself!'

Gavril caught sight of a flicker of shadow within one of the cottages. He forced his chapped lips to move, tasting salt in the cracks.

'There!'

Two of the *druzhina* kicked in the door and dragged out a man, flinging him down in the trodden snow.

'M-mercy, My Lords.' The man cowered in the snow, hands raised above his head in supplication.

'This isn't Kazimir,' Jushko said. He sounded a little disappointed. 'Get up. We mean you no harm. Tell the Lord Drakhaon what's happened here.'

'L-Lord Drakhaon—' stammered the man, even

more terrified. 'S-soldiers came over the ice. Fired on us. Smoke everywhere, white smoke – made everyone sick.'

'Fan out!' Jushko ordered the *druzhina*. 'Search. Everywhere!'

'How many soldiers?' Gavril asked.

The man gave a helpless shrug. 'Difficult to – t-tell through the smoke.'

'More than my *druzhina* here?'

'Yes, oh yes.' He nodded his head weakly. 'Many more.'

'And which way did they go?' Jushko demanded.

'Couldn't see.'

'We're looking for a doctor. Calls himself Kazimir,' Gavril said.

The man gave a shrug. 'Never heard the name.'

'And where are all the villagers?' Gavril thought he had heard the faint sound of coughing again.

'Sick. The old ones and the young, very sick. Our livestock dying. White smoke – must have been poisoned—'

'Look at this, Lord Drakhaon.' One of the *druzhina* came back, balancing a twisted fragment of metal on the tip of his sabre.

Gavril took it in his gloved hand and examined it. It looked like a spent cartridge case – though larger than any ammunition he had ever come across in Smarna. The metal gleamed dully in the raw air, and it seemed as if there was a faint trace of some substance on the inner side. Cautiously he raised it to his nose and sniffed. 'Faugh!' He let it drop to the snow. 'That's not gunpowder.' The dried powdery deposit had given off an unpleasant odour, not dissimilar to some of the poisonous chymical compounds he used to mix to make his oil paints.

A feeble wail came from the open door of the cottage. Gavril turned and saw a young girl-child leaning against the doorframe, face sickly pale.

'Da—' she said, extending her arms shakily towards the man. The weak cry turned into a retching cough that went on and on.

'Go back in the warm, Milla.' The man hurried to her and gathered her up in his arms. The child was wheezing uncontrollably now, thin ribs heaving as she struggled to breathe.

Why had the attackers fired on harmless villagers? Gavril turned away, clenching his fists.

'You heard, Lord Drakhaon?' Jushko murmured in his ear. 'They came over the ice? These soldiers have come from Tielen.'

One of the scouts came slithering down the rocks at the far end of the cove.

'We've found tracks! Heading north.'

Jushko gave the fragment of metal a vicious kick, sending it spinning far out over the snow.

'Let's get after them,' Gavril said.

As they followed the scouts, leading the horses along the windblown sands, Gavril found himself tormented by a tumult of premonitions and forebodings. That dangerous, volatile mood gripped him again as it had outside Klim. He could – and might – do anything. And the consequences . . .

Stay in control.

He forced himself to concentrate on his surroundings.

Such a bleak, rocky shore, the crags and boulders white with a rime of frozen salt . . . .

Beyond the shore stretched the sea that should have crashed against the rocks with the energy of great breakers but lay inert, a sheet of frozen water. And beyond, far across the Saltyk Sea, a distant suggestion of land that Jushko told him was Tielen . . .

'Where's Kazimir?' muttered Jushko, scanning the vast expanse of grey-green ice.

'Over here!' One of the *druzhina* who had gone on ahead appeared from behind a large rock further up the beach.

Something lay, half-hidden from view, camouflaged beneath driftwood and canvas.

'Looks like some kind of craft,' Jushko said, pulling away the concealing branches and canvas. 'See, this canvas has been used as a sail.'

'It's not a boat,' Gavril said, kneeling down to look more closely. 'The bottom's flat. More like a giant sledge. Or ice-craft . . .'

'A Tielen ice-craft? Kazimir's craft?'

Before Gavril could reply, there came a sudden sharp retort, as if the ice were cracking. And then another and another . . .

Bullets whizzed into the rock. Chips of grazed rock flew into the air.

'Ambush! Get down, My Lord!' hissed Jushko, grabbing Gavril and pulling him down.

Explosion of bright pain, then darkness.

One of the *druzhina* rolled, groaning, on the sands, clutching at his shoulder. Another lay still, face-down, where he had fallen. The others hastily ran for cover, ducking behind boulders to avoid the hail of bullets.

'Where are they?' Jushko muttered between

clenched teeth. 'And why didn't we spot 'em?'

Gavril shook his head, trying to clear the last dizzying vestiges of the brutally shattered blood-bond. He didn't need to look at the blood trickling into the sand to know one man was dead.

'Kazimir, eh? We fell for this one!' Jushko began to laugh, a dry self-deprecatory chuckle. 'What fools the Tielens must think we are. Easier to lure into a trap than woodcocks.'

'We don't stand a chance here, not against their carbines. They can pick us off, one by one.' Gavril peered up at the cliffs behind them, listening for the telltale click of carbines being reloaded.

'Our scouts are still up on the cliff—'

'Ssh,' Gavril whispered. 'Listen.'

'Can't hear a thing.'

'Exactly. If they were going to fire again, we'd have heard them priming their weapons.'

Jushko had said there were scouts close by. Gavril closed his eyes, searching for them with his mind.

'*Druzhina. I'm under attack. Come to my aid.*'

They had not heard him in the distant mountains. But now, he thought he sensed a faint response and caught a twitch of movement amongst the frozen gorse bushes high on the clifftop.

'Our men are on the cliffs, Jushko.' He rose to his feet. 'Come out, Tielens!' he yelled in the common tongue. 'You're surrounded. Show yourselves!'

Jushko walked out to stand beside him, arms contemptuously folded, as though daring the the unseen attackers to fire on them. And then he let out a low whistle. 'Well now . . . would you look at that.'

The crumbling base of the cliff rippled, as if a snow mist were suddenly melting away.

Where there had seemed to be nothing but bare cliff rock, Gavril saw men, uniformed soldiers, each one pointing a carbine at him. He swallowed down a sudden surge of panic.

'I am Gavril Nagarian. I was told to come here to meet with Altan Kazimir. Where is he?'

Gavril saw the soldiers glance uneasily at their commanding officer. He was young, not much older than himself, with a wild shock of ice-pale hair, barely confined beneath his tricorne.

Had they understood him? Gavril wondered. Did his name mean anything to them?

Slowly he stretched out one hand towards them. Claws blue as slivers of sapphire glittered in a sudden shaft of cold winter sun.

'Tell your men to throw down their weapons.' Little shocks of sensation ran up and down his arm.

I will not lose control. It was taking all his willpower to subdue the dark impulse which threatened to overwhelm him.

The Tielens gazed uncertainly back at him. The young officer raised his hand too. The front column dropped to one knee, levelling their carbines at him. This was not what he had anticipated at all . . .

The officer's hand dropped suddenly. 'Now!' Gavril heard him shout, and the word was almost muffled in a fusillade of shots.

'Look out!' Jushko grabbed hold of him, trying to fling him out of the line of fire.

Bullets thudded past them, exploding against the rocks behind.

One bullet, larger than the rest, landed close to Gavril's feet – and, to his astonishment, opened up like a flower.

'What in God's name—'

A strange fizzing sound drowned his words. Clouds of white smoke came hissing from the opened shell and blew across the shore like sea-mist, obscuring the Tielens from view. A dry alchymical smell poisoned the air.

'Cover your faces!' Gavril yelled. Pulling out his handkerchief, he clapped it over his nose and mouth.

All he knew now was that they were under attack.

He must retaliate – or die.

Gavril battled his way forwards, head down, through the white vapours that billowed over the sands.

His eyes stung. The dry, bitter taste of the alchymical smoke was in his mouth. Yet still he forged stubbornly on.

Behind him he could hear his own men coughing and spluttering as they inhaled the fumes.

But beyond the clearing smoke he saw indistinct figures hurrying away. The Tielens were retreating under the cover of their poisoned smokescreen.

The people of Narvazh had offered no resistance, yet the Tielens had fired on them indiscriminately, men, women and children alike. Now it was their turn to pay.

A plume of flame spurted from Gavril's fingertips, luminous, blue as a kingfisher's wing.

As the blue flame pierced the last drifts of smoke, they spotted him coming towards them.

'Fire!' Gavril heard the young officer scream the command aloud – but as if from a great distance away.

Aim at their weapons, not at the men . . .

He raised his hand – and sent the blue flame streaking towards the Tielens.

Bullets whizzed close past his head, but many went wide as his attack met its mark.

His head swam with churning heat, sparks danced before his eyes, blue fireflies, and still the pressure was building within him . . .

'Enough!' he cried. He must keep control. He must not let the Drakhaoul take him over again.

He dropped to his knees on the frozen sand.

His ears rang with dizziness.

On the beach below the last wisps of smoke lifted from the sands, drifting away out across the frozen sea.

Where there had been soldiers, living men, lay several charred heaps of blackened ash and bone. He had aimed at their carbines – but even at this range, his power had been too great.

'You should – have surrendered – while you could—' whispered Gavril.

Jushko led the *druzhina* off along the shore to search for survivors. Those who had inhaled the Tielens' smoke still coughed and retched miserably as they went.

Gavril sat watching, hugging his knees close to his chest. His whole body ached and his skull felt as if it had been seared in a furnace.

He heard the *druzhina* calling to each other as they searched the rocks and caves.

The face of the young Tielen officer, eyes wide with fear and anger, flashed into his mind. He had not wanted to die.

A cloud of guilt overwhelmed Gavril, blacker than the drifting smoke.

And yet he had only acted to defend his men. He had offered terms of surrender – and they had been flung back in his face.

From further down the beach he heard Jushko calling to the other *druzhina*, his voice gravel-dry from the effects of the smoke.

'These prints here, in the sand. Looks like some got away, after all.'

He came back towards Gavril, his lean face twisted into a frown of incomprehension.

'How the devil did they escape? And why didn't we see them go?'

'Their weapons are far superior to ours,' Gavril said slowly, hearing his own voice as if from a great distance away. 'Bullets that release poisonous smoke. We don't stand a chance against them.'

'But we have you, My Lord.' Jushko squatted beside him in the sand and passed him his water-flask. The water was ice-cold and tinged with a dash of aquavit to keep the taste clean. Gavril gulped it down, hoping to ease the burning in his throat and mouth. He did not acknowledge what Jushko had said; the effort of controlling the outburst of power had exhausted him. Already he could feel the return of the dark, searing thirst that would not be quenched by water or aquavit.

His situation was hopeless. If he allowed himself to become the war-leader the *druzhina* wanted him to be, it would be at the cost of his own soul. The creature that inhabited him would force him to give in to its monstrous appetites and desires. His own humanity would be slowly eaten away. Even now he knew he was losing touch with his true self, forgetting the little things that had once been so important to him: the hue of Astasia's eyes, dark as the velvety petals of a viola, or the sound of his mother's laughter as they played shuttlecock together on the overgrown lawns of the Villa Andara...

He would become nothing but a shell for the Drakhaoul.

Two of the *druzhina* flung their prisoner onto the sand in front of Gavril.

'Doctor Kazimir, Lord Drakhaon.'

The man who lay sprawled at Gavril's feet was mud-stained, wet and ragged. Gavril glanced at Jushko for confirmation of the prisoner's identity; Jushko nodded his head.

'D-don't hurt me—' The doctor was shaking, his hands clasped over his head as if to ward off blows.

'We found him hiding in a sea-cave.'

Slowly the doctor dragged himself to his knees, head drooping forwards. His fair hair hung in damp rats' tails about his face.

'You have instructions for me,' Gavril said.

Kazimir fumbled in the inside of his stained jacket and drew out a leather folder. As he took the folder from Kazimir, Gavril saw with a sudden quickening of the heart that the Orlov crest was tooled on the leather.

Was there some communication inside for him from Astasia?

Tearing open the ribbons, he unwrapped three crumpled papers, two of which bore his mother's characteristically bold, looping handwriting.

'From my mother,' he said, unable to hide the

emotion in his voice. News – after so many long weeks of absence. Now that he held the longed-for letters in his hands, he could hardly bear to open them.

The first was Kazimir's safe-conduct, but the second was addressed to him:

Dearest Gavril,
   We have so much to talk of. I cannot wait to
see you. I have missed you so much!

Blinking the tears from his eyes, he read on, devouring her words, then returned to the beginning to read them again more slowly. And then he looked sternly at Altan Kazimir who crouched trembling in the sand at his feet.

'I don't understand. This reads as if my mother were on her way to see me.'

Kazimir fumbled in his pocket and brought out a pair of twisted spectacles which he balanced on the bridge of his aquiline nose, winding the wires round about his ears. He glanced at the letter and nodded.

'Your mother has been severely misled in this whole affair. Duped. She came to Tielen with me on the understanding she would be granted safe passage to Azhkendir. And now she is Eugene's prisoner.'

'So it *is* true?'

'It's explained in the other letter.'

The third letter was sealed in glossy blue wax with the sign of a swan. Gavril broke the seal and swiftly scanned the contents:

To Gavril Nagarian, Lord Drakhaon of
Azhkendir:

By the time you read this, my armies will have crossed onto Azhkendi soil.

My terms are these: first, that you allow my armies safe passage through Azhkendir; second, that you relinquish all rights to the throne of Azhkendir in favour of Jaromir Arkhel, rightful Lord of Azhkendir, and third, that the said Lord Arkhel is restored to me, unharmed.

In return, I guarantee the release of your mother, Elysia Andar, and a safe passage to permanent exile in Smarna.

Eugene of Tielen

Jaromir, Eugene's protégé? Gavril slowly lowered the paper, staring unseeing at the distant horizon. He knew himself to be outmanoeuvred. Betrayed. And by the man to whom he had sworn an oath of friendship.

'Well, My Lord?' demanded Jushko impatiently. 'What does it say?'

Gavril could not speak. He stared at the words as they swam before his smoke-stung eyes. Eventually he said, 'It says we are to offer no resistance to Eugene's armies. If we do, my mother's life will be forfeit.'

Jushko swore. 'Does Eugene expect us to stand idly by whilst his armies ride roughshod through our lands?'

'But if we resist, they'll kill her.'

The sound of hoofbeats made him glance round. An Azhkendi scout was riding down along the cliff-path, making for the beach.

'Lord Drakhaon!' The rider leaped down from the saddle. 'A mighty army crossing the ice—'

'Mighty?' Jushko caught hold of the scout by the shoulders. 'What d'you mean, mighty?'

'Hundreds upon thousands. Men, horses, cannon—'

'So we've been duped,' Gavril said. 'These men were merely decoys, sent ahead to distract us, whilst the main body of Eugene's army has just marched into Azhkendir, unhindered.'

35

The troops came riding over the snowy hills, regiment after regiment, the faint winter sunlight glittering on boot buckles, harnesses, swords and pistols.

Elysia watched in growing dismay as hundreds, thousands of soldiers assembled on the bleak shingle shore below. Eugene was sending the might of his Northern Army against her son, and there was nothing she could do to prevent it.

A day and a night had passed since Kazimir had sped off across the ice – and in that time, a vast invasion force had gathered along the coastline. Imprisoned in the inn on the cliff, she had watched the troops assembling ice-yachts, their breath steaming in the brittle air as they laboured.

She had recovered a little of her self-composure. Yesterday she had been furious that she had allowed herself to be so easily duped. By night she was furious with those who had betrayed her. How could she have allowed herself to be deceived by Feodor Velemir? Even thinking of her foolishness brought the colour flooding to her face. He had seen her as easy prey: a middle-aged woman, aware that her charms were fast fading, too readily swayed by the attentions of a cultured, urbane diplomat.

What a fool she had been to listen to him and not to her own common sense.

Sitting at the inn window, her cheek resting against her hand, she stared out into the fast-gathering gloom and saw Eugene's troops lighting flares and torches until the whole icy shore glimmered with lights like a fairground.

A carriage appeared out of the darkness, drawing to a halt outside the inn. Orders were barked and the soldiers on guard duty stood swiftly to attention, carbines on shoulders. The door opened and Prince Eugene came in, followed by several of his officers, shuffling in their haste to escape the icy cold and blowing on their frozen fingers.

Elysia rose. Here was her captor, the man who had given the order to keep her from her son. She forgot about protocol and court etiquette. Head held high, she walked straight up to him.

'Madame Andar,' he said, briefly acknowledging her. His aide-de-camp hurried forwards to usher her away.

'How dare you keep me a prisoner here, Your Highness!' she said, shaking the aide's hand from her arm. 'I demand to be released.'

Eugene handed his gloves and fur-rimmed tricorne to his aide-de-camp.

'I have made arrangements that you be taken

back to Swanholm, madame. You should be more comfortable there.'

'Comfortable!' Elysia was almost speechless. 'I don't care about comfort, Highness. You are keeping me here against my will. I came here in good faith to plead for my son.'

He looked at her then and she felt the chill of his gaze; the cold, determined look of a man whose strength of purpose is unshakable.

'The situation has altered, madame. We have declared war on Azhkendir. You are our hostage. And will remain so until your son has surrendered. No – not merely surrendered – until he has agreed to all our terms and conditions.' He bowed his head to her and continued on through into a further fire-lit chamber, followed by his officers.

Elysia stared after them. When the door was shut, she found that her legs were trembling so violently that she had to sit down.

'Oh Gavril, Gavril, what have I done?' she whispered, her mind an agony of apprehension. 'I thought I was saving your life – and all I've done is deliver you into the hands of your enemies.'

Later Elysia wondered if she had dreamed it. The hushed voices in the darkness, the sudden glow of a dark light, red as heart's blood.

'You're certain?' The voice was Eugene's, but so different from the formal, commanding tone she had heard earlier. This was the voice of a man riven with hope and fear, a man as vulnerable as her own son.

'Look, Highness, look how brightly it burns. He *is* alive.'

'Then pray. Pray we may not be too late.'

And the crimson bloodlight had abruptly disappeared as if concealed and the voices did not speak again.

Voices, men's voices, cracked out orders.

Elysia blinked awake. She had fallen asleep in a chair by the fire and, as she tried to get up, stiffness almost paralysed her. She hobbled over to the window, peering out through the ice-flowered glass, breathing hard onto the ice to try to melt a peephole.

A dull dawn was breaking over the frozen sea, but the sky was lit with torches and their light turned the grey-green ice to gold. Hundreds upon hundreds of Eugene's men were setting out across the ice, some on ice-yachts, some leading horses.

How could the ice sustain such a great weight, the weight of a whole army?

Amidst the officers leading their men out, she picked out the tall, broad-shouldered figure of Eugene, walking alongside his men just as if he were a common soldier.

Is that the secret of his success? she wondered. The common touch? The sharing of his men's hardships, fighting beside them, shoulder to shoulder?

The Tielen army advanced so efficiently, so purposefully, towards the shores of Azhkendir. The indisciplined rabble of mountain-brigands Volkh had called his *druzhina* would not stand a chance against such a well-oiled military machine.

'Madame Andar.'

She turned – and saw with a shiver that Kaspar Linnaius was watching her.

'You do not go with them, Magus.'

He smiled. 'An old man such as myself would only hinder their progress. No, I return to Swanholm. The Prince has requested that you accompany me. A sleigh is waiting for us . . .'

Outside, Elysia huddled down under the furs in the sleigh opposite the Magus. The dawn air was so cold each breath she drew burned bitter-cold in her nostrils and throat.

As the driver touched the sleigh-horses with his whip and they began to glide away across the hard-packed snow, she looked back and saw an extraordinary sight: where there had been desolate, frozen sea, she could see nothing but soldiers and horses, as if Prince Eugene had decided to hold military manoeuvres on the ice instead of the parade ground.

If Elysia had entertained any ideas of escape, they were soon dashed.

The sleigh was met by an escort of armed cavalry at the northern gates to the Swanholm estate.

Snow had fallen on Swanholm in the night and transformed it into a shimmering edifice of snow and ice. The soft autumn colours of the birchwoods had been blotted out by the bleak whiteness of the snow. The lake glimmered grey amidst the formal parterres, the dark topiary of the yews like black chessmen on a white board.

More true winter palace than the Orlovs' glittering confection of glass, gilt and marble, Elysia thought bitterly, gazing down as the carriage road took them through the leafless alleys of chestnuts. How fitting for a prison. My prison.

An officer of the Household Guard led her to

the rooms she had occupied before their departure.

'I have orders from His Highness that you are to be treated with all courtesy, madame,' he said, saluting her. 'Please inform the guard if you need anything.'

Elysia stood on the threshold of the room, gazing about her. A fire burned in the grate. The elegant furniture, the pretty silk hangings, all seemed to belie the fact that she was a prisoner. And yet in her absence, they had fitted iron bars to the window.

She shook her head.

'Only my freedom,' she whispered.

Gavril pushed aside the bowl of dark red beetroot soup which the landlord had brought him. He had no appetite for food or drink.

He had killed again. And this time it had not been steppe wolves but men. He had looked into their faces, he had seen their fear – and still he had used his powers to destroy them. And even though he had killed in self-defence, he felt a profound sense of self-loathing.

He stumbled outside to the inn stables where the horses were being fed and watered. Water. He needed water: ice-cold well-water to quench his burning thirst. At the back of the stables, nausea overcame him and he kneeled in the snow, vomiting up the pitchy contents of his stomach.

'My Lord? Are you all right?'

Still queasy, he looked up to see a young serving-girl bending over him. The light from the stable lanterns gilded her soft skin, glinted tawny-gold in her brown hair.

'You're sick. Can I help you?' She placed her

hand on his shoulder. A tantalizingly delicious fragrance wafted towards him, the fragrance of her young body and her warm, sweet blood. He found himself overwhelmed by a desire to possess, to crush, to rend ...

'N-no!' Gavril jerked round, knocking her hand away. 'Leave me alone!' He must not let her near him. In this dangerous state, he was not sure what he might do.

'Your *eyes*—'

He saw her draw back, staring. And then she turned and ran, almost tripping over her skirts in her haste.

He sat in the snow, shivering, until the cravings had died down a little. Then, feverish and light-headed, he forced himself to go back into the overheated taproom.

Kazimir sat in a corner staring into a mug of ale which he held cupped between his shackled hands. The *druzhina* were warming hands and feet at the fire and dipping rye bread into bowls of soup.

Gavril went over to him.

'Tell me what's been going on in the world outside, Doctor.'

Kazimir looked up, blinking. 'You mean Prince Eugene?'

'Why invade Azhkendir?'

'Eugene is building himself an empire. Only you stand between him and Muscobar. With young Andrei Orlov drowned, there's no-one left but you to stop him marching into Mirom and—'

'Andrei Orlov *drowned*?'

'In a storm in the Straits. Pity poor Muscobar.

People starving in Mirom, Eugene and his war-hounds baying at the gates . . .'

'But what about Astasia?' All his own troubles forgotten, Gavril could only think of Astasia, alone and in desperate need of comfort, mourning the loss of her beloved brother.

'And when have you ever heard of a woman ruling Muscobar? She's engaged to marry Eugene. They're planning some ludicrously expensive wedding ceremony in Mirom . . . parasites, all blood-sucking parasites, these aristocrats, preying on the poor to—' Kazimir broke off. 'I – I do beg your pardon, Lord Drakhaon, I quite forgot myself.'

Astasia was to marry Eugene? Gavril had hardly heard the rest of Kazimir's rambling. Now he felt doubly betrayed.

'Lilias's device told me that you come as Eugene's envoy, Doctor. I must do exactly as you say, or it will go ill with my mother.'

'Lilias?' Kazimir glanced around uneasily. 'Wh-where is she?'

'She seduced one of my men and fled,' Gavril said, watching the doctor's face, remembering what Kostya had told him of Kazimir's feelings for Lilias Arbelian. He was in no mood to be sensitive. 'But we discovered her communications device. That was how we knew you were on your way.'

Kazimir slowly nodded.

'She used your elixir to poison my father. Did you know that?'

Kazimir nodded again. 'I – guessed as much.' He seemed utterly crushed.

'And now they've sent you to poison me, too.'

'No, My Lord. Not poison. Cure. Heal.'

'What', Gavril said, 'is the difference, precisely?'

'It's a . . . scientific thing,' Kazimir said, as though casting around for the right words.

'The man who spoke to us using the device called himself Feodor. Do you know who he is?'

'Feodor Velemir,' Kazimir said in a whisper. Gavril could see from his expression that it was not a name he felt kindly about.

Suddenly he was back in Lilias's rooms, the aromatic scent of herbal tea perfuming the air. Bewitching green eyes gazed into his.

'Count Velemir, an old friend . . . introduced me to your father . . .'

'Spymaster to the House of Orlov,' said Kazimir with distaste. 'And now, it seems, friend and advisor to Prince Eugene. Double agent. Traitor.'

'And Lilias's "old friend"?'

'She started her career as his mistress,' Kazimir said vindictively, 'until he grew tired and found a better use for her.'

A bitter rind of moon shed a thin light over the dark snowflats as Gavril and his *druzhina* rode back to Kastel Drakhaon.

The horses were weary and the last miles of the journey, toiling on through the freezing night, seemed to last for ever.

At last they passed under the ivied archway into the torchlit courtyard of the kastel.

Sosia hurried down the steps to greet them.

'Lord Gavril, that cursed contraption of Lilias's. It keeps asking for you. Over and over again. Something about Doctor Kazimir—' She gave a little yelp of surprise. 'Oh! He's here.'

Gavril swung down from the saddle and flung his reins to Ivar. 'Jushko, bring the doctor.'

As they entered Lilias's rooms, Gavril saw Kazimir give an involuntary shiver and glance uneasily about him, almost as if he expected her still to be there.

'*Lord Drakhaon.*' The faint voice swelled out of the low, intermittent hum.

'I'm here. Who is this, and what do you want?' Gavril said brusquely.

'*Is Doctor Kazimir with you?*'

'He is.'

'*Let him speak for himself.*'

'You promised me I could speak with my mother.' Gavril was in no mood to bandy words. 'I want proof she is alive.'

'*Not until Kazimir has identified himself.*'

Gavril glanced at the doctor. 'Speak to them. And be quick.'

Jushko pushed Kazimir forward.

'I – I am Altan Kazimir. All is in order.'

There was no reply. Gavril saw Kazimir nervously wipe his hand across his glistening brow.

'*Very well,*' came the reply at last.

'*Gavril.*' It was a woman's voice, speaking the Smarnan tongue. '*Gavril, is it you?*'

Gavril's heart had begun to race at the sound of the distant voice. 'Mother?' he said hesitantly.

'*Gavril – I'm so, so sorry.*' It *was* her, he knew it, in spite of the crackling and distortion.

'Are they treating you well?'

'*Believe me, dear Gavril—*' Elysia's words were breaking up. '*I never intended this to—*'

'Are you all right, Mother?' Gavril cried,

clutching the glass case. 'Tell me you're all right!'

There was no reply.

'Mother!' he shouted into the glittering crystal.

'If you wish to see your mother alive, My Lord, you will submit to Doctor Kazimir's treatment.' The man's voice, infuriatingly calm, came through again. *'He will inform us by this device when it has taken effect. Then – and only then – will we enter into any negotiations as to the precise conditions relating to the release of your mother.'*

'I want assurances that she is well,' Gavril said, his voice rough with despair. 'I want to speak with her again.'

There was a pause.

'Stand by for further instructions.'

The voice ceased abruptly and the low hum died away.

Suppose he lost all control of himself and attacked the main Tielen army? Gavril clenched his fists, willing the thought away. Nails, sharp as chips of lapis, dug into his palms. By the time he had come back to his senses, Elysia would be dead. The thought chilled him to the depths of his soul.

'My Lord?'

'Don't know – how long I can control – myself—' Slowly he felt the darkness recede. With a grimace of pain, he unclenched his fists and saw the deep lacerations he had inflicted, saw the blood well up, smearing his palms with its unnatural hue of purple-blue.

There was only one way to make sure it never happened.

'Doctor, I want you to set up your apparatus in the Kalika Tower. If you need anything – fresh water, fire – my servants will supply you. Jushko, see to it.'

Jushko hesitated, then relented.

'As you command, Lord Drakhaon.'

'We'll review our plans in the morning. Meet me at dawn, in Kostya's room.'

Gavril dreams:

He is standing on the roof of the Kalika Tower.

Dark mist drifts behind him, rolling in over the mountains, soft, silent, stifling, until the land beneath is obscured. There are particles of darkness in the mist, glittering like powdered crystal as they fall on Gavril's upturned face.

Dust of dead stars . . .

Suddenly the sky is filled with wings.

Sparkling, spangled wings, luminescent, veins pulsing with jewelled fire, daemon-creatures dart and dive about him, fanning his face with their searing breath.

He opens his mouth to cry out in wonder – but the rush of air, the beat of the great wings, muffle his voice and he is rising, rising into the sky . . .

He is flying.

Now the kastel is so far below it seems no more than an insignificant pebble on a barren shore. He circles above his home, the wind keen as ice on his skin. The others are turning, wheeling away towards the distant horizon, already far, so far away.

'Wait – wait for me—'

He wants to go with them. But some force is pulling him back down towards the kastel below, sucking him back into a whirling vortex of dark mist . . .

He woke to a grey dawn – and an ache of emptiness that he could not understand – that he had been left behind. Marooned.

Abandoned.

'You promised me news of Lilias, Lord Drakhaon.'

Gavril saw Jaromir standing over his bed, watching him.

'How did you—' Gavril's mind still whirled with the rush of air, the throbbing heartbeat of wings.

Jaromir gestured briefly towards the tapestry that concealed the door to the deserted East Wing. 'I thought it better your *druzhina* didn't see me. After all, they still believe you killed me up on the mountain,' he added with a wry, twisted smile.

Jaromir Arkhel. Gavril gazed at the man Eugene of Tielen had elected to depose him, trying to quell the simmering bitterness in his heart.

'What time is it?' He had fallen asleep in his travelling clothes. Servants must have come in to light the fire, but no-one had woken him.

'About seven in the morning.'

'Seven already?' Gavril went over to the wash-basin and poured in water, plunging his face into the bowl, coming up dripping, gasping at the icy shock of the cold. He had to test Jaromir. 'Jaromir, Azhkendir is under attack.' He made a play of fumbling for a towel, closely watching Jaromir's reactions. 'Eugene of Tielen has launched an invasion across the ice.'

'Eugene?'

A look of anguished concern passed across Jaromir's face.

'No, no,' Gavril heard Jaromir mutter, almost to himself, 'surely he wouldn't venture so much just for my sake, surely not . . .'

'For your sake?'

If Jaromir was play-acting, then he was extra-ordinarily gifted.

'Eugene has been my mentor, my protector, my friend, ever since Yephimy smuggled me out of Azhkendir. I have spent the last years in Tielen at his court. I – I owe him everything.'

'And yet this man is holding my mother hostage.' Gavril was unable to hide the rawness of betrayal in his voice. 'My mother, Jaromir.'

Jaromir looked blankly at him.

'Lilias has some kind of voice transference device in her rooms.'

'One of Linnaius's inventions? The Vox Aethyria?'

Gavril shrugged. 'All I know is that a dis-embodied voice has been telling me that my mother is Eugene's prisoner and will be executed unless I do exactly as I am instructed.'

'And the instructions?'

'Read this.' Gavril thrust Eugene's letter into Jaromir's hand. 'I am ordered to submit myself to the disabling effects of Doctor Kazimir's elixir. And hand over the governing of Azhkendir to you.'

Jaromir looked up from the paper, his eyes clouded.

'That was Eugene's original intention, yes, for me to replace Volkh. But that was before he – or I – was aware you were alive.'

Gavril said nothing.

Jaromir moved closer to him.

'You've got to believe me, Gavril,' he said, his

voice low and urgent. 'Yes, I knew about the Vox Aethyria. But this invasion plan, the threats to your mother, this is all news to me.'

Anger began to smoulder in Gavril's mind, dark as distant smoke.

'You should never have come back,' he said quietly. 'If there's to be a game of hostages, then you're in grave danger.'

'So you'd use me to bargain for your mother's life?' Jaromir said with bitter amusement.

'I'd rather have you as my ally, believe me, Jaro. But if you mean so much to Eugene—'

'I came to plead for Lilias and my son.' Jaromir gave a dry little laugh. 'And I find myself a hostage.'

Gavril gazed at him, torn between his fear for Elysia and his reluctance to betray the enemy who had become his friend. He would be no better than the Tielens if he stooped to the same tactic of threat-making and hostage-taking.

'There has to be another way,' he said. 'Wait for me here. I won't be long.'

The acrid smell of Sosia's steeping wound-herbs made Gavril's eyes sting as he entered Kostya's sickroom.

'Kostya,' Gavril said, leaning close to the old soldier's pillow. 'I need your advice.'

'What?' Kostya jerked awake. A hint of a smile curled his lips. 'And when did My Lord ever need to consult old Kostya about anything?'

'We're at war,' Gavril said. 'Eugene of Tielen has invaded us from the west.'

'War, eh?' A wolfish gleam lit Kostya's eyes and he struggled to sit up. Gavril leaned forwards to help him, plumping pillows at his back.

'They've taken my mother hostage. They say they'll kill her if we retaliate.' Gavril tried to keep the rising sense of desperation from his voice. 'What do I *do*, Kostya?'

Jushko appeared in the doorway.

'Map, Jushko!' ordered Kostya with a spark of his old vitality.

Jushko unrolled a painted leather map on the bedclothes.

'They're coming across the ice here.' He traced the route with a chipped and grimy fingernail. 'And making for Muscobar.'

Kostya forced himself up, irritably shaking off Jushko's hand when he tried to help him. For a while he stared at the map, tunelessly humming under his breath.

'Well?' Gavril said, unable to control the growing tension any longer.

Kostya turned to him. He was smiling again, a cruel, triumphant smile.

'Eugene's scared of you, lad.'

'Scared? Of me?' Gavril echoed incredulously. 'Of one man?'

'Why else take your mother hostage?' Kostya gave a dry chuckle that degenerated into a racking cough. Jushko eased him back onto the pillows and gave him a sip of water.

'So my hands are tied,' Gavril said, choked with frustration, 'and I must stand by and watch Eugene capture Azhkendir – then Muscobar?' And he had hoped – against hope – that Kostya would have devised some plan, some subtle military strategy, to rescue Elysia.

'Did I say that?' Kostya rasped. 'You must use his fear of you – and what you might do – against him.'

'But at the slightest sign of retaliation, he says he'll have her killed.'

'There are other ways to retaliate.' The same cruel glint still lit Kostya's fever-dry eyes. 'Whilst he and his armies are away from Tielen, who is keeping his palace and his family safe?'

Gavril stared at him.

'Surely he'll have left his home well-guarded. Surely . . .' And then as the implications of Kostya's words began to make sense, he fell silent, thinking, calculating.

There might yet be a way . . .

'Jushko, I want the Tielens shadowed all the way through Azhkendir.' Kostya was giving his orders. 'I want reports of their movements at all hours of the day and night.'

'Bogatyr!' Jushko saluted with alacrity.

'Warn them – keep out of sight at all times. We have the advantage here; we know the terrain. These Tielen boys're going to have a hard and dangerous climb through the southern ranges before they come down into Muscobar.'

'And Lilias Arbelian?' Gavril interrupted.

'We're still looking,' Jushko said defensively.

'I want more search-parties out there,' Gavril said. 'I want Lilias Arbelian. See to it, Jushko.'

'And Jushko,' Kostya added, 'pass me down my crossbow.'

Jushko glanced questioningly at the old warrior, but Kostya gave him such a furious glare that he went to the wall and took down the weapon from where it hung.

'Don't forget the bolts,' Kostya said, running his hand lovingly along the shaft of the crossbow. 'If the Tielens attack, I want to be ready for 'em.'

'You took your time!' Jaromir leaped up as Gavril came back into his bedchamber.

'There's no news. They're still searching for her.'

'Listen, Gavril.' Jaromir put his hand on Gavril's shoulder, his touch warm, reassuring. 'All I want is Lilias and the child.'

'Even though she fled, leaving you to the mercy of my *druzhina*?'

'She used me; I see that now. But she's also the mother of my son. My heir.'

'And Eugene's plans for Azhkendir?'

Gavril saw Jaromir shiver. 'Azhkendir has too many ghosts. If I could take them away with me, far from here, if we could start a new life together in some distant country, Francia, maybe, or Allemande, where no-one knew or cared about Arkhels or Nagarians—'

'You want me to pardon her?'

'If you don't, your *druzhina* will pursue us wherever we go, and the blood-feud will never be over.'

Gavril gazed at Jaromir, wondering how he could still feel so strongly for treacherous Lilias. Surely he deserved better?

'You know I'd do anything to ensure your safety,' he said. 'I owe you my life. But Lilias . . .'

'Just find her, Gavril. Then I'll go speak to Eugene. I can make him release your mother. He will do anything for me.'

Gavril nodded, wanting to believe Jaromir – yet doubting that Eugene's imperial ambitions could be swayed by the pleas of one man.

'Lord Drakhaon!' Jaromir glanced round uneasily as there came a rap at the door.

'Wait!' Gavril called out. What new complication could it be this time? He turned back to Jaromir. 'It's not safe for you in Kastel Drakhaon. Go back to the monastery. I'll get word to you when—'

Jaromir shook his head. 'I want to be here for her. I'll be in the East Wing if you need me. I've hidden there enough times before.' He slipped beneath the gilded tapestry and Gavril heard the concealed door click shut behind him just as his own door opened and one of the *druzhina* marched in.

'Did I give you permission to enter?' Gavril turned on him, his heart beating overfast. A few seconds sooner and Jaromir would have been discovered . . .

'Sorry, My Lord.' Beneath the over-large helmet, Gavril saw the face of the youngest of the *druzhina*, Semyon, freckled cheeks flushed red with mortification.

'What is so urgent that you have to enter without permission?'

'Doctor Kazimir sends his compliments, Lord Drakhaon. He's ready for you in the Kalika Tower.'

The fugitives huddled round the meagre fire in the brazier, rubbing their frozen fingers together over the blaze.

'How long are we to keep skulking here in this hovel?' Lilias demanded. She was cradling a fretful Artamon – but not too close, as he was badly in need of a bath and clean clothes.

'Till it's safe,' Michailo said, scowling.

Artamon started to grizzle. Lilias promptly

556

handed him over to Dysis who tried to distract him, jiggling him up and down on her shoulder.

'You need to talk terms with Kastel Drakhaon,' she said, impatient. She had misjudged him. He had seemed so full of potential, but now she was beginning to think he had not a single cunning thought in his head; he was all muscle and ill-temper. She would have to do the thinking for all of them.

'What? And give away our whereabouts? I think not. Where's Grisha got to? He's been gone too long.'

'And there are bugs in our bedding,' she said, willing herself not to scratch. There were angry red bites on her arms and legs. 'I need clean clothes. For the baby.'

'You could have had clean clothes if you'd stayed,' he said sullenly.

At first she had found this habitual sullenness attractive, the way his fair brows knotted over light blue eyes, cold as winter skies. Now it only irritated her. He might be ambitious, but he lacked the imagination to bring his plans to fruition.

The door to the hut scraped open; Michailo was on his feet in an instant, axe in hand. It was Grisha Bearclaws.

'Grisha.' Michailo slowly lowered the axe. 'I could have split your head in two—'

'Soldiers,' Grisha babbled. 'A whole army. Coming this way.'

'What kind of soldiers?'

'Not our own. Foreigners. Grey and blue uniforms. Very neat, very orderly. All carrying muskets. Column after column.'

Lilias had not missed a word. 'In grey and blue?'

557

she said. 'That sounds like the Tielens.' She glanced at Dysis. 'Has Velemir sent a rescue party at last?'

'Too many just to rescue us,' Dysis said, still jiggling Artamon on her knee.

'But they'll give us protection. We must make contact with them.'

'Are you mad, woman?' cried Michailo. 'They're not interested in us; they're off to war. And if we contact them, we risk making our position known to the Drakhaon's *druzhina*.'

She went over to Michailo. 'Don't you see, Michailo? They're our only hope of safe passage out of here.' If only she had had time to bring the Vox Aethyria with her, she could have contacted Velemir and the Tielen commanders, arranged a rendezvous . . .

'Let me go talk to them, then. You can hide in the bushes if you're so scared you'll be seen.'

'No, and that's an end to it.'

She clenched her fists in vexation, fingernails biting into her palms. She must talk Michailo round. Not such an easy task as he was so jumpy and bad-tempered, almost as if he regretted what he had done – although it was too late now for regrets.

'Michailo,' she said in her softest, sweetest voice. 'You have risked everything for my sake. Please don't think I don't appreciate the sacrifice you've made. But I have friends, influential friends, at the court of Tielen. It would be foolish not to ask for their help. Just imagine . . . our own escort of armed soldiers, safe passage beyond the reach of Lord Gavril. A new life . . .'

'I'll think about it.'

* * *

Volkh's study in the Kalika Tower glittered with phials, alembics and tubes, a brittle edifice of glistening glass. As Gavril entered, he saw Kazimir, intent on connecting another slender tube to the precarious construction.

'How soon will the elixir be ready?'

Kazimir turned to Gavril, his eyes narrowed in his bruised face. 'My Lord, this process cannot be rushed or you may die.'

'Look at me.' Gavril thrust his hands before Kazimir's face. 'It has begun again. Soon I may not be able to control my actions.'

Kazimir took his hands in his, examining the claw-nails and the glittering scales of blue skin with intense concentration. 'Fascinating,' he muttered. 'You are remarkable beings, you Nagarians. It seems a crime to suppress what is happening to you. You are unique. Your gift makes you more than human. We scientists should learn from you, not destroy.'

'You call this curse a gift?' Gavril withdrew his hands. 'I just want to be rid of it. Do what you have to do, Doctor – and be quick about it.'

Kazimir reached into his bag and withdrew a glass phial with a long needle protruding from the end. He uncorked a bottle of clear spirit and swiftly cleansed the needle.

'I will need to take samples of blood, My Lord.'

Gavril made a grimace. 'Of course.' He rolled up his sleeve. 'What is *that*?'

'A syringe. For the drawing out of fluids. Magus Linnaius gave it me.'

Gavril held out his bare arm. Kazimir came towards him, and then hesitated.

Gavril looked at him, frowning. 'What's wrong?'

'You've treated me well, Lord Gavril,' Kazimir said, 'and in return, I feel it only right and fair that I should warn you, as I warned your mother. This "cure" is highly risky. What worked for your father may not work for you. It will prove debilitating; it might prove fatal.'

'Just do it,' Gavril said, averting his eyes as Kazimir pressed with his thumb for the vein in the soft crease of his elbow. The Magus's needle pierced his skin, and his life's blood began to flow into the glass tube, blue as indigo.

36

Elysia sat in the window-seat, gazing out through the bars over Swanholm's bleak snow-covered hills and woods. All day she had sat there as she had sat the days before, staring out at the winter's gloom and the black crows in the bare branches of the parkland trees. The dull, cold weather mirrored her despairing mood all too well.

Prisoner. And all because of my own gullibility, allowing myself to be flattered and fooled!

But now she saw a sleigh speeding down the snowy road towards Swanholm, escorted by uniformed outriders.

She sat up, wondering who the new arrival might be.

The horses drew the sleigh into the courtyard below and one of the outriders jumped down to help the passengers out. First was a young woman, well-wrapped against the cold in a cape and hat of silver fur. She stood, as though amazed, gazing up at the wide sweep of the palace buildings. Elysia leaned closer against the bars, her breath misting the cold panes. There was something familiar about the lithe and graceful way the young woman moved . . .

Wigged servants appeared on the steps, raising lanterns high to brighten her way through the dwindling daylight.

As the young woman came forward into the lanterns' soft gleam to enter the palace, Elysia gave a little cry of recognition.

It was Astasia.

Astasia untied her cloak and peeled off her fur gloves. A servant silently spirited her snow-damp outer clothes away; another servant ushered her into a salon hung with yellow silks where she was served with almond biscuits and hot tea laced with aquavit. And all the time she was staring around her, astonished at the austere splendour of Eugene's palace.

'Altessa. I trust your journey was not too cold?'

She looked up and saw Count Velemir in the doorway.

'I came as soon as I received your message, Count.' She rushed over to him, pulling him into the salon. 'But why the secrecy? Surely if it's news about Andrei, my mother and father should be the first to know.'

'Your father is in a—' he hesitated, 'fragile state of mind. And your mother has never been robust. I thought it better to bring you here to your fiancé's home where you will be safe.'

'Safe?' She did not understand.

'Sit down, child.'

He had never dared to call her child before; it was oddly affectionate – yet over-familiar. Surprised, she sat down and he sat beside her, taking her hand in his.

'It's bad news, then.' A dull feeling of dread overwhelmed her. Had they found Andrei's body?

'The world has begun to change, Altessa. It was best that you were as far from Mirom as possible.'

'Mirom? I thought this was about Andrei—'

'Prince Eugene is at this moment crossing the ice into Azhkendir with his armies. From Azhkendir, he will enter Muscobar. At the same time his fleet will sail up the Nieva to Mirom.'

She snatched her hands from his, rising to her feet.

'What are you telling me? What's happening?'

'There will be some resistance in Mirom, but Eugene's armies will easily subdue the city.'

'He's invading Mirom? My home?'

'Altessa, the days of the House of Orlov are over. Your father is a broken man. He has lost the confidence of the people. And you – with all greatest respect – are too young, too inexperienced, to rule.'

Astasia stared at him in disbelief.

'But we have allies. Azhkendir. There was an agreement—'

'Altessa,' he said gently, 'you are a very fortunate young woman. You are betrothed to marry the most powerful man in the whole continent. The man who will soon be crowned Emperor. You will be Empress at his side.'

'But I don't want to be Empress!' she cried. 'And you, Velemir, I thought you were my father's trusted servant, his ambassador, what are *you* doing here?

What of the vows you made to the House of Orlov?'

'Your father asked me to arrange this marriage; I am acting on his instructions.'

'I'm not staying here a moment longer. I'm going back to Mama in Mirom. She'll need me.'

Astasia began to walk quickly towards the door. Velemir was the quicker; he barred her way.

'Return is not only inadvisable, it is impossible.'

'What? You mean to hold me here – a prisoner?'

A gold and marble horloge struck the hour in a tinkling chime of bells.

'A guest in your future home, Altessa. It is no longer safe to make the sea crossing; at any moment now, the Tielen fleet will start to sail up the Nieva. Doubtless the Muscobar fleet will retaliate. I anticipate a ferocious and decisive sea battle.'

She looked at him with loathing. She had never trusted him – and now, too late, she knew her instincts had been right.

'But just imagine how your people will welcome you back when the wedding is celebrated in Saint Simeon's. Their own Altessa marrying Eugene of Tielen.'

'How does it feel, Count,' she said coldly, 'to betray your country?' She no longer cared if she offended him. He was beneath contempt. 'Are you utterly lacking in any sense of loyalty?'

'Indeed, Altessa, I have always regarded myself as a patriot,' Velemir said smoothly. 'I have only acted in Muscobar's best interests. Your father is a weak and ineffectual ruler. The people detest him.'

She let out a little cry of outrage.

'What would you rather – to see Mirom torn apart by revolution, the Winter Palace burned and you and your family executed? Or peaceful rule restored and a new empire forged, with you and Eugene at its head?'

'If my brother were here—' she began, tears pricking her eyes.

'Andrei is dead. Drowned,' Velemir said with brutal candour.

'Where is Madame Andar?' Astasia turned from him, hoping he had not seen her tears, determined not to cry in front of him. 'No, don't tell me. She has already left for Azhkendir.'

He said nothing.

'So I am trapped. Alone. Except for my maid.'

'You will want for nothing here, Altessa. Swanholm is a marvel. Your future husband is a man of taste and refinement, and he has provided for your every need.'

This time it was she who did not reply, staring out over the formal gardens and ice-bound lake already shrouded in twilight mists. She heard the door click discreetly open and the sound of his footsteps receding down the corridor.

'Andrei,' she whispered to the grey gardens. 'Oh, Andrei . . .'

Eugene raised the telescope and scanned the landscape. The moorlands of Azhkendir stretched away to all sides, stained the cinder colours of winter: white, grey and brown. Jaro had told him of the wasteland Volkh Nagarian had created when he scorched the Arkhel lands to ashes – but he had not imagined the desolation could stretch so far. Even now, years after the attack, little grew here, only knotted grasses and stunted thorn bushes, crushed by the weight of successive snowfalls.

Now the snowy wastes were filled with marching Tielen men; horse-drawn carts lumbered behind, drawing cannons. There was no sign of the Drakhaon or his *druzhina* – and nowhere for them to hide on this bleak plain.

And then through the telescope lens he spotted movement. A man, far off, ragged as a peasant, dragging himself through the snow. One of Gavril Nagarian's spies, sent to track their progress?

'There's a man following us. Over there.' He gestured with the telescope to two of his aides. 'Bring him to me.'

He heard distant shouts as his aides caught hold of the spy and brought him to his knees. Strange. The few words he caught seemed to be in their own language, Tielen.

He climbed back onto Cinnamor and rode towards them.

'Highness! Highness!' cried the prisoner, hands outstretched. 'Tell them who I am!'

One of the aides struck him. 'Wait for His Highness to speak to you.'

Eugene gazed down at the man. He was in poor shape; his face was smeared with sweat and blood, his uniform was charred and filthy, and yet his eyes, pale and defiant, were familiar.

'Oskar Alvborg,' Eugene said.

The man sagged in his captors' grip. 'Yes,' he whispered.

'He's one of ours. Bring him to the camp and get him cleaned up.'

* * *

Oskar Alvborg sat hunched in a corner of a hospital wagon. He was wrapped in blankets but his teeth still chattered.

'Can't get much from him, Highness,' murmured the surgeon. 'Seems to be in shock. He's been quite badly burned. Lost most of his hair.'

Burned. Uneasy now, Eugene approached the patient. 'What happened, Alvborg?' he asked. 'And where are your men?'

'Dead,' muttered Alvborg, staring into nothingness. 'Dying. Don't know.'

'And who attacked you?'

Alvborg's shoulders began to shake. Eugene thought at first that he was weeping – and then he heard low, dry laughter. Pale eyes glinted at him, bright with malicious amusement.

'Can't you guess, Highness?'

'The Drakhaon?' Eugene had risked everything on the success of this campaign. He had to know his adversary.

The laughter died away. There was anger in Alvborg's pale gaze now – and something else that Eugene could not yet define.

'We did exactly as you ordered, Highness. We played the decoys. We led the Drakhaon and his men away from the invasion force. And what did we get for our pains?'

'Who fired first?'

'They were too close. We had to defend ourselves.'

'*You* fired on the Drakhaon?' He had taken a calculated risk in choosing Alvborg for this mission, and Alvborg had failed him. 'You fool. Your orders were to distract him, not attack.'

'He looked just like a man, an ordinary man.' Alvborg seemed to be talking to himself now, forgetting Eugene was there. 'But what ordinary man can make fire bloom from his fingertips? Fire, blue as burning brandy . . .'

The surgeon looked at Eugene over Alvborg's bandaged head. 'He's feverish, rambling,' he said. 'He should rest, Highness—'

'I need to know.' Eugene gripped Alvborg by the shoulders, forcing him to look into his face. 'So even the Magus's inventions were no match for his powers?'

Alvborg flinched. 'My men were burned to charred bone with one flick of his fingers.'

Eugene let go of Alvborg. His mind was buzzing. The success of his Azhkendi strategy now hinged on one man: Altan Kazimir. He knew now for sure the armies would never reach Mirom unless Gavril Nagarian was crushed.

'You have sorely disappointed me, Lieutenant Alvborg,' he said, rising to his feet. 'I expected more from you. When you are recovered from your injuries, you will have to answer to a military court.'

Alvborg said nothing. But from under swollen lids whose lashes had been singed away, he shot Eugene a look of virulent resentment.

'And you—' Eugene turned on the surgeon. 'All you heard here today was the incoherent ravings of a sick man. Nothing is to be repeated, understand?'

The man nodded, eyes lowered.

Eugene pushed open the canvas flap of the wagon and jumped down to the ground.

Morale was high amongst the troops. They were days away from a great victory. They knew they were rewriting the history of the whole continent. He would let nothing tarnish their hopes now.

'*Poison . . .*'

Gavril stared blind into darkness, sweat chill on his skin.

'*I'm dying. Poisoned. Want . . . to . . . live . . .*'

He felt sick and faint. Voices welled up in his mind, insidious fever voices. Screaming, shouting –

He clutched his hands to his head, trying to shut the voices out.

'*It's too late to divide us . . .*'

Not voices now, but one voice alone. One voice that spoke out of his nightmares, so clearly that he was sure someone else must be in the room.

'*Kill me, and you kill part of yourself.*'

He had been dreaming again. The dream images, vivid, violent, still veered before his eyes in a lurid procession.

Creatures of coloured light and shadow swoop and dart about him on wide translucent wings.

Eyes, slanted, alien – yet somehow familiar – gaze curiously into his, dazzling him with their glittering stare.

The air shimmers with the heat from their flared nostrils as they hover closer.

'*What are you?*' he whispered.

'*Save. Preserve. Protect.*'

The words whirl around his mind as the sky lights up with slashes of fire. Tall bronze-clad warriors, their faces too bright, too vengeful to look upon, stand below. And from the tips of their fingers shiver bolts of flame.

Too late the winged creatures spin around in the air.

Too late blue fire shoots from their flared nostrils towards the golden-eyed warriors.

The flame-bolts sizzle – and catch alight. In a wild whirling of wings, the burning creatures begin to thrash, to flail about – to crash to the earth. Viscous liquid sprays onto him where he stands; viscous, thick and sticky as blood – yet blue as the phosphorescent gleam of their eyes. The air is rent with their cries, terrible howling cries of agony . . .

'Protect.'

The elixir must be working. It was giving him these nightmares, making him hear voices. It was purging his system of all the toxins that enabled the being he called Drakhaoul to inhabit his body. He lay back, unable to control the shaking in his limbs.

'*Don't let me die . . .*' the dark, dry voice whispered in his brain. '*There is so much more I have to give you.*'

'You're part of my dream. I'm still dreaming.' Gavril, trying to exorcize the phantom dreamvoice, pressed his fingers into his temples until the self-inflicted pain made him squirm.

'*I am the last of my kind,*' it said with sudden clarity. '*You must protect me. Preserve me.*'

'How do you feel this morning, My Lord?' enquired Altan Kazimir.

Gavril sat slumped in a chair. He hadn't even enough energy to get up.

'Kostya drugged me when he abducted me from Smarna,' he said, each word an effort. 'I feel much the same as I did then. Sick. Dizzy. Confused.'

'Hm.' Kazimir slipped his fingers around his wrist, feeling for his pulse.

570

'And I kept hearing this voice in my sleep last night.' Gavril tried to focus his aching eyes on the doctor's face. 'Am I going mad? Or was it like this for my father?'

'There are dangerous toxins to be purged from your bloodstream.' Kazimir produced the syringe again, pushing up Gavril's sleeve.

Gavril groaned. 'Not more blood. You'll bleed me dry.'

There came a sudden clamour of voices outside. Kazimir jumped, startled, and the syringe fell to the floor and broke.

'Lord Drakhaon!'

'You're not to disturb him, Juri!' Sosia's voice, shrill with annoyance, only made Gavril's head ache more.

'This news can't wait.' The door burst open and one of the elder *druzhina* strode in, Sosia clinging to his arm in a vain attempt to stop him.

'There's been another sighting!' he said, hoarse for lack of breath.

'Where?' Gavril said.

'In the southern foothills. We were shadowing the Tielens, just as you ordered. And suddenly we sensed one of our own was close by.' Juri's voice dried in his throat and Sosia poured him a mug of small beer. Juri swallowed the beer down in one gulp, swiping the last drops from his greying moustache with the back of his hand. 'Grisha. It was Grisha Bearclaws. Who else can climb with such agility? He was watching the Tielens – like us – and he was so intent on his watch, he didn't even know we were there. But he was high, high up, in a narrow gully. If we had gone after

571

him, we'd have given ourselves away to the Tielens.'

'You let him go!' said Gavril in exasperation. Kazimir was on his knees, trying to pick up the slivers of glass, muttering to himself under his breath.

'He can't have gone far. I'd guess Michailo's hiding out somewhere close by.'

'We have a lead on Michailo?' cried Jushko from the open doorway. Kazimir flinched at the sight of him and dropped the shards of glass.

'So it seems.' Gavril had not forgotten his promise to Jaromir to find Lilias; now at last there was a chance he could fulfil it. 'I want Lilias Arbelian and her baby caught and brought back unharmed,' he said. 'Do you understand me, Jushko? They're of vital importance to us.'

'We'll do what we can,' Jushko said grudgingly. 'But it won't be easy with those cursed Tielens everywhere.'

'Unharmed, Jushko!' Gavril tried to push himself to his feet – but the room spun about him and he reeled, grabbing at the chair arm. Jushko lunged forwards and caught hold of him.

'What are you doing to him?' he cried, rounding on Kazimir. 'He looks half-dead! My Lord – I beg you – stop this cure before it kills you.'

'I gave my word,' Gavril whispered, sinking back into the chair.

Eugene reined Cinnamor to a standstill and gazed back at the column of men winding away through the narrow gorge. Beneath them a dark mountain river foamed and churned over boulders stained brown with minerals. The humble beginnings of the great Nieva? he wondered. He must consult his charts . . .

A thin stinging sleet had begun to fall.

'What a wretched country, Anckstrom,' he said, turning his collar up to keep out the sleet. 'Good thing our men are well used to adverse conditions.'

'Well-trained, Highness,' Anckstrom said dourly. His nose glowed crimson with the cold.

'We should make camp for the night.' Eugene glanced up at the fast-darkening sky.

'Isn't this place a little too exposed?' Anckstrom gestured up at the overhanging crags high above. 'They could ambush us from at least a hundred points.'

'And we could tramp on another ten miles and find it just the same. We knew it would be hard-going through the mountains. Post extra sentinels – and issue an extra ration of aquavit to keep out the cold.'

Eugene's aides hastily began to erect his field tent. Eugene dismounted and handed Cinnamor's reins to his groom. Then he went amongst the men as they began setting up their tents for the night, exchanging a word and a joke here, an ounce of tobacco there. Linnaius's fire-sticks were put to good use, intense flames of scarlet springing up in the gathering gloom.

When he returned to the tent, he found that Anckstrom had set up Linnaius's Vox Aethyria on the little table beside a half-unfurled map of the whole continent.

'Any news?'

Anckstrom looked up. 'We've just had word from the fleet. They've met little resistance from the

Muscobites. Exchanged a few broadsides. Sank two frigates, shot the flagship's mainmast in two. Admiral Janssen expects to be outside Mirom by noon tomorrow.'

'But no word from Jaromir? No word at all?' Eugene could not put his mind to the other matters until he was certain Jaromir was safe.

'Everything's going according to plan, Highness. We've encountered no resistance from the Azhkendi.'

'By God, if anything's happened to him, I'll make them pay.' The news of the fleet's victory did not excite Eugene; it was the least he had expected of Admiral Janssen.

'They've kept to their part of the bargain thus far. They've been watching us. From a safe distance.'

Eugene nodded curtly. 'I've seen them.'

'Biding their time?'

One of the aides brought them glasses of hot lingonberry brandy, dark red and fruitily alcoholic.

'Ah,' said Anckstrom, appreciatively smacking his lips. 'That drives out the chill.'

A burst of shouting rang out, then the crack of shots.

Eugene and Anckstrom grabbed their pistols and tugged open the tent flap.

'Stay back, Highness!' Anckstrom tried to block the tent entrance, pushing Eugene behind him, but Eugene, pistols primed, thrust him aside.

'What's happened? Have we been attacked?'

One of his aides came hurrying over, torch in hand.

'Not precisely, Highness. There's some kind of skirmish further up in the gorge. Captain Olsven has gone up to investigate.'

* * *

Lilias caught sight of the Tielen camp-fires in the gorge far below, little red flowers of light springing up one by one in the gathering darkness. Now she could think of nothing but the comfort of lying in a proper bed again, the warmth of perfumed hot water on her skin, hot food and wine, fine wine to drink . . .

She was tired of being a fugitive. She was tired of Michailo and his surly moods. She wanted a bath.

She set out down the narrow stony track, heedless of the noise made by the pebbles she dislodged as she walked.

Michailo came hurrying after her, grabbing her by the arm.

'Are you mad, Lilias? Anyone can see you out here! There's no cover!'

'Let go of me!' she hissed, trying to shake herself free. 'Down there, that's our only hope of getting out of Azhkendir alive.'

'Oh, so you think you can just walk straight in past their sentries, without getting shot on sight? That's an invading army, Lilias, or hadn't you noticed? They're not on manoeuvres now.'

'Michailo!' Grisha shouted. 'Look out!'

Michailo grabbed hold of her, pulling her down into the snow-covered bracken as an arrow rasped over her head. One of Michailo's men let out a hoarse scream as another arrow ripped through his throat and he pitched forwards into the gully. Another arrow and another thudded into the gorse a foot away, a shower of razor-barbed, long-stemmed shafts. *Druzhina* arrows.

'Stupid bitch. They've tracked us!' He began to

575

crawl forwards on his belly over the frozen ground, axe in hand.

'My baby—' She tried to struggle up but he shoved her back into the scrub.

'Keep low. D'you want to be skewered?'

'You're surrounded, Michailo!' The voice, hard as iron-stone, rang out across the steep hillside. 'Throw down your weapons. Give yourselves up.'

Michailo kept moving stealthily onwards through the bracken. Lilias caught the dull glint of his throwing knife as he withdrew it from his boot.

'Here I am, Jushko!' Michailo jeered. 'Come and get me!'

Shadowy figures appeared from behind boulders and stone outcrops. The *druzhina* had been lying in wait for them.

Lilias saw Michailo fling the knife with deadly accuracy – then hurl himself forward, whirling his axe about his head.

The barren hillside rang with the scything clash of steel on steel and the grunts and yells of the combatants.

Where were Dysis and the baby? Lilias began to edge away down the track. And where were Eugene's sentinels? Surely they must have heard the commotion by now.

Shots rang out. Shouts in a foreign tongue. Tielen soldiers were running up the track towards the fracas.

Lilias leaped out in their path, waving her arms.

'Help me, oh please help me!' she cried. 'They've got my baby.'

Two of the infantrymen stopped, bayonets levelled at her throat. She raised her hands high in the air.

Her mind went blank with terror, and then she remembered one of the few phrases in the Tielen language that Feodor Velemir had taught her long ago.

'Take me to your commanding officer,' she said, stumbling over the pronunciation. 'Please.'

They stared at each other, baffled. Behind her, she heard the high-pitched wail of a baby rising above the shots and cries.

'My baby!' she said. Tears sprang to her eyes, unfeigned. 'Save my baby!' She was a negligent mother, she knew it, but Artamon was her only child and at that moment she knew she would fight to the death to protect him.

'Madame, madame, you're safe!'

Dysis came stumbling down the steep track towards her, carrying a furiously yelling bundle. Lilias forgot about the bayonets and grabbed Artamon from her, clasping him close, feeling his hot little fists beat against her and tear at her hair, amazed at his strength and fury.

'There, there, baby, it's all right, Mama's got you now . . .'

'It's terrible up there, madame,' Dysis wept. 'It's a massacre. First the *druzhina*, now these soldiers. Blood on the snow. I wish I hadn't seen it.' Her face was streaked with tears and dirt, her hair had come down about her shoulders.

'This way,' one of the infantrymen said stiltedly in the common tongue, gesturing with his carbine down the track towards the camp.

'Yes, yes,' Lilias said above Artamon's crying. 'We're coming. We're coming.'

* * *

'Not one word of farewell. Not even goodbye. Just up and away.' Kiukiu paced beneath the bare branches in the frosty monastery orchard. 'Do I matter so little to him?'

Her memories of what had happened on the mountainside were as fleeting as fever-dreams. Yet one moment had stayed with her, so vivid that she was certain she had not dreamed it: the moment he had spoken her name, leaning close to stroke her face, and she had heard the catch in his voice. He had feelings for her, she was sure of it – so why had he gone away?

The monastery bells began to clang out. Startled pigeons tumbled out of the bell-tower in a flurry of grey wings.

Kiukiu hurried towards the courtyard, wondering why the brothers were ringing the bells when there was no act of worship to be observed until dusk.

The brothers came running out from the infirmary, the library and the kitchens, assembling in front of the church. Kiukiu followed them.

Abbot Yephimy climbed to the top of the steps, turning to address them as the clamour of the bells died.

'Grave news, my brothers,' he said. 'Azhkendir has been invaded by the Tielen army.'

Kiukiu stared at the Abbot. Were they at war with Tielen? Was Lord Gavril in danger?

'There's no news yet of any hostilities, but we must prepare to receive and tend casualties. Brother Hospitaller . . .'

The assembly broke up as the monks gathered around Brother Hospitaller who began to issue orders.

Kiukiu drew her cloak about her more closely, pulling the hood down over her head, and made for the gates.

She felt a firm hand clamp on her shoulder and, looking round, saw Abbot Yephimy behind her.

'Where are you going, child?'

'They need me at Kastel Drakhaon.'

'You'll be far safer here in the monastery. Stay with your grandmother. She needs you too.'

'I don't care about the danger,' she said, surprised at the coolness of her words. 'I have to go help. In any way I can.'

Must escape. I must escape.

Elysia took out the third of her hairpins and began again to try to bend it. Two had snapped in her first lockpicking experiments so this time she had warmed the metal first at the grate before setting to work.

Velemir must have anticipated that she would try to escape, for the only cutlery she was given with her meals were spoons and a blunt knife – and the servant was ordered not to leave unless every one had been returned.

Soon she would be obliged to tie her hair back with a ribbon for there were only three pins left to support the loose chignon into which she had wound her hair. Would her gaolers notice? Velemir had not been to see her in over a day . . .

As she worked at her improvised lockpick, she forced herself to plan what she would do if she succeeded. She had already discounted stealing a horse from the stables and riding off into the snows. She must find out where in the palace Astasia was installed and beg her protection. There was no other course of action.

Her crude efforts had bent the pin enough to risk a third attempt. She knelt down at the keyhole and slid the crude lockpick in, jiggling it about until it encountered resistance.

Careful now . . .

It was at this moment that the last two hairpins had broken. Gingerly, she applied a little more force – and then something – a lever? – began to give.

Just a little more pressure . . .

Her teeth bit into her lower lip as she concentrated all her efforts into this delicate manoeuvre –

Too hard. Suddenly the pin-shaft snapped and her fingers were gashed by the sudden movement against the edge of the keyhole, slicing a little of the flesh away. Blood dripped onto the polished boards.

All those hours of work for nothing. Elysia wrapped her handkerchief around her cut finger to try to staunch the bleeding.

Suddenly she found she was weeping. Tears of anger and frustration trickled down her cheeks.

I never cry! Not over something so trivial as a cut finger.

Yet still the tears kept coming. She could not stop them. She flung herself down on the boards and wept like a child.

37

'One of the prisoners keeps asking to see you, Highness. Says she has news of Lord Jaromir.'

The despatches dropped from Eugene's hands. 'Bring her to me.'

When his aide had gone, he rose and paced about the cramped tent, repeatedly striking his fist against his palm, trying to diffuse the growing sense of frustration.

The tent flap was raised and a woman was led in. To his surprise, she sank into a full court curtsey, head bowed.

'Your Highness,' she said in stumbling Tielen.

'Rise, madame,' he said in the common tongue, 'and tell me who you are.'

'My name is Lilias Arbelian. I once had the honour to be presented to Your Highness by Feodor Velemir.'

Arbelian? Her face was dirt-streaked, her clothes were torn and filthy, her red hair dishevelled – and yet there was something in her bearing and voice that signified she was no common camp-follower.

'Velemir has an agent called Arbelian,' he said, placing the name at last. 'How can I be certain you are she and not an Azhkendi impostor, sent to spy?'

'You can let me speak with Feodor using your Vox Aethyria.' She nodded her head wearily in the direction of the device. 'I lost mine when I was forced to flee Kastel Drakhaon.'

So she knew of the Vox Aethyria – and had used its correct name. He would have to risk trusting her.

'You have news of Lord Jaromir,' he said, trying to keep any hint of emotion from his voice. 'When did you last see him?'

'At Kastel Drakhaon.'

'He is a prisoner?' Dear God, if Jaro had fallen into the *druzhina*'s clutches, what atrocities had they committed? Was that why his light-flame burned so faintly? 'Tell me everything you know!'

'He came to rescue me from the *druzhina*,' she said, 'but we were caught escaping. Michailo managed to save me, but Jaromir . . .' Her voice faltered and she swayed on her feet, one hand fluttering to her forehead.

Eugene lunged forwards and caught her as she fell.

'Aquavit for Madame Arbelian,' he called. 'And be quick!' He eased her down into one of the folding camp-chairs, propping a velvet cushion behind her drooping head.

'Forgive me, Highness,' she whispered.

The aide came in with a little crystal glass of aquavit and Eugene kneeled, holding it to Lilias Arbelian's lips, tipping the clear liquid into her mouth. She swallowed a few drops, then nodded her head weakly, waving the glass away.

'You must be hungry,' Eugene said. 'Bring some broth for madame.'

He waited in an agony of apprehension as she drank some hot broth and ate a little bread. Her skin, beneath the film of dirt, seemed a little less pale, her eyes less dull.

'Now, madame,' he said, sitting opposite her. 'Tell me everything you know.'

As he listened to her account, he felt himself growing more and more agitated. It seemed that the last she had seen of Jaromir was two of the Drakhaon's *druzhina* dragging him away. And Jaromir had not caught up with them in their flight from the Drakhaon. Lord Gavril had already used his powers to destroy a wolf-horde, burning them to ashes. She feared . . .

Anckstrom came in towards the end of her tale and listened, arms folded across his broad chest, saying nothing. When she had finished, he leaned forward and whispered in Eugene's ear.

'It accords – roughly – with what we've been able to get from the other prisoners.'

Eugene rose and beckoned Anckstrom outside the tent.

'Come. Walk with me.'

Watchfires glimmered along the borders of the camp. The night air was bitterly cold.

'Accords roughly? Explain.'

'Seems we've run into two feuding factions within the *druzhina*. Your Madame Arbelian was being pursued by the Drakhaon's men. Would you care to interrogate one of them yourself?'

583

* * *

The prisoner was shackled to an interrogation post, hands high above his head. He was a tall, gaunt man, with a shaven head. His skin, where it was not covered with the blue and purple whorls of tattooed clanmarks, was rutted with old scars. What barbarians, Eugene thought with distaste.

When one of Eugene's interrogators tugged on the chains, forcing the prisoner to raise his head, Eugene saw that he had lost an eye. The lids had been sewn tightly together across the empty socket, giving his expression a perpetually ironic cast.

'Do what you will,' the prisoner said, voice faint yet defiant, 'I'll never betray My Lord Drakhaon.' Fresh wounds to his forehead and side had been bandaged, but a stain of scarlet was already leaking through the bindings.

'You Azhkendis may employ barbaric methods of torture to extract information,' Eugene said, 'but we are more civilized in Tielen. Have you administered the truth-tincture, Sergeant?' he asked the interrogator.

'It should be taking effect now, Highness.'

'What – have you done – to me?' As Linnaius's drug took effect, the prisoner began to slur his words, and what had started as a protest subsided into a confused mumble.

'Now you will tell us everything we wish to know,' Eugene said, signing to his clerk to start recording the prisoner's testimony. 'What is your name and rank?'

'Jushko. Acting commander – of the *druzhina*.' The prisoner sounded like a man murmuring in his sleep.

Anckstrom and Eugene exchanged a look.

'And what, Commander Jushko, was your mission?'

'To capture . . . Lilias . . . and the rebels . . . Bring her back . . . alive . . .'

Anckstrom nodded to Eugene.

'And where is Lord Jaromir Arkhel?'

There was a pause.

'Dead.'

'*Dead!*' Eugene's heart seemed to have stopped beating. He could see only the prisoner's ravaged face, and his dull, drugged eye. 'How can he be dead! He was taken prisoner at the kastel. Madame Arbelian saw him—'

'Escaped,' Jushko said thickly. 'Lord Gavril – went after him. Shot him. How else – lay Lord Volkh's ghost?'

'The man's babbling nonsense!' Eugene cried. 'You've given him too much of the tincture.'

'Easy, Eugene.' Anckstrom laid one hand on his arm.

'He says Jaro is dead. How can he be dead?' Eugene rounded on Anckstrom. 'The life-flame still burns. You've seen it, Anckstrom—'

'I'm sure there is a logical explanation here,' Anckstrom said calmly.

'Proof. I need proof.' Eugene pulled away from Anckstrom and went up to the prisoner, grabbing him by the shoulders and shaking him. 'Did you see the body? Answer me! Did anyone see the body!'

'Up . . . in . . . mountains.' Jushko's head slumped drunkenly forwards. 'Fell . . . down crevasse . . .'

'If this is true,' Eugene's mind was whirling with the implications of Jushko's statement, 'then the Andar woman dies.'

585

'We don't know it to be true,' said Anckstrom guardedly. 'And she is our best negotiating ploy.'

It seemed to Eugene that all the colours had leached from the tent, the warm gold from the lamplight, the scarlet from the glow of the brazier. Everything had become grey.

'Revive him,' he said, pointing to Jushko. 'He's going to lead us to Kastel Drakhaon. We're going to find out the truth.'

'But what about Muscobar?' said Anckstrom in an undertone. 'The fleet's awaiting your orders. We mustn't lose our advantage. All your work, Highness, your plans, your men—'

'Muscobar', Eugene said curtly, 'can wait.'

'Who are you?' The voice was high and clear, a child's voice.

Startled, Astasia whirled around and saw a young girl. The child, no more than six or seven years of age, was standing staring at her with probing curiosity. There was something odd about the way she stood, one shoulder hunched higher than the other.

'You startled me. How did you get in?'

'Are you going to be my new mama?' the child asked with utter directness.

Astasia did not know how to reply. She went over to the girl, kneeling down beside her. Close to, she could see that her nightgown was made of the finest cream silk, trimmed with ivory lace. With her golden curls, she was as pale and pretty as a porcelain doll – but a doll that has been violently thrown down, its limbs twisted grotesquely out of shape.

'Are you Prince Eugene's daughter?'

'My name is Karila. But you may call me Kari, if you like.'

'Does anyone know you're here, Kari? Is your governess looking for you? Shouldn't you be in bed?'

'I had bad dreams. And when I called out, no-one came.'

'Let me take you back to bed.'

Kari shook her head vehemently. 'Don't want any more bad dreams.'

'I know how to banish bad dreams. You show me the way.'

The child took Astasia's hand and led her out into the candlelit corridors.

'The dragon came again in my dream. Its breath burned me.' Her grip was hot and sticky, as if she were feverish; no wonder, Astasia thought, she had been dreaming of burning.

Suddenly Karila stopped, her hand squeezing Astasia's.

'Why is that lady crying?'

Astasia listened. Now she could hear the faint sound of someone weeping.

'It must be one of the servants, Kari.'

'No. It's the foreign painter lady. They put bars on her windows. I think she is sad because she wants to go home and Papa won't let her.'

'Bars? She's a prisoner?' So Elysia was still here! What other lies had Velemir told her? 'Show me.'

'Doctor Kazimir has made his delivery, as promised, Highness.' Eugene's aide reined in his horse to fall into step with Cinnamor.

587

Eugene pulled Cinnamor aside from the head of the column of men.

'Let me see it.'

The aide withdrew a little glass phial from his uniform jacket.

'This is all?' Eugene held the phial up to the pale winter sunlight, tipping it so that the viscous liquid slid to one end and then the other. In the light it glowed a dull blue, more like ink than blood. Drakhaon's blood.

'All that he could extract before administering the . . . other substance.'

'Where is the doctor now?'

'Awaiting Your Highness's instructions.'

'Bring him to me.'

A few minutes later the aide returned followed by Kazimir, whey-faced and breathless.

'How do I know this doesn't contain poison?' Eugene said curtly.

'I – I would never presume to—' stuttered Kazimir.

'Take some yourself.' Eugene thrust the phial into Kazimir's hands.

'A few drops on the tongue, that's all you need to protect yourself, Highness, from the Drakhaon's poisonous breath.' Kazimir did as he was bid, pulling a grimace at the taste.

Eugene watched. Kazimir had not hesitated. He took back the phial and tipped some of the contents into his mouth.

A shimmer of thunder, black and electric blue, shuddered through his mind.

He blinked. For a moment he had glimpsed something quite alien to his own experience. A touch of darkness that left his skin crawling.

He had tasted the blood of the creature that had killed Jaromir.

He felt tainted. Polluted.

He looked at Kazimir. 'You have done well, Doctor. But there is one thing more you will do for me. There is an urgent despatch to be delivered to the Drakhaon.'

The doctor's face crumpled like old parchment.

'No, Highness. Don't make me go back. I beg you. Please don't make me.'

Eugene turned away. He found the doctor's pleading embarrassing.

'Do you wish to live?'

'B-but they'll kill me if they find out I've—'

'That is a risk you will have to take.'

Elysia dried her eyes. What was the use of weeping? She was cross with herself now to have shown such weakness, and all over a little cut. She examined her finger and saw that the bleeding had stopped.

She would just have to start again with her fourth hairpin.

She went to the wash-bowl and with her left hand poured cold water into the bowl, dabbing some around her eyes to reduce the redness.

'Madame Andar?'

Someone had called her name.

'Elysia?'

She picked up a candle and hurried into her bed-chamber to see Astasia standing there, holding a fair-haired little girl by the hand.

'How did you—' she began, but before she could finish, Astasia threw herself into her arms, hugging her tight.

'Oh Madame Andar, I'm so pleased to see you. Velemir told me you had gone to Azhkendir. If it were not for Kari, I would have gone on believing it.'

'But how did you get past the guards?'

'I know all the secret passages,' said a small, clear voice proudly.

'Princess Karila?' Elysia curtseyed to the child.

'Now can we have a story?' Karila said, yawning. 'I'm tired.'

'Take us back to your rooms, Kari,' Astasia coaxed, 'and I'll tell you a story from Muscobar.'

'But not a sad story. I don't want to have bad dreams.'

'This one will have a blissfully happy ending,' Astasia said, smiling at Elysia over Karila's head.

Elysia watched in astonishment as Karila walked over to the marble mantelpiece and touched one of the carved acanthus leaves. A panel slid to one side, just wide enough for a child to walk through without bumping her head.

'Follow us,' said Astasia, beckoning.

Elysia tucked Princess Karila into her gilded bed and Astasia began to tell Karila the tale of the young prince and his mother washed up on the shores of a magical island. Elysia observed Astasia's mobile face, her dark eyes bewitchingly alight with every nuance of the story, and wondered if she should pinch herself to make certain she was not dreaming.

By the time Astasia reached the musical squirrel and the bumblebee, Karila was yawning, and long before the swan princess made her appearance, the little girl had fallen asleep.

The two women retreated into the princess's

dressing-room and talked in whispers, so as not to wake Karila.

'Velemir has treated us both shamefully,' Astasia said when Elysia had finished her tale. 'Your life is in danger, Madame Andar. We have to get you away from here.'

'The palace is surrounded by an invisible protective ward,' Elysia said, shaking her head. 'I fear we would not get far.'

'You speak as if we were on that magical island in the story!'

'Eugene employs a magus to protect him. He is a man of considerable powers. We must not underestimate what he can do.'

Astasia gave an impatient little shrug. 'Then we must play Velemir at his own game—'

'Aiii!' The child's scream pierced their whispering. They hurried back into Karila's bedchamber to see the little girl sitting upright in her bed, staring fixedly into the dim light.

Elysia put her arms around her, hugging her close. 'It's all right, Kari, it was only a dream.'

Karila's body was hot, soaked with sweat. She clutched Elysia tightly.

'It flew right over the palace,' she said in a small, toneless voice. 'I saw its eyes. Blue. Like the blue at the heart of a flame. Dragon eyes.'

Dragon eyes . . .

Gouts of red spattered Gavril's dreams. He woke with the taste and stink of spilled blood rank in his throat and nostrils. He woke knowing something had gone wrong. He had no idea what hour of the night it was, only that he could smell death.

'My Lord!' The door to his chamber burst open and Juri staggered in, collapsing to his knees. His scalp was glazed with half-dried blood. 'Forgive us. We've failed you.'

'What's happened?' Gavril struggled to get up. His head spun, his limbs felt weak and sinewless.

'Tielens have taken Jushko. We'd got Michailo cornered. A neat little ambush. But the Tielens were below in the gorge, and when they heard the noise, they returned fire. Michailo fell, Grisha—'

'Michailo was shot?'

'Didn't stand a chance. Came to . . . saw them taking away Jushko. Tielens were bayoneting anyone on the ground . . . dragged myself into the gorse . . . or I'd be lying up there with the rest, food for kites—'

'But Lilias!' Gavril cried. 'Did they find Lilias?'

'It looks bad, My Lord. Very bad—'

A sudden clanging drowned out his voice. A warning bell, frantically dinning from one of the watchtowers.

'Now what?' Gavril pulled a morning-robe over his nightshirt and hurried out onto the landing to find the kastel filled with running men.

'They're coming this way!' someone shouted from the hall below.

Gavril caught hold of one of the *druzhina*. 'Who's coming?'

'The Tielen army, My Lord.' It was young Semyon; his eyes were wide with fear.

'It can't be!' Gavril gripped the balcony rail to steady himself.

He had fulfilled Eugene's conditions. Why had the Tielens broken their bond?

38

Gavril wavered in the keen wind as he clambered out onto the Kalika Tower roof. His father's telescopes were still there. If only he didn't feel so weak, weak enough for a strong gust of wind to blow him right off the roof . . .

He staggered as he caught hold of the larger telescope and struggled to take the lens cover off; it seemed to be rusted on.

In the courtyard far below Askold was mustering the kastel *druzhina*, ordering them to defend the outer walls and the watchtowers.

'Up – about forty-five degrees to the left,' Gavril muttered, squinting down the lens, trying to focus the great telescope on the white blur of moorlands.

And then he saw them.

Line upon line of uniformed soldiers were marching over the moorlands towards the kastel, led by officers on horseback. There were cannon, drawn by horses; blue and grey standards rippled in the wind.

The Tielen army.

'Save us, Lord Drakhaon.' Ninusha clutched at Gavril's sleeve, her eyes filled with tears. 'Please save us.'

Gavril looked round at his assembled household: the women, children and elderly men who had served him and his father so faithfully. They looked back at him, their eyes wide with fear, hope – and trust. They were counting on him to protect them. And he knew in that moment that he could not sacrifice them to Eugene's troops.

'You must go into the East Wing and hide in the tunnels,' he said, forcing confidence into his voice. 'Stay underground until it's all over.'

'There's ghosts in the East Wing,' cried one of the children, bursting into terrified sobs.

Bugle fanfares, militarily dry and precise, rang out in the distance.

'Go,' Gavril said. 'Go now.'

'This way! Follow me.' Sosia began to lead the way towards the boarded-up door.

'I'm s-so frightened.' Ninusha stood trembling, rooted to the spot. Ilsi grabbed hold of Ninusha's hand and dragged her away.

'Where's Kostya?' Sosia cried, turning back. 'We can't leave Kostya!'

The fanfares rang out again.

'Leave Kostya to me,' Gavril said, pushing her gently towards the others. 'Ilsi, take care of Sosia.'

He set out towards Kostya's rooms.

A deafening explosion rocked the whole building.

Gavril swayed, clutching at a doorframe to right himself. He heard the crash of falling masonry.

They were bombarding the kastel.

Kostya, moustaches bristling, was trying to pull on his old leather campaign jacket over his nightshirt.

'Kostya, you must come with me. Down to the East Wing. You can't stay here.'

Kostya swore. 'If you think I'm going to hide with the women and children, you're mistaken. My place is with my men.'

'And I'm not leaving you here to be killed in your bed.'

'In my bed?' Kostya let out a withering stream of curses and swung his legs over the side of the bed. 'Hand me my crossbow. I may not be much use, but I'll be damned if I don't take a few of these Tielens with me to the Ways Beyond.' He stood up unsteadily, only to sink down again.

Gavril went to help him up but Kostya glared at him, shaking the proffered hand away.

'And if you were your father's son, you'd use your powers and fry the Tielen army to a crisp! Just pass me my bow.'

Gavril went from room to room, searching in vain for Altan Kazimir.

There must be something the doctor could do to restore his powers. At the least, some of his waning strength . . .

He flung open his bedchamber door. Jaromir Arkhel stood there, holding a blade to Altan Kazimir's throat.

'Jaro, what's going on?'

'The good doctor here has some explaining to do. Ask him where he's been,' said Jaromir, stern-voiced. His hair glinted darkly golden in the winter morning light. 'I found him sneaking back in through the summerhouse tunnel.'

Kazimir began to babble a stream of half-coherent words.

'F-forgive me, Lord Gavril. I – I didn't have any choice. Linnaius – p-poisoned me—'

'Calm yourself, Doctor,' Gavril said, 'you're making no sense at all.'

Jaromir lowered his blade.

'Th-they made me agree to a rendezvous. With one of the Prince's aides. I w-was to give him samples of your blood. In exchange, Magus Linnaius would give me the antidote. But they forced me to come back. With this despatch.' With shaking hands he fumbled in his jacket and drew out a sealed parchment, handing it to Gavril.

Gavril opened the despatch. It was written in a bold, official hand in the common script:

Know this, Gavril Nagarian, that you have failed to fulfil the last of our conditions, namely the restoration of Lord Jaromir Arkhel to his rightful place as ruler of Azhkendir – but instead are commonly reported to have murdered the same Lord Arkhel and usurped his title. As a consequence, we require you to surrender yourself and your kastel to us. Any resistance will be met with merciless retribution.

Eugene of Tielen

'All this because Eugene believes I'm dead?' Jaromir

turned to Gavril, eyes blank with bewilderment.

'One of my *druzhina* must have told him so.' Gavril stared at the blunt wording of the despatch. *Merciless retribution.* His lie, told with the best of intentions to preserve a forbidden friendship, had rebounded with disastrous consequences.

'And that's not all,' Jaromir said. 'Show us the other phial you have hidden in your jacket. The one that stinks of Magus Linnaius's sorceries.'

'There is no other phial—'

Jaromir pushed him back against the wall. 'Do I have to strip the jacket from your back?'

Kazimir glared balefully at Jaromir. With one hand he delved into the lining of his jacket and brought out a little phial. Jaromir took it from him and held it to the light. It glimmered faintly with a pale, grey luminescence.

'What does this contain?'

'You're not scientists,' Kazimir said. 'You wouldn't understand.'

'The truth, Kazimir. Or it will go ill with you.'

'A – a sedative. To enable the effects of the elixir.'

'To disable Lord Gavril. To poison him!'

'To subdue the creature that lives inside him, that feeds off his life-force,' snapped Kazimir. 'The thing your father called Drakhaoul.'

'Only in destroying the Drakhaoul,' Gavril said slowly, 'you're also poisoning me.'

A cannonball came whizzing high over the outer walls and smashed with a dull thud into the kastel. Kazimir flinched.

'And is there any antidote to this mage-poison you've been feeding me?' Gavril demanded.

Kazimir shook his head. 'Only to wait for its effects to be fully excreted from the system.'

'You call yourself a scientist.' He had trusted this man to help him and he had betrayed him, as he had betrayed his father. 'Is it beyond your abilities to find one?'

'I – I—'

'Then go back to your laboratory and get working!'

A fresh barrage of cannonballs thudded into the kastel. The building shook and a fine plaster dust showered down from the ceiling. Kazimir whimpered with fear.

'Up in the T-Tower?'

'Where else?'

'I must go to Eugene and make him stop the bombardment,' Jaromir said, brushing the dust from his coat.

'How?' Gavril rounded on Jaromir. 'You'll be blown to bits before you get anywhere near him! Your mentor seems determined to raze this kastel to the ground.'

'Let me use the Vox Aethyria.'

'You said it could only be tuned to one other glass. And this one is tuned to Count Velemir's.'

'Then let me speak to Velemir.'

'Fire.' Eugene stood above the cannon and watched with grim satisfaction as the next round of cannonades ripped into the outer bastion walls of the Drakhaon's stronghold.

He had stationed cannon and mortars around the whole perimeter. They had been met with crossbow fire from the walls and several of his less vigilant troopers had fallen, pierced by crossbow bolts and barbed arrows from longbows. Crude, unsophisticated weapons, but effective enough to kill.

For that insolence, he had blasted one of the watchtowers and seen it crumble, the men inside blown to bloody fragments by the destructive power of Linnaius's munitions.

Now they were loading the mortars, ramming the charges into the metal tubes, aiming them at the living quarters of the kastel.

Eugene folded his arms, narrowing his eyes against the white glare of the snows. He felt nothing but the wintercold of loss numbing his heart.

Jaromir was dead. And Azhkendir would pay dearly for his death. Gavril Nagarian would see his *druzhina* die, one by one . . .

'Ready, Highness.'

He slowly raised one white-gloved hand.

'Fire.'

'Keep back, or I'll shoot,' growled a hoarse voice.

Oleg, a bottle in each hand, wavered on the threshold of the Bogatyr's room as Kostya levelled a crossbow at his chest.

Oleg took a wobbling step backwards, one bottle raised to fend off any attack. 'It'sh me, Koshtya. Old Oleg. You don't want to kill old Oleg, do you?'

The crossbow slowly lowered. 'You're drunk,' Kostya said in tones of withering disapproval. 'Drunk on duty.'

'And it's the besht in the cellar!' Oleg thrust the bottle under Kostya's nose. 'Go on. Try. You – won't regret it. Got to finish it, you see,' he confided, 'before those Tielen bastards steal it.'

Kostya said nothing.

'Come *on*, Koshtya.' Oleg took a swig from his bottle of vintage Smarnan brandy. 'You're to come with me. Drakhaon says. Down – down – to – the—' He searched for the word, couldn't find it, and took another swig of the brandy to see if that would jog his memory.

'If you think I'm going to go hide in the cellar with the women—'

A mortar screamed overhead. Plaster thudded down from the ceiling, great chunks, leaving bare rafters and lathes exposed. The explosion threw Oleg off-balance, and the brandy bottle fell from his hands and shattered on the floor. He dropped to his knees and tried to salvage the broken pieces, wet and slippery with the spilled brandy.

'Volkh's best. Too good for those Tielen swine. Damn you all to hell!' he bawled, shaking his fist at the gaping window. 'C'mon now, Koshtya.' He swung around – only to see that Kostya lay prone on the bed, the crossbow beside him. A large chunk of plaster had fallen on his head. 'Koshtya!' he repeated, panicking. The Bogatyr did not move.

A cannonball crashed into the outer wall. Oleg clapped his hands to his ears. Cries and screams came from outside. Kostya was dead. And he would be dead if he stayed here any longer.

'Dead. Koshtya's dead!' Weeping noisily, Oleg stumbled from the Bogatyr's rooms towards the East Wing.

As Gavril and Jaromir ran into Lilias's rooms, another cannon blast rocked the kastel, followed by the crash of shattered rooftiles and beams.

The crystal glass trembled in its case on the mantelpiece.

'That was too close,' Jaromir said, lifting the delicate device down and putting it on the floor.

'You know how to make it work?' Gavril crouched down beside him as he opened the case.

'Velemir. Velemir! Respond!' Jaromir's voice was harsh with tension.

'Is it broken?'

No sound came from the device; it seemed to be dead.

'Velemir!' Jaromir kept repeating in a low, insistent voice, all the time rotating the central crystal, an open-petalled flower on its stem.

'Or could the bombardment have disabled it?'

A mortar whistled overhead, exploding on the terrace outside. The oriel window panes blew in, showering them both with broken glass. Gavril was thrown onto the floor by the force of the blast. Jaromir flung his arms around the device, covering it with his body.

'Are you all right?' Gavril, ears ringing from the explosion, rose up unsteadily, brushing the fragments of glass from his clothes and hair.

A faint crackle issued from the device.

'Velemir!' Jaromir shouted. 'This is Jaromir Arkhel! Respond!' A splinter of glass had grazed his temple and a thin line of blood, like a scarlet thread, trickled down one side of his face.

And at last a voice vibrated feebly from the crystal, the words distorted and indistinct.

'*Is this – a – joke? A – trick? Jaromir Arkhel is – reported – dead.*'

'I am in Kastel Drakhaon and very much alive.

But I won't be for long, if this bombardment continues. Tell Eugene. Tell him to stop the attack. Stop the attack!'

'*How – do I know – for sure?*'

'You don't! You'll just have to—'

A second mortar whistled past, hitting the terrace with a deafening explosion. Gavril felt his head vibrate with the force of the blast. Chips of shattered stone and dust were hurled high in the air.

'*Velemir!*' Jaromir gripped the device, but the tenuous link was broken.

'What now?' Gavril said in frustration. 'Wait till Eugene blasts us to extinction?'

Another mortar came whining overhead, exploding against the wall. The stones quivered, shuddered, and the whole of the oriel window-bay collapsed inwards. Gavril threw himself onto Jaromir, trying to push him out of the way as glass, stone and timbers thudded into the room.

Cold air was sucked in from outside. Rags and tatters of Lilias's fine brocade curtains flapped in the wind. Pages from her torn books of verse and philosophy fluttered away into the garden.

Gavril opened his mouth to speak and drew in a lungful of plaster dust.

'The – device—' Choking, he dragged himself from Jaromir on hands and knees.

Jaromir rolled over; plaster dust had powdered his clothes and face. Beyond him lay the Vox Aethyria, its crystal perfection shattered.

'That's that, then,' he said flatly. A trickle of red blood on the white plaster gave his face the bizarre look of a circus clown.

'Must get out,' Gavril managed, wheezing.

'Another blast – like the last – and the whole wing will collapse.'

Coughing, they began to crawl towards the door, which gaped open on its hinges.

'If I can – make it through the tunnels,' Jaromir said, 'maybe I can reach Eugene—' He broke off. 'Listen.'

Gavril listened. His ears were still ringing from the explosions, but there was no sound to be heard.

'The bombardment's stopped.'

'They're reloading.'

Jaromir gripped his arm tight. 'No. This is different.'

'It's a trap. To lure us out into the open.'

'Or Velemir's relayed my message.'

Gavril stared at him, desperately wanting to believe it to be so.

'Let me go out to him, Gavril.'

'No. It's too dangerous.' They picked their way through the debris brought down in the bombardment, making towards the main entrance.

'What is there to fear? Eugene won't fire on me.'

'And how will he know it's you? One man walking out alone from an enemy stronghold.'

'If only that last blast hadn't shattered the Vox . . .'

They had reached the entrance hall. *Druzhina* crouched beside every window, bows and crossbows trained on the courtyard outside.

'Get down, My Lord!' cried one of the men, leaping up to cover him.

'But it's stopped,' Gavril said, recognizing Askold, Jushko's younger brother, by his shaven head and single braid.

603

'For the time being.' Only now Askold noticed that Gavril was not alone. 'And who's this?' he asked suspiciously, levelling his crossbow at Jaromir.

'Our salvation,' Gavril said, gazing round at the faces of his *druzhina*, who were all staring at them both with distrust. He chose his words with care. 'This man is to bear a message to Prince Eugene that will save all our lives.'

'We're not surrendering!' said one. 'Not to Tielen.'

'You must hold your fire,' Gavril said, ignoring him, 'whilst my messenger walks over to the Tielen side. No-one must fire. Not one single shot. Or all will be lost. Is that understood?'

They nodded sullenly. He could sense their fear and their uncertainty. Lord Volkh, one was sure to say soon, would never have sent a messenger. He would have led the counter-attack from the air.

'One of you – Semyon –' Gavril chose the youngest, knowing he would argue less, 'relay my orders to all the other posts and watchtowers. They're to hold their fire. No retaliation. As soon as you return, I'll know it's time to proceed.'

'Young Sem'll be easy pickings for those Tielen marksmen,' grumbled one of the others.

'Then I'll go myself!'

'No, My Lord. You chose me.' Semyon sped away.

Jaromir had been brushing the dust from his clothes. 'Well,' he said, suddenly flashing Gavril a grin, 'wish me luck.'

Gavril suddenly found himself reaching out, flinging his arms around Jaromir, hugging him as warmly as if he were one of his oldest, dearest friends.

'Take care,' he said. 'We're all depending on you.'

'I know.' Jaromir grasped him by the shoulder and gazed into his eyes. 'Trust me.' Then he let Gavril go and, without a backwards glance, went out into the courtyard.

'Can we be sure it's true?'

'Velemir said the message came from within the kastel. They were cut off by what sounded like an explosion.' Anckstrom had just emerged from the communications wagon. He handed Eugene his spyglass.

Eugene scanned the kastel below from watchtower to watchtower. Smoke was billowing from one of the towers. Most of the glass in the windows was gone. Ragged holes gaped in the walls and the roofs.

'It could all be a trick, to give them time to retaliate.'

'And the life-flame?' Eugene handed Anckstrom back the spyglass and took the little phial out from within his breast pocket. It glowed darkly in the winter light, red as a flame of blood.

'There's someone coming out!' Anckstrom tried to adjust the spyglass to get a clearer view. 'A man. Alone.' And then he swore. 'Deuce take it. Could it be—'

Eugene seized the spyglass again.

'Jaromir,' he whispered. And then he started out down the snowy hill, shouting, 'Jaromir! *Jaromir!*'

'For God's sake, hold your fire!' He dimly heard Anckstrom barking an abrupt order to his officers and men. He saw only the single figure walking calmly, unhurriedly, towards the massed ranks of his troops, cannon, mortars, carbines, all levelled at him.

605

He ran on, down the mud-churned tracks and the rutted, hard-frozen snow towards him. Jaromir stopped, shading his eyes against the brightness of the daylight.

'Eugene?' he said uncertainly.

Eugene reached him at last and awkwardly, fervently, caught him in his arms, hugging him close.

'You're safe, Jaro,' he said into Jaromir's bronze-bright hair. 'You're alive.' The words stifled in his throat and he found he was unable to speak for joy. He didn't care what the army thought of this impulsive, utterly uncharacteristic show of affection. 'The flame didn't lie.'

Holding Jaromir at arm's length, he scanned his face intently, trying to read every minute change, taking every detail in. Jaromir looked fit, weather-burned, but Eugene, a seasoned campaigner, saw from the way his right arm hung awkwardly that he had been injured. 'What's happened to your arm? Your hand?' He gently raised Jaromir's right hand in his own to look more closely. The snowlight showed only too clearly the darkened, burned skin, the clawed fingers. Old injuries, ill-healed.

'Who did this to you?' he said, staring up at the kastel behind him. 'By God, I swear they'll pay dearly for making you suffer . . .'

'The man who did this to me is dead,' Jaromir said. 'I killed him. The debt is paid, Eugene.'

Eugene looked into his eyes and saw that the shadows had gone, finally exorcized. The Jaromir who had left Swanholm a tormented boy had become whole. A man.

'Gavril Nagarian is not like his father. You must believe me. He doesn't deserve this.' Jaromir gestured to the smouldering kastel behind him. 'I want you to promise me that you'll stop the bombardment, Eugene.'

Must. Want. There was a new fire in his eyes – and a directness that surprised Eugene.

'And you must order the release of his mother. She is innocent of any crime.'

'Come up to the tent.' Eugene took him by the arm and led him back up the hill, past the cannon emplacements and the waiting, watching soldiers who stared at the two in puzzlement.

'Is Lilias here?' Jaromir asked eagerly, gazing up at the Tielen tents. 'Lilias Arbelian?'

'How the devil did you find out we had the Arbelian woman?' Eugene was beginning to realize how little he knew about what had happened to his protégé in the lost months.

'But can I see her? And the child?'

'Jaro.' Eugene stopped, placing both hands on the young man's shoulders. Such concern for Lilias. Was the child Jaromir's? He guessed that Jaro would tell him the truth when he felt the time was right. Now was not the moment for probing too deeply. 'I left her and her son back at the other camp in the gorge. This is no place for a woman with a baby.'

'Are they safe?' Jaromir's eyes clouded with concern.

'They're well-protected, don't worry.'

They reached the brow of the incline and Anckstrom strode over to greet them.

'General Anckstrom!' Jaromir said, his face creasing into a wide smile.

'Glad to see you safe, lad!' Anckstrom said

gruffly. Other officers came crowding up, saluting, shaking hands with Jaromir. Eugene looked on, unable to keep from smiling, overcome by a feeling of ineffable happiness.

'On to Muscobar, eh!' Anckstrom said. 'What's to stop us now?'

'You must free Madame Nagarian first.' Jaromir detached himself from the other young officers and came hurrying back. 'You gave your word, Eugene.'

The adjutants and aides standing nearby exchanged shocked glances. Any other young lord speaking so freely to him would have been sharply admonished. But Eugene merely nodded. 'See that it's done, Anckstrom.'

'And Gavril Nagarian?'

Eugene felt an unaccountable uneasiness at the mention of the Drakhaon's name. Gazing down over the battered kastel, he saw all the signs of defeat. But Linnaius had warned him. The Drakhaons were possessed by a dark and dangerous spirit. There was no proof that Kazimir's elixir had worked.

'I want you in command here, Jaromir. Not the young Nagarian.'

'He's no threat. In all truth, Eugene,' and again this new, frank-spoken Jaromir faced him, dark eyes intense, 'whatever Linnaius persuaded Kazimir to dose him with has made him very sick. Wouldn't it have been enough to reduce his powers without resorting to alchymical poisons?'

Eugene stared at him coldly a moment. 'Whatever method of treatment was agreed between Linnaius and Doctor Kazimir is no concern of mine. My only concern was that it worked.'

'I gave my word that I would negotiate for a truce. A truce without conditions.'

'But you should be Drakhaon. Or Arkhaon – the old, true title of the rulers of Azhkendir before the Nagarians began their reign of terror.'

Jaromir shook his head. 'I don't want to usurp what is rightfully Gavril's title. Besides, his *druzhina* will never accept an Arkhel in his place.'

'They will accept what they are told to accept.' For a moment, Eugene was tempted to order the bombardment to begin again. To blast the stubborn Azhkendi into submission.

'A communication from Admiral Janssen!' One of the aides came from the tent, waving a paper.

Eugene took the note from him.

'"We have Mirom blockaded by land and sea. Minimal resistance encountered so far. Awaiting your instructions."'

Eugene passed the message to Anckstrom.

'Time to move south, Highness?' Anckstrom said, smiling broadly as he read.

'Break the siege!' Eugene said, turning to his officers.

'We should let Lord Gavril know it's over,' Jaromir said. 'If his men see any movement from our forces, they may misinterpret your intentions—'

'Then we'll send a message via Velemir.' Eugene put one arm around Jaromir's shoulders, trying to lead him towards the tent. 'This calls for a toast. Lars, wine for all my officers! Extra schnaps for the men.'

'The kastel Vox Aethyria is broken,' Jaromir said, standing his ground. 'You'd better let me take the news back to Gavril. Then I'll ride with you to Mirom.'

609

Gavril. Not Lord Nagarian. There was more here, so much more than he had realized. Eugene let his arm drop from Jaromir's shoulders. He could see from Jaromir's determined expression that his ward was not to be dissuaded.

'Go back, then. We'll drink that toast when you've said your farewells.'

At the entrance to the courtyard, Jaromir turned around and lifted his sound arm high to wave. There was so much confidence, so much exuberance, in the wave that Eugene found himself smiling broadly as he returned the gesture.

All would be well now. He would ride into Mirom with Jaro at his side.

Kostya came slowly back to his senses. He was lying face down on his bed. And he was covered in debris: plaster, splintered wood, broken glass. His window had been blown in. And when he tried to raise his head, the sky seemed to implode again. Something – or someone – had hit him a stunning blow to the back of the head and now his whole skull throbbed with the pain of it.

Kastel under attack!

He reached out blindly and his hands closed on the shaft of his crossbow.

At least he was still armed. At least he could still do his duty to the Drakhaon.

He checked – yes, there was still one bolt in the bow. One only. Must find more. He tried to stand up – but sank back. Something wrong with his eyes. A blackness – like a crow's wing – kept flapping into his vision, blocking out half the room.

Have to make do with half-sight, then. It hadn't stopped Jushko One-Eye.

Crossbow in hand, he fumbled through the debris to the window, sinking to his knees at the sill, peering out at the empty courtyard.

The dazzle of daylight made his aching head swim.

No guns now. No cannon.

All silent.

Ceasefire? Tielen subterfuge? Or surrender? He felt a clawing pain in his chest at the very thought. No surrender.

He propped the crossbow on the window-ledge, angling it so that the first Tielen to enter the courtyard from the road would die.

He blinked.

Damn it all, there was one coming now. A man approaching from the enemy lines. The insolence of it, just calmly walking in. What did it mean?

Kostya screwed up his eyes, trying to see more clearly.

And now the damned Tielen was turning to give a signal to the others. A single wave of the hand. It could only mean one thing.

Attack.

A ray of winter sunlight suddenly illuminated the intruder.

That colour of hair. Bronzed gold. Arkhel gold. Cursed Arkhel gold.

'Stavyor Arkhel!' Kostya reared up with the last of his strength, crossbow aimed. 'Now it is your turn!'

The golden-haired Arkhel heard him shout, turned back, a look of puzzlement on his face.

Kostya squeezed the lever. The lethal metal bolt flew – its aim true – and hit its target.

Stavyor Arkhel clutched at his chest – stumbled – and crashed to the ground.

'Yes!' Kostya shouted, fist raised in a gesture of triumph.

Winter sunlight suddenly flooded from a fissure in the clouds – and Jaromir was bathed in its glow of gold.

Eugene, hand still raised in an answering wave, saw a man suddenly appear at a kastel window. For a moment, he could not believe what he saw. And then – late, too late – he realized.

'Look out!' he yelled.

Something flashed in the sunlight.

Eugene saw Jaromir stagger. Saw him pitch forward onto the muddy ground, hands clutching at the metal shaft protruding from his chest.

He seized a carbine from the soldier next to him. Raised it. Aimed. Fired.

He hit the crossbowman full in the forehead. And saw him topple over the edge of the broken window to crash to the courtyard below.

Then he was running down the hill towards Jaromir, all the cold calm of the execution gone – and nothing but a winter of desolation raging in his heart.

39

Eugene dropped to his knees on the frozen snow and turned Jaromir over onto his side.

'Cover the Prince!' he heard Anckstrom yell. All around him his soldiers appeared, carbines trained on the walls of the kastel, a human shield.

Blood stained the snow, a spreading stain of blood soaked Jaromir's jacket, blood trickled from one corner of his mouth. He was still breathing – but any soldier of Eugene's experience, well used to the injuries of war, could see that those faint, shuddering breaths would soon fade. Eugene gently raised his head, supporting it against his knee, smoothing the bronze-gold hair from Jaromir's forehead.

'A surgeon!' he shouted, hearing his own voice crack with desperation.

'Eugene . . .' Jaromir whispered. His face was grey except for the red stain of blood on his lips. 'Promise me . . . take care of . . . Lilias . . .'

'Hold on now, Jaro,' Eugene urged, his voice shaking. 'For God's sake, hold on.' He could see Jaromir's dark eyes no longer stared into his but through him, as if he were gazing into another distant dimension. If only words were enough. If only . . .

'Jaro,' he said brokenly. 'My Jaro.'

Jaromir's head lolled limply back against his knee.

'Oh, Jaro,' Eugene whispered. He laid the body down, then bent to kiss the bloodstained lips . . . and with trembling fingers closed Jaromir's eyes.

The surgeon came hurrying through the cordon of soldiers, bag in hand.

'You're too late,' Eugene heard himself say. He rose to his feet unsteadily, gazing at Kastel Drakhaon. He was aware that the whole hillside was silent, that all his men were staring at him.

The blood-red flame in the lifeglass wavered, faded, and went out.

'Show them no mercy. Use the poison-shells. Raze Kastel Drakhaon to the ground.'

Kiukiu stopped on the forest path, listening. For a while now the ominous rumble of cannon-fire had ceased. It was a sound unlike any she had heard in her life before: the unnatural whine of mortars, whistling and screaming in the distance like grotesque predatory birds – and the earth-shaking rumble of explosions.

And now it had stopped.

She hefted the heavy gusly bag onto her other shoulder. The strings gave off a soft, dark shimmer of sound. She had set out, eager to use her gifts to help Lord Gavril defend the kastel against the Tielen invaders.

But what use were her gifts against such terrible weapons? She could sing long-dead warrior spirits into the *druzhina* to inspire them to feats of great courage, but all her efforts would be in vain if these terrible cannonades brought the kastel walls crashing down on them.

The silence was all the more eerie after the cacophony of the cannon. She walked swiftly on between the great ivy-wreathed tree-trunks, the sound of her feet muffled by the soft carpet of dry leaves and leaf-mould.

Malusha – still too frail to leave her bed – had forbidden her to come. But she had come anyway. If Gavril was in danger, then she wanted to be at his side, to share the danger. She could not bear to think of him facing these hazards alone.

And then she felt a bright stab of pain about her heart. The forest went chill and dark about her. All the colour leached from the day and she stood alone in a cold, desolate place, grey as drifting ash.

She blinked – and the colours returned. But not the emptiness in her heart.

Death. She had felt it as if it had been her own. Someone close to her had died. Lord Gavril? Loss and panic gripped her. No, it could not have been Gavril. His death would have left her so bereft she would not have been able to think or act. Neither was it Malusha. She closed her eyes a moment, trying to sense the aura of the soul she had felt brush past her on its journey into the Ways Beyond.

She sensed warmth, honour, friendship, regret . . . a vivid brightness all too swiftly extinguished, a flame that should have lit Azhkendir.

'Jaromir?' she cried out in anguish. 'Oh no, no . . .'

One moment Jaromir had been hurrying eagerly back towards the kastel, the winter sun bright in his hair. The next Gavril had seen him clutch at his chest – and fall.

The bolt that felled him had come from Kastel Drakhaon.

What followed seemed to flash past so swiftly – and yet each agonized moment etched itself, cut by cut, on Gavril's mind.

The sharp crack of a pistol-shot split the silence.

'Jaro!' he called uselessly. 'Jaromir!' He started out across the courtyard, heedless of any danger to himself. He had to get to Jaromir, to tell him that someone had countered his orders, that he had not ordered his death.

'No, My Lord!' Askold ran out after him, caught hold of him, restraining him, trying to drag him back. 'They'll kill you!'

'Who?' he yelled into the stillness. 'Who dared to disobey me?'

And then he saw Kostya's broken body – the crossbow lying beside him – blood leaking out from his shattered skull onto the cobbles.

'*Kostya?*' he whispered.

Across the divide he saw Eugene slowly rise from where Jaromir's still figure lay. Turn to stare at him. Even from this distance he could sense the menace and hatred in that long, cold look.

Show them no mercy.

'My Lord!' The *druzhina* dragged him back towards the doorway, stumbling over the fallen

616

debris in their haste. 'There's nothing to be done. It's too late.'

Tears streamed down his cheeks. He did not care who saw. The only man who had shown him true friendship in Azhkendir – his enemy – lay dead. Slain by his Bogatyr, his right-hand man.

A cannon-shell came whizzing above their heads – then another and another.

They tumbled back inside the doorway, hands pressed to their ears as the shells exploded and the kastel shook to its foundations.

'We're done for,' one of the men shouted above the crash of tumbling masonry.

Gavril crouched amidst the dust and rubble, paralysed with grief and shock. All Jaromir had wanted was to preserve the kastel and the people in it – and with one ill-judged crossbow bolt, Kostya had undone everything he had striven to achieve.

'Lord Drakhaon!' Semyon chose that moment to come speeding across from the nearest watchtower just as more shells burst in the courtyard outside.

Gavril glanced up and saw one of the tall barley-sugar chimney stacks wavering, starting to topple down above the boy's head.

'Look out!' Gavril dived to grab Semyon's legs, bringing him down just as the stack came crashing onto the cobbles.

Brick, tiles and stone spattered them. For a moment they lay entangled, hands still clasped to their heads as the dust settled, not daring to move.

'Th-thank you, My Lord,' Semyon said, crawling out, winded. 'You saved me—'

Another cannon-shell whined overhead.

'Inside, quick.' Gavril heaved Semyon to his feet

and dragged him inside as the shell exploded with a fizzing hiss.

Clouds of milk-white smoke billowed into the hallway. It gave off a bitter, chymical odour, quite unlike the earlier sulphurous gunpowder fumes. The men began to cough and retch, staggering around, disoriented. Gavril found his eyes stinging from the thin, milky smoke. This was the same gas the Tielens had used to disable them at Narvazh. It stank of alchymy.

'Cover your mouths!' he yelled. 'It's poisoned! They're trying to smoke us out!' He pulled up a corner of his jacket across his nose and mouth. 'Retreat!' he ordered, backing away down the hall. 'Follow me!'

And then he saw her. Standing lost, confused, in the hallway, clutching her gusly to her to protect it from the falling rubble.

And he had thought her safe.

'Kiukiu?' he cried. She ran towards him – and another blast shook the building, throwing her forwards. He caught her as she fell, steadying her against him.

'Where now, My Lord?'

'Into the cellar!'

The *druzhina* kicked open the door and they fumbled their way through the smoke down the kitchen stairs to the fusty darkness of Oleg's wine cellar. One of the older *druzhina* collapsed to his knees, vomiting and wheezing.

'We'll – be trapped here – like rats!' spluttered Askold.

'We – need to – breathe!' Gavril gasped. His tongue and throat burned. 'Who knows what this smoke does to your lungs?'

Askold swore. 'If it gets down into the East Wing tunnels . . . what of the women and children? They'll stifle to death.'

'Why, Kiukiu? Why did you come back?' Gavril gazed at Kiukiu, his heart torn by mingled feelings of fear and joy. 'You were safe at the monastery.'

'I came to help,' she said staunchly.

'Jaro's d-dead.' He stumbled over the words, feeling the grief surge up again, a wave that could not be suppressed.

'I felt him die,' she said. He gazed into her eyes and saw his own desolation and uncomprehending loss mirrored there. She – she alone of all his household – understood. She had always understood. She had come back to be with him, heedless of the danger. And there was nothing for her here but destruction – and death.

'Kiukiu,' he said brokenly. He put his arms around her and pulled her to him again, holding her pressed tightly against his heart. She did not resist, but let herself be drawn into his embrace, nestling her golden head against his shoulder.

'Lord Drakhaon.' Semyon, trying to staunch the blood streaming from a gash on the cheek with his kerchief, turned to him. 'Save us.'

Another cannon-shell exploded overhead with a dull thud that made the wine bottles clink and shudder on their racks.

'This is no fair fight,' Askold cried. 'What use are our weapons against these cannon? We're outnumbered. Outmanoeuvred.'

'Only you can save us, Lord Drakhaon.'

Gavril looked around at the exhausted, battered men sitting slumped against wine racks and barrels in the gloom of the cellar. He looked down at Kiukiu, felt the beat of her heart close to his.

'Your father would have destroyed those cursed Tielens,' said Askold accusingly.

'I gave my word,' Gavril said, 'against my mother's life.'

'What do they care for your mother? She's probably dead already.'

Elysia dead? Gavril felt the cellar grow cold about him. Suppose what Askold said was true and she had been executed by Eugene's troops in Tielen, so far from home, and all on his account . . .

'They've played us false, My Lord,' said old Guaram, shaking his head, 'on every turn.'

'But we broke the agreement.'

'Did you invite them in? They have no right to be here!'

When the steppe wolves had attacked, the Drakhaoul had woken deep inside him and caused the devastating conflagration. But the Drakhaoul still lay dormant, drugged by Kaspar Linnaius's treacherous elixir.

'Kazimir! Where is Doctor Kazimir?' he cried.

'I have Count Velemir, as you requested, Highness.' Eugene's adjutant beckoned him to the Vox Aethyria, which had been placed on a folding table for safe-keeping during the bombardment.

'*Highness.*' Velemir's voice was barely audible above the crack and rumble of the cannonfire.

'I have new instructions for you.' Eugene heard his own voice as if it were miles away, speaking with arid detachment. 'We are at war with Azhkendir. Madame Elysia Nagarian is to be executed. Firing squad.'

There was silence.

'Velemir?' Eugene tapped the crystal, wondering if the bombardment was interfering with their communication.

'*Madame Nagarian – to be shot?*' Even at such a distance Velemir sounded stunned by the instruction. 'B-but why?'

'As a spy. A foreign agent. Report to me when it is done.' Eugene straightened up and signed to his adjutant to terminate the connection. He stalked out of the tent and went back to watch the destruction of Kastel Drakhaon.

A gaping hole had been blasted in the side of the Kalika Tower. Gavril clambered up the broken stair to his father's study over rubble and twisted metal, feeling the tower tremble to its foundations as the merciless bombardment went on, cannonade after cannonade.

As he pushed open the door, another blast flung him to the floor. The floor was covered with shards of broken chymical equipment. Many of Kazimir's elaborate glass structures lay shattered.

'Kazimir!' he yelled. '*Kazimir!*'

'H-here.' Kazimir was crouched under the desk, white-faced and shaking, clutching a vodka bottle.

'Come out!'

'No.'

Gavril caught hold of him by the ankles and tugged him out from under the desk.

'Do you want to live?'

Kazimir nodded, lower lip trembling like a child's.

'You said you could reverse the effects of Linnaius's drug!' Gavril grabbed the doctor by the lapels, thrusting his face close to his. Kazimir's eyes were bloodshot and his breath stank of vodka.

'N-not enough time,' babbled Kazimir.

'Where's my antidote?'

'Hasn't been scientifically t-tested.'

'It's our only chance.'

'All my experiments – ruined—' Kazimir gestured lamely at the smashed glass with the bottle.

Gavril caught hold of him and prised the bottle from his fingers.

'No more vodka for you till you've given me the antidote.'

Kazimir lurched away, broken glass crunching beneath his feet. A colourless liquid was slowly filtering, drop by drop, into a phial. He disconnected the phial and held it up to the light.

'It c-could kill you—'

'And we'll all die anyway if I don't try. Give it here.' Gavril seized it from him and swallowed it down in one gulp.

'Ahh – it burns, it burns . . .' He dropped to his knees as a wave of dark flame shivered through his body. And then every vein, every blood vessel, seemed to pulse with molten fire.

He gave a hoarse cry as the Drakhaoul awoke within him, a cry that rasped from his throat, wild and inhuman.

He saw Kazimir fall back, hands upraised to cover his face.

All was heat now, unbearable heat and fury. His mind danced with white flames. He tore from the room, clambering up the broken stair, making for the roof and the cold, clean air of day.

Half the parapet had been blown away. He teetered on the edge of a deadly drop, the winter's wind chill on his burning skin.

Where was Eugene, his enemy?

He gazed down through the blue heat-haze misting his sight. His skin crackled; his eyes blazed.

The broken walls of his kastel lay below him. Here and there he caught sight of bodies, the bodies of his *druzhina*, lying where they had fallen at their posts. One watchtower had been completely demolished. Smoke and flames besmirched the pale winter clouds overhead.

And beyond, the massed ranks of the Tielen army on the hillside, immaculate in their grey uniforms, row after row of cannon firing in perfect synchronization. The sight of such well-organized destruction enraged him. What had his household done to incur such a brutal response? Faces flashed through his mind: tart-tongued Sosia, weeping at the loss of her cat Adzhika; silly, flirty Ninusha; young Ivar from the stables, always bursting with eagerness to help; doddering Guaram, veteran of countless campaigns, with his meandering stories, 'now when your father was a boy . . .'

And Kiukiu. His heart twisted within his breast at the thought of her hurrying back to be at his side, into this chaos of destruction.

He had thought he cared nothing for these people. And now he knew – in spite of himself – they mattered to him. They counted on him. They trusted him. And he must repay that trust.

The white flames burned his mind clear of all other thoughts. He saw with utter lucidity what he had to do.

There was only one possible way to attack Eugene – and that was from above.

The Kalika Tower reared eight dizzying floors above the courtyard. A drop half as far would smash a man to a broken, bloody pulp.

He walked slowly forward until he stood on the edge of the parapet. An icy wind whipped his hair. If he had miscalculated . . .

'Drakhaoul,' he whispered into the wind. 'I am Drakhaoul.'

And then he stepped out into nothingness.

For one moment Gavril was falling, tumbling helplessly through the air to smash to his death on the icy ground far below, and the next he felt a shuddering convulsion twist his body.

'*At last!*'

Some essence of darkness burst out from deep within him, almost tearing him apart.

No longer falling, he was soaring upwards on powerful wingbeats that thrummed through his whole body.

He was flying.

Eugene stared at Kastel Drakhaon with cold indifference, hands clasped behind his back, as another watchtower burst into flame and rubble. The cries and shrieks of the men who spilled from its burning shell were as insignificant to him as the distant calls of moorland birds. Behind him Jaromir's body lay in his tent, covered in the sky-coloured silk and gold thread of the Tielen flag. The highest honour he could bestow on a man fallen in battle for his country, and yet it seemed meaningless now, a mere mockery.

At Eugene's side Anckstrom levelled a telescope to check the effects of the bombardment, scanning the kastel walls for signs of a breach.

'Stubborn brutes, these Azhkendis,' he grunted. And then he swore. 'What in hell's name is *that*?'

Eugene blinked. Anckstrom was pointing at one of the ruined towers. Something dark flapped from the roof of the tower. He seized the telescope from Anckstrom, twisting the lens to try to see more clearly.

'Dear God,' he said under his breath.

He had never seen its like before. As it moved, it seemed to radiate a shimmer of darkness, each powerful wingstroke leaving a trail of iridescent smoke.

'Gavril Nagarian,' he murmured under his breath. '*Drakhaon.*'

And then the seasoned soldier in him recovered. Whatever the creature was, it must be destroyed before it reached his men.

'Concentrate your fire!' he ordered. 'Take aim!' His orders were repeated by his officers, cracked out along the rows and rows of cannon and infantry. 'Fire at will!'

The sky grew darker with each flap of its wings. Cannon blasted their shells into the air but still the Drakhaon came on, darting and diving in the darkening air to avoid the exploding shells. Nothing seemed to touch it, even though the sky filled with sulphur smoke and the bright stars of the exploding ammunition. Now it paused, poised overhead as though gathering itself, the dark glitter of its wings blotting out the light, fanning scorch-dry heat towards them.

'Your Highness, please move further off,' Anckstrom urged.

'I have never run from an enemy in my life. I do not intend to do so now.' Eugene gazed up into the sky. 'Show me your face, Drakhaon,' he whispered, challenging it. He was beyond fear. This creature of darkness had somehow survived Linnaius's mage-poisons – unless Altan Kazimir had played him false?

'Show me your face!' he cried aloud.

It turned its head, fixing him with a flame-blue stare that seared through him like a firebolt. Drakhaon eyes stared down at him, bright as cobalt.

And then it loosed a wave of fire. Fire crackled from its flared nostrils, flowed from its claws, rippling down from the darkened sky in a dazzle of glittering light.

For a moment everything – troops, cannon, kastel – was silhouetted starkly black against the white glare.

And then came the roar of the heat, the searing, scorching burn of the incandescent wave flowing over the hillside.

Blinded, Eugene flung himself to the ground, hands clutched to his burning face. He began to crawl up the hillside, squirming on his belly like a serpent. And then he felt the wave of heat ripple over him.

He was drowning in a sea of blue fire.

The rolling fire-swell crests, breaks over his head. Caught in the undertow, Eugene sees the Tielen standard fluttering over the broken walls of Khitari's citadel, Karila playing with her ball on Swanholm's green lawns, Jaromir, Margret, his father Karl turning to greet him with dark, dead eyes...

Drowning men see their lives flash through their minds before they die...

Gasping for air, Eugene broke from the ebbing sea of fire.

All around him a terrible sound dinned in his ears, the shriek of hundreds of men and horses dying in an agony of flames.

The smell of charring human flesh choked his nostrils, mingled with the chymical stink of molten metals.

Inching slowly forward, he began to drag himself from the inferno.

The Drakhaon hovered on dark-glittering wings above the scorched hillside. Not much that was recognizably human remained of Eugene's army. Twisted, melted knots of metal, still glowing hot, were all that remained of the cannon. Blackened piles of bone-ash blew where men had crouched behind the great guns.

Glittering particles drifted in the slowly rising smoke, smoke that reeked of bitter chymicals.

The part of him that had been human gazed down in silent, wordless horror.

Such devastation. Such destruction.

What have I done?

And then the Drakhaoul whispered, dark as smoke, in his head, '*Elysia. Mother.*'

40

'Would you like to go for a ride in a sleigh, Karila?' Astasia asked. 'It's a beautiful, crisp day. I'd love you to show me your father's estates.'

'A ride in a sleigh? Oh yes, yes!' the little girl cried. And then the eagerness faded from her voice. 'But Marta will never agree. She'll say the cold wind will make me cough.'

'I'm sure if you're wrapped up warmly in furs, Marta will agree. After all, she is only a servant and you are a princess.'

Elysia had listened to the exchange from her hiding-place in the princess's schoolroom which opened off her bedchamber. She rose as Astasia came in, carefully shutting the door behind her.

'You heard?'

'Yes,' Elysia said. 'But is it right to use the child? Her health is weak. I wouldn't want her to fall sick on my account—'

'I can see no other way for us to escape,' Astasia

said. 'Besides, they won't dare fire on us with Eugene's daughter in the sleigh.' Her dark eyes glittered with determination; Elysia glimpsed something of her brother Andrei's devil-may-care attitude.

'*Kidnap* the princess?'

'Look. Here's Marta's cloak.' Astasia took the dark-blue cloak from where it hung on a hook on the schoolroom door and draped it around Elysia, pulling the voluminous hood well over her head. 'Now, Nurse Marta, no-one will even give you a second glance.'

'Very well,' Elysia said unhappily.

The sleigh was brought to the inner courtyard, the runners clattering over the icy flagstones.

The coachman lifted Karila up into the sleigh so that the child should not have to strain her twisted leg climbing in. Elysia, the capuchin hood well pulled down to conceal her face, followed. She kept her head low as she tucked the little girl into the soft furs. Astasia came last, glancing swiftly around the courtyard to see if anyone had remarked on the little excursion.

'A tour of the Palace Gardens in the snow!' she cried merrily, settling herself next to Karila. 'What fun!'

The coachman whistled to the horses and the sleigh rattled off underneath the archway towards the formal gardens.

She can be a consummate actress when she wants to, Elysia thought, watching as Astasia chattered merrily away to Karila. *She gives no hint of the nerves she must be feeling.* She settled back in the sleigh, trying to ignore the churning in her own stomach.

The blue morning air sparkled, brittle with frost. Fresh snow had fallen in the night on the lawns and parterres. The horses trotted over the snow, following the carriage-road, moving steadily away from the palace.

'Coachman,' Astasia called, 'the view of the palace must be superb from the brow of the hill. Take us up there!'

'Beyond the grounds, Highness?' The coachman sounded uncertain. 'I haven't His Highness's authorization to take the Princess outside the palace ward.'

'Just for a few minutes,' coaxed Astasia. 'It's such a beautiful morning.'

The coachman nodded, directing the horses' heads towards the incline. At the brow of the hill stood a lodge and a great gate manned by the soldiers of Eugene's Household Guard.

Elysia held her breath as they approached and the two guardsmen on duty lowered their carbines.

'Halt!'

The coachman slowed the horses to a standstill as the guardsmen approached the sleigh. On recognizing Karila, they both saluted.

'Highness!'

'We're on an outing,' Karila told them happily. 'Astasia says we're going to have a snowball fight.'

'And your official authorization?' said the older of the two guardsmen.

'Surely we don't need authorization for a little pleasure trip?' Astasia said. Elysia heard her force laughter into her voice.

'And then we're going to have hot chocolate when

we get back,' continued Karila, 'with sponge fingers!'

The two guardsmen glanced at each other.

'Very well.' They opened the gate and waved them through.

Astasia sat back amongst the furs and let out pent-up breath. 'Oof. I thought they'd never let us through.'

'I'd like some hot chocolate now,' Karila said.

'Would you?' Astasia glanced at Elysia over the little girl's head. 'Maybe there's a village nearby. Coachman,' and she leaned forward in the sleigh, 'take us to the next village. Her Highness wants hot chocolate.'

'Better to go back to Swanholm, it's far closer than—' the coachman began.

'You heard my order,' Astasia said, suddenly sounding as imperious as her mother Sofia. 'Now obey!'

The coachman touched the horses with his whip and, bells jingling, they sped off along the snowy track.

'Wheee!' cried Karila, clutching the rail.

They were out of the palace grounds, but there was still a long, long way to go. Elysia remembered she had no money, no belongings, only the clothes she was wearing. One woman alone in a foreign country would have to use all her wits to escape.

Yet anything was preferable to being a prisoner. She would think of something. As soon as she reached a port, she would talk her way onto a ship, any ship headed far from Tielen.

Astasia smiled and Elysia saw for a moment a reflection of drowned Andrei's reckless, carefree grin.

'Thank you, Altessa,' she said, pressing Astasia's hand.

'Don't thank me! I do believe I'm enjoying this.'

The track had been winding upwards through bare birch coppices, noisy with crows; now they came out onto flatter, more gently sloping ground, where ploughed ruts could just be seen beneath the covering of snow. Farmland, Elysia thought, glimpsing a wooden farmhouse in the distance. How reassuringly normal – a world away from the bizarre masque of court politics in which she had been trapped.

And then she heard the sound of hoofbeats.

Turning around, she saw a troop of horsemen galloping up the hill towards them. And leading them, one who rode far ahead of the rest, forcing his horse to catch up with them.

'Slow down, coachman!' he cried.

'Oh no,' whispered Astasia, anguished, glancing at Elysia over Karila's golden head.

'It's Papa's Household Cavalry,' said Karila, kneeling up. 'They've come to escort us home!'

Troopers encircled the sleigh, forcing it to a standstill. How immaculate they looked, Elysia thought irrelevantly, with their white gloves and glossy boots.

'You're under arrest, coachman,' said the officer in charge.

'Spare me, Excellencies!' The coachman threw himself to his knees in the snow, hands clasped in supplication. 'I was only following orders, I had no idea—'

'Altessa.' The foremost of the riders wheeled his horse around, swung down from the saddle and walked towards the sleigh.

Elysia recognized – with a sinking of the heart – Feodor Velemir.

'Count Velemir.' Astasia glared at him coldly. 'What does this mean?'

'I have good reason to believe you are assisting the escape of an enemy of Tielen.'

'What?' Astasia cried.

'Madame Nagarian,' Velemir said. His face looked grey and pinched in the clear daylight. A muscle twitched at the corner of his mouth. He spoke in an odd, clipped way, quite unlike his usual relaxed tones. 'I regret to inform you that Prince Eugene has given orders for your arrest. You are accused of high treason.'

The Drakhaon flew on through the dark towards the brilliant glitter of the winter stars.

Night air rushed past him, but its icy chill could no longer harm him. A dark, sinister fire burned deep inside, fuelling the anger that drove him onwards.

Elysia. Mother.

Instinct – and the memory of Volkh's carefully drafted maps – directed him towards Tielen. Northwards, then west across the frozen sea.

Beneath him snow-covered mountains shimmered blue in the waning light of the setting moon. Peaks jagged as broken teeth loomed up out of the night, the coastal range, a fastness of rock and ice.

And then he was high above the grey wastes of the frozen sea. And a sliver of light appeared on the eastern horizon, tingeing the clouds an ominous red, as the sun rose. Dawn. He had flown all night.

* * *

'High treason?' Elysia echoed, staring at Velemir in disbelief.

'There must be some mistake, Velemir.' Astasia's words rang out clear and defiant on the morning air. 'Madame Nagarian is my dear friend and companion. I will not allow you to take her from me.'

'This really doesn't concern you, Altessa.' Velemir's voice was cold and dismissive.

'At least tell me the reason for my arrest!' Elysia was genuinely frightened now – but equally determined not to give Velemir the satisfaction of seeing her distress.

'Your son, madame, has viciously attacked the Prince and the Tielen army in Azhkendir. We are at war.'

'*Gavril* attacked?' Elysia gripped the side of the sleigh, her own plight forgotten. 'How? What do you mean?'

Karila suddenly let out a shrill, toneless scream.

'Highness?' Elysia turned back and saw that the child was staring up into the cloudless sky, one finger pointing.

'It's coming,' Karila whispered. 'Can't you hear its wings?'

'There, there.' Elysia put her arms around her, hugging her close. The child had gone rigid with fear and did not respond, did not even seem to feel her touch.

'Get out of the sleigh, madame,' said the officer curtly, 'and move away from the Princess.'

Elysia let go of Karila who still sat staring at the sky, oblivious to what was going on around her.

'You can take Princess Karila back to Swanholm,' Astasia began, trying to clamber out of the sleigh, 'but I will not leave Madame Nagarian's side until I am assured—'

Velemir nodded to the coachdriver and the sleigh pulled away with a jolt, throwing Astasia back amidst the furs.

'Stop!' she screamed out, but the sleigh did not even slow its hectic pace.

'It is my regrettable duty to inform you, madame,' said the officer to Elysia, 'that the Prince has authorized your execution.'

'My execution?' she repeated in disbelief.

He unrolled a paper and read in clipped tones:

'"If any act of hostility is directed against the Tielen army, all Azhkendi hostages are to be executed. Eugene."'

'Feodor?' Elysia stared at him, aghast. 'Will you just stand by and let them execute me?'

'I'm sorry, Elysia.' Velemir did not meet her eyes. 'It's out of my hands. There's nothing I can do.' He swung back up into the saddle and rode off after the sleigh.

Was this all their friendship had meant to him? All those professed confidences, those shared moments of intimate conversation, and he could do nothing to help her?

'*Sorry!*' she called after Velemir, her voice dry with contempt. 'Spare me your apologies, Feodor!'

'Come, madame.' The officer put his hand on Elysia's shoulder.

Velemir kicked his heels hard into his horse's flanks and drove it across the frozen snow after the sleigh.

The icy wind numbed his face, but not the turmoil of his thoughts.

'Count Velemir.' Astasia appealed to him as he drew level with the sleigh. 'You can't allow this to happen! You know she's innocent.'

Velemir did not reply, but her words seared his conscience.

He had accustomed himself to live with the knowledge that he was a traitor to his own country. He had reasoned with himself that the only way to bring lasting peace to Muscobar was to depose the ineffectual Orlovs and substitute Eugene as emperor, ruler of the whole continent.

But Elysia Nagarian was another matter. He had never intended that she should be harmed. He had not foreseen that Eugene would use her quite so ruthlessly in his power-game.

From the first moment they had met, he had felt an undeniable attraction – although he had determined not to let himself be seduced into any kind of liaison or intrigue until Eugene was crowned emperor.

And now he – who had prided himself on his detachment – could not think of anything but how he had deceived her, brought her here to die amongst strangers in this grey, chill country so far from the warmth of her native Smarna.

'Hiii!' Karila screamed again, pointing up at the empty sky. She fell back amongst the furs, eyes staring, fixed on some invisible terror.

'Look to the Princess, Altessa,' he said curtly, and spurred his horse ahead of the sleigh.

There must be something he could do to prevent it, to stall the brutal efficiency of Eugene's military machine.

* * *

The Tielen sky was blue and cloudless but an intense cold still shimmered in the clear air. Gavril could see his winged shadow, darker than a cloud, scudding over the snowy fields and hills below. He was tiring now, exhausted by the long flight, yet he knew he could not stop until he had found her.

Mother, where are you? He sought to sense her presence, his Drakhaoul-infected mind drawing on new, unfamiliar skills. *Let me not be too late. Please.*

They led Elysia out into the bare barracks courtyard and tied her hands behind her back. A Tielen priest, austere in robes of dark grey, mumbled words from a prayer-book.

Were these meant to be her last rites?

The blank, empty windows in the rear walls of the palace stared back at her. She was utterly alone now. Not even Astasia could save her.

Numb with shock, she could not believe this was happening. And happening so fast.

'I demand to see a lawyer!' she cried. 'I have rights. I am a citizen of Smarna!'

But instead a column of soldiers was being marched smartly in, carbine rifles on shoulders. At a gruffly barked order from an officer, they halted and faced her.

A firing-party.

Astasia ran through the palace in a last, desperate search for anyone with any authority who might help, rapping furiously on shut doors, not caring who disapproved. She was met with surprise and polite indifference from the palace staff. They seemed not to understand her requests. There was, she was informed by the Prince's personal secretary, no-one who could help her at Swanholm. Chancellor Maltheus was the only man who could revoke the execution order – and he was far away in a parliament session in the city of Tielborg.

And then the sky suddenly darkened.

Marta, Karila's nurse, burst into the secretary's office.

'She's gone! The Princess is missing!'

The officer came up to Elysia, a blindfold in his hands. He fumbled as he tried to tie it around her eyes, catching a strand of hair, mumbling an apology for his clumsiness. She caught a little of the telltale odour, sweat and soap mingled, that told her he was young, maybe as young as Gavril, and flustered, plunged into matters of state way over his head.

This isn't the end of it all, she kept telling herself. It can't be.

'Firing squad,' barked the officer, 'present arms!'

She heard the unmistakable click of the carbine rifles.

'Take aim!'

'Gavril?' she whispered. 'Gavril, where are you?'

A great building lay far below, a graceful curve of pale stone and grey slates powdered in snow.

Eugene's palace?

He circled lower, in slow, wide circles, letting the Drakhaoul control his descent.

He was dropping faster now. He could see landscaped groves of trees looming up to his right, a formal lake straight ahead. The lake was a smooth

sheen of green ice, covered with a crystalline frost-
ing of frozen snow. Now he could see terraces,
columns, carved balustrades.

Swanholm.

He detected movement in one of the many courtyards behind the fine sculpted façade of the palace.
A barracks lay behind the stable-blocks, orangeries
and kitchens.

And what was this?

A row of soldiers lined up in the furthest courtyard, carbines levelled at one solitary figure, a
woman who stood tied to a post, a blindfold over
her eyes.

'*Mother!*'

Astasia and Marta came flying down the stairs only
to encounter a tide of servants and soldiers fleeing
in the opposite direction. They were shouting,
screaming one word. It seemed to be – *dragon*.

Astasia glanced at Marta. Dragon? That was what
Karila had kept repeating in the sleigh. Had the
Princess known what was about to happen, had she
'seen' some terrible natural disaster?

'Don't go that way!' a lackey yelled at her. 'For
God's sake, get clear!'

Astasia pushed on through the crowd, even more
determined to find the little girl. In this stampede,
she could easily be knocked to the ground and
trampled. She grabbed a musket from a guardsman
and marched across the inner courtyard towards the
barracks, Marta staunchly following behind.

Gavril's shadow darkened the sky as he swooped
down, blotting out the daylight.

And felt the shock as he encountered an unseen barrier, soft yet stronger than silk. Some invisible and powerful force had been placed here to keep him out. His bruised body tingled with the shock and his mind went blank.

Mage-mischief.

Dark anger flared in his heart.

They were going to kill his mother. And they dared to try to keep him out!

He flung himself back at it, diving head first, and felt the silken barrier pulsate, then rip asunder.

He was in.

'Wait!' Elysia heard a man's voice ring out, brusque on the bitter air. Someone was hastening across the yard; she could hear the clatter of elegant court shoes over the cobbles, crisp and formal. 'Hold your fire!'

'Feodor,' she whispered, overwhelmed. 'You came back.'

And at that moment she sensed the darkness, even through the blindfold, as the beat of great wings gusted a hot, dry wind across the yard.

The men gasped in disbelief.

'Fire!' yelled the officer in a panic.

She steeled herself. *Fire*. Even Velemir's last-minute intervention would not save her. Any second now the bullets would hit her and nothing would matter any more.

But the shots – when they came – were not aimed at her. A creature cried out, a hoarse bellow of fury, neither animal nor human yet with an unmistakably familiar timbre to it.

'Gavril?' she cried. 'Gavril, is it you?'

* * *

The Drakhaon's wingtips grazed the soldiers' heads as he descended, dark as a whirling stormcloud.

They swung around, firing up at him. Lead bullets grazed his skin. With a flick of wings and tail, he knocked them flying, heard their shots go wide, peppering the surrounding buildings, shattering window-glass.

He saw only the blindfolded woman, hands tied behind her back, waiting bemusedly for death. He recognized the faded auburn of her autumn-bright hair, and felt a storm of rage, grief and recognition overwhelm his heart. They had done this to her – to punish him.

'Mother!'

He alighted in the courtyard, placing himself between Elysia and the terrified soldiers. The darkness of his anger throbbed about him like a thunderstorm.

Out of the corner of his eye he glimpsed a twitch of movement. Someone had dared to move . . .

A man. Coming towards his mother.

Had they not understood? If anyone so much as tried to harm one hair of her head, they would die.

Feodor Velemir gazed up at the Drakhaon. And felt his whole body go chill.

He realized – to his surprise – that he was afraid. Mortally afraid. And all his adult life he had been afraid of nothing.

This creature had swooped down out of his childhood nightmares, a winged dragon-daemon with the blue-burning eyes of a man cursed mad with grief. A shimmer of dark heat radiated from its body.

The secret of Azhkendir's invulnerability and power stood before him.

'*Magnificent,*' he murmured in spite of himself.

The Drakhaon heard him and swivelled its head towards him. Its nostrils flared. For a moment he felt the crazed brilliance of its flame-blue gaze pierce him, a clean, bright pain that lit up the yard.

From somewhere far away he heard a woman scream, 'No, Gavril. No!'

And then he began to burn.

Karila crept into the open doorway that led to the barracks yard and stared. No-one noticed her in the confusion, a child cowering in the shadows.

There it was: the flame-eyed dragon of darkness who had haunted her dreams. Marta had told her her nightmares were only bad dreams, they would never come true. But Marta was wrong! *Marta was wrong!*

The yard suddenly filled with the brightness of a terrible conflagration. A man was on fire. She heard his scream of terror. She watched, speechless, as the flames obliterated him: a blinding dazzle of white-blue fire, and at the heart, a blackened skeletal thing dropped to the ground and crumbled away to charred ash.

Then there was silence. Karila could hear her own heart beating, thudding against her ribs as the courtyard filled with a foul-smelling, choking smoke.

And then through the smoke she heard the soldiers calling out to one another.

'Fetch the cannon!'

Did they *still* not understand? The dragon had not come to destroy them. It was wounded beyond reason, mad with grief and confusion, as twisted in mind as she was in body. She could sense its terrible rage, blue-black like a thundercloud. If they fired on it, they would only enrage it the more.

'Dragon,' she said to it aloud. And knew it heard her, was suddenly aware of her.

'*Drakhaoul*,' a voice, dark as smoke, corrected her.

'I am coming, Drakhaoul,' she said, setting out into the courtyard. 'Coming to help you.'

The brightness of Velemir's burning scored itself against Elysia's lids, even through the thickness of the blindfold. But she scarcely felt the scorching pain of the flame-dazzle, she felt only numbing shock.

This creature that was – and was not – her son had killed a man, had seared him to an agonizing death by fire. Now she relived with vivid intensity all the horrors Volkh had tried to shield her from, that she had forced herself to forget all these years.

My son has become a monster.

And then she felt the Drakhaon's breath on her face, her neck, but now it no longer seared; it was warm as a caress. And a voice of darkness spoke with Gavril's well-loved inflections – but whether within her mind or aloud, she could not be sure.

'*Mother – we must get out of here. Climb on my back, quick.*'

'I – I can't,' she stammered, 'my hands are tied.'

The shadow loomed over her and she felt something – a Drakhaon's claw? – grate gently against the ropes that bound her wrists until they fell away.

'*Hurry. They are coming.*'

She rubbed at her rope-chafed wrists, then grimly raised one hand to tug away the blindfold, to see what she must – but dreaded to – see.

The Drakhaon stood over her protectively, wings outstretched, a great shadow-dragon, cloaked in a shimmer of darkness that issued like smoke from its nostrils. But beyond it she saw the soldiers levelling cannon at them, she saw the little flames of their fuse-matches.

'Gavril,' she said, hoping it understood her, 'they're going to fire—'

'Aim,' yelled an officer, 'on my mark—'

And then she saw a small figure coming hesitantly towards them across the smoke-filled yard.

A little girl in a white frock.

'The Princess!' she heard the officer shout. 'Hold your fire!'

The Drakhaoul sensed the child before it saw her, smelled the sweet, clean fragrance of her young body.

The Drakhaon body it had fashioned for the man it possessed was weakening, its resources depleted by the night's long flight and that last, furious burst of fire. Hunger would soon drive it to seek out fresh, untainted human blood.

Yet this child was different. Her body might be warped, deformed, but her mind burned with a white radiance, bright as a starflame. She knew its crazed pain, its utter loneliness.

'Drakhaoul,' she said aloud in her child's voice, grave and clear.

* * *

644

Astasia came dashing down the stone stairs that led out to the barracks yard, Marta following, and almost fell over a great cannon.

'Stay back, Altessa.' Guards barred her way. They were busy loading the cannon with shot and powder.

Gauzy wisps of smoke drifted from the courtyard. Glittering smoke. The vile smell of burning flesh tainted the air. She could sense heat: a dark, dry, intense heat.

'What's happening?' She pushed forward. 'Let me through. Let me see for myself—'

And then she spotted Karila. A child, vulnerable and alone, gazing up at the daemon of darkness which gazed back at her with all the madness of its flame-blue eyes.

'Karila!' she cried, starting out towards her.

'Altessa, no!' The officer tried to hold her back but, long used to chase games with Andrei, she ducked nimbly under his outstretched arms and emerged in the yard.

Slowly the creature swivelled its head, wisps of smoke, blue as indigo, issuing from its wild-flared nostrils.

It saw her.

Astasia.

How often he had sketched her beloved face from memory, trying to recall accurately every last detail. And now those liquid, dark eyes which had haunted his dreams stared at him in shock and disbelief.

He saw her pale lips open, framing a word, a name.

'Gavril,' she said in the stillness.

She knew him. Even though he was clothed in this monstrous form, she had recognized him.

645

That part of the Drakhaon which was still Gavril remembered who he was and felt a shudder of remorse shake his great daemon-body.

That she should see him like this . . .

A burning pain seared through his heart. The dreams of their love, dreams which had sustained him through the long desperate winter in Azhkendir, all fizzled to dust and smoke in that one brief moment of recognition. He saw stretching ahead a loveless, lonely future . . .

'Gavril.' He heard his mother's voice, low and urgent, close to his ear. 'They're aiming cannon at us.'

The smell of immediate danger brought him back to himself. Tired, injured as he was, he must get Elysia safely away from Tielen. A myriad little flames glinted under the arches. Cannon-fuses.

And then the girl-child turned to the soldiers cowering beneath the arches behind their great guns.

'You must let them go,' she said in her small, clear voice. 'You must hold your fire.' She came closer to him with her twisted, limping gait and stared imploringly into his eyes.

'Stay back, Kari,' called Astasia, her voice trembling.

'Take me with you, Drakhaoul,' the child said. 'I want to fly like you. I want to be free.'

Elysia reached out one shaking hand, placing it on the burning scales of the creature that was and yet was not her son, hoping her touch, her voice, would reach him, steady him. Her own safety forgotten, she only wanted to ensure he did not harm little Kari.

'Gavril,' she murmured, 'don't touch the child.

Don't even let her near. You're not in your right mind, you don't want to do anything you might regret . . .'

The Drakhaon Gavril did not answer her. She could sense how troubled he was, how unpredictable; the least distraction might spark him into another violent reaction.

Beyond Kari and Astasia, the fuses gleamed brighter in the shadows, the waiting soldiers hovering nervously, waiting for the command to fire. To blast them both to eternity.

'Let's go, Gavril. We must flee for our lives whilst we can.'

Still no response. Had he even heard her? And if he had, would he pay any attention to her words? He seemed mesmerized by the little Princess, his burning blue eyes fixed on Karila as she drew nearer.

'Gavril,' Elysia said, desperation making her voice crack. She gripped hold of the creature's broad bony shoulders, hoisted her skirts about her knees and clambered awkwardly up onto its scaly back. 'We must go!'

And only now did she see that another spectator had joined the terrified crowd. Silent, still, the Magus Linnaius stood at an open window watching Gavril with eyes grey as shadows. She saw him slowly raise his hands, the skin so translucent that the finger bones could be seen beneath, skeletal hands concentrating an energy so intense she could see the air around him tremble.

Her heart began to flutter in her breast with fear. They were so close to freedom . . .

'Gavril!' she cried. '*Now!*'

Astasia stood, helpless, speechless, as Karila walked towards the Drakhaon.

Emotions tumbled through her mind: fear; disbelief; betrayal.

Why had no-one warned her that Gavril was no longer human? She had never imagined that Elysia's veiled references to 'changing' could mean this hideous metamorphosis.

She watched, as if in a dream, Elysia climb on the creature's glittering back, saw Karila limp towards it, arms outstretched, heard Elysia cry out, 'Now!'

The Drakhaon seemed to gather itself and, unfurling its wings, leaped into the air.

Karila let out a cry. 'Don't go!'

Pulsations of light glittered across the scaly sheen of its skin: blue, green, oil-black, as it rose into the sky.

The beat of its great wings fanned gusts of burning air across the yard.

Arms still yearningly outstretched, Karila spun around to watch as the Drakhaon circled upwards into the blue sky.

And then Astasia saw her freeze, stabbing her finger at an upper window.

'Linnaius!' the child screamed out, her voice raw. An old man was standing at the open window, gnarled hands raised towards the Drakhaon. '*No!* I forbid you!'

The old man paused. A look passed between them. And then slowly he lowered his hands.

'I will come back for you, Karila,' the Drakhaon's voice drifted back, dark as drifting smoke, 'one day.'

'I know.' Suddenly Karila collapsed to her knees

on the cobbles, sobbing bitterly. Astasia hurried to her and flung her arms about her, holding her close, feeling her cling tightly.

'There, there, Kari, it's all right, the horrid dragon has gone. It's not going to hurt you, I'll never let it hurt you—'

'No,' Karila gasped, raising her tear-stained face to Astasia's, 'you don't understand. None of you understand!'

'*I will come back for you.*' Astasia had heard the Drakhaon's dark words roll around the yard. Was it a threat or a promise? Why had it spoken only to Kari with no word for her?

'I – I want to go with them,' sobbed Karila, inconsolable. 'I want to fly.'

41

Dazed and disoriented, Kiukiu wandered aimlessly through the ruined halls of Kastel Drakhaon.

From time to time she passed other kastel people, faces white with plaster dust and shock, sitting amidst the rubble staring into nothingness. No-one seemed able to help anyone else.

The merciless bombardment had ceased at the moment the Drakhaon had attacked the Tielen army.

And then she had felt them die. So many living souls extinguished in that one deadly breath of flame, so many human hopes, fears, aspirations. The rolling tide of blue fire seared the skies blinding white, and then black as starry night with glittering smoke.

Drowning, dragged into the undertow by the dying, she was washed to the very portals of the Ways Beyond. Floundering in the choking black tide, she had been forced to use all her strength to strike back towards the light.

She had opened her eyes and found it was night. Bitter-chill night. A thin wind whined through the broken walls. Her cheeks were stiff and cold with dried tears.

She must have been out of her body for many hours.

Out on the blackened hillside, she saw lantern-flames, flickering like corpse-candles. Drawn against her better judgement, Kiukiu found herself picking her way over rubble and broken beams towards the lights.

Far to the east there was a glimmer of light on the horizon. Dawn was breaking over the battlefield. Monks from Saint Sergius moved amongst the ashes, searching for survivors.

Incense censers swung, burning cleansing angel-smoke; the monks sprinkled holy water over the remains, muttering prayers as they went about their task.

But in spite of the sweetly aromatic tang of angel-smoke, the lingering smell of burned flesh made her eyes water, making her want to gag. She wound her headscarf across nostrils and mouth and went doggedly on, forcing herself to look on the worst of the damage Lord Gavril had inflicted on the enemy. Every now and then she caught a glimpse of some charred remnant on the edge of the firestrike, just recognizably human: blackened toes protruding from a boot, a clenched fist burned almost to the bone.

Gavril, Gavril, she whispered in her aching heart, *how could you have done such a terrible thing?*

'You're alive, Kiukiu!' Yephimy, leaning on his abbot's crook, hailed her. 'We feared we'd lost you.'

651

'I came to help,' she said, 'but . . .'

'There's nothing to be done for these wretched souls but pray.'

'Here, Lord Abbot!' The cry came from further up the hillside.

Yephimy turned and strode upwards through the last dispersing wisps of smoke; Kiukiu hitched up her skirts and followed, hurrying to keep up with the Abbot's brisk pace.

On the top of the ridge she saw the scorched canvas of a cluster of military tents, the ragged shreds of a Tielen standard still fluttering above the largest. It seemed as if the Drakhaon's lethal breath had only singed those furthest from the cannon; all his rage had been concentrated on the heavy artillery on the lower slopes.

As she approached she saw a huddle of monks, all gathered together, murmuring in low, awed voices. Impossible, surely, that they had found any survivors from that cataclysmic firestorm?

And then she heard a groan: faint, agonized, but recognizably human.

'Ease him onto the stretcher,' Brother Hospitaller was urging. 'Careful now—'

Kiukiu crept closer.

'Water . . .' The voice was parched, barely a whisper.

She peeped between the monks as they dripped drinking-water into the injured man's mouth – and closed her eyes in horror at what the lantern-light revealed. Drakhaon's Fire had seared his face and neck. His hair was all burned away – and half his face was a red, weeping weal, as was the hand that he raised shakily as the Abbot approached.

'Look,' said Brother Hospitaller in an undertone, nudging the brother at his side. 'The ring. The signet ring.' Kiukiu saw them exchange glances. 'What do you think, Lord Abbot?'

Yephimy gazed down at the burned man on the stretcher.

'Is it really he?' Brother Hospitaller whispered.

Yephimy did not reply but kneeled down beside the stretcher. Kiukiu saw the burned hand reach out feebly towards him.

'Yephimy.' The burned lips moved, struggling to pronounce the Abbot's name.

'Your Highness,' the Abbot said, 'this is a sad day for Azhkendir.'

'And ... for Tielen ...' The words were barely audible.

'If you permit, Highness, we will take you to Saint Sergius. Brother Hospitaller has salves that will relieve your pain.'

As the monks gently lifted the stretcher, the man let out an involuntary moan. Kiukiu bit her lip, trying not to imagine how intense his suffering must be as they carried him away towards a waiting cart.

'I don't understand,' Yephimy was saying, shaking his head. 'Everyone else has perished ... save the Prince. How did he survive?'

'That man is Prince Eugene?' Kiukiu said, forgetting that she was not supposed to be listening. 'You're going to heal him? After what he did to us?'

Yephimy turned to her, his eyes stern beneath bristling iron brows.

'He is a man, like any other. He needs our help. God will judge him.'

A horseman had appeared at the top of the ridge; he sat very still, scanning the desolation. The rising sun gleamed on his polished buttons, epaulettes and boot buckles. A Tielen scout.

'Look,' Kiukiu breathed. 'They've sent reinforcements!'

Far below she glimpsed Askold trying to muster his meagre forces in the kastel yard. He too had spotted the horseman on the ridge. The few remaining *druzhina* stood shoulder to shoulder, brandishing what weapons they could lay their hands on: pitchforks; axes; mallets.

The horseman dismounted and walked slowly towards the monks. Kiukiu glared at him, at his clean-shaven face, his spotless uniform.

'Where is the Prince?' the horseman asked in the common tongue.

'Here,' she said sullenly, pointing.

She watched the young man remove his tricorne and kneel down beside the Prince's stretcher. To her surprise, his face registered no emotion; he seemed as stiff and formal as if he were on parade. Could he not see how badly injured his master was?

'An urgent message from Field Marshal Karonen, Highness.'

'Read it – to me – Lieutenant . . .' came the faint answer.

' "Mirom surrounded. Awaiting your instructions." '

There came the sound of a sigh . . . almost, Kiukiu thought, a sigh of satisfaction.

'Tell Karonen – to – take the city.'

'B-but who—' Only now did the young messenger falter. 'Who will command in your stead?'

'Tell him – I will meet him there—'

'And Azhkendir?' The lieutenant had not once mentioned Eugene's regiments, though he must have smelled defeat and death in the smoke that still rose from the charred hillside. She held her breath, wondering what the Prince would say. Would he give the order for their annihilation? There was no Drakhaon to protect them now.

'There will be no – further – resistance—' Eugene whispered. 'And . . . no reprisals . . .'

'He's tiring. He must rest,' interjected Brother Hospitaller.

'But not here.' The lieutenant stood up, facing the monk over the stretcher.

'Indeed not here. At our monastery where I can tend his wounds properly.'

'Is that what His Highness wishes?'

'It is . . .' came the fading voice from the stretcher.

'I will send an escort.'

Kiukiu looked up and saw that the ridge was now lined with horsemen. Eugene's men must have been keeping silent vigil, pistols primed, in case of further trouble from Kastel Drakhaon.

The lieutenant gave a curt wave of one grey-gloved hand, and one by one the horsemen slowly began to move towards them.

'No reprisals,' the Abbot repeated sternly. 'You heard what His Highness said.'

'An escort, that's all.' The lieutenant swung back up into the saddle and gave a curt wave of the hand to the waiting men to follow.

Kiukiu watched the horsemen fall slowly into line behind the monks' cart as it rumbled away up the track towards the forest. Last in line, Abbot Yephimy paused, gazing at her with drawn brows.

'Are you coming back to the monastery with us, Kiukiu?'

'Not yet,' she said, scanning the pale skies. 'There's someone I must wait for here.'

'He is no longer the Gavril you knew,' Yephimy said, as though reading her thoughts, his voice heavy with warning. 'This creature of darkness has taken control of him.'

'Then I shall exorcize it,' she said defiantly, 'and set Lord Gavril free.'

Yephimy looked at her, a long, troubled look. 'I must advise you most strongly not to attempt it, child,' he said. 'For no-one – not even the most skilled Guslyar – has ever achieved what you intend.'

The Drakhaon flew wearily eastwards towards Azhkendir. Each powerful wingstroke was an effort now; he felt the strain shudder through his whole body.

He hardly saw the winter brilliance of the blue Tielen sky or the crisp snow on the hills far below.

He saw only Astasia – and the look of revulsion and fear that had clouded her face. Now she knew him for what he truly was – a monster. Possessed by a daemon of darkness, twisted into this distortion of his true self.

She must have seen him kill. And it had not been a noble killing, no duel of equals, but the last, enraged act of a creature driven mad beyond endurance. Small wonder she had looked at him with such horror.

Now they were over the frozen sea, a frosted

expanse of shimmering grey and white ice. And he was so mortally tired and heart-sick he could no longer see why he should fly onwards.

'Stir yourself, Kiukiu!' Sosia snapped. 'There's more people need soup and, heaven knows, we've little enough to go round.'

A makeshift cooking fire had been lit in the great fireplace of the Hall; little matter that the roof gaped open to the sky. Sosia, ever-resourceful, had rescued vegetables and a few strips of salt pork from the rubble in the kitchen. Now soup – of a kind – was bubbling in a dented cooking-pot over the hearth and the serving-girls were ladling it out into cups, bowls, even upturned *druzhina* helmets.

Kiukiu stared up into the sky overhead. Something was different. A tingle in the cold air, an iridescent glimmer, blue as frost. She shivered, the ladle drooping forgotten in one hand.

'What's up with you now, girl?'

'He's coming back,' she said in a whisper. 'Can't you sense it?'

'Who? Not Eugene, God forbid!' Sosia cried, clutching her shawl to her throat.

'Lord Gavril,' Kiukiu said, dropping the ladle back into the pot and running out onto the lawns.

High above the kastel grounds she saw him. At first he was no more than a swirl of dark smoke. Then, as he flew slowly nearer, she saw the shimmer of scales and the obsidian gleam of cruel, hooked talons. Now she could feel the dry heat from his body, could smell the chymical burn of his steaming breath . . .

'There's someone with him!' The people from the

657

kastel were hurrying out from the ruins, clustering together to watch, pointing and whispering.

Now Kiukiu could see what they were pointing at: a windswept figure clung on, as the Drakhaon circled, arms clasped tight around the Drakhaon's neck.

A woman.

The Drakhaon plummeted the last few feet, righting himself to land with a hiss of steam in the soft snow in the gardens. The woman passenger slithered from his back, collapsing to her hands and knees. The servants glanced uneasily at each other, not knowing what to do.

'Who *is* she?' Ilsi said.

Kiukiu's eyes were fixed only on the Drakhaon. She forced herself to look at the dark daemon-beast that possessed Lord Gavril, even though the sight seared her eyes with heat.

A convulsion twisted the great dragon-body where it lay in the snow, the tail lashing like a whip.

The Drakhaon wrapped its shadow-wings around itself like a cocoon . . . and dwindled before her eyes, melting like smoke into its body.

A man lay sprawled in the vast winged imprint in the snow.

Kiukiu forgot all caution, all propriety, and hurtled towards him, skidding to her knees in the snow at his side. He was almost naked. A few torn shreds and tatters remained of his clothes.

'Gavril?' The woman he had brought kneeled on the other side, her hands reaching out to caress his forehead.

How *dare* she touch him? Kiukiu glanced jealously up at her rival, and saw from the lines scoring her pale face, the streaks of grey in her auburn hair, that the woman was of middle years. Too old, surely, to be a lover?

'Who are you?' she demanded.

'I am Elysia Nagarian,' the woman said, her voice ragged with exhaustion. 'Gavril's mother.'

Malusha stiffened, sniffing the wind, sensing trouble.

'Powerful,' she whispered. 'Ah, so very powerful.' She hurried out into the monastery courtyard, eyes fixed on the sky.

'Malusha?'

She looked up and saw she had almost collided with the Abbot on his way to the chapel.

'What's wrong?' the Abbot asked, bending down to steady her.

'Why does he have to come now?' she said, irritably shaking herself free of the Abbot's helping hand.

'Who are you talking about?'

'You should never have brought that foreign Prince here, Yephimy. Look!'

There were clouds in the sky, but scudding faster than a cloud came a craft the like of which Malusha had never seen – or imagined – in all her long life.

'What in Sergius's name—' Yephimy shaded his eyes.

'A ship. A little sky-ship,' she murmured.

Now that it was coming nearer, she could hear the creak of its rigging, the swish of the unnatural mage-wind that propelled it along. The ship itself was no bigger than a lake-coracle, light and flimsy – but above it billowed a vast balloon. And steering it, she caught a glimpse of the pilot, one man alone, head protected from the elements by a plain, tight-fitting leathern cap tied beneath his chin.

Gusts of wild wind eddied above their heads, almost toppling them over as the wind-craft began to descend, circling slowly down above the monastery spires. Eventually it bumped along the monastery courtyard, grazing across the frozen ground until it came to a stop. With a loud exhalation of air, the balloon slowly deflated, collapsing like a spent sail on a windless day.

The sky-sailor had tethered his craft to a mounting post and was unfastening his leathern cap by the time Malusha reached him.

For a moment, a long moment, they stared at each other, assessing. He was old, she saw to her surprise, much older than she, with only a few wisps of white hair still clinging to his smooth, narrow-domed head. Yet in spite of his years and his mild demeanour, she knew she stood close to the cool, calculating mind she had sensed earlier, emanating its chill aura of sorcerous glamour.

'You're not wanted here,' she said.

'Where is Prince Eugene?' he said, ignoring her. His voice was smooth and quiet – a bland voice, all the more dangerous for its deceptive ordinariness.

The monks came out of the chapel. Yephimy went straight up to the stranger.

'You have disturbed our morning prayers. Who are you, and what do you want?'

'My name is Linnaius. I am Court Artificier to Prince Eugene.' The stranger gestured to the sky-craft. 'I have come to take him home.'

'Artificier?' Yephimy frowned.

'A scholar of the natural sciences, if you prefer,' Linnaius said calmly.

'Fancy words!' Malusha spat. 'I know what you are.' The stranger might call himself scholar, Artificier and other titles which would deceive ordinary folk, but she recognized a fellow sorceror when she encountered one.

'I have come for Prince Eugene,' repeated Linnaius.

'I'll take you to him, but I fear you'll find he is still too badly injured to be moved.'

Prince Eugene lay in a cell within the Infirmary.

Such a tall, broad-shouldered man, Malusha noted. *And well-favoured too, I'd guess, before his encounter with the Drakhaon. If he recovers, he'll bear such a deep and bitter grudge against Azhkendir that I dread to think what manner of revenge he will take on us all . . .*

The Prince's burned face and hands had been smeared with Brother Hospitaller's glossy healing salve, and the salve's pungent, bitter odour filled the cell.

As Linnaius and Yephimy approached his bed, Malusha saw the Prince's eyes flick open, eyes that seemed startlingly pale against the red of his swollen lids and seared skin.

'Highness,' said Linnaius in his quiet voice.

'Linnaius?' Eugene managed a whisper. 'Why are you here? Is Karila—'

'The Princess is well, Highness. I have come to take you wherever you wish to go. Home to Swanholm, or on to victory in Mirom.'

'Dead,' Lilias repeated. 'What do you mean, all dead?'

The regiments which had remained in the gorge awaiting the Prince's orders stood silent, dumbfounded, as the officer relayed the news of the defeat. They had seen the blinding light crackle through the sky, turning the snow-covered rocks from white to dazzling blue. They had sensed the vastness of the surge of power that shook all Azhkendir to its foundations. They had not fully understood its import until now.

'All dead but His Highness the Prince, whom God in his mercy has spared.'

A murmur ran around the massed ranks of men.

'Prince Eugene has ordered us on to Mirom. We are to strike camp and join our forces in Muscobar.'

Lilias stood clutching little Artamon to her, Dysis at her side, as the Tielen soldiers hurried about them, taking down the tents.

'And what of us? You're not going to abandon us here?'

The officer shrugged. It was obvious he had other priorities than two women with a squalling baby.

'The Prince promised me protection. He promised!'

He hesitated. 'You can hitch a ride in the baggage train. You'll have to fend for yourselves as best you can.'

A man's cry, hoarse and agonized, echoed through the kastel walls. It twisted in Kiukiu's breast, sharp as the blade of a knife.

'Doesn't anyone know what to do?' she said

again, turning from Sosia to Askold and back again.

'Only the Bogatyr, and he's dead,' said Askold, roughly blunt.

They had locked Gavril in the Kalika Tower for fear he would harm himself – or anyone who came near him.

'Someone must remember! He's saved all our lives, and we can do *nothing* to help him?'

'Kostya Torzianin was the only man Lord Volkh would let come near when the madness was on him.'

Another cry shivered through the ruined kastel, raw with desperation.

'Doctor Kazimir, then,' Kiukiu said. 'What about his elixir?'

Sosia let out a little tut of disapproval.

'Seems like the doctor's helped himself to a different kind of elixir,' Askold said, mouth wryly twisted. 'He must have crawled down into the wine-cellar during the bombardment. Judging by the state of him, he'll be sleeping it off for days.'

'The Drakhys, his mother?'

'Let the poor lady sleep a little longer; she's exhausted,' chided Sosia. 'Have you seen the state of her hands? Rubbed almost raw. I've put salve on them but they'll take a while to heal.'

Again the agonized cry shuddered through the kastel.

Kiukiu bit her lip. How could they stand by discussing so dispassionately whilst Lord Gavril was suffering such agony? She started to edge away.

'And where d'you think you're going, my girl?' Sosia had guessed what she was intending. She went up to Kiukiu and took hold of her, staring into her face with eyes sharp as pine-needles. 'Don't even think of it.'

'But no-one's—'

'That's because no woman in her right mind would go near him until he's come back to himself again.'

Thirst. Burning, excoriating thirst. The black taste of pitch fouled his mouth, his throat.

Gavril squirmed forwards, trying to drag himself across the floor towards the bowl of water they had left for him. Every movement was an agony, every torn sinew ached, sending shivers of fire through his body. It was as if he had been stretched on a rack and each of his limbs had been wrenched from its socket.

He plunged his face into the cool water and gulped down mouthfuls, feeling it sizzle down his throat.

The next moment he was doubled over again, retching up the stinking tarry sludge that had clogged his lungs and stomach.

Groaning, he lay back on the floor. Tears of self-pity leaked from his eyes, hot as sulphur springs, and trickled down his cheeks.

'*You are weak*,' the Drakhaoul's voice, smoke-dark with scorn, whispered. '*Weak-willed. Unworthy to be Drakhaon.*'

Another wave of nausea rippled through his whole body. He convulsed again, vomiting up a burning slime that smirched his throat and mouth. At last the spasm passed and he rolled over onto his back, gasping. The inside of his throat was dry, sand-dry as a baking desert under a merciless sun.

There was not an ounce of moisture left in his veins. He was parched, a living mummy.

'*Still thirsty?*' the Drakhaoul asked slyly.

'You . . . know I am . . .'

'*And you think water will quench your thirst?*'

'What . . . else is there?'

'*Remember the young men and women who used to model for you at the College of Art? Those naked limbs, so seductively posed, that you sketched in Life Class, day after day? Remember the tantalizingly sweet scent of their fragrant flesh?*'

Gavril remembered the burnished light of Smarnan summer gilding flame-haired Amalia as she posed for the students, remembered freckled throat and shoulders, stippled like tiger-lilies, yet so soft, so smooth to the touch . . .

'Amalia . . .'

'*You're dying, Gavril. A slow, agonizing death.*'

'Dying . . . ?' Gavril repeated. His own voice seemed so faint, so far away.

'*If you want to live, you must replenish yourself. You know what you need. Go; take it.*'

'No,' Gavril whispered, knowing only too well what it meant, 'I can't do it. Don't make me—'

There came the metallic grating sound of a key turning in the lock. The door opened.

A girl stood in the doorway.

Kiukiu blinked, eyes watering at the stench filling the tower room; vomit and hot pitch mingled into a dry, burning vapour.

Lord Gavril lay in the slimed shreds of his torn clothes, hair fouled with his own vomit. Her first instinct was to back away – and yet she forced herself to confront it. It was not as if she hadn't seen the like before, especially on winter solstice nights when the *druzhina* drank themselves stupid on Oleg's home-distilled spirits. Was it his fault that he was so sick? She took a tentative step into the room.

'Kiukiu?' The voice was barely recognizable as his; a smoke-dry whisper, seared by internal fires too intense for her to imagine. 'Go away. For God's sake, go away.'

So he was ashamed that she should see him in this state; at least that meant he was no longer possessed by the Drakhaoul.

'Let's get you cleaned up,' she said, forcing the unwanted tremor from her voice. It was time to be practical. She had brought a bucket of hot water, clean linen and soap from the kitchen.

'You mustn't come near me.' He tried to move further away, drawing himself into a corner. 'I – I'm not yet – in control – of myself—'

'That's nothing to be ashamed of,' she said, going closer. 'I've cleaned up after the men here many times before. Though if you were Ivar or Semyon, I'd tell you to go stick your head under the water pump for a half-hour or so.'

'You – don't understand . . .' He kept shaking his head.

'Hush, now.' Kiukiu immersed one of the linen cloths in the hot soapy water, wrung it out and, kneeling beside him, began to wipe his face with gentle yet firm strokes. The soiled shirt was so badly ripped there was little to do but peel the last tatters from his shoulders.

'There,' she said briskly, as if speaking to a sick child, 'that's better, isn't it?'

He sat huddled up, knees drawn to his chest, shuddering at the touch of the hot cloth as if he had a fever. His breathing came hard and fast and his eyes gleamed, blue-bright as star-fire, under dark-bruised lids.

'There's still time,' he said hoarsely. 'You can still go. Please, Kiukiu, please go.'

She hesitated, hearing the urgency in his voice.

'You want to be alone. But perhaps it's not good for you to be alone.'

'Alone?' A bitter laugh escaped his lips. 'But I shall never be alone now. Not until I die.'

She sat back on her heels, looking at him uncertainly. The dry laughter was tinged with scorn. Maybe they were right and this was not the same Gavril she had known . . .

'You mean . . . ?'

'*Drakhaoul,*' he said. 'That's what it calls itself. That's what you saw. My own dark daemon.'

His eyes still gleamed in the darkness: blue, dangerous. They were no longer human eyes but weirdly striated, enamelled cobalt glinting with veins of molten gold. Why had she not noticed before?

'Daemons can be cast out,' she said defiantly. 'Why don't you let me try?'

'You?' A look of hope flickered briefly across his drawn face, and for a moment she glimpsed again something of the Gavril she remembered – but deeply hurt and painfully vulnerable. Then just as swiftly, it was gone. 'No. It's no use. It's too late for me, as it was for my father. It's made itself a part of me; it's gone too deep.'

'Is that you talking, Lord Gavril,' she said, 'or the daemon?'

He did not reply, but she heard him draw in a long, thin breath between gritted teeth, as though still in pain.

'What's wrong?' She laid her hand on his shoulder; his skin was burningly hot to the touch. She snatched her fingers away as if they had been singed.

'Ahh.' He shook his head, eyes squeezed shut, hands clenched into fists as though trying to control a sudden spasm.

'Lord Gavril, what's wrong?'

He doubled up, arms crossed, knees drawn up, hugging the pain into himself. Alarmed, she drew back, hardly able to bear to see him suffering like this.

'I'll go get help.'

'Yes. Go. Go *now*.' Each word was forced out.

She rose to her feet and hurried across the room. But at the door she stopped, looking back. She saw him lying slumped on the floor, and she knew what she had to do.

She went back over to him, kneeling beside him, raising his head till she could support it against her breast.

'Why – have you come back?' he whispered.

'I know what you need,' she said simply.

'No, Kiukiu.' He tried to push her away. 'I've little control left. I don't want to hurt you—'

'I'm young, I'm strong. Let me help you.'

He turned his face away from her. 'No. I can't do it. I won't.'

'Gavril,' she said, gently touching his face, running one fingertip across his lips as if to silence his protests. There. She had dared to say his name as if they were equals.

And suddenly his eyes glimmered bright, blue wildfire in the gathering shadows. His taloned fingers gripped her shoulders. He reared up and pressed his mouth to hers. She tasted the flicker of fire on his tongue, felt the scorching heat of his body against hers. The swiftness, the violence, of his response caught her off-guard, and she felt a flutter of panic overwhelm her.

Visions of past, dead Drakhaons' Brides clustered in the shadows of her mind. Tender white bodies streaked with traceries of living scarlet; dark, dead eyes staring warningly at her . . .

But wasn't this what she'd always wanted? To be his?

'Drink. Take what you need from her.' The smoke-dry voice burned through Gavril's skull, searing away all rational thoughts. *'Do you want to die? Without her blood, you'll die, a horrible, protracted death, starved of nourishment. And I can't let you die.'*

Gavril's dry lips moved from her mouth to her throat, seeking the sweet succour the Drakhaon promised.

One taste of the blood leaking from her broken flesh – and it was a cooling, healing sweetness that flooded his parched body with life-giving moisture. He could not help himself. He had to have more.

'More,' breathed the Drakhaoul.

And then he felt Kiukiu shudder in his arms. He raised his head from her breast and saw that her eyes were rolling upwards. She slumped fainting against him, her unbound hair soft against his chest like a skein of gold silk, pale autumn gold.

And suddenly he was shocked back into himself.

'Kiukiu?' He said her name, but she did not respond.

'*You have not taken enough.*'

'I've taken too much!' There was blood on his lips. Her blood. What had he done? Weak as he was, he couldn't bear to begin to imagine what obscene act he had committed.

'*She's given herself to you. Willingly. Why won't you take what's yours?*'

'No!' Gavril, faint and sick, tried to block out the Drakhaoul's serpent-voice.

'*Take her.*' Gavril felt the Drakhaoul rear up within his mind, its dark puissance threatening to overmaster his will.

'I can't!' Gavril cried out with the last of his strength. 'And you can't make me. I won't be your puppet any longer!'

'*I must survive! And I need your body to do so . . .*'

The room spun. There was a rushing sound in his ears; he was losing consciousness. Yet one simple truth suddenly burned bright in his heart.

'I – I love her,' he said in a whisper. 'And – I won't let you destroy her. Without her I'd be – nothing.'

'*Then – be – nothing.*'

Nothing. Gavril, exhausted by the battle of wills, felt himself sucked slowly down into a vortex of blackness.

Nothing . . .

A cold dawn, chill as melting ice, woke Gavril, and for a while he lay staring up at the lead-lighted window, wondering bemusedly where he was and why most of the little glass panes were broken.

Fragments of broken glass were scattered on the floor beside him. And disjointed fragments tumbled through the void of his memory.

The kastel was under siege. Tielen cannons and mortars had blasted the towers, shaking the building to its foundations . . .

He listened, holding his breath. There was no sound of cannonfire now.

Was it all over?

He looked around him and saw that he was in his father's study with Kiukiu sprawled across him.

'Kiukiu?' he whispered. He levered himself up on his elbows, until he could touch her hair, her face.

Had the tower been hit by the cannonfire and they both been knocked unconscious? He was almost naked; the blast must have been very violent to have stripped his clothes from his body. And Kiukiu – beneath the curtain of her long golden hair, he saw that her simple linen shift was torn.

'Kiukiu!' he said again, louder this time. Why didn't she reply? She lay so heavily across him, a dead-weight, almost as if she were—

'Kiukiu!' He leaned forwards and lifted her, turning her gently over. Her head lolled back against his shoulder, and as her white breasts and neck were exposed, he saw to his horror the ragged wound, still leaking beads of blood, shockingly red against the pallor of her skin.

Soft white flesh, so fragrantly sweet to kiss, to taste . . .

'Oh no, no, no . . .' he murmured. For now it

seemed to him that ragged gash was where he had pressed his burning mouth, seeking succour.

He put his ear to her lips, listening for the faintest hint of a breath, cradling her limp body close.

What have I done?

42

A white dove wings through the dark woods of Malusha's dreams, white as innocence.

'Come to me, little pretty one,' Malusha croons, raising her hands to catch the dove.

But before it can alight, eyes gleam blue in the darkness. Some creature of darkness comes writhing out from the thorn-shadows and seizes the dove in its claws, rending it, tearing its soft flesh.

'*No!*' cries Malusha, but it is too late. One bloodied white feather flutters down to her . . .

'Kiukiu!' Malusha awoke, sitting bolt upright in her chair. Lady Iceflower, who had been roosting on the back of the chair, gave a squawk of surprise and flew straight up into the air.

'She's in trouble,' Malusha said to Lady Iceflower. 'I can sense it. Fond, foolish girl, just like her father. Drawn to that cursed House of Nagarian against all her grandmother's warnings . . .' All the while she was muttering to the owl she was busying herself, pulling a thick shawl about her shoulders, forcing her callused feet into her walking boots, picking up the gusly in its embroidered bag and slinging it over her shoulder.

The white dove struggles in the coils of a glittering serpent, its torn feathers strewn about the dark, dank leaves like snow. Its wings flutter feebly as it struggles for life . . .

'If he's laid one finger on my grandchild, I'll send him and his daemon straight to hell!'

Gavril laid Kiukiu gently down on his bed. The embroidered bedspread was covered in a film of plaster dust so he slid it away from underneath her, pulling out the fine linen sheet beneath to cover her.

All the glass had been shattered in the diamond window-panes and the bedchamber was freezing cold.

He kneeled beside her, at a loss to know what to do, uselessly stroking her limp hand, talking, as if talking could bring her back.

'Why didn't you listen to me, Kiukiu? I told you to get out. Why did you stay?'

Her skin was so white it looked almost translucent. White as death.

Tears welled in his eyes, tears hot with grief and guilt.

I've killed her.

The sight of her pale, still face blurred as the tears spilled over, trickling down his cheeks.

He leaned forwards, blinded by his tears, and gently kissed her chill mouth.

Was that a faint breath escaping her lips, so faint it was hardly even a sigh?

'Kiukiu.' He called her name, his voice tremulous with hope. 'Oh Kiukiu, please open your eyes—'

Suddenly he knew there was one thing only to be done. No matter what it cost to himself, he must see it through.

'If this is what it means to be Drakhaon, then I want no more of it!'

But first he must make his mind a blank, for if *it* once sensed his intention, it would seek to prevent him with all its guile and power.

He hastily pulled on a jacket and breeches and then wrapped the sheet gently, tenderly around Kiukiu.

Then, gathering her up in his arms, he climbed the broken stair to the roof of the Kalika Tower.

He became vaguely aware of distant shouts below, of people pointing upwards.

Malusha. He was taking her to Malusha the swiftest way he knew how.

He walked to the edge, feeling the wind cold on his face.

Don't fail me now, Drakhaoul.

Closing his eyes, holding Kiukiu tightly to him, he drew in a deep breath.

And stepped off into the void.

'Malusha?' The Abbot peered down at her in the dreary early-morning light.

Malusha cursed under her breath. Why did Yephimy have to interfere? She was sure he'd try to stop her.

'Where are you going so early?'

'To Kastel Drakhaon. Kiukiu needs me.'

'Let us take you there in the cart. It's a long walk.'

Malusha gave a snort. 'I can't wait for the cart to be made ready. She needs me now!' And then she stopped, sensing an unfamiliar presence approaching, faster than a stormwind. She shivered, feeling a sudden unmistakable tingle of warning in her bones.

'What's wrong?' the Abbot asked, bending down to steady her.

The sky grew dark.

'Too late now, Abbot!' Malusha gazed up into the turbulent sky. 'He's here.'

The Drakhaon circled the white cluster of monastery buildings, searching for somewhere to alight. Below, monks appeared, running around, pointing up at him. Faint voices and cries of alarm carried up to him as he swooped lower.

Holding the unconscious girl close, he came to a halt in front of Saint Sergius's chapel, claws scraping over the frozen ground.

Monks surrounded him. Some threw holy water at him, others brandished spades, axes, hoes, improvised weapons, snatched from their daily chores to defend the holy shrine.

'*Fools*.' The dry voice of the Drakhaoul echoed faintly through Gavril's mind. '*Do they think they can defeat us with gardening tools?*'

'Don't attack!' Yephimy came striding through the throng, staff in hand. 'Can't you see it's got the girl?'

'Kiukiu!' A little old woman pushed past the Abbot and planted herself in front of him, arms akimbo. Her eyes glittered with fury in her wrinkled face: she alone was not afraid of him. 'Give me my grandchild, Drakhaon!'

'*Destroy the old woman.*'

'No.' Gavril struggled to regain control of his mind. His thoughts were clouded in smoke and shadow. Yet he knew there was a reason he had come this far. His salvation, his immortal soul, depended upon it. 'I must talk with her.'

'*The old woman is dangerous. Powerful. She seeks to harm us.*'

'Ma-Malusha. Help me,' Gavril gasped aloud. 'Help me rid myself of this daemon—'

'*Gavril!*' The Drakhaoul let out a roar of warning that seared his mind like a lightning-spear. It knew now what he intended. It would fight him all the way.

'Give me my grandchild,' repeated Malusha, standing before him, arms outstretched.

Kiukiu. He still held her in his arms. White and gold, her aura, gold and white, a pale flame burning so faintly . . .

He knew then there was a chance, but he must hazard all to save her life.

'*Destroy her.*'

'No.' With all his strength Gavril locked his mind to the voice of the Drakhaoul. He willed himself to shrug off the dark-winged daemon-body that imprisoned him. He must slough it off as if he were a snake shedding its skin, a dragonfly emerging from its larval case.

'Kiukiu,' he said aloud. He strove to keep her brightness of spirit illuminating his mind, forcing the cloaking shadows to melt away from him, the great wings to fold into his body. The dark haze of heat clouding his vision dispersed.

He collapsed to his knees – a man again, still holding Kiukiu close.

'Quick!' he gasped. 'I haven't long.'

Yephimy dropped his staff and bent to take Kiukiu from him, gathering her up in his strong arms.

'Bring Lord Gavril to the shrine,' Malusha said to the monks, 'and tie him down. The daemon will fight us every inch of the way.'

A thunderclap resounded through Gavril's mind. Pain-stars of blue and black glittered in his brain. Gavril clapped his hands to his head, fighting to keep the Drakhaoul from regaining control.

'*Why do you betray me, Gavril?*' Each dark word was etched on his mind in fire. '*We are one now. Divide us and you will go insane.*'

'That—' Gavril managed to rasp out, 'is – a risk – I gladly take – to be finally rid of you!'

Malusha watched as the monks threw themselves upon Lord Gavril, wrestling to secure him with ropes. Daemon-possessed, he fought back, snarling, tearing at them with his taloned nails and bared teeth. But in the end they bore him down and bound his wrists and legs securely; yet still he lashed his head frenziedly from side to side.

They dragged him into Saint Sergius's shrine and she followed, drawing the gusly from her shoulder bag.

She looked dispassionately down at the young Drakhaon as the monks bound him to a stone slab.

Had she misjudged him?

He had come of his own free will – and at unimaginable risk to his own life – to beg her help to exorcize the Drakhaoul. He was voluntarily giving up his powers, powers so great that other men would kill to possess them.

Maybe Kiukiu had been right and this one was different from all the other Nagarians before him.

She struck a jagged jangle of notes on the gusly, hearing them echo and re-echo round the candlelit shrine.

Gavril felt his consciousness fading far from the shrine. The glimmer of the candles slowly receded and he found himself floating on a soft fluff of snowclouds: white, shot through with winter-gold, suspended in a moment beyond time.

Malusha stood opposite him – only she was no longer a shrunken old woman, but young, tall and strong, her brown hair blown by the soft breeze of this other plane beyond the world of the living.

'I can only control it a little while,' she said. 'Do what you must, and be quick.'

Gavril gazed down and even as she spoke it seemed as if his body melted to translucence . . .

There it lay, coiled tightly around his heart like a serpent. Slender filaments, pulsing bright star-blue, extended throughout his whole body and into his brain, a delicate tracery, thin as spidersilk. It had insinuated itself into every part of his being, inextricably intermingling itself.

Gavril steeled himself, and plunged his hands into his own breast, clutching hold of the Drakhaoul.

It was like clawing himself apart, rending, tearing his own flesh and sinew. And as his fingers took hold of the creature, he felt a shock sizzle through his whole body. Searing pain burned across his mind, white-blue as Drakhaoul's Fire.

'Don't let go!' Malusha cried.

'*Gavril.*' The Drakhaoul spoke to him now, its soft voice riven with agony. '*Why are you destroying me? I am the last of my kind. Can you live with my death on your conscience?*'

'Don't listen to it.'

'*I made you strong. I made you powerful. Without me you are nothing!*'

'I would rather – be – nothing.' Gavril clung on, tugging, feeling the slender filaments snap, one by one, as it slowly relinquished its stranglehold.

'*You think you can live without me, but without me you'll go mad. Insane.*'

Gavril gritted his teeth and tugged with all his strength. Suddenly he felt the Drakhaoul slither out of him and he fell, wrestling with a vast shadow-daemon, meshed in its serpentine coils.

'Malusha!' he cried, his voice half-stifled. '*Now!*'

Malusha gazed at the Drakhaoul.

She saw it in all its alien glamour: terrible yet possessed of a glittering beauty, a spirit-creature from the Ways Beyond, a stranger alone, abandoned in her world, unimaginably far from its own kind. For a moment she stood, pierced by sadness at its plight.

And then she remembered. This was the daemon that had ruined her life, destroying her lord and his household. This was the daemon that had ruled Azhkendir for centuries by fear.

She opened her mouth and a strong, dark note

emerged from deep within her throat, an ear-splitting resonance that tolled with the crackling intensity of rolling thunder.

In a flicker of darkness, the Drakhaoul reared round, like a snake about to strike. Eyes of blue and gold scanned her. She flinched. It was as if it had clawed through her mind, exposing her deepest, most intimate thoughts.

'Can't – control it much longer—' Gavril still clung on.

And then she found it. The pitch at which its very being, its essence, vibrated. Suddenly she was in tune with it, suddenly *she* was in control.

Light was sucked from the air. Buzzing darkness smothered Gavril. Glimmers of blue phosphorescence lit the shadows. He could no longer breathe, he was suffocating . . .

A convulsive shudder rippled through the strangling coils of the Drakhaoul.

He felt it cry out.

'*Ahh, Gavril—*'

The cry scored across his mind, a terrifying ululation of fury and loss.

He was flung down as the creature lifted from him, spinning helpless in a vortex of cloud and star-shadow.

'Be gone.' Malusha stood over him, one arm raised.

And the glittering shadow-vortex blew away across the heavens, shredding clouds like dark feathers in its wake.

43

The instant Gavril opened his eyes and recognized the frescos of Saint Sergius's shrine, he knew the Drakhaoul was gone from him.

He felt exhausted. Drained.

Empty.

He no longer saw the world through Drakhaoul-enhanced sight. Everything looked drab and dull.

Malusha stood over him, the gusly still clasped in her arms.

'You can untie him,' she said. 'He's no threat to you now.'

Monks appeared and busied themselves untying the ropes that bound Gavril; he sat up, rubbing his chafed wrists and ankles.

'Has it really left me, Malusha?'

'Oof. I'm tired.' She sat down on a bench and laid the gusly beside her.

'I feared it might have harmed you—'

'Who, me?' She looked up, her brown eyes fierce

in her wrinkled face. 'No, I'm made of stronger stuff. Besides, you did most of the work, Gavril Nagarian. That took courage. Great courage.'

A tremor of guilt and loss shivered through him. He heard it cry out again, '*I am the last of my kind.*'

'Where has it gone? Where did you send it?'

'In all truth, I don't know. Far from here. Far, far from here.'

The monks silently helped Gavril down from the slab where he had been confined.

He stood – alone for the first time in many months – and looked at Malusha.

'I owe you so much,' he said, voice unsteady with emotion. And then he saw that the gusly was broken and the strings snapped, with all the ancient painted decorations charred. 'Your instrument—'

'You can start by getting it mended,' she said wearily. 'And no slapdash job. This instrument was my mother's and her mother's before her.'

'No-one but the most skilled craftsmen from Azhgorod shall be allowed to touch it, I promise.'

Kiukiu drifted back to consciousness to see Lord Gavril sitting beside her. He looked pale, gaunt, unshaven, and there were dark shadows beneath his eyes. But those eyes were the deep summer-blue she remembered from his portrait, deep as the warm seas she had never seen but dreamed about so often. There was no alien glitter any longer, only the sad, distant look of one who has lost something of great personal significance.

'My Lord?' she said, puzzled.

He started. 'Kiukiu? How are you?'

Without fully knowing what she was doing, she

683

found herself touching the ragged wound at the base of her throat.

'I'm healing.' She nodded. 'Yes. Healing well.'

'I – I hurt you,' he said falteringly. 'I never intended to do you harm, Kiukiu.'

'I know.' She put out one hand towards him. 'I know.'

He looked at her hand as if uncertain what to do. Then she felt his fingers curl around hers, felt the warmth of his grip.

'The Drakhaoul is . . . gone?' she said wonderingly.

'Gone. For good.'

She forgot her weakness. She knew only that they were both alive, they had both survived. And a surge of happiness overwhelmed her.

This was a curious kind of homecoming, Elysia thought as she ventured out from her room, to wander the dusty corridors, as she had so often done in dreams. Once as a young bride, she had been chatelaine of this desolate domain of snow and shadows. Now the towers of the kastel lay half-ruined, blasted by Eugene's cannon, and with them the memories of her life with Volkh.

She had slept more than two days and nights, Sosia told her, utterly exhausted by the journey from Swanholm. The flight had taken its toll. Her hands had been rubbed almost raw with clinging on to the Drakhaon's scaly back, and though Sosia had salved them and bound them with clean linen, they were still stiff and painful.

All she wanted was to reassure herself that Gavril was all right – but no-one seemed to know where he was.

At the end of the dusty hall two figures appeared: a man and a girl, hand in hand. And the man – even with the daylight behind him – looked very familiar.

'Gavril?' Elysia said uncertainly.

When he saw her, his face lit with recognition, and he came running towards her, arms outstretched to hug her tight.

'Look at me, Mother!' He held her at arm's length, gazing intently into her eyes. 'I'm cured. The Drakhaoul is gone.'

She raised her bandaged hands to his face, searching for any lingering signs. She saw none. He looked weary – and in need of a good wash – but she recognized him as her son once more. She hugged him a second time, just to make certain – and knew what he said to be true. Somehow, without the aid of the elixir, he had broken free and was whole, his old self again.

And then she remembered that they were not alone. The fair-haired young woman was still there, standing shyly behind him.

'But who is this, Gavril?' Elysia turned to her with a smile, sensing there was some special connection between them.

'This is Kiukiu. I owe her my life.'

Elysia held out her hands to Kiukiu, who – after a moment's hesitation – came forward and allowed herself to be kissed. Elysia glanced from one to the other – and, feeling tears of relief pricking at her eyes, wrapped one arm around each of them, clasping them close to her.

She did not trust herself to speak yet, for fear she would weep. There were so many things to be said, so many questions to be answered – but all that could wait till later.

EPILOGUE

A storm-dark whirlwind passed over the northern wastes of Azhkendir, devastating all in its trail, blotting out the brief, pale light of the winter sun, casting noon into night.

Shafts of lightning crackled blue as the electric shimmer of the northern lights as it swept across the frozen Saltyk Sea and tore down through Tielen.

Those who witnessed its violence said afterwards that the shrieking of the wind had sounded like a Lost Soul, a soul in agony, howling for salvation. Some even claimed they had heard words wailed on the wind.

Princess Karila was working hard at her cross-stitch. She and Marta were making a wedding sampler for Papa and her new Mama which read: 'Good health and long life.'

And then she sensed a sudden quiver of darkness in the air. She started and pricked her finger. A tiny drop of blood marred the immaculate linen.

'Now I'll have to start all over again. I hate needlework!' She threw down the crumpled sampler and the skein of royal blue silk and limped to the window.

'So dark,' she said, gazing up at the sky. 'And it's not even teatime.'

'It's only another snowstorm coming, Highness,' said Marta with a sigh.

Karila felt the little golden hairs prickling on her arms. Shivers of intense cold ran through her whole body.

'Drakhaoul,' she whispered. 'Drakhaoul, what's wrong?' She raised her arms, imploring, hands extended. It was free. Free, yet filled with rage and confusion. It did not understand its freedom. Cast out into a world it did not comprehend, it knew only that it was alone – and vulnerable.

How could it understand her yearning? To move untrammelled through the air? No longer to be encumbered with this twisted, clumsy body but to fly as free, as graceful, as the wild white swans?

The sky grew dark as night and a chill wind stirred the bare branches in the park.

Karila looked up into the smoky stormclouds and saw eyes of electric blue piercing the dark haze.

'Use me, Drakhaoul. Let me help you.'

'*Use you?*' There was scorn in the words that sizzled through her brain. '*What use are you to me? You are too small, too weak, to sustain my powers.*' She sensed its frenzied despair; it was dying. '*I would sear you to a cinder.*'

'I would risk it and gladly,' she whispered, knowing what she said to be true, 'to save you from destruction.'

687

But the dying Drakhaoul was already whirling away from her.

Karila stood staring after it, her cheeks wet with tears of frustration and pity.

Another watcher silently observed the Drakhaoul's passing from his laboratory window.

Kaspar Linnaius followed its wild flight with his telescope until it had blown out of sight beyond the distant horizon.

Then he went to the Vox Aethyria and established a link with Mirom.

'Chancellor Maltheus? I have urgent news for the Emperor. Tell him Lord Gavril is no longer Drakhaon. Azhkendir is defenceless.'

THE END

PRISONER OF THE IRON-SEA TOWER
THE TEARS OF ARTAMON BOOK TWO
is the spellbinding
new novel from
Sarah Ash

Here's a taster . . .

Prologue

Gavril Nagarian, Lord Drakhaon of Azhkendir, opened the door to Saint Sergius's shrine. Candle flames from ochre beeswax candles shimmered in the chill gloom. The air smelt of bitter incense and honeyed candlesmoke.

In the gloom the radiant figure of the Blessed Sergius glimmered, staff upraised to defend his flock from the dark Drakhaon. Even the saint's face had been covered with gold leaf by the artist. In contrast, only the Drakhaon's eyes glinted in the candlelight, jewelled with chips of blue glass, the rest of his winged daemon-form painted black as a shadow.

'Now it is finally gone – and I am alone.' His words went echoing up into the shadows of the vaulted roof, where the angelic hosts of heaven stared down at him from their painted eyes.

The last of his strength suddenly drained out of him and he sank to his knees before the saint's stone tomb.

The heavy nail-studded door to the shrine was flung open with such force that it crashed into the stone wall. Candle flames wavered in the fierce draught and some blew out, guttering trails of smoke.

Warriors of his *druzhina* stood in the doorway. Foremost amongst them was Bogatyr Askold, first officer and commander of his bodyguard, who came striding down the aisle towards him.

'What have you done to yourself, My Lord?' Askold's voice was harsh with grief and accusation. 'What have you done!'

The others crowded in on him, so close he could smell the

pungent odour of their fur cloaks and the sweat of their bodies.

'Is it true, then? Is it true, Bogatyr?'

Askold seized hold of Gavril.

'Let go!' Gavril tried to wrench himself free but, all his strength exhausted, he could not break away.

'Forgive me, My Lord, but it's the only way to be certain,' muttered Askold, twisting one arm behind his back. Gavril heard the whisper of steel against leather as Askold drew a knife from his boot.

Did they mean to kill him? A flash of fear flickered through his mind. In this dangerous mood, his own men could turn against him.

And then he winced as Askold drew the knife-blade across his wrist in one small, expert stroke, the sharp kiss of steel slicing his skin open.

The warriors crowded closer, staring as blood began to well up, to trickle from the shallow incision, to drip onto the flagstones.

Gavril stared too.

Red blood. Crimson-red. Human-red. Without a trace of daemon-purple.

A shuddering sigh echoed around the shrine.

'So the Drakhaoul is gone,' Askold let go of him. 'And with it, all your powers.'

'You broke the bond! You broke the blood-bond that binds us to you!' cried out scarred Gorian. 'You betrayed us!'

'I did what I had to,' Gavril said wearily. 'I did what should have been done centuries ago.

'Azhkendir was safe,' said Barsuk Badger-Beard, his gruff voice unsteady. 'No-one dared attack us. Now it's gone, who knows what will happen—'

'You call yourselves my *druzhina*?' Gavril raised his head and stared at them, challenging. 'Then act like warriors!'

Eyes stared back at him, dark with hostility. He could see the glint of their unsheathed sabres in the guttering candle-light. If he did not win back their allegiance now, he was as good as dead.

'We've driven Eugene of Tielen out of Azhkendir. Now we must learn to fight without daemonic powers to protect us. To fight like men.'

'Didn't you hear what Lord Gavril said?' A younger voice rang out, passionate with anger. Gavril saw Semyon, the newest member of the *druzhina*, his freckled face flushed hot red. 'I swore to defend you, My Lord. I haven't forgotten how you saved my life in the siege. My oath still holds good.'

'Aye – and mine too,' said Askold. He knelt at Gavril's feet. 'Forgive us, My Lord.'

Gavril knelt down too and placed his hands on Askold's shoulders, raising him to his feet.

'We've much to do,' he said. 'Kastel Drakhaon is in ruins. Will you work with me to rebuild it?'

It was not until he left the shrine to walk across the monastery courtyard with Semyon and Askold at his side, that he heard again the far-distant echo of the Drakhaoul's dying voice, each word etched in fire on his mind:

'*Why do you betray me? Divide us and you'll go insane . . .*'

* * *

He did not remember his name. He did not know where he was. He knew only that the old fisherman Kuzko and his wife who had dragged him from the sea had cared for him as if he were their own lost son, Tikhon, drowned years before in another night of terrible storms.

They had found him lying on the seashore, so battered by the waves and the rocks that his clothes were torn to shreds. For days he wandered between life and death – and when he returned to himself, he no longer knew who he was. The sea had stolen his memories from him. The only distinguishing feature was a signet ring on his broken right hand . . . but the device had been worn so smooth by the sea and the rocks that it was impossible to tell with any certainty what it had been.

So they called him Tikhon after their dead son and nursed him slowly back to health. Many weeks later when he could walk again, he began to help with a task or two: mending nets, carrying wood for the fire. Everything had to be relearned, even speech; he seemed like a great child, limping slowly after Kuzko, speaking awkwardly, as if his tongue would not obey his brain. And he seemed cheerful enough in spite of his deficiencies – although sometimes he was suddenly overcome with a terrible wordless raging which could not be assuaged.

Tikhon was helping old Kuzko mend the boat, caulking a leak in the storm-battered hull with a stinking mess of oakum and pitch that Kuzko had boiled up over a driftwood fire.

The wind blew keen and raw across the bleak island shore. Nothing to be seen here for miles and miles but sea and rocks. The sky was pale with scudding clouds. Until Kuzko noticed one cloud blowing towards them, darker than the rest, moving faster than all the others.

'Storm coming,' he shouted to Tikhon. 'Best find shelter till it passes!' He gazed up into the sky – and saw that this was no ordinary stormcloud, it was moving too fast, its course erratic and unpredictable. And as it tumbled nearer, the light began to fade from the sky and the shoreline turned black as night.

Tikhon stumbled after his adopted father – but his damaged body betrayed him and with a gargling cry, he fell on his face on the pebbled beach.

'Come on, lad!' The old fisherman started back towards him.

The dark cloud hovered overhead. Lightning crackled – and Kuzko dropped back, covering his eyes.

Tikhon let out another cry of terror as he cowered in the lightning's beam.

Kuzko watched, helpless, as with a sudden, sinuous movement, the cloud dropped like a dark shroud around Tikhon. The lad convulsed, his body wracked by violent shudders, twisting this way and that as though struggling with some invisible shadow-creature.

And then the struggle ceased. The darkness had disappeared – and the sun's pale winter light pierced the scudding clouds.

Kuzko slowly picked himself up. 'Tikhon,' he stammered. The lad lay still, unmoving.

Tears welled in his eyes. He had seen his son taken from him once – was he to have to endure it all again?

'Tikhon?' he said, extending a shaking hand to touch his shoulder.

Tikhon's eyes opened. He sat up. Each movement was lithe, precise, controlled. He looked at Kuzko and said, 'Where am I?' His voice was no longer slurred.

'Are you all right?' quavered Kuzko.

The young man looked down at himself, frowning. 'I think so.'

'You're cured. It's a m-miracle.' Kuzko felt weak now. 'Come, Tikhon, let's go tell Mother—'

'Tikhon?' The young man slowly shook his head. 'I think you must have me confused with someone else. My name is Andrei.'

Chapter 1

Astasia Orlova leaned on the rail of the Tielen ship that was carrying her back home to Muscobar across the Straits. Cold seaspray blew into her face, her hair, but she did not care.

She was bearing Count Velemir's ashes back to Mirom. It was Feodor Velemir who had brought her to Tielen on the pretence that wreckage from her brother Andrei's command, the *Sirin*, had been washed up on the shore. She had gone, eager that there might be the faintest glimmer of hope that Andrei was not drowned but lying injured in some remote fisherman's hut, only to find there was no news of Andrei. It had all been a ruse to display her charms to the Tielen court and council, to persuade them that she would make a suitable bride for Prince Eugene.

Well, Count, she thought, gazing into the rolling sea mists that hid the coastline of Muscobar from view, *you have paid the ultimate price for your treachery. You used me heartlessly.*

You lied, you twisted the truth to further your own ends. And now you are dead.

Even now she was not sure she believed the evidence of her own eyes. What she had witnessed in the snowy palace yard had shaken her to the very core of her being.

There crouched a dark-winged creature, veiled in a blue shimmer of heat. And – most horrible of all – the burning remains of something that had once been Feodor Velemir, Muscobar's ambassador to Tielen, lay in a charred, smoking heap at its clawed feet.

Drakhaon.

In that one moment all certainties had been seared away.

'Altessa!' Nadezhda, her maid, came up to her, carrying a woollen shawl. 'You'll catch a chill up here in this bitter wind.'

'Don't fuss, Nadezhda. I'm fine.'

Nadezhda took no notice and draped the shawl over Astasia's shoulders. 'Please come below and warm yourself.'

'Not yet,' Astasia said distantly. 'In a while . . .'

The cloudy sky and the choppy sea beneath mirrored her mood. She felt numbed.

Whenever she tried to sleep, she saw the Drakhaon of Azhkendir rear up out of the darkness and then, oh then—

The one moment she could not forget. The moment when the dragon-winged daemon had turned its piercing blue gaze on her and she had recognized Gavril Andar.

Elysia Andar had tried to warn her and she had refused to listen. And now she knew it to be true. Gavril, the one man she had ever allowed to hold her, to kiss her, was possessed by a dragon-daemon—

'Altessa.'

She turned to see that one of the Tielen officers had come up on deck.

'We have received an urgent message from Mirom, Altessa, that concerns you. Will you please come below?'

Reluctantly, Astasia followed him below decks to the captain's anteroom. Chancellor Maltheus had sent an escort of the Household Guard to protect her . . . or to prevent her from running away?

A group of officers were gathered around a small, glittering device which she at first took to be some kind of naval chronometer or barometer.

'Is there a storm coming?' she asked, taking off her shawl. The fine mist of seaspray still clung to her hair. 'Should we seek harbour and sit it out?'

'The message comes from Field-Marshal Karonen, Altessa. He reports there is rioting in Mirom. It seems that your parents have been trapped in the Winter Palace by a mob of dissidents who are threatening to torch the Palace and all inside.'

Astasia gripped the edge of the table to steady herself. 'Dissidents?' she repeated.

'Your father has requested our help. It seems the situation is quite desperate.'

'My father asking for help?' Astasia was shocked at this unexpected turn of events.

'The Field-Marshal is ready to lead a rescue force into the city, Altessa. Just give the word and he will liberate the Palace.'

Astasia gazed warily around at all the Tielen officers. She could not help noticing the detailed map of Mirom that lay outspread on the table. They seemed so well prepared . . .

'We understand there has been unrest in the city for some months,' said one.

'Well, yes—' she began and then broke off. How could she have been so blind? Maltheus had sent the soldiers with her as part of the invasion force. What better way to infiltrate Tielen soldiers into the heart of the city? Dissidents or no, Muscobar was about to be swallowed up into the growing Tielen Empire.

'Prince Eugene is determined to quell any last stirrings of rebellion before your wedding takes place.'

'Of course,' she said coldly. They were still looking at her expectantly – and she realized that they were waiting for her command.

'Tell the Field-Marshal,' she said, knowing she had no choice, 'to put down the rebellion – and with my blessing.'

Astasia struggled up on deck against the fierce prevailing wind, into a raw, red dawn.

As the ship sailed up the broad Nieva, she noticed that the gilded dome of the Senate House had been reduced to a smouldering shell.

At first she had believed the red glare in the sky to be the rising sun, but surely no dawn could glow that brightly—

The West Wing of the Palace was on fire.

She heard the crackle of the flames, the tinkle of breaking glass as panes burst with the heat, saw the haze of smoke sullying the freshness of the dawn.

They were burning her home.

'No!' she cried aloud, gripping the rail to steady herself.

Now she could hear shouts from the shore; a confusion of people was swarming over the neatly clipped boxes and yews. Guards leaned from the windows, aiming muskets at the rabble, firing. A ragged rat-tat of fusillades answered.

'You must go below deck, Altessa!' One of the Tielen officers came towards her, pistol in hand. 'It's not safe up here!'

Screams carried on the wind, shrill above the rattle of gunfire. There were running silhouettes at the West Wing windows, dark against the blaze of the flames. Where were Mama and Papa? Where was her governess, poor, dear Eupraxia? She would be so flustered by the panic and the fire—

'There are people trapped in there!' she said to the officer, grabbing his arm and stabbing her finger at the burning building. 'We must get them out!'

A musket ball whizzed over their heads, grazing the nearest mast, showering them with sharp splinters of wood.

'We're doing all we can,' he said, hurrying her towards the hatch.

The battle for the Winter Palace between the insurgents and the Tielen army lasted little more than an hour. Astasia crept back up on deck and watched as more and more Tielen soldiers swarmed into the gardens, driving the rebels before them, rounding them up at musket-point.

By now the West Wing was well alight, and she saw looters risking the Tielen guns to carry away brocade curtains, pictures, fine porcelain from the ravages of the fire. Too late came the servants forming a bucket-chain, pumping water from the river. Flames burst through the roof. Rafters cracked and the whole roof collapsed inwards with a crash like rolling thunder.

Shocked beyond speech, she stood mute, hands clutched to her face. The smell of burning overwhelmed her.

'I've made some tea, Altessa.' She had not noticed that Nadezhda had emerged from below decks. 'You've eaten nothing for hours. You need to keep up your strength.'

'Mama,' Astasia whispered into the billowing smoke, 'Papa . . .'

'Tea with a drop of brandy, that'll warm you up.' Nadezhda took her by the arm and steered her back below.

At about four in the afternoon, a party of Muscobar officers came on board and asked to speak with her. Sick with worry, she hurried to meet them.

'Colonel Roskovski!' she cried, so glad to see a familiar face that she wanted to run up and hug him.

'Altessa,' he said, clicking his heels and saluting her. He looked haggard; he was unshaven and his immaculate white uniform jacket was covered in smears of soot. 'Thank God you're safe.'

'Is there any news of my parents?' she asked, almost speechless with anxiety.

'They are under the protection of Field-Marshal Karonen,' he said stiffly.

'But they're alive?'

'I believe so. Altessa—' and he hesitated, 'I have been obliged to surrender control of the city to the Field-Marshal.' She saw now that not only was he exhausted but there were tears in his smoke-reddened eyes, tears of humiliation and defeat. 'I am dishonoured. I have failed your father.'

'Not surrender, Colonel,' she said, dismayed that such a

proud and experienced soldier should openly weep with shame in front of her. 'I'm sure you and your men did all and more to save the city. But the odds were overwhelming. Without Tielen's help . . .'

'Altessa Astasia!' One of the Tielen officers came running up. 'The Field-Marshal requests a meeting with you.'

Her heart began to beat over-fast, a butterfly trapped in her breast. This was to do with her parents, she was sure of it. How would she find them? Even if they were physically unharmed, the last few days would have taken a terrible toll on Mama's nerves. And Papa . . .

'Colonel,' she said, 'please accompany me.'

It seemed that there were Tielen soldiers everywhere: lining the quay as Astasia disembarked, guarding the Water Gate and patrolling the outer walls where the rebels had smashed down the iron railings as they stormed the Palace.

Even though the officers steered a carefully chosen path, Astasia's quick eye saw the sights they sought to shield her from. Soldiers carrying out bodies from the courtyards and piling them onto carts.

'Were many killed?' she asked, determined that she should not be treated like a child.

'Enough,' Roskovski said tersely.

The city lay quiet now in the winter dusk, eerily quiet after the din of riot. Smoke still rose from the ruins of the West Wing; the choking smell of ash and cinders singed the evening air.

'Where are you taking me?' she asked the Tielen officer as they passed through the inner courtyard and entered the Palace by an obscure door. A stone stair led down into a dank subterranean passageway, lit by links set in the wall.

'This is no place to bring the Altessa,' protested Roskovski.

A smell of mould pervaded the stale air and the floor was puddled with water; Astasia lifted her skirts high, wondering uneasily whether she had walked into some Tielen trap.

At the end of the tunnel they came out into a small room: at a desk sat a tall, broad-shouldered man in Tielen uniform, poring over despatches by lantern-light. When he stood up to greet her, he had to stoop, as the ceiling was so low.

'Karonen at your service, Altessa.'

'My parents,' Astasia burst out. 'Where are they?'

Karonen cleared his throat, evidently uncomfortable. 'That is why I requested your presence in this wretched place, Altessa. This is where the insurgents imprisoned them. Now they are reluctant to come out, fearing further ill treatment. I hoped you might persuade them that the insurrection is at an end . . .'

They sat, side by side, on a wooden bench, blinking in the lantern-light in a cramped, windowless cell. At first Astasia did not even recognize her mother in the lank-haired, listless woman who stared blankly at her.

'Mama, Papa,' she said, her voice trembling, her arms out-stretched.

The Grand Duke half-rose from the bench.

'Tasia? Little Tasia?' he said, his voice trembling too.

'Yes, Papa, it's really me!' Astasia flung her arms around him and hugged him tightly.

'Look, Sofie, it's Tasia,' the Grand Duke said.

The Grand Duchess looked at her, her face still expressionless.

'Mama,' Astasia said, kneeling beside her mother, 'we're all safe now.'

'Safe?' the Grand Duchess said with a little shiver. 'Did they molest you, Tasia? Did they lay hands on you?'

'No, Mama. I'm fine. But you're not. You must come out of this cold, damp place and warm yourself.'

The Grand Duchess shrank back, cowering behind her husband. 'No, no, it's not safe. They're in the Palace. They're everywhere. They want to kill us.'

'Mama, look who's with me.' Astasia took her mother's chill hand and pressed it between her own. 'It's Field-Marshal Karonen of Tielen. He has taken the city from the rebels. He has rescued us all.'

'Tielen?' said the Grand Duchess distantly. 'Now I remember. You were betrothed to Eugene of Tielen, weren't you, child?'

699

'Come, Mama,' coaxed Astasia. 'Come with me. Wouldn't you like some hot bouillon? And clean clothes?'

The Grand Duchess glanced nervously at the officers standing in the doorway to the cell. Then she clasped Astasia's hand. 'All right, my dear,' she said in a wavering voice, 'but only if you're certain it's safe.'

Safe? Astasia thought as her mother ventured out of the cell, leaning heavily on her arm. *Poor, foolish Mama. If I've learned one thing in the past few weeks, it's that nowhere is safe any more.*

Astasia stood in an anteroom in the East Wing, gazing around her. Lies – hateful, obscene lies – had been daubed in red paint across its pale blue and white walls. The window-panes has been smashed. And she did not want to look too closely at what had been smeared over the polished floors. The rioters had slashed or defaced everything in their path that they had been unable to carry away with them; everywhere she saw the evidence of their hatred. At least the building was intact and her parents were being warmed, cosseted and fed by the few faithful servants who had not fled.

But she was not in any mood to be comforted. Her home had been violated. She could still sense the blind, senseless hatred that had caused this eruption of vandalism. She hugged her arms around herself, chilled by an all-pervading feeling of desolation.

Feodor Velemir had foreseen all this. Had she judged him too harshly? Had he anticipated the coming storm and sought to prevent it?

'Altessa.'

She swung around to see the broad-shouldered bulk of Field-Marshal Karonen filling the doorway.

'I have news of His Highness for you, from Azhkendir.' He came in, followed by several of his senior officers. The winter-grey and blue colours of the Tielen army filled the antechamber.

'News?'

'Prince Eugene has been gravely wounded,' said Karonen

700

brusquely, 'in a battle with the Drakhaon.'

The daemon-shadow of the Drakhaon suddenly billowed up, dark as smoke, in her mind.

'Ah,' she said carefully, aware they were all watching for her reaction. 'Wounded – but not killed?'

'We've lost many men, but the Prince is alive. Magus Linnaius is tending his injuries. The Prince was most anxious to ensure that you were unharmed. He would like to speak with you.'

'With me?' Astasia looked at him, uncomprehending. 'But how?'

When he showed her the Vox Aethyria, she wondered if the Field-Marshal had taken leave of his senses. She saw only an exquisite crystal flower, a rose, perhaps, encased in an elaborate tracery of precious metals and glass.

'It's very pretty, Field-Marshal, but—'

'You must approach the device and speak very slowly and clearly. The crystal array will transmit your voice through the air to His Highness.'

'What should I say?'

'I believe His Highness has a question he is most eager to ask you . . .'

'The Altessa will not be disappointed, Highness.' The valet straightened the blue ribbon of the Order of the Swan on Eugene's breast, gave one final tweak to the fine linen collar, a last spray of cologne, and withdrew from the Prince's bedchamber, bowing.

Eugene of Tielen forced himself to confront his reflection in the cheval mirror. At first he had ordered all mirrors in the palace to be covered, hating to see the ravages that his encounter with the Drakhaon had wrought. Now that he was almost recovered, he forced himself to look every day. After all, he reasoned, his courtiers were obliged to put up with the sight of his disfigurement so why shouldn't he?

He had never been vain. He had known himself to be strong-featured, certainly no handsome fairy-tale prince from one of Karila's stories. But it still pained him to see the ravages of the Drakhaon's Fire, the scarred and reddened skin that pitted one hand and one whole side of his face and head. And his hair had not yet grown back as he had hoped, though there were signs of a soft, pale fuzz the colour of ash, all colour bleached away.

How would Astasia react? Would she shrink from him, forced by court protocol to make public show of tolerating what, in her heart, she looked on with revulsion? Or was she made of stronger stuff, prepared to search deeper than superficial appearances?

He squared his shoulders, bracing himself. He had conquered a whole continent; what had he to fear from one young woman?

He pushed open the double doors and went to meet his betrothed for the first time.

The East Wing music room of the Winter Palace had escaped the worst of the ravages of the insurgents. Built for intimate concerts and recitals, it was crammed to overflowing with the military dignitaries of the Tielen royal household, leaving little room for the Orlov family and their court.

Astasia sat on a dais between her parents; a fourth gilt chair stood empty beside hers. First Minister Vassian stood silently behind her, waiting. Still in mourning for her drowned brother Andrei, her family and the court were sombrely dressed in black and violet. A tense silence filled the room; the Mirom courtiers seemed too bewildered by the rapid succession of events that had led to the annexation of Muscobar to even whisper behind their black-gloved hands.

A blaze of military trumpets shattered the air.

'His Imperial Highness, Eugene of Tielen!' announced a martial voice.

The Tielen Household Guard came marching in, spurs clanking. Astasia felt her mother shrink away in her seat.

'It's all right, Mama,' she whispered, patting her hand, trying to suppress her own nervousness. And then she saw all the heads in the room bowing, the women sinking into low curtseys.

He was here.

She rose to her feet, pressing her hands together to stop them shaking.

Prince Eugene came in, accompanied by Field-Marshal Karonen. She noted that he too wore a black velvet mourning band. Was it as a sign of respect for their loss, or had he too lost someone dear to him in the fighting?

They had warned her about his injuries. She was not squeamish but she steeled herself nevertheless, hoping she would not let anything of what she might feel show on her face.

He stood before her, but still she stared at the golden Order of the Swan glittering on his breast, unwilling to meet his eyes.

'Welcome, Your Highness,' she said, dropping into a full court curtsey, one hand extending in formal greeting.

She sensed a slight hesitation, and then a gloved hand took hers in a firm grip, raising her to her feet.

Still she did not dare to look at him, even as she felt him lift her hand to his lips.

Look, you must look, she willed herself, aware that everyone in the room was watching them with bated breath.

'You are every bit as beautiful as your portrait, Altessa.' His voice was strong, confident, coloured by a slight Tielen accent. He still held her hand in his.

She could no longer keep her gaze lowered. She looked at him then, forcing herself to concentrate on his eyes. Blue-grey eyes, clear and cold as a winter's morning, gazed steadily back. But all the skin around his eyes was red, blistered and damaged. She was looking into the ruin of a face.

Gavril did this, a voice whispered at the back of her mind. *How cruel*.

'You flatter me, Your Highness,' she answered, forcing firmness into her voice. She must not forget that this was also the man who had ruthlessly ordered Elysia's execution. 'Please . . .' She gestured to the gilt chair that had been set for him beside hers.

He stepped up onto the dais, towering above her. He

703

bowed to the Grand Duke and Duchess, to Vassian, and then sat down.

Astasia cleared her throat. This was the part of the ceremony she had been dreading the most, the more because it signalled to the world the end of the Orlov dynasty.

Her father rose from his chair and took her hand in his.

'My – my daughter has a gift to you, Your Highness,' he said. His voice faltered. 'A gift from the heart of Muscobar. Accept it – and with it her hand in marriage, freely given, so that our two countries may be united as one.'

Astasia took the jewelled casket from her father and knelt before Prince Eugene, offering it with both hands raised.

The Prince opened the casket. The Mirom Ruby glowed in his fingers like a flame as he held it aloft: a victory trophy.

'The last of Artamon's Tears!' His voice throbbed now with an intensity of emotion that startled Astasia. 'Now the Imperial crown is complete.' He helped her to rise and took her hand, closing it over the ancient ruby clutched in his fingers.

'Today a new empire rises from the ashes of Artamon's dreams. Altessa, from the day we are married in the Cathedral of Saint Simeon, you will be known as Astasia, Empress of New Rossiya.'

He drew her close and she felt – as if in a waking dream – the pressure of his burned lips hot and dry on her forehead, and then her mouth.

Field-Marshal Karonen turned to the astonished court.

'Long live the Emperor Eugene – and Empress Astasia!'

After a short, startled silence, the cheers began. Astasia, her hand still in Eugene's, glanced at her father – and saw the Grand Duke surreptitiously wiping away a tear.

Read the complete book – coming soon from Bantam Press.